65 PROOF

JA KONRATH

CONTENTS

INTRODUCTION

I'VE BEEN WRITING STORIES for as long as I've been able to hold a pen.

I love writing.

My love of writing stems from a love of reading, and my favorite things to read have always been short stories. Maybe because they don't demand a hefty time commitment. Maybe because, like a buffet, they offer variety and allow you to sample new things. Or maybe because some of the greatest ideas are best presented in 5000 words or less.

In my younger days I'd devour Ellery Queen's Mystery Magazine, visit the library to check out Alfred Hitchcock anthologies, and buy Charles Grant's Shadows anthologies and Year's Best Horror Stories paperbacks. I discovered many new writers by reading shorts, including Anthony Boucher, Ray Bradbury, Stephen King, Lawrence Block, Richard Matheson, Woody Allen, Bill Pronzini, Dave Barry, and John D. MacDonald, masters all.

I learned my craft by studying and imitating these authors, and did so much writing as a kid that my parents bought me a word processor as a birthday gift.

By the time I was out of college I had written over two hundred short stories, and deemed myself ready to write a novel.

From that moment until my first sale took twelve years.

Whiskey Sour, my debut Jack Daniels novel, was published in

2003. I've done six more books in the series since then (Bloody Mary, Rusty Nail, Dirty Martini, Fuzzy Navel, Cherry Bomb, and Shaken.)

Though Whiskey Sour was the first thing I ever sold, it was actually my tenth book. The previous nine never found a publisher. Neither did any of my early short stories. Between 1990 and 2002 I wrote over a million words, without earning a single dime. All I earned were rejection letters. Over five hundred of them.

My early work apparently sucked.

Luckily, my new book contract allowed me to write full time. Since writing became my main source of income, and that income depended on people buying my books, I spent every waking hour trying to think up ways to enlarge my audience. It took me years to reach that point, and I intended to do everything I could to make sure my books didn't flop.

In sales vernacular, that meant immersing myself in self-promotional marketing to spread name-recognition through increased brand awareness.

In layman's terms, I had to find readers.

One of the main things I did to promote myself was write and sell short stories. Magazines, websites, and anthologies can reach thousands, hundreds of thousands, even millions of people. And as I learned from my youthful reading experiences, there's no better advertisement for an author than a sample of his writing.

So I looked through my stack of old shorts, rewrote a select few, and sent them out. I also began to write new stories, many of them featuring characters from my novels.

In order to reach as many markets as possible, I wrote about a wide variety of subjects. Some stories were geared toward mystery and crime readers. Others, since my novels have scary parts, were aimed at horror fans. I also penned some straight comedy stories and essays, because the Jack Daniels books contain a lot of humor.

Since 2003, I've sold and/or published over fifty stories and articles. Many new readers have found me by reading my short stuff, and have gone on to become fans of my books.

Which leads us to 65 Proof.

Over the years, a lot people have contacted me, asking where they could get copies of old magazines or anthologies I've been in. Unfortunately, some of my published stories are out-of-print, foreign, defunct, sold-out, or otherwise difficult to find.

Not anymore.

This collection brings all of my published works together in one package, and it's a lot cheaper than spending hundreds of dollars buying every single magazine and anthology that features a JA Konrath story, though bless you folks who have tried to do just that.

For reading convenience, I've divided 65 Proof into four sections.

JACK AND FRIENDS. These are stories that directly tie into my series novels. They stand alone, and don't need to be read in any particular order, nor do they fit into any specific timeline in the Jack Daniels universe.

CRIME STORIES. These are mystery and thriller yarns that don't have anything to do with Jack and company. They range in tone from extremely hardboiled noir, to light-hearted satire, to solve-it-yourself mini mysteries.

HORROR STORIES. Scary tales, some funny, some extremely dark. This is where you'll find monsters, vampires, ghosts, aliens, and assorted things that go bump in the night.

FUNNY STUFF. Shorts and essays in various genres, intended to provoke smiles.

While I enjoy writing the Jack books, I have even more fun writing shorts. The short form is liberating. It allows me to experiment, to be goofy, to take risks. I believe within these fifty-five stories is some of my best work.

I encourage you to skip around these pages and sample the different tones and styles. Think of it as a buffet where you can pick and choose.

And thank you for reading. Thank you more than you'll ever know…

Jack and Friends

THERE HAVE BEEN SEVEN Jack Daniels novels so far (Whiskey Sour, Bloody Mary, Rusty Nail, Drity Martini, Fuzzy Navel, Cherry Bomb, and Shaken.)

The continuing cast of characters in the Jack Daniels books are one of the reasons I enjoy writing them so much. Having established early on that the series is a mixture of humor, scares, mystery, and thrills, I have complete freedom to write short stories in any and all of these sub-genres.

I use shorts to take my characters in places they wouldn't normally go in the novels. Jack can function as a traditional sleuth, solving crimes like Sherlock Holmes or Miss Marple. But she can also star in nail-biting thrillers without any element of mystery. She can even be delegated to sidekick role, letting someone else take center stage.

Harry McGlade can be even goofier in short stories than he is in the books. When I write a McGlade short, I play it for laughs and cross over into parody, which would never work in the novels.

Phineas Troutt is ideal for hardboiled tales. Because he's a criminal, I can walk on the dark side with him, and have him do things that Jack, with her moral compass, would never do.

Plus, I can get away with things in short stories that I can't in my books. I don't have to worry about having lines cut, or having my characters' motivations questioned. For a writer, it's the ultimate indulgence, and the ultimate freedom.

It also allows me to do some pretty fun shit.

On the Rocks

After landing my first three-book deal, I started writing short stories like crazy, trying to get my name out there. I always liked locked-room mysteries, and decided to do one featuring my newly published detective, Lt. Jacqueline "Jack" Daniels of the Chicago Police Department. Here, Jack takes a break from serial killers to solve a classic whodunnit. This sold to Ellery Queen Mystery Magazine, *and was placed in their Department of First Stories, which thrilled me because*

"SHE SURE BLED A LOT."

I ignored Officer Crouch, my attention focused on the dead woman's arm. The cut had almost severed her left wrist, a flash of pink bone peeking through. Her right hand was curled around the handle of a utility knife.

I'd been in Homicide for more than ten years, and still felt an emotional punch whenever I saw a body. The day I wasn't affected was the day I hung up my badge.

I wore disposable plastic booties over my flats because the shag carpet oozed blood like a sponge wherever I stepped. The apartment's air conditioning was set on freeze, so the decomposition wasn't as bad as it might have been after a week—but it was still pretty bad. I got down on my haunches and swatted away some blowflies.

On her upper arm, six inches above the wound, was a bruise.

"What's so interesting, Lieut? It's just a suicide."

In my blazer pocket I had some latex gloves. I snapped them on.

The victim's name was Janet Hellerman, a real estate lawyer with a private practice. She was brunette, mid thirties, Caucasian. Her satin slip was mottled with drying brown stains, and she wore nothing underneath. I put my hand on her chin, gently turned her head.

There was another bruise on her cheek.

"Johnson's getting a statement from the super."

I stood up, smoothed down my skirt, and nodded at Herb, who had just entered the room. Detective First Class Herb Benedict was my partner. He had a gray mustache, Basset hound jowls, and a Santa Claus belly. Herb kept on the perimeter of the blood puddle; those little plastic booties were too hard for him to get on.

"Johnson's story corroborates?"

Herb nodded. "Why? You see something?"

I did, but wasn't sure how it fit. Herb had questioned both Officer Crouch and Officer Johnson, and their stories were apparently identical.

Forty minutes ago they'd arrived at apartment 3008 at the request of the victim's mother, who lived out of state. She had been unable to get in touch with her daughter for more than a week. The building superintendent unlocked the door for them, but the safety chain was on, and a sofa had been pushed in front of the door to prevent anyone from getting inside. Crouch put his shoulder to it, broke in, and they discovered the body.

Herb squinted at the corpse. "How many marks on the wrist?"

"Just one cut, deep."

I took off the blood-soaked booties, put them in one of the many plastic baggies I keep in my pockets, and went over to the picture window, which covered most of the far wall. The view was expensive, overlooking Lake Shore Drive from forty stories up. Boaters swarmed over the surface of Lake Michigan like little white ants, and the street was a gridlock of toy cars. Summer was a busy time for Chicagoans—criminals included.

I motioned for Crouch, and he heeled like a chastened puppy. Beat cops were getting younger every year; this one barely needed to shave. He had the cop stare, though—hard eyes and a perpetual scowl, always expecting to be lied to.

"I need you to do a door-to-door. Get statements from everyone on this floor. Find out who knew the victim, who might have seen anything."

Crouch frowned. "But she killed herself. The only way in the apartment is the one door, and it was locked from the inside, with the safety chain on. Plus there was a sofa pushed in front of it."

"I'm sure I don't need to remind you that suicides are treated as homicides in this town, Officer."

He rolled his eyes. I could practically read his thoughts. How did this dumb broad get to be Homicide Lieutenant? She sleep with the PC?

"Lieut, the weapon is still in her hand. Don't you think..."

I sighed. Time to school the rookie.

"How many cuts are on her wrist, Crouch?"

"One."

"Didn't they teach you about hesitation cuts at the Academy? A suicidal person usually has to work up the courage. Where was she found?"

"On the floor."

"Why not her bed? Or the bathtub? Or a comfy chair? If you were ending your life, would you do it standing in the middle of the living room?"

He became visibly flustered, but I wasn't through yet.

"How would you describe the temperature in this room?"

"It's freezing."

"And all she's wearing is a slip. Little cold for that, don't you think? Did you read the suicide note?"

"She didn't leave a note."

"They all leave notes. I've worked these streets for twenty years, and never saw a suicide where the vic didn't leave a note. But for some strange reason, there's no note here. Which is a shame because maybe her note would explain how she got the multiple contusions on her face and arm."

Crouch was cowed, but he managed to mumble, "The door—"

"Speaking of doors," I interrupted, "why are you still here when you were given an order to start the door-to-door? Move your ass."

Crouch looked at his shoes and then left the apartment. Herb raised an eyebrow.

"Kinda hard on the newbie, Jack."

"He wouldn't have questioned me if I had a penis."

"I think you have one now. You took his."

"If he does a good job, I'll give it back."

Herb turned to look at the body. He rubbed his mustache.

"It could still play as suicide," he said. "If she was hit by a sudden urge to die. Maybe she got some terrible news. She gets out of the shower, puts on a slip, cranks up the air conditioning, gets a phone call, immediately grabs the knife and with one quick slice…"

He made a cutting motion over his wrist.

"Do you buy it?" I asked.

Herb made a show of mulling it over.

"No," he consented. "I think someone knocked her out, sliced her wrist, turned up the air so the smell wouldn't get too bad, and then…"

"Managed to escape from a locked room."

I sighed, my shoulders sagging.

Herb's eyes scanned the view. "A window washer?"

I checked the window, but as expected it didn't open. Winds this high up weren't friendly.

"There's no other way in?" Herb asked.

"Just the one entryway."

I walked up to it. The safety chain hung on the door at eye level, its wall mounting and three screws dangling from it. The doorframe where it had been attached was splintered and cracked from Crouch's entrance. There were three screw holes in the frame that matched the mounting, and a fourth screw still remained, sticking out of the frame about an inch.

The hinges on the door were dusty and showed no signs of tampering. A black leather sofa was pushed off to the side, near the doorway. I followed the tracks that its feet had made in the carpet. The sofa had been placed in front of the door and then shoved aside.

I opened the door, holding the knob with two fingers. It moved easily, even though it was heavy and solid. I closed it, stumped.

"How did the killer get out?" I said, mostly to myself.

"Maybe he didn't get out. Maybe the killer is still in the apartment." Herb's eyes widened and his hand shot up, pointing over my shoulder. "Jack! Behind you!"

I rolled my eyes.

"Funny, Herb. I already searched the place."

I peeled off the gloves and stuck them back in my pocket.

"Well, then there are only three possibilities." Herb held up his hand, ticking off fingers. "One, Crouch and Johnson and the superintendent are all lying. Two, the killer was skinny enough to slip out of the apartment by going under the door. Or three, it was Houdini."

"Houdini's dead."

"Did you check? Get an alibi?"

"I'll send a team to the cemetery."

While we waited for the ME to arrive, Herb and I busied ourselves with tossing the place. Bank statements told us Janet Hellerman made a comfortable living and paid her bills on time. She was financing a late model Lexus, which we confirmed was parked in the lot below. Her credit card debt was minimal, with a recent charge for plane tickets. A call to Delta confirmed two seats to Montana for next week, one in her name and one in the name of Glenn Hale.

Herb called the precinct, requesting a sheet on Hale.

I checked the answering machine and listened to thirty-eight messages. Twenty were from Janet's distraught mother, wondering where she was. Two were telemarketers. One was from a friend named Sheila who wanted to get together for dinner, and the rest were real estate related.

Nothing from Hale. He wasn't on the caller ID either.

I checked her cell phone next, and listened to forty more messages; ten from mom, and thirty from home buyers. Hale hadn't left any messages, but there was a 'Glenn' listed on speed dial. The phone's call log showed that Glenn's number had called over a dozen times, but not once since last week.

"Look at this, Jack."

I glanced over at Herb. He set a pink plastic case on the kitchen counter and opened it up. It was a woman's toolkit, the kind they sold at department stores for fifteen bucks. Each tool had a cute pink handle and a corresponding compartment that it snugged into. This kit contained a hammer, four screwdrivers, a measuring tape, and eight wrenches. There were also two empty slots; one for needle nose pliers, and one for something five inches long and rectangular.

"The utility knife," I said.

Herb nodded. "She owned the weapon. It's looking more and more like suicide, Jack. She has a fight with Hale. He dumps her. She kills herself."

"You find anything else?"

"Nothing really. She liked to mountain climb, apparently. There's about forty miles of rope in her closet, lots of spikes and beaners, and a picture of her clinging to a cliff. She also has an extraordinary amount of teddy bears. There were so many piled on her bed, I don't know how she could sleep on it."

"Diary? Computer?"

"Neither. Some photo albums, a few letters that we'll have to look through."

Someone knocked. We glanced across the breakfast bar and saw the door ease open.

Mortimer Hughes entered. Hughes was a medical examiner. He worked for the city, and his job was to visit crime scenes and declare people dead. You'd never guess his profession if you met him on the street—he had the smiling eyes and infectious enthusiasm of a television chef.

"Hello Jack, Herb, beautiful day out." He nodded at us and set down a large tackle box that housed the many particular tools of his trade. Hughes opened it up and snugged on some plastic gloves and booties. He also brandished knee pads.

Herb and I paused in our search and watched him work. Hughes knelt beside the vic and spent ten minutes poking and prodding, humming tunelessly to himself. When he finally spoke, it was high-pitched and cheerful.

"She's dead," Hughes said.

We waited for more.

"At least four days, probably longer. I'm guessing from hypovolemic shock. Blood loss is more than forty percent. Her right zygomatic bone is shattered, pre-mortem or early post."

"Could she have broken her cheek falling down?" Herb asked.

"On this thick carpet? Possible—yes. Likely—no. Look at the blood pool. No arcs. No trails."

"So she wasn't conscious when her wrist was cut?"

"That would be my assumption, unless she laid down on the floor and stayed perfectly still while bleeding to death."

"Sexually assaulted?"

"Can't tell. I'll do a swab."

I chose not to watch, and Herb and I went back into the kitchen. Herb pursed his lips.

"It could still be suicide. She cuts her wrist, falls over, breaks her cheek bone, dies unconscious."

"You don't sound convinced."

"I'm not. I like the boyfriend. They're fighting, he bashes her one in the face. Maybe he can't wake her up, or he thinks he's killed her. Or he wants to kill her. He finds the toolbox, gets the utility knife, makes it look like a suicide."

"And then magically disappears."

Herb frowned. "That part I don't like."

"Maybe he flushed himself down the toilet, escaped through the plumbing."

"You can send Crouch out to get a plunger."

"Lieutenant?"

Officer Crouch had returned. He stood by the kitchen counter, his face ashen.

"What is it, Officer?"

"I was doing the door-to-door. No one answered at the apartment right across the hall. The superintendent thought that was strange—an old lady named Mrs. Flagstone lives there, and she never leaves her home. She even sends out for groceries. So the super opens up her door and…you'd better come look.

Mrs. Flagstone stared up at me with milky eyes. Her tongue protruded from her lips like a hunk of raw liver. She was naked in the bathtub, her face and upper body submerged in foul water, one chubby leg hanging over the edge. The bloating was extensive. Her white hair floated around her head like a halo.

"Still think it's a suicide?" I asked Herb.

Mortimer Hughes rolled up his sleeve and put his hand into the water. He pressed her chest and bubbles exploded out of her mouth and nose.

"Didn't drown. Her lungs are full of air."

He moved his hand higher, prodding the wrinkled skin on her neck.

"I can feel some damage to the trachea. There also appears to be a lesion around her neck. I want to get a sample of the water before I pull the drain plug."

Hughes dove into his box. Herb, Crouch, and I left him and went into the living room. Herb called in, requesting the forensics team.

"Any hits from the other tenants?" I asked the rookie.

He flipped open his pad. "One door over, at apartment 3010, the occupant, a Mr. Stanley Mankowicz, remembers some yelling coming from the victim's place about six days ago."

"Does he remember what time?"

"It was late, he was in bed. Mr. Mankowicz shares a wall with the vic, and has called her on several occasions to tell her to turn her television down."

"Did he call that night?"

"He was about to, but the noise stopped."

"Where's the super?"

"Johnson hasn't finished taking his statement."

"Call them both in here."

While waiting for them to arrive, I examined Mrs. Flagstone's door. Like Janet's, it had a safety chain, and like Janet's, it had been ripped from the wall and the mounting was hanging from the door. I found four screws and some splinters on the floor. There were no screws in the door frame.

A knock, and I opened the door. Officer Johnson and the super. Johnson was older than his partner, bigger, with the same dead eyes. The superintendent was a Pakistani man named Majid Patel. Mr. Patel had dark skin and red eyes and he clearly enjoyed all of this attention.

"I moved to this country ten years ago, and I have never seen a dead body before. Now I have seen two in the same day. I must call and tell my mother. I call my mother when anything exciting happens."

"We'll let you go in a moment, Mr. Patel. I'm Lt. Jack Daniels, this is Detective Herb Benedict. We just have a few…"

"Your name is Jack Daniels? But you are not a man."

"You're very observant," I deadpanned. "Did you know Janet Hellerman?"

Patel winked at me. Was he flirting?

"It must be hard, Lt. Jack Daniels, to be a pretty woman with a funny name in a profession so dominated by male chauvinist pigs." Patel offered Herb a look. "No offense."

Herb returned a pleasant smile. "None taken. If you could please answer the Lieutenant's question."

Patel grinned, crooked teeth and spinach remnants.

"She was a real estate lawyer. Young and good looking. Always paid her rent on time. My brother gave her a deal on her apartment, because she had nice legs." Patel had no reservations about openly checking out mine. "Yours are very nice too, Jack Daniels. For an older lady. Are you single?"

"She's single." Herb winked at me, gave me an elbow. I made a mental note to fire him later.

"Your brother?" I asked Patel.

"He's the building owner," Officer Johnson chimed in. "It's the family business."

"Did you know anything about Janet's personal life?"

"She had a shit for a boyfriend, a man named Glenn. He had an affair and she dumped him."

"When was this?"

"About ten days ago. I know because she asked me to change the lock on her door. She had given him a key and he wouldn't return it."

"Did you change the lock?"

"I did not. Ms. Hellerman just mentioned it to me in the elevator once. She never filled out the work order request."

"Does the building have a doorman?"

"No. We have security cameras."

"I'll need to see tapes going back two weeks. Can you get them for me?"

"It will not be a problem."

Mortimer Hughes came out of the bathroom. He was holding a closed set of tweezers in one hand, his other hand cupped beneath it.

"I dug a fiber out of the victim's neck. Red, looks synthetic."

"From a rope?" I asked.

Hughes nodded.

"Mr. Patel, we'll be down shortly for those tapes. Crouch, Johnson, help Herb and I search the apartment. Let's see if we can find the murder weapon."

We did a thorough toss, but couldn't find any rope. Herb, however, found a pair of needle nose pliers in a closet. Pliers with pink handles.

"They were neighbors," Herb reasoned. "Janet could have lent them to her."

"Could have. But we both doubt it. Call base to see if they found anything on Hale."

Herb dialed, talked for a minute, then hung up.

"Glenn Hale has been arrested three times, all assault charges. Did three months in Joliet."

I wasn't surprised. All evidence pointed to the boyfriend, except for the damned locked room. Maybe Herb was right and the killer just slipped under the door and…

Epiphany.

"Call the lab team. I want the whole apartment dusted. Then get an address and a place of work on Hale and send cars. Tell them to wait for the warrant."

Herb raised an eyebrow. "A warrant? Shouldn't we question the guy first?"

"No need," I said. "He did it, and I know how."

Feeling, a bit foolishly, like Sherlock Holmes, I took everyone back into Janet's apartment. They began hurling questions at me, but I held up my hand for order.

"Here's how it went," I began. "Janet finds out Glenn is cheating, dumps him. He comes over, wanting to get her back. She won't let him in. He uses his key, but the safety chain is on. So he busts in and breaks the chain."

"But the chain was on when we came in the first time," Crouch complained.

Herb hushed him, saving me the trouble.

"They argue," I went on. "Glenn grabs her arm, hits her. She falls to the floor, unconscious. Who knows what's going through his mind? Maybe he's afraid she'll call the police, and he'll go to jail—he has a record and this state has zero tolerance for repeat offenders. Maybe he's so mad at her he thinks she deserves to die. Whatever the case, he finds Janet's toolkit and takes out the utility knife. He slits her wrist and puts the knife in her other hand."

Five inquisitive faces hung on my every word. It was a heady experience.

"Glenn has to know he'd be a suspect," I raised my voice, just a touch for dramatic effect. "He's got a history with Janet, and a criminal record. The only way to throw off suspicion is to make it look like no one else could have been in the room, to show the police that it had to be a suicide."

"Jack," Herb admonished. "You're dragging it out."

"If you figured it out, then you'd have the right to drag it out too."

"Are you really single?" Patel asked. He grinned again, showing more spinach.

"If she keeps stalling," Herb told him, "I'll personally give you her number."

I shot Herb with my eyes, then continued.

"Okay, so Glenn goes into Janet's closet and gets a length of climbing rope. He also grabs the needle nose pliers from her toolbox and heads back to the front door. The safety chain has been ripped out of the frame, and the mounting is dangling on the end. He takes a single screw," I pointed at the screw sticking in the door frame, "and puts it back in the doorframe about halfway."

Herb nodded, getting it. "When the mounting ripped out, it had to pull out all four screws. So the only way one could still be in the doorframe is if someone put it there."

"Right. Then he takes the rope and loops it under a sofa leg. He goes out into the hall with the rope, and closes the door, still holding both ends of the rope. He tugs the rope through the crack under the door, and pulls the sofa right up to the door from the other side."

"Clever," Johnson said.

"I must insist you meet my mother," Patel said.

"But the chain…" Crouch whined.

I smiled at Crouch. "He opens the door a few inches, and grabs the chain with the needle nose pliers. He swings the loose end over to the door frame, where it catches and rests on the screw he put in halfway."

I watched the light finally go on in Crouch's eyes. "When Mr. Patel opened the door, it looked like the chain was on, but it really wasn't. It was just hanging on the screw. The thing that kept the door from opening was the sofa."

"Right. So when you burst into the room, you weren't the one that broke the safety chain. It was already broken."

Crouch nodded rapidly. "The perp just lets go of one end of the rope and pulls in the other end, freeing it from the sofa leg. Then he locks the door with his own key."

"But poor Mrs. Flagstone," I continued, "must have seen him in the hallway. She has her safety chain on, maybe asks him what he's doing. So he bursts into her room and strangles her with the climbing rope. The rope was red, right Herb?"

Herb grinned. "Naturally. How did you know that?"

"I guessed. Then Glenn ditches the pliers in the closet, makes a half-assed attempt to stage Mrs. Flagstone's death like a drowning, and leaves with the rope. I bet the security tapes will concur."

"What if he isn't seen carrying the rope?"

No problem. I was on a roll.

"Then he either ditched it in a hall, or wrapped it around his waist under his shirt before leaving."

"I'm gonna go check the tapes," Johnson said, hurrying out.

"I'm going to call my mother," Patel said, hurrying out.

Herb got on the phone to get a warrant, and Mortimer Hughes dropped to his hands and knees and began to search the carpeting, ostensibly for red fibers—even thought that wasn't his job.

I was feeling pretty smug, something I rarely associated with my line of work, when I noticed Officer Crouch staring at me. His face was projecting such unabashed admiration that I almost blushed.

"Lieutenant—that was just…amazing."

"Simple detective work. You could have figured it out if you thought about it."

"I never would have figured that out." He glanced at his shoes, then back at me, and then he turned and left.

Herb pocketed his cell and offered me a sly grin.

"We can swing by the DA's office, pick up the warrant in an hour. Tell me, Jack. How'd you put it all together?"

"Actually, you gave me the idea. You said the only way the killer could have gotten out of the room was by slipping under the door. In a way, that's what he did."

Herb clapped his hand on my shoulder.

"Nice job, Lieutenant. Don't get a big head. You wanna come over for supper tonight? Bernice is making pot roast. I'll let you invite Mr. Patel."

"He'd have to call his mother first. Speaking of mothers…"

I glanced at the body of Janet Hellerman, and again felt the emotional punch. The Caller ID in the kitchen gave me the number for Janet's mom. It took some time to tell the whole story, and she cried through most of it. By the end, she was crying so much that she couldn't talk anymore.

I gave her my home number so she could call me later.

The lab team finally arrived, headed by a Detective named Perkins. Soon both apartments were swarming with tech heads—vacuuming fibers, taking samples, spraying chemicals, shining ALS, snapping pictures and shooting video.

I filled in Detective Perkins on what went down, and left him in charge of the scene.

Then Herb and I went off to get the warrant.

Whelp Wanted

Harry McGlade dates back to 1985, when I was 15. I've been a mystery fan since I was nine years old, and I thought it would be a fun genre to parody. On a summer afternoon at my friend Jim Coursey's house, we sat at his Apple IIe (with the green phosphorus monitor) and giggled like fiends writing one stupid PI cliché after another. I picked the name Harry McGlade out of a phone book. For the next dozen years, I wrote over a hundred McGlade short stories. None of them were any good, but they did garner me my very first rejection letters, including one in 1989 from Playboy. *This story was sold to the now-defunct* Futures Mysterious Anthology Magazine. *I wrote it just after my first novel came out in 2004.*

I WAS HALFWAY THROUGH a meatball sandwich when a man came into my office and offered me money to steal a dog.

A lot of money.

"Are you an animal lover, Mr. McGlade?"

"Depends on the animal. And call me Harry."

He offered his hand. I stuck out mine, and watched him frown when he noticed the marinara stains. He abruptly pulled back, reaching instead into the inner pocket of his blazer. The suit he wore was tailored and looked expensive, and his skin was tanned to a shade only money can buy.

"This is Marcus." His hand extended again, holding a photograph. "He's a Shar-pei."

Marcus was one of those unfortunate Chinese wrinkle dogs, the kind that look like a great big raisin with fur. He was light brown, and his face had so many folds of skin that his eyes were completely covered.

I bet the poor pooch walked into a lot of walls.

"Cute," I said, because the man wanted to hire me.

"Marcus is a champion show dog. He's won four AKC competitions. Several judges have commented that he's the finest example of the breed they've ever seen."

I wanted to say something about Marcus needing a good starch and press, but instead inquired about the dog's worth.

"With the winnings, and stud fees, he's worth upwards of ten thousand dollars."

I whistled. The dog was worth more than I was.

"So, what's the deal, Mr…"

"Thorpe. Vincent Thorpe. I'm willing to double your usual fee if you can get him back."

I took another bite of meatball, wiped my mouth on my sleeve, and leaned back in my swivel chair. The chair groaned in disapproval.

"Tell me a little about Marcus, Mr. Thorpe. Curly fries?"

"Pardon me?"

I gestured to the bag on my desk. "Did you want any curly fries? Potatoes make me bloaty."

He shook his head. I snatched a fry, bloating be damned.

"I've, um, raised Marcus since he was a pup. He has one of the best pedigrees in the sport. Since Samson passed away, there has quite literally been no competition."

"Samson?"

"Another Shar-pei. Came from the same littler as Marcus, owned by a man named Glen Ricketts. Magnificent dog. We went neck and neck several times."

"Hold on, a second. I'd like to take notes."

I pulled out my notepad and a pencil. On the first piece of paper, I wrote, "Dog."

"Do you know who has Marcus now?"

"Another breeder named Abigail Cummings. She borrowed Marcus to service her Shar-pei, Julia. When I went to pick him up, she insisted she didn't have him, and claimed she didn't know what I was talking about."

I jotted this down. My fingers made a grease spot on the page.

"Did you try the police?"

"Yes. They searched her house, but didn't find Marcus. She's insisting I made a mistake."

"Did Abigail give you money to borrow Marcus? Sign any contracts?"

"No. I lent him to her as a favor. And she kept him."

"How do you know her?"

"Casually, from the American Kennel Club. Her Shar-pei, Julia, is a truly magnificent bitch. You should see her haunches."

I let that one go.

"Why did you lend out Marcus if you only knew her casually?"

"She called me a few days ago, promised me the pick of the litter if I lent her Marcus. I never should have done it. I should have just given her a straw."

"A straw?"

"Of Marcus's semen. I milk him by..."

I held up my palm and scribbled out the word 'straw.' It was more info than I wanted. "Let's move on."

Thorpe pressed his lips together so tightly they lost color. His eyes got sticky.

"Please, Harry. Marcus is more than just a dog to me. He's my best friend."

I didn't doubt it. You don't milk a casual acquaintance.

"Maybe you could hire an attorney."

"That takes too long. If I go through legal channels, it could be months before my case is called. And even then, I'd need some kind of proof that she had him, so I'd have to hire a private investigator anyway."

I scraped away a coffee stain on my desk with my thumbnail.

"I'm sorry for your loss, Mr. Thorpe. But hiring me to bust into someone's home and steal a dog...I'm guessing that breaks all sorts of laws. I could have my license revoked, I could go to jail—"

"I'll triple your fee."

"I take cash, checks, or major credit cards."

Night Vision Goggles use a microprocessor to magnify ambient light and allow a user to see in almost total blackness.

They're also pricey as hell, so I had to make due with a flashlight and some old binoculars.

It was a little past eleven in the evening, and I was sitting in the bough of a tree, staring into the backyard of Abigail Cummings. I'd been there for almost two hours. The night was typical for July in Chicago; hot, sticky, and humid. The black ski mask I wore was so damp with sweat it threatened to drown me.

Plus, I was bloaty.

I let the binocs hang around my neck and flashed the light at my notepad to review my stake-out report.

> 9:14pm—Climbed tree.
> 9:40pm—Drank two sodas.
> 10:15pm—Foot fell asleep.

Not too exciting so far. I took out my pencil and added, "11:04pm—really regret drinking those sodas."

To keep my mind off of my bladder, I spent a few minutes trying to balance the pencil on the tip of my finger. It worked, until I dropped the pencil.

I checked my watch. 11:09. I attempted to write "dropped my pencil" on my notepad, but you can guess how that turned out.

I was all set to call it a night, when I saw movement in the backyard.

It was a woman, sixty-something, her short white hair glowing in the porch light.

Next to her, on a leash, was Marcus.

"Is someone in my tree?"

I fought panic, and through Herculean effort managed to keep my pants dry.

"No," I answered.

She wasn't fooled.

"I'm calling the police!"

"Wait!" My voice must have sounded desperate, because she paused in her race back to the house.

"I'm from the US Department of Foliage. I was taking samples of your tree. It seems to be infested with the Japanese Saganaki Beetle."

"Why are you wearing that mask?"

"Uh…so they don't recognize me. Hold on, I need to ask you a few sapling questions."

I eased down, careful to avoid straining myself. When I reached ground, the dog trotted over and amiably sniffed at my pants.

"I'm afraid I don't know much about agriculture."

From the tree, Ms. Cummings was nothing to look at. Up close, she made me wish I was still in the tree.

The woman was almost as wrinkly as the dog. But unlike her canine companion, she had tried to fill in those wrinkles with make-up. From the amount, she must have used a paint roller. The eye shadow alone was thick enough to stop a bullet. Add to that a voice like raking gravel, and she was quite the catch.

I tried to think of something to ask her, to keep the beetle ploy going. But this was getting too complicated, so I just took out my gun.

"The dog."

Her mouth dropped open.

"The what?"

"That thing on your leash that's wagging its tail. Hand it over."

"Why do you want my dog?"

"Does it matter?"

"Of course it does. I don't want you to shoot me, but I also don't want to hand over my dog to a homicidal maniac."

"I'm not a homicidal maniac."

"You're wearing a ski mask in ninety degree weather, hopping from one foot to the other like some kind of monkey."

"I had too much soda. Give me the damn leash."

She handed me the damn leash. So far so good.

"Okay. You just stand right here, and count to a thousand before you go back inside, or else I'll shoot you."

"Aren't you leaving?"

"Yeah."

"Not to second-guess you, Mr. Dognapper, but how can you shoot me, if you've already gone?"

Know-it-all.

"I think you need a bit more blush on your cheeks. There are some folks in Wisconsin who can't see it from there."

Her lips down turned. With all the lipstick, they looked like two cartoon hot dogs.

"This is Max Factor."

"I won't tell Max if you don't. Now start counting."

I was out of there before she got to six.

After I got back to my office, I took care of some personal business, washed my hands, and called the client. He agreed to come right over.

"Mr. McGlade, I can't tell you how...oh, yuck."

"Watch where you're stepping. Marcus decided to mark his territory."

Thorpe made an unhappy face, then he took off his shoe and left it by the door.

"Mr. McGlade, thank you for...yuck."

"He's marked a couple spots. I told you to watch out."

He removed the other shoe.

"Did you bring the money?"

"I did, and I—wait a second!"

"You might as well just throw away the sock, because those stains..."

"That's not Marcus!"

I looked at the dog, who was sniffing around my desk, searching for another place to make a deposit.

"Of course it's your dog. Look at that face. He's a poster boy for Retin-A."

"That's not a he. It's a she."

"Really?" I peeked under the dog's tail and frowned. "I'll be damned."

"You took the wrong dog, Mr. McGlade. This is Abigail's bitch, Julia."

"It's an honest mistake, Mr. Thorpe. Anyone could have made it."

"No, not anyone, Mr. McGlade. Most semi-literate adults know the difference between boys and girls. Would you like me to draw you a picture?"

"Ease up, Thorpe. When I meet a new dog, I don't lift up a hind leg and stick my face down there to check out the plumbing."

"This is just...oh, yuck."

"The garbage can is over there."

Thorpe removed his sock, and I wracked my brain to figure out how this could be salvaged.

"Any chance you want to keep this dog instead? You said she was a magnificent broad."

"Bitch, Mr. McGlade. It's what we call female dogs."

"I was trying to put a polite spin on it."

"I want Marcus. That was the deal."

"Okay, okay, let me think."

I thought.

Julia had her nose in the garbage can, sniffing Thorpe's sock. If I could only switch dogs somehow.

That was it.

"I'll switch dogs somehow," I said.

"What are you talking about?"

"Like a hostage trade. I'll call up Ms. Cummings, and trade Julia for Marcus."

"Do you think it'll work?"

"Only one way to find out."

I picked up the phone.

"Ms. Cummings? I have your dog."

"I know. I watched you steal him an hour ago."

For someone who looked like a mime, she was sure full of comments.

"If you'd like your dog back, we can make a deal."

"Is my little Poopsie okay? Are you taking care of her?"

"She's fine. I can see why you call her Poopsie."

"Does Miss Julia still have the trots? Poor thing."

I stared at the land mines dotting my floor. "Yeah. I'm all broken up about it."

"Make sure she eats well. Only braised liver and the leanest pork."

Julia was currently snacking on a tuna sandwich I'd dropped under the desk sometime last week.

"I'll do that. Look, I want to make a trade."

I had to play it cool here, if she knew I knew about Marcus, she'd know Thorpe was the one who hired me.

"What kind of trade?"

"I don't want a female dog. I want a male."

"Did Vincent Thorpe hire you?"

Dammit.

"Uh, never heard of him."

"Mr. Thorpe claims I have his dog, Marcus. But the last time I saw Marcus was at an AKC show last April. I have no idea where his dog is."

"That's not how he tells it."

Nice, Harry. I tried to regroup.

"Look, Cummings, you have twelve hours to come up with a male dog. I also want sixty dollars, cash."

Thorpe nudged me and mouthed, "Sixty dollars?"

I put my hand over the mouthpiece. "Carpet cleaning."

"I don't know if I can find a male dog in just 12 hours, Mr. Dog-napper."

"Then I turn Julia into a set of luggage."

I heard her gasp. "You horrible man!"

"I'll do it, too. She's got enough hide on her to make two suitcases and a carry-on. The wrinkled look is hot this year."

I scratched Julia on the head, and she licked my chin. Her breath made me teary-eyed.

"Please don't hurt my dog."

"I'll call you tomorrow morning with the details. If you contact the police, I'll mail you Julia's tail."

"I…I already called the police. I called them right after you left."

Hell. "Well, don't call the police again. I have a friend at the Post Office who gives me a discount rate. I'm there twice a week, mailing doggie parts."

I hit the disconnect.

"Did it work?" Thorpe asked.

"Like a charm. Go home and get some rest. In about twelve hours, you'll have your dog back."

The trick was finding an exchange location where I wouldn't be conspicuous in a ski mask. Chicago had several ice rinks, but I didn't think any of them allowed dogs.

I decided on the alley behind the Congress Hotel, off of Michigan Avenue. I got there two hours early to check the place out.

Time crawled by. I kept track of it in my notepad.

> 9:02am—Arrive at scene. Don't see any cops. Pull on ski mask and wait.
> 9:11am—It sure is hot.
> 9:33am—Julia finds some rotting fruit behind the dumpster. Eats it.
> 10:01am—Boy, is it hot.
> 10:20am—I think I'm getting a heat rash in this mask. Am I allergic to wool?
> 10:38am—Julia finds a dead rat. Eats it.
> 10:40am—Sure is a hot one.
> 11:02am—Play fetch with the dog, using my pencil.

Julia ate the pencil. I was going to jot this down on the pad, but you can guess how that went.

"Julia!"

The dog jerked on the leash, tugging me to my feet. Abigail Cummings had arrived. She wore a pink linen pants suit, and more make-up than the Rockettes. All of them, combined. I fought the urge to carve my initials in her cheek with my fingernail.

Dog and dog owner had a happy little reunion, hugging and licking, and I was getting ready to sigh in relief when I noticed the pooch Abigail had brought with her.

"I'm no expert, but isn't that a Collie?"

"A Collie/Shepherd mix. I picked him up at the shelter."

"That's not Marcus."

Abigail frowned at me. "I told you before, Mr. Dognapper. I don't have Vincent Thorpe's dog."

Her bottom lip began to quiver, and her eyes went glassy. I realized, to my befuddlement, that I actually believed her.

"Fine. Give me the mutt."

Abigail handed me the leash. I stared down at the dog. It was a male, but I doubted I could fool Thorpe into thinking it was Marcus. Even if I shaved off all the fur and shortened the legs with a saw.

"What about my money?" I asked.

She dug into her purse and pulled out a check.

"I can't take a check."

"It's good. I swear."

"How am I supposed to remain incognito if I deposit a check?"

Abigail did the lip quiver thing again.

"Oh my goodness, I didn't even think of that. Please don't make Julia into baggage."

More tears.

"Calm down. Don't cry. You'll ruin your…uh…make-up."

I offered her a handkerchief. She dabbed at her eyes and handed it back to me.

It looked like it had been tie-dyed.

"I think I have two or three dollars in my purse," she rasped in her smoker voice. "Is that okay?"

What the hell. I took it.

"I'll take those Tic-Tacs, too."

She handed them over. Wint-O-Green.

"Can we go now?"

"Go ahead."

She turned to leave the alley, and a thought occurred to me.

"Ms. Cummings! When the police came to visit you to look for Marcus, did you have an alibi?"

She glanced over her shoulder and nodded vigorously.

"That's the point. The day Vincent said he brought the dog to my house, I wasn't home. I was enjoying the third day of an Alaskan Cruise."

Vincent Thorpe was waiting for me when I got back to my office. He carefully scanned the floor before approaching my desk.

"That's not Marcus! That's not even a Shar-pei!"

"We'll discuss that later."

"Where's Marcus?"

"There have been some complications."

"Complications?" Thorpe leaned in closer, raised an eyebrow. "What happened to your face?"

"I think I'm allergic to wool."

"It looks like you rubbed your cheeks with sandpaper."

I wrote, "I hate him" on my notepad.

"Look, Mr. Thorpe, Abigail Cummings doesn't have Marcus. But I may have an idea who does."

"Who?"

"First, I need to ask you a few questions…"

My face was too sore for the ski mask again, so I opted for a nylon stocking.

It was hot.

I shifted positions on the branch I was sitting on, and took another look through the binoculars.

Nothing. The backyard was quiet. But thirty feet away, next to a holly bush, was either a small, brown anthill, or evidence that there was a dog on the premises.

I took out my pencil and reviewed my stake-out sheet.

> 9:46pm—Climbed tree.
> 9:55pm—My face hurts.
> 10:07pm—It really hurts bad.
> 10:22pm—I think I'll go see a doctor.
> 10:45pm—Maybe the drug store has some kind of cream.

I added, "11:07pm—Spotted evidence in backyard. Remember to pick up some aloe vera on the way home."

Before I had a chance to cross my Ts, the patio door opened.

I didn't even need the binoculars. A man, mid-forties with short, brown hair, was walking a dog that was obviously a Shar-pei.

Though my track-team days were far behind me (okay, non-existent), I still managed to leap down from the tree without hurting myself.

The man yelped in surprise, but I had my gun out and in his face before he had a chance to move.

"Hi there, Mr. Ricketts. Kneel down."

"Who are you? What do…"

I cocked the gun.

"Kneel!"

He knelt.

"Good. Now lift up that dog's back leg."

"What?"

"Now!"

Glen Ricketts lifted. I checked.

It was Marcus.

"Leash," I ordered.

He handed me the leash. My third dog in two days, but this time it was the right one.

Now for Part Two of the Big Plan.

"Do you know who I am, Glen?"

He shook his head, terrified.

"Special Agent Phillip Pants, of the American Kennel Club. Do you know why I'm here?"

He shook his head again.

"Don't lie to me, Glen! Does the AKC allow dognapping?"

"No," he whimpered.

"Your dog show days are over, Ricketts. Consider your membership revoked. If I so much catch you in the pet food isle at the Piggly Wiggly, I'm going to take you in and have you neutered. Got it?"

He nodded, eager to please. I gave Marcus a pat on the head, and then turned to leave.

"Hold on!"

Glen's eyes were defeated, pleading.

"What?"

"You mean I can't own a dog, ever again?"

"Not ever."

"But…but…dogs are my life. I love dogs."

"And that's why you should have never stole someone else's."

He sniffled, loud and wet.

"What am I supposed to do now?"

I frowned. Grown men crying like babies weren't my favorite thing to watch. But this joker had brought it upon himself.

"Buy a cat," I told him.

Then I walked back to my car, Marcus in tow.

"Marcus!"

I watching, grinning, as Vincent Thorpe paid no mind to his expensive suit and rolled around on my floor with his dog, giggling like a caffeinated school boy.

"Mr. McGlade, how can I ever repay you?"

"Cash is good."

He disentangled himself from the pooch long enough to pull out his wallet and hand over a fat wad of bills.

"Tell me, how did you know it was Glen Rickets?"

"Simple. You said yourself that he was always one of your closest competitors, up until his dog died earlier this year."

"But what about Ms. Cummings? I talked to her on the phone. I even dropped the dog off at her house, and she took him from me. Wasn't she involved somehow?"

"The phone was easy—Ms. Cummings has a voice like a chainsaw. With practice, anyone can imitate a smoker's croak. But Glen really got clever for the meeting. He picked a time when Ms. Cummings was out of town, and then he spent a good hour or two with Max Factor."

"Excuse me?"

"Cosmetics. As you recall, Abigail Cummings wore enough make-up to cause back-problems. Who could tell what she looked like under all that gunk? Glen just slopped on enough to look like a circus clown, and then he impersonated her."

Thorpe shook his head, clucking his tongue.

"So it wasn't actually Abigail. It was Glen all along. Such a nice guy, too."

"It's the nice ones you have to watch."

"So, now what? Should I call the police?"

"No need. Glen won't be bothering you, or any dog owner, ever again."

I gave him the quick version of the backyard scene.

"He deserves it, taking Marcus from me. But now I have you back, don't I, boy?"

There was more wrestling, and he actually kissed Marcus on the mouth.

"Kind of unsanitary, isn't it?"

"Are you kidding? A dog's saliva is full of antiseptic properties."

"I was speaking for Marcus."

Thorpe laughed. "Friendship transcends species, Mr. McGlade. Speaking of which, where's that Collie/Shepherd mix that Abigail gave you?"

"At my apartment."

"See? You've made a new friend, yourself."

"Nope. I've got a six o'clock appointment at the animal shelter. I'm getting him gassed."

Thorpe shot me surprised look.

"Mr. McGlade! After this whole ordeal, don't you see what amazing companions canines are? A dog can enrich your life! All you have to do is give him a chance."

I mulled it over. How bad could it be, having a friend who never borrowed money, stole your girl, or talked behind your back?

"You know what, Mr. Thorpe? I may just give it a shot."

When I got home a few hours later, I discovered my new best friend had chewed the padding off of my leather couch.

I made it to the shelter an hour before my scheduled appointment.

Street Music

Street Music is my favorite story of any I've written. Phineas Trout was the hero of my first novel, an unpublished mystery called Dead On My Feet, *written back in 1992. It was unabashedly hardboiled, and it helped me land my first agent. The book never sold, probably because it was unabashedly hardboiled. Phin starred in two more unpublished novels, and then I relegated him to the role of sidekick in the Jack Daniels series, which did wind up selling. I'm intrigued by the idea of a hero dying of cancer, and how having no hope left could erode a man's morality. I wrote this story right after selling* Whiskey Sour, *and soon after sold it to* Ellery Queen.

MITCH COULDN'T ANSWER ME with the barrel of my gun in his mouth, so I pulled it out.

"I don't know! I swear!"

If that was the truth, I had no use for it. After three days of questioning dozens of hookers, junkies, and other fine examples of Chicago's populace, Mitch was my only link to Jasmine. I was seriously jonesing; I hadn't done a line since Thursday. Plus, the pain in my side felt like a baby alligator was trying to eat its way out of my pancreas.

I gave Mitch's chin a little tap with the butt of the Glock.

"I really don't know!"

"She's one of yours, Mitch. I thought big, tough pimps like you ran a tight ship."

His black face was shiny with sweat and a little blood. Sure, he was scared. But he wasn't stupid. Telling me Jasmine's whereabouts would put a dent in his income.

I raised the gun back to hit him again.

"She went rogue on me, man! She ditched!"

I paused. If Jasmine had left Mitch, his reluctance to talk about it made some sense. Mack Daddies don't like word to get out that they're losing their game.

"How much money do you have on you?"

"About four hundos. It's yours, man. Front pants pocket."

"I'm not putting my hand in there. Take it out."

Mitch managed to stop shaking long enough to retrieve a fat money clip. I took the cash, and threw the clip—a gold emblem in the shape of a female breast–onto the sidewalk.

"You letting me go?" Mitch asked.

"You're free to pimp another day. Go run to the bus station, see if you can find some other fresh meat to bust out."

When I let go of his lapels, his spine seemed to grow back. He adjusted the collar on his velour jump suit and made sure his baseball hat was tilted to the correct odd angle.

"Ain't like that. I treat my girls good. Plenty of sweet love and all the rock they can smoke."

"Leave. Now. Before I decide to do society a favor."

He sneered, spun on his three hundred dollar sneakers, and did his pimp strut away from me.

I probably should have killed him; I had too many enemies already. But, tough as I am, shooting fourteen-year-old kids in the back isn't my style.

The four hundred was enough to score some coke, but not very much. I thought about calling Manny, my dealer, and getting a sample to help kill the pain, but every minute I wasted gave Jasmine a chance to slip farther away.

Pain relief would have to wait. I pressed my hand to my left side and exited the alley and wondered where the hell I should look next.

I'd already checked Jasmine's apartment, her boyfriend's apartment, her parent's house, her known pick-up spots, and three local crack houses.

To rule out other options, I had to call in a marker.

It was September, about seventy with clear skies, so I took a walk down the block. The first payphone I came to had gum jammed in the coin slot. The second one smelled like a urinal, but I made do.

"Violent Crimes, Daniels."

"Hi, Jack. Phineas Troutt."

"Phin? Haven't seen you at the pool hall lately. Afraid I'll kick your ass?"

My lips twisted in a tight grin. Jacqueline Daniels was a police Lieutenant who busted me a few years back. We had an on-again-off-again eight ball game Monday nights. I'd missed a few.

"I'm sort of preoccupied with something."

"Chemo again?"

"No, work. Listen, you know what I do, right?"

"You're a freelance thug."

"I prefer the term problem solver. I keep it clean."

"I'm guessing that's because we haven't caught you in the act, yet."

"And you never will. Look, Jack, I need a favor."

"I can't do anything illegal, Phin. You know that."

"Nothing shady. I just have to rule some stuff out. I'm looking for a woman. Hooker. Name is Janet Cumberland, goes by the street nick Jasmine. Any recent arrests or deaths with that name?"

There was a pause on the line. I could only guess Jack's thoughts.

"Give me half an hour," she decided. "Got a number where I can call you back?"

I killed time at a hot dog stand, sipping black coffee mixed with ten crushed Tylenol tablets; they worked faster when they were pre-dissolved.

The phone rang eighteen minutes later.

"No one at the morgue matching that name, and her last arrest was three months ago."

"Do you have a place of residence?"

Jack read off the apartment number I'd already checked.

"How about known acquaintances?"

"She's one of Mitch D's girls. Been arrested a few times with another prostitute named Georgia Williamson, street name is Ajax. Kind of an odd name for a hooker."

"She one of Mitch's, too?"

"Lemme check. No, looks like she's solo."

"Got an addy?"

Jack gave it to me.

"There's also a note in Janet's file, says her parents are looking for her. That your angle? Even if you find her, the recit rate with crack is over 95 percent. They'll stick her in rehab and a week later she'll be on the street again."

"Thanks for the help, Jack. Next time we play pool, beer's on me."

"You're on, Phin. How's the—"

"Hurts," I interrupted. "But my doc says it won't for much longer."

"The tumor is shrinking? That's great news!"

I didn't correct her. The tumor was growing like a weed. I wouldn't be in pain much longer because I didn't have much longer.

Which is why I had to find Jasmine, and fast.

She had to die first.

Georgia Williams, aka Ajax, lived on 81st and Stoney, in a particularly mean part of Chicago's South Side. Night was rolling in, bringing with it the bangers, junkies, ballers, wanna-bes, and thugs. None of them were thrilled to see a white guy on their turf, and some flashed their iron as I drove by.

Ajax's place wasn't easy to find, and asking for directions didn't strike me as a smart idea. Maybe in neighborhoods this bad, whole buildings got stolen.

Finally, I narrowed it down to a decrepit apartment without any street number. I parked in front, set the alarm on my Bronco, and made sure I had one in the chamber.

"You lost, white boy?"

I ignored the three gang members—Gangster Disciples according to their colors—and headed for the building. The front door had a security lock, but it was long broken. There was a large puddle of something in front of the staircase, which I walked around.

Ajax lived in 206. I took the stairs two at a time, followed a hall decorated with graffiti and vomit, and found her door.

"Georgia Williams? Chicago PD!"

Another door opened opposite me, fearful old eyes peeking out through the crack.

"Is Ms. Williams home?" I asked the neighbor.

The door closed again.

I kicked away a broken bottle that was near my feet, and knocked again.

"Georgia Williams! Open the door!"

"You got ID?"

A woman's voice, cold and firm. I held a brass star, $12.95 on eBay, up to the peephole.

"Where's your partner?" asked the voice.

"Watching the car. We're looking for a friend of yours. Jasmine. She's in big trouble."

"She sure is."

"Can I come in?"

I heard a deadbolt snick back. Then another. The door swung inward, revealing a black girl of no more than sixteen. She wore jeans, a white blouse. Her face was garishly made-up. Stuck to her hip was a sleeping infant.

"Can't be long. Gotta go to work."

Ajax stepped to the side, and I entered her apartment. Expecting squalor, I was surprised to find the place clean and modestly furnished. The ceiling had some water damage, and one wall was losing its plaster, but there were nice curtains and matching furniture and even some framed art. This was the apartment of someone who hadn't given up yet.

"I'll be straight with you, Georgia. If we don't find Jasmine soon, it's very likely she'll be killed. You know about Artie Collins?"

She nodded, once.

"If you know where she is, it's in her best interest to tell me."

"Sorry, cop. I don't know nothing."

I took out my Glock, watched her eyes get big.

"Do you have a license for this firearm I found on your premises, Georgia?"

"Aw, this is—"

I got in her face, sneering.

"I'll tell you what this is. Six months in County, minimum. With your record, the judge won't even think twice. And say goodbye to your baby; when I get done wrecking this place, DCFS will declare you so unfit you won't be allowed within two hundred yards of anyone under aged ten."

Her lips trembled, but there were no tears.

"You bastards are all the same."

"I want Jasmine, Ajax. She's dead if I don't find her."

I gave her credit for toughness. She held out. I had to topple a dresser and put my foot through her TV before she broke down.

"Stop it! She's with her boyfriend!"

"Nice try. I already checked Melvin Kincaid."

"Not Mel. She found a new guy. Named Buster something."

"Buster what?"

"I dunno."

I chucked a vase at the wall. The baby in her arms was wiggling, hysterical.

"I don't have his last name! But I got a number."

Georgia went for her purse on the bed, but I shoved the Glock in her face.

"I'll look."

The purse was the size of a cigarette pack, with rhinestone studs and spaghetti straps. A hooker purse. I didn't figure there could be much of a weapon in there, and was once again surprised. A .22 ATM spilled onto the bed.

"I'm sure this has a license."

Georgia didn't answer. I rifled through the packs of mint gum and condoms until I found a matchbook with a phone number written on the back.

"This it?"

"Yeah."

"Can't you shut that kid up?"

Georgia cooed the baby, rocking it back and forth, while I picked up her .22 and removed the bullets. I tossed the gun back on the bed, and put the lead and the matchbook in my pocket.

She got my evil face when I walked past her.

"If you warn her I'm coming, I'll know it was you."

"I won't say a damn thing, officer."

"I know you won't."

I fished out three of the hundreds I took from Mitch D, and shoved them into her hand. It was a lot more than the TV was worth.

"By the way, why do they call you Ajax?"

She shrugged.

"I've robbed a few tricks."

"Meaning?"

"Ajax cleans out the johns."

When I got back outside, the three Disciples had multiplied into six, and they were standing in front of my truck.

"This is a nice truck, white boy. Can we have it?"

My Glock 21 held thirteen forty-five caliber rounds. More than enough. But Jack was the one who gave me this address, and if I killed any of these bozos she'd eventually get the word.

Dying of cancer was bad enough. Dying of cancer in prison was not on my to-do list.

Stuck in my belt, nestled along my spine, was a combat baton. Sixteen inches long, made of a tightly coiled steel spring. Because it could bend, it didn't break bones.

But it did hurt like crazy.

The Disciples had apparently expected me to tremble in fear, because I clocked three of them across the heads before they went into attack mode.

The first one to draw was a thin kid who watched too many rap videos. He pulled a 9mm out of his baggy pants and thrust it at me sideways, with the back of his hand facing skyward.

Not only did this mess up your aim, but your grip was severely compromised. I gave him a tap across the back of the knuckles, and the gun hit the pavement. A second smack in the forehead opened up a nice gash. As with his buddies, the blood running into his eyes made him blind and worthless. I turned on the last two.

One had a blade. He held it underhanded, tip up, showing me he knew how to use it. After two feints, he thrust it at my face.

I turned, catching the tip on my cheek, and gave him an elbow to the nose. When he stumbled back, he also got a tap across the eyebrows.

The last guy was fifty yards away, sprinting for reinforcements.

I climbed in my Bronco and hauled out of there before they arrived.

"Hi, Jack, I need one more favor."

"You already owe me a night of beer."

"I'll also spring for pizza. I need an address to go with this number."

"Lemme have it."

I read it to her, hoping Georgia was honest with me. I didn't want to pay another visit to Stoney Island.

"Buster McDonalds. Four-four-two-three Irving Park, apartment seven-oh-six."

"Thanks again, Jack."

"Listen, Phin, I asked around about Janet Cumberland. The word on the street is that Artie Collins put a contract out on her."

"I'll be careful."

There was a long pause on the line. I cut off her thought.

"I don't work for mobsters, Jack. I don't kill people for money."

"Watch yourself, Phin."

She hung up.

I stopped at a drive-thru, filled up on grease, and had ten more aspirin. My side ached to the touch. I had stronger stuff, doctor prescribed, but that dulled the senses and took away my edge. I thought about scoring some coke, but the hundred I had left wouldn't buy much, and time was winding down.

I had to find Jasmine.

Buster's neighborhood was several rungs above Ajax's as far as quality of life went. No junkies shooting up in the alleys, hookers on the corners, or roving gangs of teens with firearms.

There were, however, lots of kids drunk out of their minds, moving in great human waves from bar to bar. The area was a hot spot for night life, and Friday night meant the partying was mandatory.

Even the hydrants were taken, so I parked in an alley, blocking the entrance. I took the duffle bag from the passenger seat and climbed out into the night air.

The temp had dropped, and I imagined I could smell Lake Michigan, even though it was miles away. There were voices, shouting, laughing, cars honking. I stood in the shadows.

The security door on Buster's apartment had a lock that was intact and functioning, unlike Ajax's. I spotted someone walking out and caught the door before it closed, and then I took the elevator to the seventh floor.

The cop impersonation wouldn't work this time; Jasmine was on the run and wouldn't open the door for anybody.

But I had a key.

It was another online purchase. There were thirty-four major lock companies in the US, and they made ninety-five percent of all the locks in America. These lock companies each had a few dozen models, and each of the models had a master key that opened up every lock in the series.

Locksmiths could buy these master keys. So could anyone with a credit card who knew the right website.

The lock on Buster's apartment was a Schlage. I took a large key ring from my duffel bag and got the door open on the third try.

Jasmine and Buster were on a futon, watching TV. I was on him before he had a chance to get up.

When he reached for me, I grabbed his wrist and twisted. Then, using his arm like a lever, I forced him face down into the carpeting.

"Buster!"

I didn't have time to deal with Jasmine yet, so she got a kick in the gut. She went down. I took out roll of duct tape and secured Buster's wrists behind him. When that was done, I wound it around his legs a few times.

"Jazz, run!"

His mouth was next.

Jasmine had curled up in the corner of the room, hugging her knees and rocking back and forth. She was a little thing, no older than Ajax, wearing sweatpants and an extra large t-shirt. Her black hair was pulled back and fear distorted her features.

I made it worse by showing her my Glock.

"Tell me about Artie Collins."

She shrunk back, making herself smaller.

"You're going to kill me."

"No one is killing anyone. Why does Artie want you dead?"

"The book."

"What book?"

She pointed to the table next to the futon. I picked up a ledger, scanned a few pages.

Financial figures, from two of Artie's clubs. I guessed that these were the ones the IRS didn't see.

"Stupid move, lady. Why'd you take these from him?"

"He's a pig," she spat, anger overriding terror. "Artie doesn't like it straight. He's a real freak. He did things to me, things no one has ever done."

"So you stole this?"

"I didn't know what it was. I wanted to hurt him, it was right there in the dresser. So I took it."

Gutsy, but dumb. Stealing from one of the most connected guys in the Midwest was a good way to shorten your life expectancy.

"Artie is offering ten thousand dollars for you. And there's a bonus if it's messy."

I put the book in the duffle bag, and then removed a knife.

Artie Collins was a slug, and everyone knew it. He had his public side; the restaurants, the riverboat gambling, the night clubs, but anyone worth their street smarts knew he also peddled kiddie porn, smack cut with rat poison, and owned a handful of cops and judges.

Standing before me, he even looked like a slug, from his sweaty, fat face, to the sharkskin suit in dark brown, of all colors.

"I don't know you," he said.

"Better that way."

"I like to know who I'm doing business with."

"This is a one time deal. Two ships in the night."

He seemed to consider that, and laughed.

"Okay then, Mystery Man. You told my boys you had something for me."

I reached into my jacket. Artie didn't flinch; he knew his men had frisked me earlier and taken my gun. I took out a wad of Polaroids and handed them over.

Artie glanced through them, smiling like a carved pumpkin. He flashed one at me. Jasmine naked and tied up, the knife going in.

"That's a good one. A real Kodak moment."

I said nothing. Artie finished viewing my camera work and carefully stuck the pics in his blazer.

"These are nice, but I still need to know where she's at."

"The bottom of the Chicago river."

"I meant, where she was hiding. She had something of mine."

I nodded, once again going into my jacket. When Artie saw the ledger I thought he'd crap sunshine.

"She told me some things when I was working on her."

"I'll bet she did," Artie laughed.

He gave the ledger a cursory flip through, then tossed it onto his desk. I took a breath, let it out slow. The moment stretched. Finally, Artie waggled a fat, hot dog finger at me.

"You're good, my friend. I could use a man of your talents."

"I'm freelance."

"I offer benefits. A 401K. Dental. Plus whores and drugs, of course. I'd pay some good money to see you work a girl over like you did to that whore."

"You said you'd also pay good money for whoever brought you proof of Jasmine's death."

He nodded, slowly.

"You sure you don't want to work for me?"

"I don't play well with others."

Artie made a show of walking in a complete circle around me, checking me out. This wasn't going down as easy as I'd hoped.

"Brave man, to come in here all by yourself."

"My partner's outside."

"Partner, huh? Let's say, for the sake of argument, I had my boys kill you. What would your partner do? Come running into my place, guns blazing?"

He chuckled, and the two goons in the room with us giggled like stoned teenagers.

"No. He'd put the word out on the street that you're a liar. Then the next time you need a little favor from the outside, your reputation as a square guy would be sullied."

"Sullied!" Artie laughed again. He had a laugh like a frog. "That's rich. Would you work for a man with a sullied reputation, Jimmy?"

The thug named Jimmy shrugged, wisely choosing not to answer.

"You're right, of course." Artie said when the chuckles faded. "I have a good rep in this town, and my word is bond. Max."

The other thug handed me a briefcase. Leather. A good weight.

"There was supposed to be a bonus for making it messy."

"Oh, it's in there, my friend. I'm sure you'll be quite pleased. You can count it, if you like."

I shook my head.

"I trust you."

I turned to walk out, but Artie's men stayed in front of the door.

If Artie was more psychotic than I guessed, he could easily kill me right there, and I couldn't do a damn thing to stop him. I lied about having a partner, and the line about his street rep was just ego stroking.

I braced myself, deciding to go for the guy on the left first.

"One more thing, Mystery Man," Artie said to my back. "You wouldn't have made any copies of that ledger, maybe to try and grease me for more money sometime in the future?"

I turned around, gave Artie my cold stare.

"You think I would mess with you?"

His eyes drilled into me. They no longer held any amusement. They were the dark, hard eyes of a man who has killed many people, who has done awful things.

But I'd done some awful things, too. And I made sure he saw it in me.

"No," Artie finally decided. "No, you wouldn't mess with me."

I tilted my head, slightly.

"A pleasure doing business with you, Mr. Collins."

The thugs parted, and I walked out the door.

When I got a safe distance away, I counted the money.

Fifteen thousand bucks.

I dropped by Manny's, spent two gees on coke, and did a few lines.

The pain in my side became a dim memory.

Unlike pills, cocaine took away the pain and let me keep my edge.

These days, my edge was all I had.

I didn't have to wait for someone to leave Buster's apartment this time; he buzzed me in.

"Jazz is in the shower," he told me.

"Did you dump the bag?"

"In the river, like you told me. And I mailed out those photocopies to the cop with the alcohol name."

He gave me a beer, and Jasmine walked into the living room, wrapped in a towel. Her face and collarbone were still stained red from the stage blood.

"What now?" she asked.

"You're dead. Get the hell out of town."

I handed her a bag filled with five thousand dollars. She looked inside, then showed it to Buster.

"Jesus!" Buster yelped. "Thanks, man!"

Jasmine raised an eyebrow at me. "Why are you doing this?"

"If you're seen around here, Artie will know I lied. He won't be pleased. Take this and go back home. Your parents are looking for you."

Jasmine's voice was small. The voice of a teenager, not a strung-out street whore.

"Thank you."

"Since you're so grateful, you can do me one a small favor."

"Anything."

"Your friend. Ajax. I think she wants out of the life. Take her with you."

"You got it, Buddy!" Buster pumped my hand, grinning ear to ear. "Why don't you hang out for a while? We'll tilt a few."

"Thanks, but I have some things to do."

Jasmine stood on her tiptoes, gave me a wet peck on the cheek. Then she whispered in my ear.

"You could have killed me, kept it all. Why didn't you?"

She didn't get it, but that was okay. Most people went through their whole lives without ever realizing how precious life was. Jasmine didn't understand that.

But someday she might.

"I don't kill people for money," I told her instead.

Then I left.

All things considered, I did pretty good. The blood, latex scars, and fake knife cost less than a hundred bucks. Pizza and beer for Jack came out to fifty. The money I gave to Ajax wasn't mine in the first place, and I already owned the master keys, the badge, and the Polaroid camera.

The cash would keep me in drugs for a while.

It might even take me up until the very end.

As for Artie Collins…word on the street, his bosses weren't happy about his arrest. Artie wasn't going to last very long in prison.

I did another line and laid back on my bed, letting the exhilaration wash over me. It took away the pain.

All the pain.

Outside my window, the city sounds invaded. Honking horns. Screeching tires. A man coughing. A woman shouting. The el train rushing past, clackety-clacking down the tracks louder than a thunder clap.

To most people, it was background noise.

But to me, it was music.

The One that Got Away

Brilliance Audio does the books on tape for the Jack series, and every year they let me read an extra short story to include with the audio version. Sort of like a DVD bonus. This was included on the audio of Whiskey Sour. *I thought it would be interesting to revisit the Gingerbread Man, the villain from that book, through the point-of-view of a victim.*

A STEEL CROSSBEAM, FLAKING brown paint.

Stained PVC pipes.

White and green wires hanging on nails.

What she sees.

Moni blinks, yawns, tries to turn onto her side.

Can't.

The memory comes, jolting.

Rainy, after midnight, huddling under an overpass. Trying to keep warm in hot pants and a halter top. Rent money overdue. Not a single john in sight.

When the first car stopped, Moni would have tricked for free just to get inside and warm up.

Didn't have to, though. The guy flashed a big roll of twenties. Talked smooth, educated. Smiled a lot.

But there was something wrong with his eyes. Something dead.

Freak eyes.

Moni didn't do freaks. She'd made the mistake once, got hurt bad. Freaks weren't out for sex. They were out for pain. And Moni, bad as she needed money, wasn't going to take a beating for it.

She reached around, felt for the door handle to get out.

No handle.

Mace in her tiny purse, buried in condoms. She reached for it, but the needle found her arm and then everything went blurry.

And now…

Moni blinks, tries to clear her head. The floor under her is cold. Concrete.

She's in a basement. Staring up at the unfinished ceiling.

Moni tries to sit up, but her arms don't move. They're bound with twine, bound to steel rods set into the floor. She raises her head, sees her feet are also tied, legs apart.

Her clothes are gone.

Moni feels a scream building inside her, forces it back down. Forces herself to think.

She takes in her surroundings. It's bright, brighter than a basement should be. Two big lights on stands point down at her.

Between them is a tripod. A camcorder.

Next to the tripod, a table. Moni can see several knives on top. A hammer. A drill. A blowtorch. A cleaver.

The cleaver is caked with little brown bits, and something else.

Hair. Long, pink hair.

Moni screams.

Charlene has long pink hair. Charlene, who's been missing for a week.

Street talk was she'd gone straight, quit the life.

Street talk was wrong.

Moni screams until her lungs burn. Until her throat is raw. She twists and pulls and yanks, crying to get free, panic overriding the pain of the twine rubbing her wrists raw.

The twine doesn't budge.

Moni leans to the right, stretching her neck, trying to reach the twine with her teeth.

Not even close. But as she tries, she notices the stains on the floor beneath her. Sticky brown stains that smell like meat gone bad.

Charlene's blood.

Moni's breath catches. Her gaze drifts to the table again, even though she doesn't want to look, doesn't want to see what this freak is going to use on her.

"I'm dead," she thinks. "And it's gonna be bad."

Moni doesn't like herself. Hasn't for a while. It's tough to find self-respect when one does the things she does for money. But even though she ruined her life with drugs, even though she hates the twenty-dollar-a-pop whore she's become, Moni doesn't want to die.

Not yet.

And not like this.

Moni closes her eyes. She breathes in. Breathes out. Wills her muscles to relax.

"I hope you didn't pass out."

Every muscle in Moni's body contracts in shock. The freak is looking down at her, smiling.

He'd been standing right behind Moni the whole time. Out of her line of sight.

"Please let me go."

His laugh is an evil thing. She knows, looking at his eyes, he won't cut her free until her heart has stopped.

"Keep begging. I like it. I like the begging almost as much as I like the screaming."

He walks around her, over to the table. Takes his time fondling his tools.

"What should we start with? I'll let you pick."

Moni doesn't answer. She thinks back to when she was a child, before all of the bad stuff in her life happened, before hope was just another four-letter word. She remembers the little girl she used to be, bright and full of energy, wanting to grow up and be a lawyer like all of those fancy-dressed women on TV.

"If I get through this," Moni promises God, "I'll quit the street and go back to school. I swear."

"Are you praying?" The freak grins. He's got the blowtorch in his hand. "God doesn't answer prayers here."

He fiddles with the camcorder, then kneels between her open legs. The torch ignites with the strike of a match. It's the shape of a small fire extinguisher. The blue flame shooting from the nozzle hisses like a leaky tire.

"I won't lie to you. This is going to hurt. A lot. But it smells delicious. Just like cooking bacon."

Moni wonders how she can possibly brace herself for the oncoming pain, and realizes that she can't. There's nothing she can do. All of the mistakes, all of the bad choices, have led up to this sick final moment in her life, being burned alive in some psycho's basement.

She clenches her teeth, squeezes her eyes shut.

A bell chimes.

"Dammit."

The freak pauses, the flame a foot away from her thighs.

The bell chimes again. A doorbell, coming from upstairs.

Moni begins to cry out, but he guesses her intent, bringing his fist down hard onto her face.

Moni sees blurry motes, tastes blood. A moment later he's shoving something in her mouth. Her halter top, wedging it in so far it sticks to the back of her throat.

"Be right back, bitch. The Fed-Ex guy is bringing me something for you."

The freak walks off, up the stairs, out of sight.

Moni tries to scream, choking on the cloth. She shakes and pulls and bucks but there's no release from the twine and the gag won't come out and any second he'll be coming back down the stairs to use that awful blowtorch…

The blowtorch.

Moni stops struggling. Listens for the hissing sound.

It's behind her.

She twists, cranes her neck around, sees the torch sitting on the floor only a few inches from her head.

It's still on.

Moni scoots her body toward it. Strains against the ropes. Stretches her limbs to the limit.

The top of her head touches the steel canister.

Moni's unsure of how much time she has, unsure if this will work, knowing she has less than a one-in-a-zillion chance but she has to try something and maybe dear god just maybe this will work.

She cocks her head back and snaps it against the blowtorch. The torch teeters, falls onto its side, and begins a slow, agonizing roll over to her right hand.

"Please," Moni begs the universe. "Please."

The torch rolls close–too close–the flame brushing Moni's arm and the horrible heat singeing hair and burning skin.

Moni screams into her gag, jerks her elbow, tries to force the searing flame closer to the rope.

The pain blinds her, takes her to a place beyond sensation, where her only thought, her only goal, is to make it stop make it stop MAKE IT STOP!

Her arm is suddenly loose.

Moni grabs the blowtorch, ignoring the burning twine that's still wrapped tightly around her wrist. She points the flame at her left hand, severs the rope. Then her feet.

She's free!

No time to dress. No time to hide. Up the stairs, two at a time, ready to dive out of a window naked and screaming and–

"What the hell?"

The freak is at the top of the stairs, pulling a wicked-looking hunting knife out of a cardboard box. He notices Moni and confusion registers on his face.

It quickly morphs into rage.

Moni doesn't hesitate, bringing the blowtorch around, swinging it like a club, connecting hard with the side of the freak's head, and then he's falling forward, past her, arms pinwheeling as he dives face-first into the stairs.

Moni continues to run, up into the house, looking left and right, finding the front door, reaching for the knob…

And pauses.

The freak took a hard fall, but he might still be alive.

There will be other girls. Other girls in his basement.

Girls like Charlene.

Cops don't help whores. Cops don't care.

But Moni does.

Next to the front door is the living room. A couch. Curtains. A throw rug.

Moni picks up the rug, wraps it around her body. Using the torch, she sets the couch ablaze, the curtains on fire, before throwing it onto the floor and running out into the street.

It's early morning. The sidewalk is cold under her bare feet. She's shaken, and her burned arm throbs, but she feels lighter than air.

A car stops.

A john, cruising. Rolls down the window and asks if she's for sale.

"Not anymore," Moni says.
She walks away, not looking back.

With a Twist

Another locked room mystery, this one even more complicated. What's fun about Jack is that I can put her in different sub genres without changing her character. She can function as Sherlock Holmes, or Spenser, or Kay Scarpetta, depending on the story. This won 2nd place in the Ellery Queen *Reader's Choice Contest.*

"HIS SKULL IS SHATTERED, and his spinal column looks like a Dutch pretzel." Phil Blasky straightened from his crouch and locked eyes with me, his expression neutral. "This man has fallen from a great height."

I glanced up from my notepad, not having written a word. "You're positive?"

"I've autopsied enough jumpers in my tenure as ME to know a pancake when I see one, Jack."

I stared at the body, arms and legs akimbo, splayed out on a living room carpet damp with bodily fluids. On impulse I looked up, focusing on a ceiling that couldn't be any higher than eight feet.

"Maybe he jumped off the couch." This from my partner, Detective First Class Herb Benedict. His left hand scratched his expansive stomach, his light blue shirt dotted with mustard stains. It was 11am, so how the mustard got there was anybody's guess.

I frowned at Herb, then located a patch of dry beige carpeting and knelt next to the corpse, careful not to stain my heels or pants. The victim was named Edward Wyatt, and this was his house. He was Caucasian, 67 years old, and as dead as dead can be. The smell wasn't too bad—this was a fresh one—but the wake would definitely be a closed casket.

"What do you make of the blood spatters, Phil?"

"Unremarkable star-configuration, arcing away from the nexus of the body in all directions. Droplets coating the walls and ceiling. Notice the double pattern—see the large spot here, next to the body? It has it's own larger radius of spatters."

"Meaning?"

"Meaning he bounced once, when he hit the carpet. Consistent with jumpers, leaving a primary then a secondary spatter."

Benedict cleared his throat. "You're telling us this is authentic? That he fell five stories into a living room?"

"I'm telling you it looks that way."

I've been with the Chicago Police Department for twenty years, half of those with the Violent Crimes unit, and have seen a few things. But this was flat-out weird. I almost ordered my team to do a house sweep for Rod Serling.

"Could somebody have dumped him here? After he died someplace else?"

"That seems reasonable, but I don't notice any tissue or fluid missing. If he were scraped off the street, there would be blood left behind. If anything, there's too much blood in this room."

I would have asked how it was possible for him to know that, but Phil knew more about dead people than Mick Jagger knew about rock and roll.

"Also," Phil motioned us closer, "take a look at this."

He crouched, holding some tweezers, and used a gloved hand to gently lift the corpse's head. After some prodding and poking, he removed a small fiber.

"Beige carpeting, deeply embedded in his flesh. The deceased has hundreds of these fibers in the skin, consistent with..."

I finished the sentence for him. "...falling from a great height."

"However improbable it seems. It's as if someone took off the roof, and he jumped out of a plane and landed in his living room. And don't forget about the doors."

I felt a headache coming on. The house had two entry points, the front door and the rear door. Each had been dead-bolted from the inside—no outside entry was possible. The locks were privacy locks, similar to the ones on hotel rooms; there were no keyholes, just a latch. The first officers on the scene had to break through a window to get in; the windows had all been locked from the inside.

"Lt. Daniels?" A uniform, name of Perez, motioned me over to a corner of the room. "There's a note."

I watched my step, making my way to the room-length book shelf, crammed full of several hundred paperbacks. Their spines were splashed with blood, but I could make out some authors: Carr, Chandler, Chesterton. Perez pointed to a pristine sheet of white typing paper, tacked to the shelf between Sladek and Stout. The handwriting on it was done in black marker. I snugged on a pair of latex gloves I keep in my blazer pocket, and picked up the note.

God doesn't understand. Eternal peace I desire. The only way out is death. Answers come to those who seek. Can't get through another day. Let me rest. Until we meet in heaven. Edward.

I pondered the message for a moment, then returned to Benedict and Blasky.

"What about a steamroller?" Herb was asking. "That would crush a body, right?"

"It wouldn't explain the spatters. Also, unless there's a steamroller in the closet, I don't see how…"

I interrupted. "I'm looking around, Herb. When the techies get here, I want video of everything."

"That a suicide note?" Herb pointed his chin at the paper I held.

"Yeah. Strange, though. Take a peek and let me know if you spot the anomaly."

"Anomaly? You've been watching too many of those cop shows on TV."

I winked at him. "I'll let you know if I find the steamroller."

Notebook in hand, I went to explore the house. It was a modest two bedroom split-level, in a good neighborhood on the upper north side. Nine-one-one had gotten an anonymous call from a nearby payphone, someone stating that he'd walked past the house and smelled a horrible stench. The officers who caught the call claimed to hear gunshots, and entered through a window. They discovered the body, but found no evidence of any gun or shooter.

I checked the back door again. Still locked, the deadbolt in place. The door was old, its white paint fading, contrast to the new decorative trim around the frame.

I checked the linoleum floor and found it clean, polished, pristine.

Running my finger along the door frame, I picked up dust, dirt, and some white powder. I sniffed. Plaster. The hinges were solid, tarnished with age. The knob was heavy brass, and the deadbolt shiny steel. Both in perfect working order.

I turned the deadbolt and opened the door. It must have been warped with age, because it only opened 3/4 of the way and then rubbed against the kitchen floor. I walked outside.

The backyard consisted of a well-kept vegetable garden and twelve tall bushes that lined the perimeter fence, offering privacy from the neighbors. I examined the outside of the door and found nothing unusual. The door frame had trim that matched the interior. The porch was clean. I knelt on the welcome mat and examined the strike panel and the lock mechanisms. Both were solid, normal.

I stood, brushed some sawdust from my knee, and went back into the house.

The windows seemed normal, untampered with. There was broken glass on the floor by the window where the uniforms had entered. Other than being shattered, it also appeared normal.

The front door was unlocked; after breaching the residence through the window, the uniforms had opened the door to let the rest of the crew inside. I examined the door, and didn't find anything unusual.

The kitchen was small, tidy. A Dell puzzle magazine rested on the table, next to the salt and pepper. Another sat by the sink. The dishwasher contained eight clean mason jars, with lids, and a turkey baster. Nothing else. No garbage in the garbage can. The refrigerator was empty except for a box of baking soda. The freezer contained three full trays of ice cubes.

I checked cabinets, found a few glasses and dishes, but no food. The drawers held silverware, some dishtowels, and a full box of Swedish Fish cherry gummy candy.

I left the kitchen for the den, sat at the late Edward Wyatt's desk, and inched my way through it. There was a bankbook for a savings account. It held $188,679.42—up until last month when the account had been emptied out.

I kept digging and found a file full of receipts dating back ten years. Last month, the victim had apparently toured Europe, staying in London, Paris, Rome, and Berlin. Bills for fancy restaurants abounded. The most recent purchases included several hundred dollars at a local hardware store, a dinner for two at the 95th Floor that cost over six-hundred dollars, a one week stay at the Four Seasons hotel in Chicago, a digital video recorder and an expensive new stereo, and a bill for wall-to-wall carpeting; the beige shag Mr. Wyatt was currently staining had been installed last month.

I also found several grocery lists, and the handwriting seemed to match the handwriting on the suicide note.

Next to the desk, on a cabinet, sat a Chicago phonebook. It was open to BURGLAR ALARMS.

The den also had a cabinet which contained some games (Monopoly, chess, Clue, backgammon) and jigsaw puzzles, including an old Rubik's Cube. I remember solving mine, back in the 1980s, by pulling the stickers off the sides. This one had also been solved, and the stickers appeared intact.

I left the den and found the door to the basement. It was small, unfinished. The floor was bare concrete, and a florescent lamp attached to an overhead beam provided adequate light. A utility sink sat in a corner, next to a washer and dryer. On the other side was a workbench, clean and tidy. The drawers contained the average assortment of hand tools; wrenches, hammers, screwdrivers, saws, chisels. Atop the workbench was an electric reciprocating saw that looked practically new.

A closet was tucked away in the corner. Inside I found an old volleyball net, a large roll of carpet padding, a croquet set, some scraps of decorative trim, and half a can of blue paint. Also, hanging on a makeshift rack, were three badminton rackets, an extra-large super-soaker squirt gun, and a plastic lawn chair.

After snooping until there was nothing left to snoop, I met Herb back in the living room.

"Find anything?" Herb asked.

I described through my search, ending with the Swedish Fish.

"That was the only food?" Herb asked.

"Seems to be."

"Are we taking it as evidence?"

"I'm not sure yet. Why?"

"I love Swedish Fish."

"If I poured chocolate syrup on the corpse, would you eat that too?"

"You found chocolate syrup?"

I switched gears. "You figure out the note?"

Herb smiled. "Yeah. Funny how the note is perfectly clean when everything around it, and behind it, is soaked in blood."

"Find anything else?"

"I tossed the bedrooms upstairs, found some basics; clothes, shoes, linen. Bathroom contained bathroom stuff; towels, toiletries, a lot of puzzle magazines. Another bookshelf—non-fiction this time. Some prescription meds in the cabinet." Benedict checked his pad. "Diflucan, Abarelix, Taxotere, and Docetexel."

"Cancer drugs," Phil Blasky said. He held Wyatt's right arm. "That explains this plastic catheter implanted in his vein and this rash on his neck. This man has been on long term chemotherapy."

A picture began to form in my head, but I didn't have all the pieces yet.

"Herb, did you find any religious paraphernalia? Bibles, crucifixes, prayer books, things like that?"

"No. There were some books upstairs, but mostly philosophy and logic puzzles. In fact, there was a whole shelf dedicated to Free-Thinking."

"As opposed to thinking that costs money?"

"That's a term atheists use."

Curiouser and curiouser.

"I found receipts for a new stereo and camcorder. Were they upstairs?" I asked.

"The stereo was, set-up in the bedroom next to that big bay window. I didn't see any camcorders."

"Let me see that note again."

The suicide letter had been placed in a clear plastic bag. I read it twice, then had to laugh. "Quite a few religious references for a Free-Thinker."

"If he was dying of cancer, maybe he found God."

"Or maybe he found a way to die on his terms."

"Meaning?"

"The terms of a man who loved mysteries, games, and puzzles. Look at the first letter of each sentence."

Herb read silently, his lips moving. "G-E-T-A-C-L-U-E. Cute. You know, I became a cop because it required very little lateral thinking."

"I thought it was because vendors gave you free donuts."

"Shhh. Hold on…I'm forming a hypothesis."

"I'll alert the media."

Phil Blasky snorted. "You guys have a drink minimum for this show?"

Herb ignored us. "Wyatt obviously had some help, because the note was placed on top of the blood. But was his help in the form of assisted suicide? Or murder?"

"It doesn't matter to us—they're treated the same way."

"Exactly. So if this is a game for us to figure out, and the clues have been staged, will the clues lead us to what really happened, or to what Wyatt or the killer would like us to believe really happened?"

The word 'game' made me remember the cabinet in the den. I returned to it, finding the Parker Brothers classic board game, Clue. Inside the box, instead of cards, pieces, and a game board, was a cryptogram magazine.

"I'm going out to the car to get my deermilker cap," Herb said.

"It's deerstalker. While you're out there, call the Irregulars."

I removed the magazine and flipped through it, noting that all of the puzzles had been solved. Nothing else appeared unusual. I went through it again, slower, and noticed that page 20 had been circled.

"Herb, grab all puzzle magazines you can find. I'll meet you back here in five."

I did a quick search of the first floor and gathered up eight magazines. Each had a different page number circled. Herb waddled down the stairs a moment later.

"I've got twelve of them."

"Did he circle page numbers?"

"Yeah."

We took the magazines over to the dining room table and spread them out. Herb made a list of the page number circled in each issue.

"Let's try chronological order," I said. "The earliest issue is February of last year. Write down the page numbers beginning with that one."

I watched Herb jot down 7, 19, 22, 14, 26, 13, 4, 19, 12, 16, 13, 22, 4, 7, 12, 12, 14, 6, 24, and 19.

Herb rubbed his mustache. "No number higher than twenty-six.

Could be an alphabet code." He hummed the alphabet, stopping at the seventh letter. "Number seven is G."

"Yeah, but nineteen is S and twenty-two is V. What word starts with GSV?"

"Maybe it's reverse chronological order. Start with the latest magazine."

I did some quick calculating. "That would be SXF. Not too many words begin like that."

"Are you hungry? I'm getting hungry."

"We'll eat after we figure this out."

"How about reverse alphabet code? Z is one, Y is two, and so on."

I couldn't do that in my head, and had to write down the alphabet and match up letters to numbers. Then I began to decode.

"You nailed it, Herb. The message is T-H-E-M-A-N-W-H-O-K-N-E-W-T-O-O-M-U-C-H. The Man Who Knew Too Much."

"That Hitchcock movie. Maybe he's got a copy lying around."

We searched, and didn't find a single video or DVD. My hands were pruning in the latex gloves. I snapped the gloves off and stuffed them in my pocket. The air felt good.

"Was it based off a book?" Herb asked. "The guy's got plenty of books."

"Could have been. Let me ask the expert." I pulled out my cell and called the smartest mystery expert I knew; my mother.

"Jacqueline! I'm so happy to hear from you. It's about time I get out of bed."

I felt a pang of alarm. "Mom, it's almost noon. Are you okay?"

"I'm fine, dear."

"But you've been alone in bed all day…"

"Did I say I was alone?" There was a slapping sound, and my mother said, "Behave, it's my daughter."

I felt myself flush, but worked through it.

"Mom, do you remember that old Hitchcock movie? The Man Who Knew Too Much?"

"The Leslie Banks original, or the Jimmy Stewart remake?"

"Either. Was it based off a book?"

"Not that I'm aware of. I can check, if you like. I have both versions."

"Can you? It's important."

Herb nudged me. "Can I have that Swedish Fish candy?"

I nodded, and Herb waddled off.

"Jacqueline? On the Leslie Banks version, the back of the box lists the screenwriter, but doesn't mention it is based on a book. And…neither does the Jimmy Stewart version."

Damn.

"Can you give me the screenwriter's name?"

"Two folks, Charles Bennett and D.B. Wyndham-Lewis. Why is this so important?"

"It's a case. I'll tell you about it later. I was hoping The Man Who Knew Too Much was a book."

"It is a book. By G.K. Chesterton, written in the early 1920s. But that had nothing to do with the movie."

"Chesterton? Thanks, Mom."

"Chesterton was a wonderful author. He did quite a few locked-room mysteries. Not too many writers do those anymore."

"I'll call you tonight. Be good."

"I most certainly won't."

I put away the phone and went to the blood-stained bookshelf. The Chesterton book was easy to find. I put the gloves back on and picked it up. Wedged between pages sixty-two and sixty-three was a thin, plastic flash video card, a recent technology that was used instead of film in digital video cameras. And camcorders…

I met Herb in the kitchen. He had his mouth full of red gummy candy. I held up my prize.

"I found a video card."

Herb said something that might have been, "Really?" but I couldn't be sure with his teeth glued together.

"Is your new laptop in your car?"

He nodded, chewing.

"Do you have a card reader?"

He nodded again, shoving the candy box into his pants pocket and easing though the back door.

Two minutes later Herb's laptop was booting up. I pushed the flash card into his reader slot, and the appropriate program opened the file and began to play the contents.

On Herb's screen, a very-much-alive Edward Wyatt smiled at us.

"Hello," the dead man said. "Congratulations on reaching this point. I thought it fitting, having spent my life enjoying puzzles, to end my life with a puzzle as well. Though I commend you for your brainpower thus far, I regret to say that this video won't be providing you with any clues as to how this seemingly impossible act was committed. But I will say it has been done of my own, free will. My oncologist has given me less than a month to live, and I'm afraid it won't be a pleasant month. I've chosen to end things early."

"Pause it," I said.

Herb pressed a button. "What?"

"Go back just a few frames, in slow motion."

Herb did. I pointed at the screen. "See that? The camera moved. Someone's holding it."

Herb nodded. "Assisted suicide. I wonder if he moved the camera on purpose, to let us know he had help."

"Let it finish playing."

Herb hit a button, and Wyatt began again.

"Undoubtedly, by this point you know I've had help."

Benedict and I exchanged a look.

"Of course," Wyatt continued, "I wouldn't want to put my helper in any legal jeopardy. This friend graciously helped me fulfill my last wish, and I'd hate for this special person to be arrested for what is entirely my idea, my wishes, my decision, and my fault. But I also know a little about how the law works, and I know this person might indeed become a target of Chicago's finest. Steps have been taken to make sure this person is never found. These steps are already in motion."

Herb paused the recording and looked at me. "I'm fine stopping right here. He says it was suicide, I believe him, let's clear the case and grab a bite to eat."

I folded my arms. "You're kidding. How did the body get inside when everything was locked? How could he have jumped to his death in his living room? Who's the helper? Don't you want answers to these questions?"

"Not really. I don't like mysteries."

"You're fired."

Herb ignored me. I fire him several times a week. He let the recording play.

"However," Wyatt went on, "all good mysteries have a sense of closure. With me dead, and my helper gone, how will you know if you've figured out everything? There's a way. If you're a sharpie, and you've found all the clues, there will be confirmation. Good luck. And don't be discouraged…this is, after all, supposed to be fun."

Benedict snorted his opinion on the matter. The recording ended, and I closed my eyes in thought.

"Herb—the stereo upstairs. Was it on or off?"

"Off."

"Fully off? Or on standby?"

"I'll check."

Benedict wandered out of the kitchen, and I went back into the basement. I found a hammer in the workbench drawer and brought it to the back door. Once again, when I opened the door, it caught on the linoleum flooring. The floor remained shiny, even where the door touched it.

The lack of scuff marks struck me as a pretty decent clue.

Since the door looked old, but the decorative trim around the frame appear new, I decided to remove a section of trim. After a full thirty seconds of searching for a nail to pull, I realized there were no nails holding the trim on.

How interesting.

Using the claw end of the hammer, I wedged off a piece of side trim. And in doing so, I solved the locked-room part of the mystery.

Three gunshots exploded from the floor above, shattering my smugness. I tugged my .38 from my shoulder holster and sprinted up the stairs, flanked by Perez.

"Herb!"

Three more gunshots, impossibly loud. Coming from the room at the end of the hall. I crouched in the doorway, my pistol coming up.

"Jack! All clear!" Herb stood by the stereo, a CD clutched in one hand, the other grasping his chest. "Damn, you almost gave me a heart attack."

I put two and two together quickly enough, but Officer Henry Perez wasn't endowed with the same preternatural detecting abilities.

"Where's the gun?" he croaked, arms and legs locked in full Weaver stance. "Who's got the gun?"

"Easy, Officer." I put a hand on his elbow and eased his arms down. "There is no gun."

Perez's face wrinkled up. "No gun? That sounded just like…"

Herb finished his sentence, "…the gunshots you heard when you arrived on the scene. I know. It's all right here."

Herb held up the CD.

"It's a recording of gunshots," I told Perez. "It was used to get you to break into the house. Probable cause. Or else you never would have gone in—the 911 call talked about a bad smell, but the corpse is fresh and there is no smell."

Perez seemed reluctant to holster his weapon. I ignored him, holding out my hand for the CD. It was a Maxell recordable CD-R. On the front, in written black marker, was the number 209. I held the disc up to the light, checking for prints. It looked clean.

"Maybe this is one of those clues the dear, departed Edward Wyatt mentioned in his video." Herb said. "You ready to get some lunch?"

"I figured out how the doors were locked from the inside," I said.

We went downstairs and I showed Herb the fruits of my labors, prying off another piece of trim.

"Smart. What made you think of it, Jack?"

"The trim is glued on, rather than nailed. Which made me wonder why, and what it covered up."

"Impressive, Oh Great One. Did you also happen to notice the number?"

"What number?"

"Written on the back of the trim, in black marker." Herb pointed at the number 847.

"What did Wyatt say in his recording? About being a sharpie? What's the most popular black marker?"

"A Sharpie." Herb grunted his disapproval. "Wyatt's lucky he's dead, because if he were still alive I'd smack him around for making us jump through these hoops."

"Are you saying you'd rather be interviewing a domestic battery?"

"I'm saying my brain hurts. I'm going to need to watch a few hours of prime time to dumb myself back down. Isn't that reality show on tonight? The one where the seven contestants eat live bugs on a tropical island to marry a millionaire who's really a janitor? My IQ drops ten points each time I watch that show."

I stared at the black marker writing. "Eight four seven is a local area code. The two zero nine could be a prefix."

"Almost a phone number. Maybe there's another clue with the last four digits."

We went back to the game of Clue, but nothing was written on or inside the box. Another ten minutes were wasted going through the pile of puzzle magazines.

"Okay, what have we figured out so far?" I said, thinking out loud. "We figured out the gunshots that brought us to the scene, and we figured out the locked room part. But we still don't know how he fell to his death in the living room."

"He must have jumped off a building somewhere else, and then his partner brought the body here and staged the scene."

I rubbed my eyes, getting a smudge of eyeliner on my gloves.

"It's a damn good staging. ME said the blood spatters indicate he fell into that room. Plus there are carpet fibers embedded in his face."

"Maybe," Herb got a gleam in his eye, "he jumped onto that carpet at another location, then both the carpet and the body were put back into the room."

"The entire living room is carpeted, Herb."

"Maybe the helper cut out a section, then put it back in."

We went back into the living room, wound plastic food wrap around our shoes and pants, and spent half an hour crawling over the damp carpet, looking for seams that meant it had been cut out. It was a dead end.

"Damn it." Herb stripped off some bloody cling wrap. "I was sure that's how he did it."

I shrugged. My neck hurt from being on all fours, and some of the blood had gotten through the plastic and stained my pants. "Maybe the fibers embedded in the body won't match the fibers from this carpet."

Herb sighed. "And maybe the blood found squirted all over the room won't match, either. But we both know that everything will match. This guy was so meticulous…"

"Hold it! You said 'squirted.'"

"It's a perfectly good word."

"I think I know why the living room looks that way. Come into the kitchen."

I opened the dishwasher, showing Herb the mason jars and turkey baster. Herb remained dubious.

"That turkey baster wouldn't work. Not powerful enough."

"But what about one of those air-pump squirt guns? The kind that holds a gallon of water, and can shoot a stream twenty feet?"

I led Herb into the basement closet, holding up the squirt gun I'd seen earlier. Written on the handle, in black marker, was the word 'Charlie.'"

"Okay, so we've got two three-digit numbers, and a name. Now what? We still don't know how the fibers got embedded in the victim."

Herb rubbed his chin, thinking or doing a fair imitation of it. "Maybe the helper embedded the fibers by hand after death?"

"Phil would have caught that. I think Wyatt actually leapt to his death and landed on carpeting."

"I've got it," Herb said. He explained.

"Herb, that's perfect! But there's no way you can put black marker on something that isn't here. What else do we have?

"Got me. That revelation taxed my mental abilities for the month."

"The only other obvious clue is the Swedish Fish candy."

Herb pulled the box out of his pocket. The package, and contents, seemed normal. So normal that Herb ate another handful.

I racked my brain, trying to find something we'd missed. So far, all the clues made sense except for that damn candy.

"I'm going back upstairs," Herb said. "Want to order a pizza?"

"You're kidding."

"I'm not kidding. I have to eat something. We might be here for the rest of our lives."

"Herb, you can't have a pizza delivered to a crime scene."

"How about Chinese food? I haven't had Mu Shu Pork since Thursday. You want anything?"

"No."

"You sure?"

"I'm sure."

"You're not getting any of mine."

"Get me a small order of beef with pea pods."

"That sounds good. How about a large order and we split it?"

"What about the Mu Shu pork?"

Herb patted his expansive belly. "I'll get that too. You think I got this fat just looking at food?" He turned, heading for the stairs. "Where's Wyatt's phone book?"

"It's on his desk." Insight struck. "Herb! That might be another clue!"

"Chinese food?"

"The phone book! It's open to a page."

I squeezed past my portly partner and raced up the stairs. The phone book was where I left it, BURGLAR ALARMS covering the left-hand page. I went through each of the listings, put there was no black marker. I checked the other page, and didn't see anything unusual. But on the very top of the right hand page was spillover from the previous entry. A listing called CHARLIE'S, with the phone number 847-209-7219.

When I noted what subject came alphabetically before BURGLAR ALARMS in the phonebook, I grinned like an idiot. Then I pulled out my cell and called the number. After four rings and a click, a male voice answered.

"This is Charlie."

"This is Lieutenant Jack Daniels of the Chicago Police Department."

"That was fast. Edward would have been pleased."

"You helped murder him?"

"No. He killed himself. I helped set up all of the other stuff, but I had nothing to do with killing him. I've got proof, too. Footage of him jumping to his death."

"Off of your crane. Or platform. What is it you use?"

"A hundred foot platform. He went quick—in less than four seconds. He preferred it to the agony of cancer."

Herb sidled up to me, putting his ear next to the phone.

"How did Wyatt find you?" I asked Charlie.

"The want ads. He saw I was selling my business. I guess that's how he came up with this whole idea. Pretty clever, don't you think? He bought me out, plus paid me to assist in setting up the scene. Nice guy. I liked him a lot."

"You know, of course, we'll have to arrest you."

"I know. Which is why my office phone forwarded this call to my cell. I'm on my way out of the country. Edward paid me enough to lay low for a while."

"One hundred and eighty-eight thousand dollars." I remembered the number from the empty bank account.

"No, not nearly. Edward lived very well for the last month of his life. He spent a lot of money. And good for him—what good is a life savings if you can't have some fun with it?"

"Not much," Herb said.

I shushed him.

"Can I assume, Lieutenant, that you've figured everything out? Found all the clues? If you know everything, I'm supposed to give you a reward. Edward has this list of questions. Are you ready?"

Not knowing what else to say, I agreed.

"Okay, question number one; how were the doors locked from the inside?"

"You removed the entire door and frame while the door was already locked. Edward, or you, used a reciprocating saw to cut around the door frame. Then one of you glued new trim to the inside of the frame. When the door was pulled back into place, the trim covered the inside cut marks. Then you nailed the frame in place from the outside, and put more trim around the edges to cover the outside cut."

"What gave it away?"

"Sawdust on the outside matt, a receipt from the hardware store, a new electric saw in the basement, and extra trim in the closet. Plus, the door didn't open all the way."

"Edward purposely left all the clues except that last one. The door was heavy, and I couldn't fit it back in the hole perfectly. Question number two; how did it appear Edward jumped to his death in his living room?"

"He'd been drawing his own blood for a few weeks, using the catheter in his arm, and saving it in the refrigerator in mason jars. Then he used a turkey baster to fill a super soaker squirt gun with his blood, and sprayed the living room. I assume he read enough mysteries to know how to mimic blood spatters. He even faked the bounce that happens when a jumper hits."

"Excellent. How did the carpet fibers get on the body?"

"He visited Charlie's Bungee Jumping Emporium in Palatine and did a swan dive onto a pile of carpet remainders. We found carpet padding in the basement, but no remainders, and usually the installers give you all the extra pieces. A clue by omission."

"Very good. Question number three; where did the gunshots come from?"

"The stereo upstairs. That was also a new purchase. The stereo faced the window, so you must have hit the PLAY button from the street, using the remote."

"I did. The remote is in a garbage can next to the payphone I called from, if anyone wants it back. Did you find anything else interesting?"

I explained the suicide note, the Clue game, and the puzzle magazines.

"How about the Swedish Fish candy?" he asked.

"We have no idea what that means."

"That was Edward's favorite clue. I'd tell you, but I'm sure you'll figure it out eventually. Anyway, there's a surprise for you in John Dickson Carr's book The Three Coffins. Don't bother calling me back—I'm throwing away this phone as soon as I hang up. Goodbye, Lieutenant."

And he was gone.

We found the Carr book without difficulty. In the pages were a folded cashier's check, and another flash card. We played the card on Herb's computer.

Edward Wyatt, standing atop a large bungee platform, smiled at the camera, winked, and said, "Congratulations on figuring it out. In order to make absolutely, positively sure that there's no doubt I'm doing this of my own free will, without assistance or coercion, I give you this proof."

He jumped. The camera followed him down onto a pile of beige carpet remainders. I winced when he bounced.

"So that's it?" Herb whined. "We spend our entire afternoon, without any food, on a plain, old suicide?"

"I don't think this one qualifies as plain or old. Plus, a twenty grand check for the KITLOD Fund is a nice return for our time."

"I think I'd rather be killed in the line of duty than forced to go through one of these again. And he didn't tell you the reason for the

Swedish Fish?"

"No. It doesn't seem to fit at all. Almost as if…" I began to laugh.

"What's funny?"

"Don't you get it? Wyatt planted a box of little red candy fish, knowing it would confuse us. It was meant to throw us off the trail."

"I still don't get it."

"You need to read more mysteries, Herb."

"So, you're not going to tell me?"

"You'll figure it out. Now let's go grab that Chinese food." I smiled, pleased with myself. "Preferably a place that sells herring."

Epitaph

I've been a longtime David Morrell fan, so when he co-founded the International Thriller Writers organization and asked me to join, I complied even though I'm not much of a joiner. I'm glad I did, because they published an anthology called Thriller, *edited by James Patterson, and I won a wild card spot among the many bestselling authors in the collection. This story was later nominated for a British Dagger award, but what excited me most was to share the covers with F. Paul Wilson's Repairman Jack, Phin's literary ancestor.*

THERE'S AN ART TO getting your ass kicked.

Guys on either side held my arms, stretching me out crucifixion-style. The joker who worked me over swung wildly, without planting his feet or putting his body into it. He spent most of his energy swearing and screaming when he should have been focusing on inflicting maximum damage.

Amateur.

Not that I was complaining. What he lacked in professionalism, he made up for in mean.

He moved in and rabbit-punched me in the side. I flexed my abs and tried to shift to take the blow in the center of my stomach, rather than the more vulnerable kidneys.

I exhaled hard when his fist landed. Saw stars.

He stepped away to pop me in the face. Rather than tense up, I relaxed, trying to absorb the contact by letting my neck snap back.

It still hurt like hell.

I tasted blood, wasn't sure if it came from my nose or my mouth.

Probably both. My left eye had already swollen shut.

"Hijo calvo de una perra!"

You bald son of a bitch. Real original. His breath was ragged now, shoulders slumping, face glowing with sweat.

Gang-bangers these days aren't in very good shape. I blame TV and junk food.

One final punch—a half-hearted smack to my broken nose—and then I was released.

I collapsed face-first in a puddle that smelled like urine. The three Latin Kings each took the time to spit on me. Then they strolled out of the alley, laughing and giving each other high-fives.

When they got a good distance away, I crawled over to a Dumpster and pulled myself to my feet. The alley was dark, quiet. I felt something scurry over my foot.

Rats, licking up my dripping blood.

Nice neighborhood.

I hurt a lot, but pain and I were old acquaintances. I took a deep breath, let it out slow, did some poking and prodding. Nothing seemed seriously damaged.

I'd been lucky.

I spat. The bloody saliva clung to my swollen lower lip and dribbled onto my T-shirt. I tried a few steps forward, managed to keep my balance, and continued to walk out of the alley, onto the sidewalk, and to the corner bus stop.

I sat.

The Kings took my wallet, which had no ID or credit cards, but did have a few hundred in cash. I kept an emergency fiver in my shoe. The bus arrived, and the portly driver raised an eyebrow at my appearance.

"Do you need a doctor, buddy?"

"I've got plenty of doctors."

He shrugged and took my money.

On the ride back, my fellow passengers made heroic efforts to avoid looking at me. I leaned forward, so the blood pooled between my feet rather than stained my clothing any further. These were my good jeans.

When my stop came up, I gave everyone a cheery wave goodbye and stumbled out of the bus.

The corner of State and Cermak was all lit up, twinkling in both English and Chinese. Unlike NY and LA, each of which had sprawling Chinatowns, Chicago has more of a Chinablock. Blink while you're driving west on 22nd and you'll miss it.

Though Caucasian, I found a kind of peace in Chinatown that I didn't find among the Anglos. Since my diagnosis, I've pretty much disowned society. Living here was like living in a foreign country—or a least a square block of a foreign country.

I kept a room at the Lucky Lucky Hotel, tucked away between a crumbling apartment building and a Chinese butcher shop, on State and 25th. The hotel did most of its business at an hourly rate, though I couldn't think of a more repulsive place to take a woman, even if you were renting her as well as the room. The halls stank like mildew and worse and the plaster snowed on you when you climbed the stairs and obscene graffiti lined the halls and the whole building leaned slightly to the right.

I got a decent rent; free—as long as I kept out the drug dealers. Which I did, except for the ones who dealt to me.

I nodded at the proprietor, Kenny-Jen-Bang-Ko, and asked for my key. Kenny was three times my age, clean-shaven save for several black moles on his cheeks that sprouted long, white hairs. He tugged at these hairs while contemplating me.

"How is other guy?" Kenny asked.

"Drinking a forty of malt liquor that he bought with my money."

He nodded, as if that was the answer he'd been expecting. "You want pizza?"

Kenny gestured to a box on the counter. The slices were so old and shrunken they looked like Doritos.

"I thought the Chinese hated fast food."

"Pizza not fast. Took thirty minutes. Anchovy and red pepper."

I declined.

My room was one squeaky stair flight up. I unlocked the door and lumbered over to the bathroom, looking into the cracked mirror above the sink.

Ouch.

My left eye had completely closed, and the surrounding tissue bulged out like a peach. Purple bruising competed with angry red swelling along my cheeks and forehead. My nose was a glob of strawberry jelly, and blood had crusted black along my lips and down my neck.

It looked like Jackson Pollack kicked my ass.

I stripped off the T-shirt, peeled off my shoes and jeans, and turned the shower up to scald.

It hurt, but got most of the crap off.

After the shower I popped five Tylenol, chased them with a shot of tequila, and spent ten minutes in front of the mirror, tears streaming down my face, forcing my nose back into place.

I had some coke, but wouldn't be able to sniff anything with my sniffer all clotted up, and I was too exhausted to shoot any. I made do with the tequila, thinking that tomorrow I'd have that codeine prescription refilled.

Since the pain wouldn't let me sleep, I decided to do a little work.

Using a dirty fork, I pried up the floorboards near the radiator and took out a plastic bag full of what appeared to be little gray stones. The granules were the size and consistency of aquarium gravel.

I placed the bag on the floor, then removed the Lee Load-All, the scale, a container of gunpowder, some wads, and a box of empty 12 gauge shells.

Everything went over to my kitchen table. I snapped on a fresh pair of latex gloves, clamped the loader onto my counter top, and spent an hour carefully filling ten shells. When I finished, I loaded five of them into my Mossberg 935, the barrel and stock of which had been cut down for easier concealment.

I liked shotguns—you had more leeway when aiming, the cops couldn't trace them like they could trace bullets, and nothing put the fear of god into a guy like the sound of racking a shell into the chamber.

For this job, I didn't have a choice.

By the time I was done, my nose had taken the gold medal in throbbing, with my eye coming close with the silver. I swallowed five more Tylenol and four shots of tequila, then laid down on my cot and fell asleep.

With sleep came the dream.

It happened every night, so vivid I could smell Donna's perfume. We were still together, living in the suburbs. She was smiling at me, running her fingers through my hair.

"Phin, the caterer wants to know if we're going with the split pea or the wedding ball soup."

"Explain the wedding ball soup to me again."

"It's a chicken stock with tiny veal meatballs in it."

"That sounds good to you?"

"It's very good. I've had it before."

"Then let's go with that."

She kissed me; playful, loving.

I woke up drenched in sweat.

If someone had told me that happy memories would one day be a source of incredible pain, I wouldn't have believed it.

Things change.

Sun peeked in through my dirty window, making me squint. I stretched, wincing because my whole body hurt—my whole body except for my left side, where a team of doctors severed the nerves during an operation called a chordotomy. The surgery had been purely palliative. The area felt dead, even though the cancer still thrived inside my pancreas. And elsewhere, by now.

The chordotomy offered enough pain relief to allow me to function, and tequila, cocaine, and codeine made up for the remainder.

I dressed in some baggy sweatpants, my bloody gym shoes (with a new five dollar bill in the sole), and a clean white T-shirt. I strapped my leather shotgun sling under my armpits, and placed the Mossberg in the holster. It hung directly between my shoulder blades, barrel up, and could be freed by reaching my right hand behind me at waist-level.

A baggy black trench coat went on over the rig, concealing the shotgun and the leather straps that held it in place.

I pocketed the five extra shells, the bag of gray granules, a Glock 21 with two extra clips of .45 rounds, and a six inch butterfly knife. Then I hung an iron crowbar on an extra strap sewn into the lining of my coat, and headed out to greet the morning.

Chinatown smelled like a combination of soy sauce and garbage. It was worse in the summer, when stenches seemed to settle in and stick to your clothes. Though not yet seven in the morning, the temperature already hovered in the low 90s. The sun made my face hurt.

I walked up State, past Cermak, and went east. The Sing Lung

Bakery had opened for business an hour earlier. The manager, a squat Mandarin Chinese named Ti, did a double-take when I entered.

"Phin! Your face is horrible!" He rushed around the counter to meet me, hands and shirt dusty with flour.

"My mom liked it okay."

Ti's features twisted in concern. "Was it them? The ones who butchered my daughter?"

I gave him a brief nod.

Ti hung his head. "I am sorry to bring this suffering upon you. They are very bad men."

I shrugged, which hurt. "It was my fault. I got careless."

That was an understatement. After combing Chicago for almost a week, I'd discovered the bangers had gone underground. I got one guy to talk, and after a bit of friendly persuasion he gladly offered some vital info; Sunny's killers were due to appear in court on an unrelated charge.

I'd gone to the Daly Center, where the prelim hearing was being held, and watched from the sidelines. After matching their names to faces, I followed them back to their hidey-hole.

My mistake had been to stick around. A white guy in a Hispanic neighborhood tends to stand out. Having just been to court, which required walking through a metal detector, I had no weapons on me.

Stupid. Ti and Sunny deserved someone smarter.

Ti had found me through the grapevine, where I got most of my business. Phineas Troutt, Problem Solver. No job too dirty, no fee too high.

I'd met him in a parking lot across the street, and he laid out the whole sad, sick story of what these animals had done to his little girl.

"Cops do nothing. Sunny's friend too scared to press charges."

Sunny's friend had managed to escape with only ten missing teeth, six stab wounds, and a torn rectum. Sunny hadn't been as lucky.

Ti agreed to my price without question. Not too many people haggled with paid killers.

"You finish job today?" Ti asked, reaching into his glass display counter for a pastry.

"Yeah."

"In the way we talk about?"

"In the way we talked about."

Ti bowed and thanked me. Then he stuffed two pastries into a bag and held them out.

"Duck egg moon cake, and red bean ball with sesame. Please take."

I took.

"Tell me when you find them."

"I'll be back later today. Keep an eye on the news. You might see something you'll like."

I left the bakery and headed for the bus. Ti had paid me enough to afford a cab, or even a limo, but cabs and limos kept records. Besides, I preferred to save my money for more important things, like drugs and hookers. I try to live every day as if it's my last.

After all, it very well might be.

The bus arrived, and again everyone took great pains not to stare. The trip was short, only about two miles, taking me to a neighborhood known as Pilsen, on Racine and 18th.

I left my duck egg moon cake and my red bean ball on the bus for some other lucky passenger to enjoy, and then stepped out into Little Mexico.

It smelled like a combination of salsa and garbage.

There weren't many people out—too early for shoppers and commuters. The stores here had Spanish signs, not bothering with English translations: *zapatos, ropa, restuarante, tiendas de comestibles, bancos, teléfonos de la célula.* I passed the alley where I'd gotten the shit kicked out of me, kept heading north, and located the apartment building where my three amigos were staying. I tried the front door.

They hadn't left it open for me.

Though the gray paint was faded and peeling, the door was heavy aluminum, and the lock solid. But the jamb, as I'd remembered from yesterday's visit, was old wood. I removed the crowbar from my jacket lining, gave a discreet look in either direction, and pried open the door in less time than it took to open it with a key, the frame splintering and cracking.

The Kings occupied the basement apartment to the left of the entrance, facing the street. Last night I'd counted seven—five men and two women—including my three targets. Of course, there may be other people inside that I'd missed.

This was going to be interesting.

Unlike the front door, their apartment door was a joke. They apparently thought being gang members meant they didn't need decent security.

They thought wrong.

I took out my Glock and tried to stop hyperventilating. Breaking into someone's place is scary as hell. It always is.

One hard kick and the door burst inward.

A guy on the couch, sleeping in front of the TV. Not one of my marks. He woke up and stared at me. It took a millisecond to register the gang tattoo, a five pointed crown, on the back of his hand.

I shot him in his forehead.

If the busted door didn't wake everyone up, the .45 did, sounding like thunder in the small room.

Movement to my right. A woman in the kitchen, in panties and a Dago-T, too much make-up and baby fat.

"Te vayas!" I hissed at her.

She took the message and ran out the door.

A man stumbled into the hall, tripping and falling to the thin carpet. One of mine, the guy who held my right arm while I'd been worked over. He clutched a stiletto. I was on him in two quick steps, putting one in his elbow and one through the back of his knee when he fell.

He screamed falsetto.

I walked down the hall in a crouch, and a bullet zinged over my head and buried itself in the ceiling. I kissed the floor, looked left, and saw the shooter in the bathroom; the guy who held my other arm and laughed every time I got smacked.

I stuck the Glock in my jeans and reached behind me, unslinging the Mossberg.

He fired again, missed, and I aimed the shotgun and peppered his face.

Unlike lead shot, the gray granules didn't have deep penetrating power. Instead of blowing his head off, they peeled off his lips, cheeks, and eyes.

He ate linoleum, blind and choking on blood.

Movement behind me. I fell sideways and rolled onto my back. A kid, about thirteen, stood in the hall a few feet away. He wore Latin

Kings colors; black to represent death, gold to represent life.

His hand ended in a pistol.

I racked the shotgun, aimed low.

If the kid were old enough to be sexually active, he wasn't anymore.

He dropped to his knees, still holding the gun.

I was on him in two steps, driving a knee into his nose. He went down and out.

Three more guys burst out of the bedroom.

Apparently I'd counted wrong.

Two were young, muscular, brandishing knives. The third was the guy who'd worked me over the night before. The one who called me a bald son of a bitch.

They were on me before I could rack the shotgun again.

The first one slashed at me with his pig-sticker, and I parried with the barrel of the Mossberg. He jabbed again, slicing me across the knuckles of my right hand.

I threw the shotgun at his face and went for my Glock.

He was fast.

I was faster.

Bang bang and he was a paycheck for the coroner. I spun left, aimed at the second guy. He was already in mid-jump, launching himself at me with a battle cry and switchblades in both hands.

One gun beats two knives.

He took three in the chest and two in the neck before he dropped.

The last guy, the guy who broke my nose, grabbed my shotgun and dove behind the couch.

Chck chck. He ejected the shell and racked another into the chamber. I pulled the Glock's magazine and slammed a fresh one home.

"Hijo calvo de una perra!"

Again with the bald son of a bitch taunt. I worked through my hurt feelings and crawled to an end table, tipping it over and getting behind it.

The shotgun boomed. Had it been loaded with shot, it would have torn through the cheap particle board and turned me into ground beef. Or ground hijo calvo de una perra. But at that distance, the granules didn't do much more than make a loud noise.

The banger apparently didn't learn from experience, because he tried twice more with similar results, and then the shotgun was empty.

I stood up from behind the table, my heart a lump in my throat and my hands shaking with adrenalin.

The King turned and ran.

His back was an easy target.

I took a quick look around, making sure everyone was down or out, and then went to retrieve my shotgun. I loaded five more shells and approached the downed leader, who was sucking carpet and whimpering. The wounds in his back were ugly, but he still made a feeble effort to crawl away.

I bent down, turned him over, and shoved the barrel of the Mossburg between his bloody lips.

"You remember Sunny Lung," I said, and fired.

It wasn't pretty. It also wasn't fatal. The granules blew out his cheeks, and tore into his throat, but somehow the guy managed to keep breathing.

I gave him one more, jamming the gun further down the wreck of his face.

That did the trick.

The second perp, the one I'd blinded, had passed out on the bathroom floor. His face didn't look like a face anymore, and blood bubbles were coming out of the hole where his mouth would have been.

"Sunny Lung sends her regards," I said.

This time I pushed the gun in deep, and the first shot did the trick, blowing through his throat.

The last guy, the one who made like Pavarotti when I took out his knee, left a blood smear from the hall into the kitchen. He cowered in the corner, a dishrag pressed to his leg.

"Don't kill me, man! Don't kill me!"

"I bet Sunny Lung said the same thing."

The Mossberg thundered twice; once to the chest, and once to the head.

It wasn't enough. What was left alive gasped for air.

I removed the bag of granules from my pocket, took out a handful, and shoved them down his throat until he stopped breathing.

Then I went to the bathroom and threw up in the sink.

Sirens wailed in the distance. Time to go. I washed my hands, and then rinsed off the barrel of the Mossberg, holstering it in my rig.

In the hallway, the kid I emasculated was clutching himself between the legs, sobbing.

"There's always the priesthood," I told him, and got out of there.

My nose was still clogged, but I managed to get enough coke up there to damper the pain. Before closing time I stopped by the bakery, and Ti greeted me with a somber nod.

"Saw the news. They said it was a massacre."

"Wasn't pretty."

"You did as we said?"

"I did, Ti. Your daughter got her revenge. She's the one that killed them. All three."

I fished out the bag of granules and handed it to her father. Sunny's cremated remains.

"Xie xie," Ti said, thanking me in Mandarin. He held out an envelope filled with cash.

Ti looked uncomfortable, and I had drugs to buy, so I took the money and left without another word.

An hour later I'd filled my codeine prescription, picked up two bottles of tequila and a skinny hooker with track marks on her arms, and had a party back at my place. I popped and drank and screwed and snorted, trying to blot out the memory of the last two days. And of the last six months.

That's when I'd been diagnosed. A week before my wedding day. My gift to my bride-to-be was running away so she wouldn't have to watch me die of cancer.

Those Latin Kings this morning, they got off easy. They didn't see it coming.

Seeing it coming is so much worse.

Taken to the Cleaners

Harry is my favorite character to write for. I love the idea of an idiotic, selfish jerk as a protagonist. He's too obnoxious and unsympathetic to carry a book on his own, but I think he makes a great foil for Jack, so he appears in every novel. Some readers hate him. Some readers adore him. This story sold to The Strand Magazine *in 2005.*

"I WANT YOU TO kill the man that my husband hired to kill the man that I hired to kill my husband."

If I had been paying attention, I still wouldn't have understood what she wanted me to do. But I was busy looking at her legs, which weren't adequately covered by her skirt. She had great legs, curvy without being heavy, tan and long, and she had them crossed in that sexy way that women cross their legs, knee over knee, not the ugly way that guys do it, with the ankle on the knee, though if she did cross her legs that way it would have been sexy too.

"Mr. McGlade, did you hear what I just said?"

"Hmm? Yeah, sure I did, baby. The man, the husband, I got it."

"So you'll do it?"

"Do what?"

"Kill the man that my husband—"

I held up my hand. "Whoa. Hold it right there. I'm just a plain old private eye. That's what is says on the door you just walked through. The door even has a big magnifying glass silhouette logo thingy painted on it, which I paid way too much money for, just so no one gets confused. I don't kill people for money. Absolutely, positively, no way." I leaned forward a little. "But, for the sake of argument, how much money are we talking about here?"

"I don't know where else to turn."

The tears came, and she buried her face in her hands, giving me the opportunity to look at her legs again. Marietta Garbonzo had found me through the ad I placed in the Chicago phone book. The ad used the expensive magnifying glass logo, along with the tagline, Harry McGlade Investigators: We'll Do Whatever it Takes. It brought in more customers than my last tagline: No Job Too Small, No Fee Too High, or the one prior to that, We'll Investigate Your Privates.

Mrs. Garbonzo had never been to a private eye before, and she was playing her role to the hilt. Besides the short skirt and tight blouse, she had gone to town with the hair and make-up; her blonde locks curled and sprayed, her lips painted deep, glossy red, her purple eye shadow so thick that she managed to get some on her collar.

"My husband beats me, Mr. McGlade. Do you know why?"

"Beats me," I said, shrugging. Her wailing kicked in again. I wondered where she worked out. Legs like that, she must work out.

"He's insane, Mr. McGlade. We've been married for a year, and Roy always had a temper. I once saw him attack another man with a tire iron. They were having an argument, Roy went out to the car, grabbed a crow bar from the trunk, then came back and practically killed him."

"Where do you work out?"

"Excuse me?"

"Exercise. Do you belong to a gym, or work out at home?"

"Mr. McGlade, I'm trying to tell you about my husband."

"I know, the insane guy who beats you. Probably shouldn't have married a guy who used a tire iron for anything other than changing tires."

"I married too young. But while we were dating, he treated me kindly. It was only after we married that the abuse began."

She turned her head away and unbuttoned her blouse. My gaze shifted from her legs to her chest. She had a nice chest, packed tight into a silky black bra with lace around the edges and an underwire that displayed things to a good effect, both lifting and separating.

"See these bruises?"

"Hmm?"

"It's humiliating to reveal them, but I don't know where else to go."

"Does he hit you anywhere else? You can show me, I'm a professional."

The tears returned. "I hired a man to kill him, Mr. McGlade. I hired a man to kill my husband. But somehow Roy found out about it, and he hired a man to kill the man I hired. So I'd like you to kill his man so my man can kill him."

I removed the bottle of whiskey from my desk that I keep there for medicinal purposes, like getting drunk. I unscrewed the cap, wiped off the bottle neck with my tie, and handed it to her.

"You're not making sense, Mrs. Garbonzo. Have a swig of this."

"I shouldn't. When I drink I lose my inhibitions."

"Keep the bottle."

She took a sip, coughing after it went down.

"I already paid the assassin. I paid him a lot of money, and he won't refund it. But I'm afraid he'll die before he kills my husband, so I need someone to kill the man who is after him."

"Shouldn't you tell the guy you hired that he's got a hit on him?"

"I called him. He says not to worry. But I am worried, Mr. McGlade."

"As I said before, I don't kill people for money."

"Even if you're killing someone who kills people for money?"

"But I'd be killing someone who is killing someone who kills people for money. What prevents that killer from hiring someone to kill me because he's killing someone who is killing someone that I…hand me that bottle."

I took a swig.

"Please, Mr. McGlade. I'm a desperate woman. I'll do anything."

She walked around the desk and stood before me, shivering in her bra, her breath coming out in short gasps through red, wet lips. Her hands rested on my shoulders, squeezing, and she bent forward.

"My laundry," I said.

"What?"

"Do my laundry."

"Mr. McGlade, I'm offering you my body."

"And it's a tempting offer, Mrs. Garbonzo. But that will take, what, five minutes? I've got about six loads of laundry back at my place, they take an hour for each cycle."

"Isn't there a dry cleaner in your neighborhood?"

"A hassle. I'd have to write my name on all the labels, on every sock, on the elastic band of my whitey tighties, plus haul six bags of clothes down the street. You want me to help you? I get five hundred a day, plus expenses. And you do my laundry."

"And you'll kill him?"

"No. I don't kill people for money. Or for laundry. But I'll protect your guy from getting whacked."

"Thank you, Mr. McGlade."

She leaned down to kiss me. Not wanting to appear rude, I let her. And so she didn't feel unwanted, I stuck my hand up her skirt.

"You won't tell the police, will you Mr. McGlade?"

"Look, baby, I'm not your priest and I'm not your lawyer and I'm not your shrink. I'm just a man. A man who will keep his mouth shut, except when I'm eating. Or talking, or sleeping, because sometimes I sleep with my mouth open because I have the apnea."

"Thank you, Mr. McGlade."

"I'll take the first week in advance, Visa and MasterCard are fine. Here are my spare keys."

"Your keys?"

"For my apartment. It's in Hyde Park. I don't have a hamper, so I leave my dirty clothes all over the floor. Do the bed sheets too—those haven't been washed since, well, ever. Washer and dryer are in the basement of the building, washer costs seventy-five cents, dryer costs fifty cents for each thirty minutes, and the heavy things like jeans and sweaters take about a buck fifty to dry. Make yourself at home, but don't touch anything, sit on anything, eat any of my food, or turn on the TV."

I gave her my address, and she gave me a check and all of her info. The info was surprising.

"You hired a killer from the personal ads in Famous Soldier Magazine?"

"I didn't know where else to go."

"How about the police? A divorce attorney?"

"My husband is a rich and powerful man, Mr. McGlade. You don't recognize his name?"

I flipped though my mental Rolodex. "Roy Garbonzo? Is he the

Roy Garbonzo that owns Happy Roy's Chicken Shack?"

"Yes."

"He seems so happy on those commercials."

"He's a beast, Mr. McGlade."

"The guy is like a hundred and thirty years old. And on those commercials, he's always laughing and signing and dancing with that claymation chicken. He's the guy that's abusing you?"

"Would you like to see the proof again?"

"If it isn't too much trouble."

She grabbed my face in one hand, squeezing my cheeks together.

"Happy Roy is a vicious psycho, Mr. McGlade. He's a brutal, misogynist pig who enjoys inflicting pain."

"He's probably rich too."

Mrs. Garbonzo narrowed her eyes. "He's wealthy, yes. What are you implying?"

"I like his extra spicy recipe. Do you get to take chicken home for free? You probably have a fridge stuffed full of it, am I right?"

She released my face and buttoned up her blouse.

"I have to go. My husband gets paranoid when I go out."

"Maybe because when you go out, you hire people to kill him."

She picked up her purse and headed for the door. "I expect you to call me when you've made some progress."

"That includes ironing," I called after her. "And hanging the stuff up. I don't have any hangers, so you'll have to buy some."

After she left, I turned off all the office lights and closed the blinds, because what I had to do next, I had to do in complete privacy.

I took a nap.

When I awoke a few hours later, I went to the bank, cashed Mrs. Garbonzo's check, and went to start earning my money.

My first instinct was to dive head-first into the belly of the beast and confront Mrs. Garbonzo's hired hitman help. My second instinct was to get some nachos, maybe a beer or two.

I went with my second instinct. The nachos were good, spicy but not so much that all you tasted was peppers. After the third beer I hopped in my ride and headed for the assassin's headquarters, which turned out to be in a well-to-do suburb of Chicago called Barrington. The development I pulled into boasted some amazingly huge houses, complete with big lawns and swimming pools and trimmed bushes that looked like corkscrews and lollipops. I double-checked the address I'd scribbled down, then pulled into a long circular driveway and up to a home that was bigger than the public school I attended, and I came from the city where they grew schools big.

The hitman biz must be booming.

I half expected some sort of maid or butler to answer the door, but instead I was greeted by a fifty-something woman, her facelift sporting a deep tan. I appraised her.

"If you stay out in the sun, the wrinkles will come back."

"Then I'll just have more work done." Her voice was steady, cultured. "Are you here to clean the pool?"

"I'm here to speak to William Johansenn."

"Billy? Sure, he's in the basement."

She let me in. Perhaps all rich suburban women were fearless and let strange guys into their homes. Or perhaps this one simply didn't care. I didn't get a chance to ask, because she walked off just as I entered.

"Lady? Where's the basement?"

"Down the hall, stairs to the right," she said without turning around.

I took a long, tiled hallway past a powder room, a den, and a door that opened to a descending staircase. Heavy metal music blared up at me.

"Billy!" I called down.

My effort was fruitless—with the noise, I couldn't even hear myself. The lights were off, and squinting did nothing to penetrate the darkness.

Surprising a paid assassin in his own lair wasn't on the list of 100 things I longed to do before I die, but I didn't see much of a choice. I beer-belched, then went down the stairs.

The basement was furnished, though furnished didn't seem to be the right word. The floor had carpet, and the walls had paint, and there seemed to be furniture, but I couldn't really tell because everything was covered with food wrappers, pop cans, dirty clothing, and discarded magazines. It looked like a 7-Eleven exploded.

William "Billy" Johansenn was asleep on a waterbed, a copy of Creem open on his chest. He had a galaxy of pimples dotting his forehead and six curly hairs sprouting from his chin.

He couldn't have been a day over sixteen.

I killed the stereo. Billy continued to snore. Among the clutter on the floor were several issues of Famous Soldier, along with various gun and hunting magazines. I poked through his drawers and found a cheap Rambo knife, a CO2 powered BB gun, and a dog-eared copy of the infamous How to be a Hitman book from Paladin Press.

I gave the kid a shake, then another. The third shake got him to open his eyes.

"Who the hell are you?" he said, defiant.

"I'm your wake-up call."

I slapped the kid, making his eyes cross.

"Hey! You hit me!"

"A woman hired you to kill her husband."

"I don't know what you're—"

He got another smack. "That's for lying."

"You can't hit me," he whined. "I'll sue you."

I hit him twice more; once because I didn't like being threatened by punk kids, and once because I didn't like lawyers. When I pulled my palm back for threesies, the kid broke.

"Please! Stop it! I admit it!"

I released his t-shirt and let him blubber for a minute. His blue eyes matched those of the woman upstairs. Not many professional killers lived in their mother's basement, and I wondered how Marietta Garbonzo could have been this naive.

"I'm guessing you never met Mrs. Garbonzo in person."

"I only talked to her on the phone. She sent the money to a P.O. Box. That's how the pros do it."

"So how did she get your home address?"

"She wouldn't give me the money without my address. She said if I didn't trust her, why should she trust me?"

Here was my proof that each new generation of teenagers was stupider than the last. I blame MTV.

"How much did she give you?"

He smiled, showing me a mouth full of braces. "Fifty large."

"And how were you going to do it? With your BB gun?"

"I was going to follow him around and then…you know…shove him."

"Shove him?"

"He's an old guy. I was thinking I'd shove him down some stairs, or into traffic. I dunno."

"Have you shoved a lot of old people into traffic, Billy boy?"

He must not have liked the look in my eyes, because he shrunk two sizes.

"No! Never! I never killed anybody!"

"So why put an ad in the magazine?"

"I dunno. Something to do."

I considered hitting him again, but didn't know what purpose it would serve.

I hit him anyway.

"Ow! My lip's caught in my braces!"

"You pimple-faced little moron. Do you have any idea what kind of trouble you're in right now? Not only did you accept money to commit a felony, but now you've got a price on your head. Did Mrs. Garbonzo tell you about the guy her husband hired to kill you?"

He nodded, his Adam's apple wiggling like a fish.

"Are-are you here to kill me?"

"No."

"But you've got a gun." He pointed to the butt of my Magnum, jutting out of my shoulder holster.

"I'm a private detective."

"Is that a real gun?"

"Yes."

"Can I touch it?"

"No."

"Come on. Lemme touch it."

This is what happens when you spare the rod and spoil the child.

"Look kid, I know that you're a loser that nobody likes, and that you're a virgin and will probably stay one for the next ten years, but do you want to die?"

"Ten years?"

"Answer the question."

"No. I don't want to die."

I sighed. "That's a start. Where's the money?"

"I've got a secret place. In the wall."

He rolled off the bed, eager, and pried a piece of paneling away from the plaster in a less-cluttered corner of the room. His hand reached in, and came out with a brown paper shopping bag.

"Is it all there?"

Billy shook his head. "I spent three hundred on a wicked MP3 player."

"Hand over the money. And the MP3 player."

Billy showed a bit of reluctance, so I smacked him again to help with his motivation.

It helped. He also gave me fresh batteries for the player.

"Now what?" he sniffled.

"Now we tell your parents."

"Do we have to?"

"You'd prefer the cops?"

He shook his head. "No. No cops."

"That blonde upstairs with the face like a snare drum, that your mom?"

"Yeah."

"Let's go have a talk with her."

Mrs. Johansenn was perched in front of a sixty inch television, watching a soap.

"Nice TV. High definition?"

"Plasma."

"Nice. Billy has something he wants to tell you."

Billy stared at his shoes. "Mom, I bought an ad in the back of Famous Soldier Magazine, and some lady gave me fifty thousand dollars to kill her husband."

Mrs. Johansenn hit the mute button on the remote, shaking her head in obvious disappointment.

"Billy, dammit, this is too much. You're a hired killer?"

"Sorry," he mumbled.

"You're father is going to have a stroke when he hears this."

"Do we have to tell Dad?"

"Are you kidding?"

"I gave the money back."

"Who are you?" Billy's mom squinted at me.

"I'm Harry McGlade. I'm a private eye. I was hired to find Billy. Someone is trying to kill him."

Mrs. Johansenn rolled her eyes. "Oh, this gets better and better. I need to call Sal."

"You husband?"

"My lawyer."

"Ma'am, a lawyer isn't going to do much to save Billy's life, unless he's standing between him and a bullet."

"So what then, the police?"

"Not the cops, Mom! I don't want to go to jail!"

"He won't survive in prison," I said. "The lifers will pass him around like a bong at a college party. They'll trade him for candy bars and cigarettes."

"I don't want to be traded for candy bars, Mom!"

Mrs. Johansenn frowned, forming new wrinkles. "Then what should we do, Mr. McGlade?"

I paused for a moment, then I grinned.

"I get five-hundred a day, plus expenses."

I celebrated my recent windfall with a nice dinner at a nice restaurant. I was more of a burger and fries guy than a steak and lobster guy, but the steak and lobster went down easy, and after leaving a 17% tip I headed to Evanston to visit the Chicken King.

Roy Garbonzo's estate made the Johansenn's look like a third world mud hut. He had his own private access road, a giant wrought iron perimeter fence, and a uniformed guard posted at the gate. I was wondering how to play it when the aforementioned uniformed guard knocked on my window.

"I need to see Roy Garbonzo," I told him. "My son choked to death on a Sunny Meal toy."

"He's expecting you, Mr. McGlade."

The gate rolled back, and I drove up to the mansion. It looked like five mansions stuck together. I parked between two massive Doric columns and pressed the buzzer next to the giant double doors. Before anyone answered, a startling thought flashed through my head.

How did the guard know my name?

"It's a set up," I said aloud. I yanked the Magnum out of my shoulder holster and dove into one of the hydrangea bushes flanking the entryway just as the knob turned.

I peeked through the lavender blooms, finger on the trigger, watching the door swing open. A sinister-looking man wearing a tuxedo stepped out of the house and peered down his nose at me.

"Would Mr. McGlade care for a drink?"

"You're a butler," I said.

"Observant of you, sir."

"You work for Roy Garbonzo."

"An excellent deduction, sir. A drink?"

"Uh—whiskey, rocks."

"Would you care to have it in the parlor, sir, or would you prefer to remain squatting in the Neidersachen?"

"I thought it was a hydrangea."

"It's a hydrangea Neidersachen, sir."

"It's pretty," I said. "But I think I'll take that drink inside."

"Very good, sir."

I extricated myself from the Neidersachen, brushed off some clinging leaves, and followed Jeeves through the tiled foyer, through the carpeted library, and into the parlor, which had wood floors and an ornate Persian rug big enough to park a bus on.

"Please have a seat, sir. Mr. Garbonzo will be with your shortly. Were you planning on shooting him?"

"Excuse me?"

"You're holding a gun, sir."

I glanced down at my hand, still clenched around my Magnum.

"Sorry. Forgot."

I holstered the .44 and sat in a high-backed leather chair, which was so plush I sank four inches. Waddles returned with my whiskey, and I sipped it and stared at the paintings hanging on the walls. One in particular caught my interest, of a nude woman eating grapes.

"Admiring the Degas?" a familiar voice boomed from behind.

I turned and saw Happy Roy the vicious misogynist psycho, all five foot two inches of him, walking up to me. He wore an expensive silk suit, but like most old men the waist was too high, making him seem more hunched over than he actually was. On his feet were slippers, and his glasses had black plastic frames and looked thick enough to stop a bullet.

"Her name is Degas?" I asked. "Silly name for a chick."

He held out his hand and I shook it, noticing his knuckles were swollen and bruised.

"Degas is the painter, Mr. McGlade. My business advisors thought it was a good investment. Do you like it?"

"Not really. She's got too much in back, not enough up front, and her face is a double-bagger."

"A double-bagger?"

"I'd make her wear two bags over her head, in case one fell off."

The Chicken King laughed. "I always thought she was ugly too. Apparently, this little lady was the ideal beauty hundreds of years ago."

"Or maybe Degas just liked ugly, pear-shaped chicks. How did you know I was coming, Mr. Garbonzo?"

He sat in the chair across from me, sinking in so deep he had trouble seeing over his knees.

"Please, call me Happy Roy. I've been having my wife followed, Mr. McGlade. The man I hired tailed her to your office. Does that surprise you?"

"Why should I be surprised? I remember that she came to my office."

"What I meant was, are you surprised I'm having my wife followed?"

I considered it. "No. She's young, beautiful, and you look like a Caucasian version of one of the California Raisins."

"I remember those commercials. That's where I got the idea for the claymation chicken in the Chicken Shack spots. Expensive to produce, those commercials."

"Enough of the small talk. I want you to call off your goon."

"My goon?"

"The person your wife hired to whack you, he's a teenage kid living in the suburbs. He's not a real threat."

"I'm aware of that."

"So you don't need to have that kid killed."

"Mr. McGlade, I'm not having anyone killed. I'm Happy Roy. I don't kill people. I promote world peace through deep fried poultry. I simply told my wife that I hired a killer, even though I didn't."

"You lied to her?"

Happy Roy let out a big, dramatic sigh. "When I found out she wanted me dead, I was justifiably annoyed. I confronted her, we got into an argument, and I told her that I'd have her assassin killed. I was trying to get her to call it off on her own."

I absorbed this information, drinking more whiskey. When the whiskey ran out, I sucked on an ice cube.

"Tho wmer mmmpt wooor—"

"Excuse me? I can't understand you with that ice in your mouth."

I spit out the ice. "She said you abuse her. That you're insane."

"The only thing insane about me is my upcoming promotion. Buy a box of chicken, get a second box for half price."

I wondered if I should tell him about the bruises she had, but chose to keep silent.

"What about divorce?"

"I love Marietta, Mr. McGlade. I know she's too young for me. I know she's a devious, back-stabbing maneater. That just makes her more adorable."

"She wants you dead."

"All spouses have their quirks."

I leaned forward, an effort because my butt was sunk so low in the chair.

"Happy Roy, I have no doubt that Marietta will kill you if she can. When this doesn't pan out, she'll try something else. Eventually, she'll hook up with a real assassin."

Happy Roy's eye became hooded, dark. "She's my wife, Mr. McGlade. I'll deal with her my way."

"By beating her?"

"This conversation is over. I'll have my butler show you to the door."

I pried myself out of the chair. "You're disgustingly rich, powerful, and not a bad looking guy for someone older than God. Let Marietta go and find some other bimbo to play with."

"Good bye, Mr. McGlade. Feel free to keep working for my wife."

"Are you trying to pay me off, so I drop this case?"

"No. Not at all."

"If you were thinking about paying me off, how much money would we be talking?"

"I'm not trying to pay you off, Mr. McGlade."

I got in the smaller man's face. "You might be able to afford fat

Degas and huge estates, but I'm a person, Happy Roy. And no matter how rich you get, you'll never be able to buy a human being. Because it's illegal, Happy Roy. Buying people is illegal."

"I'm not trying to buy you!"

"I'll find my own way out."

I stormed out of the parlor, through the library, into the dining room, into another parlor, or maybe it was a den, and then I wound up in the kitchen somehow. I tried to back track, wandered into the dining room, and then found myself back in one of the parlors, but I couldn't tell if it was the first parlor or the second parlor. I didn't see that painting of the naked heifer, but Happy Roy may have taken it down just to confuse me.

"Hello?" I called out. "I'm a little lost here."

No one answered.

I went back into the dining room, then the kitchen, and took another door which led down a hallway which led to a bathroom, which was fine because I needed to go to the bathroom anyway.

When the lizard had been adequately drained, I discovered some very interesting prescription drugs, just lying there, in the medicine cabinet.

And then it all made sense.

Forty minutes later I found the front door and headed back to my apartment.

Time to drop the truth on Little Miss Marietta.

At first, I thought I had the wrong place. Everything was so…clean. Not only were all of my clothes picked up, but the apartment had been vacuumed—a real feat since I didn't think I owned a vacuum cleaner.

"Mrs. Garbonzo? You here?"

I walked into the bedroom. The bed had been made, and the closet door was open, revealing over a dozen shirts on hangers.

In the kitchen, the sink was empty of dishes for the first time since I rented the place fifteen years ago. There was even a fresh smell of lilacs and orange zest in the air.

The door opened and I swung around, hand going to my gun. Mrs. Garbonzo entered, carrying a plastic laundry basket overflowing with my socks. She flinched when she saw me.

"Mr. McGlade. I didn't expect you back so soon."

"Surprised, Marietta? I thought you might be."

"Did you take care of the guy?"

"Sit down. We need to talk."

She set the basket down on my kitchen counter, and seductively perched herself on one of my breakfast bar stools. Her blouse had been untucked from her skirt, the shirt tails tied in a knot around her flat stomach.

"You lied to me, Marietta."

"Lied?" She batted her eyelashes. "How?"

There was a bottle of window cleaner next to the sink that I'd never seen before. I picked it up.

"How about opening up that shirt and letting me squirt you with this?"

"Is that what turns you on? Spraying women with glass cleaner?"

I grabbed her blouse and pulled, tearing buttons.

"I was thinking more along the lines of washing off those fake bruises. They're so fake, the purple has even rubbed off on your collar. See?"

I shot two quick streams at the marks, then used my sleeve to wipe them off.

They didn't wipe off.

I tried again, to similar effect.

Marietta sneered at me. "Are you finished?"

"So what's that purple stuff on your collar?"

"Eye shadow." She pointed at her eyes. "That's why it matches my eye shadow."

"Big deal. So you gave yourself those bruises. Or paid someone to give them to you. I met your husband today, Mrs. Garbonzo. All ninety pounds of him. He couldn't beat up a quadriplegic."

"My husband abuses me, Mr. McGlade."

"Yeah, I saw his swollen knuckles. At first, I thought they were swollen from hitting you. But he didn't hit you, did he Marietta? Roy has rheumatoid arthritis. I saw his medication. His knuckles are swollen because of his disease, and they undoubtedly cause him great pain. So much pain, he'd never be able to hit you."

Marietta put her hands on her hips.

"He beats me with a belt, Mr. McGlade."

"A belt?"

"These bruises are from the buckle. It also causes welts. See?"

She turned around, lifting her blouse. Angry, red scabs stretched across her back.

I gave them a spritz of the window cleaner, just to be sure.

"Ow!"

"Sorry. Had to check."

Marietta faced me. "I've paid you, I've done your laundry, and I've cleaned your apartment. Did you take care of the assassin for me?"

"Your husband didn't hire an assassin."

"Is that what he told you?"

"I know it for a fact. The guy you hired is a sixteen-year-old pimply-faced kid. He couldn't whack anyone. He couldn't even whack a mole."

I smiled at my pun.

Marietta made a face. "I thought he sounded young on the phone. He really won't do it?"

"He lives in his parent's basement."

The tears came. "I gave him a lot of money. Everything I've been able to hide from Roy during six years of marriage."

I thought about mentioning I got the money back, but decided against it.

"Look, Marietta, just divorce the guy."

"I can't. He threatened to kill me if I divorced him."

"You can run away. Hire a lawyer."

She sniffled. "Pre-nup."

"Pre-nup?"

"I signed a pre-nuptial agreement. If I divorce Roy, I don't get a penny. And after six years of abuse, I deserve more than that." She licked her lips. "But if he dies, I get it all."

"Don't you think killing the guy is a little extreme?"

She threw herself at me, teary-eyed and heaving. "Please, Harry. You have to help me. I'll give you half—half of the entire chicken empire. Help me kill the son of a bitch."

"Marietta…"

"I cleaned your place, you promised you'd help." She added a little grinding action to her hug. "Please kill him for me."

I looked around the kitchen. She did do a pretty good job. I wondered, briefly, if I'd make a decent Chicken King.

"I'll tell you what, Marietta. I don't do that kind of thing. But I know someone who can help. Do you want me to make a phone call?"

"Yes. Oh, yes."

I pried myself out of her grasp and picked up the phone, dialing the number from memory.

"Hi, partner. It's me. Look, I've got a woman here who wants to kill her husband. I told her I'm not interested, but I thought maybe you'd be able to set something up. Say, tomorrow, around noon? You can meet her at the Hilton. Rent a room under the name Lipshultz. No, schultz, with a U-L. Okay, she'll be there."

I hung up. "Got it all set for you, sugar."

She squeezed me tight and kissed my neck. "Thanks, Harry. Thank you so much. Is there anything I can do to repay you?" Her breath was hot in my ear. "Anything at all?"

"You can start by folding those socks. And maybe some dusting. Yeah, dusting would be good."

She smiled wickedly and caressed my cheek. "I was thinking of something a little more intimate."

"I was thinking about dinner."

"Dinner would be wonderful."

"I'm sure it will be. Have the place dusted by the time I get back."

Marietta Garbonzo called me the next night, around eight in the evening.

"You son of a bitch! You set me up! You didn't call a hitman! You called a cop!"

"You can't go around murdering people, sweetheart. It's wrong on so many levels."

"But what about all of the washing? The cleaning? The dusting? And what about after dinner? What we did? How could you betray me after that?"

"You expect me to throw away all of my principles because we spent five minutes doing the worm? It was fun, but not worth twenty to life."

"You bastard. When I get out of here I'll…"

I hung up and went back to the Sharper Image catalog I'd been thumbing through. I had my eye on one of those massaging easy chairs. That would set me back two grand. Earlier that day, I bought a sixty inch plasma TV. The money I took from William "Billy" Johansenn was being put to good use.

I plopped down in front of the TV, found the wrestling channel, and settled in to watch two hours of pay-per-view sports entertainment. The Iron Commie had Captain Frankenbeef in a suplex when I felt the gun press against the back of my head.

"Hello, Mr. McGlade."

"Happy Roy?"

"Yes. Stand up, slowly. Then turn around."

I followed instructions. Happy Roy held a four barreled COP .357, a nasty weapon that could do a lot of damage at close range.

"How'd you get in?" I asked.

"You gave a key to my wife, you moron. I took it from her last night, when she got home." His face got mean. "After you slept with her."

"Technically, we didn't do any sleeping."

The gun trembled in Happy Roy's hand.

"She's in jail now, Mr. McGlade. Because of you."

"She wanted to kill you, Happy Roy. You should thank me."

"You idiot!" Spittle flew from his lips. "I wanted to kill her myself. With my own two hands. Now I have to get her out of jail before I can do it. Do you have any idea what Johnny Cochrane charges an hour?"

"Whatever it is, you can afford it."

Happy Roy's voice cracked. "I'm practically broke. Those damn claymation commercials are costing me a fortune, and no one is buying the tie-in products. I've got ten thousand Happy Roy t-shirts, moldering away in a warehouse. Plus the burger chains with their processed chicken strips are forcing me into bankruptcy."

"Those new Wendy's strips are pretty good."

"Shut up! Put your hands over your head. No quick moves."

"What about your mansion? Can't you sell that?"

"It's a rental."

"Really? Do you mind if I ask what you pay a month?"

"Enough! We're going for a ride, Mr. McGlade. I'm going to introduce you to one of our extra large deep fryers, up close and personal."

"You told me I could keep working with your wife."

"I said you could work with her, not set her up!"

"Six of one, half a dozen of…"

"I'm the Chicken King, goddammit! I'm an American icon! Nobody crosses me and gets away with it!

I'd had enough of the Chicken King's crazy ranting, so I reached for the gun. Happy Roy tried to squeeze the trigger, but I easily yanked it away before he had the chance.

"Let me give you a little lesson in firearms, Happy Roy. A COP .357 has a twenty pound trigger pull. Much too hard to fire for a guy with arthritis."

Happy Roy reached for his belt, fighting with the buckle. "You bastard! I'll beat the fear of Happy Roy into you, you son of a bitch! No one crosses…"

I tapped him on the head with his gun, and the Chicken King collapsed. After checking for a pulse, I went for the phone and dialed my Lieutenant friend.

"Hi, Jack. Me again. Marietta Garbonzo's husband just broke into my place, tried to kill me. Yeah, Happy Roy himself. No, he doesn't look so happy right now. Can you send someone by? And can you make it quick? He's bleeding all over my carpet, and I just had it cleaned. Thanks."

I hung up and stared down at the Chicken King, who was mumbling something into the carpet.

"You say something, Happy Roy?"

"I should have stayed single."

"No kidding," I said. "Relationships can be murder."

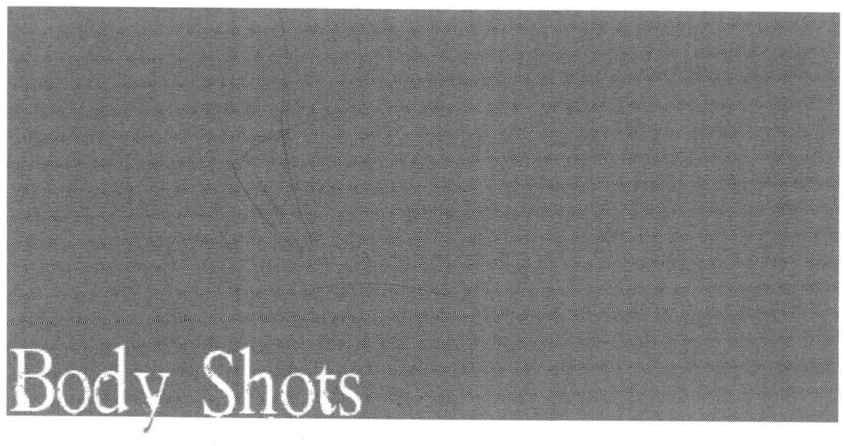

Body Shots

Amazon.com introduced a program in 2005 called Amazon Shorts, where customers could download short stories for 49 cents. I wrote this story specifically for Amazon. It was an attempt to really take Jack to the brink, by making the situation get worse and worse no matter how hard she tried to fix things. It's as dark as Jack has gotten, so far…

"AND CAN YOU MEGA-size that meal deal?"

I reach over from the passenger seat and give my partner, Sergeant Herb Benedict, a poke in the ribs, except I don't actually feel his ribs because they're encased in a substantial layer of fat—the result of many years of mega-sizing his fast food meals.

"What?" he asks. "You want me to mega-size your fat-free yogurt?"

"No. You told me to point it out whenever I saw you overeating."

"How am I overeating?"

"You just mega-sized a triple bacon cheeseburger and a chocolate shake."

Herb shrugs, multiple chins wiggling.

"So? It's just one meal."

"The mega-size french fries come in a carton bigger than your head. The shake is the size of a rain barrel."

"Be realistic here, Jack. It's only 49 cents. You can't buy anything for 49 cents these days."

"How about another heart attack? How much is that—"

My words are cut off by two quick pops from the drive-thru speaker. Though October, Chicago has been blessed with unseasonably warm weather, and my passenger window is wide open, the sound reaching me through there as well. It's coming from the restaurant.

Only one thing makes a sound like that.

Herb hits the radio. "This is Car 118, officer needs assistance. Shots fired at the Burger Barn on Kedzie and Wabash."

I beat Herb out of the car, pulling my star from the pocket of my jacket and my .38 from my shoulder holster. I'm wearing flats and a beige skirt. A cool wind kicks up and brings goosebumps to my legs. The shoes are Kate Spade. The jacket and skirt are Donna Karan. The holster is Smith and Wesson.

As I near the building, I can make out screams, followed by another gunshot. A spatter of blood and tissue blossoms on the inside of the drive-thru window, blocking my view of the interior.

I hold up my pinky—my signal to Herb that there are casualties—and hurry past the window in a crouch, stopping before the glass doors. I tug the lanyard out of the badge case and loop it over my head. On one knee, I crane my neck around the brick jamb and peek into the restaurant.

I spot a single perp, Caucasian male, mid-thirties. I can't make out his hair color because he's wearing a black football helmet complete with face gear. Jeans, black combat boots, and a gray trench coat complete the ensemble. And under the trench coat…

An ammo belt.

Two strips of leather crisscross his chest, bandolero style. Instead of bullets in the webbing, I count eight clips. Four more clips are stuck into his waistband. I assume they're for the 9mm Beretta in his hand, currently pointed at a family cowering under a plastiform table.

A mother and two kids.

Before my mind can register what is happening, he fires six times. The bullets tear through the table and into the mother's back. Blood sprays onto the children she's been shielding, and then erupts from the children in fireworks patterns.

I tear my eyes away from the horror and scan for more hostiles, but see only potential victims—at least twenty. Behind me, I hear footfalls and Herb's labored breathing.

"At least four down. One perp, heavily armed."

"You want to be old yeller?"

I shake my head and swallow. "I want the shot."

"On three."

Herb flashes one, two, three fingers, then I shove through the door first, rolling to the side, coming up in a shooting position just as Herb yells, "POLICE! DROP THE WEAPON!"

The gunman swings toward Herb, I let out a slow breath and squeeze—angle up to discourage ricochets, aiming at the body mass, no ricochet because the shot is true, squeeze, the perp recoiling and stepping back once, twice, dropping the green duffle bag that's slung over his shoulder, squeeze, screams from everywhere at once, Herb's gun going off behind me, squeeze, watching the impact but not seeing blood—

Vest.

I scream, "Vest!" and roll to the side as the gunman takes aim, firing where I was, orange tile chips peppering the side of my face like BBs.

I come up in a kneeling position behind a rectangular trash can enclosure, look at Herb and see that he's out of the line of fire, gone to ground.

I stick my head around the garbage island, watch as the perp vaults the counter, shooting a teenaged cashier who's hugging the shake machine and sobbing. The back of the teen's head opens up and empties onto the greasy floor.

"Everybody out!" I yell.

There's a stampede to the door, and I glance back and see Herb get tackled by a wall of people, then I take a deep breath and bolt for the counter.

The gunman appears, holding a screaming employee dressed in a Burger Barn uniform, using the kid as a human shield. Her face is streaked with tears, and there's a dark patch in the front of her jeans where she's wet herself. The Beretta is jammed against her forehead.

The perp says, "Drop the gun, Jack."

His voice is a low baritone, and it's eerily calm. His blue eyes lock on mine, and they hold my gaze. He doesn't seem psychotic at all, which terrifies me.

How does he know my name?

I stand up, adopt a Weaver stance, aiming for the face shot.

The gunman doesn't wait for me. He fires.

There's a sudden explosion of blood and tissue and the girl's eyes roll up and the perp ducks behind some fryers before her body hits the floor.

Too fast. This is all happening too fast.

I chance a look at the door, don't see Herb among the panicking people. I can't wait—there are probably more employees in the back. I dig into my blazer pocket and find some loose bullets, jamming them into my revolver. When I leap over the counter, my gun is at full cock.

No one by the grill. I glance left, see a body slumped next to the drive-thru window. Glance right, see a dead man on his back, most of his face gone. Stare forward, see a long stainless steel prep table. There's a young guy hiding under it. I tug him out and push him toward the counter, mouthing at him to "Run."

Movement ahead. The freezer door opens, and my finger almost pulls the trigger. It's another employee. Behind him, the perp.

The perp is grinning.

"Let's try this again," he says. "Drop the gun or I shoot."

I can't drop my gun. I'm not allowed to. It's one of the first things they teach you at the police academy.

"Let's talk this through," I say, trying to keep my voice steady.

"No talk."

He fires, and I watch another kid die in front of me.

I aim high, putting two rounds into the gunman's helmet, where they make dents and little else. He's already running away, pushing through the emergency exit, the alarm sounding off.

I tear after him, slipping on blood, falling to my hands and knees but holding onto my weapon. I crawl forward, my feet scrambling for purchase through the slickness, and then I'm opening the door, scanning the parking lot left and right.

He's standing ten feet away, aiming his Beretta at me.

I throw myself backward and feel the wind of the shots pass my face.

"Jack!" Herb, from the front of the restaurant.

"He went out the back!"

My hands, slippery with blood and sweat, are shaking like dying birds. I force myself to do a slow count to five, force my bunched muscles to relax, then nudge open the back door.

He's waiting for me.

He fires again, the bullet tugging at my shoulder pad, stinging like I've been whacked with a cane. I scoot backward on my ass, turn over, and crawl for the counter, more shots zinging over me before the back door closes under its own weight, having to climb over the girl he just killed, the scent of blood and death running up my nostrils and down the back of my throat.

I lean against the counter, pull back my jacket, feeling the burn, glancing at my wound and judging it superficial.

A soft voice, muffled, to my right.

"Hey!"

I see the green duffle bag that the perp dropped.

"Hello? Are you there, Jacqueline?"

The voice is coming from the bag. I go to it, tug back the zipper.

Gun. Another Beretta. Loose bullets, more than a hundred. And a walkie-talkie.

"Jack," the walkie barks.

How the hell does he know my name?

"Can you hear me, Jacqueline?"

I look around, find some napkins on a table, pick up the radio and hit the talk button.

"Who is this?"

"I'm doing this for you, Jacqueline. This is all for you. Do you remember Washington?"

Thoughts rush at me. Seven dead so far. He knows me. The perp has over a hundred bullets left. I don't know this guy. I've never been to Washington, the state or the capitol. He knows me. Someone I arrested before? Who is he?

I press talk. "If it's me you want, come and get me."

"I can't right now," the walkie says. "I'm late for class."

I race for the front doors. When I step onto the sidewalk, I see the perp darting through traffic and running full sprint down the sidewalk.

Heading for Thomas Jefferson Middle School.

I don't hear any sirens. Too soon. Look left and right, and don't see Herb.

I rush back into the restaurant, drop the radio into the perp's bag, grab the handle and run after him.

Three steps into the street I'm clipped by a bike messenger.

He spins me around, and I land on my knees, watching as he skids down the tarmac on his helmet, a spray of loose bullets from the gunman's bag jingling after him like dropped change. A car honks. There's a screech of tires. I manage to make it to my feet, still holding the bag, still holding my gun, too distracted to sense if I'm hurt or not.

The school.

I cross the rest of the street, realize I've somehow lost a shoe, my bare right foot slapping against the cold concrete, pedestrians jumping out of my path.

An alarm up ahead, so piercing I feel it in my teeth. The metal detector at the school entrance. It's followed by two more gunshots.

"Jack!"

Herb, from across the street.

"Cars in the parking lot!" I yell, hoping he'll understand. Guy in a football helmet and ammo belts didn't walk in off the street. Must have driven.

The school rushes up at me. I push through the glass doors, the metal detector screaming, a hall monitor slumped dead in her chair, blood pooling black on the rubber mat.

I drop the bag, pocket the Beretta and a handful of brass, hit talk on the radio.

"Where are you?"

Static. Then, coming through the speaker, children's screams.

Followed by gunshots.

I run, trying to follow the echo, trying to pinpoint the cries for help, passing door after door, rushing up a staircase, hearing more gunshots, seeing the muzzle flashes coming from a classroom, going in low and fast.

"Drop the gun," he says.

His Beretta is aimed at the head of a seven-year-old girl.

A sob gets caught in my throat, but I refuse to cry because tears will cloud my vision.

I can't watch anyone else die.

I drop my gun.

The perp begins to twitch, his face wet behind the football helmet.

"Do you have children, Jack?"

I'm not able to talk, so I just shake my head.

"Neither do I," he says. "Isn't…isn't it a shame?"

He pats the girl on the head, crouches down to whisper.

"You did good, sweetheart. I don't need you anymore."

I scream my soul raw when he pulls the trigger.

The little girl drops away, her pink dress now a shocking red, and I launch myself at him just as he turns his weapon on the children cowering in the corner of the room and opens fire.

One.

Two.

Three.

He manages four shots before I body-tackle him, both hands locking on his gun arm, pushing it up and away from the innocents, my head filled with frightened cries that might be from the children but might also be mine.

I grip his wrist and tug hard, locking his elbow, dropping down and forcing him to release the gun. It clatters to the ground.

His free hand tangles itself in my hair and pulls so hard my vision ignites like a flashbulb. I lose my grip and fall to my knees, and he jerks me in the other direction, white hot pain lacing across my scalp as a patch of hair rips free.

I drive an uppercut between his legs, my knuckles bouncing off a plastic supporter, then I'm being pushed away and he's leaping for the door.

My jacket is twisted up, and I can't find my pocket even though I feel the weight of the gun, and finally my hand slips in and I tug a Beretta free and bury three shots into his legs as he runs into the hallway.

I chance a quick look at the children, see several have been hit, see blood on the wall covering two dozen construction paper jack-o-lantern pictures, then I crawl after the perp with the gun raised.

He's waiting for me in the hall, sitting against the wall, bleeding from both knees. I hear him sobbing.

"You weren't supposed to drop your gun," he says.

My breath is coming quick, and I blow it out through my mouth. I'm shaking so bad I can't even keep a bead on him. I blink away tears and repeat over and over, "he's-unarmed-don't-shoot-he's-unarmed-don't shoot-he's-unarmed-don't shoot…"

Movement to my left.

Herb, barreling down the hall. He stops and aims.

"You okay?" Herb asks.

I think I nod.

"Hands in the air!" he screams at the perp.

The perp continues to moan. He doesn't raise his hands.

"Put your hands in the air now!"

The sob becomes a howl, and the perp reaches into his trench coat.

Herb and I empty our guns into him. I aim at his face.

My aim his true.

The perp slumps over, streaking the wall with red. Herb rushes up, pats down the corpse.

"He's clean," Herb says. "No weapons."

I can hear the sirens now. I manage to lower my gun as the paramedics storm the stairs. Kids flood out of the classroom, teachers hurrying them down the hall, telling them not to look.

Many of them look anyway.

I feel my vision narrow, my shoulders quake. I'm suddenly very cold.

"Are you hurt?" Herb asks, squatting down next to me. I'm covered with the blood of too many people.

I shake my head.

"I found the car," Herb says. "Registered to a William Phillip Martingale, Buffalo Grove Illinois. He left a suicide note on the windshield. It said, 'Life no longer matters.'"

"Priors?" I ask, my voice someone else's.

"No."

And something clicks. Some long ago memory from before I was a cop, before I was even an adult.

"I think I know him," I say.

William Phillip Martingale. Billy Martingale. In my fifth grade class at George Washington Elementary School.

"When we were kids. He asked me to the Valentine's Day dance." The words feel like stale bread crust stuck in my throat. "I turned him down. I already had a date."

"Jesus," Herb says.

But there was more. No one liked Billy. He had a bad front tooth, dark gray. Talked kind of slow. Everyone teased him. Everyone including me.

I crawl past the paramedics, over to the perp, probing the ruin of his face, finding that bad tooth he'd never bothered to get fixed.

The first body is wheeled out of the classroom, the body bag no larger than a pillow.

I begin to cry, and I don't think I'll ever be able to stop.

Suffer

Another Phin story. Phin comes from a long tradition of anti-heroes, and was influenced by Mickey Spillane's Mike Hammer, Max Allan Collins' Quarry, and Richard Stark's Parker. But he's mostly a direct descendant of F. Paul Wilson's Repairman Jack, with decidedly less humanity. I wrote this story at the request of the editor for the anthology Chicago Noir. *He rejected it. So I sold it to* EQMM *and wrote another Phin story for him,* Epitaph. *He rejected that as well, and I sold that to James Patterson for the ITW* Thriller *anthology. I'm happy how things worked out.*

"I WANT YOU TO kill my wife."

The man sitting across from me, Lyle Tibbits, stared into my eyes like a dog stares at the steak you're eating. He was mid to late thirties, a few inches taller than my six feet, wearing jeans and a button down shirt that pinched his thick wrists.

I sipped some coffee and asked why he wanted his wife dead.

"Do you care?" he asked.

I shrugged. "No. As long as I get paid."

Lyle smiled, exposing gray smoker's teeth.

"I didn't think it mattered. When I called you, I heard you did anything for money."

I rubbed my nose. My nostrils were sore from all the coke I'd been snorting lately, and I'd been getting nosebleeds.

"Any particular way you want it done?"

He looked around Maxie's Coffee Shop—his choice for the meeting place—and leaned forward on his forearms, causing the table to shift and the cheap silverware to rattle.

"You break into my house, discover her home alone, then rape and kill her."

Jaded as I was, this made me raise an eyebrow.

"Rape her?"

"The husband is always a suspect when the wife dies. Either he did it, or he hired someone to do it. The rape will throw the police off. Plus, I figured, with your condition, you won't care about leaving evidence."

He made a point of glancing at my bald head.

"Who gave you my number?" I asked.

"I don't want to say."

I thought about the Glock nestled between my belt and my spine, knew I could get him to tell me if I needed to. We were on Damon and Diversey in Wicker Park, which wasn't the nicest part of Chicago. I could follow him out of the diner and put the hurt to him right there on the sidewalk, and chances were good we'd be ignored.

But truth be told, I didn't really care where he got my number, or that he knew I was dying of cancer. I was out of money, which meant I was out of cocaine. The line I'd done earlier was wearing off, and the pain would return soon.

"I get half up front, half when it's done. The heat will be on you after the job, and you won't have a chance to get the money to me. So you'll put the second half in a locker at the train station, hide the key someplace public, and then give me the info when I'm done. Call from a payphone so the number isn't traced. You fuck me, and I'll find you."

"You can trust me."

Like your wife trusts you? I thought. Instead I said, "How would you like me to do it?"

"Messy. The messier the better. I want her to suffer, and suffer for a long time."

"You've obviously been living in marital bliss."

"You have to hurt her, or else we don't have a deal."

I made a show of thinking it over, even though I'd already made my decision. I assumed this was a way to cash in on life insurance, but what life insurance policy paid extra for torture and rape?

"You have the money on you?" I asked.

"Yeah."

"Pass it under the table."

He hesitated. "Trust goes both ways, you know."

"I could just walk away."

Like hell I could. I needed a snort worse than Wimpy needed his daily hamburger. But I'm a pretty decent bluffer.

Lyle handed me the paper bag he'd brought with him. I set it on the booth next to me and peeked inside. The cash was rubber-banded in stacks of tens and twenties. I stuck my fingers in and did a quick count.

Six grand, to take a human life.

Not bad for a few hours work.

"When?" I asked.

"Tomorrow night, after 10pm. I'll be out, and she'll be home alone. I'll leave the front door open for you. I'm at 3626 North Christiana, off of Addison. Remember, rape and pain."

He seemed to be waiting for a reply so I said, "Sure."

"And Mr. Troutt..." Lyle smiled again, flashing gray. "Have fun with it."

After the diner meeting, I called a guy about securing some fake ID. Then I called my dealer and scored enough coke to keep me high for a while. I also bought some tequila and refilled my codeine prescription.

Back at my ratty apartment, Earl and I had a party.

Earl is what I call the tumor growing on my pancreas. Giving my killer a name makes it a little easier to deal with. Each day, Earl eats a little more of my body. Each day, I try to prevent Earl from doing that. There's chemo, and radiation, and occasional surgery. And in the off-times, there's illegal drugs, pharmaceuticals, and alcohol.

Earl was winning.

Luckily, being a drug abuser has some excellent side benefits, such as not caring about anything, erasing all emotion, and helping to forget the past.

Just a few months ago I had a well paying job in the suburbs, a beautiful fiancée, and a life most would be envious of. Earl changed all that. Now, not even the roaches in my tenement building were envious of me.

I drank, and popped, and snorted, until the pain was gone. Until reality was gone. Until consciousness was gone.

Earl woke me up the next morning, gnawing at my left side with jagged, rabid teeth.

I peeled myself from the floor, stripped off the jeans and underwear I'd soiled, and climbed into a shower slick with mildew. I turned the water as hot as it would go, and the first blast came out rusty and stung my eyes. I had no soap, so I used shampoo to scrub my body. I didn't eat well, if I remembered to eat at all, and I could count the ribs on my hairless chest. I made a note to eat something today. Who would hire a thug that weighed ninety pounds?

After the shower I found some fresh jeans and a white t-shirt. I did a line, choked down three painkillers, and dug out an old Chicago phone book.

"Walker Insurance."

"I had a couple questions about life insurance."

"I'll transfer you to one of our agents."

I took my cell over the fridge and listened to a Musak version of Guns N Roses while rummaging through the ice box. Nothing in there but frost.

"This is Brad, can I help you?"

"I'm thinking of taking out a life insurance policy on my wife. We live in a nice neighborhood, but she has this unrealistic fear—call it a phobia—of being raped and killed. I'm sure that would never happen, but do you have policies that cover that?"

"Accidental death includes murder, but not suicide."

"And rape?"

"Well, I've heard of some countries like India and Africa that offer rape insurance, but there's nothing like that in the US. But if she's afraid of being attacked, a good life insurance policy can help bring some peace of mind."

"What if she doesn't like the idea of insurance? Could I insure her without her knowing it?"

"For certain types of insurance, the person covered doesn't need to sign the policy. You can insure anyone you want. Would you like to schedule an appointment to talk about this further?"

I thought about asking him if he covered people dying of cancer, but I resisted and hung up. My next call was to the 26th District of the Chicago Police Department.

"Daniels."

"Hi, Jack. It's Phineas Troutt."

"Haven't seen you at the pool hall lately. What's up?"

"I need a favor. I'm looking for paper on a guy named Lyle Tibbits."

"And I should help you because?"

"Because you're a friend. And because he owes me money. And because I probably won't live to see Christmas."

Jack arrested me a few years back, but she'd been cool about it, and we had an on-again-off-again eight ball game on Monday nights. I'd missed a few lately, too stoned to leave my apartment. But I'd helped Jack out a few times, and she owed me, and she knew it.

"Let's see what Mr. Computer has to say. Lyle Tibbits. Prior arrest for—it looks like trafficking kiddie porn. Did a nickel's worth at Joliet. Paroled last year."

"Anything about a wife or kids?"

"Nope."

"Address?"

"Roscoe Village, on Belmont."

She gave me the numbers, and I wrote them down.

"Nothing on Addison?"

"Nope."

"Can you give me his vitals?"

Jack ran through his birth date, social security number, mother's maiden name, and some other choice info cops are privy to.

"You coming this Monday?" she asked when the litany ended. "I finally bought my own cue."

"A Balabushka?"

"A custom stick on my salary? More like Wal-Mart."

"I'll try to make it. Thanks, Jack."

"Take care, Phin."

I tucked the Glock into my pants, pocketed my set of master keys and a pair of S & W handcuffs, and hit the street. It was cool for July, in the low seventies, the sun screened by clouds or smog or both. I grabbed some sweet and sour chicken at a local shop, and then spent an hour at a place on Cermak filling out paperwork. When I finished, I hopped in a cab and took it to Roscoe Village.

Lyle's apartment had a security door, which I opened on the

fourth try. One of my first acts as a criminal had been to rob a locksmith, earning me a set of sixty master keys. They opened ninety percent of the locks in the US. It was much easier than learning how to use picks and tension wrenches, which is something I didn't have the time to learn anyway.

The halls were empty, befitting midday. I found Lyle's apartment number and knocked twice, holding my pistol behind my back.

No answer.

I got through this door on the second try, set the security chain so no one could pop in on me, and began my search.

In the living room were six double DVD recorders, all which seemed to be running. In a box next to the TV were a hundred plastic clamshell boxes, and a spindle of blank recordable DVD-Rs. In the corner of the room were three digital camcorders and a PC. I powered up the computer, spent ten minutes trying to get his password, then gave up and turned it off.

The kitchen revealed a smorgasbord of junk food—he had enough sugar in here to put an elephant into a diabetic coma. On the counter, next to the phone, was a receipt for a glazier, the total more than five hundred bucks. Stuck to the fridge with a banana-shaped magnet was a picture of Lyle drinking a beer. I put the picture in my pocket.

In the bedroom, I found an extensive collection of porno DVDs. Bondage, watersports, S/M, D/s, extreme spanking, and even a kink new to me; latex vacuum mummification. All legal.

I found his illegal stuff in a padlocked trunk, in the back of the bedroom closet. The lock opened with the seventh key I tried.

Child porn. Movies with titles like "See Billy Cry" and "Maxie's Birthday Surprise." Some of the covers had pictures.

I tried not to look.

There were also a few other illegal movies, along with a bag full of cash. Over twenty grand worth.

I took the money, locked the trunk back up, and left the apartment.

Satisfied that I knew who I was dealing with, I bided my time until 10pm.

Then I could finish the job.

As promised, Lyle had left the door open for me.

The house was dark and quiet, just like the neighborhood. I walked down Christiana and up the porch stairs without encountering a soul. Once inside, I locked the door behind me and held my breath, listening for sounds of life.

Nothing.

The lights were on in the living room, and I held my Glock before me and did a quick search of the first floor. The furnishings leaned towards the feminine side; pink drapes and flower patterns on the couch. On the end table, copies of Glamour and Cosmo. In the kitchen, a half-eaten container of lowfat yogurt sat on the counter, a spoon alongside it. I checked the back door, found it locked, and then crept over to the staircase.

The stairs were carpeted, but they squeaked with my weight. I paused after every two steps, ears open. I didn't hear a damn thing.

The second floor revealed an empty bathroom, an empty guest room, and a bedroom.

The bedroom was occupied.

A woman was tied to the bed, naked and spread-eagled. She was white, late twenties, her blond hair tangled up in the red leather ball gag buckled around her mouth. Leather straps around her ankles and wrists twisted around the four bedposts. Her eyes were wide with terror, and she screamed when she saw me, the sound lost in her throat.

There was a note next to her head.

Give it to her. And leave the gag in, or she'll wake the neighbors.

The room was unusually well-lit. Besides the ceiling light, there were lamps on either side of the bed, one in the corner next to the mirrored closet, and an extra work-light—the portable kind that clips to things—attached to the bed canopy.

"Hello," I said to the woman.

She screamed again.

"Shh. I'll be with you in just a minute."

I took two steps backwards, toward the closet, and then spun around, facing the mirrored sliding door. My free hand pulled back the handle while my business hand jammed the Glock into the closet, into the chest of Lyle Tibbits.

Lyle yelped, dropping the camcorder and trying to push me away.

I brought the gun up and clipped him in the teeth with the butt.

He fell forward, spitting blood and enamel. I gave him another chop on the back of the head, and he ate the floor.

"Dontkillmedontkillme!"

I put my foot on his neck and applied some weight, glancing back to check the rest of the closet. Empty. The mirror was one-way, and I could see the bed through the door's glass. The original mirror rested against the rear wall.

"Who is she, Lyle?"

He yelled something, the carpet muffling his words. I eased up some of the pressure from my foot.

"I just met her last week!"

"She's not your wife."

"No! She's just some chick I'm dating!"

"And you hired me to rape and kill her so you could videotape it. I saw the other films back at your apartment. Does snuff sell for more than kiddie porn?"

Lyle wiggled, trying to crane his neck around to look at me.

"It's worth a fortune! I'll cut you in, man! It's enough money for both of us!"

I glanced at the woman, tied up on the bed.

"How much money?" I asked.

"I've got over half a mil in advance orders! We'll be rich, man!"

"That's a lot of money, Lyle. But I'm not greedy. I don't need that much."

"How much do you want? Name the price!"

"You're worth eighty grand to me."

"Eighty grand? No problem! I can—"

I knelt on his back, cutting off his breath. Pressing the Glock to the back of his head, I yanked the handcuffs out of my pocket.

"Put your left hand behind your back, Lyle."

He complied. I yanked his arm back in a submission hold, slapped on the cuffs, then climbed off.

"Let's go into the bathroom, Lyle."

I was a bit too eager helping him to his feet, because I hyper-extended his arm and felt it snap at the elbow.

Lyle howled loud enough to hurt my ears, and I gave his broken arm a twist and told him to shut the hell up. In the bathroom, I chained him to the drainage pipe under the sink, then I went back into the bedroom.

"You're safe," I told the woman. "No one can hurt you now. I'm going to call the police. Are you okay to talk to them?"

She nodded, frantic. I took off her gag.

"He was gonna kill me."

"I know." I picked up the phone next to the bedside and dialed 911, then placed it on the bed next to her mouth.

I walked out of the room as she began talking.

I was in a drugged haze when Jack called on my cell.

"Missed you on Monday."

"Sorry. Been busy."

"Remember that guy you called me about? Lyle Tibbits? He got picked up a few days ago."

"Is that a fact?"

"It seems as if Mr. Tibbits was planning on making a snuff film, but someone came and rescued the snuffee."

I wiped some blood off my nose. "Sounds like she got lucky."

"She said it was a bald man."

"Poor guy. It's tough being bald. Society discriminates."

"It would help the case if this mysterious bald man came forward and testified."

"If I see him, I'll let him know. But you probably don't need him. If you check out Lyle's apartment, you might find plenty of reasons to lock him up for good."

"We did that already. Mr. Tibbits will be eligible for parole when he's four hundred years old."

"So why the call?"

"The woman who was saved wants to thank her hero. In person."

An image flashed through my head of Linda, my fiancée. I'd left her because I didn't want her to see me suffer and die.

No one should be subjected to that. To me.

"That's not possible," I told Jack.

"I'll let her know. Pool Monday?"

"I'll try to make it. Jack?"

"Yeah?"

"They holding Tibbits over at Cook County?"

"Yeah. Why?"

"General population?"

"I think so. He's in for kidnapping and attempted murder. The State's Attorney is putting together the illegal porn case."

"Thanks, Jack."

I staggered to the bathroom and rinsed the blood and powder off my face. Then I threw on some clothes, left my apartment, and staggered to the corner news vendor. The daily paper set me back a buck. I sat on the curb and read the police blotter until I found what I needed. Then I picked up three cartons of Marlboros and took a cab to Cook County Jail on 26th and California.

I spent two hours waiting before I was able to see Jerome Johnston. He was black, twenty-two years old, a member of the Gangsta Disciples. Jerome was being held for first degree murder.

"Who the hell are you, cracker?" he said upon meeting me in the visitation room.

"I've got a deal for you, Jerome. A good deal." I handed him the three cartons of smokes that the guards had already searched. "This is for your valuable time."

"What do you want?"

"There's a white boy in your division. Name of Lyle Tibbits. He's a baby raper. Likes to have sex with five-year-old boys and girls." I stared hard into Jerome's lifeless eyes. "I want you to spread the word. Anyone who takes care of him will get twenty cartons of cigarettes. He'll be an easy mark—he's got a broken arm. Here's a picture."

I handed him the photo I'd taken from Lyle's apartment.

"How do you know me?" Jerome asked.

"I don't. Just read about your drive-by in the paper. Thought you'd be the right man for the job. Are you, Jerome?"

Jerome looked at the picture, then back at me. "Hell yeah, dog."

"One more thing. It can't happen until tomorrow. Okay?"

"I'm straight."

I left the jail and cabbed it back home. In my room I did more coke, ate some codeine, and stared at the eighty-thousand dollar life insurance policy I'd taken out on Lyle Tibbits, which I'd bought posing as his brother, using fake identification. It would become effective tonight at midnight.

Eighty grand would buy a lot of pain relief. It might even be enough to help me forget.

I drank until I couldn't feel Earl anymore, and then I drank some more.

When Monday rolled around I cashed my policy and met Jack at Joe's Pool Hall and whipped her butt with my new thousand dollar Balabushka custom-made pool cue.

Overproof

My friend Libby Fischer Hellmann edited an anthology called Chicago Blues, *published by Bleak House in 2007. I wrote a Jack story for her, based on a premise I thought of while stuck in traffic downtown. Why do cars get gridlocked? Here's one possible answer…*

THE MAN SAT IN the center of the southbound lane on Michigan Avenue, opposite Water Tower Place, sat cross-legged and seemingly oblivious to the mile of backed-up traffic, holding a gun that he pointed at his own head.

I'd been shopping at Macy's, and purchased a Gucci wallet as a birthday gift for my boyfriend, Latham. When I walked out onto Michigan I was hit by the cacophony of several hundred honking horns and the unmistakable shrill of a police whistle. I hung my star around my neck and pushed through the crowd that had gathered on the sidewalk. Chicago's Magnificent Mile was always packed during the summer, but the people were usually moving in one direction or the other. These folks were standing still, watching something.

Then I saw what they were watching.

I assumed the traffic cop blowing the whistle had called it in—he had a radio on his belt. He'd stopped cars in both directions, and had enforced a twenty meter perimeter around the guy with the gun.

I took my .38 Colt out of my purse and walked over, holding up my badge with my other hand. The cop was black, older, the strain of the situation heavy on his face.

"Lt. Jack Daniels, Homicide." I had to yell above the car horns. "What's the ETA on the negotiator?"

"Half hour, at least. Can't get here because of the jam."

He made a gesture with his white gloved hand, indicating the gridlock surrounding us.

"You talk to this guy?"

"Asked him his name, if he wanted anything. Told me to leave him alone. Don't have to tell me twice."

I nodded. The man with the gun was watching us. He was white, pudgy, mid-forties, clean shaven and wearing a blue suit and a red tie. He looked calm but focused. No tears. No shaking. As if it was perfectly normal to sit in the middle of the street with a pistol at your own temple.

I kept my Colt trained on the perp and took another step toward him. If he flinched, I'd shoot him. The shrinks had a term for it: suicide by cop. People who didn't have the guts to kill themselves, so they forced the police to. I didn't want to be the one to do it. Hell, it was the absolute last thing I wanted to do. I could picture the hearing, being told the shooting was justified, and I knew that being in the right wouldn't help me sleep any better if I had to murder this poor bastard.

"What's your name?" I asked.

"Paul."

The gun he had was small, looked like a .380. Something higher caliber would likely blow through both sides of his skull and into the crowd. This bullet probably wasn't powerful enough. But it would do a fine job of killing him. Or me, if he decided he wanted some company in the afterlife.

"My name is Jack. Can you put the gun down, Paul?"

"No."

"Please?"

"No."

That was about the extent of my hostage negotiating skills. I dared a step closer, coming within three feet of him, close enough to smell his sweat.

"What's so bad that you have to do this?"

Paul stared at me without answering. I revised my earlier thought about him looking calm. He actually looked numb. I glanced at his left hand, saw the wedding ring.

"Problems with the wife?" I asked.

His Adam's apple bobbled up and down as he swallowed. "My wife died last year."

"I'm sorry."

"Don't be. You married?"

"Divorced. What was your wife's name, Paul?"

"Doris."

"What do you think Doris would say if she saw you like this?"

Paul's face pinched into a sad smile. My Colt Detective Special weighed twenty-two ounces, and my arm was getting tired holding it up. I brought my left hand under my right to brace it, my palm on the butt of the weapon.

"Do you think you'll get married again?" he asked.

I thought about Latham. "It will happen, sooner or later."

"You have someone, I'm guessing."

"Yes."

"Does he like it that you're a cop?"

I considered the question before answering. "He likes the whole package."

Paul abruptly inhaled. A snort? I couldn't tell. I did a very quick left to right sweep with my eyes. The crowd was growing, and inching closer—one traffic cop couldn't keep everyone back by himself. The media had also arrived. Took them long enough, considering four networks had offices within a few blocks.

"Waiting for things to happen, that's a mistake." Paul closed his eyes for a second, then opened them again. "If you want things to happen, you have to make them happen. Because you never know how long things are going to last."

He didn't seem depressed. More like irritated. I took a slow breath, smelling the cumulative exhaust of a thousand cars and buses, wishing the damn negotiator would arrive.

"Do you live in the area, Paul?"

He sniffled, sounding congested. "Suburbs."

"Do you work downtown?"

"Used to. Until about half an hour ago."

"Do you want to talk about it?"

"No."

"Can you give me more than that?"

He squinted at me. "Why do you care?"

"It's my job, Paul."

"It's your job to protect people."

"Yes. And you're a person."

"You want to protect me from myself."

"Yes."

"You also want to protect these people around us."

"Yes."

"How far away are they, do you think? Fifteen feet? Twenty?"

A strange question, and I didn't like it. "I don't know. Why?"

Paul made a show of looking around.

"Lot of people here. Big responsibility, protecting them all."

He shifted, and my finger automatically tensed on the trigger. Paul said something, but it was lost in the honking.

"Can you repeat that, Paul?"

"Maybe life isn't worth protecting."

"Sure it is."

"There are bad people in the world. They do bad things. Should they be protected too?"

"Everyone should be protected."

Paul squinted at me. "Have you ever shot anyone, Jack?"

Another question I didn't like.

"When I was forced to, yes. Please don't force me, Paul."

"Have you ever killed anyone?"

"No."

"Have you ever wanted to?"

"No."

Paul made a face like I was lying. "Why not? Do you believe in God? In heaven? Are you one of those crazy right-to-lifers who believe all life is sacred? Do you protest the death penalty?"

"I believe blood is hard to get off of your hands, even if it's justified."

He shifted again, and his jacket came open. There was a spot of something on his shirt. Something red. Both my arms were feeling the strain of holding up my weapon, and a spike of fear-induced adrenalin caused a tremor in my hands.

"What's that on your shirt, Paul? Is that blood?"

He didn't bother to look. "Probably."

I kept my voice steady. "Did you go to work today, Paul?"

"Yes."

"Did you bring your gun to work?"

No answer. I glanced at the spot of blood again, and noticed that his stomach didn't look right. I'd first thought Paul was overweight. Now it looked like he had something bulky on under his shirt.

"Did you hurt anyone at work today, Paul?"

"That's the past, Jack. You can't protect them. What's done is done."

I was liking this situation less and less. That spot of blood drew my eyes like a beacon. I wondered if he was wearing a bullet proof vest under his business suit, or something worse.

"I don't want to go to jail," he said.

"What did you do, Paul?"

"They shouldn't have fired me."

"Who? Where do you work?"

"Since Doris died, I haven't been bringing my 'A Game.' That's understandable, isn't it?"

I raised my voice. "How did you get blood on your shirt, Paul?"

Paul glared at me, but his eyes were out of focus.

"When you shot those people, did they scream?" he asked.

I wasn't sure what he was after, so I stayed silent.

He grinned. "Doesn't it make you feel good when they scream?"

Now I got it. This guy wasn't just suicidal—he was homicidal as well. I took a step backward.

"Don't leave, Jack. I want you to see this. You should see this. I'm moving very slow, okay?"

He put his hand into his pocket. I cocked the hammer back on my Colt. Paul fished out something small and silver, and I was a hair's breadth away from shooting him.

"This is a detonator. I've got some explosives strapped to my chest. If you take another step away, if you yell, I'll blow both of us up. And the bomb is strong enough to kill a lot of people in the crowd. It's also wired to my heartbeat. I die, it goes off."

I didn't know if I believed him or not. Explosives weren't easy to get, or to make. And rigging up a detonator—especially one that was hooked into your pulse—that was really hard, even if you could find the plans on the Internet. But Paul's eyes had just enough hint of psychosis in them that I stayed put.

"Do you doubt me, Jack? I see some doubt. I work at LarsiTech, out of the Prudential Building. We sell medical equipment. That's where I got the ECG electrode pads. It's also where I got the radioactive isotopes."

My breath caught in my throat, and my gun became impossibly heavy. Paul must have noticed my reaction, because he smiled.

"The isotopes won't cause a nuclear explosion, Jack. The detonator is too small. But they will spread radioactivity for a pretty good distance. You've heard of dirty bombs, right? People won't die right away. They'll get sick. Hair will fall out. And teeth. Skin will slough off. Blindness. Leukemia. Nasty business. I figure I've got enough strapped to my waist to contaminate the whole block."

All I could ask was, "Why?"

"Because I'm a bad person, Jack. Remember? Bad people do bad things."

"Would Doris…approve…of this?"

"Doris didn't approve of anything. She judged. Judged every little thing I did. I half expected to be haunted by her ghost after I shot her, telling me how I could have done a better job."

I didn't have any saliva left in my mouth, so my voice came out raspy.

"What happened today at LarsiTech?"

"A lot of people got what was coming to them. Bad people, Jack. Maybe they weren't all bad. I didn't know some of them well enough. But we all have bad in us. I'm sure they deserved it. Just like this crowd of people."

He looked beyond me.

"Like that woman there, pointing at me. Looks nice enough. Probably has a family. I'm sure she's done some bad things. Maybe she hits her kids. Or she stuck her mom in a nursing home. Or cheats on her taxes. We all have bad in us."

His Helter Skelter eyes swung back to me.

"What have you done that's bad, Jack?"

A cop's job was to take control of the situation, and somehow I'd lost that control.

"You're not thinking clearly, Paul. You're depressed. You need to put down the detonator and the gun."

"You have five seconds to tell me something bad you've done, or I press the button."

"I'll shoot you, Paul."

"And then a lot of people will die, Jack. Five..."

"This isn't a game, Paul."

"Four..."

"Don't make me do this."

"Three..."

Was he bluffing? Did I have any options? My .38 pointed at his shoulder. If I shot him, it might get him to drop the detonator. Or it might kill him and then his bomb would explode. Or it might just piss him off and get him to turn his gun on me.

"Two..."

It came out in a spurt. "I cheated on my boyfriend with my ex husband."

The corners of Paul's eyes crinkled up.

"Does your boyfriend know, Jack?"

"Yes."

"He found out, or you told him?"

I recalled the pained expression on Latham's face. "I told him."

"He forgave you?"

"Yes."

Paul chewed his lower lip, looking like a child caught with his hand in the cookie jar.

"Did it feel good to hurt him, Jack?"

"No."

Paul seemed to drink this in.

"You must have known it would hurt him, but you did it anyway. So some part of you must not have minded hurting him."

"I didn't want to hurt him. I just cared more about my needs than his."

"You were being selfish."

"Yes."

"You were being bad."

The word stuck like a chicken bone in my throat. "Yes."

His thumb caressed the detonator, and he licked his lips.

"What's the difference between that and what I'm doing right now?"

The gun weighed a hundred pounds, and my arms were really starting to shake.

"I broke a man's heart. You're planning on killing a bunch of people. That's worse."

Paul raised an eyebrow. "So I'm a worse person than you?"

I hesitated, then said, "Yes."

"Do you want to shoot me?"

"No."

"But I'm bad. I deserve it."

"Bad things can be forgiven, Paul."

"Do you think your boyfriend would forgive me if I killed you?"

I pictured Latham. His forgiveness was the best gift I'd ever gotten. It proved that love had no conditions. That mistakes weren't deal breakers.

I wanted to live to see Latham again.

Regain control, Jack. Demand proof.

"Show me the bomb," I said to Paul. My tone was hard, professional. I wasn't going to neutralize the situation by talking. Paul was too far gone. When dealing with bullies, you have to push back or you won't gain their respect.

"No," he said.

Louder, "Show me the bomb!"

At the word bomb a collective wail coursed through the crowd, and they began to stampede backward.

He began to shake, and his eyes became mean little slits. "What did I say about yelling, Jack?"

Paul's finger danced over the detonator button.

"You're bluffing." I chanced a look around. The perimeter was widening.

"I'll prove I'm not bluffing by blowing up the whole—"

I got even closer, thrusting my chin at him, steadying my gun.

"I'm done with this, Paul. Drop the gun and the detonator, or I'm going to shoot you."

"If you shoot me, you'll die."

"I'm not going to believe that unless you show me the goddamn bomb."

Time stretched out, slowed. After an impossibly long second he lowered his eyes, reaching down for his buttons.

I was hoping he was bluffing, praying he was bluffing, and then his shirt opened and I saw the red sticks of dynamite.

Son of a bitch. He wasn't bluffing.

I couldn't let him press that detonator. So I fired.

Thousands of hours on the shooting range meant the move was automatic, mechanical. His wrist exploded in blood and bone, and before the scream escaped his lips I put one more in the opposite shoulder. He dropped both his gun and the detonator. I kicked them away, hoping I hadn't killed him, hoping he'd be alive until help came.

I stared at his chest, saw two electrode pads hooked up to his heart. His waist was surrounded by explosives, and in the center was a black box with a radiation symbol on it.

Paul coughed, then slumped onto his back. His wrist spurted, and his shoulder poured blood onto the pavement like a faucet. Each bullet had severed an artery. He was doomed.

I shrugged off my jacket, pressed it to the shoulder wound, and yelled, "Bomb! Get out of here!" to the few dozen idiots still gawking. Then I grabbed Paul's chin and made him look at me.

"How do I disarm this, Paul?"

His voice was soft, hoarse. "…you…you killed me…"

"Paul! Answer me! How can I shut off the bomb!"

His eyelids fluttered. My blazer had already soaked through with blood.

"…how…"

"Yes, Paul. Tell me how."

"…how does…"

"Please, Paul. Stay with me."

His eyes locked on mine.

"…how does it feel to finally kill someone?"

Then his head tilted to the side and his mouth hung open.

I felt for the pulse in his neck. Barely there. He didn't have long.

I checked the crowd again. The traffic cop had fled, and the drivers of the surrounding cars had abandoned them. No paramedics rushed over, lugging life-saving equistaent. No bomb squad technicians rushed over, to cut the wires and save the day. It was only me, and Paul. Soon it would be only me, and a few seconds later I'd be gone too.

Should I run, give myself a chance to live? How much contamination would this dirty bomb spread? Would I die anyway, along with hundreds or thousands of others? I didn't know anything about radiation. How far could it travel? Could it go through windows and buildings? How much death could it cause?

Running became moot. Paul's chest quivered, and then was still.

I knew even less about the inner working of the human body than I did about radiation. If I started CPR, would that trick the bomb into thinking Paul's heart was still beating?

I didn't have time to ponder it. Without thinking I tore off the electrodes and stuck them up under my shirt, under my bra, fixing them to my chest, hoping to find my heartbeat and stop the detonation.

I held my breath.

Nothing exploded.

I looked around again, saw no help. And none could get to me, with the traffic jam. I needed to move, to get to the next intersection, to find a place where the bomb squad could get to me.

But first I called Dispatch.

"This is Lieutenant Jack Daniels, from the 26th District. I'm on the corner of Michigan and Pearson. I need the bomb squad. A dirty bomb is hooked up to my heartbeat. I also need someone to check out a company downtown called LarsiTech, a medical supply company in the Prudential Building. There may have been some homicides there."

I gave the Dispatch officer my cell number, then grabbed Paul's wrist and began to drag him to the curb. It wasn't easy. My grip was slippery with blood, and the asphalt was rough and pulled at his clothes. I would tug, make sure the electrodes were still attached, take a step, and repeat.

Halfway there my cell rang.

"This is Dispatch. The bomb squad is on the way, ETA eight minutes. Are you sure on the company name, Lieutenant?"

"He said it several times."

"There's no listing for LarsiTech in the Prudential Building. I spelled it several different ways."

"Then where is LarsiTech?"

"No place I could find. Chicago had three medical supply companies, and I called them all. They didn't report any problems. The phone book has no LarsiTech. Information has no listing in Illinois, or the whole nation."

I looked down at Paul, saw the wires had ripped out of the black box. And that the black box had a local cable company's name written on the side. And that the radiation symbol was actually a sticker that was peeling off. And that the dynamite was actually road flares with their tops cut off.

Suicide by cop.

I sat down in the southbound lane on Michigan Avenue, sat down and stared at my hands, at the blood caked under the fingernails, and wondered if I'd ever be able to get them clean.

Bereavement

In 2005 I decided that I knew so many thriller authors I should edit an anthology. It developed into a collection of hitman stories called These Guns For Hire. *I'm hugely proud of that antho, which was published in 2006 by Bleak House. I also discovered that the easiest way to get published is to stick one of your own stories in the anthology that you're editing.*

"Why should you care? Guys like you got no scruples."

If I had any scruples, I would have fed this asshole his teeth. Or at least walked away.

But he was right.

"Half up front," I said. "Half at the scene."

He looked at me like flowers had suddenly sprouted out of my bald head, Elmer Fudd-style.

"At the scene?"

I'd been through this before, with others. Everyone seemed to want their spouse dead these days. Contract murder was the new black.

I leaned back, pushing away the red plastic basket with the half-eaten hot dog. We were the only customers in Jimmy's Red Hots, the food being the obvious reason we dined alone. The shit on a bun they served was a felony.. If my stomach wasn't clenched tight with codeine withdrawal spasms, I might have complained.

"You want her dead," I said, fighting to keep my voice steady. "The cops always go after the husband."

He didn't seem to mind the local cuisine, and jammed the remainder of his dog into his mouth, hoarding it in his right cheek as he spoke.

"I was thinking she's home alone, someone breaks in to rob the place, gets surprised and kills her."

"And why weren't you home?"

"I was out with friends."

He was a big guy. Over six feet, neck as thick as his head so he looked like a redwood with a face carved into it. Calloused knuckles and a deep tan spoke of a blue collar trade, maybe construction. Probably considered killing the little lady himself, many times. A hands-on type. He seemed disappointed having to hire out.

Found me through the usual channels. Knew someone who knew someone. Fact was, the sicker I got, the less I cared about covering my tracks. Blind drops and background checks and private referrals were things of the past. So many people knew what I did I might as well be walking around Chicago wearing a sandwich board that said, "Phineas Troutt–He Kills People For Money."

"Cops will know you hired someone," I told him. "They'll look at your sheet."

He squinted, mean dropping over him like a veil.

"How do you know about that?"

The hot dog smell was still getting to me, so I picked up my basket and set it on the garbage behind out table.

"Let me guess," I said. "Battery."

He shrugged. "Domestic bullshit. Little bitch gets lippy sometimes."

"Don't they all."

I felt the hot dog coming back up, forced it to stay put. A sickening, flu-like heat washed over me.

"You okay, buddy?"

Sweat stung my eyes, and I noticed my hands were shaking. Another cramp hit, making me flinch.

"What are you, some kinda addict?"

"Cancer," I said.

He didn't appear moved by my response.

"Can you still do this shit?"

"Yeah."

"How long you got?"

Months? Weeks? The cancer had metastasized from my pancreas, questing for more of me to conquer. At this stage, treatment was bullshit. Only thing that helped was cocaine, tequila, and codeine. Being broke meant a lot of pain, plus withdrawal, which was almost as bad.

I had to get some money. Fast.

"Long enough," I told him.

"You look like a little girl could kick your ass."

I gave him my best tough-guy glare, then reached for the half-empty glass bottle of ketchup. Maintaining eye contact, I squeezed the bottle hard in my trembling hands. In one quick motion, I jerked my wrist to the side, breaking the top three inches of the bottle cleanly off.

"Jesus," he said.

I dropped the piece on the table and he stared at it, mouth hanging open like a fish. I shoved my other hand into my pocket, because I cut my palm pretty deep. Happens sometimes. Glass isn't exactly predictable.

"You leave the door open," I told him. "I come in around 2am. I break your wife's neck. Then I break your nose."

He went from awed to pissed. "Fuck you, buddy."

"Cops won't suspect you if you're hurt. I'll also leave some of my blood on the scene."

I watched it bounce around behind his Neanderthal brow ridge. Waited for him to fill in all the blanks. Make the connections. Take it to the next level.

His thoughts were so obvious I could practically see them form pictures over his head.

"Yeah." He nodded, slowly at first, then faster. "That DNA shit. Prove someone else was there. And you don't care if you leave any, cause you're a dead man anyway."

I shrugged like it was no big deal. Like I'd fully accepted my fate.

"When do we do this?"

"When can you have the money ready?"

"Anytime."

"How about tonight?"

The dull film over his eyes evaporated, revealing a much younger man. One who had dreams and hopes and unlimited possibilities.

"Tonight is great. Tonight is perfect. I can't believe I'm finally gonna be rid of the bitch."

"Till death do you part. Which brings me to the original question. Why don't you just divorce her?"

He grinned, showing years of bad oral hygiene.

"Bitch ain't keeping half my paycheck for life."

Ain't marriage grand?

He gave me his address, we agreed upon a time, and then I followed him outside, put on a baseball cap and some sunglasses, escorted him down a busy Chinatown sidewalk to the bank, and rammed a knife in his back the second after he punched his PIN into the enclosed ATM.

I managed to puncture his lung before piercing his heart, and he couldn't draw a breath, couldn't scream. I put my bleeding hand under his armpit so he didn't fall over, and again he gave me that look, the one of utter disbelief.

"Don't be surprised," I told him, pressing his CHECKING ACCOUNT button. "You were planning on killing me tonight, after I did your wife. You didn't want to pay me the other half."

I pressed WITHDRAW CASH and punched in a number a few times higher than our agreed upon figure.

He tried to say something, but bloody spit came out.

"Plus, a large ATM withdrawal a few hours before your wife gets killed? How stupid do you think the cops are?"

His knees gave out, and I couldn't hold him much longer. My injured palm was bleeding freely, soaking into his shirt. But leaving DNA was the least of my problems. This was a busy bank, and someone would be walking by any second.

I yanked out the knife, having to put my knee against his back to do so because of the suction; gravity knives don't have blood grooves. Then I wiped the blade on his shirt, and jammed it and the cash into my jacket pocket.

He collapsed onto the machine, and somehow managed to croak, "Please."

"No sympathy here," I told him, pushing open the security door. "Guys like me got no scruples."

Pot Shot

A lot of my readers like Herb, but for some reason I don't enjoy using him in shorts as much as Jack, Harry, and Phin. This is a rare exception. I originally wrote this as a chapbook, to give away at writing conferences. It deals with Herb's retirement, a topic later covered in greater detail in my novel Dirty Martini.

"How did you know pot roast is my favorite?"

Detective First Class Herb Benedict stepped into the kitchen, following the aroma. He gave his wife Bernice a peck on the cheek and made a show of sniffing deeply, then sighing.

"I've been making pot roast every Friday night for the past twenty-two years, and you say that every time you come home."

Herb grinned. "What happens next?"

"You pinch me on the bottom, change into your pajamas, and we eat in the family room while watching HBO."

"Sounds pretty good so far." He gently tugged Bernice away from the stove and placed his hands on her bottom, squeezing. "Then what?"

Bernice gave Herb's ample behind a pinch of its own.

"After HBO we go upstairs, and I force you to make love to me."

Herb sighed. "A tough job, but I have to repay you for the pot roast."

He leaned down, his head tilted to kiss her, just as the bullet plinked through the bay window. It hit the simmering pot with the sound of a gong, showering gravy skyward.

Herb reacted instinctively. His left hand grabbed Bernice and pulled her down to the linoleum while his right yanked the Sig Sauer from his hip holster and trained it on the window.

Silence, for several frantic heartbeats.

"Herb..."

"Shh."

From the street came the roar of an engine and screaming tires. They quickly blended into Chicago traffic. Herb wanted to go have a look, but a burning sensation in his hip stopped him. He reached down with his free hand, feeling dampness.

"Herb! You're been shot!"

He brought the fingers to his mouth.

"No—it's juice from the pot roast. Leaked down the stove."

Motioning for his wife to stay down, Herb crawled over to the window and peered out. The neighborhood was quiet.

He turned his attention to the stove top. The stainless steel pot had a small hole in the side, pulsing gravy like a wound.

Herb wondered which was worse; his Friday night plans ruined, or the fact that someone just tried to kill him.

He looked into the pot and decided it was the former.

"Dammit. The bastards killed my pot roast."

He tore himself away from the grue and dialed 911, asking that they send the CSU over. And for the CSU to bring a pizza.

Officer Dan Rogers leaned over the pot, his face somber.

"I'm sorry, Detective Benedict. There's nothing we can do to save the victim."

Herb frowned around a limp slice of sausage and pepperoni. Over two dozen gourmet pizza places dotted Herb's neighborhood, and the Crime Scene Unit had gone to a chain-store. The greasy cardboard box the pie came in probably had more flavor.

"You might think you're amusing, but that's an eighteen dollar roast."

"I can tell. Look at how tender it is. It's practically falling off the bone. And the aroma is heavenly. It's a damn shame."

Officer Hajek snapped a picture. "Shouldn't let it go to waste. When you're done, can I take it home for the dog?"

Herb watched Roberts attack the roast with gloved hands and wanted to cry at the injustice of it all. Another slice of pizza found its way into Herb's mouth, but it offered no comfort.

"And…gotcha, baby!"

Rogers held up his prize with a pair of forceps. The slug was roughly half an inch long, shaped like a mushroom and dripping gravy.

It looked good enough to eat.

"I think it's a 22LR. Must have been a high velocity cartridge. Punched a hole through the window without shattering it."

Herb and Rogers exchanged a knowing look, but didn't speak aloud because Bernice was nearby. Your typical gang member didn't bring a rifle on a drive-by shooting. Twenty-two caliber long range high speeds were favored by hunters.

And assassins.

Herb's mind backtracked over his career, of all the men he'd put away who held a grudge. After thirty-plus years on the force, there were too many to remember. He'd have to wade through old case files, cross-reference with recent parolees…

"Herb?"

"Hmm? Yes, Bernice?"

His wife's face appeared ready to crack. Herb had never seen her so fragile before.

"I…I called the glazier. They're open twenty-four-hours, so they're sending someone right away to fix the window, but they might not be here until late, and I don't know if—"

Herb took her in his arms, rubbed her back.

"It's okay, honey."

"It's not okay."

"You don't have to worry. Look how big a target I am, and they still missed."

"Maybe we should put an APB out for a blind man," Hajek offered.

Bernice pulled away, forcefully.

"This isn't a joke, Herb. You don't know what it's like, being a cop's wife. Every morning, when I kiss you before you go to work, I don't know if…"

The tears came. Herb reached for her, but Bernice shoved away his hands and hurried out of the kitchen.

Herb rubbed his eyes. No pot roast, no HBO, and certainly no nookie tonight. The evening's forecast; lousy pizza and waiting around for the glass man.

Being a cop sure had its perks.

The alarm went off, startling Herb awake.

Bernice's side of the bed remained untouched. She'd stayed in the guest room all night.

He found her in the kitchen, frying eggs. The stainless steel pot with the hole in it rested on top of their wicker garbage can, too large to fit inside.

"Smells good. Denver omelet?"

Bernice didn't answer.

"The glass guy said that homeowner's insurance should cover the cost. If you have time later today, can you give our agent a call? The bill is by the phone."

Bernice remained silent, but began to furiously stir the eggs. They went from omelet to scrambled.

"There will be a squad car outside all day. Let me give you their number in case…"

"In case of what?" Bernice's red eyes accused him. "In case someone tries to kill me? No one's after me, Herb. I don't have any enemies. I'm a housewife."

Herb wanted to get up and hold her, but knew she wouldn't allow it.

"I'll also have an escort, all day. It's standard procedure."

"I don't care about procedure."

"There's nothing more I can do, Bernice."

"Yes there is. You can retire."

Herb let the pain show on his face.

"I've got six more years until full pension."

"Forget the full pension. We've got our savings. We've got our investments. We can make it work."

"Bernice…"

"This isn't about money, and you know it. You'll never leave the Force. Not until they kick you out or…"

Bernice's eyes locked on the holey pot.

Herb had no reply. He skipped breakfast, showered, shaved, and began to dress. Normally, Bernice laid out an ironed shirt for him.

Not today.

"I'll be at the Center all day."

Her voice startled Herb. She stood in the bedroom doorway, arms folded.

"I'd prefer if—"

"If I stay home? You go on with your life, and I have to hide in the house?"

Herb sighed.

"It's my job, Bernice."

"I see. Volunteering doesn't count as a job because I'm not getting paid."

"I didn't say that."

Bernice walked away. Herb took a shirt from the hanger and put it on, wrinkles and all. He instructed the team outside to follow Bernice wherever she went, and then waited for his escorts to arrive to take him to work.

"It could be a thousand different people."

Herb's partner, Lt. Jacqueline Daniels, looked up over the stack of printouts. Jack wore her brown hair up today, revealing gray roots. Her hands cradled a stained coffee mug.

"You only have yourself to blame, Herb. If you were a lousy cop, this pile would be a lot smaller."

Herb blinked at the case files, a career's worth, propped on the desk. Though the amount was substantial, it didn't seem big enough. He opened another Twinkie and eased it in, wishing it was a Denver Omelet.

"I always wanted to be a cop. Even as a kid. I blame Dragnet. Joe Friday was my hero. I used to talk like him all the time. Drove my parents crazy."

"You've got some Twinkie filling in your mustache, Mr. Friday."

Herb wiped at his face. "Maybe I should transfer to Property Crimes. They never get death threats."

"You just pushed it over two inches."

Herb used his sleeve.

"What do you think, Jack?"

"Better, but now some of it is up your nose. Want to use my hand mirror?"

"I meant about the transfer."

Jack set aside the report she'd been reading. "Seriously?"

"I'm a fin away from retirement. These are supposed to be my golden years. I should be golfing and taking cruises."

"You hate golf. And the ocean."

"I also hate getting shot at."

Herb picked up a case file from a few years ago, gave it a token glance, and tossed it in the maybe pile. He could feel Jack staring at him, so he met her gaze.

"You think I'm crazy, don't you? You think after two weeks at Property Crimes I'll be going out of my mind with boredom."

Jack smiled, sadly.

"Actually, I think Property Crimes will be very lucky to get you."

Herb let her reply sink in. The more he thought it over, the more confident he felt. This was right.

"I'm going to tell Bernice."

"Good idea. But before you do, wipe the sugar out of your nose."

The Burketold Center was a dirty, crumbling building many years older than the senior citizens it catered to. Funded by tax dollars, the Center served as a game room/social area/singles mixer for the area's ten-plus nursing homes. Buses came several times a day, dropping off seniors for bingo, swing dancing, and craft classes.

The Center provided these services free of charge, the only condition being attendees had to be over sixty years old.

Herb walked through the automatic doors and took everything in.

To the left, four elderly men sat around a table as rickety as they were, noisily playing cards. In the pot, along with a pile of chips, were a set of dentures.

To the left, a solitary old woman twisted the knobs on a foosball table. She mumbled to herself, or perhaps to an imaginary opponent.

A TV blared in the corner, broadcasting the Food Network to three sleeping ladies. To the right, an ancient man with pants hiked up to his chest repeatedly kicked a Coke machine. Herb approached him.

"Did the machine take your money, sir?"

The old man squinted at Herb with yellow eyes.

"No, it did not take my money. But if you kick it in the right spot, it spits out free sodas. I've gotten six Mountain Dews so far today."

Herb left the guy to his larceny. In just a few short years, Herb would be turning sixty. Then he, too, would be able to join the fun for free. The thought didn't comfort him.

He located the front desk and found a cheerful-looking man holding down the fort. The man wore a loose fitting sweater with a stag's head stitched into the pattern, and his smile was so wide it looked to crack his face. Herb placed him in his early fifties.

"May I help you?"

"I'm looking for Bernice Benedict."

"Oh. And you are…?"

"Her husband, Herb."

Smiling Guy hesitated, then extended a hand.

"Pleased to meet you, Herb. Bernice has told me a lot about you. I'm Phil Grabowski."

Herb took the hand and found it plump and moist. He vaguely recalled Bernice mentioning the name Phil before.

"Hi, Phil. Great work you're doing here."

"Thanks. We try to do our part. It's a real heartbreaker reaching the autumn years and finding there's no one to share them with."

Phil chuckled, but it sounded painfully forced. Perhaps being around geriatrics all the time wrecked havoc on one's social skills.

"Is Bernice around?"

"She's calling bingo in room 1B, through that door and down the hall."

"Thanks." Herb nodded a good-bye and began to turn away.

"Bernice…she mentioned what happened last night. Terrible thing."

Herb's first reaction was annoyance. Bernice shouldn't have been relating police matters. But shame quickly overcame irritation.

Of course Bernice would mention it to her friends at work. As she should. What other outlet did she have?

Herb could feel himself flush. Bernice had worked at the Center for seven years, and he'd never visited once. This man, Phil, was obviously a close friend of hers, and he didn't know a thing about him.

Herb wondered how much harm he'd done to his marriage by putting his job first.

He also wondered if it was too late to make it up to her.

"Yeah, well, that won't be happening anymore."

Phil offered another face-splitting smile. "Really?"

It went against Herb's private nature to share his intentions with a stranger, but he thought it was a step in the right direction.

"I'm transferring to a different division." He almost bit his tongue. "I'm also reducing my hours."

"Why, that's wonderful. Bernice will be thrilled. She's…she's quite the trophy, you know."

"Nice to meet you, Phil."

Phil grinned wildly. Herb headed off in search of 1B, his wife's voice guiding him.

"G-15. That's G-15. You've got a G-15 on your card there, Mrs. Havensatch. Right under the G, dear. There it is."

Herb paused in the doorway, watching her. Love, pride, and responsibility all balled-up together to form a big lump in his throat. He rapped his knuckle on the frame and walked in.

"Bernice?"

"Herb?" His wife appeared surprised, but the anger from this morning had gone from her face. "What are you doing here? Is everything okay?"

"Look, honey, can we talk for a second?"

"I'm in the middle of bingo."

Herb felt a dozen pairs of eyes on him. He rubbed the back of his neck.

"I'm transferring to Property Crimes. And reducing my hours."

Bernice blinked.

"You're kidding."

"I'm not."

"When are you going to do this?"

"I already talked to Jack. Tomorrow morning, first thing."

Herb had expected a dozen different reactions form his wife, but crying wasn't one of them. She took several quick steps to him, and folded herself into his arms.

"Oh, Herb. I've wanted this for so long."

"So you're happy?"

"Yes."

"Bingo!"

A geriatric in the front row held her card above her head and cackled madly.

"I'll be with you in just a moment, Mrs. Steinmetz."

Herb stroked her hair. All of his indecision melted away. He'd made the right choice. Her friend Phil was right. Bernice was a real trophy.

Trophy. The word snagged in his mind. People won trophies in sports, but they also shot trophies. Like that ten point buck on Phil's sweater.

"Bernice—your friend Phil. Is he a hunt…"

The bullet caught Herb in the meaty part of his upper shoulder, spinning him around. Before hitting the floor, he glimpsed Phil, clutching a rifle in the doorway.

Screams filled the room, Bernice's among them. Herb tugged at his hip holster, freeing his Sig. His left arm went numb from his finger tips to his armpit, but he could feel the spreading warmth of gushing blood, and he knew the wound was bad.

"Drop the gun, Herb!"

Phil had the .22 pointed at Herb's head. Herb hadn't brought his gun around yet. Maybe, if he rolled to the side…

Too late. Bernice stepped in his line of fire.

"Phil! Stop it!"

"I'm doing it for you, Bernice! He's no good for you!"

Herb chanced a look at his shoulder wound. Worse than he thought. If he didn't stop the bleeding soon, he wouldn't make it.

"I love him, Phil."

"Love him? He's never home, and when he is, you said it's just the same, boring routine!"

"I like the same, boring routine. And I like my husband. Stop acting crazy and put down the gun."

Bernice took a step towards him, her hands up in supplication.

"Bernice…" Herb's voice radiated strength. "He won't shoot you. Walk out and call the police."

"Shut up!"

Bernice turned and looked at Herb. He nodded at his wife, willing her to move.

"I'll kill her! I'll kill both of you!"

Bernice stepped to the side. Phil's gun followed her.

Herb's gun followed Phil.

Detective First Class Herb Benedict fired four shots, three to the chest and one to the head.

All of them hit home.

Phil dropped, hard. Bernice rushed to her husband.

"Herb! Herb, I'm so sorry!"

Herb's eyes fluttered twice, and then closed.

"Bingo!" Mrs. Steinmetz yelled.

The food redefined horrible, but Herb ate everything. Even the steamed squash. Assuming it was steamed squash.

"I can't wait to get out of here and eat some real food."

Bernice stroked his arm, below the IV.

"We need to talk, Herb."

Herb didn't like the tone of her voice. She sounded so sad. He shook his head, trying to clear the codeine cloud, trying to concentrate.

"Bernice, honey, I'll make it up to you. I know I haven't been there. I know I've been spending too much time at work. Give me a chance, and I'll change."

Bernice smiled.

"That's what I want to talk to you about." Bernice took a deep breath. "I don't want you to transfer to Property Crimes."

Herb did a damn good impression of confused.

"But I thought…"

"When you told me you wanted to transfer, it was a dream come true for me. But then, with Phil…"

Herb reached out with his good hand, held hers.

"You're a good cop, Herb Benedict. It would be selfish of me to keep you from that."

"That's okay. You're allowed to be selfish."

Bernice's eyes glassed over.

"You know, every day when you go to work, I worry about you. But seeing you in action…"

Herb smiled.

"Was I dashing?"

"You were magnificent. You saved more than me and you. Phil had…problems."

"No kidding."

After his death, a search of Phil Grabowski's apartment uncovered a large cache of weapons and eighteen notebooks full of handwritten, paranoid ranting. Herb was only one name on a long list of targets.

"I can't deprive you of your job, Herb. And I can't deprive Chicago of you. You've got six years left to do good for this city. I want you to use those years well."

Herb pulled Bernice close and held her tight, despite the twenty-odd stitches in his shoulder.

"You know, the doctor says I'll be out of here by next Friday."

Bernice touched his cheek.

"Just in time for pot roast."

"Pot roast is my favorite, you know."

"I think you've mentioned that before."

"But this Friday, why don't we go out to eat instead? Someplace nice, romantic."

Bernice's eyes lit up. She looked like a teenager again.

"I'd like that."

"And then afterwards, maybe some nookie."

"That sounds perfect, but you know what?"

"What?"

Bernice grinned, and it was positively wicked.

"We don't have to wait until Friday for that."

She closed the door to the room and turned out the light.

Last Request

Phin has been in four of the six Jack Daniels books so far, Whiskey Sour, Rusty Nail, Fuzzy Navel, *and* Cherry Bomb. *In those books, Jack tempers some of Phin's darker moments. Not so in this story. This is also my favorite first line of anything I've written.*

I picked up a transsexual hooker named Thor, all six feet of her, at the off ramp to Eau Claire, Wisconsin, as I was driving up north to kill a man.

She had on thigh-high black vinyl boots, red fishnet stockings, a pink mini skirt, a neon green spandex tube top, and a huge blonde wig that reminded me of an octopus. I could have spotted her from clear across the county.

"You looking for action?" she said after introducing herself.

"I'm always looking for action."

"Tonight's your lucky night, handsome. I'm getting out of this biz. You give me a ride, you can have whatever you want for free."

I opened the door, rolled up the window, and got back on the road.

Thor spent five miles trying to pay for her ride, but the painkillers had rendered me numb and useless in that area, and eventually she gave up and reclined her seat back, settling instead for conversation.

"So where are you headed?" she asked. She sounded like she'd been sucking helium. Hormone therapy, I guessed. I couldn't tell if her breasts were real under the tube top, but her pink micro mini revealed legs that were nice no matter which sex she was.

"Rice Lake."

I yawned, and shifted in my seat. It was past one in the morning, but the oppressive July heat stuck around even when the sun didn't. I had the air conditioning in the Ford Ranger cranked up, but it didn't help much.

"Why are you going to Rice Lake?" she asked.

I searched around for the drink holder, picked up the coffee I'd bought back in the Dells, and forced down the remaining cold dregs, sucking every last molecule of caffeine from the grit that caught in my teeth.

"Business."

She touched my arm, hairless like the rest of me.

"You don't look like a businessman."

The road stretched out ahead of us, an endless black snake. Mile after mile of nothing to look at. I should have gotten a vehicle with a manual transmission, given my hand something to do.

"My briefcase and power ties are in the back seat."

Thor didn't bother to look. Which was a good thing.

"What sort of business are you in?"

I considered it. "Customer relations."

"From Chicago," Thor said.

She noticed the plates before climbing in. Observant girl. I wondered, obliquely, how far she'd take this line of questioning.

"Don't act much like a businessman, either."

"How do businessmen act?" I said.

"They're all after one thing."

"And what's that?"

"Me."

She tried to purr, and wound up sounding like Mickey Mouse. Personally, I didn't find her attractive. I had no idea if she was pre-op, post-op, or a work in progress, but Thor and I weren't going to happen, ever.

I didn't tell her this. I might be a killer, but I'm not mean.

"Where are you headed?" I asked.

She sighed, scratching her neck, posture changing from demure seductress to one of the guys.

"Anywhere. Nowhere. I don't have a clue. This was a spur of the moment thing. One of my girlfriends just called, said my former pimp was coming after me."

"How former?"

"I left him yesterday. He was a selfish bastard."

She was quiet for a while. I fumbled to crank the air higher, forgetting where the knob was. It was already up all the way. I glanced over at Thor, watched her shoulders quiver in time with her sobs.

"You love him," I said.

She sniffled, lifted up her chin.

"He didn't care about me. He just cared that I took his shit."

This got my attention.

"You holding?" I asked. Codeine didn't do as good a job as coke or heroin.

"No. Never so much as smoked a joint, if you can believe it."

I would have raised an eyebrow, but they hadn't grown back yet. Maybe I'd be dead before they did.

"It's true, handsome. Every perverted little thing I've ever done I've done stone cold sober. Lots of men think girls like me are all messed up in the head. I'm not. I have zero identity issues, and my self esteem is fine, thank you."

"I've never met a hooker with any self esteem," I said.

"And I've never met a car thief on chemotherapy."

I glanced at her again. Waited for the explanation.

"You couldn't find the climate control," Thor said. "And you're so stoned on something you never bothered to adjust the seat or the mirrors. Vicodin?"

I nodded, yawned.

"You okay to drive?"

"I managed to pick you up without running you over."

Thor clicked open a silver-sequined clutch purse and produced a compact. She fussed with her make-up as she spoke, dabbing at her tears with a foundation sponge.

"So why did you pick me up?" she asked. "You're not the type who's into transgender."

"You're smart. Figure it out."

She studied me, staring for almost a full minute. I shifted in my seat. Being scrutinized was a lot of work.

"You stole the car in Chicago, so you've been on the road for about six hours. You're zonked out on painkillers, probably sick from chemotherapy, but you're still driving at two in the morning. I'd say you just robbed a bank, but you don't seem jumpy or paranoid like you're running from something. That means you're running to something. How am I doing so far?"

"If I had any gold stars, you'd get one."

She stared a bit longer, then asked.

"What's your name?"

"Phineas Troutt. People call me Phin."

"Sort of a strange name."

"This from a girl named Thor."

"My father loved comic books. Wanted a tough, macho, manly son, thought the name would make me strong."

I glanced at her. "It did."

Thor smiled. A real smile, not a hooker smile.

"Are you going to Rice Lake to commit some sort of crime, Phin?"

"That isn't the question. The question is why I picked you up."

"Fair enough. If I still believed in knights in shining armor, I'd say you picked me up because you felt bad for me and wanted to help. But I think your reason was purely selfish."

"And that reason is?"

"You were falling asleep behind the wheel, and needed something to keep you awake."

I smiled, and it morphed into a yawn.

"That's a damn good guess."

"But is it true?"

"I'm definitely enjoying the company."

She kept watching me, but it was more comfortable this time.

"So who are you going to kill in Rice Lake, Phin?"

I stayed quiet.

"No whore ever gets into a car without checking the back seat," Thor said. "A forty dollar trick can turn into a gang rape freebie, a girl's not careful."

I wondered what she meant, then remembered what was lying on the back seat. What I hadn't bothered to put away. "You saw the gun."

"People normally keep those things hidden. You should try to be inconspicuous."

"I'm not big on inconspicuous."

"That box of baby wipes. Are you a proud papa, or are they for something else?"

"Sometimes things get messy." Which was an understatement. "So if you saw the gun, why did you get in?"

Thor laughed, throaty and seductive. She could shrug the whore act on and off like it was a pair of shoes.

"The streets are dangerous, Phin. A working girl has to carry more protection than condoms."

She reached into the top of her knee high black vinyl boot, showed me the butt of a revolver.

"Mine's bigger," I said.

"Mine's closer."

I nodded. The road stretched onward, no end in sight.

"So how much do you charge, for your services?" Thor asked.

"Depends."

"On what?"

"The job. How much I need the money."

"Does it matter who the person is?"

"No."

"Don't you think that's cold?"

"Everyone has to die sometime," I said. "Some of us sooner than others."

Another stretch of silence. Another stretch of road.

"I've got eight hundred bucks," Thor said. "Is that enough?"

"For your pimp. The selfish bastard."

"He is. I earned this money. Earned every cent. But in this area, every whore, from the trailer girls to the high class escorts, has to pay Jordan a cut."

"And you didn't pay."

"He knows how important my transformation is. One more operation, and I'm all woman. Holding out was the only way I could make it."

"I thought you loved him."

"Just like he says, love and business are two separate things."

Her breathing sped up. Over the hum of the engine, I thought I heard her heart beating. Or maybe it was mine.

"Why don't you kill him yourself, with your little boot revolver." I said.

"Jordan has the cops in his pocket. They'd catch me."

"Unless you had an alibi when it happened."

Thor nodded. "Exactly. You drop me off at a diner. I spend three hours with a cup of coffee. We both get something we need."

I considered it. Eight hundred was twice as much as I was making on this job. Years ago, if someone told me that one day I'd drive twelve hours both ways to kill a man for a lousy four hundred bucks, I would have laughed it off.

Things change.

The pinch in my side, growing bit by bit as the minutes passed, would eventually blossom into a raw explosion of pain. I was down to my last three Vicodin, and only had twenty-eight cents left to my name. I needed more pills, along with a bottle of tequila and a few grams of coke.

Codeine for the physical. Cocaine and booze for the mental. Dying isn't easy.

"So what do you say?" Thor asked.

"What kind of man is Jordan?"

"You said it doesn't matter. Does it?"

"No."

I waited. The car ate more road. The gas gage hovered over the E.

"He's a jerk. A charming jerk, but one just the same. I thought I loved him, once. Maybe I did. Or maybe I just loved to have a good looking man pay attention to me, make me feel special."

"Murder will pretty much ruin any chance of you two getting back together."

"I'll try to carry on," she said, reapplying her lipstick.

Gas station, next exit. I made up my mind. A starving dog doesn't question why his belly is empty. His only thought is filling it.

"I'll do it," I said.

"Really?"

"Yes."

Thor smiled big, then gave me a hug.

"Thanks, Phin. You're my knight in shining armor after all."

"I'll need the money up front," I said. "You got it on you?"

"Yeah. Take this exit. There's a Denny's. You can drop me off there."

I took the exit.

We pulled into the parking lot. It was close to empty, but I killed the lights and rolled behind the restaurant near the Dumpsters, so no one would see us together. When I hit the breaks, Thor stayed where she was.

"Second thoughts?" I asked.

"How do I know you won't take my money and run?"

"All I have left is my word," I said.

She considered it, then fished a roll of bills from her purse. When she was counting, I put my hand on her leg.

Thor smiled at me.

"I didn't think you were into me," she said. "Finish the job, and then I'll throw in a little bonus for you."

"I just need to finish my other job first," I told her.

"I understand."

My hand moved down her knee, found the revolver, and tugged it out.

With the windows closed I doubt anyone heard the gunshots, even though they were loud enough to make my ears ring.

I took the cash, hit the button to recline Thor's seat until she was out of sight, and rolled down her window. I hated to let the heat in, but the glass was conspicuously spattered with her blood, and I didn't need to make any more mistakes. Then I pulled out of the parking lot and got back on the highway, heading south.

Jordan had told me, over the phone, that I'd find Thor working the Eau Claire off ramp. He said to dump the body somewhere up the road, then meet him in the morning. The few hours wait were so he could establish an alibi.

A few miles up the road I pulled over, yanked Thor out of the car, and got behind the wheel again before another car passed. Then I grabbed the box of baby wipes in the back seat. As I drove I cleaned up my hands, then the passenger side of the vehicle. There wasn't too much of a mess. Small gun, small holes. I was lucky Thor got in the car at all, after spying the gun I'd sloppily left in plain sight. Stupid move on my part.

Hers, too.

When I reached Eau Claire I headed to where I thought Jordan would be. He'd be angry to see me so soon, but that wouldn't last very long. Just until I shot him in the head.

I had nothing against Jordan. I had nothing against Thor, either. But a deal is a deal, and as I told the lady, all I had left was my word.

Planter's Punch

A Lt. Jack Daniels/Duffy Dombrowski Mystery by JA Konrath & Tom Schreck

Duffy

My face hurt like a toothache.

The boxer I'd just fought—a fat guy from Gary, Indiana who was supposedly slow and easy to hit—could punch. I hit him a lot, easily, but he countered well, and every time he did it felt like getting banged with a fabric-covered cinder block. Enough of those and it makes your head ring. Not a pleasant dull throb, but a crackling pain going through from your forehead to your jaw.

Incidentally, I won the fight—six rounds to two in an eight rounder that left me a thousand dollars richer. Now, my true reward; a trip to AJ's for a beer. I fought at the Armory, a two minute car ride to the bar, and got the shock of my life when I came through the front door.

The place had a crowd.

That never happened. Usually, the crowd, and I use that term loosely, consisted of the Fearsome Foursome, Kelley the cop, me and maybe, on a good night, a couple of cab drivers. Tonight other people had invaded my refuge.

Luckily, the Foursome had their usual seats at the bar and saved me one. Kelley, one away from that, was also in. Maybe not so luckily, the Foursome had already started.

"They wrapped her tits in ace bandages, you know." TC said.

"She sprain 'em?" Jerry Number One said.

Fuck, they were arguing about the Wizard of Oz again. TC loved to talk about how Judy Garland had her breasts wrapped to look younger in her famous role.

"Jed Clampett got sick making that flick," Rocco said. It silenced the room for a second while the others stared. I took my seat, put a hand up to my face. No swelling, yet.

"The glue on the lion outfit gave him the hives," Rocco said with confidence.

"Bulger." Jerry Number Two.

"It is not Bulger, it's the truth," Rocco said.

AJ, the owner and only bartender, slid a bottle of Schlitz in front of me. I took a long pull and held the rest of it to my forehead.

"Let me get a Beam, too." I said. AJ lifted his eyebrows but said nothing and put a sidecar of the brown elixir next to the Schlitz.

"Buddy Epson got allergic to the silver paint. Ray Bulger played the lion," I said. "You fuckin' guys had this discussion a month ago."

The Fearsome Foursome—Jerries One and Two, Rocco and TC—all stared at me.

"Sorry, fellas," I said, realizing I'd snapped at them. "My head hurts."

The unusual silence from the crew called my attention to the crowd in the bar for the first time. There were three strangers on stools on the end by the TV. They didn't look like the usual cab drivers who drifted in. Foreign, maybe eastern block, each in a suit worth more than my payday. They seemed familiar, and it dawned on me they were at the fight. I saw them in the dressing room hanging out with Wilkerson, the fight promoter. They also had front row seats.

I figured they probably followed me here for a drink, but then realized they were here before me. Unusual. Behind them, another group chatted quietly while sipping their drinks. A fat balding guy ate an AJ's cheeseburger, getting mustard, ketchup and grease on his face. He didn't bother with a napkin and instead dragged his sleeve in an upward motion across his mouth.

He talked to a forty-something woman in a very sharp suit—way too sharp for AJ's. No spring chicken, but hot enough in that self-confident, cougarish way.

I reached for the whiskey, letting it burn down my throat.

"Be cool, Duffy. Any second now, they're going to approach you, make thc offer."

I cocked an eyebrow at Kelley. "What the hell are you talking about? Did I just walk into a bad spy novel?"

"Lower your voice, dumb ass. I said stay cool."

I was going to give Kelley more shit but his eyes made me think better. I took another pull on the Schlitz and played along.

"You wearing the wire?" I asked.

I guess I was going to give Kelley shit after all. But he surprised me by saying, "No. You are. Joint effort with the Chicago cops. Stick this in your pocket."

He passed something into my hand. I glanced down. Looked like a pen drive.

Kelley wasn't the practical joker type. He wouldn't crack a smile on his birthday in a room full of clowns. Maybe my fat opponent had jarred something loose in my head, because I truly had no idea what was going on.

"Pocket," Kelley said. "Here they come. Tell them yes."

I felt movement to my right. The three well-dressed foreign-types were standing over me.

"Matching Rolexes," Jerry Two said. The Fearsome Foursome were appraising the new arrivals. "Daytonas. Platinum bands."

"White gold," Rocco said.

"Platinum."

"I thought white gold and platinum were the same thing, just different colors." This from KC.

"Different elements," said Jerry Two. "Platinum is heaver."

"No it ain't, zipper-head. Gold is."

"Platinum. That's why it's more, you know, pricier."

The tallest of the men, the guy who stood in the middle, smiled at me. Dark hair, dark eyes, five o-clock shadow coming in strong even though he smelled like aftershave. He had something on his front tooth. A diamond.

"Mr. Dombrowski," he said. His accent was Russian. "May we have a word with you?"

"You know how to tell a fake Rolex?" Jerry One. "If it's got a ticking second hand. The real thing sweeps, don't tick."

"Another dead giveaway is the plastic band with Fred Flintstone on the face," said Rocko.

Titters from the Foursome. I rubbed the pen drive recorder in my hand, and still couldn't figure out what exactly was going on here. Were these the Chicago cops Kelley mentioned?

"You guys were at the fight," I said. Seemed like a smart thing to say. "Ringside."

"Yes. Your performance was..." he smiled, the diamond glinting blue from the neon beer sign, "acceptable. Now can we have a word?" His eyes flitted over to the Foursome, then back to me. "In private?"

In between fights, I made my living as a counselor. Over the years I got pretty good at reading people. These three didn't look like cops, sound like cops, or act like cops. But their expensive suits had bulges under their left armpits, which meant concealed weapons, and Kelley did insist I say yes to them. So I nodded, finished my beer, and stood up.

The trip wasn't a long one. I followed them over to their table.

"Please, Mr. Dombrowski. Sit."

"I'd rather stand."

Bling Tooth made a dismissive gesture, but he and his buddies stayed standing too.

"You put on a pretty good show tonight," he said. His accent seemed to get thicker. "Your opponent, however... the show he put on was much better."

I waited, not liking where this was going, but not jumping to conclusions.

"We paid him ten thousand dollars to put on that show."

I felt the burn coming up my neck, to my ears. I'd gone eight rounds with the fat guy, but all of my energy had suddenly returned, tenfold. It all clicked what Kelley wanted from me, but I couldn't hold back the anger and my fists clenched involuntarily, which probably wouldn't be good for the voice recorder in my palm.

"I've heard the rumors," I said, making sure my rage wasn't in my voice. "New guys in town. Russians. Paying fighters to take falls. But the guy tonight, he hit back. Hard. I know him from the circuit. He's legit. You're telling me you owned him?"

"We can be... persuasive."

I wondered how much his diamond tooth was worth, and where I could pawn it after I knocked it out of his mouth. But they had guns, and like an idiot I was standing between them and Kelley, my back-up. Plus, Kelley'd told me to say yes. Get it on tape, they go to jail, win-win. All I had to do was swallow my pride and agree to take a dive.

But then Bling Tooth made a big mistake. Two fingers scissored into his vest pocket and removed a photograph.

"We hope you agree to help us, Mr. Dombrowski. Or else we'd be forced to hurt someone you care very much about."

He flashed the picture at me. It was Al, my basset hound.

These fuckers had my dog.

It didn't sink in right away. It had already been a long night of getting punched in the head. I looked up to see Bling Tooth smile at me.

"You want I send you a floppy ear for proof?" he said. He went to smile but before the corners of his mouth turned something went bad inside me and I hit him with a straight left. It caught part nose and part upper lip. He went down hard, grasping his face. Blood already spurted from between his fingers, and I guessed it was nose blood by the way it shot.

I sat on the bastard's chest and grabbed his thorax with my right. My grip remained sore from the eight rounder, so it wasn't as tight as I would have liked.

"Listen mother—" I didn't get to finish.

I heard a series of clickety-clacks and realized his two buddies held guns pointed at my head.

Then one of them bent down next to me, picking something up off the floor.

I'd dropped the pen drive recorder.

Jack

The trail led us to Crawford, about fifty miles out of New York City. When a murderer crossed state lines, the Feds had jurisdiction. At least, they were supposed to. But neither Herb nor I gave them a call. We didn't even tell our boss, Captain Bains, we were leaving Chicago.

Sometimes being a law enforcement officer meant tip-toeing around the law.

Our suspect, a Russian mobster named Vladimir Polchev, had skipped town before we could haul him in. Polchev had made two big mistakes.

First, he'd murdered a friend of mine. Dirk Wendt, a semi-pro boxer who happened to be my taekwondo instructor for the last six years.

Second, he'd done it on my turf.

The Russians scared the crap out of people, so most weren't willing to talk. But when I've got my mean on, I can be pretty damn persuasive. Herb and I shook down a pimp owned by the mob, got word that Polchev was paying off fighters to throw matches. If they didn't play along, his crew killed them. Wendt was a Chicagoan, but it didn't take much research to find two other murders that matched Polchev's signature.

A tip took us to New York. We called ahead, playing nice with the locals, and were invited to visit as part of a joint task force. It seemed Polchev was a person of interest in several recent murders. The NY fuzz put a tail on him, checked with their informants, and learned Polchev was planning to put the squeeze on a boxer named Dombrowski. We met the lead investigator, Kelley, at a dive bar, to supervise a sting operation. Kelley informed us, in no uncertain terms, that this was not our collar, and we were to maintain a hands-off policy.

Herb and I had no problem with this. I wanted Polchev, bad. It didn't matter to me which city locked him up, as long as someone did.

"This is an excellent burger," Herb said. There was so much of it on his face, shirt, and tie, I was dubious he'd gotten any of it into his mouth.

"I'll take your word for it."

"You should eat something, Jack. The food is good."

My stomach was still a bit queasy from our flight. The pilot called it "a little bit of turbulence," but it had been enough to knock the ice out of my complimentary cup of water. Besides, I had a rule never to eat in a place where the main source of lighting was neon.

I checked my watch, then glanced over at the bar. In my left side peripheral vision, Polchev and two cronies sat, drinking top shelf vodka. Polchev was the one with the diamond in his front tooth. To my right, four men argued about the merits and detriments of toothpaste.

"You know fluoride is poisonous?"

"Is not."

"Is so, Jerry. They don't use fluoride toothpaste in space."

"You can't brush your teeth in space, dumb ass. It's a vacuum."

"You mean it can clean your rugs?"

"There's no air in space. You tried to brush your teeth, your brain would slurp out your nose."

"I mean on the space shuttle. No fluoride in the toothpaste, because astronauts have to swallow it."

"Makes sense. If they spit it out, it would float after them, following them around all mission."

I tuned them out. Or tried to, at least. I turned back to Herb, took a sip of my club soda and lime, glancing casually at Polchev. He and his men were all armed. Kelley said nothing was going to go down here, and I hoped he was right. The bar was crowded, and shooting would be a catastrophe. I hoped that this Dombrowski guy was good at keeping his cool. Kelley said he was a social worker. Interesting combination, social work and boxing.

Herb finished licking his fingers and dug out the paperback he was reading. Afraid, by Jack Kilborn. He'd read a good portion of it on the plane, every once and a while pausing to whisper, "Jesus H. Christ." Apparently, the book was supposed to be scary.

"Jesus H. Christ," Herb whispered again.

I hated it when people did that, because of course I had to ask what was so upsetting.

"This girl is hanging upside down over a pile of dead bodies," Herb said.

"Sounds like fun."

"You gotta read this, Jack."

"I will. Right after I order a burger."

The four next to us segued into The Wizard of Oz.

"The horse of a different color died. The color they used on him was toxic."

"Was not. They used gelatin. He kept licking it off."

"You're thinking of the tin man."

"The tin man licked off his paint?"

"No, dummy. The horse."

"The tin man licked the horse?"

"You guys know it's impossible to lick your own elbow?"

They all tried to do just that. I shook my head and inwardly wept for the gene pool.

The front door swung open, and a guy walked in. Athletic build, not bad looking, a bit old for a boxer. But I knew it was Dombrowski by the way he walked. Economical, no movement wasted, but coiled, like he was waiting for something to happen.

Dombrowski played it cool, walking up to the four nitwits, having a drink and joining in the conversation. Then he had a few private words with Kelley that I missed in the bar chatter.

When Polchev and his goons approached him, I told Herb to put away the book and pay attention. He tucked it into his inside jacket pocket.

Dombrowski seemed confused about everything happening, and I wondered if Kelley had bothered to inform him what exactly was going down.

Then everything went to hell. The boxer hit the mobster, and the other mobsters drew their guns. If that wasn't bad enough, one of the goons picked up the recorder Dombrowski had dropped. A simple sting operation, where no one was supposed to get hurt, was moments away from turning into a bloodbath. I wanted to smack the shit out of Kelley for staging this in a public place, but before I could, instinct took over and I had my .38 in my hand, pointing it at the thugs.

"Police! Drop the weapons!"

The bar went silent. No one moved. I could hear my heart beating, and sensed Herb draw his gun next to me, and Kelley draw his as well.

"That's one damn sexy cop," said one of the four. I think it was one of the Jerrys.

"Drop them, hands in the air," I ordered. "Or we will shoot you."

There was a bad moment when I thought they might be stupid enough to point their guns my way. But the moment passed, and the mobsters let their weapons fall to the floor.

"Chick cop is wearing Armani," said one of the four.

"You sure? Could be Fendi."

"It's Armani," I said. "Now shut the fuck up or I'll shoot you guys, too."

Dombrowski must have noticed he didn't have any guns aimed at his head anymore, because he resumed pounding the crap out of Polchev.

Kelley got to him before we did.

"Cool it, Duff. We got him."

"Asshole has my dog." Punch. "He's going to tell me where A is." Punch. "Or he's going to spend the rest of his life eating his meals through a straw." Punch.

Herb grabbed the recorder, zip-tied the other two mobsters hands behind their backs, and I asked everyone in the bar to kindly step outside.

"Everyone, get the fuck out, now!"

Okay, maybe it wasn't so kindly.

"Duffy, ease up, man." Kelley was trying to hold Dombrowski's arm back, and not doing a very good job. Polchev looked like someone dropped a lasagna, extra sauce, on his face.

I pointed the gun at the boxer.

"Shit, the Fendi cop is gonna shoot Duff."

"Armani. She said Armani."

"That the designer guy, got shot?"

"That was Versace."

"Think she's the one who shot Versaci?"

Apparently, the Four Stooges hadn't left when I'd ordered them to.

"Mr. Dombrowski, stop hitting the mobster and get your hands up over your head."

Kelley stared at me. "Lieutenant, he's one of the good guys."

"And I'm trying to save him from a murder rap. Get ahold of yourself, Mr. Dombrowski."

The boxer looked at me. There was anger in his features, but some sadness too.

"He took my dog, Al."

"We'll get your dog back," I said. "I promise."

He nodded. But before he got up, he punched Polchev one more time, in the kidneys.

Kelley slapped the cuffs on Polchev, and Mirandized all three suspects. I heard sirens in the distance. Back-up, and probably an ambulance. I looked for Dombrowski, but he was moving toward the front door, staring at something in his hands.

A wallet. Polchev's wallet.

"Duffy!" I yelled. "Don't leave the bar!"

He glanced over at me, then ran out the entrance.

Duffy

My fist hurt, but I pushed back the pain and headed for my car. When I punched Bling Tooth in the kidneys, I reached around and swiped his wallet. I had the asshole's address. For his sake, the dog had better be there.

I bolted to my El Dorado, my mind racing. Al saved my life, he'd been there through some of my toughest times. I couldn't deal with someone mistreating him. It happened once before. Nightmares of the incident still woke me in the middle of the night.

The wallet told me the guy lived in Wilmette, Illinois. But it also held a key card for the Crawford Holiday Inn.

Picturing Polchev, with his thousand dollar suit, he wasn't the type to take Al to his fancy house. The hotel sounded like a better bet. I adjusted my course.

The V-8 moaned and I didn't stop for lights or slow down through Jefferson Park or worry about one way signs. Thankfully, the Eastern Block scumbag whose blood covered my shirt kept the key card in the original cardboard holder. Room 116 awaited, as did a merciless beat down for anyone unlucky enough to be in it.

I turned on to Washington Ave at the end of the park and a patrol car's flashing lights fired up behind me.

"Get in line," I mumbled to myself, pinning the gas pedal.

A glance into the rearview confirmed two cars fell in behind the police cruiser. Fuck 'em. Take it minute by minute. Just like I told me AA clients.

I hit the brakes near the entrance to the motel. I had six blocks on my pursuers and wasted no time exiting the car and sliding the room key into the lobby door. I looked at the arrows that pointed rooms 101-125 and sprinted as fast as I could. My heart pounded in time with my head, and my nerves had almost caught up with my rage.

Almost.

In front of 116 I paused just for a second, hearing a television tuned to CNN coming from inside. No dog sounds. Was he even in there?

My neck twitched, a telltale sign of a looming battle. I slid the card into the electronic lock, took a deep breath, and burst into the room, ready for anything.

The room was empty.

An unmade bed, a leash, a rawhide bone, an open suitcase. A teddy bear sat on the floor in front of me. I realized sweat had soaked my shirt and I began to hyperventilate. The next thing I saw kicked all that up a notch.

The sheets of the bed were soaked in dark crimson. Blood drenched the carpet. I also noticed that the leash—Al's leash—was caked with gore.

I threw up on the floor in front of me.

Jack

This cop Kelley could drive.

I sat up front and Herb took the back, sticking his head through the space between the front seats so he could be in the conversation.

"So, your pal Duffy, he's a little nuts?" Herb said. As he spoke he dug the nail of his index finger deep into his mouth to release some ground beef from a molar.

"More than a little," Kelley said.

"Would you say he's a danger to himself and others?"

"Depends on the day."

I raised my eyebrows, ready to launch into an argument about civilians screwing up investigations. But I was close to one thousand miles from home, and had no authority here, so I held my tongue. The siren of the cruiser helped mask the awkward silence. That is, until Herb spoke up.

"So if he's committing a crime, are you willing to use force to stop him?" Herb looked hard at Kelley, adding, "Lethal force?"

Kelley took us around a curve, pinning me against the passenger door.

"He may be nuts, but he's a good man. You need to cut him some slack."

I glanced back at Herb, who seemed to be thinking the same thing I was. Kelley's personal relationship with Dombrowski might result in a bad ending for all concerned.

In the distance, a Holiday Inn appeared. I noticed Dombrowski's Cadillac double-parked in front.

As we screeched into the motel lot a call came over the radio. The dispatcher announced, "All units we have a missing girl, probable abduction. Four years old, light brown hair, in red striped pajamas. The girl has Down Syndrome and has the facial features associated with that condition. She was last seen in the vicinity of the Crawford Holiday Inn."

Kelley sighed through his teeth, then radioed Dispatch to say he was on the scene. When he pushed open this door I grabbed his shoulder.

"Kelley, this changes things. Your friend isn't the priority anymore."

"I know."

"If the girl is here, and he gets in the way…"

Kelley hooded his eyes and shook out of my grasp. "I know how to do my job, Lieutenant.

Duffy

The blood trailed down the hallway, a few drips and dribbles hard to make out on the dark carpet. I followed after it best I could.

Through the windows on the wall that bordered the rooms I saw flashing red lights fill the parking lot. At least three patrol cars pulled in. Kelley got out of one, followed by the two cops from AJ's. The fat guy spotted me through the window and the three of them ran toward the entrance.

I had no intention of waiting for them to haul me away so I

picked up the pace on the blood trail. It stopped at an unmarked door. A faint hand print, tiny fingers outlined in blood, was near the knob.

I opened it and found myself in an unlit corridor. I went in running, my hands on the wall, feeling my way. After four steps I bumped into something waist high. It rocked on contact and as it did I felt a string run across my face. I grabbed the string and pulled. I sixty watt bulb went on and I realized I was in the laundry room. I'd bumped into a cart full of dirty towels and sheets.

My shoes squeaked on the tile floor. I looked down.

A pool of blood was at my feet.

Noise from behind. I spun, fists clenched, and saw three figures appear.

"Duff, its Kel, Hold up."

I was all out of time.

Jack

Dombrowski's shirt was soaked through with blood and sweat, and he looked somewhere between panic and determination.

"They got Al. I gotta find 'em."

"Let us take it from here, Dombrowski." I put a hand on his chest arm, not rough, but not gentle either.

He slapped my hand away, his neck twitching.

"Just settle down," I said. "We're going to find the dog. We got guns, we're cops, let us do it."

He went to push past me. I grabbed his right arm, leveraged my hip into his groin and flipped him to the ground. I heard the breath whoosh out of his lungs.

Kelley backed me away, reached down for his friend. "Duff, please, let us take care of this."

Duffy nodded, seeming to calm down. Kelley helped him up. He looked down at his shoes, wiped his hands on his pants, and then the son of a bitch shoved me aside and ran for the hallway.

He was fast. Real fast.

But I'm fast, too.

I stretched out, hooking my foot around his ankle, tripping him forward. Duffy caught himself against the wall, whipping around to face me. Herb blocked his side of the hallway. My partner was reaching for his gun, but I gave him a stern head shake.

"I know you're upset, Mr. Dombrowski. But this is a police matter. You have to let us handle it."

He pretended to go left, then went right, not telegraphing the move at all. I threw a roundhouse after him, aiming for his ear, but he anticipated the punch and bunched up his shoulder. It was like hitting a side of beef, but it staggered him enough to bounce him into the opposite wall.

Duffy shook his head and looked at me.

"I don't fight women. I'm just trying to find my dog."

I unconsciously widened my stance, kicking off my heels and planting my feet on the carpet, my left slightly ahead of my right.

"I sympathize. But there's more at stake here than just your dog. And if you try to run away again, I'll take you down."

Something flashed in his eyes, something that looked vaguely like amusement. And though he said he didn't fight women, I noticed he'd adopted a stance similar to mine, feet wide, hands in front of him.

Then he threw a very fast uppercut.

I flinched back, but his punch was just a feint, and he again tried to take off. I whipped my foot around, snapping my leg back in a spin kick, catching him on the side of his head.

He staggered but didn't go down.

"Duff..." I heard Kelley say.

I didn't pay attention to the local cop, following up my kick with a one-two combination to the body. Duffy braced his stomach muscles, dancing away from my blows, and then threw a combination of his own, each one stopping short of its mark.

He had pulled the punches. Dombrowski didn't want to hurt me, but he was showing me he could.

But I'd beaten faster, stronger guys before, and the fact that he wasn't willing to hit me made my job a lot easier. I faked a lunge kick, got in close, and clipped him under the chin with an elbow. Then I reared back my knee, ready to punt his balls up into his neck.

Duffy grabbed my leg, blocking the blow, and held it while he looked into my eyes.

"Not on the first date," he said.

I smiled, batted my eyelashes, and gave him all I had, right in his kidney.

Duffy doubled over.

I reared back, ready to break his nose, when Herb cried out.

"Jack!"

Before Kelley or I could react, a flash of darkness bolted up the hallway.

A man. A sprinting man, covered in blood. Coming right at us.

I heard a thwak, and then Herb went down.

My partner had a knife in his chest.

Duffy

The tough broad from Chicago got off me to tend to the fat guy. He had a throwing knife sticking out of his chest.

I paused, wondering if I could do anything to help, but realized she'd take care of him, and I needed to find Al, so I ran down the hallway after the dark figure.

He staggered and wobbled a bit, and by the time he reached the doorway for the stairwell I was within ten feet of him. He made it through the stairway door before me and tried to slam it shut. I blocked it with my foot and got in behind him. He sprinted up four or five steps but fell hard, rolled over and then slid down toward me.

I slammed my knee into his chest, and then punched him square in the nose. The familiar crack let me know I broke it.

He didn't move. Dead or passed out, I didn't care. His shirt was covered with blood. Al's blood?

"Duff!"

Kelley, coming up behind me. I didn't have time for him right now.

Above where the guy collapsed the blood trail continued. I took off after it. At the second floor I found another bloody hand print on the wall. I got to the hallway, turned and headed to my left.

Then the trail died. No more blood. No more hand prints.

I cupped my hands around my mouth. "Al! Boy, where are you? Al!"

I listened for an answer. None came.

If that son of a bitch had hurt my dog, and I'd killed him on the stairs, I'd go back, revive him, and kill him again. Images of Al flashed, unbidden, through my head, and I felt my knees begin to give out, like someone had just socked me in the temple.

"Al," I whispered.

That's when I heard it. A muffled bark.

I felt my heart rate kick up again, hope spurring me toward the sound.

But the bark tapered off, followed by a terrifying, gagging wheeze.

The same sound Al made when he almost choked to death eating the foam rubber off my sofa.

"Al!"

I ran to the cubby with the soda and ice machines. There was Al, drenched in blood, lying next to a curled-up little girl.

Jack

As Kelley cuffed the guy on the stairs, I ran to the second floor and saw Dombrowski turn in by the ice machine. My gun was drawn, just in case. From ahead came a choking noise. I reached the corner and spun fast, clutching my .38 in a two-handed Weaver stance.

There were all three of them. Dombrowski, the dog, and the missing little girl. All were spattered with blood.

The dog, a portly basset hound, was coughing and retching. Dombrowski sat next to the mutt, its head on his lap. I knelt down and felt the girl's neck.

"She's just asleep," Duffy mumbled. He stroked the dog's nose. "C'mon, Al. C'mon and be okay. Be okay."

Dombrowski had tears running down his face. The fat pooch opened its mouth as wide as an alligator's and dry-heaved with an awful, disgusting sound. He seemed to be in a really bad way.

"I'm sorry," I told Duffy. "Can we move him? Get him to a vet?"

I heard wheezing from behind me. Herb had finally caught up.

"Aw, jeez," he said, staring at the bloody dog. To Duffy he said, "Ambulance on the way. What the hell did you do to that guy on the stairs, man? Did you see his hand?"

The boxer's face went grim. "Whatever it was, he deserved that and more."

"What the hell did you do? Bite him?"

Duffy looked up at us, confused. "What?"

Then Al made the most revolting sound yet, sort of a cross between a wet-vac sucking up water and the world's loudest belch. Something long and covered in mucus shot from the dog's mouth, plopping onto the floor.

"Oh, there it is," Herb said. "One of the scumbag's fingers. The guy on the stairs was missing a few."

"How many?" I asked, both fascinated and repulsed.

"Three."

Herb nudged the digit with his toe, and then the dog gagged again and threw up the other two on Herb's shoe.

"And there they are. I think he's giving you the finger, Duffy."

"You okay, boy?" Duffy said, cradling the dog's head in his hands.

Al licked him, wagging his tail.

"All that blood in his fur must be from the perp," Herb laughed. "Your dog's a hero."

I now had the sleeping little girl in my arms. She wasn't bleeding either. The hound had gone to town on the bad guy, and all of the blood seemed to be from him.

Al bayed, howling like the wolfman, and the girl opened her eyes.

"Nice doggy," she said, yawning.

Dombrowski had lifted the dog and kissed him on the back of the head. Kelley came down the hall.

"The guy's alive but he's lost a lot of blood. He..." He didn't finish, staring at Herb. "Hold it, didn't you take a knife to the chest?" Kelley's face blanched like he was standing in front of a big fat ghost.

Herb reached in to his jacket and pulled out a paperback. Afraid by Jack Kilborn was written across the cover in bright red.

"Best book I ever bought." Herb said. The book had a two inch rip in the cover that went three quarters through the thickness. "If it wasn't filled with so many pages of unrelenting horror, the knife would have gone through and killed me." Herb grinned. "God bless authors who write long descriptions of gratuitous violence."

"We should all go out right now and buy copies," I said.

"I'm buying two," said Kelley.

Al barked in agreement.

Duffy

Turns out, the little kid was the daughter of Wilkerson, the fight promoter. They reunited tearfully in the parking lot. Al, messy with blood, remained as healthy as an eighty-five pound hound could be. The scumbag and his three buddies from AJ's got arrested. Things got even worse for them when Kelley found a shoe box full of heroin in the hotel room. They wouldn't taste free air again for quite some time.

I cleaned Al up with a thick Holiday Inn towel. He began to bark incessantly, his polite way of telling me he was hungry. I guess finger food wasn't enough for him.

The cops took reports and interviews and I changed into a pair of sweats and a hoodie I had in the trunk.

The chick cop in the fancy suit came over to the Cadillac. She reached down and scratched Al under the chin, then looked up at me.

"No hard feelings." She extended her hand.

"No hard feelings."

Her hand may have lingered just a bit. Or maybe mine did. She was much cuter when she wasn't trying to kick my ass.

"Akido?" I asked.

"A little. Training's in taekwondo, but I've tried to pick up as much as I can." She smiled, which softened her features even more.

"Not bad. You ever box?"

"Nah. Too rough for me."

"Somehow I doubt that."

She looked down at Al. "Your dog protected that kid, didn't he?"

"Probably." I thought about it for a second. "Might've been something else too."

She wrinkled her brow. "What?"

"He doesn't like bullies, and there's something inside him that goes bad when he sees someone getting mistreated."

She nodded and stood up. "He's not the only one."

We stared at each other, maybe for a little longer than we needed to, and then she turned to leave.

"You know…" I said. She paused. "Every once and a while I'm on a fight card in the Windy City. If you'd be interested, I can get you some tickets."

"I'd like that." She reached into her purse pulled out a business card, and handed it to me, offering one last smile before walking back over to the fat guy.

I looked down at the card.

Lt. Jack Daniels.

And for all these years, I'd been drinking Jim Beam.

Maybe I'd have to give Jack Daniels a try.

But first I had to go out and buy that book everyone was talking about. Afraid by Jack Kilborn.

Al loved a good book, too. He'd already eaten most of mine.

I tucked the card into my pocket, herded Al into the Caddy, and headed straight to my nearest all-night bookstore. If your town doesn't have an all-night bookstore, you can also order Afraid at many fine online retailers.*

Konrath put that ending in. In the ending I wrote, Duffy takes Jack back to his place and rocks her world—Schreck*

****I like my ending better. And I'm Jack Kilborn, if you haven't figured it out—Konrath*

Truck Stop

TRUCK STOP takes place before the events portrayed in AFRAID by Jack Kilborn, SERIAL UNCUT by Jack Kilborn & Blake Crouch, and FUZZY NAVEL by JA Konrath. Reading the authors' previous work isn't necessary to enjoy TRUCK STOP, though both authors encourage you to buy everything they've written. They also encourage you to buy them beer.

"He who is unjust, let him be unjust still; he who is filthy, let him be filthy still; he who is righteous, let him be righteous still…" —REVELATION 22

-1-

TAYLOR LIKED TOES.

He wasn't a pervert. At least, not *that* kind of pervert. Taylor didn't derive sexual gratification from feet. Women had other parts much better suited for that type of activity. But he was a sucker for a tiny foot in open-toed high heels, especially when the toenails were painted.

Painted toes were yummy.

The truck stop whore wore sandals, the cork wedge heels so high her toes were bent. She had small feet — they looked like a size five — and her nails matched her red mini skirt. Taylor spotted her through the windshield as she walked over to his Peterbilt, wiggling her hips and wobbling a bit. Taylor guessed she was drunk or stoned.

Perhaps both.

He climbed out of his cab. When his cowboy boots touched the pavement he reached his hands up over his head and stretched, his vertebrae cracking. The night air was hot and sticky with humidity, and he could smell his own sweat.

The whore blew smoke from the corner of her mouth. "Hiya, stranger. My name's Candi. With an I."

"I'm Taylor. With a T."

He smiled. She giggled, then hiccupped.

Even in the dim parking lot light, Candi with an I was nothing to look at. Mid-thirties. Cellulite. Twenty pounds too heavy for her skirt and halter top. She wore sloppy make-up, her lipstick smeared, making Taylor wonder how many truckers she'd already blown on this midnight shift.

But she did have very cute toes. She dropped her cigarette and crushed it into the pavement, and Taylor licked his lower lip.

"Been on the road a long time, Taylor?"

"Twelve hours in from Cinci. My ass is flatter than roadkill armadillo."

She eyed his rig. He was hauling four bulldozers on his flatbed trailer. They were heavy, and his mileage hadn't been good, making this run much less profitable than it should have been.

But Taylor didn't become a trucker to get rich. He did it for other reasons.

"You feeling lonely, Taylor? You looking for a little company?"

Taylor knew he could use a little company right now. He could also use a meal, a hot shower, and eight hours of sleep.

It was just a question of which need he'd cater to first.

He looked around the truck stop lot. Pretty full for late night in Bumblefuck, Wisconsin. Over a dozen rigs and just as many cars. The 24 hour gas station had a line for the pumps, and *Murray's Eats*, the all-night diner, appeared full.

On either side of the cloverleaf there were a few other restaurants and gas stations, but *Murray's* was always busy because they boasted more than food and diesel. Besides the no-hassle companionship the management and local authorities tolerated, *Murray's* had a full-size truck wash, a mechanic on duty, and free showers.

After twelve hours of caffeine sweating in this muggy Midwestern

August, Taylor needed some quality time with a bar of soap just as badly as he needed quality time with a parking lot hooker.

But it didn't make sense to shower first, when he was only going to get messy again.

"How much?" he asked.

"That depends on —"

"Half and half," he cut her off, not needing to hear the daily menu specials.

"Twenty-five bucks."

She didn't look worth twenty-five bucks, but he wasn't planning on paying her anyway, so he agreed.

"Great, sugar. I just need to make a quick stop at the little girls' room and I'll be right back."

She spun on her wedges to leave, but Taylor caught her thin wrist. He knew she wasn't going to the washroom. She was going to her pimp to give him the four Ps: Price, preferences, plate number, parking location. Taylor didn't see any single men hanging around; only other whores, and none of them were paying attention. Her pimp was probably in the restaurant, unaware of this particular transaction, and Taylor wanted to keep it that way.

"I'm sorta anxious to get right to it, Candi." He smiled wide. Women loved his smile. He'd been told, many times, that he was good-looking enough to model. "If you leave me now, I might just find some other pretty girl to spend my money on."

Candi smiled back. "Well, we wouldn't want that. But I'm short on protection right now, honey."

"I've got rubbers in the cab." Taylor switched to his brooding, hurt-puppy dog look. "I need it bad, right now, Candi. So bad I'll throw in another ten spot. That's thirty-five bucks for something we both know will only take a few minutes."

Taylor watched Candi work it out in her head. This john was hot to trot, offering more than the going rate, and he'd probably be really quick. Plus, he was cute. She could probably do him fast, and pocket the whole fee without having to share it with her pimp.

"You got yourself a date, sugar."

Taylor took another quick look around the lot, made sure no one was watching, and hustled Candi into his cab, climbing up behind her and locking the door.

The truck's windows were lightly tinted — making it difficult for anyone on the street to see inside. Not that Candi bothered to notice, or care. As soon as Taylor faced her she was pawing at his fly.

"The bedroom is upstairs." Taylor pointed to the stepladder in the rear of the extended cab, leading to his overhead sleeping compartment.

"Is there enough room up there? Some of those spaces are tight."

"Plenty. I customized it myself. It's to die for."

Taylor smiled, knowing he was being coy, knowing it didn't matter at this point. His heart rate was up, his palms itchy, and he had that excited/sick feeling that junkies got right before they jabbed the needle in. If Candi suddenly had a change of heart, there wasn't anything she could do about it. She was past the point of no return.

But Candi didn't resist. She went up first, pushing the trap door on the cab's ceiling, climbing into the darkness above. Taylor hit the light switch on his dashboard and followed her.

"What is this? Padding?"

She was on her hands and knees, running her palm across the floor of the sleeper, testing its springiness with her fingers.

"Judo mats. Extra thick. Very easy to clean up."

"You got mats on the walls too?" She got on her knees and reached overhead, touching the spongy material on the arced ceiling, her exposed belly jiggling.

"Those are baffles. Keeps the sound out." He smiled, closing the trap door behind him. "And in."

The lighting was subdued, just a simple overhead fixture next to the smoke alarm. The soundproofing was black foam, the mats a deep beige, and there was no furniture in the enclosure except for an inflatable rubber mattress and a medium-sized metal trunk.

"This is kind of kinky. Are you kinky, Taylor?"

"You might say that."

Taylor crawled over to the trunk at the far end of the enclosure. After dialing the combination lock, he opened the lid. Then he moved his Tupperware container aside and took out a fresh roll of paper towels, a disposable paper nose and mouth mask, and an aerosol spray can. He ripped off three paper towels, then slipped the mask on over his face, adjusting the rubber band so it didn't catch in his hair.

"What is that, sugar?" Candi asked. Her flirty, playful demeanor was slipping a bit.

"Starter fluid. You squirt it into your carburetor, it helps the engine turn over. Its main ingredient is diethyl ether."

He held the paper towels at arm's length, then sprayed them until they were soaked.

"What the fuck are you doing?" Candi looked panicked now. And she had good reason to be.

"This will knock you out so I can tie you up. You're not the prettiest flower in the bouquet, Candi with an I. But you have the cutest little toes."

He grinned again. But this wasn't one of his attractive grins. The whore shrunk away from him.

"Don't hurt me, man! Please! I got kids!"

"They must be so proud."

Taylor approached her, on his knees, savoring her fear. She tried to crawl to the right and get around him, get to the trap door. But that was closed and now concealed by matting, and Taylor knew she had no idea where it was.

He watched her realize escape wasn't an option, and then she dug into her little purse for a weapon or a cell phone or a bribe or something else that she thought might help but wouldn't. Taylor hit her square in the nose, then tossed the purse aside. A small canister of pepper spray spilled out, along with a cell phone, make-up, Tic-Tacs, and several condoms.

"You lied to me," Taylor said, slapping her again. "You've got rubbers."

"Please…"

"You lying little slut. Were you going to pepper spray me?"

"No… I…"

"Liar." Another slap. "I think you need to be taught a lesson. And I don't think you'll like it. But I will."

Candi's hands covered her bleeding nose and she moaned something that sounded like, "Please… My kids…"

"Does your pimp offer life insurance?"

She whimpered.

"No? That's a shame. Well, I'm sure he'll take care of your children for you. He'll probably have them turning tricks by next week."

Taylor knocked her hands away and pressed the cold, wet paper towels to her face. Not hard enough to cut off air, but hard enough that she had to breathe through them. Even though he wore a paper face mask, some of the pungent, bitter odor got into Taylor's nostrils, making his hairs curl.

It took the ether less than a minute to do its job on the whore. When she finally went limp, Taylor placed the damp towels in a plastic zip-top bag. Then he took several bungee cords out of the trunk and bound Candi's hands and arms to her torso. Unlike rope, the elastic bands didn't require knots, and were reusable. Taylor wrapped them around Candi tight enough for her to lose circulation, but that didn't matter.

Candi wouldn't be needing circulation for very much longer.

While the majority of his murder kit was readily available at any truck stop, his last piece of equipment was specially made.

It looked like a large board with two four-inch wide holes cut in the middle. Taylor flipped the catch on the side and it opened up on hinges, like one of those old-fashion jail stocks that prisoners stuck their heads and hands into. Except this one was made for something else.

Taylor grabbed Candi's left foot and gingerly removed her wedge. Then he placed her ankle in the half-circle cut into the wood. He repeated the action with her right foot, and closed the stock.

Now Candi's bare feet protruded through the boards, effectively trapped.

He locked the catch with a padlock, and then set the stock in between the floor mats, where it fit snuggly into a brace, secured by two more padlocks.

Play time.

Taylor lay on his stomach, taking Candi's right foot in his hands. He cupped her heel, running a finger up along her sole, bringing his lips up to her toes.

He licked them once, tasting sweat, grime, smelling a slight foot odor and a faint residue of nail polish. His pulse went up even higher, and time seemed to slow down.

Her little toe came off surprisingly easy, no harder than nibbling the cartilage top off a fried chicken leg.

Taylor watched the blood seep out as he chewed on the severed digit — a blood and gristle-flavored piece of gum — and then swallowed.

This little piggy went to market.

He opened up his mouth to accommodate the second little piggy, the one who stayed home, when he realized something was missing.

Where was the screaming? Where was the begging? Where was the thrashing around in agony?

He crawled around the stock, alongside Candi's head. Ether was a pain in the ass to get the dose right, and he'd lost more than one girl by giving her too big a whiff. Luckily, Candi was still breathing. But she was too deeply sedated to let some playful toe-munching wake her up.

Taylor frowned. Like sex, murder was best with two active participants. He gathered up the whore's belongings, then rolled away from her, over to the trap door.

He'd get a bite to eat, maybe enjoy one of *Murray's* famous free showers. Hopefully, when he got back, *Sleeping Homely* would be awake.

Taylor used one of the ether-soaked paper towels to wipe the blood off his chin and fingers, stuffed them back into the bag, then headed for the diner.

-2-

"WHERE ARE YOU?"

"I have no idea." My cell was tucked between my shoulder and my ear as I drove. "I think I'm still in Wisconsin. Wouldn't there be some kind of sign if I entered another state?"

"Don't you have the map I gave you?" Latham asked. "The directions?"

"Yeah. But they aren't helping."

"Are you looking at the map right now?"

"Yes."

The map might have done me some good if I'd been able to see what was on it. But the highway was dark, and the interior light in my 1989 Nova had burned out last month.

"You can't see it, can you?"

"Define see."

I heard my fiancée sigh. "I just bought you a replacement bulb for that overhead lamp. I saw you put it in your purse. It's still in your purse, isn't it?"

"Maybe."

"And you can't replace the bulb now, because it's too dark."

"That's a good deduction. You should become a cop."

"One cop in this relationship is enough. Why didn't you take my GPS when I insisted?"

"Because I didn't want you to get lost."

A billboard was coming up on my right. MURRAY'S – NEXT EXIT. That was nice to know, but I had no idea what *Murray's* was, or how far the exit was. Not a very effective advertisement.

"*My* interior light works, Jackie. I could have used Mapquest."

"Mapquest lies. And don't call me Jackie. You know I hate it when people call me Jackie."

"And I hate it when you say you'd be here three hours ago, and you're still not here. You could have left at a reasonable hour, Jack."

He had a point. This was my first real vacation — and by that I mean one that involved actually travelling somewhere — in a few years. Latham had rented a cabin on Rice Lake, and he had driven there yesterday from Chicago to meet the rental owners and get the keys. I was supposed to go with him, and we'd been planning this for weeks, but the murder trial I'd been testifying at had gone longer than expected, and since I was the arresting officer I needed to be there. As much as I loved Latham, and as much as I needed some time away from work, my duty to put criminals away ranked slightly higher.

"Your told-you-so tone isn't going to get you laid later," I said. "Just help me figure out where I am."

Another sigh. I shrugged it off. My long-suffering boyfriend had suffered a lot worse than this in order to be with me. I figured he had to be incredibly desperate, or a closet masochist. Either way, he was a cutie, and I loved him.

"Do you see the mile markers alongside the road?"

I didn't see any such thing. The highway was dark, and I hadn't noticed any signs, off-ramps, exits, or mile markers since I'd left Illinois. But I hadn't exactly been paying much attention, either. I was pretty damn tired, and had been zoning out to AM radio for the last hour. FM didn't work. Sometimes I wish someone would shoot my car, put it out of my misery.

"No. There's nothing out here, Latham. Except *Murray's*."

"What's *Murray's*?"

"I have no idea. I just saw the sign. Could be a gas station. Could be a waterpark."

"I don't remember passing anything called *Murray's*. Did the sign have the exit number?"

"No."

"Are you sure?"

I made a face. "The defense attorney never asked me if I was sure. The defense attorney took me at my word."

"He should have also made you take my GPS. You see those posts alongside the road with the reflectors on them?"

"Yeah."

"Keep watching them."

"Why should —" The next reflector had a number on top. "Oh. Okay, I'm at mile marker 231."

"I don't have Internet access here at the cabin. I'll call you back when I find out where you are. You're okay, right? Not going to fall asleep while driving?"

I yawned. "I'm fine, hon. Just a little hungry."

"Stop for something if it will keep you awake."

"Sure. I'll just pull over and grab the nearest cow."

"If you do, bring me a tenderloin."

"Really? Is your appetite back?" Latham was still recovering from a bad case of food poisoning.

"It's getting there."

"Aren't you tired? You should rest, honey."

"I'm fine."

"Are you sure?"

"I'm sure. I'll call soon with your location."

My human GPS unit hung up. I yawned again, and gave my head a little shake.

On the plus side, my testimony had gone well, and all signs pointed to a conviction.

On the minus side, I'd been driving for six straight hours, and I was hungry, tired, and needed to pee. I also needed gas, according to my gauge.

Maybe Murray could take care of all my needs. Assuming I could find Murray's before falling asleep, running out of fuel, starving to death, and wetting my pants.

The road stretched onward into the never-ending darkness. I hadn't seen another car in a while. Even though this was a major highway (as far as I knew), traffic was pretty light. Who would have thought that Northern Wisconsin at two in the morning on a Wednesday night was so deserted?

I heard my cell phone ring. My hero, to the rescue.

"You're not on I-94," he said. "You're on 39."

"You sound annoyed."

"You went the wrong way when the Interstate split."

"Which means?"

"You drove three hours out of the way."

Shit.

I yawned. "So where do I go to get to you?"

"You need some sleep, Jack. You can get here in the morning."

"Three hours is nothing. I can be there in time for an early breakfast."

"You sound exhausted."

"I'll be fine. Lemme just close my eyes for a second."

"That's not even funny."

I smiled. The poor sap really did care about me.

"I love you, Latham."

"I love you, too. That's why I want you to find a room somewhere and get some rest."

"Just tell me how to get to you. I don't want to sleep alone in some cheap hotel with threadbare sheets and a mattress with questionable stains. I want to sleep next to you in that cabin with the big stone fireplace. But first I want to rip off those cute boxer-briefs you wear and… hello? Latham?"

I squinted at my cell. No signal.

Welcome to Wisconsin.

I yawned again. Another billboard appeared.

MURRAY'S FAMOUS TRUCK STOP. FOOD. DIESEL. LODGING. TRUCK WASH. SHOWERS. MECHANIC ON DUTY. TEN MILES.

Ten miles? I could make ten miles. And maybe some food and coffee would wake me up.

I pressed the accelerator, taking the Nova up to eighty.

Murray's here I come.

-3-

TAYLOR PAUSED AT THE diner entrance, taking everything in. The restaurant was busy, the tables all full. He spotted three waitresses, plus two cooks in the kitchen. Seated were various truckers, two with hooker companions. Taylor knew the owners encouraged it, and wondered what kind of cut they got.

He saw what must have been Candi's pimp, holding court at a corner table. Rattleskin cowboy boots, a gold belt buckle in the shape of Wisconsin, fake bling on his baseball cap. He was having a serious discussion with one of his whores. The rest of the tables were occupied by truckers. Taylor didn't see any cops; a pimp in plain sight meant they were being paid off.

The place smelled terrific, like bacon gravy and apple pie. Taylor's stomach grumbled. He located the emergency exit in the northeast corner, and knew there was also a back door that led into the kitchen; Taylor had walked the perimeter of the building before entering.

With no tables available, he approached the counter and took a seat there, between the storefront window and a pudgy, older guy nursing a cup of coffee. It was a good spot. He could see his rig, and also see anyone approaching it or him.

Taylor hadn't been to Murray's in over a year, but the printed card sticking in the laminated menu said their specialty was meatloaf.

"Meatloaf is good," the old guy leaned over and said.

"I didn't ask for your opinion."

"You were looking at the card. Thought I'd be helpful."

He examinedthe man, a grandfatherly type with thinning gray hair and red cheeks. Taylor wasn't in the best of moods—one toe was barely an appetizer for him—and he was ready to tell Grandpa off. But starting a scene meant being remembered, and that wasn't wise.

"Thank you," Taylor managed.

"You're welcome."

A waitress came by, wearing ugly scuffed-up gym shoes. Taylor ordered coffee and the meatloaf. The coffee was strong, bitter. Taylor added two sugars.

"Showers are good here too," his fat companion said.

Taylor gave him another look.

Is this guy trying to pick me up?

The man sipped his coffee and didn't meet Taylor's stare.

"Look, buddy. I just want to eat in peace. No offense. I've been on the road for a long time."

"No offense taken," the fat man said. He finished his coffee, then signaled the waitress for a refill. "Just telling you the showers are good. Be sure to get some quarters. They've got a machine, sells soap. Useful for washing off blood."

All of Taylor's senses went on high alert, and he felt himself flush. This guy didn't look like a cop—Taylor could usually spot cops. He wore baggy jeans, a plaid shirt, a Timex. On the counter next to his empty cup was a baseball cap without any logo. A few days' worth of beard graced his double chin.

No, he wasn't law. And he wasn't cruising him, either.

So what the hell does hewant?

"What do you mean?" Taylor asked, keeping his tone neutral.

"Drop of blood on your shirt. Another spot on your collar. Some under your fingernails as well. You wiped them with ether, but it didn't completely dissolve. Did you know that ether was first used as a surgical anesthetic back in 1842? Before that, taking a knife to a person meant screaming and thrashing around." The man held a beefy hand to his mouth and belched. "'Course, some people might like the *screaming and thrashing around* part."

Taylor bunched his fists, then forced himself to relax. Had this guy seen him somehow? Did he know about Candi in the sleeper?

No. He couldn't have. Tinted windows on his cab. No windows at all in the sleeping compartment.

He took a casual glance around, trying to spot anyone else watching. No one seemed to be paying either of them any attention.

Taylor dropped his hand, slowly reaching for the folding knife clipped to his belt. He considered sliding it between this guy's ribs right there and getting the hell out. But first Taylor needed to know what Grandpa knew. Maybe he could lead him to the bathroom, get him into a stall…

Taylor froze. His knife was missing.

"Take it easy, my friend," said the old, fat man. "I'll give you your knife back when we're through."

Taylor wasn't sure what to say, but he believed everyone had an angle. This guy knew more than he should have. But what was he going to do with his information?

"Who are you?" Taylor asked.

"Name's Donaldson. And you probably meant to ask *What are you?* You've probably figured out I'm not a cop, not a Fed. Thanks, Donna." He nodded at the waitress as she refilled his coffee. "Actually, I'm just a fellow traveler. Enjoying the country. The sites. The *people*." Donaldson winked at him. "Same as you are."

"Same as me, huh?"

Donaldson nodded. "A bit older and wiser, perhaps. At least wise enough to not use that awful ether anymore. Where do you even get that these days? I thought ether and chloroform were controlled substances."

"Starter fluid," Taylor said. This conversation was getting surreal.

"Clever."

"So what is it exactly you do, Donaldson?"

"For work? Or do you mean with the people I encounter? I'm a courier, that's my job. I travel all around, delivering things to people who need them faster than overnight. As for the other—well, that's sort of personal, don't you think? We just met, and you want me to reveal intimate details of my antisocial activities? Shouldn't we work up to that?"

So far, Donaldson had been the embodiment of calm. He didn't seem threatening in the least. They might have been talking about the weather.

"And you spotted me because of the blood and the ether smell?"

"Initially. But the give-away was the look in your eyes."

"And what sort of look do my eyes have, Donaldson?"

"This one." Donaldson turned and looked at Taylor. "The eyes of a predator. No pity. No remorse. No humanity."

Taylor stared hard, then grinned. "I don't see anything but regular old eyes."

Donaldson held the intense gaze a moment longer, then chuckled.

"Okay. You caught me. The eyes don't tell anything. But I caught you casing the place before you walked in. Looking for cops, for trouble, for exits. A man that careful should have noticed some spots of blood on his shirt."

"Maybe I cut myself shaving."

"And the ether smell?"

"Maybe the rig was giving me some trouble, so I cleaned out the carburetor."

"No grease or oil under your nails. Just dried blood."

Taylor leaned in close, speaking just above a whisper.

"Give me one good reason I shouldn't kill you, Donaldson."

"Other than the fact I have your knife? Because you should consider this a golden opportunity, my friend. You and I, we're solitary creatures. We don't ever talk about our secret lives. We never share stories of our exploits with anyone. I've been doing this for over thirty years, and I've never met another person like us. A few wannabes. More than a few crazies. But never another hunter. Like we are. Don't you think this is a unique chance?"

The meatloaf came, steaming hot. But Taylor wasn't hungry anymore. He was intrigued. If Donaldson was what he claimed to be, the fat man was one hundred percent correct. Taylor had never talked about his lifestyle with anyone, other than his victims. And then, it was only to terrify them even more.

Sometimes, Taylor had fantasies of getting caught. Not because he harbored any guilt, and not because he wanted to be locked up. But because it would be nice, just once, to be open and honest about his habits with the whole world. To let a fellow human being know how clever he'd been all these years. Maybe have some shrink interview him and write a bestselling book.

How interesting it would be to talk shop with someone as exceptional as he was.

"So you want to swap stories? Trade tactics? Is that it, Donaldson?"

"I can think of duller ways to kill some time at a truck stop."

Taylor cut the meatloaf with his fork, shoved some into his mouth. It was good.

"Fine. You go first. You said you don't like ether. So how do you make your—" Taylor reached for the right words "—*guests* compliant."

"Blunt force trauma."

"Using what?"

"Trade secret."

"And what if you're too... *aggressive*... with your use of blunt force?"

"An unfortunate side-effect. Just happened to me, in fact. Just picked up a tasty little morsel, but her lights went out before I could have any fun with her."

"Picked up? Hitcher?"

Donaldson sipped more coffee and grinned. "Didn't you know about the dangers of hitchhiking, son? Lots of psychos out there."

Taylor shoved more meatloaf into his mouth, and followed it up with some mashed potatoes. "Hitchers might be missed."

"So could truck stop snatch."

Taylor paused in mid-bite.

"Your fly is open. And I saw how you were measuring the resident pimp." Donaldson raised an eyebrow. "Have you relieved him of one of his steady sources of income?"

Now it was Taylor's turn to grin. "Not yet. She'll be dessert when I'm done with this meatloaf."

"And once you're finished with her?"

Taylor zipped up his fly. "I like rivers. Water takes care of any trace evidence, and it's tough for the law to pinpoint the location where they were dumped in. You?"

"Gas and a match. First a nice spritz with bleach. Bleach destroys DNA, you know."

"I do. Got a few bottles in the truck."

Taylor still couldn't assess what sort of threat Donaldson posed. But he had to admit, this was fun.

"So, here's the ten-thousand dollar question," Donaldson asked. "How many are you up to?"

Taylor wiped some gravy off his mouth with a paper napkin. "So that's where we stand? Whipping out our dicks and seeing whose is bigger?"

"I've been at this a very long time." Donaldson belched again. "Probably since before you were born. I've read about others like us; I love those true crime audiobooks. They help pass the time on long trips. I collect regular books, too. Movies. Newspaper articles. If you've done the same research I have, then you know none of our American peers can prove more than forty-eight. That's the key. *Prove.* Some boast high numbers, but there isn't proof to back it up."

"So are you asking me how many I've done, or how many I can prove?"

"Both."

Taylor shrugged. "I lost count after forty-eight. Once I had one in every state, it became less about quantity and more about quality."

"You're lying," Donaldson said. "You're too young for that many."

"One in every state, old man."

"Can you prove it?"

"I kept driver's licenses, those that had them. Probably don't have more than twenty, though. Not many whores carry ID."

"No pictures? Trophies? Souvenirs?"

Taylor wasn't going to share something that personal with a stranger. He pretended to sneer. "Taking a trophy is like asking to get caught. I don't plan on getting caught."

"True. But it is nice to relive the moment. Traveling is lonely, and memories unfortunately fade. If it wasn't so dangerous, I'd love to videotape a few."

That would be nice, Taylor thought, finishing the last bit of meatloaf. *But mytrophy box will have to suffice.*

"So how many are you up to, Grandpa?"

"A hundred twenty-seven."

Taylor snorted. "Bullshit."

"I agree with you about the danger of keeping souvenirs, but I have Polaroids from a lot of my early ones."

"Dangerous to carry those around with you."

"I've got them well hidden." Donaldson stared at him, his eyes twinkling. "Would you be interested in seeing them?"

"What do you mean? One of those *I'll show you mine if you show me yours* deals?"

"No. Well, not exactly. I'm not interested in seeing your driver's license collection. But I would be interested in paying a little visit to your current guest."

Taylor frowned. "I'm not big on sharing. Or sloppy seconds."

Donaldson slowly spread out his hands. "I understand. It's just that… you know how it is, when you get all worked up, and then they quit on you."

Taylor nodded. Having a victim die too soon felt like having something precious stolen from him.

"You don't seem like the shy type," Donaldson continued. "I thought, perhaps, you wouldn't mind doing your thing when someone else was there to watch."

Taylor smiled. "Aren't you the dirty old man."

Donaldson smiled back. "A dirty old man who doesn't have the same distaste of sloppy seconds as you apparently have. I see no problem in going second. As long as there's something left for me to enjoy myself with."

"I leave all the major parts intact."

"Then perhaps we can come to some sort of arrangement."

"Perhaps we can."

Donaldson's smile suddenly slipped off his face. He'd noticed the same thing Taylor had.

A cop had walked into the restaurant.

Woman, forties, well built, a gold star clipped to her hip. But even without the badge, she had that swagger, had that *look*, that Taylor had spent a lifetime learning to spot.

"Here comes trouble," Donaldson said.

And, as luck would have it, trouble sat down right next to them.

-4-

AFTER FILLING MY GAS tank and emptying my bladder, I went in search of food.

The diner was surprisingly full this late at night. Truckers mostly. And though I hadn't worked Vice in well over a decade, I was pretty sure the only women in the place were earning their living illegally.

Not that I judged, or even cared. One of the reasons I switched from Vice to Homicide was because I had no problems with what consenting adults did to themselves or each other. I'd done a few drugs in my day, and as a woman I felt I should be able to do whatever I wanted with my body. So the scene in the diner was nothing more to me than local color. I just wanted some coffee and a hot meal, which I believed would wake me up enough to get me through the rest of my road trip and into the very patient arms of my fiancée.

I expected at least one or two catcalls or wolf whistles when I entered, but didn't hear any. Sort of disappointing. I was wearing what I wore to court, a brown Ann Klein pantsuit, clingy in all the right places, and a pair of three inchKate Spade strappy sandals. The shoes were perhaps a bit frivolous, but the jury couldn't see my feet when I took the stand. I left for Wisconsin directly from court, and wore the shoes because Latham loved them. I had even painted my toenails to celebrate our vacation.

Maybe the current diners were too preoccupied with the hired help to know another woman had entered the place. Or maybe it was me. Latham said I gave off a "cop vibe" that people could sense, but he assured me I was stillsexy. Still, a Wisconsin truck stop at two in the morning filled with lonely, single men, and I didn't even get a lecherous glance. Maybe I needed to work-out more.

Then I realized I still had my badge clipped to my belt. Duh.

I quickly scoped out the joint, finding the emergency exit, counting the number of patrons and employees, identifying potential trouble. An absurdly dressed man in expensive boots and a diamond studded John Deere cap stared hard at me. He gave me a look that said he hated cops, and I gave him a look that said I hated his kind even more. While I tolerated prostitutes, I loathed pimps. Someone taking the money you earned just because they were bigger than you wasn't fair.

But I didn't come here to start trouble. I just wanted some food and caffeine.

I walked the room slowly, feeling the cold stares, and found counter space next to a portly man. I eased myself onto the stool.

"Coffee, officer?"

I nodded at the waitress. She overturned my mug and filled it up. I glanced at the menu, wondering if they had cheese curds—those little fried nuggets of cheddar exclusive to Wisconsin.

"The meatloaf is good."

I glanced at the man on my left. Big and tall, maybe fifteen years older than I was. He had a kind-looking face, but his smile appeared forced.

"Thanks," I replied.

I sipped some coffee. Nice and strong. If I got two cups and a burger in me, I'd be good to go. The waitress returned, I ordered a cheeseburger with bacon, and a side of cheese curds.

"Never seen you here before."

The voice, reeking of alpha male, came from behind me. I could guess who it belonged to.

"Passing through," I said, not bothering to turn around.

"Well, maybe you can hurry it along, little lady. Your kind isn't good for business."

I carefully set down my mug of coffee, then slowly swiveled around on my stool.

The pimp was sticking his chest out like he was being fitted for a bra, a few stray curly hairs peeking through his collar. One of his women, strung out on something, clung unenthusiastically to his side. Her concealer didn't quite cover up her black eye.

"I'm off duty, and just stopped in for coffee and some cheese curds, which I can't get in Illinois. I suggest you mind your own business. This isn't my jurisdiction, but I'm guessing the local authorities wouldn't mind if I fed you someof your teeth."

The older fat guy next to me snorted. The pimp wasn't so amused.

"The *local authorities,*" he said it in a falsetto, obviously trying to mimic me, "and I have an arrangement. That arrangement means no cops." He gave me a rough shove in the shoulder. "And I'm sure they wouldn't mind if I fed you—"

I drove the salt shaker into his upper jaw with my palm, breaking both the glass and the teeth I'd promised. Besides being hard and having weight, the shards and the salt did a number on the pimp's gums. Must have hurt like crazy.

He dropped to his knees, clutching his face and howling, and three of his women dragged him out of there. I did a slow pan across the room, looking for other challengers, seeing none. Then I brushed my hand on my pants, wiping off the excess salt, and went back to my coffee, trying to control the adrenalin shakes. I hated violence of any kind, but once he touched me, I didn't have any other recourse. I didn't want to play footsie with the local cops he was paying off, trying to get an assault charge to stick. Or worse, wind up in the hospital because some asshole pimp thought he could treat me the same way he treated the women who worked for him.

Better to nip it in the bud and drop him fast. Though I didn't have to feel good about it.

I took a deep, steadying breath, and managed to sip some coffee without spilling it all over myself, all the while keeping one eye on the entrance. I'd hurt the pimp bad enough to require an emergency room visit, but if he were tougher and dumber than I'd guessed, he might return with a weapon. I set my purse on the counter, my .38 within easy reach, just in case.

"You're Lieutenant Jack Daniels, aren't you?"

I glanced at the fat man again. Even though I'd been on the news many times, I didn't get recognized very often in Chicago, and it never happened away from home.

"And you are?" My voice came out higher than I would have liked.

"Just a fan. You got that serial killer Charles Kork, the one they called the Gingerbread Man. How many women did he kill?"

"Too many." I turned back to my coffee.

"I saw the TV movie. The one that became the series. You're much better looking than the actress who played you."

I was in no mood to be idolized. Plus, there was something creepy about this guy.

"Look, buddy, I don't want to be rude, but I'm really not up for conversation right now."

The fat man didn't take the hint. "And you got Barry Fuller. He killed over a dozen, didn't he? He was both a serial killer and a mass murderer, due to all those Feds he took out at that rest stop."

I sighed. The waitress came by with my cheese curds. She set down the basket and winked at me. "These are on me."

"Thanks. I could use some salt."

I tried a curd. Too hot, so I spit it back out into my palm and played hot potato until it cooled off. My biggest fan refused to give up.

"There were others in the Kork family as well, weren't there? A whole group of psychos. I heard they killed over forty people, total."

I really didn't want to think about the Kork family, and I really didn't want to have a late-night gabfest with a cop groupie.

But, on the plus side, knocking out that pimp's teeth really woke me up.

When the waitress brought me the salt, I asked for my meal to go. The fat guy apparently didn't like that, because he gave me his back and had an intense whisper exchange with his buddy; a younger, attractive man in a flannel shirt. The young guy nodded, got up, and left.

"Just one last question, Lieutenant, and then I promise I'll leave you alone."

I sighed again, glancing at him. "Go ahead."

"Did you ever try to take on two serial killers at once?"

"I can't say that I have."

He smiled, lopsided. "Too bad. That would have been cool."

The fat guy threw down some money, then followed his buddy out.

No longer pestered, I decided to eat there, and settled in to eat my cheese curds.

-5-

TAYLOR HADN'T EVER KILLED a cop. He came close once, a few years ago, when a state trooper pulled him over, and asked him to step out of his truck. Taylor had been ready to pull his knife and gut the pig, but the cop only wanted him to do a field sobriety test. Taylor wouldn't ever risk driving drunk, and he easily passed, getting let off with a warning and pulling away with a dead hooker in his sleeping compartment.

But he was itching to get at this cop. Taylor liked strong women. He liked when they fought him, refusing to give up. They were so much fun to break. Especially when they had such adorable feet.

As Donaldson suggested, Taylor had left the diner and gone back to his rig to grab the ether. Candi with an I was still out cold, but she held far less fascination for Taylor than this new prospect.

I'm going tohave a little nip of Jack Daniels, he thought, smiling wildly. *Maybe more than one. And maybe not so little.*

For helping out, he'd let Donaldson have Candi. While Taylor wasn't into the whole *voyeur* scene, it might be interesting to watch another pro do his thing. Hopefully, it didn't involve any sort of sex, because he had zero desire to see Donaldson's flabby, naked ass.

Taylor grabbed the plastic bag—the ether-soaked paper towels still moist—and met Donaldson in the parking lot.

"The best spot is here, in the shadow of this truck," Donaldson said.

Taylor didn't like him calling the shots, but he heard the man out.

"She thinks I'm a fan," Donaldson continued, "so I'm going to call her over here, ask for an autograph. Then you come up behind her with the ether."

"She's armed. Her purse was too heavy to only be carrying a wallet and make-up."

"I saw that, too. I'll grab her wrists, you get her around the neck. We can pull her to the ground here, out of sight. How close is your truck?"

"The red Peterbilt, a few spaces back."

"When she's out, we throw her arms around our shoulders, walk her over there like she's drunk."

Taylor shook his head. "Only when we're sure no one is watching. I don't want a witness getting my plate number."

"Fine. We can walk her around until we're sure we're clear."

Taylor stared at Donaldson for a moment, then said, "She's mine."

Donaldson didn't respond.

"I'll give you the whore for helping me, Donaldson. But the cop is mine."

Donaldson eventually nodded. "Fair enough. Is the whore cute?"

"Too old, fat thighs, saggy gut from popping out kids."

Donaldson raised his eyebrow. "She's got kids?"

Taylor laughed. "You into kiddies, Donaldson?"

"Any port in the storm. But you can have fun with kids in other ways. Did the whore have a cell phone?"

"Yeah."

"Give it here."

Interested in where Donaldson was going with this, Taylor dug the phone out of his pocket and handed it over. Donaldson scrolled through the address book.

"Calling home," Donaldson told him.

"Can't calls be traced?"

"They can be traced to this cell phone, but not to our current location. To do that requires some highly sophisticated equipment—which I highly doubt the local constabulary possesses."

"Put it on speaker."

Donaldson hit a button, and Taylor heard ringing.

"Hello?" A child's voice, pre-teen.

"This is Detective Donaldson. I'm sorry to inform you that your mommy is dead."

"What?"

"Mommy is dead, kid. She was horribly murdered."

"Mommy's dead?" The child began to cry.

"It's an occupational hazard. Your mom was a whore, you know. She had sex with strange men for money. One of those men killed her."

"Mommy's dead!"

Donaldson hit the disconnect button.

Taylor shook his head, smiling. "Man, that is low."

"I'll call him back later, see how he's doing. This phone has a camera, too. Maybe I'll send him some pictures of Mommy when I'm done with her."

"What about the babysitter sending the cops here?"

"You think the babysitter knows what Mom's job is? And even if she calls the cops, Murray's pays them to stay away. Besides, we'll be in your truck by then."

Taylor thought it was reckless. But still, calling up a kid and saying his mother was dead was pretty funny. Taylor considered all of the cell phones he'd thrown away, and cursed himself for the fun he'd missed.

Donaldson dug into his pocket and produced a pair of small binoculars. He held them to his face and looked at the diner.

"The cop is still working on her burger. She is a sweet piece of pie, isn't she? *Jack fucking Daniels.* What a lucky day indeed. It's a small world, my friend."

"Not when you're driving from L.A. to Boston."

"Funny you should mention that. One of the reasons I'm a courier is to have a wide area to hunt in. I'm assuming you got into trucking for the same reason."

"The wider the better. You shouldn't shit where you eat."

"I agree. I don't think I'm even on the Fed's radar. And cops don't talk to each other from state to state. A man could keep on doing this for a very long time, if he plays it smart."

"So, what's your thing?" Taylor asked.

Donaldson lowered the binocs. "My thing?"

"What you do to them."

Donaldson did the eyebrow raise again, which was starting to get annoying. "Have we reached that point in our relationship where we can share our methods? You haven't even told me your name."

"It's Taylor. And I want to know, before I invite you into my truck, that you aren't into some sick shit."

"Define *sick*."

"Guts are okay, but don't puncture the intestines. That smell takes forever to go away."

"I'm not into internal organs."

"How about rape?"

Donaldson smiled. "I *am* into rape."

"I don't want to see it. No offense, but naked guys are not a turn-on for me."

"That's fair enough. We can take turns, give each other some privacy. My *thing*, as you put it, is to cut off their faces. One little piece at a time. A nostril. An ear. An eye. A lip. And then I feed their faces to them, bit by bit. You?"

"Biting. Toes and fingers, to start. Then all over."

"How long have you kept one alive for?"

"Maybe two days."

Donaldson nodded. "See, that's nice. I do all my work outdoors, different locations, so I never have time to make it last, enjoy it. You've got a little murder-mobile, you can take your time."

"That's the reason I'm a trucker, not a courier."

Donaldson got a wistful look. "I'm thinking of renting a shack out in the woods. Out in the middle of nowhere. Then I could bring someone there, really drag it out. You remember that old magic trick? The girl in the box, and the magician sticks swords in it?"

Taylor nodded. "Yeah."

"I'd love to build one of those. Except there's no trick. Wouldn't that be fun? Sticking the swords in one at a time?"

Taylor decided it would.

Donaldson peered through the binocs again. "Here she comes.

Let's get in position."

Taylor nodded. He felt the excitement building up again, but a different kind of excitement. This time, he was sharing the experience with another person. It was oddly fulfilling, in a way his dozens of other murders hadn't been.

Maybe tag-team was the way to go.

He clenched the ether-soaked paper towels, crouched behind a bumper, and waited for the fun to start.

-6-

THE BURGER WAS GOOD. The coffee was good. The cheese curds were heavenly. I had no idea why they weren't served in Chicago.

I paid, left a decent tip, then tried calling Latham to tell him I felt good enough to keep driving.

Still no signal. I needed to switch carriers, or get a new phone. It especially bugged me because I saw other people in the diner talking on their cell phones. If that *Can you hear me now?* guy walked into the restaurant, I would have bounced my cell off his head.

The parking lot had decent lighting, but all of the big trucks cast shadows, and I knew more than most the dangers of walking in shadows. I pulled my purse on over my head and tucked it under my arm, then headed for my car while staying in the light. The last thing I needed was the pimp to make a play for me. Or that—

"Lieutenant Daniels!"

—fat guy from the diner, who approached me at a quick pace, coming out from behind one of the rigs. I stopped, my hand slipping inside my purse and seeking my revolver. Something about this man rubbed me the wrong way, and at over two hundred and fifty pounds he was too big to play around with.

He slowed down when I reached into my handbag—a bad sign. People with good intentions don't expect you to have a gun. I felt my heart rate kick up and my legs tense.

"Don't come any closer," I commanded, using my cop voice.

He stopped about ten feet in front of me. His hands were empty. "I wanted to ask you for your autograph."

My fingers wrapped around the butt of my .38. Confrontation, even with over twenty years of experience, was always a scary thing. Ninety-nine percent of the time, de-escalation was the key to avoiding violence. Take control of the situation, be polite but firm, apologize if needed. It wouldn't have worked on the pimp, who was showing off for the crowd, but it might work here.

"I'm sorry, I don't give autographs. I'm not a celebrity."

"It would mean a lot to me." He held up his palms and took another step forward.

I was taught that you never pull out your weapon unless you intend to use it.

I pulled out my weapon.

"I told you not to come any closer."

"You're kidding, right?" Another step. He was six feet away from me.

I pointed my gun at his chest. "Does it look like I'm kidding?"

He put on a crooked grin. "Is this how you treat your fans, Lieutenant? I don't mean any harm. You want to shoot an innocent civilian?"

"I don't want to. But I will, if I feel threatened. And right now I feel threatened. Where's your buddy?"

"My buddy?"

He was lying, I could see it on his face, and I swirled around, sensing something behind me. I caught a flash of movement, someone ducking between two parked cars. I spun again, storming up to the fat guy, grabbing two of his outstretched fingers and twisting. My action was fast, forceful, and I gained enough leverage to bend his arm to the side and drive him onto his knees, my gun trained on his head.

"Get on the pavement, face down!"

He pitched forward, and I had to let him go or fall with him. Rather than face-first, he dropped onto his side and swung his leg at me.

I should have fired, but a small part of me knew I could be killing a guy whose only crime was wanting my autograph, and I had enough of an ego to think I could still handle the situation. I sidestepped his leg and rammed my heel into his kidney, hard enough to show him this wasn't a joke.

That's when his partner dove at me.

He hit me sideways, knocking me off my feet in a flying tackle that drove me to the asphalt, shoulder-first. His weight squeezed the air out of me, his hand pawing at my face, a cold, wet hand covering my mouth and nose, flooding my airway with harsh chemicals. I held my breath, bringing my weapon up, squeezing the trigger—

The trigger wouldn't squeeze. The gun didn't fire.

Now the paper towels were in my eyes, the sting a hundred times worse than chlorine, making me squeeze my eyelids shut in pain. I felt my gun being wrestled away, and the small part of my brain that wasn't panicking knew the perp had grabbed my .38 by the hammer, his grip preventing me from shooting.

I still refused to breathe, knowing that whatever was on my face would knock me out, knowing when that happened I was dead. That made me panic even more, thrashing and pushing against my unseen assailant. I tried to kick my feet, get them under me to gain some leverage, but then they were weighed down the same as my upper body—the fat guy had joined the party.

So I went for the fake-out, letting my body go limp.

The seconds ticked by, each one a slice of eternity since I was oxygen-deprived. I could hold my breath for over a minute under ideal conditions. But terrified and with two psychos on top of me, I wouldn't be able to last a fraction of that…

One second at a time, Jack. Just don't breathe.

I felt that vertigo sensation in my head, my mind seeming to stretch out and twist around.

"Is anyone coming?"

"It's clear."

Stay still. Don't breathe.

My eyes were stinging like crazy, and I wanted to put my hands to my face, rub the pain away.

Don't. Move. Don't. Breathe.

My chest began to spasm, my diaphragm convulsing and begging for air. In moments it wouldn't be under my control anymore. I would breathe in those toxic fumes whether I wanted to or not.

Hold it in don't breathedon't breathe DON'T BREATHE—

"Too much and you'll kill her." The fat guy talking.

The hand over my face eased up, the noxious rag being pulled away. I wanted to gasp, to suck in air like a marathon runner, but I managed to take a slow, silent breath through my nose.

The fumes still clinging to my face smelled like gasoline, and by sheer will I didn't sneeze or cough. I kept my breathing slow, like I was sleeping, even though my heart pounded so loud and fast I could hear it.

"She's out. Grab an arm."

I felt myself lifted into an upright position, my arms over their shoulders. Then I was dragged, my feet scraping against the asphalt, which tore at my bare toes like sandpaper. I bit my inner cheek. If I made a peep, they'd use the rag again.

"Her feet! Watch her feet! I don't want them messed up!"

"Shh! Lift higher."

Then I was completely off the ground. I tried to peek, to see where we were, but everything was blurry and opening my eyes made the pain worse. I could feel the weight of my purse still hanging at my side, and I had a dull throb in my shoulder where I'd hit the pavement, but it didn't seem dislocated or broken.

"It's this one."

My body was shifted, and I heard the jingle of keys and a vehicle door opening.

"I'll get in first, pull her up."

"Check around for witnesses."

"We're alone out here, brother."

Another shift, and then strong hands under my armpits, pulling me up, hands on my ankle, my right shoe coming off, and then…

Something warm and wet on my big toe.

Jesus… he's got my toein his mouth.

His tongue circled it, once, twice, and then I felt the suction. Heard the slurping. Heard him moan.

This freak is sucking my toe.

Wet and sloppy, like a popsicle. I wanted to flinch. I wanted to scream.

Stay still, Jack. Don't kick him. Don't move.

His teeth locked on, scraping along the top and bottom, not enough to break the skin but enough to hurt, the pressure increasing…

I felt a surge of revulsion unlike any I've ever experienced, and my muscles involuntarily locked and my stomach churned, threatening to upload the burger and curds. I was half-hanging out of a truck, and I couldn't see, but I was going to take my chances and kick this bastard in the face, hopefully burying my shoe heel into his eye socket. It was two on one, and they had my gun, but I wasn't going to let him chew my toe off without a fight.

"Taylor, let's hold off until we get her inside."

My toe was abruptly released, and then I was violently shoved upward onto the fat guy's lap. I assumed he was sitting in the driver's seat of a semi. I felt his hot breath on my ear, and then the clammy touch of his lips. One hand pawed at my chest, tugging at my bra through my shirt. The other slid up my leg.

"Such a pretty lady," he said, nuzzling my neck. "I'm going to love feeding you your face."

When his lips touched my cheek it was like a taser shock, and my bile began to rise again.

"Take her in the back," Taylor said. "We'll bring her up to the sleeper."

The fat man gave my knee a final squeeze, then grunted as he hefted me up in his arms and shifted his bulk. Once again I was lifted, tugged, and pushed. I chanced a peek, everything dark and blurry, wanting so badly to rub my eyes, and all I could make out was a ladder of some sort.

"There's a handle on the trap door. Turn it."

"Where?"

"Right above your head."

I was shoved through an opening in the ceiling of the cab, then dropped unceremoniously onto a mat. It was hot. I smelled bleach, cheap perfume, and the copper-pennies stench of fresh blood. Also, underneath everything, was an odor that scared me to my core, an odor I recognized from hundreds of cases from more than twenty years or cases. A cross between meat gone bad and excrement that all the bleach on the planet couldn't ever fully erase.

The stink of dead bodies.

People havedied in this room.

"Warm up here."

"When we get started, I'll put the air conditioning on. I've also got recessed stereo speakers, for mood music, and an AC outlet up by the fire alarm, if you want to plug in any power tools."

"I like power tools."

"Give yours a tap, see if she's awake yet."

I heard a slapping sound, skin on skin, and then a feminine whine.

"She's still groggy."

"She'll be up soon. I know she's not much to look at, but that really doesn't matter once you get started, does it?"

"Actually, Taylor, as grateful as I am to you for inviting me into your home, I've been reading about Jack Daniels for years. She's every killer's wet dream."

There was a long pause.

"What are you saying?" Taylor said.

"I'm saying I want the cop."

"We already agreed, she's mine."

"You can have her feet. I want her face."

"Maybe I want the whole thing."

Donaldson laughed. "You know, you remind me of my younger brother. I miss that kid, so much that I sometimes regret killing him. But I remember something my father used to say when we were fighting over a toy. He said, *If you can't share, then neither of you can haveit.*"

Then I heard the unmistakable sound of my .38 being cocked.

-7-

STANDING ON THE LADDER, with his upper half through the trap door, Taylor stared at the gun in the kneeling fat man's hand. It was pointed at the cop's head, but Donaldson's eyes were focuses on him.

Goddammit, why did I let him grab the gun?

Taylor felt himself go dead inside, like his body turned to ice. He chose his words carefully, keeping his voice even. "You know what, Donaldson? Maybe you're right. Sharing seems like a fair thing to do, and it might even be fun. Besides, it would be a shame to deprive such a famous lady of either of our company. But I have to say that seeing you holding a gun makes me a bit nervous. We don't want to make enemies of each other, do we?"

Donaldson smiled, shrugged, and then uncocked the gun and shoved it into his front pocket. "I appreciate your generosity, Taylor. Really, I do. And normally I wouldn't be so ungracious to a fellow traveler. But this woman just *does*something to me. I haven't been this excited in years."

"I can see that." Taylor was eye-level with Donaldson's crotch. "Or maybe that's the gun."

"So let's have a meeting of the minds."

"Fine."

Taylor relaxed a notch now that the weapon was out of play, but he had no doubt Donaldson would use it again. His original fantasy of tag-team action had been replaced by the unpleasant image of Donaldson tying him up and feeding him his own face. When there are too many foxes in the henhouse, the foxes kill each other. A shame, because Taylor was starting to like the older man.

"Since you agree to sharing," Donaldson said, "would you be adverse to both of us going at her at the same time? You take the bottom half, I take the top?"

Taylor reached a hand behind his back and touched the folding knife clipped to his belt—Donaldson had given it back to him in the parking lot. Killing him right now would probably be the best bet, but the guy was big, and the knife blade was short. Unless he died quick, Donaldson would fight back and be able to grab his gun.

No, the knife wasn't the way to go.

But Taylor did have a sawed-off shotgun under his passenger seat. All he needed to do was jump down, lock the trap door, and grab it.

"Sharing would be okay." Taylor tried to look thoughtful. "But I want to look her in the eyes when I'm doing my thing. Be tough to do if her eyes were gone."

"They wouldn't be gone. They'd be in her mouth."

Taylor shook his head. "That wouldn't be good for me."

"I could leave her eyes alone. Maybe just take off her eyelids so she'd be forced to look. It could work. We could do a trial run on the whore, here."

Donaldson kicked Candi in her side. She moaned.

Taylor figured there were three steps beneath him. He would need to grab the door and tug it closed before Donaldson pulled his gun. He didn't know if the cop's bullet would go through the half inch steel the sleeper was made out of, but his shotgun slugs certainly would. Lots of damage, though, and it would make a lot of noise.

"I'm not exactly keen on a two on one. If you promise to leave her eyes alone, and that she'll stay conscious and not die on you, I could let you go first."

Donaldson's face remained blank for a moment, then he raised his eyebrow.

"I appreciate your offer. I sincerely do. But I can't help but think that while I'm doing my thing, you might make some sort of effort to do me harm. Or perhaps lock me in here."

Taylor began to wish he never parked at this truck stop.

"We seem to be at an impasse."

"No," Donaldson shook his head. "I believe we can work this out. I have no desire to harm you, Taylor. And I am grateful for this opportunity. I shouldn't have flashed the gun. That was a mistake. I've been playing this game solo for so long, I wasn't thinking clearly. I know you have a knife on you, and probably some other weapons in the truck, and I fear I just began a war of escalation."

"I don't want to kill you either." It was the truth. Not that he had any real affection for Donaldson, but trying to muscle the dead fat man out of his sleeper and drag him to a river didn't seem like a fun time.

"We don't know each other well yet. But we're kindred spirits. Maybe we could even become friends."

"It's possible."

"How long will the cop be out for?" Donaldson asked.

"A few minutes, probably more. Pinch her, see if she flinches. When they're really under, they don't flinch."

Donaldson leaned over Jack Daniels and squeezed her breast. She didn't move.

"She's out. You have some rope?"

"More bungee cords in the trunk."

Neither man moved to get them. Eventually, Donaldson raised an eyebrow. "Are you a gambling man, Taylor?"

"I've been known to play the odds."

"Let's flip a coin. Winner gets first crack at the cop."

Taylor considered it. "I'd be up for that, if it were a fair toss."

"We could go in the diner, have our waitress do the flipping. I'll even let you call it. Would be good to get out in the fresh air, clear our heads."

"Let's say I agree. You still have me at a disadvantage."

Donaldson nodded. "The gun. Firing it wouldn't be smart for either of us. Cops might already be on their way, after what Lieutenant Daniels did to that pimp."

"I've got a solution."

"I'm listening."

"An empty gun isn't a threat. Hand me the bullets. But do it slowly, or else I might get nervous and lock you up here for a few days with no air conditioning or water."

"Fair enough."

Donaldson gently reached back into his pants and removed the gun. He held it upside-down by the trigger guard, and swung out the cylinder. Then he dumped the rounds onto his palm and handed them to Taylor.

Taylor grinned.

Maybe this tag-team thing willwork out after all.

"Are we good?" Donaldson asked.

"We're good. Let's hogtie this pig."

Taylor climbed into the sleeper, and after an uneasy moment of sizing each other up, the two of them began to bind the cop. Donaldson quickly got the hang of it, and they soon had Jack suitably trussed.

"You sure she's safe here?" Donaldson asked, admiring their handiwork.

"Never had an escape. Bungee cords are tighter than rope. The enclosure is steel, the lock on the door is solid. She's not going anywhere."

Taylor grabbed the cop's purse, wound it over his shoulder, and crawled down out of the sleeper after Donaldson. He made sure the trap door was locked, took what he wanted from the purse, and together they walked back to the diner.

-8-

THE MOMENT THEY WERE gone I rolled onto my belly and

inch-wormed up to my knees. My hands were behind my back, the bungee cords so tight my fingers were tingling. I strained against the elastic, trying to twist my wrists apart, but couldn't free myself.

More cords wound around my chest and upper arms, and encircled my knees and ankles. I flopped onto my side, wincing at the pain. My shoulder still hurt, and there was a throb in my left breast where Donaldson had pinched me. If he'd done it for a few seconds longer, I would have screamed.

Pretending to be unconscious seemed like a better choice than really being unconscious, but when they tied me up I realized that maybe fighting back and yelling for help when I had the chance might have been the better move.

Panic threatened to overwhelm me, and I began to hyperventilate. Fear and I were old adversaries. There was no way to squelch it, but if I kept my focus I could work through the fear. The goal was to not think about any potential outcome to this situation other than escape.

Still unable to open my eyes because of the stinging, I rolled to my left, hoping to bump into anything that would help me free myself. I hit something soft. I brushed my cheek against it. Foam of some kind. I rolled right instead, eventually coming up against something more suitable. Something hard, stuck into the floor. After maneuvering around onto my knees, I rubbed my hands against the object.

It felt like a board, only two feet tall, and thin. Midway down the side was some sort of protrusion. Though my hands were quickly getting numb, I could tell by the sound when I jiggled it that it was a padlock.

I got my wrists under the lock, trying to wedge it in between my arms and the bungee cords. Then I took a deep breath and violently tugged my arms forward.

The elastic caught, stretched.

I pulled harder, feeling like my arms were pulling out of their sockets.

Then, abruptly, my hands were free, and I pitched forward onto my face, bumping my forehead against the padded floor.

I spent a few seconds wiggling my fingers, wincing as the blood came back, and made quick work of the other cords around my arms. Then I spit in my hands and rubbed them against my eyes. The stinging eased up enough for me to have a blurry look around the enclosure. There was moderate lighting, from an overhead fixture. I saw beige mats. A black slanted ceiling covered with sound baffles. A trunk. And a bound woman, her feet in some sort of wooden stock, my wrist bungee cord wound around a padlock on the side.

I unwound my legs, tugged off my remaining shoe, and crawled over to her, unhooking her bindings. "Can you hear me?"

The woman moaned softly, and her eyelids fluttered.

"You need to wake up." I gave her a shake. "We're in trouble."

"My… foot… hurts…"

"What's your name?"

"My… foot…"

I cupped her chin in my hand, made her look at me.

"Listen to me. I'm a cop. We're in a truck sleeper and some men are trying to kill us. What's your name?"

"Candi. I… I can't move my feet. It hurts."

I turned my attention to the stock. I crawled around to the other side, wincing when I saw the blood. I took a closer look because I had to assess the damage, then wished I could erase the image from my mind.

"What's wrong with my foot?"

"You're missing your little toe."

"My… *toe?*"

I studied the stock. Heavy, solid, the padlock and latch unbreakable. So I looked at the hinge on the other side. Six screws held it in place.

I scooted away from the stock, on my butt, and reared back my right heel.

"Stay still, Candi. I'm going to try to break the hinge."

I shot my leg out like a piston, striking the top of the stock once, twice, three times.

The stock stayed solid, the screws tight. And if I tried kicking any harder I'd break my heel.

"Don't you have a gun?"

I ignored her, turning my attention to the trunk in the corner of the enclosure. I crawled over to see if there was anything inside I could use.

"Don't leave me!"

"I won't leave you. I promise."

I found paper towels, paper masks, starter fluid, plastic bags, and a large Tupperware container. The lid had brown stains on it—dried blood—and I got an uneasy feeling looking at it. Fighting squeamishness, I pulled the top off.

It was filled with rock salt. But I could make out something brown peeking through. I shook the box, and it revealed a few of the brown things, small and wrinkled. They looked like prunes.

Then I realized what they were, and came very close to throwing up. I pulled away, covering my mouth. There had to be dozens, maybe over a hundred, of them in there.

That sick bastard…

"Did you find anything?"

"Nothing helpful," I said, closing the lid.

"What's in that box you were holding?"

Taylor was smart. He didn't leave any tools, weapons, or keys lying around. I eyed the starter fluid.

"Candi, do you smoke?"

"Yeah."

"Do you have matches on you? A lighter?"

"In my purse. He took it."

Dammit. But starting a fire in the enclosed space probably wasn't a good idea anyway. However, the chest itself had possibilities. It was made of wood, with metal reinforced corners. I picked it up, figuring it weighed at least fifteen pounds.

"What was in the box!"

I muscled the chest over to Candi and knelt next to her.

"Hold still," I said. "If I miss I could break your leg."

I reared back, clenched my teeth, and shoved the chest into the top of the stock. There was a loud *crack*, but both objects stayed intact.

I did it again.

And again.

And again.

And again.

My shoulder began to burn, and the corners of the chest were coming apart, but the hinge on the stock was bending.

Two more times and the chest burst open, spilling its contents onto the mat, the Tupperware container bouncing next to Candi.

I hit the stock one last time. The chest broke into several large pieces. I grabbed one of the slats used to make the chest, and wedged it in the opening I'd made between the top and bottom of the stock. I used it like a crowbar, levering at the hinge.

It was slowly giving… giving…

Then the stock popped open like a shotgun blast.

Candi sat up abruptly, grabbing her ankle to see her injury for herself. Then the tears hit, fast and hard.

"Ah shit… that fucker."

"We need to find a way out of here."

"My toe…" she sobbed.

"Candi! Focus!"

Her eyes locked on mine.

"We need to start rolling up the mats," I ordered, "find the way out of here before they come back."

She sniffled. "They? I only know one. Taylor."

"He's got a buddy now." I made a face. "And they're armed."

I watched Candi's face do an emotion montage. Anger, pain, despair, then raw fear.

"I have kids," Candi whispered. "A boy and a girl."

"Then we need to find the exit, fast. Start pulling up the mats."

"What time is it? My man, Julius, he'll come looking for me when I don't report back."

I thought about the pimp, running out of the diner with his teeth in his hand.

"Julius, uh, probably won't be coming to the rescue. Do the mats. Now."

She wiped her nose on her arm, and then reached for the Tupperware container.

"Candi…"

"I want to see."

She popped off the lid and squinted at the objects in the rock salt.

"What are these things?"

"We need to look for the exit, Candi."

"Are those… *aw, Jesus…*"

"Don't worry about that now."

"Don't worry? Do you know what these are?"

"Yes."

"These are... *nipples.*"

"I know, Candi. That's why we need to get the hell out of here."

That seemed to spur her to action. I joined Candi in pulling up mats, and we soon found the trap door. I pulled on the recessed handle.

Locked.

I tugged as hard as I could, until the cords on my neck bulged out and I saw stars.

It wouldn't budge.

"We're going to die up here." Candi was hugging her knees, rocking back and forth.

I blew out a breath. "No, we're not."

"He's going to bite off our toes. Then our tits, to add to his collection."

I reached up overhead, tugging at the baffling stuck to the ceiling. Under it was heavy aluminum. I did a 360, looking at all the walls.

There was no way out. We were trapped up here.

Then we both felt it. The truck cab jiggle.

Oh, shit. They're back.

-9-

FRAN THE WAITRESS WAS happy to flip a coin for the two gentlemen who had tipped her so well.

"Tails," Taylor called.

Fran caught the quarter, slapped it against her wrist.

"Tails it is. Congrats, handsome."

Taylor gave her a polite nod, then turned to judge Donaldson's reaction. There wasn't one. The fat man's face was blank. Taylor left the diner, his cohort in tow. It was still hot and muggy outside, and the lot was still almost full, but there weren't any people around.

"Are we cool?" Taylor asked as they walked to his truck.

"Yeah. Fair is fair. You'll let me watch?"

Taylor shrugged like it didn't matter, but secretly he was thrilled at the idea of an audience.

"Sure."

"And you'll let me do her face?"

"Her face is all yours."

"You should try it once. The face. You peel enough of the flesh away, you can see the skull underneath. I bet Jack Daniels has a beautiful skull."

Taylor stopped and stared at him. "You've really got a hard-on for this cop, don't you?"

"I'd marry her if she'd have me. But I'll settle for a bloody blow-job after I knock her teeth out. Do you still have Jack's phone?"

Taylor had pocketed her phone and wallet. He tugged the cell out.

"Does Officer Donaldson want to inform the next of kin?" Taylor grinned as he handed it over.

"That's a possibility. Might also be fun to call up her loved ones while you're working on her, let them hear her screams."

"You've got a sick mind, my friend."

"Thank you, kindly. Let's see who our favorite cop talked to last. The winner is… *Latham.* And less than an hour ago. Shall we see if Latham is still up?"

"Put it on speaker."

The phone rang twice, and a man answered.

"Jack? I was worried."

"And you have good reason to be," Donaldson said. "Is this Latham?"

"Who is this?"

"I'm the man about to murder Jack Daniels. She's going to die in terrible pain. How do you feel about that?"

There was silence.

"What's wrong, Latham? Don't you care that…" Donaldson squinted at the phone. "Dammit, lost the signal."

Donaldson hit redial. The call didn't go through.

They stood there for a moment, neither of them saying anything.

"I hate dropped calls," Taylor finally offered. "Drives me nuts."

"Cops."

"I hate cops, too."

"Behind you."

Taylor spun around and froze. A Wisconsin squad car rolled up next to them. Its lights weren't on, but the driver's side window was open and a pig was leaning out. White male, fat, had something on his upper lip that an optimist might call a mustache.

"Did you men happen to witness a disturbance in the diner earlier?"

Taylor thought fast. But apparently so did Donaldson, because he spoke first.

"What disturbance?"

"Seems an Illinois cop got into a tussle with one of the locals."

"We're just passing through," Donaldson said. "Didn't see anything."

The pig nodded, then pulled up next to the diner. He let his fellow cop out, then began to circle the parking lot.

"I had to lie," Donaldson said, "or else we'd have to give statements. I don't want my name in any police report."

"I'm with you. But now we've got a big problem. One of them is going to talk to our waitress, and she'll mention us. The other is taking down plate numbers. He'll find Jack's car, realize she's still here, and start searching for her."

"We need to move our vehicles. Right now."

Taylor nodded. "There's an oasis thirty miles north on 39. I'll meet you there in half an hour. You've got the whore's phone, right?"

"Yeah."

"Give me the cop's," Taylor said. "We'll exchange numbers if we need to get in touch."

After programming their phones, Donaldson offered his hand. Taylor shook it.

"See you soon, fellow traveler."

Then they parted.

Taylor hustled into his cab, started the engine, and pulled out of Murray's parking lot. He smiled. While he still didn't fully trust Donaldson, Taylor was really starting to enjoy their partnership. Maybe they could somehow extend it into something fulltime. Teamwork made this all so much more exciting.

Taylor was heading for the cloverleaf when he saw the light begin to flash on the dashboard.

It was the fire alarm. The smoke detector in the overhead sleeper was going off.

What the hell?

Taylor pulled onto the shoulder, set the brake, and tugged his sawed-off shotgun out from under the passenger seat. Then he headed for the trap door to see what was going on with those bitches.

-10-

THE MOMENT THE CAB jiggled, I began to gather up bungee cords and hook them to the handle on the trap door, pulling them taut and attaching them to the foot stock. When that door opened, I wanted it to stay open.

Then the truck went into gear, knocking me onto my ass. Moving wasn't going to help our situation. At least at Murray's we were surrounded by people. If Taylor took us someplace secluded, our chances would get even worse.

I looked around the sleeper again, and my eyes locked on the overhead light. Next to it, on the ceiling, was a smoke alarm. I doubted it would be heard through all the soundproofing, but there was a good chance it signaled the driver somehow.

"Candi! Press the test button on the alarm up there!"

She steadied herself, then reached up to press it. The high-pitched beeping was loud enough to hurt my ears. But would Taylor even be aware of it?

Apparently so, because a few seconds later, the truck stopped.

I reached for the Tupperware container and a broken slat from the chest, and crawled over to the side of the trap door. Then I waited.

I didn't have to wait long. The trap door opened up and the bungee cords worked as predicted, tearing it out of Taylor's grasp. The barrel of a shotgun jutted up through the doorway. I kicked that aside and threw a big handful of salt in Taylor's eyes. He screamed, and I followed up with the wooden slat, smacking him in the nose, forcing him to lose his footing on the stepladder.

As he fell, I dove, snaking face-first down the opening on top of him, landing on his chest and pinning the shotgun between us.

He pushed up against me, strong as hell, but I had gravity on my side and I was fighting for my life. My knee honed in on his balls like it lived there, and the first kick worked so well I did it three more times.

He moaned, trying to keep his legs together and twist away. I grabbed the shotgun stock and jerked. He suddenly let go of the weapon, and I tumbled backwards off of him, the gun in my hands, and my back slammed into the step ladder. The wind burst out of me, and my diaphragm spasmed. I tried to suck in a breath and couldn't.

Taylor got to his knees, snarling, and lunged. I raised the gun, my fingers seeking the trigger, but he easily knocked it away. Then he was straddling me, and I still couldn't breathe—a task that became even more difficult when his hands found my throat.

"You're gonna set a world fucking record on how long it takes to die."

Then Candi dropped onto his back.

Taylor immediately released his grip, trying to reach around and get her off. But Candi clung on like a monkey, one hand around his neck, the other pressing a wet paper towel to his face.

He fell on all fours and bucked rodeo bull-style. Candi held tight. I blinked away the stars and managed to suck in some air, my hands seeking out the dropped shotgun. It was too dangerous to shoot him with Candi so close, so I held it by the short barrel, took aim, and cracked him in the temple with the wooden stock.

Taylor crumpled.

I gasped for oxygen, my heart threatening to break through my ribs because it was beating so hard. Candi kept the rag on Taylor's face, and part of me wanted to let her keep it there, let her kill him. But my better judgment took over.

"Candi." I lightly touched her shoulder. "It's over."

"It'll be over when I bite one of his goddamn toes off."

I shook my head. "Give me the rag, Candi. He's going away for the rest of his life. Depending on the jurisdictions, he might even get the death penalty."

She looked at me. Then she handed over the rag and burst into tears.

That's when Donaldson stepped into the cab. He took a quick look around, then pointed my gun at me.

"Well what do we have here? How about you drop that shotgun, Lieutenant."

I looked at him, and then got a ridiculously big grin on my face.

"You gave him the bullets, asshole."

Donaldson's eyes got comically wide, and I brought up the shotgun and fired just as he was diving backward out the door. The dashboard exploded, and the sound was a force that punched me in my ears. Candi slapped her hands to the sides of her head. I ignored the ringing and pumped another slug into the chamber, already moving after him.

Something stopped me.

Taylor. Grabbing my leg.

Candi pounced on him, tangled her fingers in his hair, and bounced his head against the floor until he released his grip.

I stumbled out of the cab, stepping onto the pavement. My .38 was on the road, discarded. I looked left, then right, then under the truck.

Donaldson was gone.

A few seconds later, I saw a police car tearing up the highway, lights flashing, coming our way.

-11-

"THANK YOU, HONEY."

I took the offered wine glass and Latham climbed into bed next to me. The fireplace was roaring, the chardonnay was cold, and when Latham slipped his hand around my waist I sighed. For a moment, at least, everything was right with the world. Candi had been reunited with her children. Taylor was eagerly confessing to a string of murders going back fifteen years, and ten states were fighting to have first crack at prosecuting him. No charges were filed against me for my attack on the pimp, because Fran the waitress had sworn he shoved me first. My various aches and pains were all healing nicely, and I even got all of my things back, including my missing shoe. It was five days into my vacation, and I was feeling positively glorious.

The only loose end was Donaldson. But he'd get his, eventually. It was only a matter of time until someone picked him up.

"You know, technically, you never thanked me for saving your life," Latham said.

"Is that what you did?" I asked, giving him a playful poke in the chest. "I thought I was the one who did all the saving."

"After that man called me, I called the police, told them you were at Murray's and someone had you."

"The police arrived after I'd already taken control of the situation."

"Still, I deserve some sort of reward for my cool-headedness and grace under pressure, don't you think?"

"What have you got in mind?"

He whispered something filthy in my ear.

"You pervert," I said, smiling then kissing him.

Then I took another sip of wine and followed his suggestion.

-Epilogue-

DONALDSON KEPT ONE HAND on the wheel. The other caressed the cell phone.

The cell phone with Jack Daniels's number on it.

It had been over a week since that fateful meeting. He'd headed southwest, knowing there was a nationwide manhunt going on, knowing they really didn't have anything on him. A description and a name, nothing more.

He'd been aching to call the Lieutenant. But it wasn't the right time yet. First he had to let things cool down.

Maybe in another week or so, he'd give her a ring. Just to chit-chat, no threats at all.

The threats would come later, when he went to visit her.

In the meantime, he'd been so busy running from the authorities, covering his tracks, Donaldson hadn't had any time to indulge in his particular appetites. He kept an eye open for likely prospects, but they were few and far between.

The hardest thing about killing a hitchhiker was finding one to pick up.

Donaldson could remember just ten years ago, when interstates boasted a hitcher every ten miles, and a discriminating killer could pick and choose who looked the easiest, the most fun, the juiciest. These days, cops kept the expressways clear of easy marks, and Donaldson was forced to cruise off-ramps, underpasses, and rest areas, prowl back roads, take one hour coffee breaks at oases. Recreational murder was becoming more trouble than it was worth.

He'd finally found one standing in a Cracker Barrel parking lot. The kid had been obvious, leaning against the cement ashtray near the entrance, an oversize hiking pack strapped to his back. He was approaching every patron leaving the restaurant, practicing his grin between rejections.

A ripe plum, ready to pluck.

Donaldson tucked the cell phone into his pocket and got out of the car…

For a continuation of Donaldson's adventures, read SERIAL by Jack Kilborn & Blake Crouch.

For a continuation of Jack's adventures, read FUZZY NAVEL by J.A. Konrath.

For a continuation of Taylor's adventures, read AFRAID by Jack Kilborn.

CRIME STORIES

THE FIRST GROWN-UP books I ever read, at the age of nine, were mysteries. This had more to do with them being on my mother's bookshelf than any particular design on my part. But I fell in love with them. Spenser and Travis McGee were my first literary heroes. I really enjoyed Ed McBain's 87th Precinct, and the Remo Williams Destroyer series by Richard Sapir and Warren Murphy.

Then I got into hardboiled and noir. Mickey Spillane. Max Allan Collins. Lawrence Block. Ross MacDonald. Donald Westlake and Richard Stark. Chandler and Hammet. Andrew Vachss. Reading about cops and PIs was cool, but reading about criminals was cool too.

In my teen years, I was floored by Red Dragon and Silence of the Lambs, and that started me on a serial killer binge. I devoured John Sandford, James Patterson, Robert W. Walker, David Wiltse, and Ridley Pearson.

Which is probably why my novels are such a mishmash of different genre styles.

When I sit down to write a short story, it's for one of two reasons. First, because someone asked me for one. Second, because I have an idea that begs to be written. If I'm writing to fill an anthology slot or crack a market, I usually start with a few lines, which leads me to a premise, which leads to conflict, which leads to action. But if I already have an idea, it usually springs full blown from my head and onto the page as fast as I can type.

Often, I have story ideas that won't fit into the Jack Daniels universe. Sometimes these are horror stories, or straight humor, or sci-fi, or a combination of different styles.

Sometimes they're crime stories

THE BIG GUYS

This was one of three stories written for Small Bites, *an anthology of flash fiction to benefit horror author and editor Charles Grant, who needed assistance paying some hefty medical bills. Flash fiction is a story of 500 words or less. Strange as it sounds, writing shorter is sometimes harder than writing longer, because you have less words to fit all of the story elements in.* Small Bites *used three of my flash fiction shorts. This piece won a Derringer Award.*

"I'M SURPRISED YOU ASKED me here, Ralph. I didn't think you liked me."

Ralph grinned over the wheel. "Don't be silly, Jim." He cut the engines and glanced over the starboard bow. There was some chop to the sea, but the yacht had a deep keel and weathered it well.

"Well, we've been neighbors for almost ten years, and we haven't ever done anything together."

Ralph shrugged. "I work crazy hours. Not a lot of free time. But I've always considered you a good friend, Jim. Plus, our wives are close. I thought this would give us a chance to get to know each other. Belinda mentioned you like to fish."

Jim nodded. "Mostly freshwater. I haven't done much deep sea fishing. What are we going for, anyway?"

Ralph adjusted his captain's cap.

"I was originally thinking salmon or sailfish, but it's been a while since I went for the big guys."

"Big guys?"

"Sharks, Jim. You up for it?"

"Sure. Just tell me what I need to do."

"First step is getting into the harness." Ralph picked up a large life vest, crisscrossed with straps and latches. "This clips onto the rod, so you don't lose it, and this end is attached to the boat, in case you get pulled overboard."

Jim raised an eyebrow. "Has that ever happened?"

"Not yet, but it pays to be careful. These are Great White waters, and some of those bad boys go over two thousand pounds."

Ralph helped Jim into the vest, snugging it into place.

"What next?"

"We have to make a chum slick."

"I've heard of that. Fish blood and guts, right?"

"Yep. It's a shark magnet. You want to get started while I prepare the tackle?"

"Sure."

Ralph went to the cooler and took out the plastic bucket of chum. Even refrigerated, it stank to high heaven. He handed it to Jim, with a ladle.

"Toss that shit out there. Don't be stingy with it."

Jim began to slop chum into the blue waters.

Ralph swiveled his head around, scanning the horizon. No other boats.

"So," Jim asked, "what's the bait?"

Ralph gave Jim a deep poke in the shoulder with a fillet knife, then shoved his neighbor overboard.

Jim surfaced, screaming. Ralph ladled on some guts.

"Not very neighborly of you, Jim. Screwing my wife while I was at work."

"Ralph! Please!"

Jim's hands tried to find purchase on the sides of the yacht, but they were slippery with blood. Ralph dumped more onto his head, making Jim gag.

"Keep struggling." Ralph smiled. "The big guys love a moving target."

"Don't do this, Ralph. Please. I'm begging you."

"You'd better beg fast. I see that we already have some company."

Jim stared across the open water. The dorsal fin approached at a brisk pace.

"Please! Ralph! You said you considered me a good friend!"

"Sorry…wrong choice of words. I actually meant to say I considered you a good chum."

It took a while for Ralph to stop laughing.

THE AGREEMENT

I wrote this in college, and never tried to publish it because I considered it too violent. But after selling several stories to Ellery Queen, I still couldn't crack its sister publication, Alfred Hitchcock. After a handful of rejections, I sent them this, and they bought it. I liked the last line so much I've reused it a few times in other stories.

HUTSON CLOSED HIS EYES and swallowed hard, trying to stop sweating. On the table, in the pot, thirty thousand dollars worth of chips formed a haphazard pyramid. Half of those chips were his. The other half belonged to the quirky little mobster in the pink suit that sat across from him.

"I'll see it."

The mobster pushed more chips into the pile. He went by the street nick Little Louie. Hutson didn't know his last name, and had no real desire to learn it. The only thing he cared about was winning this hand. He cared about it a great deal, because Bernard Hutson did not have the money to cover the bet. Seven hours ago he was up eighteen grand, but since then he'd been steadily losing and extending his credit and losing and extending his credit. If he won this pot, he'd break even.

If he didn't, he owed thirty thousand dollars that he didn't have to a man who had zero tolerance for welchers.

Little Louie always brought two large bodyguards with him when he gambled. These bodyguards worked according to a unique payment plan. They would hurt a welcher in relation to what he owed. An unpaid debt of one hundred dollars would break a finger. A thousand would break a leg.

Thirty thousand defied the imagination.

Hutson wiped his forehead on his sleeve and stared at his hand, praying it would be good enough.

Little Louie dealt them each one more card. When the game began, all six chairs had been full. Now, at almost five in the morning, the only two combatants left were Hutson and the mobster. Both stank of sweat and cigarettes. They sat at a greasy wooden card table in somebody's kitchen, cramped and red-eyed and exhausted.

One of Louie's thugs sat on a chair in the corner, snoring with a deep bumble-bee buzz. The other was looking out of the grimy eighth story window, the fire escape blocking his view of the city. Each men had more scars on their knuckles than Hutson had on his entire body.

Scary guys.

Hutson picked up the card and said a silent prayer before looking at it.

A five.

That gave him a full house, fives over threes. A good hand. A very good hand.

"Your bet," Little Louie barked. The man in the pink suit boasted tiny, cherubic features and black rat eyes. He didn't stand over five four, and a pathetic little blonde mustache sat on his upper lip like a bug. Hutson had joined the game on suggestion of his friend Ray. Ray had left hours ago, when Hutson was still ahead. Hutson should have left with him. He hadn't. And now, he found himself throwing his last two hundred dollars worth of chips into the pile, hoping Little Louie wouldn't raise him.

Little Louie raised him.

"I'm out of chips," Hutson said.

"But you're good for it, right? You are good for it?"

The question was moot. The mobster had made crystal clear, when he extended the first loan, that if Hutson couldn't pay it back, he would hurt him.

"I'm very particular when it comes to debts. When the game ends, I want all debts paid within an hour. In cash. If not, my boys will have to damage you according to what you owe. That's the agreement, and you're obliged to follow it, to the letter."

"I'm good for it."

Hutson borrowed another five hundred and asked for the cards to be shown.

Little Louie had four sevens. That beat a full house.

Hutson threw up on the table.

"I take it I won," grinned Little Louie, his cheeks brightening like a maniacal elf.

Hutson wiped his mouth and stared off to the left of the room, avoiding Little Louie's gaze.

"I'll get the money," Hutson mumbled, knowing full well that he couldn't.

"Go ahead and make your call." Little Louie stood up, stretched. "Rocko, bring this man a phone."

Rocko lifted his snoring head in a moment of confusion. "What boss?"

"Bring this guy a phone, so he can get the money he owes me."

Rocko heaved himself out of his chair and went to the kitchen counter, grabbing Little Louie's cellular and bringing it to Hutson.

Hutson looked over at Little Louie, then at Rocko, then at Little Louie again.

"What do you mean?" he finally asked.

"What do you mean?" mimicked Little Louie in a high, whiny voice. Both Rocko and the other thug broke up at this, giggling like school girls. "You don't think I'm going to let you walk out of here, do you?"

"You said…"

"I said you have an hour to get the money. I didn't say you could leave to get it. I'm still following the agreement to the letter. So call somebody up and get them to bring it here."

Hutson felt sick again.

"You don't look so good." Little Louie furrowed his brow in mock-concern. "Want an antacid?"

The thugs giggled again.

"I…I don't have anyone I can call," Hutson stammered.

"Call your buddy, Ray. Or maybe your mommy can bring the money."

"Mommy." Rocko snickered. "You ought to be a comedian, boss. You'd kill 'em."

Little Louie puffed out his fat little chest and belched.

"Better get to it, Mr. Hutson. You only have fifty-five minutes left."

Hutson took the phone in a trembling hand, and called Ray. It rang fifteen times, twenty, twenty-five.

Little Louie walked over, patted Hutson's shoulder. "I don't think they're home. Maybe you should try someone else."

Hutson fought nausea, wiped the sweat off of his neck, and dialed another number. His ex-girlfriend, Dolores. They broke up last month. Badly.

A man answered.

"Can I speak to Dolores?"

"Who the hell is this?"

"It's Hutson."

"What the hell do you want?"

"Please let me speak to Dolores, it's real important."

Little Louie watched, apparently drinking in the scene. Hutson had a feeling the mobster didn't care about the money, that he'd rather watch his men inflict some major pain.

"Dolores, this is Hutson."

"What do you want?"

"I need some money. I owe a gambling debt and…"

She hung up on him before he got any farther.

Hutson squeezed his eyes shut. Thirty thousand dollars worth of pain. What would they start with? His knees? His teeth? Jesus, his eyes?

Hutson tried his parents. They picked up on the sixth ring.

"Mom?" This brought uncontrollable laughter from the trio. "I need some money, fast. A gambling debt. They're going to hurt me."

"How much money?"

"Thirty grand. And it need it in forty-five minutes."

There was a lengthy pause.

"When are you going to grow up, Bernard?"

"Mom…"

"You can't keep expecting me and your father to pick up after you all the time. You're a grown man Bernard."

Hutson mopped his forehead with his sleeve.

"Mom, I'll pay you back, I swear to God. I'll never gamble again."

An eternity of silence passed.

"Maybe you'll learn a lesson from this, son. A lesson your father and I obviously never taught you."

"Mom, for God's sake! They're going to hurt me!"

"I'm sorry. You got yourself into this, you'll have to get yourself out."

"Mom! Please!"

The phone went dead.

"Yeah, parents can be tough." Little Louie rolled his head around on his chubby neck, making a sound like a crackling cellophane bag. "That's why I killed mine."

Hutson cradled his face in his hands and tried to fight back a sob. He lost. He was going to be hurt. He was going to be very badly hurt, over a long period of time. And no one was going to help him.

"Please," he said, in a voice he didn't recognize. "Just give me a day or two. I'll get the money."

Little Louie shook his head. "That ain't the deal. You agreed to the terms, and those terms were to the letter. You still have half an hour. See who else you can call."

Hutson brushed away his tears and stared at the phone, praying for a miracle. Then he had an idea.

He called the police.

He dialed 911, then four more numbers so it looked like it was a normal call. A female officer answered.

"Chicago Police Department."

"This is Hutson. This is a matter of life and death. Bring 30,000 dollars over to 1357 Ontario, apartment 506."

"Sir, crank calls on the emergency number is a crime, punishable by a fine of five hundred dollars and up to thirty days in prison."

"Listen to me. Please. They want to kill me."

"Who does, sir?"

"These guys. It's a gambling debt. They're going to hurt me. Get over here."

"Sir, having already explained the penalty for crank calls…"

The phone was ripped from Hutson's hands by Rocko and handed to Little Louie.

"I'm sorry. It won't happen again." Little Louie hung up and waggled a finger at Hutson. "I'm very disappointed in you, Mr. Hutson. After all, you had agreed to my terms."

Hutson began to cry. He cried like a first grader with a skinned knee. He cried for a long time, before finally getting himself under control.

"It's time." Little Louie glanced at his watch and smiled. "Start with his fingers."

"Please don't hurt me…"

Rocko and the other thug moved in. Hutson dodged them and got on his knees in front of Little Louie.

"I'll do anything," he pleaded. "Anything at all. Name it. Just name it. But please don't hurt me."

"Hold it boys." Little Louie raised his palm. "I have an idea."

A small ray of hope penetrated Hutson.

"Anything. I'll do anything."

Little Louie took out a long, thin cigarillo and nipped off the end, swallowing it.

"There was a guy, about six years ago, who was in the same situation you're in now."

He put the end of the cigar in his mouth and rolled it around on his fat, gray tongue.

"This guy also said he would do anything, just so I didn't hurt him. Remember that fellas?"

Both bodyguards nodded.

"He finally said, what he would do, is put his hand on a stove burner for ten seconds. He said he would hold his own hand on the burner, for ten whole seconds."

Little Louie produced a gold Dunhill and lit the cigar, rolling it between his chubby fingers while drawing hard.

"He only lasted seven, and we had to hurt him anyway." Little Louie sucked on the stogie, and blew out a perfect smoke ring. "But I am curious to see if it could be done. The whole ten seconds."

Little Louie looked at Hutson, who was still kneeling before him.

"If you can hold your right hand on a stove burner for ten seconds, Mr. Hutson, I'll relieve you of your debt and you can leave without anyone hurting you."

Hutson blinked several times. How hot did a stove burner get?

How seriously would he be hurt?

Not nearly as much as having thirty thousand dollars worth of damage inflicted upon him.

But a stove burner? Could he force himself to keep his hand on it for that long?

Did he have any other choice?

"I'll do it."

Little Louie smiled held out a hand to help Hutson to his feet.

"Of course, if you don't do it, the boys will still have to work you over. You understand."

Hutson nodded, allowing himself to be led into the kitchen.

The stove was off-white, a greasy Kenmore, with four electric burners. The heating elements were each six inches in diameter, coiled into spirals like a whirlpool swirl. They were black, but Hutson knew when he turned one on it would glow orange.

Little Louie and his bodyguards stepped behind him to get a better look.

"It's electric," noted Rocko.

Little Louie frowned. "The other guy used a gas stove. His sleeve caught on fire. Remember that?"

The thugs giggled. Hutson picked the lower left hand burner and turned it on the lowest setting.

Little Louie wasn't impressed.

"Hey, switch it up higher than that."

"You didn't say how high it had to be when we made the agreement." Hutson spoke fast, relying on the mobster's warped sense of fairness. "Just that I had to keep it on for ten seconds."

"It was inferred it would be on the hottest."

"I can put it on low and still follow the deal to the letter."

Little Louie considered this, then nodded.

"You're right. You're still following it to the letter. Leave it on low then."

It didn't matter, because already the burner was firey orange. Rocko leaned over and spat on it, and the saliva didn't even have a chance to drip through the coils before sizzling away and evaporating.

"It think it's hot," Rocko said.

Hutson stared at the glowing burner. He held his trembling hand two inches above it. The heat was excruciating. Hutson's palm began to sweat and the hair above his knuckles curled and he fought the little voice in his brain that screamed get your hand away!

"Well, go ahead." Little Louie held up a gold pocket watch. "I'll start when you do. Ten whole seconds."

"Sweet Jesus in heaven help me," thought Hutson.

He bit his lip and slapped his hand down on to the burner.

There was an immediate frying sound, like bacon in a pan. The pain was instant and searing. Hutson screamed and screamed, the coils burning away the skin on his palm, burning into the flesh, blistering and bubbling, melting the muscle and fat, Hutson screaming louder now, smoke starting to rise, Little Louie sounding off the seconds, a smell like pork chops filling Hutson's nostrils, pain beyond intense, screaming so high there wasn't any sound, can't keep it there anymore, jesus no more no more and…

Hutson yanked his hand from the burner, trembling, feeling faint, clutching his right hand at the wrist and stumbling to the sink, turning on the cold water, putting his charred hand under it, losing consciousness, everything going black.

He woke up lying on the floor, the pain in his hand a living thing, his mouth bleeding from biting his lower lip. His face contorted and he yelled from the anguish.

Little Louie stood over him, holding the pocket watch. "That was only seven seconds."

Hutson's scream could have woken the dead. It was full of heart-wrenching agony and fear and disgust and pity. It was the scream of the man being interrogated by the Gestapo. The scream of the woman having a Caesarean without anesthetic. The scream of a father in a burning, wrecked car turning to see his baby on fire.

The scream of a man without hope.

"Don't get upset." Little Louie offered him a big grin. "I'll let you try it again."

The thugs hauled Hutson to his feet, and he whimpered and passed out. He woke up on the floor again, choking. Water had been thrown in his face.

Little Louie shook his head, sadly. "Come on Mr. Hutson. I haven't got all day. I'm a busy man. If you want to back out, the boys can do their job. I want to warn you though, a thirty grand job means we'll put your face on one of these burners, and that would just be the beginning. Make your decision."

Hutson got to his feet, knees barely able to support him, breath shallow, hand hurting worse than any pain he had ever felt. He didn't want to look at it, found himself doing it anyway, and stared at the black, inflamed flesh in a circular pattern on his palm. Hardly any blood. Just raw, exposed, gooey cooked muscle where the skin had fried away.

Hutson bent over and threw up.

"Come on, Mr. Hutson. You can do it. You came so close, I'd hate to have to cripple you permanently."

Hutson tried to stagger to the door to get away, but was held back before he took two steps.

"The stove is over here, Mr. Hutson." Little Louie's black rat eyes sparkled like polished onyx.

Rocko steered Hutson back to the stove. Hutson stared down at the orange glowing burner, blackened in several places where parts of his palm had stuck and cooked to cinder. The pain was pounding. He was dazed and on the verge of passing out again. He lifted his left hand over the burner.

"Nope. Sorry Mr. Hutson. I specifically said it had to be your right hand. You have to use your right hand, please."

Could he put his right hand on that burner again? Hutson didn't think he could, in his muddied, agony-spiked brain. He was sweating and cold at the same time, and the air swam around him. His body shook and trembled. If he were familiar with the symptoms, Hutson might have known he was going into shock. But he wasn't a doctor, and he couldn't think straight anyway, and the pain, oh jesus, the awful pain, and he remembered being five years old and afraid of dogs, and his grandfather had a dog and made him pet it, and he was scared, so scared that it would bite, and his grandfather grabbed his hand and put it toward the dog's head…

Hutson put his hand back on the burner.

"One..............two.............."

Hutson screamed again, searing pain bringing him out of shock. His hand reflexively grabbed the burner, pushing down harder, muscles squeezing, the old burns set aflame again, blistering, popping…

"..............three.............."

Take it off! Take it off! Screaming, eyes squeezed tight, shaking his head like a hound with a fox in his teeth, sounds of cracking skin and sizzling meat…

"……………four……………five……………"

Black smoke, rising, a burning smell, that's me cooking, muscle melting and searing away, nerves exposed, screaming even louder, pull it away!, using the other hand to hold it down…

"……………six……………seven……………"

Agony so exquisite, so absolute, unending, entire arm shaking, falling to knees, keeping hand on burner, opening eyes and seeing it sear at eye level, turning grey like a well-done steak, meat charring…

"Smells pretty good," says one of the thugs.

"Like a hamburger."

"A hand-burger."

Laughter.

"……………eight……………nine……………"

No flesh left, orange burner searing bone, scorching, blood pumping onto heating coils, beading and evaporating like fat on a griddle, veins and arteries searing…

"……………ten!"

Take it off! Take it off!

It's stuck.

"Look boss, he's stuck!"

Air whistled out of Hutson's lungs like a horse whimpering. His hand continued to fry away. He pulled feebly, pain at a peak, all nerves exposed–pull dammit! –blacking out, everything fading…

Hutson awoke on the floor, shaking, with more water in his face.

"Nice job Mr. Hutson." Little Louie stared down at him. "You followed the agreement. To the letter. You're off the hook."

Hutson squinted up at the mobster. The little man seemed very far away.

"Since you've been such a sport, I've even called an ambulance for you. They're on their way. Unfortunately, the boys and I won't be here when it arrives."

Hutson tried to say something. His mouth wouldn't form words.

"I hope we can gamble again soon, Mr. Hutson. Maybe we could play a hand or two. Get it? A hand?"

The thugs tittered. Little Louie bent down, close enough for Hutson to smell his cigar breath.

"Oh, there's one more thing, Mr. Hutson. Looking back on our agreement, I said you had to hold your right hand on the burner for ten seconds. I said you had to follow that request to the letter. But, you know what? I just realized something pretty funny. I never said you had to turn the burner on."

Little Louie left, followed by his body guards, and Bernard Hutson screamed and screamed and just couldn't stop.

A FISTFUL OF COZY

Satire, written for the webzine ShotsMag.uk at their request. This pokes gentle fun at the sub-genre of zero-violence cozy mysteries, with their quirky but spunky amateur sleuths.

"THIS IS SIMPLY DREADFUL!"

Mrs. Agnes Victoria Mugilicuddy blanched under a thick layer of rouge. Her oversized beach hat, adorned with plastic grapes and lemons, perched askew atop her pink-hued quaff.

Barlow, her graying manservant, placed a hand on her pointy elbow to steady her.

"Indeed, Madam. I'll call the police."

"The police? Why, Barlow, think of the scandal! Imagine what Imogene Rumbottom, that busy-body who writes the Society Column, will say in her muck-raking rag when she discovers the Viscount de Pouissant dead on my foyer floor."

"I understand, Madam. Will you be solving this murder yourself, then?"

"I have no other choice, Barlow! Though I'm a simple dowager of advancing years and high social standing, my feisty determination and keen eye for detail will no doubt flush out this dastardly murderer. Where is Miss Foo-Foo, the Mystery Cat?"

"She's in her litter box, burying some evidence."

"Miss Foo-Foo!" Agnes's voice had the pitch and timbre of an opera soprano. "Come immediately and help Mumsy solve this heinous crime!"

Miss Foo-Foo trotted into the foyer, her pendulous belly dragging along the oriental rug. Bits of smoked salmon clung to her whiskers.

"Barlow!" Agnes commanded, clapping her liver-spotted hands together.

Barlow bent down and picked up the cat. He was five years Mrs. Agnes's senior, and his back cracked liked kindling with the weight of Miss Foo-Foo.

Agnes patted the cat on the head as Barlow held it. Miss Foo-Foo purred, a sound not unlike a belch.

"We have a mystery to solve, my dearest puss-puss. If we're to catch the scoundrel, we must be quick of mind and fleet of foot. Barlow!"

"Yes, Madam?"

"Fetch the Mystery Kit!"

"Right away, Madam."

Barlow turned on his heels.

"Barlow!"

Barlow turned back.

"Yes, Madam?"

"First release Miss Foo-Foo."

"Of course, Madam."

Barlow bent at the waist, his spine making Rice Krispie sounds. Miss Foo-Foo padded over to Agnes and allowed herself to be patted on the head.

Straightening up was a painful affair, but Barlow managed without a grunt. He nodded at Mrs. Agnes and left the room.

"To think," Agnes mused, "only ten minutes ago the Viscount was sipping tawny port and regaling us with ribald tales of the gooseberry industry. Just a waste, Miss Foo-Foo."

Agnes's eyes remained dry, but she removed a handkerchief from the side pocket on her jacket and dabbed at them nonetheless.

Barlow returned lugging a satchel, its black leather cracked with age. He undid the tarnished clasps and held it open for Mrs. Agnes. She removed a large, Sherlock Holmes-style magnifying glass.

"The first order of business is to establish the cause of death." Mrs. Agnes spoke to the cat, not to Barlow. "It's merely a hunch, but I'm compelled to suggest that perhaps the lovely port the Viscount had been sipping may have been tampered with."

"An interesting hypothesis, Madam, but perhaps instead it has something to do with that letter opener?"

"'The letter opener, Barlow?"

"The one sticking in the Viscount's chest, Madam."

Agnes squinted one heavily mascaraed eye and peered through the glass with the other.

"Miss Foo-Foo, your hunch proved incorrect. The poor, dear Viscount appears to be impaled through the heart with some kind of silver object. But what can it be, puss-puss?"

"A letter opener, Madam?"

"Could it be a knife, Miss Foo-Foo? Perchance some rapscallion gained entry to the den though the window, intent on robbing the rich Viscount? Perhaps a fight ensued, resulting in the bloodthirsty criminal tragically ending the Viscount's life with this vaguely Freudian symbol of male power?"

Barlow peered at the body.

"It appears to be the letter opener you bought me for my anniversary, Madam. The gift you presented to me for fifty years of loyal service."

"Miss Foo-Foo!" Agnes bent over the fallen Viscount and lightly touched the handle of the protruding object. "Why, this is no knife! It's Barlow's letter opener! I can see the engraving."

"'How lucky you must feel to have served me for so many years.'" Barlow intoned.

"This changes everything!" Mrs. Agnes placed the magnifying glass back into the satchel, her gnarled fingers latching onto a tin of fingerprint powder. "Some heathen must have stolen Barlow's lovely gift—"

"Sterling silver plated," Barlow said.

"—with the intent to frame our loyal manservant! Barlow!"

"Yes, Madam?"

"Open this tin so I may dust the offending weapon!"

"Yes, Madam."

Mrs. Agnes used the tiny brush to liberally apply a basecoat of powder to the letter opener's handle.

"Why, look, puss-puss! There's nary a print to be found! The handle has been wiped clean!"

"Perhaps the murderer wore gloves, Madam?" Barlow reached for the powder tin with a gloved-hand.

"Or perhaps, Miss Foo-Foo, the killer wore gloves! This fiend is no mere street malcontent. This seems premeditated, the result of a careful and calculating plot. But why the Viscount?"

"Perhaps he was a witness, Madam? To another murder?"

Mrs. Agnes squinted at her manservant.

"That's daft, Barlow. Even for a lowly servant such as yourself. Do you see another victim in this room?"

"Indeed I do, Madam."

Barlow removed the cheese grater from his vest pocket, a gift from Mrs. Agnes for his forty year anniversary, and spent forty minutes grating off the old dowager's face.

The old bat still had some life left in her after that, so he worked on her a bit with his thirtieth-year-anniversary nutcracker, his twentieth-year-anniversary potato peeler, and finally the fireplace poker, which wasn't a gift, but was handy.

When she finally expired, he flipped the gory side face-down and spent a leisurely hour violating her corpse—something he couldn't have managed if she were alive and yapping. Sated, Barlow stood on creaky knees and picked up the bored Miss Foo-Foo.

"You have a date with the microwave, puss-puss. And then I'm the sole heir to Madam's fortune."

Miss Foo-Foo purred, making a sound like a belch.

Three minutes and thirteen seconds later, she made a different kind of sound. More like a pop.

CLEANSING

"THERE'S A LINE."

A long line, too. Thirty people, maybe more.

Aaron cleared his throat and spat the result onto a rock. He could feel the desert heat rising up through the leather of his sandals. An unforgiving sun blew waves of heat into their faces.

"It seems to be moving."

Aaron squinted at Rebekah, fat and grimy. The wrap around her head was soaked with sweat and clung to her scalp in dark patches. Her eyes were submissive, dim. A bruise yellowed on her left cheek.

Looking at her, Aaron felt the urge to blacken it again.

"I cannot believe I let you drag me here."

"You promised."

"A man should not have to keep the promises he makes to his wife. In another nation, you'd be property. Worth about three goats and a swine. Perhaps less, an ugly sow such as you."

Rebekah turned away.

Aaron set his jaw. A proper wife did not turn her back on her husband. He clutched at Rebekah's shoulder and spun her around.

"I could have you stoned for insolence, you worthless bitch."

He raised his hand, saw the fear in her eyes.

Liked it.

But Rebekah did not finch this time, did not cower.

"I will tell my father."

The words made Aaron's ears redden. Her father was a land owner, known to the Roman court. A Citizen. On his passing, Aaron would inherit his holdings.

Aaron lowered his fist. He tried to smile, but his face would not comply.

"Tell your father—what? Any husband has the right to discipline his wife."

"Shall I open my robe to show him the marks from your discipline?"

Aaron bit the inside of his cheek. This sow deserved all that and more.

"Our marriage is our business, no one else need intrude."

"And that is why we are here, Husband. I will not tell Father because you consented to this. It is the only way."

Aaron spat again, but his dry mouth yielded little. The line moved slowly, the sun baking their shadows onto the ground behind them.

As they approached the river, Aaron's throat constricted from thirst.

But this river was not fit to drink. Shallow and murky, the surface a skein of filth.

"Perhaps I should tell your father that his daughter has been seduced by a cult."

"My father knows. He was cleansed a fortnight past."

"Your father?" Aaron could not believe it. Her father had clout and status. Why would he jeopardize that by fooling around with fanatics?

Aaron stared at the river, confused. Another person waded into the center. Unclean, smelling of work and sweat, someone's servant.

The man known as the Baptist laid hands on the zealot's shoulders and plunged him underneath the scummy waves.

Then the Baptist yelled in a cracked voice, about sin and rebirth and Jehovah. A few seconds later the servant was released, gasping for air.

"He has been saved," Rebekah said. "John has cleansed his soul."

Aaron frowned. The man did not look saved. He looked muddy and disoriented.

"You are a fool, Rebekah. This talk of souls and one god is illegal and dangerous."

"It works, Aaron. I have heard the tales. Healing the lame. The sick. Purging anger and hatred from men's hearts."

"I will not let that fool dunk my head in that putrid water."

"Good day, Father."

Aaron followed her eye line, turned.

Rebekah's father Mark smiled at Aaron, clapping a hand on his shoulder.

"There is nothing to fear, Aaron. The stories are true. At my baptism, I felt as if released from bondage. I felt my soul shrug off the chains of sin and soar like a bird."

Aaron stared into Mark's twinkling, smiling eyes and calmed a bit.

"I am not afraid, Mark."

"Good. You are next."

Rebekah and her father stepped onto the bank with Aaron. The warm water lapped against his toes.

"Am I to go alone?"

"We are family," Rebekah said. "We shall all go together."

She took his hand, a gesture that she had not made since their wedding day. As a unit, they waded over to the man called John.

"Are you ready to cast aside sin and be reborn in the glorious love of your Father, Jehovah?"

Aaron looked at Rebekah's father. The older man smiled, nodded.

"Yes," Aaron said. A quick dunk and it would be over.

John put his hands upon Aaron's shoulders and shoved him downward.

The water was hot, alive against his skin. Aaron's shoulders were pressed down to the bottom and the muck parted to accept him.

He held his breath, straining to hear the words John would speak.

But John spoke nothing.

Aaron shifted, placing a hand on John's thick wrist. He gave it small squeeze, a signal to begin.

The wrist did not yield.

Aaron felt another hand upon him, and then a weight against his chest.

He grasped at it.

A foot.

Alarm coursed through Aaron. Something was wrong. He opened his eyes, peered up through the murk.

John held him firm, Rebekah hunched beside him. Her eyes were venom, and it was her foot that pinned down Aaron's chest.

Aaron tried to twist and thrash, but he had no leverage. A burst of precious air escaped his lungs, bubbling violently up through his field of vision in an endless stream.

This crazy cult was going to murder him.

He reached out his hand, grasping at Rebekah's father. He could not allow this.

Mark caught his wrist, held it tight…and pushed Aaron deeper into the mud.

Aaron screamed, sucked in a breath. The water tasted sour and burned the inside his lungs as if they'd inhaled fire instead. He pried at John's fingers with his free hand, and a moment of clarity flashed through the chaotic panic in his mind.

This was not John the Baptist. He'd seen this man before. He was a servant of Rebekah's father.

The crowd by the river. They'd all been Mark's servants.

And through the weighty distortion of the water, he could hear them cheering.

LYING EYES

The following four stories were all written for the magazine Woman's World. Every week it publishes a 1000 word mini mystery, in the tradition of Donald Sobol. The story provides the clues to solve the crime, then the solution is explained. I wrote four of these for Woman's World before finally selling one. This one was a reject, but was later published in the magazine Twisted Tongue. Can you solve the mystery?

It was a textbook kidnapping, or so they thought…

BILLIONAIRE DAVID MORGAN DIDN'T look anything like he did on television. His distinguished face appeared worn and tired, and his piercing blue eyes were bloodshot from lack of sleep.

"I just want her to be okay," he said, for the hundredth time.

Detective Starker patted his should.

"I know, Mr. Morgan. The kidnapper said he'll call with your wife's location."

Morgan's eyes released another tear.

"Are you sure they have the money?" he asked.

"We're sure."

Starker thought back to the money drop, and his insides burned. One million dollars in unmarked bills, left in a suitcase in a parked car. The kidnapper had warned the police that any attempts to stop him or track him would result in the death of Celia Morgan, David's young wife.

Nonetheless, Starker had made sure there was a tiny transmitter in the suitcase, housed in the lining and impossible to detect.

But at the money drop, Starker had watched the kidnapper transfer the cash into a large plastic bag, leaving the suitcase and the tracking device behind in the parking garage, leaving the authorities with no way to find him.

Now Celia's only hope was that the kidnapper was a man of his word, and would reveal her location.

"What if he doesn't call?" Morgan asked, voice trembling. "When Margaret, my first wife, passed away, I never thought I'd love again. I couldn't bear…"

His words were lost to another crying spell. Starker gave the millionaire another pat on the back.

"Don't worry, Mr. Morgan. We'll get her. Let's go over your list of enemies again."

"Enemies? I told you before. I'm the CEO of one of the largest manufacturing companies on the planet. I've been in this business for forty years. I have more enemies than there are names in the Manhattan phonebook."

"Does anyone stand out? Someone who felt you wronged them? Someone wanting money from you?"

"You saw the list. Everyone on it hates me. I told you before, Detective, that line of investigation is hopeless."

"How about around your home? Fired any of the help lately? Landscapers? Maids? Chauffeurs?"

"Celia handles all of that. Wait—I did have to fire the pool cleaner a month ago. I came home from work early and found him in our living room, watching television. Fired him on the spot."

"What was his name?"

"I don't remember. Celia will know…oh dear…"

The mention of his wife's name brought fresh tears. Starker felt awful for the man.

"Where did you meet Celia, Mr. Morgan?"

"She…she was one of my house cleaners. I pretty much ignored her for the first few weeks she worked for me. But she always had a kind word, a bright thing to say. Soon, I began to linger before going to the office, chatting with her over morning coffee. I know she's barely a third of my age, but she makes me feel young."

The phone rang, startling Starker. He nodded at Morgan to pick it up.

"Hello? Is she okay? Where is she?"

Starker, listening in on an extension, wrote down the address for the storage facility where the kidnapper claimed he'd left Celia Morgan.

"Let's move," Starker told his people.

Super Value Storage was across town, but Starker arrived in record time. He led his team, and the anxious David Morgan, to storage locker 116. It was a large sized unit, used for storing furniture, and the door had a combination lock on it. One of the cops used the bolt cutters, and Starker raised the door, a chemical stinging his eyes and making him squint.

He shone his flashlight inside, revealing a terrified-looking Celia Morgan.

She sat in the dark, tied to an office chair, a gag in her pretty mouth. Behind her were two empty buckets of something called sodium bisulfate, and a large empty cardboard box that had BROMINE written on the side.

David Morgan rushed to his wife, white granules crunching under his feet.

"Mr. Morgan!" Starker shouted. "Don't touch anything until we've collected evidence!"

Starker stepped in, snapping on a pair of latex gloves, removing the gag from Celia's perfectly made-up face. She was a strong one—her mascara hadn't even run. He then used a utility knife to cut the clothesline that securely bound her, careful to leave the knots for the crime lab to analyze.

"Celia, my love!"

David Morgan embraced his wife, and she kissed his cheek.

"I'm okay, David. He didn't hurt me."

Starker motioned for his team to come in, and he reached overhead and fumbled with the bare bulb hanging overhead, burning his fingers before eventually finding the pull cord and bathing the area in light.

"Did you have a chance to see your kidnapper?" Starker asked the woman.

"No. I'm sorry. I never saw his face," she said, her clear blue eyes drilling into him. "I've been sitting here in the dark for hours."

"Hours?" Starker repeated.

"Yes."

Starker gave Morgan a final pat on the back, and then separated the married couple.

"I'm sorry, Mr. Morgan, but I'm going to have to arrest your wife…as an accomplice in her own kidnapping."

How did Starker know?

SOLUTION: Celia's make up was perfect. If she'd been in that room for hours, locked up with chemicals that made Starker's eyes sting, her own eyes would have been red she would have been crying. Plus, when Starker reached up to turn on the light, the bulb was hot, meaning it had recently been on. Thus, Celia had just gotten there, and was lying to them. Since bromine and sodium bisulfate are pool cleaning chemicals, Starker suspected Celia was in on the scheme with the pool cleaner Morgan had fired a month previously.

PERFECT PLAN

Another Woman's World rejection. Though these are short, fast reads, they took a bit of thought to produce. They were a fun exercise in the mystery tradition of seeding clues.

The heist was flawless, except for one large detail…

MARTY HAD BEEN WATCHING them for over a month. The Richardsons were an attractive young couple, wealthy by chance—they had rich parents on both sides. Five nights a week they prowled the town, dressed in fancy clothes and expensive jewelry. Sometimes to the theater. Sometimes to a five star restaurant. But they enjoyed riverboat gambling the most.

Mrs. Richardson's weakness was hundred dollar slots. She could go through ten thousand dollars an hour. For Mr. Richardson, the allure of blackjack proved irresistible. He was what casino folks called a 'whale,' betting more money on a single hand than Marty earned in the last three years—and Marty held down two jobs and couldn't even afford a car. By day, Marty drove a school bus. At night, he cleaned casino ashtrays and emptied trash cans.

But if Marty's plan worked out, he'd never work another shift at either job.

Marty had seen the Richardsons gamble many times, reckless in the way the very rich tended to be. Mostly, they lost. But sometimes they won, and won big. When they did, they took their spoils in cash.

On those big win days, the casino sent an armed escort with the Richardsons, to make sure they arrived home safely.

Marty watched, and waited, polishing slot machines and vacuuming gaudy plush carpeting. He was biding his time until the Richardsons hit it big, because the next time they did, he would relieve them of their winnings.

Marty had followed them all around town, many times. He'd made frequent, secret visits to their house. In the past four weeks, Marty had learned a great deal about the Richardsons.

He knew they had an electric fence, but he had a plan to deal with the electric fence. He knew they had a dog, but he had a plan to deal with the dog. He knew they had a burglar alarm, but he had a plan to deal with the burglar alarm. He knew they had a safe, but he had a plan to deal with the safe. He even had a way to deal with the Richardsons themselves, if they woke up during the robbery. Marty had a gun, and would use it if he had to.

Marty had planned every tiny detail.

All Marty needed was for the Richardsons to win big, and that night, it happened. Mrs. Richardson hit the Double Diamond Jackpot—a cool half a million dollars.

The Richardsons celebrated, cheering and laughing. The casino manager came by to congratulate them both. The couple left with two satchels full of cash, accompanied by two armed guards.

Marty followed.

The Richardsons lived exactly 6.3 miles away from the riverboat. They always took the same route, but just to be sure they didn't deviate from their routine, Marty kept them in sight. He tailed them up to their estate and parked across the street. Once the Richardsons were through their electric fence, the armed guards waved farewell and drove away.

Which left Marty alone to do his work.

He kept his tools in a large satchel under his seat. After setting the parking brake, he grabbed the bag and exited his vehicle through the rear door.

The electrified gate crackled in the night air. From the bag, Marty removed some heavy rubber gloves and galoshes. Rubber didn't conduct electricity, and Marty climbed over the fence safely.

The mansion stood three stories high, boasting dozens of rooms. Marty located the five bullhorns attached to the outside of the building. Any unauthorized person trying to get in through a door or window would trigger these sirens. He filled each bullhorn with a can of aerosol insulating foam—the kind homeowners use in their attics to reduce drafts. The foam filled every crack and crevice, quickly hardening into a solid material. The sirens would still go off, but they wouldn't be any louder than a whisper.

With the alarm system beaten, Marty located the living room window and pushed a plumber's plunger onto the surface. Using a diamond edged tool, he cut around the plunger until he could remove the glass.

When he had a hole in the window, he took a thermos from his bag and shook out a ball of raw hamburger.

Scruffy, the Richardson's harmless but noisy pug, came running into the room. Before the dog could begin barking, Marty stuck his hand through the hole in the window, holding the hamburger. Mixed in with the meat were sleeping pills.

The dog gobbled up the treat, then stared at Marty, waiting for more. Marty gave the dog a rawhide bone. Scruffy chewed for five full minutes, then closed his eyes and began to snore harmlessly.

Marty felt for the latch and opened the window. He listened closely for the Richardsons, hearing a TV in another part of the house.

The safe, Marty knew from his many reconnaissance visits, was behind a large painted portrait of Mrs. Richardson. Marty crept up to it in the darkness, removing a cordless drill and a feather pillow from his bag. Unzipping the pillow, he placed the drill inside until just the large bit protruded, and then began drilling the safe, the sound muffled by the feathers.

He'd barely begun when the lights suddenly switched on. Marty spun around, reaching for his pistol, but decided against it when he saw the room was filled with cops.

Marty dropped the drill and raised his hands.

"How did you get here so fast?" Marty asked. "My plan was perfect!"

The lead detective answered. "The casino helped the Richardsons set up the phoney slot machine payoff tonight, to lure you here. We've been waiting for you for over an hour. You made one very big mistake."

What was Marty's mistake?

SOLUTION: Marty didn't own a car, so every time he followed the Richardsons and parked near their house, it was using his work vehicle...a school bus. The Richardsons spotted it easily, and knew something was going on because there are no school buses that run at night.

PIECE OF CAKE

This is the Mini Mystery that Woman's World finally bought. I still have no idea why they preferred this one over the other three. It's actually my least favorite.

Some folks will do anything to win…

THE BITSY FARMER ROCKY Mountain Cake Bake-Off had played host to many wonderful desserts over the past ten years, but this was the first time it played host to a criminal.

Bitsy stared at the five finalists and frowned. When she began the contest a decade ago, it was to help new chefs. But things had gotten ugly. Really ugly.

Bitsy's skills in the kitchen had given rise to a multi-million dollar cake-mix company. Always the innovator, Bitsy used the Rocky Mountain Cake Bake-Off to encourage amateur cooks. The winner received ten thousand dollars, plus her recipe would be sold through Bitsy's company. But never before had Bitsy been faced with this dilemma.

An anonymous phone caller had informed Bitsy that one of the remaining contestants was planning to sabotage her competitors. Not only was that unfair, but the scandal could hurt the integrity of the event—an integrity Bitsy had spent years building.

Bitsy knew she had to figure out who the villain was, before the competition was ruined.

She walked over to Contestant #1, Suzi Snow. The elderly Ms.

Snow reminded Bitsy of her grandmother; hair up in a gray bun and always smiling.

"Hello, Ms. Snow. What are you baking for us today?"

Ms. Snow grinned, showing off super-white dentures.

"My famous angel food cake, with a fresh raspberry glaze. I have a secret ingredient, passed down through six generations."

"What is it?" Bitsy asked, curious.

Ms. Snow winked. "I'll only share it if I win."

Bitsy wished her luck, and walked through the kitchen studio over to Contestant #2, Maureen Hamilton. Maureen was Bitsy's age, but shorter and perpetually scowling. She looked to be in a mood when Bitsy approached.

"The altitude is murderous," Maureen moaned. "It will be a miracle if this chocolate cake turns out. Plus I don't think this oven is calibrated correctly. I don't want to lose because of faulty equipment."

"I'll send a technician over to check it out," Bitsy said. She spoke into her walkie-talkie and asked someone to come by.

Maureen frowned and kept mixing.

Contestant #3 was Maria Espinoza. She'd brought her teenaged daughter with to assist, which the rules allowed. Both wore white latex gloves, which was definitely sanitary, but somewhat unusual.

"This will be the best angel food cake you've ever eaten," Maria beamed.

Bitsy noticed that Maria's daughter was opening a package of raspberries.

"Are you making a raspberry glaze?" she asked.

"Yes. I know that other lady is making a similar cake, but mine will be better. You'll see."

Bitsy bid her good baking and moved on the Contestant #4, Holly Doolittle. Holly was opening up packages of cream cheese, and Bitsy noted that her counter top was covered with graham cracker crumbs.

"Bitsy! I'm so excited to meet you! You're my idol!"

"Thank you," Bitsy said, a little embarrassed.

"I only hope my cake is half as good as one yours. You've got the be the best baker in all of Colorado. Boy, I just love you!"

Bitsy endured a hug, then moved along to the final contestant,

Georgia Peters.

"Ms. Peters, I…"

"Shhh!" Georgia put a finger in front of her lips. "The first layer of my quadruple golden layer cake is in the oven. With this elevation, I can't take any chances."

"Sorry," Bitsy whispered, somewhat mollified. "Good luck."

"I don't need luck," Georgia whispered back. "This cake will win for sure."

Bitsy's walkie-talkie squawked. Georgia shot Bitsy an evil look at the intrusive sound, and Bitsy hurried away.

"What is it?" she asked into the radio.

"We found something." It was Niki James, Bitsy's assistant. "You'd better come and look."

"Where are you?"

"In the hospitality suite.

Bitsy flew through the kitchen, down the hallway, and to the suite. When she arrived, Niki was as pale as cake flour.

"It was under the sofa, in a plain paper bag."

She pointed to the table, and Bitsy gasped when she saw a gun laying next to a bowl of chips.

"When I became your assistant, I never knew I'd have to deal with anything more dangerous than a spatula," Niki said. "Who would bring a gun to a bake-off?"

"Did you touch it?" Bitsy asked.

Niki nodded. "I didn't know what was inside, so I reached in."

"No name on the bag?"

"It's just a regular paper lunch sack," Niki said.

"How about on the gun?"

"I didn't look close enough."

Bitsy thought out loud. "How long has the hospitality suite been open?"

"It's been open all night. I know for a fact that every contestant has been in here, some several times."

Bitsy rubbed her temples. She couldn't believe that one of the women she'd just met would commit murder just to win.

"Should we call the police?" Niki asked.

"Yes. We'll have to cancel the bake-off."

"The negative publicity will be devastating."

"I know. But there's nothing—"

Bitsy's voice trailed off when her eyes locked on the gun. There was something unusual about it. She crept closer to get a better look.

"This isn't a regular gun," she said. "Look at the writing on the side."

Niki came over and read the word engraved into the stock.

"Starter pistol? What's that?"

"It's used for races. It doesn't fire real bullets. Only makes a loud noise."

As the words left Bitsy's mouth, she smiled.

"Call security. I know who the saboteur is."

Who is the saboteur, and how did Bitsy know?

SOLUTION: Bitsy believed Holly Doolittle had brought the starter gun. A loud noise, especially at the high altitude in the Colorado Rockies, would cause flour-based cakes to collapse. Holly was making a cheesecake, which would be unharmed by the loud bang, ensuring a win. Holly had bragged about her plan to her next door neighbor, who placed the anonymous call to Bitsy.

ANIMAL ATTRACTION

After I sold Piece of Cake, I figured I had a new market that would take everything I wrote. I was wrong. After buying my previous story, Woman's World gonged this one. My hat's off to Encyclopedia Brown, because this isn't as easy as it looks.

Only obscure knowledge will lead to a killer…

THE FIRST ANNUAL SPOKANE Zoologist Convention ended on a very sour note…a murder.

To make matters even worse, no one knew who the dead man was.

"I'm sure he's a registered zoologist," said the convention organizer, Dr. Myrna Simmons, who claimed she recognized the deceased from the day before. "I checked him in at the reception table. I remember searching for his name tag. But for the life of me. I can't recall his name. The poor man."

The victim was a handsome forty-something male, wearing a blue suit and a red tie. His wallet was missing. A cheese knife pierced his back—it had apparently been taken from the hors d'oeuvres table. A napkin was wrapped around its handle, preventing the killer from leaving fingerprints.

The body had been found lying face-first on the coatroom floor. One of the convention attendees had gone to hang up her jacket, and almost tripped over him. Immediately afterward, the police had been called, and the banquet hall sealed. No one was allowed to leave without permission from the authorities.

Detective Robbie Walker personally checked the alibi of every person in attendance, and was left with four remaining suspects. During the course of his investigation, Walker cross-referenced the guest list and discovered that there was one person too many in the banquet hall. Walker deduced that this convention crasher was the murderer, and he'd taken the dead man's name tag in an attempt to blend into the crowd and escape.

None of the four suspects had any form of picture ID on them, and each was unable to confirm his identity.

Walked needed to figure out who the imposter was.

He approached the first man, an elderly fellow with a bushy white beard who claimed to be Dr. Jordan McDermott.

"Dr. McDermott, what types of animals do you specialize in?"

"I study the duck-billed platypus," McDermott said, a bit too cheerfully considering the morbid circumstances. "Its fur is among the softest in the world. It lays eggs, and after they hatch it nurses its young. The male platypus is also poisonous. Quite an amazing animal."

Walker was skeptical. "Is all of that true?" he asked the others.

They each shrugged.

"Zoology has so many specialties," said Dr. Apu Patel, a tall, thin man with penetrating brown eyes. "It's impossible to know everything about everything."

"What do you specialize in, Dr. Patel?"

"Elephants. They can smell water from three miles away. And an elephant is the only animal that cannot jump."

"Really?"

"It's true. Did you know that African elephants only have four teeth?"

"I did not know that," Walker admitted. It sounded very suspicious.

"That's nothing," said Dr. Harry Reinsdorff, a fat man with thick, round glasses. "I'm a marine biologist, and I'm studying why sharks don't get cancer. Did you know that sharks can smell a drop of blood in the water from five miles away? And besides the five senses humans have, they also have an extra sense called the Line of Lorenzo, which lets them detect electrical fields in the water."

Walker felt a headache coming on. He didn't know if any of these outrageous facts were true or false.

"How about you?" he asked Dr. Mark Kessler. "What do you specialize in?"

"I unashamedly admit that I study cockroaches," Kessler said. His bulging eyes and brown suit made him look sort of like a cockroach himself. "They're really fascinating creatures. Their blood is white, not red. They can hold their breath underwater for more than ten minutes. And did you know a cockroach can live up to two weeks with its head removed?"

"Yuck," Walker said. The other suspects echoed the sentiment.

"Let's go over your stories again. Dr. McDermott," Walker said, turning to the platypus specialist, "Where were you when the body was discovered?"

"In the bathroom," McDermott said. "I wasn't feeling very well. Too many libations last night. I tried a drink called a rusty nail. Vile stuff."

"How about you, Dr. Patel?" Walker asked the pachyderm professor.

"I was on my cell phone, checking my voice mail. I'd gotten a message from the San Diego Zoo. Apparently one of their elephants has elephant pox."

"And you, Dr. Reinsdorff?"

"I was also on the phone, confirming my reservation tonight at an expensive Japanese sushi restaurant that serves sea cucumbers. They can be poisonous, unless you remove the brain at the center."

Walker said, "Yuck," again, and then asked, "How about you, Dr. Kessler?"

"I'm afraid I was just staring out the window, doing nothing at all. I'm not a very sociable person."

Walker had no idea what to ask next, but fortunately Dr. Myrna Simmons, the convention organizer, came hurrying over.

"Detective Walker! I've got that book you wanted."

She handed him a copy of The Complete Encyclopedia of Animals. Walker thanked her, excused himself, and went into the other room for some fact-checking.

He returned ten minutes later, a broad grin on his face. With dramatic flourish, he pointed at one of the suspects.

"I've discovered that you are lying. I'm afraid you'll have to come downtown with me to answer some more questions."

Which of the suspects was lying?

SOLUTION: The so-called shark expert. Walker discovered that sharks do in fact get cancer, that they can only smell blood in the water from a quarter mile away (not five miles), and that the sense that detects electricity is called the ampullae of Lorenzini, not the Line of Lorenzo. He also discovered that sea cucumbers don't have brains, therefore their brains could not be poisonous, and the man must have been lying about his sushi restaurant reservations. Incredibly, all of the other facts strange animal facts were true. The imposter soon confessed that he had snuck into the convention and murdered Dr. Reinsdorff for having an affair with his wife.

URGENT REPLY NEEDED

Another Amazon.com short, this one in response to the email spam we all get, seemingly all the time. I've remained undecided if the last page hurts the story or helps it, and I've cut the ending many times. Here it is uncut.

WHEN CONROY SAW THE message in his INBOX, he smiled.

> **URGENT REPLY NEEDED!!!**
>
> **Allow me sir to introduce myself. My name is Dr. William Reingold, executor to the estate of Phillip Percy Jefferson III, former CEO of…**

According to the email, Dr. Reingold had 17 million dollars that he was required to distribute to Jefferson's heirs, and a detailed genealogy search had turned up Conroy.

Conroy considered his luck. Just last week, a diplomat from Nigeria had emailed him requesting assistance to help distribute 42 million dollars in charity funds, and a month prior he was contacted by an auditor general from Venezuela with 24 million in a secret arms account and a lawyer from India trying to locate the relatives of a billionaire who died in a tragic plane crash. He'd also recently become a finalist in the Acculotto International lottery in Madrid, which wanted to give him a share of a 30 million euro prize.

Conroy hadn't even bought a lottery ticket.

"Wonderful thing, the Internet," he mused.

"Playing computer solitaire again?" Ryan, from the cubicle to his right, spoke over the flimsy partition.

"Email. If I just give this fellow my bank account number, he'll wire 9 million dollars into my account."

Ryan laughed. "Spam. I got that one too."

Conroy darkened. "Did you reply?"

"Of course not. Who would reply to those things?"

"Who indeed?" Conroy thought. Then he hunched over his keyboard.

Dear Dr. Reingold, I'm very interested in discussing this with you further...

The warehouse where Dr. Reingold had scheduled their meeting was located in Elk Grove Village, a forty minute drive from Conroy's home in Elgin. The late hour troubled Conroy. Midnight. If Conroy hadn't needed the money so badly, he never would have agreed to it. Insurance barely covered half of his mother's nursing home costs, and since his layoff he'd only been able to find temp data entry work at nine dollars an hour—not even enough for one person to live on.

Conroy pulled his BMW into the warehouse driveway, his stomach fluttering. This was an industrial section of town, the area deserted after hours. Conroy wondered how often the police patrolled the area.

He switched on his interior light and reread the email he'd printed out.

Park in front and enter the red door on the side of the building.

Conroy stuffed the note into his jacket and peered at the warehouse. His headlights illuminated a sidewalk, which led to the building's west side. A few seconds of fumbling through his jacket pocket produced a roll of antacids. He chewed four, the chalky taste clinging to the inside of his dry throat.

"I don't like this at all," he whispered to himself.

Then he killed the engine and got out of the car.

The sidewalk was invisible in the dark, but Conroy moved slowly toward the warehouse until he felt it underfoot. He followed the perimeter of the building around the side, and saw a dim light above a red doorway, a hundred feet ahead.

The walk seemed to take an eternity. When he finally put his hand on the cold knob, his knees were shaking.

The door opened with a creak.

"Hello?"

Conroy peeked his head inside, almost crying out when he felt the steel barrel touch his temple.

"Hello, Mr. Conroy."

He dared not turn his head, instead peering sideways to see the thin, rat-faced man with the .38. His light complexion was pocked with acne scars, and he wore too much aftershave. Standing behind him was another, larger man, holding a baseball bat.

Conroy couldn't keep the tremor out of his voice when he said, "Where's Dr. Reingold?"

The man snickered, his laugh high-pitched and effeminate.

"Idiot. I'm Dr. Reingold."

He didn't look very much like a doctor at all.

"You bring your bank account number?"

"No, I—"

Dr. Reingold grabbed Conroy by the ear and tugged him into the room, a small office lit with a single bare bulb hanging from the ceiling.

"I told you to bring that number! Can't you follow instructions?"

Conroy didn't see the blow coming. One moment he was on two feet, the next he was flat on his back, his head vibrating with pain, his world completely dark.

"I can't find his wallet."

A different voice. Probably the big guy.

"No wallet. No check book. What a loser."

A jingle of keys.

"A Beemer. That's worth a few grand. Wasn't a total waste of time."

"In his email, he said he was rich."

"Could have been lying." There was a cold laugh. "Internet is filled with liars."

A gun cocking, close to Conroy's head.

"So let's waste him and—"

"I have money," Conroy croaked.

He managed to open his eyes, unable to focus but sensing the two men staring down at him.

Dr. Reingold nudged him with his foot. "What did you say, buddy?"

"I have a coin collection. Worth over fifty thousand dollars."

"Where is it?"

"At my house."

"Where's your house?"

"Please don't kill me."

Dr. Reingold leaned down, scowling at Conroy. "I'll do worse than kill you if you don't tell me where your house is."

Conroy cursed his own stupidity. He doubted he'd live through this.

"In Elgin. It's in a safe."

"Marty, find a pencil on that desk."

Conroy tried to touch his throbbing head, but Dr. Reingold kicked his hand away.

"The safe combination is tricky. Even if I gave it to you, you probably couldn't open in."

Dr. Reingold tapped the gun against his own cheek, apparently thinking.

"You live alone?"

"Yes."

"Any dogs? Guns? Nasty surprises?"

Conroy's eyes teared up. "No."

Dr. Reingold grinned. "Well then, Mr. Conroy, let's go see this coin collection of yours."

Conroy sat wedged between the two thugs. The big one, Marty, drove. Dr. Reingold kept the .38 pressed into Conroy's ribs, hard enough to bruise.

This wasn't supposed to happen, Conroy thought. This should have ended in a bank account deposit, not in my death.

He pictured his poor mother, who would be sent to a State nursing home if the checks stopped coming. Filthy living conditions. Nurses who stole jewelry and medication. Sexual abuse.

Conroy pushed the images out of his mind, focusing on the problem at hand.

"This it?" Marty asked.

Dr. Reingold gave Conroy's sore ribs a jab.

"Next house, on the end."

"Nice neighborhood. Real quiet. Bet you can put the TV volume all the way up, neighbors don't complain."

Conroy didn't answer.

Marty pulled the BMW into the driveway, parking next to the garage. Dr. Reingold tugged Conroy out of the car and shoved him up to the front door.

"Move it. We gotta another sucker to meet later tonight."

Conroy's hands were shaking so badly he could barely get his key into the lock. He took a deep breath before he turned the knob.

"I'd better go in first," he said, quickly pulling the door open. His house was dark, quiet.

"Easy there, speedy." Dr. Reingold had Conroy's ear again. "You're a little too eager to get inside. I think I'd better…"

The bear trap closed around Dr. Reingold's leg with a sound that was part clang, part squish. He screamed falsetto, dropping the gun and prying at the trap with both hands.

Conroy reached for the pistol, swinging it around at Marty, who watched the whole scene slack-jawed. He shot the large man four times in the chest, then raised the gun and cracked it alongside Dr. Reingold's head, silencing the screams.

Conroy was shoveling the last bit of dirt atop the grave when Dr. Reingold woke up.

"Good morning," Conroy said, wiping a sleeve across his sweaty brow.

Dr. Reingold's eyes were wide with terror, and he struggled against the chair he'd been bound to.

"You can't get away, Dr. Reingold. The knots are too tight."

"What the hell is going on?"

"You don't remember? You and your associate lured me to a warehouse in Elk Grove, using a fake email story. Right now you're in my basement."

"Where's Marty?" Dr. Reingold said, his voice creaking.

"He's right here." Conroy patted the fresh mound. "Next to him is Mr. Bekhi Kogan, a highly dubious Nigerian diplomat. One mound over is Sr. Domingo, who spoke no Spanish, though he was supposedly a Venezuelan auditor general. The third grave is Zakir

Mehmood, who had a distinct Chicago accent, even though he claimed to be from Pakistan. Behind him is a lottery commissioner from Madrid, I forget his name. Began with an L, I think."

Conroy set the shovel on the table, next to the pliers and the filet knife.

"Spammers. All of them. They all promised me riches. Just like you did, Dr. Reingold. All they wanted in return was my bank account number. Speaking of which..."

Conroy picked up the filet knife, and held it against the bound man's ear.

"...why don't you tell me your account number, Dr. Reingold?"

Dr. Reingold began to sob.

"Who...who are you?"

"I'm your most dreaded enemy, Dr. Reingold." Conroy grinned, his eyes sparkling. "I'm a spam killer."

Conroy pushed the knife forward and Dr. Reingold began to scream.

All in all, a pretty decent take. Dr. Reingold's bank account contained over seventeen thousand dollars. He'd had a little trouble remembering his routing number, but Conroy was good at helping people remember things.

Next time, he'd do things differently. He hadn't expected an Internet swindler to have a partner. Or a weapon. The ones he'd dealt with previously had been con artists, not hardened criminals.

Well, live and learn. In the future, he'd be more prepared.

After a quick shower, Conroy visited his favorite all night diner for some meatloaf and a slice of cherry pie. Late night grave digging made a man hungry.

"How are you, Mr. Conroy?"

The regular waitress, Dora, was in mid coffee pour when she sneezed, spilling some onto the table.

"Sorry about that."

Conroy grimaced.

"Sounds like you have a cold."

Dora sniffled. "Yeah. Bad one too."

"Shouldn't you be home, resting?"

"Can't. Need the money."

"I'm sorry to hear that."

Dora sneezed again, not even bothering to cover her mouth. "You want the usual?"

Conroy thought it over, then made his decision.

"Not today. I just remembered something I have to do."

Conroy left the restaurant. Instead of climbing into his car, he walked around back and waited in the alley for Dora's shift to end. His hunger had been replaced by a hunger of a different kind.

He fingered the .38 in his pocket, pleased with his newfound sense of purpose.

I'm giving myself an upgrade, he mused.

From now on, he would be Conroy Version 2.0—Spam Killer and Virus Eliminator.

BLAINE'S DEAL

Before I owned a computer, I had WebTV, which was an Internet browser that hooked up to the television. I found some online writing groups, and would regularly type stories to post for critiques. This was the first story I ever put on the world wide web.

THEY SHOOT CHEATERS AT The Nile.

Blaine lost his mentor that way, a counter named Roarke. Didn't even have a chance to get ahead before the eye in the sky locked on, videotaping skills that took years to master. Then it was burly men and a room without windows. One between the eyes, tossed out with the trash.

Poor bastard deserved better.

Blaine pushed back the worry. He was dressed like a tourist, from his sandals to his Nile Casino T-shirt. Made sure to spill some beer from the paper cup down his chin when he took a sip. Sat by a loud slot machine called Pyramids and plunked in quarters, trying to look angry when he lost. Ugly American. Probably had a job in the auto industry.

When the coins ran out, he frowned, scratched himself, and made a show of looking around. He'd had an eye on a particular Blackjack dealer for the last two hours. Surfer guy, looked like a tan version of the Hulk, too young to have been in the business long.

Blaine wandered over to the table, pretended to think it over, then sat down and fished some cash out of his shorts. Three hundred to start.

He took it slow. Six deck shoe, sixteen tens per deck. Too many to keep track of mentally. But no need to. Every counter had his tally method.

Roarke had been one of the best. Subtle. See a ten, adjust the elbow. Ace, move the foot. Depending on his body position, Roarke knew if the shoe was heavy or light with face cards.

But the silver globes in the ceiling caught him just an hour into his game. Roarke was found a few days later in an alley, the offending foot and elbow smashed. Back of his head was missing, and no one bothered to look for it.

Blaine was a counter as well, but his tally couldn't be seen by the cameras. No tapping feet or odd posture. Pit boss could be taking a dump on his shoulder, wouldn't notice a thing.

He bet small, safe. Won a few, lost a few. Turned more cash into chips and bided time until he got a nice, fat shoe. Then it was payday.

Thirty minutes. Twelve thousand dollars.

He lost a grand, on purpose, before tipping the Hulk a hundred bucks and calling it quits for the night.

Blaine walked out of the casino happy, not needing to fake that particular emotion. He'd be off this tropic isle tomorrow. Back to his wife, laden with money. A memorable and profitable trip.

The goons grabbed him in the parking lot. Nile Security. Guys with scars who were paid to give them.

"What the hell's going on?"

No answer. They dragged Blaine back inside. Past the crowd. Down a hall. To a room without windows.

Panic stitched through his veins. He fought to stay in character. Hackles and indignation.

"I'm calling the police! I'm an American!"

The door slammed. A bare bulb hung from the ceiling, casting harsh shadows. The pit boss forced Blaine to his knees. Big guy, a walrus in Armani, breath like rotten meat.

"We shoot card counters here."

"What are you talking about? I won the money fair!"

The blow knocked Blaine off his feet. Concrete was sticky under his palms. Old stains.

"Camera caught it. Under the table."

The blood in Blaine's mouth contrasted sharply with his blanched face. The pit boss reached down, pulled at Blaine's shorts, his underwear.

Blaine stared down between his naked legs. The abacus was along his thigh, taped to the right of his testicles.

The pit boss ripped it off, a thousand curly hairs screaming.

"This belong in your shorts?"

"How did that get there?" Blaine tried for confused. "I swear, I borrowed this underwear. I have no idea how that got on me."

His explanation was met with a kick in the head. Blaine kissed the mottled floor, his vision a carousel. He flashed back to Roarke's funeral, closed casket, the promise he made. "I'll beat the Nile for you, old buddy."

Should have stuck with Vegas.

The pit boss dug a hand inside his sport coat. "Never saw a guy count cards with his dick before. Man with your talent, should have gone into porno."

The gun was cool against Blaine's temple.

"No one cheats the Nile."

Blaine's wife cried for seven weeks straight when she learned of his death.

THE CONFESSION

Beware. This is a rough one. I wrote this story as a dual experiment. First, to do a serious story using only dialog. No action. No exposition. No speaker attribution. Just talking. And second, I always wondered if I could make readers squirm without relying on description. It was written for a horror issue of the webzine Hardluck Stories, at the request of Harry Shannon, and it's as nasty a story as I've ever done.

"FROM THE BEGINNING? THE very beginning?"

"Wherever you want to start, Jane."

"Wherever I want to start. Well. I guess you could say it all started when I was thirteen years old, when my father started coming into my bedroom."

"Your father molested you?"

"Molested? That sounds like he stuck his hand under my bra. My father fucked me. Made me suck him off. Called me Daddy's Little Whore. Used to write it on my forehead, in marker. I'd have to scrub it off before going to school. Wretched bastard. Went on until I ran away, at sixteen."

"And that's when you met Maurice?"

"That pimp fucker thought he was so smooth, busting out a white girl. Had no idea my old man busted me out years earlier."

"Was Maurice the one in the pit?"

"No. Maurice was the belt sander."

"Who was in the pit?"

"You want me to tell it, or answer questions?"

"Whatever you're more comfortable with."

"Okay. I'll tell it. Maurice found me at the shelter. Slimy pricks like him can probably sniff out teenage pussy. He talked sweet, hooked me on crack, and the next thing you know I'm blowing guys in their cars for twenty bucks a pop. Wasn't that bad, actually. I know I'm nothing to look at. Even before all the scars, I was fat and dumpy. Plain Fucking Jane, my mom called me. You got a cigarette?"

"Menthol."

"Beats sucking air. Thanks. Anyway, Maurice set me up with this freak. Guy took me back to his place, had a whole torture dungeon in his bedroom. That's how my face got all fucked up. Cigarette burns. Looks like acne scars, doesn't it? Kept me there for four days, then dumped me in a trash can."

"Did you know his name?"

"We'll get to that. You wanted this from the beginning, remember?"

"Take your time."

"Shit. I'm sorry, I can't smoke menthols. Do you have anything else?"

"No."

"Do I have to smoke?"

"No."

"I want to do this right for you."

"It's okay."

"Thanks…Mr. Police-man. Where was I? Oh yeah, after my face got burned, Maurice couldn't give me away. I wound up ass fucking winos in alleys for three bucks a pop. You ever have gonorrhea in your ass? Hurts like a bitch. And fucking Maurice wouldn't give me money for the clinic. Whatcha got there? A picture?"

"Is this Maurice?"

"Jesus! That's disgusting! Is that real?"

"Is this Maurice?"

"Yeah. That's him. Doesn't look too good there, does he? Heard he might live."

"We don't know yet."

"Ha! Be damn tough for him to testify. But I'm getting ahead of myself. After a while, the VD got so bad I couldn't walk. Maurice beat the shit out of me, left me for dead. That's when Gordon found me."

"Reverend Gordon Winchell?"

"He's no reverend. No church would have him. He was just another preacher, screaming scripture at drunks in soup kitchens. Saved my life, probably. Got me to the hospital. Actually came to visit me during my recovery. Seemed like an actual decent guy for a while. Until I learned his kink."

"What did he do to you?"

"On the day of my release, the good Reverend took me to his apartment, tied me to the bed, and began biting me."

"Biting you?"

"Look at this —"

"You don't need to —"

"Don't get all prude on me. See? Nothing there. Bit my nipples right off. If I wasn't in handcuffs I'd show you what he did to my twat."

"Jesus."

"You okay, Mr. Police-man? You don't look so good. You want to take a break?"

"How did you get away?"

"He had it all worked out in his head that he'd kill me. But he couldn't. Didn't have the balls. So he dumped me in front of the same hospital he brought me home from."

"Did you call the police?"

"Are you fucking kidding me? I called fucking everybody. When my dad was raping me, I called DCFS, and he paid the assholes off. When that freak burned my face, I filed a complaint, and you guys didn't do shit. Gordon eats my private parts, one of your finest told me to have my pimp take care of it. Is this turning you on?"

"Stick to the story."

"This is some pretty sick shit."

"Stick to the story!"

"Okay. Sorry. Where was I? I lost my place."

"The cops didn't help you."

"Right. Okay, here it is. That was it for me. I had enough of playing the victim."

"Is that when you started…?"

"Is that when I started grabbing these sons of bitches? Yeah. When I got out of the hospital the second time, I tracked down the freak, watched his house until he was asleep, and then broke in. Used his own handcuffs on him. And his own blowtorch. It was hard to restrain myself, lemme tell you. But even holding back, his balls turned black and fell off after only three days."

"This was John McSweeny?"

"Yeah. He sure was a screamer. Screamed so much, his throat actually started to bleed. Know what the weird part is? He smelled great! Like honey baked ham. When I burned off his face I was actually drooling. Is that funny or what?"

"You stabbed Mr. McSweeny."

"The hell I did. I never killed no one. After a week or so, I uncuffed one of his hands, and gave him a steak knife. Fucker cut his own throat, and that's God's truth."

"After McSweeny came Maurice."

"Nope. Next came my father. I invited him over, got all weepy on the phone saying I forgave him. Hit him with a tire iron when he walked in the door. The freak, McSweeny, had all of these ropes and pulleys and shit, so I stripped Dad naked and hung him up. Then I lowered him down on that hat rack. Right up his ass. Funniest damn thing you ever saw. The more he moved, the lower he sunk, the higher the pole went up his poop chute. He lasted almost a month. I'd bring him food and water. That pole got about two feet up him before he finally died."

"That's murder, Jane."

"That's gravity, cop. If he stayed perfectly still, he would have lived. Blame Isaac Newton."

"Then Maurice?"

"Then Maurice. When I was honey baking McSweeny, he was anxious to make the pain stop. Gave me all sorts of things. His bank account. His stocks. His car. I went to the dealer who used to sell me crack, bought a needle of H, snuck up on Maurice."

"You mentioned you used a belt sander."

"It takes all the skin off, but then gets real slippery. I kept buying belt after belt, until I figured out I could improve the traction if I threw salt on him."

"How long did you torture Maurice?"

"A few weeks. He'd scab over, then I'd start on him again."

"So…the guy in the pit?"

"That was the good Reverend Gordon. He got a heroin poke too, and when he woke up, he was chained up in the hole."

"What did you do to him?"

"Poetic justice. Fucker liked to bite, so I gave him a taste of his own medicine. I went to the pet store, bought a big box of rats. Put them in the pit with him. They were tame at first, but when they got hungry they began to nibble nibble. They started on the soft parts — look, do I have to read anymore?"

"Stick to the script."

"But you've still got your clothes on. You don't seem into this at all."

"I pay the money. I make the rules. I want you to finish reading."

"Look, sugar, I'm the best. Why do you want me to sit here and read when I can make you feel good?"

"Please don't…"

"Are you crying? Don't cry, baby. It's okay. Don't be afraid. Let me just get these pants off."

"I don't want to…"

"I like shy boys. Are you a shy boy? Let's see how shy you are — Jesus!"

"You…you were supposed to stick with the script."

"Where's your cock? You don't have a fucking cock!"

"You read the story."

"The story?"

"Reverend…Reverend Gordon."

"But that was all bullshit, right? Some freaky shit you made up?"

"He…liked to bite…"

"You're bullshitting me."

"I'm…a whore…"

"I'm leaving. Open this door."

"Daddy's Little Whore…"

"Open this fucking door or I'll start to scream!"

"McSweeny's house. Soundproof."

"You psychotic fucking freak! Let me out!"

"I won't hurt you. I want you to understand."

"Get the fuck away from me!"

"You're a prostitute. You're a victim too."

"Let me go!"

"Someone hurt you, right?"

"I want to leave. Please let me leave."

"You didn't choose this. You didn't choose to fuck men for money."

"I…want to leave."

"Who hurt you? Your father? Your pimp? You can tell me."

"I…don't…"

"I won't judge you. It's okay."

"No…"

"Who was it?"

"Don't…"

"Who was the monster that made you this way?"

"My…uncle."

"Your uncle?"

"He'd babysit me. Make me do things."

"I'm sorry."

"I…didn't mean to call you a freak."

"I know. It's okay."

"Jesus, I thought my life was shit. But all you went through…"

"It's okay. From now on, we're both okay. Come on, I want to show you something."

"I…I don't wanna go down there."

"Trust me. I would never hurt you."

"What's that smell?"

"I told you. Smells like ham."

"That was all true?"

"Most of it. Except they're all still alive. Meet Mr. John McSweeny."

"Oh my god…"

"Looks tasty, doesn't he? I use that wire brush on his burns. Still can coax a few screams out of him. Watch your step, there's the pit."

"Oh Jesus…"

"I see the rats finished off most of your face, Gordon. And congratulations! Looks like they also had a litter of hungry babies!

You're a papa!"

"What…what is that?"

"That's Maurice. Can't even tell he's a black guy anymore, can you? That belt sander is quite a tool. Want me to pour some vinegar on him, wake him up?"

"This is all…I can't believe…"

"I know. It's a lot to take in. But here's who I really wanted you to meet. Say hello to my father. The person who turned me into the man I am today. Go on, say hello."

"Um…hello."

"He can't talk, because of the gag. But if you want him to answer, just give the pole a little shake. Like this. Hear that? I think he likes you."

"He's…crying."

"Of course he is. He's got two feet of hat rack up his ass. Probably punctured all sorts of vital stuff. You want to give the pole a little shake?"

"No…"

"Go ahead. Not too much, though. Just a little tap like this. See? You can hear him screaming in his throat.

"I don't want to."

"Yes you do. You're a victim, just like me. The only way to stop being a victim is to fight back. Go on."

"I really don't…"

"Stop playing the victim."

"But…"

"Fight back. It's the only way you'll be able to live with yourself. Put your hand on the pole."

"This isn't right."

"Raping children isn't right. Pretend it's your uncle hanging there. Remember all the things he did to you."

"My uncle. That fucking son of a bitch."

"Whoa! Hold on! You're going to kill him, shaking it that hard. Ease back."

"I'm sorry. I didn't mean to…"

"Yes you did. Felt good didn't it?"

"I…I thought of killing him so many times."

"Death is too good for men like that. He doesn't need killing. He needs to be shown the error of his ways. Oh…don't cry. It's okay. No one is ever going to hurt you, ever again. I promise. There there."

"Can we…can we…"

"Can we find your uncle and bring him here?"

"Yeah."

"Of course we can, dear. Of course we can."

Horror Stories

I'M A HUGE HORROR movie fan, dating back to the creature features and Twilight Zone reruns on UHF Channel 32 in the mid-seventies. If you ever visit a Jaycee's haunted house on Halloween, or ride a roller coaster, you'll hear both screams and laughter. The two emotions are closely tied.

Since writing is about provoking emotion in the reader, I try to use as much fear and as much humor as I can in my stories. Fear is universal. It connects us as human beings. And being scared is a blast.

My bookcase is filled with thousands of horror novels and anthologies, from the traditional standbys of King and Koontz, to the splatterpunk gorefests of Jack Ketchum and Ed Lee, to the British shocks of Graham Masterton and James Herbert.

I tend to jump around sub-genres when writing horror. I don't mind going for the gross out, but I also like to poke fun and make jokes. Even my darkest horror stories could be classified as black comedy if you look hard enough. Though I write some scary and disturbing stuff, it's always done with a wink.

My Lt. Jacqueline "Jack" Daniels thrillers all contain healthy doses of horror. Jack chases some pretty frightening criminals, and if reading those scary sections doesn't make you lock your doors and turn on all your lights you probably have a heart made of stone.

In 2009, I wrote a horror novel called *Afraid* under the pen name Jack Kilborn. Since then I've written two other Kilborn books (they'll be released eventually.) In the meantime, here's a big dose of primal fear, aimed right at your jugular. Make sure your doors are locked…

Finicky Eater

This is my very first published story, which was published right after I sold Whiskey Sour. It centers on a theme I've gone back to often in my fiction. This appeared in the magazine Horror Garage, which featured a girl on the cover with her face soaked in blood. My mom didn't pass out copies at her job.

"EAT IT."

Billy pushed his plate away.

"I'm not hungry anymore."

A pout appeared on his shiny little face. A miniature version of Josh's. Marge could remember when it used to be cute.

"You haven't even tried it. I made it different today. Just take a bite."

"No."

Marge could feel the tension build in her neck, like cables beneath the skin.

"Billy, honey, you need to eat. Look how skinny you're getting."

"I want an apple."

"We've been over this Billy. There are no apples. There won't be any apples ever again."

He crossed his arms. So thin. His elbows and wrists looked huge.

"I want a Twinkie."

Marge's mouth quivered, got wet.

"Billy, please don't…"

"I want McDonald's french fries, and a Coke."

A deep breath.

"Billy, we don't have any of those things anymore. Since they dropped all those bombs, we have to make do with what's available. Now please, you need to eat."

She pushed the plate back towards her son. His portion of meat was small, scarcely the size of a cracker. Pale and greasy. Marge eyed it and felt her stomach rumble.

It's for Billy, she chastened herself.

But if he didn't want it…

Marge killed the thought and looked away for some distraction.

She failed.

After three months in the shelter, there was nothing left to distract herself with.

She knew every inch of the tiny room like she knew her own body. The shelves, once stocked with canned goods, were empty. The TV and radio didn't work. The three dirty cots smelled like body odor, and the sump hole in the corner had long overflowed with urine and feces. No view, no entertainment, no escape.

Josh had built the shelter because he wanted his family to live. But was this living?

Marge turned to her son, the tears coming. "We're going to make it, Billy. I promise. But you need to eat. Please."

"No." Billy's own eyes began to glaze. "I want Daddy."

"I know you do. But Daddy left, Billy. He knew we didn't have enough food. So he made a sacrifice for you and me."

"I wish Daddy was here."

Tears burned her cheeks.

"He's here, Billy." She patted her chest. "He's here, inside of us, and he always will be."

Billy narrowed his eyes. "You hit Daddy on the head."

Marge recoiled as if slapped.

"No, Billy. Your father made a sacrifice."

"He did not. You hit him on the head while he was asleep."

Billy picked up the small piece of meat and threw it at his mother.

"I don't want to eat Daddy anymore!"

Marge scooped up the meat, sobbing. It tasted salty. She didn't want to take food from her son, but she needed the strength for what came next.

She silently cursed her husband. Why didn't he properly stock this place? Getting nuked would have been better than this.

Her hand closed around the fire axe.

The scream woke her up.

Marge's face burned with fever. Infection, she knew. In a way, a blessing. Consciousness was far too horrible.

"Billy?"

Whimpering. Marge squinted in the darkness.

"Mommy?"

She shifted, the pain in her legs causing her to cry out. She unconsciously reached down to touch them, but felt nothing.

They'd eaten her legs last week.

"What's the matter, Billy? Are you hungry, honey?"

"I made a sacrifice, Mommy."

He crawled out of the shadows, handing Marge his tiny, dirty foot.

The drool that leaked from her mouth had a mind of its own.

"You…you have to do it, Billy."

Billy was crying.

"You have to do it for Mommy. Mommy can't cut off her second arm. I can't hold the axe."

"I wish Daddy were here."

"Daddy!" Marge's face raged with anger, madness. "Your father did this to us! He got off lucky!"

She stared a her baby boy, legless, pulling himself along on his hands. Damn the world, and damn God, and damn Josh for letting this…

There was a noise coming from the door.

It was a knock! Someone was knocking!

"Billy! Do you hear it! We're going to be…"

Billy swung the axe.

"This one's still alive!"

Officer Carlton leaned over the small boy, checking his pulse. He was awful to look at, legless and caked with blood. His mouth was a ruin of ragged flesh.

No — not a ruin. The flesh wasn't his.

"Jesus."

His partner, Jones, made a face.

"Looks like the kid ate his mom. There's another body over here. My guess it's the homeowner. Why'd they come down here?"

Carlton shrugged. "The father had a history of paranoid behavior. Maybe he convinced them it was a nuclear war."

He squinted at the father's corpse. The bones had been broken to get at the marrow inside. Carlton shivered.

"There's a hidden room back here. Look, the shelf swings away."

The hinged shelf moved inward, revealing a large pantry, stocked with canned goods. Enough for years.

"Now, Billy!"

Carlton caught the movement and spun around, in time to see the little creature with the axe bring it down on his partner's head.

Carlton's jaw dropped. The woman — the gory, limbless torso that they thought was dead — was undulating across the floor towards him like a gigantic worm.

He drew his gun. The axe hit him in the belly.

"We're saved!" the mother-thing cried.

Her voice was wet with something. Blood?

When she bit into his leg, he realized it was drool.

Marge slithered away from the light. It was too bright outside. There was probably radiation coming in, but she didn't pay it any mind.

Her only motivation was hunger. And the food was in the hidden room.

Part of her brain recognized the can goods around her, recognized that they contained edible things. But her attention was focused on the police officer, cowering in the corner, holding the pumping wound in his gut.

Her mouth got wet.

She crawled, inch-worm style, up to him.

"Get away, lady!"

Billy crawled past her, faster because he still had arms. The cop screamed, and Billy hacked at his flailing legs like kindling.

A sound mixed in with the screams, and Marge realized it was laughter.

Her son was laughing.

"Billy! Don't play with your food!"

"You killed Daddy."

Billy had his mouth full of something purple, and his eyes were far away.

"Yes I did, Billy. I killed him so you could have food. But we have enough food now for weeks. And these men have families, who will come looking for them. We'll never be hungry again."

Billy chewed and spit out something hard.

"Daddy is inside me."

"That's right."

"You're a little inside me, too. Your legs and arms."

Marge almost smiled at the child's analogy.

"That's right. Mommy is a little inside you."

Billy narrowed his eyes.

"I want all of you inside me."

Marge watched her son drag himself over to the axe.

Billy opened his eyes. The sheets were soaked with sweat. He turned in bed and shook his wife, who was snoring softly.

"Jill! Wake up!"

Her eyelids fluttered. "What's wrong, Billy?"

"Get the baby!" Billy rolled over and strapped on his prosthetic legs, snugging the belts tight. "It's happening!"

Jill sat up. The air raid siren cut through their bedroom like a scream.

"The bombs are dropping, Jill! We have to get down to the shelter! Hurry!"

He hobbled out of the room, Jill joining him on the stairs with their six month old son. The siren was louder in the night air. On the horizon was a horribly bright light, and a pluming cloud in the shape of a mushroom.

He opened the door to the underground shelter, ushering his wife and son down the stairs, frightened and anxious and…salivating.

The Screaming

This is from the first anthology I ever appeared in, The Many Faces of Van Helsing, which had nothing to do with the Hugh Jackman film but was released at the same time to capitalize on it. I don't do many period pieces, and don't do many stories set in foreign countries. I also don't do many vampire stories, even though I love to read them. This is set in England in the 1960s, and I paid a lot of attention to vernacular, trying to get it to sound right.

"THREE STINKING QUID?"

Colin wanted to reach over the counter and throttle the old bugger. The radio he brought in was brand new and worth at least twenty pounds.

Of course, it was also hot. Delaney's was the last pawnbroker in Liverpool that didn't ask questions. Colin dealt with them frequently because of this. But each and every time, he left the shop feeling ripped off.

"Look, this is state of the art. The latest model. You could at least go six."

As expected, the old wank didn't budge. Colin took the three coins and left, muttering curses under his breath.

Where the hell was he going to get more money?

Colin rubbed his hand, fingers trailing over dirty scabs. His eyes itched. His throat felt like he'd been swallowing gravel. His stomach was a tight fist that he couldn't unclench.

If he didn't score soon, the shakes would start.

Colin tried to work up enough saliva to spit, and only half-managed. The radio had been an easy snatch; stupid bird left it on the window ledge of her flat, plugged in and wailing a new Beatles tune. Gifts like that don't come around that often.

He used to do okay robbing houses, but the last job he pulled left him with three broken ribs and a mashed nose when the owner came home early. And Colin'd been in pretty good shape back then. Now-frail and wasted and brittle as he was-a good beating would kill him.

Not that Colin was afraid to die. He just wanted to score first. And three pounds wouldn't even buy him a taste.

Colin hunkered down on the walk, pulled up the collar on his wool coat. The coat had been nice once, bought when Colin was a straighty, making good wage. He'd almost sold it many times, but always held out. English winters bit at a man's bones. There was already a winter-warning chill in the air, even though autumn had barely started.

Still, if he could have gotten five pounds for it, he'd have shucked it in an instant. But with the rips, the stains, the piss smell, he'd be lucky to get fifty p.

"Ello, Colin."

Colin didn't bother looking up. He recognized the sound of Butts's raspy drone, and couldn't bear to tolerate him right now.

"I said, ello, Colin."

"I heard you, Butts."

"No need to be rude, then."

Butts plopped next to him without an invite, smelling like a loo set ablaze. His small eyes darted this way and that along the sidewalk, searching for half spent fags. That's how he'd earned his nickname.

"Oh, lucky day!"

Butts grinned and reached into the street, plucking up something with filthy fingers. There was a lipstick stain on the filter, and it had been stamped flat.

"Good for a puff or two, eh?"

"I'm in no mood today, Butts."

"Strung out again, are we?"

Butts lit the butt with some pub matches, drew hard.

"I need a few more quid for a nickel bag."

"You could pull a job."

"Look at me, Butts. I weigh ten stone, and half that is the coat. A small child could beat my arse."

"Just make sure there's no one home, mate."

"Easier said," Colin thought.

"You know"—Butts closed his eyes, smoke curling from his nostrils"—I'm short on scratch myself right now. Maybe we could team up for something. You go in, I could be lookout, we split the take."

Colin almost laughed. He didn't trust Butts as far as he could chuck him.

"How about I be the lookout?"

"Sorry, mate. You'll run at the first sign of trouble."

"And you wouldn't?"

Butts shrugged. His fag went out. He made two more attempts at lighting it, and then flicked it back into the street.

"Sod it, then. Let's do a job where we don't need no lookout."

"Such as?"

Butts scratched his beard, removed a twig.

"There's this house, see? In Heysham, near where I grew up. Been abandoned for a long time. Loaded with bounty, I bet. That antiquey stuff fetches quite a lot in the district."

"It's probably all been jacked a long time ago."

"I don't think so. When I was a pup, the road leading up to it was practically invisible. All growed over by woods, you see. Only the kids knew about it. And we all stayed far away."

"Why?"

"Stories. Supposed to have goblins. Bollocks like that. I went up to it once, on a dare. Got within ten yards. Then I heard the screaming."

Colin rolled his eyes. He needed to quit wasting time with Butts and think of some way to get money. It would be dark soon.

"You think I'm joshing? I swear on the head of my lovely, sainted mother. I got within a stone's throw, and a god-fearful scream comes out of the house. Sounded like the devil his self was torturing some poor soul. Wet my kecks, I did."

"It was probably one of your stupid mates, Butts. Having a giggle at your expense."

"Wasn't a mate, Colin. I'm telling you, no kid in town went near that house. Nobody did. And I've been thinking about it a lot, lately. I bet there's some fine stuff to nick in there."

"Why haven't you gone back then, eh? If this place is full of stealables, why haven't you made a run?"

Butts's roving eyes locked onto another prize. He lit up, inhaled.

"It's about fifteen miles from here. Every so often I save up the rail money, but I always seem to spend the dough on something else. Hey, you said you have a few quid, right? Maybe we can take the train and —"

"No way, Butts."

Colin got up, his thin bones creaking. He could feel the onset of tremors in his hands, and jammed them into his pockets.

"Heysham Port is only a two hour ride. Then only a wee walk to the house."

"I don't want to spend my loot on train tics, and I don't want to spend the night in bloody Heysham. Pissant little town."

Colin looked left, then right, realizing it didn't matter what direction he went. He began walking, Butts nipping at his heels.

"I got old buds in Heysham. They'll put us up. Plus I got a contact there. He could set us up with some smack, right off. Wouldn't even need quid; we can barter with the pretties we nick."

"No."

Butts put his dirty hand on Colin's shoulder, squeezed. His fingernails resembled a coal miner's.

"Come on, mate. We could be hooked up in three hours. Maybe less. You got something better to do? Find a hole somewhere, curl up until the puking stops? You recall how long it takes to stop, Colin?"

Colin paused. He hadn't eaten in a few days, so there was nothing to throw up but his own stomach lining. He'd done that, once. Hurt something terrible, all bloody and foul.

But Heysham? Colin didn't believe there was anything valuable in that armpit of a town. Let alone some treasure-filled house Butts'd seen thirty years back.

Colin rubbed his temple. It throbbed, in a familiar way. As the night dragged on, the throbbing would get worse.

He could take his quid, buy a tin of aspirin and some seltzer, and hope the withdrawal wouldn't be too bad this time.

But he knew the truth.

As far as bad decisions went, Colin was king. One more wouldn't make a dif.

"Fine, Butts. We'll go to Heysham. But if there's nothing there, you owe me. Big."

Butts smiled. The three teeth he had left were as brown as his shoes.

"You got it, mate! And you'll see! Old Butts has got a feeling about this one. We're going to score, and score big. You'll see."

By the time the rail spit them out at Heysham Port, Colin was well into the vomiting.

He'd spent most of the ride in the loo, retching his guts out. With each purge, he forced himself to drink water, so as not to do any permanent damage to his gullet.

It didn't help. When the water came back up, it was tinged pink.

"Hang in there, Colin. It isn't far."

Bollocks it wasn't far. They walked for over three hours. The night air was a meat locker, and the ground was all slope and hill. Wooded country, overgrown with trees and high grass, dotted with freezing bogs. Colin noticed the full moon, through a sliver in the canopy, then the forest swallowed it up.

They walked by torchlight; Butts had swaddled an old undershirt around a stick. Colin stopped vomiting, but the shivering got so bad he fell several times. It didn't help that Butts kept getting his reference points mixed up and changed directions constantly.

"Don't got much left, Butts."

"Stay strong, mate. Almost there. See? We're on the road."

Colin looked down, saw only weeds and rocks.

"Road?"

"Cobblestone. You can still see bits of curbing."

Colin's hopes fell. If the road was in such disrepair, the house was probably worse off.

Stinking Heysham. Stinking Butts.

"There it is, mate! What did I tell you?"

Colin stared ahead and viewed nothing but trees. Slowly, gradually, he saw the house shape. The place was entirely obscured, the land so overgrown it appeared to be swallowing the frame.

"Seems like the house is part of the trees," Colin said.

"Was like that years ago, too. Worse now, of course. And lookit that. Windows still intact. No one's been inside here in fifty years, I bet."

Colin straightened up. Butts was right. As rundown as it was, the house looked untouched by humans since the turn of the century.

"We don't have to take everything at once. Just find something small and pricey to nick now, and then we can come back and —"

The scream paralyzed Colin. It was a force, high pitched thunder, ripping through him like needles. Unmistakably human, yet unlike any human voice Colin had ever heard.

And it was coming from the house.

Butts gripped him with both hands, the color fleeing his ruddy face.

"Jesus Christ! Did you hear that? Just like when I was a kid! What do we do, Colin?"

A spasm shook Colin's guts, and he dry-heaved onto some scrub brush. He wiped his mouth on his coat sleeve.

"We go in."

"Go in? I just pissed myself."

"What are you afraid of, Butts? Dying? Look at yourself. Death would be a blessing."

"My life isn't a good one, Colin, but it's the only one I've got."

Colin pushed past. The scream was chilling, yes. But there was nothing in that house worse than what Colin had seen on the street. Plus, he needed to get fixed up, bad. He'd crawl inside the devil's arse to get some cash.

"Hold up for me!"

Butts attached himself to Colin's arm. They crept towards the front door.

Another scream rattled the night, even louder than the first. It vibrated through Colin's body, making every nerve jangle.

"I just pissed myself again!"

"Quiet, Butts! Did you catch that?"

"Catch what?"

"It wasn't just a scream. I think it was a word."

Colin held his breath, waiting for the horrible sound to come again. The woods stayed silent around them, the wind and animals still.

The scream cut him to the marrow.

"There! Sounded like hell."

Butts's eyes widened, the yellows showing.

"Let's leave, Colin. My trousers can't hold anymore."

Colin shook off Butts and continued creeping towards the house.

Though naive about architecture, Colin had grown up viewing enough castles and manors to recognize this building was very old. The masonry was concealed by climbing vines, but the wrought iron adorning the windows was magnificent. Even decades of rust couldn't obscure the intricate, flowing curves and swirls.

As they neared, the house seemed to become larger, jutting dormers threatening to drop down on their heads, heavy walls stretching off and blending into the trees. Colin stopped at the door, nearly nine feet high, hinges big as a man's arm.

"Butts! The torch!"

Butts slunk over, waving the flame at the door.

The knob was antique, solid brass, and glinted in the torchlight. At chest level hung a grimy knocker. Colin licked his thumb and rubbed away the patina.

"Silver."

"Silver? That's great, Colin! Let's yank it and get out of here."

But Colin wouldn't budge. If just the door knocker was worth this much, what treasures lay inside?

He put his hand on the cold knob. Turned.

It opened.

As a youth, Colin often spent time with his grandparents, who owned a dairy farm in Shincliffe. That's how the inside of this house smelled; like the musk and manure of wild beats. A feral smell, his grandmum had often called it.

Taking the torch from Butts, he stepped into the foyer, eyes scanning for booty. Decades of dust had settled on the furnishings, motes swirling into a thick fog wherever the duo stepped. Beneath the grime, Colin could recognize the quality of the furniture, the value of the wall hangings.

They'd hit it big.

It was way beyond a simple, quick score. If they did this right, went through the proper channels, he and Butts could get rich off of this.

Another scream shook the house.

Butts jumped back, his sudden movement sending clouds of dust into the air. Colin coughed, trying to wave the filth out of his face.

"It came from down there!" Butts pointed at the floor, his quivering hand casting erratic shadows in the torchlight. "It's a ghost, I tell you! Come to take us to hell!"

Colin's heart was a hummingbird in his chest, trying to find a way out. He was scared, but even more than that, he was concerned.

"Not hell, Butts. It sounded more like help."

Colin stepped back, out of the dust cloud. He thrust the torch at the floor, looking for a way down.

"Ello! Anyone down there?"

He tapped at the wood slats with the torch, listening for a hollow sound.

"Ello!"

The voice exploded up through the floorboards, cracking like thunder.

"PRAISE GOD, HELP ME!"

Butts grabbed Colin's shoulders, his foul breath assaulting his ear.

"Christ, Colin! There's a wraith down there!"

"Don't be stupid, Butts. It's a man. Would a ghost be praising God?"

Colin bent down, peered at the floor.

"What's a man doing under the house, Colin?"

"Bugger if I know. But we have to find him."

Butts nodded, eager.

"Right! If we rescue the poor sap, maybe we'll get a reward, eh?"

Colin grabbed Butts by the collar, pulled him close.

"This place is a gold mine. We can't let anyone else know it exists."

Butts gazed at him stupidly.

"We have to snuff him," Colin said.

"Snuff him? Colin, I don't think —"

Colin clamped his hand over Butts's mouth.

"I'll do it, when the time comes. Just shut up and follow my lead, got it?"

Butts nodded. Colin released him and went back to searching the floor. "Ello! How'd you get down there!"

"There is a trap door, in the kitchen!"

Colin located the kitchen off to the right. An ancient, wood burning stove stood vigil in one corner, and there was an icebox by the window. On the kitchen table, slathered with dust, lay a table setting for one. Colin wondered, fleetingly, what price the antique china and crystal would fetch, and then turned his attention to the floor.

"Where!"

"The corner! Next to the stove!"

Colin looked around for something to sweep away the dust. He reached for the curtains, figured they might be worth something, and then found a closet on the other side of the room. There was a broom inside.

He gave Butts the torch and swept slowly, trying not to stir up the motes. After a minute, he could make out a seam in the floorboards. The seam extended into a man-sized square, complete with a recessed iron latch.

When Colin pulled up on the handle, he was bathed in a foul odor a hundred times worse than anything on his grandparent's farm. The source of the feral smell.

And it was horrible.

Mixed in with the scent of beasts was decay; rotting, stinking, flesh. Colin knelt down, gagging. It took several minutes for the contractions to stop.

"There's a ladder." Butts thrust the torch into the hole. His free hand covered his nose and mouth.

"How far down?" Colin managed.

"Not very. I can make out the bottom."

"Hey! You still down there!"

"Yes. But before you come down, you must prepare yourselves, gentlemen."

"Prepare ourselves? What for?"

"I am afraid my appearance may pose a bit of a shock. However, you must not be afraid. I promise I shall not hurt you."

Butts eyed Colin, intense. "I'm getting seriously freaked out. Let's just nick the silver knocker and —"

"Give me the torch."

Butts handed it over. Colin dropped the burning stick into the passage, illuminating the floor.

A moan, sharp and strong, welled up from the hole.

"You okay down there, mate?"

"The light is painful. I have not born witness to light for a considerable amount of time."

Butts dug a finger into his ear, scratching. "Bloke sure talks fancy."

"He won't for long." Colin sat on the floor, found the rungs with his feet, and began to descend.

The smell doubled with every step down; a viscous odor that had heat and weight and sat on Colin's tongue like a dead cat. In the flickering flame, Colin could make out the shape of the room. It was a root cellar, cold and foul. The dirt walls were rounded, and when Colin touched ground he sent plumes of dust into the air. He picked up the torch to locate the source of the voice. In the corner, standing next to the wall, was…

"Sweet Lord Jesus Christ!"

"I must not be much to look at."

That was the understatement of the century. The man, if he could be called that, was excruciatingly thin. His bare chest resembled a skeleton with a thin sheet of white skin wrapped tight around, and his waist was so reduced it had the breadth of Colin's thigh.

A pair of tattered trousers hung loosely on the unfortunate man's pelvis, and remnants of shoes clung to his feet, several filthy toes protruding through the leather.

And the face, the face! A hideous skull topped with limp, white hair, thin features stretched across cheekbones, eyes sunken deep into bulging sockets.

"Please, do not flee."

The old man held up a bony arm, the elbow knobby and ball-shaped. Around his wrist coiled a heavy, rusted chain, leading to a massive steel ball on the ground.

Colin squinted, then gasped. The chain wasn't going around this unfortunate's wrist; it went through the wrist, a thick link penetrating the flesh between the radius and ulna.

"Colin! You okay?"

Butts's voice made Colin jump.

"Come on down, Butts! I think I need you!"

"There is no need to be afraid. I will not bite. Even if I desired to do so."

The old man stretched his mouth open, exposing sticky, gray gums. Both the upper and lower teeth were gone.

"I knocked them out quite some time ago. I could not bear to be a threat to anyone. May I ask to whom I am addressing?"

"Eh?"

"What is your name, dear sir?"

Colin started to lie, then realized there was no point. He was going to snuff this poor sod, anyway.

"Colin. Colin Willoughby."

"The pleasure is mine, Mr. Willoughby. Allow me. My name is Dr. Abraham Van Helsing, professor emeritus at Oxford University. Will you allow me one more question?"

Colin nodded. It was eerie, watching this man talk. His body was ravaged to the point of disbelief, but his manner was polite and even affable.

"What year of our Lord is this, Mr. Willoughby?"

"The year? It's nineteen sixty-five."

Van Helsing's lips quivered. His sad, sunken eyes went glassy.

"I have been down here longer than I have imagined. Tell me, pray do, the nosferatu; were they wiped out in the war?"

"What war? And what is a nosfer-whatever you said?"

"The war must have been many years ago. There were horrible, deafening explosions that shook the ground. I believe it went on for many months. I assumed it was a battle with the undead."

Was this crackpot talking about the bombing from WWII? He couldn't have been down here for that long. There was no food, no water…

"Mary, Mother of God!"

Butts stepped off the ladder and crouched behind Colin. He held another torch, this one made from the broom they'd used to sweep the kitchen floor.

"Whom am I addressing now, good sir?"

"He's asking your name, Butts."

"Oh. It's Butts."

"Good evening to you, Mr. Butts. Now if I may get an answer to my previous inquiry, Mr. Willoughby?"

"If you mean World War Two, the war was with Germany."

"I take it, because you both are speaking in our mother tongue, that Germany was defeated?"

"We kicked the krauts' arses," Butts said from behind Colin's shoulder.

"Very good, then. You also related that you do not recognize the term nosferatu?"

"Never heard of it."

"How about the term vampire?"

Butts nodded, nudging Colin in the ribs with his elbow. "Yeah, we know about vampires, don't we Colin? They been in some great flickers."

"Flickers?"

"You know. Movie shows."

Van Helsing knitted his brow. His skin was so tight, it made the corners of his mouth draw upwards.

"So the nosferatu attend these movie shows?"

"Attend? Blimey, no. They're in the movies. Vampires are fake, old man. Everyone knows that. Dracula don't really exist."

"Dracula!" Van Helsing took a step forward, the chain tugging cruelly against his arm. "You know the name of the monster!"

"Everyone knows Dracula. Been in a million books and movies."

Van Helsing seemed lost for a moment, confused. Then a light flashed behind his black eyes.

"My memorandum," he whispered. "Someone must have published it."

"Eh?"

"These vampires… you say they do not exist?"

"They're imaginary, old man. Like faeries and dragons."

Van Helsing slumped against the wall. His arm jutted out to the side, chain stretched and jangling in protest. He gummed his lower lip, staring into the dirt floor.

"Then I must be the last one."

Colin was getting anxious. He needed some smack, and this old relic was wasting precious time. In Colin's pocket rested a boning knife he kept for protection. Colin'd never killed anybody before, but he figured he could manage. A quick poke-poke, and then they'd be on their way.

"I thought vampires had fangs." Butts approached Van Helsing, his head cocked to the side like a curious dog.

"I threw them in the dirt, about where you are presently standing. Knocked them out by ramming my mouth rather forcefully into this iron weight I am chained to."

"So you're really a vampire?"

Colin almost told Butts to shut the hell up, but decided it was smarter to keep the old man talking. He fingered the knife handle and took a casual step forward.

"Unfortunately, I am. After Seward and Morris destroyed the Monster, we thought there were no more. Foolish."

Van Helsing's eyes looked beyond Colin and Butts.

"Morris passed on. Jonathan and Mina named their son after him. Quincey. He was destined to be a great man of science; that was the sort of mind the boy had. Logical and quick to question. But on his sixth birthday, they came."

"Who came?" Butts asked.

"Keep him talking," Colin thought. He took another step forward, the knife clutched tight.

"The vampiri. Unholy children of the fiend, Dracula. They found us. My wife, Dr. Seward, Jonathan, Mina… all slaughtered. But poor, dear Quincey, his fate proved even worse. They turned him."

"You mean, they bit him on the neck and made him a vampire?"

"Indeed they did, Mr. Butts. I should have ended his torment, but he was so small. An innocent lamb. I decided that perhaps, with a combination of religion and science, I might be able to cure him."

Butts squatted on his haunches, less than a yard from the old man. "I'll wager he's the one that got you, isn't he?"

Van Helsing nodded, glumly.

"I kept him down here. Performed my experiments during the day, while he slept. But one afternoon, distracted by a chemistry problem, I stayed too late, and he awoke from his undead slumber and administered the venom into my hand."

"Keep talking, old man," Colin whispered under his breath. He pulled the knife from his pocket and held it at his side, hidden up the sleeve of his coat.

"I developed the sickness. While drifting in and out of consciousness, I realized I was being tended to. Quincey, dear, innocent Quincey, had brought others of his kind back to my house."

"They the ones that chained you to the wall?"

"Indeed they did, Mr. Butts. This is the ultimate punishment for one of their kind. Existing with this terrible, gnawing hunger, with no way to relieve the ache. The pain has been quite excruciating, throughout the years. Starvation combined with a sickening craving. Like narcotic withdrawal."

"We know what that's like," Butts offered.

"I tried drinking my own blood, but it is sour and offers no relief. Occasionally, a small insect or rodent wanders into the cellar, and much as I try to resist it, the hunger forces me to commit horrible acts." Van Helsing shook his head. "Renfield would have been amused."

"So you been living on bugs and vermin all this time? You can't survive on that."

"That is my problem, Mr. Butts. I do survive. As I am already dead, I shall exist forever unless extraordinary means are applied."

Butts laughed, giving his knees a smack. "It's a bloody wicked tale, old man. But we both know there ain't no such things as vampires."

"Do either of you have a mirror? Or a crucifix, perhaps? I believe there is one in the jewelry box, on the night stand in the upstairs bedroom. I suggest you bring it here."

Now they were getting somewhere. Jewelry was easy to carry, and easier to pawn. Colin's veins twitched in anticipation.

"Go get it, Butts. Bring the whole box down."

Butts nodded, quickly disappearing up the ladder.

Colin studied Van Helsing, puzzling about the best way to end him. The old man was so frail, one quick jab in the chest and he should be done with it.

"That small knife you clutch in your hand, that may not be enough, Mr. Willoughby."

Colin was surprised that Van Helsing had noticed, but it didn't matter at this point. He held the boning knife out before him.

"I think it'll do just fine."

"I have tried to end my own life many times. On many nights, I would pound my head against this steel block until bones cracked. When I still had teeth, I tried gnawing off my own arm to escape into the sunlight. Yet every time the sun set again, I awoke fully healed."

Colin hesitated. The knife handle was sweaty, uncomfortable. He wondered where Butts was.

"My death must come from a wooden stake through my heart, or, in lieu of that, you must sever my head and separate it from my shoulders." Van Helsing wiped away a long line of drool that leaked down his chin. "Do not be afraid. I am hungry, yes, but I am still strong enough to fight the urge. I will not resist."

The old man knelt, lifting his chin. Colin brought the blade to his throat. Van Helsing's neck was thin, dry, like rice paper. One good slice would do it.

"I want to die, Mr. Willoughby. Please."

Hand trembling, Colin set his jaw and sucked in air through his teeth.

But he couldn't do it.

"Sorry, mate. I —"

"Then I shall!"

Van Helsing sprung to his feet, tearing the knife away from Colin. With animal ferocity he began to hack at his own neck, slashing through tissue and artery, blood pumping down his translucent chest in pulsing waterfalls.

Colin took a step back, the gorge rising.

Van Helsing screamed, an inhuman cry that made Colin go rigid with fear. The old man's head cocked at a funny angle, tilting to the side. His eyes rolled up in their sockets, exposing the whites. But still he continued, slashing away at the neck vertebrae, buried deep within his bleeding flesh like a white peach pit.

Colin vomited, unable to pull his eyes away.

"He's going to make it," Colin thought, incredulous. "He's going to cut off his own head."

But it wasn't to be. Just as the knife plunged into the bone of his spine, Van Helsing went limp, sprawling face first onto the dirt.

Colin stared, amazed. The horror, the violence of what he just witnessed, pressed down upon him like a great weight. After a few minutes, his breathing slowed to normal, and he found his mind again.

Colin reached tentatively for the knife, still clutched in Van Helsing's hand. The gore gave him pause.

"Go ahead and keep it," Colin decided. "I'll buy another one when —"

Alarm jolted through Colin. He realized, all at once, that Butts hadn't returned. Had the bugger run off with the jewelry box?

Colin sped up the ladder, panicked.

"Butts!"

No answer.

Using the torch, he followed Butts's tracks in the dust, into the bedroom, and then back out the front door. Colin swung it open.

"Butts! Butts, you son of a whore!"

No reply.

Colin sprinted into the night. He ran fast as he could, hoping that his direction was true, screaming and cursing Butts between labored breaths.

His foot caught on a protruding root and Colin went sprawling forward, skidding on his chin, his torch flying off into the woods and sizzling out in a bog.

Blackness.

The dark was complete, penetrating. Not even the moon and stars were visible.

It felt like being in the grave.

Colin, wracked by claustrophobia, once again called out for Butts.

The forest swallowed up his voice.

Fear set in. Without a torch, Colin would never find his way back to Heysham. Wandering around the woods without fire or shelter, he could easily die of exposure.

Colin got back on his feet, but walking was impossible. On the rough terrain, without being able to see, he had no sense of direction. He tried to head back to the house, but couldn't manage a straight line.

After falling twice more, Colin gave up. Exhausted, frightened, and wracked with the pain of withdrawal, he curled up at the base of large tree and let sleep overtake him.

"This better be it, Butts."

"We're almost there. I swear on it."

Colin opened his crusty eyes, attempted to find his bearings.

He was surrounded by high grass, next to a giant elm. The sun peeked through the canopy at an angle; it was either early morning or late afternoon.

"You've been saying that for three hours, you little wank. You need a little more encouragement to find this place?"

"I'm not holding out on you, Willie. Don't hit me again."

Colin squinted in the direction of the voices. Butts and two others. They weren't street people, either. Both wore clean clothes, good shoes. The smaller one, Willie, had a bowler hat and a matching black vest. The larger sported a beard, along with a chest big as a whiskey barrel.

Butts had taken on some partners.

Colin tried to stand, but felt weak and dizzy. He knelt for a moment, trying to clear his head. When the cobwebs dissipated, he began to trail the trio.

"Tell us again, Butts, how much loot there is in this place."

"It's crammed full, Jake. All that old, antiquey stuff. I'm telling you, that jewelry box was just a taste."

"Better be, Butts, or you'll be wearing your yarbles around your filthy neck."

"I swear, Willie. You'll see. We're almost there."

Colin stayed ten yards back, keeping low, moving quiet. Several times he lost sight of them, but they were a loud bunch and easy to track. His rage grew with each step.

This house was his big break, his shot at a better life. He didn't want to share it with anybody. He may have choked when trying to off Van Helsing, but when they arrived at the house, Colin vowed to kill them all.

"Hey, Willie. Some bloke is following us."

"Eh?"

"In the woods. There."

Colin froze. The man named Jake stared, pointing through the brush.

"Who's there, then? Don't make me run you down."

"That's Colin. He came here with me."

Damned Butts.

"He knows about this place? Jake, go get the little bleeder!"

Colin ran, but Jake was fast. Within moments the bigger man caught Colin's arm and threw him to the ground.

"Trying to run from me, eh?"

A swift kick caught Colin in the ribs, searing pain stealing his breath.

"I hate running. Hate it."

Another kick. Colin groaned. Bright spots swirled in his vision.

"Get up, wanker. Let's go talk to Willie."

Jake grabbed Colin by the ear and tugged him along, dumping him at Willie's feet.

"Why didn't you tell us about your mate, Butts?"

"I thought he'd gone. I swear it."

Jake let loose with another kick. Colin curled up fetal, began to cry.

"Should we kill him, Willie?"

"Not yet. We might need an extra body, help take back some of the loot. You hear me, you drug-addled bastard? We're going to keep you around for awhile, as long as you're helpful."

Butts knelt next to Colin and smiled, brown teeth flashing. "Get up, Colin. They're not going to kill you." He helped Colin gain his footing, keeping a steady arm around his shoulders until they arrived at the house.

In the daylight, the house's aristocratic appearance was overtaken by the many apparent flaws; peeling paint, cracked foundation, sunken roof. Even the stately iron work covering the windows looked drab and shabby.

"This place is a dump." Willie placed a finger on one nostril and blew the contents of his nose onto a patch of clover.

"It's better on the inside," encouraged Butts. "You'll see."

Unfortunately, the inside was even less impressive. The dust-covered furniture Colin had pegged as antique was damaged and rotting.

"You call this treasure?" Willie punched Butts square in the nose.

Butts dropped to the floor, bleeding and hysterical.

"This is good stuff, Willie! It'll clean up nice! Worth a couple thousand quid, I swear!"

Willie and Jake walked away from Butts, and he crawled behind them, babbling.

A moment later, Colin was alone.

The pain in his ribs sharpened with every intake of breath.

If he made a run for it, they'd catch him easily. But if he did nothing, he was a dead man.

He needed a weapon.

Colin crept into the kitchen, mindful of the creaking floorboards. Perhaps the drawers contained a weapon or some kind.

"What you doing in here, eh? Nicking silver?" Jake slapped him across the face.

Colin staggered back, his feet becoming rubber. Then the floor simply ceased to be there. He dropped, straight down, landing on his arse at the bottom of the root cellar.

Everything went fuzzy, and then black.

Colin awoke in darkness.

He felt around, noticed his leg bent at a funny angle.

The touch made him cry out.

Broken. Badly, from the size of the swelling.

Colin peeled his eyes wide, tried to see. There was no light at all. The trap door, leading to the kitchen, was closed. Not that it mattered; he couldn't have climbed up the ladder anyway.

He sat up, tears erupting onto his cheeks. There was a creaking sound above him, and then a sudden burst of light.

"I see you're still alive, eh?"

Colin squinted through the glare, made out the bowler hat.

"No worries, mate. We won't let you starve to death down there. We're not barbarians. Willie will be down shortly to finish you off. Promise it'll be quick. Right Willie?"

Willie's laugh was an evil thing.

"See you in a bit."

The trap door closed.

Fear rippled through Colin, but it was overwhelmed by something greater.

Anger.

Colin had ever been the victim. From his boyhood days, being beaten by his alcoholic father, up to his nagging ex-wife, suing him into the recesses of poverty.

Well, if his miserable life was going to end here, in a foul smelling dirt cellar, then so be it.

But he wasn't going without a fight.

Colin pulled himself along the cold ground, dragging his wounded leg. He wanted the boning knife, the one he'd left curled in Van Helsing's hand.

When Jake came down to finish him off, the fat bastard was going to get a nice surprise.

Colin's hand touched moisture, blood or some other type of grue, so he knew he was close. He reached into the inky blackness, finding Van Helsing's body, trailing down over his shoulder…

"What in the hell?"

Colin brought his other hand over, groped around.

It made no sense.

Van Helsing's head, which had been practically severed from his shoulders, had reattached itself. The neck was completely intact. No gaping wound, no deep cut.

"Can't be him."

Perhaps another body had been dumped down there, possibly Butts. Colin touched the face.

No beard.

Grazing the mouth with his fingers, Colin winced and stuck a digit past the clammy lips.

It was cold and slimy inside the mouth. Revolting. But Colin probed around for almost an entire minute, searching for teeth that weren't there.

This was Van Helsing. And he had completely healed.

Which was impossible. Unless —

"Jesus Christ." Colin recoiled, scooting away from the body.

He was trapped in the dark with a vampire.

When would Van Helsing awake? Damn good thing the bloke was chained down. Who knows what horrors he could commit if he were free?

Colin repeated that thought, and grinned.

Perhaps if he helped the poor sod escape, Van Helsing would be so grateful he'd take care of the goons upstairs.

The idea vanished when Colin remembered Van Helsing's words.

All the poor sod wanted was to die. He didn't want to kill anyone.

"Bloody hell. If I were a vampire, I'd do things —"

Colin halted mid-sentence. His works were in a sardine can, inside his breast pocket. He reached for them, took out the hypo.

It just might work.

Crawling back to Van Helsing, Colin probed until he found the bony neck. He pushed the needle in, then eased back the plunger, drawing out blood.

Vampire blood.

Tying off his own arm and finding his vein in the dark wasn't a problem; he'd done it many times before.

Teeth clenched, eyes shut, he gave himself the shot.

But there was no rush.

Only pain.

The pain seared up his arm, as if someone was yanking out his veins with pliers.

Colin cried out. When the tainted blood reached his heart, the muscle stopped cold, killing him instantly.

Colin opened his eyes.

He was still in the cellar, but he could see perfectly fine. He wondered where the light could be coming from, but a quick look around found no source.

Colin stood, realizing with a start that the pain in his leg had vanished.

So, in fact, had all of his other pain. He lifted his shirt, expecting to see bruised ribs, but there wasn't a mark on them.

Even the withdrawal symptoms had vanished.

The hypodermic was still in his hand. Colin stared at it, remembering.

"It worked. It bloody well worked."

Van Helsing still lay sprawled out on the floor, face down.

Colin looked at him, and he began to drool. Hunger surged through him, an urge so completely overwhelming it dwarfed his addiction to heroin.

Without resisting the impulse, he fell to the ground and bit into the old man's neck. His new teeth tore through the skin easily, but when his tongue touched blood, Colin jerked away.

Rancid. Like spoiled milk.

A sound, from above. Colin listened, amused at how acute his hearing had become.

"All right, then. Jake, you go downstairs and mercy kill the junkie, and then we'll be off."

Mercy kill, indeed.

Colin forced himself to be patient, standing stock-still, as the trap door opened and a figure descended.

"Well well well, look who's up and about. Be brave, I'll try to make it painless."

Jake moved forward. Colin almost grinned. Big, sweating, dirty Jake smelled delicious.

"You got some fight left in you, eh?"

Colin lunged.

His speed was unnatural; he was on Jake in an instant. Even more astounding was his strength. Using almost no effort at all, he pulled the larger man to the ground and pinned down his arms.

"What the hell?"

"I'll try to make it painless," Colin said.

But from the sound of Jake's screams, it wasn't painless at all.

This blood wasn't rancid. This blood was ecstasy.

Every cell in Colin's body shuddered with pleasure; an overwhelming rush that dwarfed the feeling of heroin, a full body orgasm so intense he couldn't control the moan escaping his throat.

He sucked until Jake stopped moving. Until his stomach distended, the warm liquid sloshing around inside him like a full term embryo.

But he remained hungry.

He raced up the ladder, practically floating on his newfound power. Butts stood at the table, piling dishes into a wooden crate.

"Colin?"

Butts proved delicious, too. In a slightly different way. Not as sweet, sort of a Bordeaux to Jake's Cabernet. Colin's tongue was a wild thing. He lapped up the blood like a mad dog at a water dish, ravenous.

"What the hell are you doing?"

Colin let Butts drop, whirling to face Willie.

"Good God!"

Willie reached into his vest, removed a small Derringer. He fired twice, both shots tearing into Colin's chest.

There was pain.

But more than pain, there was hunger.

Willie turned to run, but Colin caught him easily.

"I wonder what you'll taste like," he whispered in the screaming man's ear.

Honeysuckle mead. The best of the three.

Colin suckled, gulping down the nectar as it pulsed from Willie's carotid. He gorged himself until one more swallow would have caused him to burst.

Then, in an orgiastic stupor, he stumbled from the house and into the glorious night.

No longer dark and silent and scary, the air now hummed with a bright glow, and animal sounds from miles away were clear and lovely.

Bats, chasing insects. A wolf, baying the moon. A tree toad, calling out to its mate.

Such sweet, wonderful music.

The feeling overwhelmed Colin, and he shuddered and wept. This is what he'd been searching for his entire life. This was euphoria. This was power. This was a fresh start.

"I see you have been busy."

Colin spun around.

Van Helsing stood at the entrance to the house. His right hand still gripped Colin's bone knife. His left hand was gone, severed above the wrist where the chain had bound him. The stump dripped gore, jagged white bone poking out.

Colin studied Van Helsing's face. Still sunken, still anguished. But there was something new in the eyes. A spark.

"Happy, old man? You finally have your freedom."

"Freedom is not what I seek. I desire only the redemption that comes with death."

Colin grinned, baring the sharp tips of his new fangs.

"I'll be happy to kill you, if you want."

Van Helsing frowned.

"The lineage of nosferatu ends now, Mr. Willoughby. No more may be allowed to live. I have severed the heads of the ones inside the house. Only you and I remain."

Colin laughed, blood dripping from his lips.

"You mean to kill me? With that tiny knife? Don't you sense my power, old man? Don't you see what I have become?" Colin spread out his arms, reaching up into the night. "I have been reborn!"

Colin opened wide, fangs bared to tear flesh. But something in Van Helsing's face, some awful fusion of hate and determination, made Colin hesitate.

Van Helsing closed the distance between them with supernatural speed, plunging the knife deep into Colin's heart.

Colin fell, gasping. The agony was exquisite. He tried to speak, and blood — his own rancid blood — bubbled up sour in his throat.

"Not…not…wood."

"No, Mr. Willoughby, this is not a wooden stake. It will not kill you. But the damage should be substantial enough to keep you here for an hour or so."

Van Helsing drove the knife further, puncturing the back of Colin's rib cage, pinning him to the ground.

"I have been waiting sixty years to end this nightmare, and I am tired. So very tired. With our destruction, my wait shall finally be over. May God have mercy on our souls."

Colin tried to rise, but the pain brought tears.

Van Helsing rolled off, and sat, cross-legged, on the old cobblestone road. He closed his eyes, his thin, colorless lips forming a serene smile.

"I have not seen a sunrise in sixty years, Mr. Willoughby. I remember them to be very beautiful. This should be the most magnificent of them all."

Colin began to scream.

When sunrise came, it cleansed like fire.

Mr. Pull Ups

Prior to being published, I'd often go to open mike night and read stories at a venue called Twilight Tales in Chicago. They sporadically publish short story collections, and for their latest anthology, Tales From The Red Lion, asked me for one. This is what I gave them.

HORACE CHECKED THE ADDRESS he'd written down, then walked left on Fullerton. Chicago was dark, but far from quiet. Summer meant people stayed out late. Though it neared 10pm, the sidewalks remained packed with college kids, bar hoppers, tourists, and the occasional homeless man holding out his filthy Styrofoam change cup.

Straight ahead he saw the sign; The Red Lion. Horace contemplated walking away, realized he didn't have any choices left, and entered through the narrow door.

The bar resembled a traditional English pub, or what Horace assumed one would look like. Dark, smoky, with stools older than he was and a large selection of scotch bottles lining the wall. He scanned the room, saw one man sitting alone, and approached him cautiously, the stained hardwood floor creaking beneath his feet.

"Are you Dr. Ricardo?"

The man — old, grizzled, red-eyed — glanced up at Horace over a half-empty rocks glass. He drained the remainder and stared, not saying anything.

"My name is Horace Gelt. You're a plastic surgeon, right?"

Ricardo sniffed the empty glass, looking mournful.

"I don't like talking about the past." The doctor's voice was rough, as if he didn't use often.

Horace looked around, saw that none of the bar's four customers were paying attention to him, and sat at the table across from the doctor. He leaned forward on his elbows, getting a closer look. The results didn't impress him. Sallow pallor. Sunken eyes. A fat tongue that protruded between thin lips. The doctor looked like he'd died a month ago but no one had bothered to tell him.

Again, Horace considered walking away. Then he thought about the record book, about his life's dream, and forced himself to continue.

"I was told you might be able to help me."

Ricardo's red eyes squinted. "Help you how?"

This wasn't illegal. At least, not on Horace's end. But he still felt as if he were making a drug deal, or soliciting a prostitute.

"I need…surgery."

"I need whiskey."

Horace caught the attention of the bartender and pointed at Ricardo. A moment later, the doctor had a fresh glass in front of him.

"How about you?" Ricardo asked. "Don't drink?"

"I'm training."

Ricardo's shoulders flinched in what might have been a shrug, or a snort. He sipped his new drink and leaned forward. The smell of booze coming off this guy made Horace want to recoil, but he didn't move.

"What are you? Tranny? Want me to lop off the goods, shave the Adam's apple, give you boobies?"

Horace made a face. "No."

"I'm good at it. Making little boys into little girls. Had talent. A kind of sixth sense. They shouldn't have revoked my license. I helped a lot of people."

Horace had done his research, and didn't mention the patient that had sued Ricardo out of a license. The guy had gone into surgery expecting a nose job, and had walked out with a vagina. Rhinoplasty on the wrong protrusion.

"I don't want to be a woman." Horace pulled the book page from his pocket, unfolded it carefully. Brett Gantner's smiling face stared up at him, mocking. Horace showed the doctor.

"What is that? I don't have my glasses on."

"Page 43 from the Shawley Book of World Records. Brett Gantner is the record holder for pull-ups. Seven-hundred and forty in an hour."

"I'm sure it makes his mother proud." Ricardo leaned back and sipped more booze. The bartender returned with a basket of food — fish and chips — and set it before the doctor. Without bothering to look at it Ricardo stuck his hand in and began to munch.

"I'm second place. See?" Horace pointed at the printing. "Horace Kellerman. Seven-hundred twenty-five."

"Only missed by a few," Ricardo said, his open mouth displaying half-chewed fish. "Damn shame. Maybe you should work out."

Horace bit back his reply. He worked out all the time, eight, sometimes ten hours a day. He ate all the right foods, supplemented with the right products, treated his body like a shrine. But no matter how hard he worked, how much effort he gave, he couldn't do more than seven-hundred and twenty-five pull ups. It didn't seem humanly possible.

The quest to be number one had become such an obsession with Horace that he actually flew to Phoenix to meet Brett Gantner, to see what he had that Horace didn't.

As it turned out, it was what Brett didn't have that made him the World Record holder. Brett was missing his left leg, above the knee.

"Car accident," Gantner had told him over wheat germ smoothies. "I get around okay with the prosthesis. It hasn't slowed me down any. Don't you agree, Mr. Second Place?"

Horace felt his bile rise at the memory. Gantner had beaten him not because he was the superior athlete, but because he weighed less. About fifteen pounds less. The weight of one leg.

After that meeting, Horace had gone on a crash diet. But his body fat percentage was already dangerously low, and the diet caused him to lose muscle: he couldn't even break six hundred. That led to steroid injections, which led to heart palpitations and perpetual shortness of breath, which made him give out at just over five hundred. He finally went back to his old regimen of diet and supplements, and again regularly hit the seven hundred mark, but he couldn't reach seven-forty. The last time he tried he'd hung on the bar, tears streaming down his face, putting so much effort into his last few pull ups that he shit himself. But seven twenty-five was as high as he could go.

But then inspiration struck. Epiphany. All Horace needed was a doctor who would be willing to perform the surgery. He'd been searching for two months straight, and so far had gotten nowhere. Doctor after doctor turned down his request. One had even told him his problem wouldn't be solved by plastic surgery, but by psychiatry. Asshole.

An internet forum on body modification and voluntary amputation eventually led him to Dr. Ricardo and this dinky little bar.

Horace wasn't sure if the whack-jobs on the website were telling the truth. One guy bragged he had his hands removed. If he did, how could he be using a computer keyboard? Was he typing with his face? But if the forum people were right, Dr. Ricardo might be able to help him.

"I want you to cut off my legs," Horace told the doctor.

Ricardo didn't miss a beat. He drained his whiskey and then used a fork to roughly bisect a golden fried fillet of perch. He only answered after his mouth was full of fish.

"Ten thousand. Cash. Up front."

Horace was overcome by a surge of joy, but mingled in were feelings of wariness, and oddly, remorse.

"Five beforehand, five after the operation."

Ricardo dunked a greasy bit of fish into some mayo and popped it into his mouth.

"That's fine. But why stop at your legs? Human's have lots of unnecessary body parts weighing them down. A kidney is a few ounces. You don't need all of your liver. Appendix, tonsils, gall bladder, half your stomach and a few yards of intestines — that's several pounds of material."

Horace's face fell, and he realized that the man sitting in front of him wasn't simply an incompetent drunk — he was insane. Much as he longed for the surgery, he wasn't about to subject himself to…

Ricardo's body shook, and it took Horace a moment to realize the doctor was laughing.

"Just kidding, Mr. Kellerman. Let's talk dates. The sooner you lose those legs, the sooner you can break your record. When are you free?"

Horace stared up at the operating room lights. Actually, this was a bedroom, and the lights were the kind do-it-yourselfers used when repairing drywall. He turned his gaze to Dr. Ricardo, who was fussing with a tank of anesthetic, turning the dials this way and that.

Upon arriving at the building — a crumbling brick duplex with empty beer bottles and used syringes decorating the front porch — Horace almost decided to forget the whole thing. But the inside seemed much cleaner than the exterior, and the ersatz surgery theater was extremely white and bright and smelled like lemons; courtesy of the can of disinfectant on the counter. The doctor had walked Horace through the whole procedure, and he seemed to know what he was doing. Tourniquets would restrict massive blood loss, veins and arteries would be tied off one at a time, and an extra flap of skin would be left on each leg to cover the bone and form an attractive stump, just below the buttocks.

Dr. Ricardo poured a fresh bottle of rubbing alcohol over a hacksaw blade, and Horace looked down the table at his legs, one last time.

They were good legs, as legs went. Perhaps a bit thin, but they'd treated him well for twenty-six years. Horace felt no remorse in losing them. His goal to become the world record pull-up holder was more important than petty things, like walking. And his job had amazing disability insurance. Horace would make do in a wheelchair just fine.

"Are you ready?"

Dr. Ricardo had on his surgical mask, and to Horace's eye seemed sober as a judge. Horace nodded, and Ricardo fit the gas mask over his face.

"Take a deep breath, and count backwards from one hundred…"

Horace began to count, but not from one hundred. He began at seven hundred and forty.

By the time he reached seven hundred and twenty, he was asleep.

Recovery was harder than Horace might have guessed. The pain was minimal when he was lying down, but moving, sitting, taking a shit — these all brought agony.

Ricardo had given him drugs, both oral meds and morphine to inject into his stumps. He only used them once, and as a result slept all day. That was unacceptable. Horace couldn't afford to miss a work out.

While in bed, he stuck with barbells, but after a week he was ready to hit the pull-up bar again.

The results were impressive. On his first attempt, he hit six-hundred and fifty. Not bad after major surgery and seven days on his back. His balance was a little off, but he was thrilled by the results. Ricardo had warned him against resuming activity so soon, and Horace did manage to rip a few of his stitches, but he knew — knew — that the world record would soon be his.

A month after his double amputation, Horace felt great. His stamina was back, and constantly moving around on his hands had made his arms stronger than ever. He set up his video camera, used a step ladder to reach the pull-up bar, and prepared to break the record.

The first two hundred pull-ups were candy. They came smooth, easy. Horace didn't even break a sweat.

The next two hundred were harder, but he still felt good. No leg pain, good breathing, good stamina, and a full half an hour left on the clock.

Horace paced himself for the next two hundred. Fatigue kicked in, and the familiar muscle pain. He also felt a bit of dizziness. But he still considered himself better off than he did while still having legs, and knew he'd make it no matter what.

When he reached seven hundred, he wasn't so sure anymore. He became extremely dizzy, and nauseous. While his grip was strong, the up and down movement had begun to make his stomach lurch. Perhaps it was still too soon. Perhaps he needed more recovery time, more workouts.

At seven hundred and ten Horace threw up, lost his grip, and fell hard onto his stumps, sending lightning bolts of pain up his spine that made him throw up again.

He waited a week before giving it another shot. Made it to seven hundred and thirty, then hung there for ten minutes until the time ran out, unable to do any more.

The week after that he could only manage seven hundred and twenty-five. A few days later he ran out of time at seven hundred and thirty-two. In the following month he posted numbers of 722, 734, 718, 736, 728, 731, 734, 729, and a tantalizingly frustrating 737. But he couldn't reach seven hundred and forty. No matter how hard he tried.

Depression set in. Then anger. Then a plan. Dr. Ricardo had mentioned all of the extra organs in a human being, extras that amounted to several pounds.

If Horace were five pounds less, he could easily get over 740.

When Horace rolled up to Dr. Ricardo at his usual table in the Red Lion, the good doctor was tilted back in his chair and snoring. Horace shook him, hard.

"I need help. I still weigh too much."

Ricardo took a few seconds to focus. When he spoke, the booze on his breath burned Horace's eyes.

"I remember you. Howard something, right? You needed your legs amputated for some reason. What was it again? Some sort of fetish?"

Horace roughly grabbed Ricardo by the shirt.

"You mentioned that people have extra organs. Kidney, liver, appendix, stuff like that. I want them taken out."

Ricardo blinked, and his eyes began to glaze. Horace gave him a shake.

"Remove it, Doctor. All of it."

"Remove what?"

"Everything. Take away everything I don't need. All of the extra stuff."

"You're crazy."

Horace struck the doctor, a slap than sounded like a thunder crack. The Red Lion's three patrons all turned their way. Horace ignored them, focusing on Ricardo.

"I got a disability settlement. Half a million dollars. I'll give you ten thousand dollars for each pound of me you can remove."

Ricardo nodded. "I remember now. You want to weigh less. Some sort of world record. Sure, I can help. A few yards of intestines. Half the stomach. The arms."

"No! The arms and the muscles stay. Everything else that isn't essential to life can be removed."

"When?" Dr. Ricardo asked.

Horace smiled. "Doing anything tonight?"

Horace awoke in a drug-induced haze. Thoughts flitted across his drowsy mind, including his last instructions to the doctor.

"Leave the arms, leave the eyes. Everything else goes."

Like a fire sale on body parts.

He squinted at the table next to him, saw the mason jars lined up with bits and pieces that used to be his. Pounds and pounds of flesh and organs.

Several large loops of intestines, floating in formaldehyde.

A kidney.

A chunk of liver.

So far, so good.

An appendix and a gall bladder, though Horace didn't know which was which.

A jar of fat, suctioned from his buttocks.

Part of his stomach.

His penis and testicles.

When Horace saw that, he gasped. No sound came out — in the next jar were his tongue, his tonsils, his vocal chords, and a bloody half moon that he realized was his lower jaw.

Doctor Ricardo had gone too far. The drunken bastard had turned Horace into a monster, a hideous freak.

But…Horace still had his arms. And even as maimed and mutilated as he'd become, he could still do pull-ups, still break the…

Horace's eyes focused on the last mason jar. Horace filled his remaining lung with air and screamed, and he was absolutely sure he made some noise, even though he had no ears to hear it.

The last jar contained ten fingers.

The Shed

Just about every horror mag in the world rejected this story. I'm not sure why. Sure, it's a standard EC Comics supernatural comeuppance, but I think it's fun. It eventually sold to Surreal Magazine.

"THAT'S GOTTA BE WHERE the money is."

Rory took one last hit off the Kool and flicked the butt into a copse of barren trees. The orange firefly trail arced, then died.

Phil shook his head. "Why the hell would he keep his money locked up in a backyard shed?"

"Because he's a crazy old shit. Hasn't left the house in thirty years."

The night was cold and smelled like rotting leaves. They stood at the southern side of Old Man Loki's property, just beyond a tall hedge with thorns like spikes. The estate butted up against the forest preserve on the east and Lake Fenris on the west. Due north was Fenris Road, a winding, private driveway that eventually connected with Interstate 10 about six miles up.

Phil peered through the bramble at the mansion. It rested, dark and quiet, a mountain of jutting dormers and odd angles. To Phil it looked like something that had been asleep for a long time.

"Even crazy people know about banks."

Rory clamped a hand behind Phil's head and tugged the smaller teen closer. "If it's not money, then why the hell does he got that big lock and chain on it? To protect his lawnmower?"

Phil pulled away and glanced at the shed. It stood only a few dozen yards away, the size of a small garage. The roof was tar shingles, rain-worn to gray, and dead vines partially obscured the oversized padlock and chain hanging on the door.

"Doesn't look like it's been opened in a while."

Rory grinned, his teeth blue in the moonlight. "All the more reason to open it now."

It felt all wrong, but Phil followed Rory onto the estate grounds. A breeze cooled the sweat that had broken out on his neck. Rory pulled the crowbar from his belt and swung it at a particularly tall prickle-weed.

"Yard looks like shit. Can't he pay someone to cut his goddamned grass?"

"Maybe he's dead." Phil chanced another look at the mansion. "No lights on."

"We woulda heard about it."

"Could be recent. Could be he just died, and no one found the body yet."

Phil's words bounced small and tinny in the open air. He felt a rush of exposure, as if Old Man Loki was sitting at one of the dark windows of his house and watching their every move.

"You turning chicken shit on me? Baby need his wittle bottle?"

"Shut up, Rory. What if he is dead?"

"Then he won't mind us stealing his shit. Damn — will you check out the size of that lock!"

The padlock was almost as big as Phil's head. An old-fashioned type with a key-shaped opening on its face, securing three lengths of thick, rusty chain which wrapped around the entire shed like packing tape.

"You gonna try to bust that with just a crowbar?"

"Won't know until we try." Rory raised the iron over his head, and Phil set his jaw and cringed at the oncoming sound.

The clang reverberated over the grounds like a ghost looking for someone to haunt.

"Sonuvabitch! First try!"

The lock hung open on a rusty hinge. Rory pulled it off and the chains fell to the ground in a tangle. Phil eyed the door. It was some kind of heavy wood, black as death. Next to the doorknob was a grimy brass plaque.

"Welcome," Phil read.

"How about that shit? We're invited."

Rory laughed, but Phil felt a chill stronger than the night air. He'd heard stories about Old Man Loki. Stories of how he used to live in Europe, and how he hung around with that creepy Mr. Crowley guy Ozzy sang about.

Reflexively, Phil looked over his shoulder to see if anyone was watching.

There was a light on in the house.

"Shit! Rory, there's…"

The light winked twice, then went off.

"There's what, Phil?"

"A light. On the second floor."

Rory pulled a face and made a show of squinting at the mansion. His mouth stretched open in horror, lips snicking back over years of dental neglect.

"Run, Phil! Jesus Christ! Run!"

Phil took off in a dead sprint, fighting to keep his bladder closed. He was forty yards away when he noticed Rory wasn't next to him.

That's when he heard his friend's laughter.

Phil looked back over his shoulder and saw Rory holding his stomach, guffawing so loud that it sounded like a barking dog.

Phil felt his ears burn. He took his time walking back to the shed.

"You should have seen your face!" Rory had tears in his eyes.

"Shut up, Rory. That wasn't funny."

"I swear, you ran like that during football tryouts you woulda made the team."

Phil turned away, shoving his hands in his pockets. "I wasn't scared. You told me to run, so I did."

"Okay, tough guy — prove you aren't scared." Rory pointed at the black door. "You go in first."

Phil chewed his lower lip. If he didn't go in, Rory would never let him forget it. The teasing would last for eternity.

Why the hell did he hang out with Rory anyway?

"I knew you were chicken."

"Kiss my ass, Rory."

Phil grasped the knob and pulled.

The massive door opened with a whisper, moving smoothly despite its weight. Warm, stale air enveloped Phil, and the sound of his own breathing echoed back at him.

So quiet.

Rory switched on the flashlight. The small beam played over four bare walls.

"It's empty."

"Shine the light on the floor."

The cone of light jerked to the center of the room, bending over the edge of a large, round pit and disappearing into the darkness.

"What the hell is that?"

Rory crept up to the edge, holding his flashlight out in front of him like a sword. He peered down into the pit.

"Do you smell that?"

"Yeah. Rotten eggs. I think it's coming from the hole."

Phil glanced over his shoulder again, taking a quick peek at the house.

The light was back on.

"Rory —"

"There's a rusty ladder going down."

"The light is —"

"Shh! Do you hear that?"

Both boys held their breath. There was a quick, rhythmic thumping, coming from deep within the pit.

Bump…bump…bump…bump…bump…

"What is that? Footsteps?"

…bump…bump…bump…bump…

"It's getting louder."

The sound quickened, like a Harley accelerating.

"I think something's coming up the ladder."

Phil decided he'd had enough. This was the part in the movie where the stupid kids got their guts ripped out, and he didn't want to stick around for it. He spun on his heels and hauled ass for the entrance, just in time to see a very old man with a pulpy, misshapen face slam the door closed.

Phil grabbed for the knob and pushed, but the door held firm.

"He locked us in! Old Man Loki locked us in!"

Rory kept his focus on the pit. "I think I can see some…"

A black hairy thing sprang out of the hole and yanked Rory downward. The flashlight spun in the empty air for the briefest of seconds, and then fell into the pit after Rory, the light dimming until the room was drenched in pitch black.

Phil stood stock-still in the darkness.

A minute passed.

Five.

He heard whimpering, and realized it was his own.

This can't be happening, he thought. Why was this happening?

Bump.

A sound. Coming from the pit.

The thing was climbing the ladder.

Phil forced himself to back up until he was pressed against the door.

"Hailmaryfulofgracethelordiswithyou —"

…bump…bump…bump…bump…bump…

"—blessedartthouamong —"

The noise crescendoed, then stopped.

The silence was horrible.

Phil couldn't see anything, but he could feel the presence of something large and warm coming towards him. Something that smelled like rotten eggs and wet dog.

He screamed, and kept screaming when it wrapped its prickly tentacles around his face, a thousand hooks digging in and pulling. Phil's hands shot up to push the pain away, and similar barbs shot into his palms.

His screaming stopped when the barbs filled his open mouth.

Then, with a quick tug, Phil was dragged down into the pit.

There was a sensation of falling, skin burning and tearing away, consciousness blurring into a darkness as complete as the one that surrounded him.

And suddenly, Phil was watching a movie in his head. A shaky, black and white film of him and Rory breaking into Old Man Loki's mansion. Rory had the crowbar, and they used it on Loki, breaking his bones, bashing his face, demanding his money. Old Man Loki moaning the whole time, "The shed! The shed!" Repeating it over and over, even when Rory jammed the crowbar down the old man's throat.

The movie abruptly cut to Phil as a much older man, clad in an orange prison uniform. He was strapped to a chair, a guard swabbing electrolyte on his temples and his left leg. The switch was thrown and Phil's blood began to boil within his veins, every nerve locked in agony.

Phil watched the prison doctor pronounce him dead, watched as his own soul left his body, transporting him to Loki's estate.

A terrifying déjà vu ensued as he viewed himself acting out the same scenario he'd experienced only moments ago. Breaking into the shed — the thing grabbing Rory — getting dragged into the pit —

When Phil finally caught up with himself, he discovered he was in a small, stone dungeon.

Next to him, a forty-year-old version of Rory was chained to a medieval torture rack, naked and stretched out until his shoulders had separated. His body was a haven of slithering, spiny worms, which burrowed underneath his skin.

"Hi, buddy." Rory offered a bloody smile, his teeth filed down to exposed nerves. "Be nice to have some company."

Phil remembered that Rory had been executed eight years prior.

"What's going on? What happened to the shed?"

Rory whimpered, a worm tunneling into his ear. "Old Man Loki didn't have no shed. That's why we beat him to death. Kept saying it over and over, when we asked him where his money was."

"But we just broke into the shed."

The worm stitched out of Rory's nose, trailing crimson mucus. "The shed is the doorway to this place. I remember breaking in, too. Right after I died."

Phil squeezed his eyes shut. His temples still burned where the electrodes had been attached. But the memory of his own death dwarfed the fear he felt right now.

He opened his eyes and tried to bolt, panic surging through him. But, like Rory, he found himself tied to a rack. His eyes fell upon a fire pit, where a dozen branding irons glowed white.

A squat, hairy man entered the room. He had sharp horns sticking out of his head where ears would normally be, and his skin was a dull shade of crimson.

He picked up a hot iron and gave Phil a fanged grin. "Welcome to eternity, Phil. Let's get started."

Them's Good Eats

I had this terrible little story idea stuck in my head for almost twenty years, and finally put it down on paper for the collection Gratia Placente published by Apex Digest. One of my rare jumps into science-fiction, though this is more horrific black humor than sci-fi.

"DAMN, JIMMY BOB, THESE are damn good cracklins."

Earl's face — wrinkled and sporting three days' worth of gray whiskers — glistened with a fine sheen of lard. A hot Georgia breeze blew smells of tilled earth and manure, but the overpowering scent was pig skins, fresh from the deep fryer. Earl eagerly reached for the plate Jimmy Bob held out, a pile of pork rinds stacked onto a grease-soaked paper towel.

"Thanks, Earl," Jimmy Bob said. "Got me a new way of preparation."

"Tell me." Earl scooped two more into his mouth and chewed so fast he risked a tongue severing. "I been eating cracklins since I was weened off the tit, ain't never had any this good before."

"It's a secret."

"Chicken shit. Tell me or I'll beat it out of you."

Jimmy Bob snorted, a sound not unlike a fat bullfrog croaking. He slapped Earl on the back, hard enough to make the old man's dentures slup off his gums and out of his mouth. The teeth bounced onto the dirty wooden porch.

Jimmy Bob stared down at Earl, a man half his weight and forty years his senior, and smiled big.

"Well, I wouldn't want to take a beating, Earl. The secret, my good buddy, is skinning the piggies while they still alive and kicking."

"Doe thip?" Earl said. He'd been going for "no shit" but hadn't stuck his teeth back in yet.

Jimmy Bob held up his hand, preacherman-style. "That's the God's truth, Earl. Something about them porkers struggling and squealing before they die, tenderizes their skins and imparts that extra tangy sensation. Longer they struggle, tastier they get."

Earl wiped his falsies on his bib overalls and slurped them into his eating hole.

"You're putting me on," Earl said.

"You got a dead spider in your bridgework, Earl."

Earl picked out a dry Daddy Longlegs and flicked it over his shoulder, then repeated his prior statement.

"I'm honest as the day is scorchin', Earl. Ain't just the cracklings, neither. Bacon comes out so juicy it melts in your mouth, and you can cut the pork chop with a spoon they're so tender."

"Now I know you're funning me, Jim Bob. Ain't no way you can carve up a hog while it's still kicking. It would run like the dickens, and the blood would make it all slippery."

"I built me a hog rack, out of wood. Keeps it locked in place while I do the carving. Put on the salt and vinegar while they're still wiggling, so it soaks in. Louder then hell, but you're tasting the results. Want another one?"

"Hell yeah."

Earl was reaching for more when the big silver saucer flew out from behind a fluffy white cloud, situated itself over Jimmy Bob's porch, and hit the two men with a beam of light.

There was a moment of searing hot pain, then darkness.

Jimmy Bob awoke on his back. His head hurt. His last memory was of Earl, who had come over with a mason jar full of his rotgut corn shine, and he figured he had himself a granddaddy hangover. But Jimmy Bob couldn't remember drinking any of the shine. All he could recall was eating cracklins.

He stared up at the ceiling, and realized it wasn't his ceiling. It was silver, and curvy.

Then he noticed he was naked. Even worse, Earl was on the floor next to him, similarly declothed.

"Oh sweet Jesus, how drunk did we get?"

Jimmy Bob reached for his nether regions, but nothing down there seemed to ache from use. Thank the lord for that.

He sat up, the metal floor smooth and cool under his buttocks, and looked around. The room they were in was all silver. No furniture. No carpet. No doors or windows. No lights, even though he could see just fine. It was like being inside a giant metal can.

Then Jimmy Bob jerked, remembering the spaceship in the sky, the blinding bright light.

An unidentified flying saucer. A UFO.

Lordy, him and Earl had been ubducticated.

He nudged his old buddy.

"Earl! Get your ass up. We're in some shit."

Earl didn't move.

"Goddammit, Earl!"

He shoved Earl again. Earl remained still. Jimmy Bob noticed his friend wasn't breathing, and had taken on an unhealthy bluish tint.

Jimmy Bob knew about CPR from watching TV, and much as he didn't want to touch lips with the older man, especially since they both were nekkid, he forced Earl's mouth open and blew hard down the old geezer's throat.

His breath didn't go nowhere, no matter how hard he gusted, and Jimmy Bob squinted down and saw the big bulge in Earl's neck.

Earl has swallowed his falsies.

Jimmy Bob stuck his finger into Earl's mouth, tried to fish the teeth out, but they were down too far and Earl's throat was cold and slimy and disgusting and after ten or so seconds Jimmy Bob realized he didn't like Earl that much to begin with so he took his hand back and wiped the spit off on Earl's thick tangle of gray chest hairs.

Jimmy Bob wondered if he should say some words, but he didn't know no prayers and then he got really scared because he was alone — all alone — in an alien spaceship, so he tried to give Earl CPR again.

It didn't work no better the second time, and then Jimmy Bob got up and started pacing back and forth, terrible thoughts bouncing around in his bean.

He'd seen all the movies. Starship Troopers. Independence Day. War of the Worlds. Alien. Predator. Alien vs. Predator. No good ever came out of being abducticated. The aliens were always bad guys who wanted to take over the world or eat people's guts or hunt humans for sport or get folks pregnant in their bellies or give painful probes up the brown place.

Jimmy Bob didn't want none of that to happen to him. He wondered why those guys that made movies never made one about an alien who came to earth and gave a lucky farmer a brand new plow. He'd watch that on the cable, for sure. But instead it was always death rays and cut-off heads.

Jimmy Bob yelled for help, loud as he could, so loud his ears hurt. No one answered.

He ran to the nearest wall, pushed against it. The surface was slippery, almost like it was covered with a fine layer of grease. He grunted with effort, but the metal was solid, immobile. Jimmy Bob walked around the room, trying to find some sort of seam, some sort of crease. Everything he touched was rock solid and perfectly smooth.

Jimmy Bob sat in the center of the room and hugged his knees to his chest. He wondered if they was still flying over earth, or if they was already in another universe, about to land on some weird planet with rivers made of acid and trees that looked like rib bones. He wondered what the aliens looked like. Tall and gray with big glowin eyes? Green and scaly with sharp fangs? Or did they have fish heads, like that commander guy in Star Wars? And what did they want from him?

Was it the butt probes?

He looked at Earl. Earl got off easy, the lucky bastard. Maybe Jimmy Bob could fish out those false teeth and choke on them himself. Not a bad idea, considering. He began to crawl towards his dead friend when he heard a buzzing sound.

It sounded like a pissed off hornet, and seemed to come from everywhere at once. Jimmy Bob looked around, tried to find the source, and noticed a pinpoint of white light on the wall. First it was a real tiny, and then it grew into a larger and larger circle until it was the size of a manhole cover.

Death ray.

Jimmy Bob crabbed backwards, trying to get away from the death ray, but there was no place to go. He retreated until he was up against the opposite wall, fists and teeth clenched, waiting for the final ZAP that would make his skeleton light up then turn him into cigarette ashes.

The ZAP didn't come. In fact, the more he looked at the light, the more Jimmy Bob began to think it looked more like a door than a death ray.

Was this some kind of alien trick? If he went through the door, would he be hunted down like a deer, aliens in big orange coats chasing him through the woods? Would he have to fight in some alien gladiator battle? Would he be forced to squat on a probe the size of a fire plug?

Maybe none of those things. Maybe this was a chance to escape.

Jimmy Bob took a quick look at lumpy-throat Earl, then sprang to his feet and ran for the circle of light. He was almost upon it when something flew out the doorway at him.

It was large, and red, and hit him in the chest with the force of a football tackle. Jimmy Bob tumbled backwards, the weight of the thing pinning him down, blanketing him in a warm, wet goo.

Jimmy Bob screamed.

The thing on top of him also screamed, and Jimmy Bob bucked and pushed and got it off and scurried away, his eyes focusing on a creepy crimson alien, completely hairless, dripping head to toe with some kind of blood-like fluid.

No, it wasn't blood-like. It was actual blood.

And the creature wasn't an alien.

"No more," it whimpered. Its voice was thick and wet.

Like Jimmy Bob, it was naked. A man. A human man. Or what was left of one. Every square inch of his body was bleeding, thick and viscous like he'd been dunked in raspberry preserves. The man lay on his back, trembling, red smudges coating the floor where he had rolled.

"Hey buddy, you okay?" Jimmy Bob asked, knowing how ridiculous it must have sounded.

"No more…please…no more…"

Jimmy Bob chewed his lower lip and looked the man over. There didn't seem to be any main wound. Instead, his whole body was a wound. He hadn't been skinned — Jimmy Bob didn't see any exposed muscle or fat on the man. No, this man looked more like he'd been worked over with a cheese grater. Every square inch was raw and bloody. Even his eyelids looked scraped.

"What happened to you?" Jimmy Bob asked.

The man's chest rose and fell. "Kill me," he said.

"Who are you?"

"Please…kill me. I tried to…kill myself…by breaking open my head…but I always knock myself out first."

The bleeding man lifted his head then rammed it viciously into the floor, making a hollow pinging sound.

"Are we on an alien ship?" Jimmy Bob asked.

The man's eyes opened, startlingly white compared to the redness of his body. His eyes locked on Jimmy Bob.

"I'm begging you…kill me…"

Jimmy Bob crawled over to the man.

"Answer my questions."

"I want to die."

Jimmy Bob slapped him. The man howled like a dog with a toothache.

"Keep it together. I need to know what's going on."

Rather than reply, the man began to sob. Jimmy Bob slapped him once more. And a few times after that. It was like hitting a wet fish.

"Damn it, tell me what's going on! Answer me!"

"I'll…I'll tell you…if you promise to kill me after."

Jimmy Bob considered it. He'd never killed a man before, but if anyone needed killing, this poor bastard did. He figured he could snap his neck, if'n he got a good hold of it. Couldn't be any harder than breaking hog necks, which he did with tasty regularity.

"Deal. Now tell me what's happening."

"Appealing. It's appealing."

The man began to sob again, and Jimmy Bob smacked him on the chest to get his attention.

"What's appealing?"

"They…pulled them all off."

"You're not making sense. Start at the beginning."

"They…caught me when I was in the woods…hunting coon.

Ship. A big white light. At first I didn't know where I was…didn't know what had happened. They left me in this room. I don't know…for how long. But then…they came."

"Who?"

"Aliens. Short…like midgets. Big heads and tiny mouths. Scales instead of skin. They took me…took me to the room and…"

The man began to cry again. Jimmy Bob dug his fingernails into the man's shoulder to help him focus.

"And what?"

"And they put me…in the machine. It…it scraped my skin off."

"But why? Why torture you? Did they ask you questions?"

"No."

"Were you," Jimmy Bob winced, "probed?"

"They…they kept me in there…just long enough."

"Long enough for what?"

"For me to bleed. Then they took me here. I thought it was over. But they came back. They always come back."

"For what? What do they want?"

The buzzing sound began again, and the pinpoint light on the wall began to grow.

"Kill me! You promised!"

Jimmy Bob backed up to the other side of the room, fear oozing out of every pore. Two figures stepped through the light. They were short, green, with heads like watermelons and tiny little black eyes. True to form, they wore little silver suits, and held little silver ray guns.

"Get away from me, you stinking space iguanas!" yelled Jimmy Bob.

They shot their little guns, and Jimmy Bob was paralyzed where he stood, his muscles locked by an unpleasant tingle of electricity. Space tasers. He strained to move but couldn't.

The aliens approached, walking in a strange, waddling gait, as if their oversized heads were threatening to tip them over. Jimmy Bob noticed childlike, almost delicate, noses and mouths on their broad faces, and their black rat eyes had a glint of red to them. He watched as they went to Earl, poked him with their clawed fingers, and then spoke rapidly to each other in some foreign space language that sounded a lot like that singing chipmunk cartoon. They didn't look happy.

Jimmy Bob tried to speak, but his jaw felt like it had been wired shut and he could only manage a few grunts. If only he could talk, maybe he could get out of this. Reason with them. Or bribe them. Maybe they'd like Jimmy Bob's complete collection of state quarters, each coin in mint condition and sealed in a protective plastic case. Or maybe they'd want his grandma's antique sterling silver serving set, complete except for a single salad fork that he broke adjusting the carb on his Chevy.

Jimmy Bob tried to say, "Silverware," but only a grunt came out. They didn't seem impressed. Their little iguana claws latched onto his wrists and pulled him forward with amazing ease. Jimmy Bob noticed for the first time that he was floating a few inches about the floor, and they tugged him along as if he were a balloon. The aliens maneuvered him through the opening, and he caught a last glimpse of his bleeding cellmate, who had resumed bashing his own head into the floor.

Jimmy Bob was pulled through a large metal tube, first right, then left, then down a gradual incline sort of like those tube slides at Chuck E. Cheese. The aliens kept chittering to each other, and one of them patted Jimmy Bob on the thigh and smiled.

Maybe this will be okay, Jimmy Bob thought. Maybe they won't hurt me.

A few seconds later, Jimmy Bob was placed into a large upright box, which closed around him like a coffin and dipped him into complete darkness.

Then, agony.

At first, it felt like being burned alive. But there wasn't any heat. The pain was the same, though, every nerve in his body firing at once. It was as if someone was using a power sander on his body, scraping every inch from head to toe. There was even a probe, but it felt more like a giant drill bit, coring out his unhappy place. Jimmy Bob screamed in his throat, screamed until he was sure it bled like the rest of him.

After an unknown amount of time, Jimmy Bob passed out.

He came to while being pulled back through the hallway, and then shot, like a rocket, back through the doorway and back into the original room. He hit the floor with a wet splat, and rolled onto his belly, the pain driving him mad, eating him alive. He was no longer frozen by the ray gun taser, but he dared not twitch because even the slightest movement was torture.

"Kill me," someone said.

He glanced right, his eyes already crusting with dried blood, and saw his cellmate.

Jimmy Bob asked, "Why are they doing this?" but it came out garbled — even his tongue had been scraped raw.

"Been here…weeks…maybe months. They use…an IV…so we don't die…"

"Why?" Jimmy Bob asked again.

"Snacks."

Jimmy Bob wasn't sure he heard right.

"What?"

"We're snacks."

"How? They suck our blood?"

His cellmate sobbed.

"Scabs. They wait until we heal, then peel off the scabs and eat them. Like beef jerky."

Jimmy Bob moaned. Those little iguana bastards were going to wait until his scoured body began to scab over, and then tear off the scabs? He couldn't bear it.

"A dozen of them come in with pliers," the man said, even though Jimmy Bob didn't want to hear no more, "They peel off every last piece. They're slow eaters, too."

"Jesus, no."

"And…" the man became full blown hysterical, "they dip us in salt and vinegar so we taste better!"

Jimmy Bob squeezed his eyes shut. He could already feel the sores on his body begin to heal, begin to clot. The light on the wall appeared, and began to get bigger.

"You promised to kill me!" the man shrieked at Jimmy Bob.

A bunch of space iguanas filed in, chirping at each other like Alvin and the band, snapping gleaming metal pincers. One of them held up a bottle of hot sauce.

"NOOOOOO!" Jimmy Bob began to scream before the space taser froze his vocal parts.

Then the snacking began.

Jimmy Bob hadn't thought his pain could get any worse.

But it did.

First Time

I wrote this when I turned thirty. I never was able to sell it, perhaps because it's a bit too obvious. This is also one of the few shorts I've ever written with an omniscient narrator, popping into the heads of more than one person in the same scene.

"WERE YOU NERVOUS YOUR first time?"

Robby didn't break stride. He could clearly remember that smelly hotel room, Father paying the money, the girl naked and waiting.

"A little," he answered his brother. "Everyone's nervous the first time."

"I guess I am too. A little."

Pete looked it. Thirteen and small for his age, lost in one of Robby's old T-shirts. But that's how Robby was at thirteen, walking into that room. And ten minutes later, he walked out a man, ready to take on the whole damn world. Robby wished their father was there, then cursed himself for the thought. He was the man of the family now, since Father had gone away. It was his job to initiate Pete.

"How long do I have?" Pete asked.

"Long as it takes. Once you pay, you're there 'till it's done."

"Is it a lot different from animals?" They lived on a farm, so both boys had a lot of experience with animals.

"A lot different. Think about it. A real woman, like in one of those magazines. Naked and all yours. Maybe I'll even do one too."

"Really?" Robby knew he wouldn't. They didn't have enough money for two. Besides, Robby did it enough at home. He was eighteen, and picked up women whenever he liked. His boyish good looks, just this side of full-blown manhood, attracted girls like flies to compost. Robby was a real lady killer.

"Are we almost there Robby?"

"Almost."

The neighborhood was seedy, all cracked sidewalks and graffiti and urine soaked winos. It hadn't changed at all since Father brought him here, those years ago. He could still picture the face of his first girl — oval, with high cheek bones and bright red lipstick that made her mouth look like a wound. Her eyes were vacant, wasted on some drug, but not so wasted that she didn't moan when he stuck it in.

You never forget your first.

The boys cut through an alley, rats scurrying out of their path. Pete moved a little closer to his brother. He was nervous, but didn't want to show it. Robby was his hero. He wanted to make him proud. He relished every story Robby told him about his times with women, forever caught between awe and envy. Now it was his turn.

"Did Father watch you?" Robby asked.

"Yeah. He watched. Afterward he said he was real proud of how I gave it to her."

Pete's face bunched up.

"I don't remember Father so good. Before they took him away."

"Father's a great man. We'll see him again some day. Don't worry."

Pete looked up at his older brother. "Will you watch me, Robby?"

"If you want me too."

"I want you too."

"I will then. Here we are."

The alley door was brown and rotten. Robby kicked it twice.

"I got money!" That was what Father had said five years ago, and Robby's chest swelled saying the same words. After a moment the door inched open. A red eye peered through the crack.

"You the ones called earlier?"

The boys nodded.

"You cops?" Pete giggled.

"Hell no, we ain't cops!"

The door opened, revealing a short, thick man with hairy arms.

"Thirty bucks."

Robby took six fives from his pocket and laid them out one at a time. They quickly disappeared into the man's dirty jeans.

"You or the kid?"

"It will be Pete tonight," Robby said.

They followed the man through a hall lit with single bare bulb, down some stairs, and into a basement thick with mold. Against the wall, naked and waiting, was the girl. She was fatter than Robby's first one, with dirty knees and smeared lipstick and so much blue eye shadow she looked like a peacock. But there was some life in her eyes, a tiny spark that hadn't been totally dulled by the drugs.

"Hey, hey guys," she said, her voice slurring. "Untie me and we can party, okay?"

"You bring your own?" the man asked Pete.

Pete nodded, patting his pocket. The man spit on the floor, and then left the basement.

"What's you name, beautiful?" Robby asked. He put a hand on her cheek and she nuzzled against his touch.

"Candy. Can you untie my hands? I'm better when I can use my hands."

"Hi Candy, this is Pete. You're gonna be his first."

"Hey, Petey," she flashed him a whore's smile, a curved mouth without any trace of warmth. "Come get some Candy, baby."

Pete licked his lips and gave his brother a glance. Robby nodded his approval, and backed away.

"She's all yours, Pete. Do her good."

Pete looked at her, hanging there by her wrists, and couldn't believe this was really happening. It was almost as if he wasn't there, but rather above himself someplace, watching everything going on.

She protested when she saw the knife. The protest was soon replaced by crying. Pete made some tentative cuts at first. Her screams were so loud that it freaked him out.

"No one can hear," Robby assured him. "Just mind the blood."

Getting brave, Pete jabbed deeper and harder. It was just like Robby had told him. She cried. She begged. And every sound made Pete hate her even more. The excitement built and built, and he cut faster and harder, and finally he lost control and stuck the knife in her neck and there was a gurgling choking sound and then she wasn't moving.

Pete took a step back, his heart hammering, the thick smell of blood filling his nostrils. He was excited, but disappointed that it ended so fast. Robby patted his shoulder.

"Nice job. I'm proud of you. Father would be proud too."

"It wasn't…too quick?" Robby laughed.

"The first one is always quick. You'll be able to last longer the more you do it."

The door opened behind them. It was the short man, with a mop and bucket. Pete looked at the dead girl, wishing he could take her home as a trophy. He settled on the left breast, putting it in a plastic bag we brought with for the purpose.

"A breast man," Robby laughed. "Just like Father."

"When can I do it again, Robby?"

"Whenever you want. I'll teach you how to get women, just like Father taught me. It gets more and more fun each time. Remember to wipe off your knife. We'll ditch it down a sewer grate on the way home."

Robby made a show of eyeing the body.

"Good work. You really wrangled some screams out of her. Didn't I tell you it was more fun than slaughtering a pig?"

"A lot more fun. I'm gonna write Father in prison, tell him I finally did it."

"Good idea. He'd like that. Now I think you deserve — some ice cream!"

Pete grabbed his older brother and hugged him.

"Thanks, Robby."

Robby took a deep breath, filling his lungs with pride. He thought about Tommy and Ed and Jasper, all younger than Pete, all anxious for their first times.

"After the ice cream, let's tell our brothers. Tommy's turn is coming up in October."

"He's gonna love it," Pete said, and the two of them walked out of the basement, through the building, and down the alley, searching the seedy neighborhood for a place that sold soft serve.

Forgiveness

The toughest horror magazine to get into is Cemetery Dance, and I sent them a few things before they finally published this one. Odd thing though, they never gave me a formal acceptance, or a contract, or a check. I only knew it saw print because some guy at a writing convention brought a copy up to me to sign.

THE WOMAN PUTTING THE tube into my penis has cold hands.

She's younger than I am — everyone is younger than I am — but she betters me in the wrinkle department; scowl lines, frown lines, deep-set creases between the eyebrows. The first woman to touch my peter in fifty years, and she has to be a gargoyle.

I close my eyes, wince as the catheter inches inward, my nostrils dilating with ammonia and pine-lemon disinfectant and something else that I knew so well.

Death.

Death has many smells. Sometimes it smells like licking copper pennies out of used public washrooms. Other times it smells like cold cuts pickled in vinegar, left in the sun to rot.

On me it smells sour. Gassy and bloated and ripe.

"There you go, Mr. Parson." She pulls down my gown and covers me with the thin blanket. Her voice is perfunctory, emotionless.

She knows who I am, what I've done.

"I'd like to talk to someone."

"Who?"

"A priest."

She purses her lips, lines deepening around her mouth in cat whisker patterns.

"I'll see what I can do."

The nurse leaves.

I stare at the white cinder block walls over the hump of my distended stomach. Edema. My body can no longer purge itself of fluid, and I look ten months pregnant. The morphine drip controls the worst of the pain, the sharp stuff. But the dull, cold ache of my insides rotting away can't be dampened by any drug.

The room is cool, dry, quiet. No clock in here. No TV. No window. The door doesn't have bars, but it is reinforced with steel and only opens with a key.

As if escape is still an option.

Time passes, and I go into my mind and tried to figure out what I want to say, how to say it. So many things to straighten out.

The next thing I know the priest is sitting beside the bed, nudging me awake.

"You wanted to see me, Mr. Parson?"

Young, blond, good-looking, his Roman collar starched and bright. Youthful idealism sparkles in his eyes.

Life hasn't knocked the hope out of him yet.

"Do you know who I am, Father?"

He smiles. Even white teeth. Little points on the canines.

"I've been informed."

I watch his face. "Then you know what I've done?"

"Yes."

I see patience, serenity. Old crimes don't shock people— they have the emotional impact of lackluster history books.

But the crimes are still fresh in my mind. They're always fresh. The images. The sounds.

The tastes.

"I've killed people, Father. Innocent people."

"God forgives those who seek forgiveness."

My tongue feels big in my mouth. I speak through trembling lips. "I've been locked up in here since your parents were babies."

He rests his elbows on his knees, leaning in closer. His hair smells like soap, and he's recently had a breath mint.

"You've spent most of your life in this place, paying your debt to society. Isn't it time to pay your debt to the Lord?"

And what of the Lord's debt to me?

I cough up something wet and bloody. The priest gives me a tissue from the bedside table. I ball it up in my fist, squeeze it tight.

"What's your name, Father?"

"Bob."

"Father Bob — I've got cancer turning my insides into mush. The pain, sometimes, is unbearable. But I deserve that and more for what I've done."

I pause, meet his eyes.

"You know I was once a priest."

He pats my hand, his fingers brushing my IV.

"I know, Mr. Parson."

Smug. Was I that smug, when I was young?

"I'm in here for killing twelve people."

Another pat on the hand.

"But there were more than twelve, Father."

Many more. So many more.

His complacent smile slips a notch.

"How many were there, Mr. Parson?"

The number is intimate to me, something I haven't ever shared before.

"One hundred and sixty-seven."

The smile vanishes, and he blinks several times.

"One hundred and —"

I interrupt. "They were children, mostly. War orphans. No one ever missed them. I'd pick them up at night, offer them money or food. There was a place, out by the docks, where no one could hear the screams. Do you know how I killed them?"

A head shake, barely perceptible.

"My teeth, Father. I tied them up — tied them up naked and filthy and screaming — and I kept biting them until they died."

The priest turns away, his face the color of the walls.

"Mr. Parson, I…"

The memories fill my head; the dirty, bloody flesh, the piercing cries for help, the wharf rats scurrying over my feet and fighting for scraps…

"It isn't easy, Father, to break the skin. Human teeth aren't made for tearing. You have to nip with the front incisors until you make a small hole, then clench down hard and tug back, putting your neck and shoulders into it. It took a long time. Sometimes hours for them to die."

I sigh through my teeth.

"I'd make them eat bits of themselves…"

The priest stands, but I grab his wrist with the little strength I had left. He can't leave, not yet.

"Please, Father. I need Penance."

He takes a breath, stares at me. Watching him regain composure is like watching a drunk wake up in a strange bed. He manages it, finally, but some of that youthful idealism is gone.

"Are you sorry for what you've done?"

"I'm sorry, Father." The tears come, a rusty faucet that has gone unused for years. "I'm sorry and I beg for God's forgiveness. I'm…so…alone. I've been so alone."

He touches my face as if petting a crocodile, but I'm grateful for the touch.

The tears don't last long. I swat them away with tissue.

Together we say the Act of Contrition.

The words are familiar on my tongue, but my conscience isn't eased.

There's more.

"Rest now, Mr. Parson." He makes the sign of the cross on my forehead with his thumb, but his eyes keep flitting to the door, the way out.

"Father…"

"Yes?"

I have to proceed carefully here. "How strong is your faith?"

"Unshakable."

"What if…what if you no longer needed faith?"

"I will always need faith, Mr. Parson."

For the first time since his arrival, I allow myself a small smile. "Not if you have proof."

"What do you mean?"

"If there is proof that God exists, you'd no longer need faith. You would have knowledge— tangible knowledge."

He narrows his eyes. "You have this proof? A lapsed priest?"

"Defrocked, Father. My title was stripped."

"Of course it was. You killed…"

I sigh, wet and heavy. "You misunderstand, Father Bob. They didn't defrock me because of the murders. My vocation was taken away from me because I knew too much."

I lower my voice so he must lean closer to hear me.

"I KNOW God exists, Father."

The priest frowns, folds his arms.

"The great mystery of Faith is that we accept God without knowing. If God wanted us to truly know, he would appear on earth and touch us."

I raise my hand, point at him.

"You're wrong there, Father. He has come down and touched us. Touched me." This is the tricky part. "Would you like to see the proof?"

I almost shout with glee when he nods his head.

"Sit, Father Bob. This story takes a while."

He sits beside me, his face a mixture of interest and wariness.

My mouth is dry. I take a sip from a cup of tepid water, soak my tongue.

"Fresh from the Seminary, I was sent to Western Samoa, a group of islands in the South Pacific. It's tropical paradise, the population predominantly Christian. A garden of Eden, one of the most beautiful places on earth. Except for the hurricanes. I arrived after a particularly devastating storm wiped out most of Apia, the capitol."

It comes back in fragments, a series of faded snapshots. After a twenty hour plane ride, I landed in little more than a field. The island air and deep blue beaches were a stark contrast to the wholesale destruction throughout the land. I saw livestock rotting in trees. Overturned cars with little brown arms jutting out crookedly beneath them. Roofs in the middle of streets, and jagged pipes planted in piles of rubble where schools once stood.

Worst of all was the constant, keening sob that hung over the city like a cloud.

So many ruined lives.

"It looked like God had smashed His mighty fist down on that country. How could He have allowed this? I had to assist in the amputation of a man's legs, without anesthetic because there was none left. I had to help mothers bury their babies using gnarled traffic signs to dig graves. I gave so much blood I almost died myself."

"Natural disasters are a test of one's faith."

I shake my head.

"It didn't test mine. I was sure in my faith, like you are. But it made me question God's intent."

"We cannot question God, Mr. Parson."

"But we do anyway, don't we?"

I sip more water before I continue.

"In Western Samoa, I did God's work. I helped to heal. To rebuild. I restarted the parish. I preached to these poor, proud people about God's grace, and they believed me. Things slowly got back to normal. And then the murders began."

I close my eyes and see the first body, as if it is in the room with me now. The eyes jut out of the bloody, ruined face like two golf balls pushed into the meat of a watermelon. The flesh is peeled away, in some places exposing pink bone. A rat pokes its greasy head out of a lacerated abdomen and squeals in gluttonous delight.

"Every seven days, another mutilated body was discovered. The police didn't seem to care. Neither did my congregation. They accepted it like they accepted the hurricane; sad but unavoidable."

Father Bob folds his arms, eyebrows furrowing.

"Were you killing those people, Mr. Parson?"

"No…it turned out to be one of my parishioners. A fisherman with a wife and three kids. He came to me just after he butchered one — came into my Confessional drenched in blood, bits of tissue sticking to his nails and teeth. Begged me for forgiveness."

The man had been short, painfully thin for a Samoan. His eyes were the eyes of the damned, flickering like windblown candles, both insane and afraid.

"He claimed he was a victim of a curse. A curse that had been plaguing his island for millennia."

"Did you dismiss his superstitions?"

"At first. While Christians, the islanders had a distant connection to paganism, sometimes fell back to it. I tried to convince him the curse wasn't real, to turn himself in. I begged him that God didn't want any more killing."

I was so earnest, so full of the Word. Convinced I was doing God's work.

"He laughed at me. He said that killing is exactly what God wanted."

The priest shakes his head. He speaks with the sing-song voice of a kindergarten teacher. "God is all-loving. Killing is a result of free-will. We had the paradise of Eden, and chose knowledge instead of bliss."

I scowl at him.

"God created mankind knowing that we'd fall from grace. It's like having a child, knowing a child will be hungry, and then punishing the child for that hunger."

Father Bob leans in, apparently flustered. "God's grace…"

"God has no grace," I spit. "He's a vengeful, vindictive God. A sadist, who plays with mankind like a child pulling the wings off of flies. Samoa was Eden, Father. The real Eden, straight out of the Bible. The murderer, he showed me a mark on his scalp."

I lift up my bangs, reveal the Mark at my hairline.

"Witness, Father Bob! Proof that God truly exists!"

The priest opens his mouth. It takes a moment before words came out.

"Is that…?"

I nod. I feel inner strength, the strength that had forsaken me so long ago.

"It's the Mark of Cain, given to the son of Adam when he slew Abel. But the Bible was inaccurate on that point — Cain didn't wander the earth forever, but his curse did, passed on from man to man for thousands of years. Passed on to me from the murderer in Samoa."

The Mark grows warm on my head, begins to burn.

"This is your proof of God, Father."

He stands abruptly, his chair tumbling backwards. I grin at him.

"How does it feel to no longer need faith?"

Father Bob falls to his knees, weeping.

"My God…my sweet God…"

Abruptly, blessedly, the burning sensation disappears. I laugh,

laugh for the first time in decades, laugh with a sense of perfect relief.

Father Bob presses his hands to his forehead. He screams, just once, a soul shattering epiphany that I understand so well.

"The Lord be with you, Father Bob."

And then he falls upon me, mouth open.

I try to push him away, but am no match.

His first few bites are awkward, but he quickly learns my technique.

Nip.

Clench.

Pull.

The pain is exquisite. So much worse than cancer.

So much better…

Redux

Another story for a Twilight Tales anthology. This was the first story of mine they ever accepted, for the collection Spooks. I'm mixing genres again, this time PI noir and ghost stories.

"LET ME GET THIS straight — you want me to murder you tonight?"

She nodded. "At midnight. As violently as possible."

I leaned back, my office chair creaking in distress. The woman sitting across from me was mid-thirties, thin, well groomed. Her blonde hair, pulled back in a tight bun, held a platinum luster, and the slash of red lipstick she wore made her lips look like a wound. There was something familiar about her, or maybe it was my whiskey goggles.

I blinked at my watch. 11:00am. I'd been soused since breakfast.

"And this decision is because of your dead husband?"

"Yes."

"You want to be —" I paused. "—reunited with him?"

A tricky word to pronounce, reunited, even when sober. But being a semi-professional drunk with some serious pro potential, it came out fine.

"I need to die, Mr. Arkin."

"Call me Bert. And you haven't offered your name yet, Miss…"

"Ahh...Springfield. Doris Springfield."

"Are you trying to atone for some sin, Ms. Springfield?"

Another tough sentence, but it slid out like butter.

"No. The death has to be violent, because a person needs to die violently in order to become a ghost."

I blinked. Then I blinked again. Before my face gave anything away, I broke her stare and went looking through my desk drawer for the Emergency bottle. I took two strong pulls.

A frank look of pity, perhaps disgust, flit past her eyes.

I shrugged it off. Who was she to judge me? She was the one who came in here wanting a violent death.

The bottle went back into the drawer, and I wiped my mouth on the back of my jacket sleeve.

"It's medicinal." I didn't care if she believed it or not. "So...you want to die to become a ghost?"

"Yes. He haunts me, my husband does. Not in any of the clichéd methods you've heard about; I mean, he doesn't break dishes or rattle chains. Instead, every night, he comes to me and holds me when I'm in bed."

Her eyes went glassy, and I frowned. Tears made me uncomfortable.

"We're both so very alone, Mr. Arkin. I want to...I must...be with him."

"Ms. Springfield, I'm sorry for your loss. But murder is —"

"I have thirty-six thousand dollars."

The number gave my weak resistance pause. I could put money like that to good use.

Since I'd gotten kicked off the force, a grievous wrong since half the guys in the CPD are alkies, employment opportunities nowadays were slim. I work as a night watchman four times a week at a warehouse, and do the private investigator thing in my free time, mostly lapping up scraps that my friend Barney throws me. Barney is still on the Job, and whenever something minor comes along that the cops don't have time for, he funnels it my way. Mostly cheating spouses and runaway kids.

But Barney never sent me anyone who wanted to die.

"Just how did you find me, Ms. Springfield?"

"I...I heard about your problem."

"Which problem is that?"

Her eyes, tinged with red, locked onto me like laser sights.

"You're being haunted, too."

This time there was no hiding my reaction, and I recoiled as if slapped. My shaky hands fumbled with the desk drawer, unable to open it fast enough.

The whiskey burned going down, but I fought the pain and sucked until my eyes watered.

Rather than face her, I got up and walked over to the window. My third floor view of the alley didn't change much from winter to summer, but it did offer me a brief moment to collect my thoughts.

"Who told you?" I managed to say.

"I'd…I'd rather not say. I'm asking you to do something illegal, and if something should happen…well, I wouldn't want it getting back to him."

I searched my mental Rolodex for people I'd blabbed to about my problem. Hell, it could have been any bar jockey in any of three dozen gin joints going back two years.

When I drink, I talk.

So I wind up talking a lot.

"Does this person — the one who sent you here — know that you want to die?"

"No. I simply asked around for someone who believes in ghosts, and your name came up. Who haunts you, Mr. Arkin?"

I shut my eyes on the view.

"My mother," I lied.

"She died violently?"

"You could say that."

The booze made my tongue feel big in my mouth, and I began to forget where I was. Usually a good thing, but now…

"I can't do this, Ms. Springfield."

"There's no way to link it to you. You can use my gun."

"That's not the problem. I just don't want this kind of thing on my conscience."

"Is thirty-six thousand enough?"

"Yes. No. I don't know."

"I also have these."

I turned to look at her. She opened her purse and took out a small, white envelope.

"Diamonds, Mr. Arkin. About six carats worth. My husband was a jeweler, and he assured me they're worth over twenty thousand dollars. I was going to leave them to charity, but…"

"Look, Ms. Springfield —"

"I'll leave you the papers on these. That's almost sixty-thousand dollars, Mr. Arkin."

Sixty grand for my conscience?

Who was I kidding? My conscience wasn't worth sixty cents.

"Congratulations, Ms. Springfield. You've hired yourself a killer.

I stumbled out of Harvey's Liquor on Diversey and took a nip right there in the middle of the street.

Chicago winter wind bit at my cheeks and face, making all the broken capillaries even redder. I stuck the bottle in my jacket and climbed into my car.

Driving was a blurry, dreamlike thing, but I managed to make it home. Truth be told, I'd driven a lot worse. At least I could still see the traffic signals.

My apartment, a little shoe box in Hyde Park, had the smell to go along with the ambience. Checking the fridge revealed just a dirty pat of butter and some old pizza crusts.

So I had a liquid lunch instead.

Part of me wanted to sober up so I wouldn't make any mistakes tonight.

The other part wanted me to get drunk enough so I wouldn't remember the details later.

I took a spotty glass from the sink and poured myself three fingers and sat down at my cheap dinette set and drank.

I had to admire the lady. She had guts, and her plan looked like it would work.

At 11:45pm I arrive at her house on Christiana off of Addison. Park in the K-Mart lot across the street. Access her place from the alley; she'll leave her gate and her back door unlocked. The house will look like it had been robbed — drawers pulled out and pictures yanked off the walls. She'll be in the bedroom, hand me the gun. A quick blam-blam in the brain pan, and I can leave with the diamonds and the cash. No witnesses, no muss, no fuss.

I got to pouring another drink when the screech of tires raped my ears and made me drop the bottle.

There was a room-shaking, sickening crunch of motor vehicle meeting flesh, followed by the thump-thump of a skull cracking under the front and rear tires.

"Leave me alone, you little bitch!"

She came out of the wall and hovered before me. Her glow was soft and yellow, a flashlight bulb going dead.

I avoided looking at her face, even as she moved closer.

"You're a bad man, Mr. Arkin."

I bit the inside of my cheek, refusing to be baited.

"A very baaaaaaad man."

She touched my arm, and I jerked back, slopping my drink all over the table. Being touched by a ghost was like getting snow rubbed into your bare skin — so cold it was hot.

"Go away!"

I turned to get up, but she already stood in front of me. No more than five feet tall, her head a crushed pumpkin leaking brains instead of stringy seeds. One eye was popped out and dangling around her misshapen ear by the optic nerve. The other one stared, accusing.

"You can still turn yourself in."

I stumbled away, heading for the bedroom, bottle in hand.

"Call the police, Mr. Arkin. Confess…confess…"

I pulled the door open and screamed. My bedroom had become a winding stretch of suburban highway. Speeding at me at fifty MPH, a swerving, drunken maniac unscrewed his bottle cap rather than paid attention to the road.

Me. It was me driving.

The car hit like a slap from God, knocking me backwards, smearing my face and body against the phantom asphalt in a fifteen foot streak.

I lay there, in agony, as I watched myself get out of the car, look in my direction and vomit, and then get right back into the car and drive off.

The image faded, and I found myself lying on my stained carpet.

"Confess, Mr. Arkin."

I sought my dropped bottle, the worst of the nightly terror over for the time being.

"Confess?" I spat. "Why should I? Haven't you tortured me enough for the last two years? I ran you over once. You've done this to me how many times? Two hundred? Three?"

She stood next to me now, the loops of intestines hanging out of her belly giving me cold, wet slaps in the face.

"Go to the police and confess."

"Go to hell, or heaven, or wherever you're supposed to go."

I rolled away and struggled to my feet.

"I can't go away until my business here is done."

I drank straight from the bottle now, trying to tune her out. Confess? My ass. Going to the cops meant going to prison. And that just can't happen. I couldn't survive in prison.

They don't let you drink.

"You can't die without resolution, Mr. Arkin. If you do…"

"I know! You've said it a thousand times!"

"Your soul will be mine if you don't atone."

She cracked a bloody smile, all missing teeth and swollen tongue.

"I don't think you'll like eternity with me in charge."

I spun on her, jabbing a finger into her spongy head.

"I'll have money soon! Lots of money! I'll hire someone to exorcize your preachy little ass!"

She laughed, a full, rich, deep sound that made the hair on my arms vibrate.

"I'll be seeing you, Mr. Arkin. Soon."

And then she faded away, like a puff of cigar smoke.

I drank until I started to puke blood.

Then I drank some more.

My hands perspired in the latex gloves Ms. Springfield had provided. The alley behind her house was deserted, except for a rat scurrying into an old Pepsi box.

I walked up to her gate — it was the only one that was unlocked — and let myself into her modest backyard.

Dark ,silent, porch light off. Her back door opened with a whisper.

"Ms. Springfield?"

The door led into her kitchen. Drawers had been pulled out and silverware scattered along the floor. I avoided stepping on anything sharp, and made my way through the kitchen and into a hallway.

"Ms. Springfield? It's me."

Silence.

I took a pull from my flask, to calm my nerves. Then another, for luck.

"Ms. Springfield?"

She said to meet her in the bedroom. There were stairs to the right.

I ascended slowly, cautiously. The higher I climbed, the more this seemed like a very bad idea. Even if I could bring myself to murder her — and get away with it — who was to say she wouldn't haunt me too? One ghost was bad enough. Having two…

"Mr. Arkin?"

Her voice came as such a shock that I almost lost my balance on the steps.

"Ms. Springfield?"

"Second door on the right."

Her voice was terribly relaxed.

I took a deep breath, blew it out. Reflexively, my hand went to my hip holster, and I haven't worn a hip holster in years.

"I'll be right there," I said, more for myself than for her.

She was sitting on her bed, dressed in a white night gown. Her blonde hair hung over her shoulders. In her hand was a .38 police special.

I had a momentary flash of panic, but she turned the revolver around and handed it to me, butt first.

"I was worried you wouldn't come."

"Money makes a man do strange things."

I looked on the nightstand, next to the bed. Stacked in a neat pile, so many twenties I'd need a bag to carry them out.

So much money.

"It's almost midnight." Ms. Springfield's voice had a pleasant, almost cheerful lilt. "I want you to shoot me in the heart."

I shuffled from one foot to the other, uncomfortable.

"The head would be better."

"I don't intend joining my husband without a head to kiss him with."

Good point.

"The heart it is."

I moved closer, my gaze flickering between her and the money. Part of me wanted to just take the cash and run. I could make it to Mexico before the cops got on me.

"It's almost midnight, Mr. Arkin."

Her face — calm, so sure.

"This is what you really want, isn't it?"

For the first time since I'd met her, she smiled. "This is all I want."

She tilted her chin upward, thrust out her chest.

I extended the gun.

"This might hurt."

"Just keep firing until it's done. I want messy, remember?"

I chewed my lower lip. The gun shook in my grasp.

A drink. I needed a drink.

My free hand reached back for my flask, and Ms. Springfield's features erupted in pure anger.

"Shoot me, you worthless drunk!"

I fired.

The bullet took her in the center of the left breast, her white nightgown exploding in red fireworks. She pitched to the side, gasping like a landed fish.

I shot her in the back.

Twice.

Three times.

Still twitching. And a high-pitched, whistling wheeze from the sucking wounds in her chest.

"Aw, screw it."

I put the last two slugs in the back of her head.

She stopped moving.

Shoving the gun deep in my jacket, I went for the money. I took a bloody pillow case and began stuffing it full of stacks. The diamonds lay there too, and the papers. I grabbed them and turned to get the hell out of there, but the bedroom suddenly transformed into a highway, and for the second time today I ran myself over.

I tried to brace for the impact, but you can never brace for that kind of thing.

Even knowing it wasn't real, I screamed at the very real feeling of the impact sluicing through every nerve and fiber of my being. Spectral or not, it hurt like hell.

When I was able to move again, the pumpkin head ghost floated above my head, staring down with her one good eye.

But this time she had company.

"I believe you've met my daughter," said the ghost of Ms. Springfield. Her nightgown glowed white, peppered with ugly red starbursts. Bits of brain and bone floated above her hair like a halo.

She held a glowing .38.

The ghostly gun fired, and I felt the bullets rip into my body, gasping in pain and shock.

"It's not real," I told myself.

I lay there, listening to the slurping, keening sound of my lungs leaking air through the holes in my chest. Even though I wanted to move, I couldn't.

Even when I heard the approaching sirens.

Killing me? It would have been too easy.

Ms. Springfield knew I was the one who ran down her daughter. Her daughter told her.

The only thing stronger than the woman's grief had been her lust for revenge.

She truly did want to die, so she could join her child on the other side.

So they could be together.

So they could haunt me together.

I sat on the cold floor of my cell, hugging my knees.

I've been dry for over a month now, and it's been as bad as I thought. Shaking, vomiting, delirium tremens, pure hell.

But none of it's as bad as the ghosts.

Every day I am treated to an agonizing smearing across the highway, or having large holes blown out of my chest and head.

On some days, I get both.

And without the booze to deaden the pain…

In hindsight, I should have turned myself in after I hit that little girl.

I try to explain that to them. Try to get them to understand that I was just a scared drunk.

They show no mercy.

"And this is just a taste," Ms. Springfield repeatedly tells me. "When you die, your soul belongs to us. We have plans for you, Mr. Arkin."

They have shown me their plans.

Sometimes I cry so hard the prison doctor has to medicate me.

Life now centers on diet and exercise. I watch what I eat. I work out three times a day.

I'm in the best shape of my life.

Which is a good thing.

Because as horrifying as my life is, I want to live as long as I can.

The ghosts can run me over and gun me down a thousand times a day, and that is nothing compared to what they have in store for me after I die.

I don't want to die.

Please, God, don't let me ever die.

The Bag

I wrote this for the zombie anthology Cold Flesh. It began as a writing exercise, where someone hands your protagonist a paper bag and says don't open it until midnight. I tried to think of the absolute worst thing a paper bag could contain…

"NO THANKS."

The bum thrust the bag at me again. Brown paper, bearing the name of a local grocery store, crumpled and filthy and dripping something brown.

"Take it."

I tried to shove him away using my elbows; he was even dirtier than the bag. Strange how these people are invisible until one is in your face, reeking of garbage and body odor and piss. This is what I get for forgoing a cab and deciding to get a little exercise on the way home from work.

"Take the bag, Jimmy."

I'd pushed him an arm's-length away, but his use of my first name was like a slap.

"How did you…?"

"The answer is in the bag. Take it."

I grinned. Someone I knew must have put this poor sap up to this. Maybe Marky, from Accounting, or my cousin Ernie, who was the only forty-year-old in all of Chicago who still thought joy buzzers were funny.

"Fine. You win. Give me the bag."

The street person smiled, giving me a blast of brown teeth and fortified wine. I took the brown bag, which had surprising heft to it, and reached into my pocket for some change.

"Don't open it until the sun goes down."

"Excuse me?"

He walked away, blending into the rush hour sidewalk crowd, before I could give him his dollar.

My first impulse was to open it right then and there. But there were people all over, and if this was from Cousin Ernie, it was probably offensive or even illegal. Good old Ernie once sent a sixty-eight-year-old stripper to my office, one whose pasties hung at belly button level and whose grand finale included popping out her dentures. If this drippy, heavy thing in the bag was from Ernie, it would be best to open it when I got home.

Home was on the Lake Shore, a high rise condo with a killer view and a 24-hour doorman and mirrors in the elevator. Not too shabby for a South Side kid who used to pitch pennies in back alleys for lunch money. Money had always been the primary motivator of my life, and the stock market was a natural evolution from teenage poker games and fantasy football pools.

I did okay. Better than okay. Enough to keep me in Armani and Cristal. I was on the short list for five star restaurants, and got to bed women of fine social standing, and twice a year I'd fly my mom to Tuscany so she could visit relatives who all worshipped me as a god.

Life was fine.

My condo was cold and smelled like vanilla, some kind of stuff the maid sprayed around after her afternoon visit. I plopped the bag up on the breakfast bar and went to the bedroom to strip, shower, and change into evening wear. Tonight was Molly Wainwright, of the Barrington Wainwrights, and she was ten years younger than me and a foxy little tramp who oozed sex like her daddy oozed real estate.

If all went well, Molly would be notch number ninety-seven on the Jimmy belt. That's ninety-seven runs batted in, out of a possible two hundred-twenty. I did the math in my head.

"Score tonight, I'll be batting .440."

Damn impressive for a South Side kid. And as far a fielding went, I only had one error in my entire career. It was an experience I didn't care to repeat.

I shaved, took the dry-cleaner's plastic from my gray suit, and decided to go with the diamond stud cufflinks. By the time I was dressed and ready to roll I'd completely forgotten about the leaky paper bag on my breakfast bar.

But when I went to the fridge for Evian, there it was, perched on the counter like an old alley cat.

I checked my Bvlgari — a quarter to six. The bum warned me not to open it until the sun went down, but that sounded like stupid Ernie theatrics and I didn't have time to play around. Slowly, gently, I unrolled the top of the bag and peeled it open.

The stench hit me like a sucker punch. Rotting meat masked with something antiseptic. I got an accidental snootful, gagged, and staggered back.

The bag wiggled.

I squinted, held my breath. Whatever was in the bag was definitely dead; the smell was proof. It had to be an air current, or the contents settling, or —

It moved again.

My heart did the pitter-patter thing, like the couple times I'd been caught cheating at five card stud and a beating was about to ensue. The bag jerked to the left, then to the right, then toppled over onto its side.

A tiny red fist appeared from the top, opening and wiggling five miniature fingers.

I knew what this was. I knew, in the depths of my soul.

My fielding error.

The thing cried out, soft and wet. A bulbous, bald head emerged, large fetal eyes locking onto me.

"Daddy."

"Oh, Jesus."

It pulled itself from the bag, dragging along two undersized first-trimester legs and a slimy blue umbilical cord. Though covered in mucus, I could make out the large scars running zigzag over most of its body. Scars that had been sewn up in an ugly Frankenstein stitch.

In its tiny hand was a curved needle, trailing thread.

"Oh, sweet Jesus."

"Not until dark, Daddy. I haven't finished yet." The needle dug into its shoulder, repairing a laceration caused by the abortionist's knife. "I wanted to look pretty for you."

"It wasn't my fault," I managed. "The rubber broke."

My head swam with images of Margo Williams. Young. Sweet. Timid in bed, but I liked them that way. When she called me with news of her pregnancy, I'd had three women since her.

I mailed her a check to get rid of it, and hadn't heard anything of the matter until months later, when I found out she died from complications during the procedure.

"Not my fault," I said again.

The thing on the counter sat up and slumped forward, unable to support its oversized head.

"Mommy says hello. She sent me here so you could take care of me."

The emotions piled one top of another in my chest, fighting for dominance. Guilt. Revulsion. Amazement. Fear. Anger.

Anger won.

"Go back where you came from!"

"Don't you want me, Daddy?"

For an absurd moment, I pictured the bloody, scarred thing sitting on my lap at a baseball game, a tiny cap on its misshapen fetal skull.

"I don't want you! I paid them to take care of you!"

Its tiny face crinkled, tears clearing trails in the mucus.

My decision made, I wondered how to get rid of it. Wrap it in newspaper and drop it down the garbage chute? Flush it down the toilet? It was small enough to fit. But if it was discovered in either case, it might lead back to me. I watched TV. I knew about DNA tests.

I glanced around the kitchen, eyes flicking over possibilities. Microwave. Stove. Compactor. Freezer.

Disposal.

The thing sat right next to the sink, a sink I paid almost two grand for. The garbage disposal could grind up a turkey leg, and this thing wasn't that much bigger. One quick push and —

"Don't grind me up in the garbage disposal, Daddy."

I clenched my teeth. How could it read my thoughts?

"I'm a part of you, Daddy."

It smiled, or tried to smile, with that big scar bisecting its head.

I forced myself to act.

In one quick motion, I scooped it up and shoved it down the sink drain, hard. The bulbous head was too big to fit through the opening, so I smacked it with the edge of my fist, over and over, forcing it down.

"Daddy, don't! I'm your own flesh and blood!"

I pulled my hand free and hit the garbage disposal switch.

For a moment, nothing happened. Then everything happened at once.

The whir of the disposal was surpassed by horrible screaming.

My screaming.

It was like being attacked by hundreds of men with hatchets. My ears were the first to be stripped away, then my nose and cheeks. Clothing was flayed off my body in bloody strips, followed by the meat underneath. Fingers, knees, cock and balls, ground up in a bladed tornado. And a booming voice tore through my head, louder than my own cries.

"I'M PART OF YOU, DADDY!"

How I managed to hit the off switch, I have no idea. My eyes had been cored from my skull. Even more unbelievable, I somehow dialed 911 using only the meaty stump of my hand.

The pain was unimaginable.

It still is.

These days, my son visits me in the hospital. I can't see him, but I can feel him. He's very good at sewing. He practices on me, when the nurses sedate me at night.

I've named him Jimmy Jr.

Looks just like me, I bet.

Careful, He Bites

Another flash fiction piece for the Small Bites anthology. The guidelines were to write a were-creature tale in 500 words or less.

"CAREFUL. HE BITES."

Malcolm snorted, offering Selma a glimpse of gray teeth. His pants hung around his ankles, the condom dangling like an elephant booger.

"Bites? Damn thing don't even got no feet or wings."

Malcolm banged his palm against the canary cage, knocking the bird across the newspaper-lined bottom.

"I wouldn't do that," Selma said.

Malcolm squinted at her, ugly. "What you gonna do about it, whore?"

Selma shrugged. She swung her legs over the side of the bed and reached for the pack of smokes. Malcolm leaned over and gave her a harsh shove.

"I said, what are you gonna do about it?"

"Nothing. The bird can take care of himself."

Malcolm snorted again, the condom jiggling.

"It can, huh? Let's see what Mr. Birdy can do."

Selma stared blankly as Malcolm opened the cage and stuck in a sweaty fist. The bird tried to wiggle away, but Malcolm managed to get a hold of it quickly.

"Looks like Mr. Birdy is…DAMN!"

Malcolm dropped the bird and withdrew his hand, staring dumbly at the small spot of blood on his palm.

"Damn thing bit me!"

Selma lit a smoke.

"Told you."

Malcolm slapped her across the mouth, smearing bright red lipstick. Then he turned his attention back to the bird.

"I'm gonna…"

"You're not gonna do nothing." Selma's lower lip began to swell, but she seemed calm. "It's a full moon."

"Full moon? What the hell are you talking about?"

"Were-canary," Selma said.

Malcolm frowned, raising his hand to strike her again.

The little feathers growing out of his fingers caused him quite a shock.

Malcolm screamed, bones and tendons snapping and shrinking as the ancient curse of the were-canary mutated his adult human form into that of a tiny, yellow songbird. He perched on the nest of his tangled pants, the condom wrapped around his pointy feet.

"Tweet," Malcolm said.

Selma snatched him up and promptly broke one of his wings. Malcolm sang in agony, flopping around on the bedroom floor in tight circles.

Disoriented and wracked by pain, he didn't notice the cat under the bed until the feline had already pounced.

"He bites too," Selma said.

The next morning, Selma awoke to whimpering.

"…*please*…*kill me*…"

She stared at the man, naked and cramped in the birdcage. Roscoe, her former pimp. His legs and arms were missing; it was the only way he'd fit into the cage.

"Morning, Roscoe."

"…*please*…"

She gave him some fresh water and birdseed, then padded off to the bathroom.

The cat's litter box contained several bowling ball-sized deposits.

They didn't come out that big, but once the moon went down, things went back to normal.

That was the price she paid for having pets.

"Hey, Roscoe! How about a little song while I shower?"

"*...please...Selma...*"

"Do you want me to get the cheese grater?"

Roscoe began "Blue Moon."

Selma smiled. After all, who else had a bird that sang baritone?

Symbios

The closest I've ever come to hard science fiction. I wrote this back in college, and then polished it up a decade later when it was published by Apex Digest. It was originally called Star Vation, but I wisely changed the title.

Voice Module 195567

Record Mode:

Is this thing working?

Play Mode:

Is this thing working?

Record Mode:

This is Lieutenant Jehrico Stiles of the mining ship Darion. I've crash-landed on an unknown planet somewhere in the Eighty-Sixth Sector. Captain Millhouse Braun is dead.

I suppose I'm Captain now.

Captain Braun's last VM concerned the delays we'd been having due to a micro meteor shower while mining Asteroid 336-09 in orbit around Flaxion.

A lot has happened since then. The Brain caught the Madness.

I told Mill a thousand times we shouldn't have used an Organic, but he was willing to take the risks, as long as he had extra cargo space to carry more ore. You know the sales pitch. Why have an interstellar processor that weighs twenty six metric tons and takes up gads of space when an Organic Brain with nutrient pumps can navigate the ship while weighing only three kilograms?

Well, we did fit more ore on the ship. And now Mill and the rest of the crew are dead. When the Brain went bad it thrust the ship into Wormhole GG54 and I got spewed out here.

Mill and Johnson and the rest of the crew were fried when the Brain misfired the photon props. One moment I was watching them on the console viewer, drilling into the asteroid's cortex, and the next moment they were vaporized and the ship was being hurtled toward the wormhole.

The trailer detached before I went through, sending millions of credits worth of iron on some unknown trajectory.

I survived re-entry because the ionic suppressors run automatically and not on Brain power.

The Brain wasn't so lucky. It's dead now, the nutrient containers smashed when we hit the planet's surface. But the Brain had enough juice left in it to seal every hatch and cargo hold before its functioning ceased.

Nothing on the ship works. The com-link is dead. The homing beacon is dead. I can't even open the steel doors to the pantry, and my unrefrigerated food supply is rotting away without me being able to get to it.

The oxygen systems have malfunctioned, but the planet I'm on has an atmosphere I can breathe. The nitrogen level is high, and I'm light-headed a lot, but so far I'm still alive.

The temperature is also hospitable to human life. A bit chilly, but mostly pleasant. Days last about forty hours, and nights about twenty.

I'm surprised this Voice Module still works. It's got a crack in the case, but the batteries haven't leaked. I figure without a recharge, I've got maybe two hours of recording time left.

I'll have to use it sparingly. I've salvaged all I can from this damn ship, and I can't find a lousy pen.

Voice Module 195568

Record Mode:

This is my fourth day on the planet, and I made an impressive discovery. The terrain here tests high for ferrite, making this planet worth a fortune. If no *one* has staked a claim, I could get funding and mine this place until it's just as gutted as earth is. The planet is large enough that it might even end the Ore Crisis, perhaps for a few years.

The only problem is that I'm starving.

There's a water stream nearby, brackish but drinkable. I waded in deep and searched for hours, but couldn't find animal life in the water, or the surrounding area.

Plant life abounds. At least I think they're plants. Maybe they're fungi. They're reddish in color, lacking chlorophyll, and they have appendages that resemble leaves. The landscape is littered with hundreds of different species, some as high as buildings, some the size of grass.

None have been edible. Everything I've plucked so far contains an acidic enzyme — concentrated highly enough to burn my fingers and my tongue. Swallowing any of it would tear a hole through my stomach.

But at least I have water.

I haven't scouted very far yet, only a few kilometers. Maybe I'll be lucky and there will something to eat on the other side of that big hill that splits my horizon.

Hunger is starting to weaken me. I can't stay awake for more than seven or eight hours. Tried several times to pry open the steel pantry doors, but can't budge them a crack. I think I broke my big toe kicking the panel in frustration.

I hope for rescue, but know the odds against it. If this is truly an undiscovered planet, then no one knows it exists, and no one knows that I'm here.

And I have no way to tell them.

Voice Module 195569

Record Mode:

My hiking boots were a gift from my mother, and came with genuine antique pig-leather laces.

I boiled and ate the laces this morning. My boots won't stay on now, and I've got — I know this sounds funny — a terrible knot in my stomach. But there's nothing else to eat. The only other organic thing on the ship is the Brain, and I'm not touching that. I'd rather starve to death. I'd rather die.

Morals are what make us human.

Voice Module 195570

Record Mode:

I met my new neighbors today.

They are only knee-high, and somewhat resemble the extinct species called dogs. They're covered with a short, rough fur, have pointy ears and yellow eyes, and walk around on underdeveloped hind legs.

I was sleeping in what used to be the control bay, dreaming about food, when I felt something poke me in the ribs.

I opened my eyes, startled, and found six of them in a circle around me. They spoke to one another with high pitched yaps.

None wore clothing or carried weapons. And even when I stood, towering over them by some five feet, none seemed afraid.

One of them yipped at me in what might have been a question. I said hello, and it cocked its head, confused by my voice. I can't recall reading about any life form like these back in school. For all I know they are an undiscovered species.

They half-coaxed, half-pushed me out of my ship and led me further than I'd previously scouted, over the hill.

They took me to their home. There were no structures, just a collection of holes in the dirt. When we arrived, dozens of little brown heads popped up out of the holes to stare at me.

A short time later, I was surrounded.

A kind of collective humming sound rose up within the group, and they all came to me, holding out tiny paws to touch my legs. They took turns, their eyes locked on mine.

For a moment, I felt like a god.

When I reached out to touch them they weren't afraid. And when I did pat a head their dog lips turned into grins and they wiggled their tails.

It was like being around dozens of well-behaved children. For a while I completely forgot how hungry I was.

Voice Module 199571

Record Mode:

They eat the plants. Somehow they're immune to the acid content. They eat many different varieties, raw. Then, out of their droppings, new plants grow.

Nature's perfect symbiotic planet. Ironic that I'd wind up here, considering how my own species has trashed the earth, and the planets of the surrounding star systems.

Perhaps this is a penance of sorts.

I stayed for most of the day in the village, watching the puppies play, patting small heads. I've counted eighty-two dog people in this settlement. Maybe there are other settlements, elsewhere. Staring across the huge landscape with nothing to see but kilometers of horizon, I have to wonder.

Later I left them and tried once again to pry open the metal door that locks away all of the food in the ship's pantry. Once again I was unsuccessful.

Voice Module 199572

Record Mode:

I'm dying. My clothes hang on my body like sheets, and I know I've lost at least fifteen kilograms.

The dogs seem to understand that I'm deteriorating in some way. They try to do funny things to make me laugh, like cartwheels or jumping on me, but I can't laugh.

In fact, when I look at the dogs for too long, I start to salivate.

I wonder what they taste like.

Like that synthetic meat, locked away in the ship's pantry?

I've never had real meat. Could never afford it. My father had a cat steak once, and said it was delicious. My grandfather remembers when he was young and there were still a few cows left, and he used to get meat on holidays.

What do these little dog people taste like?

If I wanted to I could wipe out the entire village in just a few minutes. They have no weapons. They don't move very fast. Their teeth are rounded. I could kill their entire population and not even get scratched.

But I don't. I can't. I won't.

Voice Module 199573

Record Mode:

I ate the Brain today.

I thought it would be rotten, but there was no decay at all. I have a hypothesis why. Decay is caused by bacteria, and perhaps this world has none.

I boiled the Brain, picked out the glass shards, and ate with my eyes closed, trying not to think about what it was.

But I did think about it.

It shouldn't matter. After all, the Brain had ceased operation. Tissue is tissue.

Even if the tissue is human.

Besides, the volunteers who sign up for the Organic Processor Program are elderly, near the ends of their lives. Running a starship gave a brain donor dozens of extra years of sentience, of life.

And, important point, this one did go mad and kill my crew and destroy my ship.

It owed me.

There wasn't any taste to it. Not really. But when I was finished eating, I cried like a child.

Not because of what I had done.

But because I wanted more.

Voice Module 199574

Record Mode:

I can't eat an intelligent life form. Not that the dog people are particularly intelligent. No tools, no clothing, no artificial shelter, though they do have a rudimentary form of communication. I even understand some of their words now.

I can't eat things that speak.

But all I've consumed in the past fifteen days were two shoe laces and a soggy, very small Brain.

I have a few solar matches left. I could spit-roast one of these doggies using a piece of pipe.

What did my grandfather call it? A barbeque.

The village has named me. When I come by, they yip out something that sounds like "Griimmm!"

So to the dog people I am Grim.

They sleep next to me and hug my legs and smile like babies.

Please let a rescue ship find me tonight, so I don't have to do what I'm planning to do.

Voice Module 199575

Record Mode:

I ate one.

When I awoke this morning I had such a single-mindedness, such a raw craving to eat, that I didn't even try to fight it.

I went to the dog people's village, picked up the nearest one, and as it yipped "Griiimmm!" with a smile on its face, I broke its neck.

I didn't wait around to see what the others did. I just ran back to ship, drooling like a baby.

Then I skinned the little dog person with a paring knife.

It was delicious.

Roasted over an open fire. Cooked to perfection. I only left the bones.

When I was done, the feeling was euphoric. I was sated. I was satisfied.

I smacked my lips and patted my stomach and knew how grandfather must have felt. Real meat was amazing. It made the synthetic stuff seem like garbage.

Then I noticed all of dog people around me.

They stared, their eyes accusatory and sad. And they began to cry. Howling cries, with tears.

When I realized what I had done, I cried too.

Voice Module 195576

Record Mode:

Two months on this damn planet, and that's according to these sixty hour days, so it's more like half a year. I haven't recorded anything in a while, because I haven't wanted to think about what I've been doing.

I've eaten fifty-four dog people so far.

I've stopped losing weight, but I can count my ribs through my shirt. One a day isn't enough nourishment for a man my size.

I try to make it enough. I have to ration. And not because of any moral reason.

The population is dwindling.

I don't know why they haven't run away. Packed up and left.

But they haven't.

They don't fear me. Maybe they don't understand fear.

The young puppies still hug my legs when I visit the village.

Everyone else stays inside their holes.

I try not to take the young ones. Instead I dig with my hands and pluck the adults from the ground. They don't fight. In fact, they try to hug me.

I think I'm a little insane at this point.

When I grab them, and they look at me with those sad eyes and say my name…

Sometimes I wish they would run away, leaving me to starve. So I couldn't kill any more of them.

It's like eating my children.

Voice Module 199577

Record Mode:

There are just three left.

They don't even go underground anymore. It's almost as if they've accepted their own deaths.

I wonder sometimes if I deserve to live when so many have died.

But the hunger. The terrible hunger.

I know when my food supply here runs out, I'll have to search for more.

More children to eat.

How can something that sickens make my stomach rumble?

Voice Module 199577

Record Mode:

A ship!

I saw a ship orbiting.

It was night. I was staring at the constellations, trying to remember my astronomy so I could pinpoint where I was in the galaxy.

One of the stars moved.

It circled the planet twice in three hours. I hope against hope it's a manned ship, not a damned probe. Please let there be people on board. I can't last too much longer.

There is nothing left to eat. I've consumed the entire dog village, boiled their bones and eaten the hides, hair and all.

I'm so thin I look like a skeleton with my face.

Voice Module 195578

Record Mode:

The ship landed several kilometers away. I ran most of the way to it, my euphoria bordering on hysterics.

It turned to hysteria when I saw the ship.

Nothing human made it.

It was spherical and grey, like a giant pearl. At first I thought it was some type of meteorite. There were no portals or exhausts, just smooth grey curves, reflecting the world around it.

I hadn't gotten within a few steps when it opened. A hole just sort of appeared in its side. Small and blurry at first, but soon several meters wide. I hid behind an outcropping of rocks.

Then something came out of the hole.

It was twice my size. Vaguely humanoid, but lacking a head. Six yellow eyes stared out from behind the clear visor encircling its chest. The eyes moved in different directions, scanning the terrain. No arms, but under the trunk of the body were four legs, thick and each ending in three long toes.

Its skin appeared reptilian; black scales that shone as if wet.

On the lower half of its body, it wore a bizarre version of pants. Above the eyes was a large and impressive mouth. I instantly thought of old hologramsI'd seen depicting sharks. The rows of triangular jagged teeth encircled the top of the creature like a bastardized crown.

As odd as its appearance was, it seemed to exude a kind of peace. I felt as if I were looking at a fellow intelligent being rather than an enemy from space.

I took a step toward it, and it reared up on its two back legs and waved its front legs at me, making a snorting sound. I suppose my appearance unnerved it. My features probably were just as strange and grotesque to it as it was to me.

"I won't harm you," I told it.

"I won't harm you," it repeated, imitating my voice perfectly. It lowered its front legs and took a cautious step forward. I also took a step.

"Zeerhweetick," it said.

I tried to imitate the sound as best I could. It relaxed its legs and squatted when we were within a meter of each other. I also sat down.

"I won't harm you," it said again.

I recalled my astronaut training. Intelligent Lifeforms 101 was an entirely hypothetical class about the possibility of communication with an intelligent alien life form. It was in the curriculum because the World Assembly demanded that all space travelers have that training. They believed if we ever did encounter a new race, the first meeting between species would set the tone for all future relations. Making first impressions and all that crap.

Everyone considered it a joke class — we'd visited hundreds of planets, and never encountered any life form smarter than a cockroach.

Now I felt like that was the most important class I ever took.

I began by using words and miming motions. Pointing to myself I said, man. Pointing at its ship I said, ship. And so on.

It watched, and repeated, and within an hour it had picked up several verbs and began asking questions.

"Man here long?" it said in my voice. Then it pointed to the ground.

"Fifty cycles," I said. I flashed fifty fingers, then pointed at the sun, slowly moving across the horizon.

"More men?"

"No."

"Ship?"

"Broken." I pulled up a nearby weed and cracked it in half, illustrating my point.

It gestured at its own ship with a three fingered leg and also yanked a plant from the ground.

"Ship broken." It ripped the weed in two.

"Man," I said again, pointing to myself. Then I pointed at it.

"Zabzug," it said, pointing at itself.

"Hello, Zabzug."

"Hello, Man."

And so began mankind's historic first communication with an intelligent alien species.

I was so excited I wasn't even thinking about the other intelligent alien species I had just finished devouring.

Voice Module 195579

Record Mode:

After communicating for several hours, Zabzug and I went back to my ship. He moved slower than I did, sometimes tripping over foliage. One time I helped him up, getting my first close look at those teeth on his scalp. How he could imitate me so perfectly with a mouthful of fangs like that was anyone's guess.

"Thank you, Man," Zabzug said after getting back to his feet.

I smiled at him. His teeth twitched, which I took to be a smile too.

He was very excited at the sight of my ship, and began speaking rapidly in a series of grunts and snorts. I sat and watched him explore it top to bottom. He stopped in front of the pantry and stayed there a long time, snuffling, trying to open the metal door. Liquid poured down from his head and over his eye plate like tears.

"Hungry," Zabzug said. "No eat long time."

"Man hungry too," I told him.

He beckoned me over and we struggled with the pantry for a while, not budging the door a centimeter. Zabzug's drool smelled like a sour musk, and being right next to him made me realize how big he really was. Three times my mass, easy.

And those appendages of his had incredible strength behind them, putting huge dents in the thick steel door.

But it was all for nothing. The pantry stayed closed.

Voice Module 195580

Record Mode:

Zabzug explained to me how he crashed by drawing a very detailed schematic in the dirt. His ship runs on a bastardized form of fission, using a refined chemical to help control the reaction. I guess the chemical could best be described as a form of lubricant, as oil was used in combustion engines back on ancient earth.

So basically he's stranded here because he ran out of oil, stalled, and got sucked into the same wormhole as me.

We made some limited talk about putting my power supply into his ship, but the parts were so fundamentally incompatible that it proved impossible.

Zabzug tried eating some plants, doing me one better and actually swallowing a few. He became violently ill. I must admit to some perverse amusement at watching black foam erupt out of the top of his head like a volcano, but that only served to remind me how hungry I was.

Two intelligent species, meeting for the first time in history, each with the capability of interstellar travel, and both starving to death.

It might be funny if it were happening to someone else.

Voice Module 195581

Record Mode:

After a week together, I consider Zabzug a friend. He's told me much about his planet, which seems to be located in the Hermida Galaxy. Like humans, his species have used up their natural resources, and have begun scouring the universe for food, fuel, and building material.

He's much better at learning English than I am at learning his language. He's gained such a mastery of it that he made his first joke.

We were resting near his ship, talking as usual about how hungry we were, and Zabzug told me, "If you weren't so ugly, I'd consider eating you."

Funny guy, that Zabzug.

Voice Module 195582

Record Mode:

Zabzug is starving too. His skin has lost its luster, and his eyes are glazed.

We still have animated talks, but the silence often lasts as long as the chatting.

I'm hesitant to tell him about the dog people, about what I consider my genocidal crime.

But they're all I can think about.

I finally spill the story. Hopeful he won't judge. Hopeful that he might know where to search for more.

To my surprise, Zabzug seems to know what I'm speaking about, and he's able to draw an exact picture of their species.

"Hrucka," he told me. He awkwardly explained that the hrucka were like pets to his species.

It made sense. Evolution doesn't create just one species of animal in an ecosystem. The hrucka must have been put here.

Or stranded here.

Which might mean that somewhere, on the planet, there's another ship like Zabzug's.

He's very excited by this prospect, and we decide to conduct a search first thing tomorrow.

Voice Module 195583

Record Mode:

We searched for three days.

We didn't find anything.

Voice Module 195584

Record Mode:

Zabzug came into my ship at night as I slept. The viscous drool from his mouth dripped onto my face and woke me up. In one of his appendages he held a sharp piece of pipe, the one I had been using to roast dog people. Upon my awakening, he yelped and dropped the pipe, hurrying from my ship.

I suppose he's having the same problem that I had with the dog people. Respect for an intelligent life form versus the overwhelming need to survive.

But he's in for a surprise.

I'm going to eat him first.

I stayed awake the rest of the night, standing guard with the pointed pipe. He had the strength advantage. I had the speed advantage. We both seemed to be of similar intelligence, and both had the ability to use tools.

His eyes might be a weak point, but they were always covered by that face plate — Zabzug even wore it to sleep. His skin was covered with scales, and though they looked moist, they were hard, almost metallic, to the touch.

The vulnerable point was his mouth. It was crammed full of sharp teeth, but maybe I could jam something down his throat and into all the soft parts inside.

At the first peek of sunlight I'll go to Zabzug's ship with my spear.

What does alien lizard taste like?

Voice Module 195585

Record Mode:

He didn't come out all day, and I couldn't find a way in. There isn't a seam on the entire ship. No cracks or ridges or anything to pry or beat open. After several hours of trying, I decided to just wait. He'd have to come out eventually.

He wanted the same thing I wanted.

Voice Module 195586

Record Mode:

The bastard ate my hand.

Chomped it off at the wrist. I fell asleep, waiting for him to come out.

But I got him…haha…I got him…jammed the pipe down his throat, into the soft stuff.

Dead. He's dead.

Zabzug, my friend, is dead.

I used my belt as a tourniquet for my hand, but it didn't stop the bleeding.

I had to use the solar matches to close the wound.

The pain…so much pain in my wrist.

But the hunger…the need…is even stronger.

I'm going to cut him open now.

Voice Module 195587

Record Mode:

I'm full! What a wonderful feeling! For the first time since I landed on this planet, I've eaten until I'm ready to burst.

I'm so happy I don't even notice the pain.

Voice Module 195588

Record Mode:

Zabzug lasted for a whole month.

Some parts were delicious.

Some parts, not so delicious.

I ate everything. The inedible parts were boiled into soup until every calorie and nutrient was leeched out.

I even gained a few kilos.

And now, with the last of the soup gone, with the hunger pangs returning, I am afraid.

Voice Module 195589

Record Mode:

Four days since I've eaten anything. Zabzug had stretched out my belly, and I drink a lot to keep it full, to try and fool it into feeling sated.

My belly isn't fooled

I've managed to get into Zabzug's ship, using a key. It's a tiny sphere he'd been keeping in a pocket. When it touches the ship, the portal opens.

I've fully explored the interior, trying to gain an understanding of how it works. The vessel is a marvel of engineering, with a navigation system light-years ahead of ours. The technology is even more valuable than the iron-rich planet I'm stranded on.

If I can get off this rock, I'll be the wealthiest man in the universe.

The first thing I'll do is get a limb graft…no, the first thing I'll do is have a banquet. A feast that will last a month. I'll gorge myself like the ancient Romans, purging between courses so I can cram in more food.

Such a beautiful picture.

Voice Module 195590

Record Mode:

My wrist isn't healing right. It doesn't seem to be infected, but the wound keeps opening.

I think it's a symptom of starvation. My body is conserving its energy, and deems healing unnecessary.

I'm so weak it's an effort to even stand up.

I have to do something. If I stay here, I'll die. Perhaps there's food somewhere else. I've scouted at least fifty kilometers in all directions, but I need to pick one and keep moving.

I decide to follow the sunset. I'll leave tomorrow.

I have no other choice.

Voice Module 195591

Record Mode:

I don't know how far I've traveled. Perhaps a hundred or a hundred and fifty kilometers. I'm in a desert now, and ran out of water a few hours ago.

My tongue is so thick it's hard to speak.

I fear sleep, because I don't think I'll wake up.

Voice Module 195592

Record Mode:

I can't move another step. Thirst is worse than hunger. I'm hallucinating. Hearing things. Seeing things. I even had a fever-dream, imagining a space ship crashing in the distance…

Voice Module 195593

Record Mode:

A week has passed.

Obviously, I didn't die in the desert. I was rescued. Well, sort of.

That ship I'd imagined I saw — it really did exist. A salvage ship, which had made a run at retrieving the trailer full of ore we'd lost.

They also got sucked into the wormhole, and were spit out here.

Their ship is damaged beyond repair. They'd been here for only a few days, and saw my Voice Module unit glinting in the sun.

They listened to it, unfortunately.

Marta, the woman, said she didn't judge me. She understood.

The man, Ellis, didn't say a word to me.

I received fresh water, medicine for my wrist, and synth rations.

"We have enough synth rations for a month," Marta told me. "And we're hoping for a rescue."

But all three of us knew that a wormhole rescue has never been attempted. It's suicide to go near those things.

I eat, and drink, and try to regain my strength.

I'll need it.

Voice Module 195594

Record Mode:

I got them while they slept.

Ellis, with a large rock to the head.

The rock made a mess. I smothered Marta. Not bloody, but it took a while.

One month rations for three people equals three months rations for one person.

I'm sorry I had to kill them. I truly am.

I'm not a monster.

Voice Module 195595

Record Mode:

Is this thing still working?

Play Mode:

Is this thing still working?

Record Mode:

It's been…how long has it been since I used this? Many months. Perhaps years.

I stopped shaving, and my beard reaches my chest.

Where did I leave off? I think it was with Marta and that guy, I forget his name. The one I killed with the rock.

It was for their synth rations. I paced myself, ate small portions, but still finished them too quickly.

I knew what was next. I knew it from the beginning.

When the rations were finally gone, I ate the people I'd murdered.

Humans, it turns out, are the best meat. Better than dog people. Better than alien lizards.

They sustained me for a while, but then they were gone too.

I began to starve again.

Days, maybe weeks, passed, and I began to whither away. Though I knew hunger well, it didn't make the pain any easier.

At night, I watched the skies. Watched them with a yearning. Hoping for another ship to crash on this planet.

And one did.

Astronomical luck?

Hardly.

Only one survivor this time. Angela something. She explained.

The ore-filled trailer from my ship, the Darion, didn't become lost in space. It's in orbit around Wormhole GG54, daring salvage ships to try and take it.

Many ships have tried. None have succeeded. They get pulled into the wormhole and pushed out here.

It's a giant, baited trap.

According to Angela, five ships have already been lost.

There's a good chance they're somewhere on this planet.

I asked Angela how large her crew was.

She told me there were seven. All dead.

When I killed her, that made eight.

Eight.

Mmmmm.

But that's not enough. It's never enough. I always run out.

I need to find those other ships. And I think I can. The Organic Brain on Angela's ship is still functioning, and it created a partial topographical map of the planet.

The map pinpoints the other crash sites. Some, only a few kilometers away.

I need to move fast. There may be survivors.

The longer I wait, the thinner they get.

A Matter of Taste

Another flash fiction piece for Small Bites. I'm a huge fan of zombie movies, especially the Italian gut munchers. It's pretty obvious with this piece.

"FINISH YOUR BRAINS, PHILLIP."

Phillip pushed the jellied hunk away, using his stump.

"I don't want any more."

Mom squinted in his general direction; her eyes had long since dried up and fallen out.

"Don't you like brains? All little zombie boys need to eat brains. You want to become rotten and putrefied like Dad, right?"

"Arrgghhhhh," said Dad. He didn't have a bottom jaw, so pronunciation wasn't one of his strengths.

"You know I do, Mom. It's just…"

"Just what?"

Phillip folded his arms and picked his nose with the ulna protruding from his stump.

"Phillip!" Mom chided. "Manners!"

"Arrghhhh," his father concurred.

Phillip stopped picking.

"I hate brains."

Mom took a deep breath, and blew it out of the bullet holes in her lungs.

"Fine. Finish your small intestines and you can be excused."

Phillip made a face.

"I don't want to."

"But Phillip, you love intestines. Don't you remember when you rose from the grave? You'd stuff yourself with guts until they were slithering out of your little undead bottom."

Phillip stuck out his lower lip.

"I don't want to eat this stuff anymore, Mom."

"Arrghhhh," said Dad.

"See, Phillip? You're upsetting your father. Do you know how hard he works, hunting the living all day and night, to bring back fresh meat so you can eat? It isn't easy work — he can't move much faster than a limp, and most of the humans left are heavily armed and know to aim for the head."

Phillip stood up. "I don't like it! I don't like the taste! I don't like the smell! And most of all, I don't like eating people I used to go to school with! Last week we ate my best friend, Todd!"

"We're the living dead! It's what we do!"

Phillip's father shrugged, reaching for the child's plate. He dumped the contents onto the edge of the table, and then lowered his face to the organs and bumped at them with his teeth — the only way he could chew.

"I don't want to be a zombie anymore, Mom!"

"We don't have a choice, Phillip."

"Well, from now on, I'm eating something else." Phillip reached under the table and held up a plastic bag.

"What is that?" Mom demanded. "I hear roughage."

"It's a Waldorf Salad."

"Phillip!"

"I'm sorry, Mom. But this is what I'm going to eat from now on. It has apples, and walnuts, and a honey-lemon mayonnaise."

"I forbid it!"

"Arrghhhh," Dad agreed.

"I don't care!" Phillip cried. "I'm a vegan, Mom! A vegan! And there's nothing you can do about it!"

He threw the salad onto the table and shuffled off, crying.

Dad shoved a piece of duodenum down his throat, then patted his wife on the bottom.

"Arrghhhh."

"I know, dear. But what can we do? Blow off his head and eat him for lunch tomorrow?"

"Arrghhhh?"

"Good idea. I'll fetch the shotgun."

Mom limped in the general direction of the gun closet.

"Waldorf Salad? Not in my house."

Embrace

Written back in college when I thought good writing had to sound flowery and imagery was more important than story. I was wrong on both counts. I can't help noticing, looking over this collection, how many stories of mine have some sort of religious foundation or overtones. That's what happens when you're raised Catholic.

SHE COMES AT NIGHT.

I push the rocking chair to the balcony so I may watch her, antique cherry that squeaks and protests much like my old bones. This affords me a towering view of my back yard; the hedges trimmed to lollipops, the fountain cherub eternally spitting water, the ocean in the distance.

The sun takes a lazy bow and exits, raking orange and purple fingers across my acres of thick lawn. Years ago, it was champagne cocktails and croquet. Now, I can't even recall the last time I walked the grounds. An acquaintance, deceased like most, once described men as fine single malt — fiery and immature when young, mellowing with age.

I am finally palatable.

The portrait of my younger self hangs above the fireplace, stern face and eyebrows tempered with resolve. Eyebrows that have grown gray and bushy and without direction.

Once, I would settle for nothing less than crushing all opposition.

Now, I'll settle for some honey in my tea.

I watch as the mist arrives, a soft, ethereal blanket, glowing in my yard lights.

She always comes with the mist, and I feel my pulse quicken, warming me. I drop the blanket from my lap — I don't need it anymore.

The first sight of her is magic. Awe and wonder, feelings known only to the young and to me. Worth more than I have ever earned. She is clothed in translucent blue, the color of the moon, a robe that moves like silk. Her face is always peaceful, her movements sure, and I am both enthralled and pacified. Her dance is nature and life, ebb and flow. Slow, languid turns and comfortable poses, arms always beckoning, the tune known only to her.

Beneath my balcony she stops and smiles, as she has for many years.

"Dance with me."

Tonight I shall.

I grip the armrests of my rocker with gnarled hands and tremble to my feet. The thousand pains that plague my days, the gagging pills that keep me beating, the nights of disquiet — all nullified by my resolve. I finally have the strength to know I have none left. The hand has been played, and folded.

Legs shaky, a yearling, knock-kneed and wide-eyed, I lean over the railing. Into her arms I fall, and break…

And then I am free. I bow to my Lady, and take her hand. "May I have this dance?"

The music is crisp in my ears, light and airy. I embrace her, and we waltz on the mist, above my lawn, away from my empty prison. Through the cherub and the hedges, across the beach, over the sea to chase the sun.

Her mouth flutters closer to mine, soft lips parting.

Black teeth. Sharp.

I cry out, my voice muffled by her hungry kiss, ripping at my face, peeling, pulling.

I gaze up at her through lidless eyes, milky with red.

Her maw finds my soft belly, bites, probes deep.

I am tugged into the ground by looping coils of innards.

Down.

Down.

Down to heat so strong the very air sears, baking raw flesh without ever killing nerves.

We dance again on rusty nails, on white coals and fish hooks, my bowels roping us together for eternity.

For another dance.

And another dance.

Trailer Sucks

I almost didn't write this story, because the subject matter is downright disturbing. But I couldn't get the idea out of my head, so I made this humorous rather than straight horror. After writing it I put it away, convinced it would never see print. Incredibly, it was picked up by Cemetery Dance for an anthology of extreme horror. Along with The Confession, *this is something I sometimes wish I never wrote. You've been warned.*

THE NIGHT BEGAN LIKE any other night at the Galaxy Trailer Park, everyone on lawn chairs in front of Freddie's big double-wide, sharing a bottle of Evan Williams whiskey and setting fire to any squirrel stupid enough to wander into Billy's box trap.

They'd caught three so far, at the cost of one peanut per squirrel. Zeke would yank them out of the box with a leather work glove, sprinkle some of Erma Mae's fancy smelling nail polish remover on its fluffy tail, and then touch a Marlboro to the critter. Damn things ran so fast, they looked like bottle rockets shooting across the lawn, squealing all the way. One even made it all the way up a tree and into its nest, setting that ablaze, little flaming baby squirrels leaping to their deaths and bouncing when they hit the sod.

Good clean American fun.

Jim Bob walked over, a spit covered stogie dead in his lips, smiling like the way he did when he got his weekly check from the gubment, or like that one time when he shit in a box and mailed it to the local porker department because they gave him a ticket for having that rusty Ford up on blocks on his front lawn for over six years.

"Guess what I got me, fellas?"

"A small pecker?" Freddie cackled. Billy thought this was so funny he squirted Evan Williams out of his nose.

Idiots, Jim Bob thought.

"No, you jackasses. I got me a vampire."

More giggling. The giggling turned to guffaws when Zeke, in a show of wit usually reserved for men with more teeth, said, "Well, now…that really sucks."

Jim Bob waited for the laughter to die, showing extraordinary patience, especially considering he broke his ex's nose for sassing back with less conviction. He looked at each of them men in turn, giving them his quit fucking around stare. It only took a few seconds for respectful silence to ensue.

"Here's the deal," Jim Bob said. "You all know 'bout them killings, right?"

The group nodded as one. Some nutbag had been cutting off noggins–one a week–of neighborhood church-going folk. The heads hadn't been found. Last week it was dear old Mrs. Parsons who got herself killed. She had been one of the few women in the community Jim Bob respected, and he often played Mr. Fix-it in her townhouse for eight dollars an hour and homemade apple pie.

"Well, I caught me the killer," Jim Bob said. "Out in the woods, south of Rooney Lake, by that overgrown cemetery. I was hunting coon, discovered this old shack. Outside, in a rain barrel, were all eight heads from the eight people been killed."

Jim Bob paused. Every eye was locked on him, respectful.

"So I go into the shack, and it's got one of them, whatchmacallits, caskets inside. I opened it up, and sleeping in the casket was an honest-to-Christ vampire. Fangs and all. She'd been cutting off the heads, see, to hide the bite marks on the neck. Pretty slick, I gotta admit."

"What'd you do?" Zeke asked.

"You gotta put a stake through the heart," Billy said. "I saw this movie…"

"I'm telling this story," Jim Bob snapped.

"Sorry, Jim Bob. I'll shut up."

"You do that. Anyway, I was thinking the same thing. Put a stake in this bitch."

"Bitch? It was a lady vampire?"

"Hell yeah. And a pretty piece of tail too. Big old titties, and legs that looked like they could wrap around you and ride you until your balls fell off."

"So, what'd you do?"

"I'm getting to that. I was thinking about staking her, but she seemed too damn pretty to kill. Plus, since the Missus left, I haven't tagged a piece of ass."

"You cornholed the vampire?" Freddie asked.

"Can you guys shut up and let me finish the damn story? Jumpin' Jesus on a pogo stick! Do I have to staple your flappers shut?"

"Sorry, Jim Bob."

"Sheesh. Anyway, I'd been riding my 4 by 4, so I hitched a chain up to the casket and dragged it back to my trailer. It was getting dark, and I had to hurry in case the little vixen woke up."

"Did you make it?" Zeke asked.

"No, you idiot. She woke up and killed me."

Silence from the group.

"Hell yeah I made it, you jackass. And I brought her inside and tied her, nekkid, to my bed. Then I gave it to her."

"The stake?"

"The dick."

Billy cocked a head at Jim Bob. "You raped a vampire?"

"It wasn't rape. A vampire ain't alive, dummy. Ain't no laws against humping the living dead."

Zeke winked and gave Jim Bob a nudge. "So how was the little whore?"

"Like fucking an ant hill. That bitch was drier than a box of Grape Nuts. Plus, she woke up in the middle of it, started hissing and snapping those fangs. Could hardly get my nut off."

"Did you stake her?"

"Goddamn, Billy, can you shut up about the goddamn stake for five goddamn minutes?"

Billy nodded, pretending to zip his mouth closed.

Jim Bob chomped on his cigar, swallowed a little piece. "Okay, so

I got to thinking. She might be all dried up down there, but her mouth looked all warm and wet and inviting. 'Cept for those long teeth, of course. So I got my five pound rubber mallet and my chisel and I got rid of those nasty teeth. Wasn't easy, neither, bitch spitting and snapping at me the whole time."

"Did it work?" Zeke asked.

Jim Bob broke into a big grin. "Worked like an unwed mother with ten kids. That girl could suck the feathers off a jaybird."

Laughter and spontaneous back-slapping ensued.

"Can we see her?" Zeke asked.

"See her? You can take her for a test drive," Jim Bob said, to cheers. Then he added, "For five bucks."

"Five bucks?" Freddie frowned. "I thought we was buddies, Jim Bob."

"We is buddies, Freddie. But the care and feeding of a vampire costs money. I had to make a deal with Jesse Miller, the janitor over at Covington Hospital. He charges ten bucks for a pack of blood. So unless one of you guys wants to hook up a straw to your wrist, it's five bucks a bang."

Freddie had to go inside to get some cash. Billy gave Jim Bob a check. Zeke didn't have no money, but had two and a half packs of Marlboros, which Jim Bob admitted was just as good.

They all went over to Jim Bob's trailer, which stank of stale beer and rotten food because Jim Bob hadn't done much cleaning since his wife left.

"She's in my room," Jim Bob said. "It's still daytime, so she's sleeping the sleep of the undead. But the sun is gonna set soon, and then she'll be wild and buckin'."

The quartet crept, quiet as church mice, into the bedroom.

As promised, there was a naked woman tied to the bed, with big old melon titties and fat, red dick-sucking lips, which recessed a bit into her mouth seeing as she had no teeth no more.

"Goddamn!" Zeke removed his John Deere cap and smacked himself on the thigh with it. "Ain't this something!"

"I'm first." Freddie had already undid his overalls. "It's been almost three weeks for me."

"I thought Fat Sue Ellen gave you a handjob behind the church last Sunday."

"Handjobs don't count."

"Wait a second," Billy stepped in front of Freddie. "How do we know this is really a vampire or not?"

Freddie got mean eyes. "Frankly, Billy, I don't give a shit if it's a vampire, my sister, or Mother goddamn Theresa. I'm fucking it."

"You want to go to jail, Freddie? We could all go to jail for this. Is a piece of ass worth prison?"

"Hell yeah."

"Hold up, Freddie." Jim Bob smiled, put a hand on his shoulder. "Billy's right. I don't want to see my good buddies go down on no felony charges. Lemme prove to you this bitch is what I say she is. First of all, any of you see her breathing?"

The three squinted, looking for the telltale rise and fall of the nekkid girl's chest. It didn't move an inch.

"See? No breathing. Now Billy, you want to check to see if you can find a pulse?"

Billy reached out a hand, then hesitated.

"I don't want to."

"Well, shit. You want to stick your peter in her, but you're afraid to touch her wrist?"

Billy swallowed and put two fingers on her wrist, right below where the baling wire bound her to the bedpost.

"Nothing," Billy said. "And she's real cold."

"You sure this ain't just a dead body?" Zeke said. "Because I didn't just pay two packs of smokes to bugger no dead bitch."

"Does a dead body do this?"

Jim Bob reached into his jeans and took out a small silver rosary. He touched the cross to the girl's thigh.

The reaction was instant. The skin blistered and smoked, burning a cross shape into her flesh.

"Goddamn!"

Freddie sniffed the air. "Smells like bacon."

Billy grabbed Jim Bob's wrist, pulled it away from the vampire.

"Jesus, Jim Bob! You made your point. Quit marking her all up."

Jim Bob laughed. "Don't matter none. Bitch heals up the next day. You can get real rough with this little lady, and she's like that fucking battery bunny on TV. Keeps on a'going."

To prove his point, Jim Bob made a fist and punched at her ribs until the left side of her chest caved in.

"Lemme have a go," said Zeke. He picked up the rubber mallet resting on the dresser and brought it down hard on the girl's knee. There was a snapping sound, and the knee bent inwards.

"Son of a bitch! Ain't that somethin'…"

All four men jumped back as the vampire lurched in the bed, her toothless mouth stretched open, crying out like a colicky child.

But no sound came out.

"Shut the fuck up, whore," Jim Bob said, slapping the vampire across the face. She narrowed her yellow eyes at him and hissed, her fat lips flapping.

"Damn," Billy said. "That's some scary shit."

"You kidding? This is the perfect woman. Beat her ass and she can't complain."

Freddie's bibs were already around his ankles.

"I'm first. What do I do? Just stick it in her suck hole?"

Jim Bob slapped her again, then swallowed another piece of cigar. "You could, but it ain't no good. She tries to spit it out."

"Then what do I do?"

Jim Bob put the rosary back in his pants, and his hand came out with a pocket knife.

"Give yourself a little nick on the pecker with this."

Freddie hooded his eyes. "Slice open my pecker? Fuck you."

"Trust me, Freddie. This bitch drinks blood. She goes crazy for just a little taste. Just make a tiny little cut, and she'll suck your balls right out your dick hole."

"No way."

"Don't be a pussy," Zeke said. "Ain't nothing but a little prick on a little prick."

"Then you go first."

"No problem." Zeke shoved Freddie aside and dropped trou. "Gimme the damn knife."

Jim Bob handed Zeke the pocket knife and watched his friend made a tiny slit along the top of his dirty, wrinkled foreskin.

"Now what?" Zeke asked.

"Climb on and give her a taste…and get ready for the ride of your life."

Zeke got onto the bed, causing the vampire to scream again when he kneed her broken ribs. But when his bloody dick got near her lips, she stopped screaming and opened her mouth wide, straining to reach it, tongue licking the air.

"Well, lookee here. Bitch really wants it."

"Shove it in, Zeke. Let her have it."

Zeke did, and the room filled with slurping and sucking sounds. Zeke's eyes rolled up into his head and he moaned.

"Is it good, Zeke?"

"Unngh unghh unghh unghh…"

"Is that yeah?"

"Oh…fuck yeah…"

Zeke's hips were like a piston, gaining speed. Within a minute, his hairy butt clenched, his thighs spasmed, and he was crying out for his mama.

Zeke fell back with a look on his face that was positively fucking angelic.

"I've been boning since I was eleven years old, and that was the best fuck I've had in my whole entire goddamn life."

"I'm next," Freddie said.

Jim Bob handed him the knife, and Freddie gave his pecker two pokes, one on either side of the head, before jamming it in.

Freddie was even quicker than Zeke, finishing up faster than it took most guys to piss.

"That made my nose hair curl," Freddie said, laughing. "Damn, Jim Bob, I think I shot about a gallon into that bitch."

"Goddamn sloppy thirds," Billy swore. But that didn't stop him from stripping off his shit stained underwear, giving his pecker a little cut, and ramming it in those drippy fat lips.

Jim Bob had gotten it four times the night prior, but watching his buddies go at it made his cock so hard he could jack up a car with it. When Billy finished, Jim Bob gave himself a poke-poke with the knife, squeezed to get the bleeding started, and shoved it down her throat.

The sensation was no less incredible than it had been the first four times. This bitch used it all; her lips, her tongue, her cheeks, her throat. She bobbed her head so fast it was a fucking blur. Goddamn, it was good. For five dollars, this was the deal of the century. He should charge at least seven-fifty. Hell, when word got around, there'd be guys lined up out the door for a taste of this. At seventy-fifty a head, twenty people per day…

"Ouch!"

Jim Bob pulled out. While he was mouth fucking her, he felt something pinch.

Sure enough, looking down at his dick, there was more blood than there should have been.

"What the fuck?"

He tried to wipe away the blood, and then noticed the small hole near the base of his pecker.

"What happened, Jim Bob?"

Jim Bob clenched his teeth.

"Fucking bitch bit me."

"I thought you knocked out her teeth."

"I did."

Jim Bob reached over to the dresser, picked up his chisel. He shoved it in the vampire's mouth and pried her jaws open.

There it was, on her upper gums; a new goddamn tooth growing in.

"Son of a bitch!"

Jim Bob flew into a rage. He hit her in the face with the chisel, over and over, cheekbones snapping and jaw cracking. The vampire shook like unholy hell, but that just fueled his fury.

Goddamn women. Can't trust any of them. Even the undead ones.

"Jim Bob…"

Jim Bob didn't pay the boys no mind. He switched his grip on the chisel and began to stab the vampire with it, putting out one of the bitch's eyes with a slurpy pop, then the other.

"Jesus, Jim Bob!"

Someone, maybe it was Zeke, tried to pull him off. But Jim Bob wouldn't budge. After he'd turned the vampire's face into Spaghetti-O's, he began to stab at her chest, puncturing the chisel through her rib cage, driving it into her heart all the way up to the wood handle.

"Holy shit," Billy said.

The vampire began to smoke, her skin cracking and splitting open, exposing red, raw muscle and rotting organs. There was sizzling and snapping and a terrible odor like wet, burning dog.

"Stop it, Jim Bob!"

And then something hit Jim Bob in the back of the head and he was out.

"Look. He's waking up."

Jim Bob sensed people in the room with him. Without opening his eyes, he knew it was Freddie, Zeke, and Billy.

He could smell them.

His memory was hazy, but Jim Bob knew one thing for certain; I've never felt so good.

His shoulder, which had bothered him every single day since he dislocated it ten years ago hauling bags of cement, didn't hurt at all. He wiggled his big toe, which had an ingrown nail so full of puss it was nearly double the size, but there was no pain.

He felt fan-fucking-tastic.

There was only one problem; he couldn't seem to move his arms.

"Jim Bob? You awake?"

Jim Bob opened his eyes and stared his friends standing around his bed. It seemed to be very bright in his room, even though the only light was the forty watt lamp on the dresser.

"Do you understand me, Jim Bob?"

Jim Bob tried to say Of course I understand you, you idiot, but nothing came out of his mouth.

"Goddamn," Zeke said. "He doesn't understand a damn word."

Billy leaned in close. "Do you remember what happened, Jim Bob? You were killing that vampire bitch, and the Freddie hit you on the head with that mallet…"

"Sorry, man." Freddie shrugged his shoulders. "But you were destroying the best piece of ass I ever had."

Billy shook his head sadly. "Problem was, he hit you too hard."

"My bad," said Freddie.

Jim Bob tried to ask a question, but his lips moved in silence.

"You died, Jim Bob. But since that vampire girl bit you on the pecker, we figured we should keep an eye on you, case you came back. And you did."

Zeke smiled. "You should see yourself, Jim Bob. You got teeth longer than my German Shepherd, Harley. I'd hold up a mirror to show you, but it probably wouldn't do nuthin'."

A vampire? Jim Bob thought. This is crazy.

But then he touched his tongue to his teeth and felt the sharp points.

Holy shit! I'm a vampire. That must be the reason I can't talk — I'm dead, and there's no goddamn air in my lungs.

"Sorry we had to tie you up," Billy said. "But we didn't know what else to do. You…uh…want some of this blood?"

Billy held up a plump unit of plasma, one of the packs Jim Bob had bought from Jesse Miller at the hospital.

Jim Bob's mouth instantly filled with drool. He craned his neck toward the blood, licking his lips, trying to reach it. Never before had he been so hungry. He had to have that blood. Hadtohadtohadtohadto…

"Damn!" Zeke said. "Will you lookit that! I think he wants it!"

"Give it to him, Billy." Freddie nudged him.

Zeke held up a hand. "Hold on, wait a second."

"Give it to him. He's our friend."

"He ain't our friend no more. He's a goddamn monster. Look at him, snapping and slobbering."

Gimmeegimmeegimmeegimmee! I need that blood!

"So what should we do?" Billy asked. "Kill him?"

Jim Bob opened his mouth to scream, but nothing came out.

Zeke grinned, rubbing his goatee. "I got me a better idea. Jim Bob may not have big old titties, but I bet he'll be pretty good just the same."

Zeke picked up the mallet and chisel. Billy smiled, unzipping his pants.

"I got first this time!"

Markey

Flash fiction, a little slice-of-life tale that I posted on my website as a freebie.

SOMETHING IS IN MY EAR.

It crawled in when I was sleeping. Really deep. I can feel it tickle against the side of my brain.

I tried to kill it with a sharp pencil.

There was a lot of blood. But it didn't come out.

I stuck some pliers in my ear, to pull it out.

But it went in deeper.

Then it started to talk to me.

It didn't sound like words, not at first. More like chirping.

Kind of like a cricket.

But if I concentrated real hard, I could understand.

He says his name is Markey.

Markey talks to me all the time. He tells me he understands me. He knows that I'm different.

Markey says we're going to be famous one day.

He wants me to kill a little girl.

I don't want to. Killing is bad. I tried to get Markey out of my ear by banging my head into the wall, over and over.

Markey didn't like that. He made me hold my hand over the stove burner as punishment.

It hurt a lot, and I had to go to the hospital for a while. The doctors were very nice. They asked me what happened.

I told them it was an accident.

I didn't tell them about Markey.

When my hand got better, Markey was nicer to me.

For a while.

Then he started talking about killing again.

He said I should bring a little girl back to my basement and do mean things to her with a hammer.

Markey said it won't be much different than all the cats he's made me kill. Except this will be even more fun.

Markey has made me kill a lot of cats.

I have a table in my basement with straps on it. The straps are strong, so the little girl won't get away when I'm putting the nails in her head.

I drive a school bus.

It would be easy to grab a little girl.

Better than cats, Markey said.

I was so alone before Markey crawled into my ear.

He's my best friend.

I'll grab the little bitch tomorrow.

Punishment Room

Another EC Comics inspired tale that I wrote in my younger days. I polished it a decade later for an anthology that never came out, so instead I printed up copies as chapbooks and gave them away for free at horror conventions.

DOMINICK PATAGLIA TRIED TO block out the screaming coming from the Punishment Room, but the ceiling mounted speakers were at maximum volume.

The screams came at regular intervals — animal cries, sharp and shrill, only identifiable as human because they were punctuated with pleas for mercy.

Mercy was not known here.

Dominick clamped his fists over his ears, but the terrible sound penetrated the flesh and bone of his hands. From the creaking noise that underscored the screaming, Dominick guessed they were using the screws; wooden clamps, tightened on joints until the bones almost cracked.

Sometimes bones did crack, causing political bedlam in the form of inquiries and written protestations from sympathy groups.

This usually resulted in a sharp fine.

The Law plainly stated that the punishment couldn't inflict permanent damage. The Government was a stickler on that. It interfered with the education process.

Another scream, like a pig being butchered. Dominick squeezed his eyes shut. He had felt the screws before, and other things that were even more horrible.

Dominick had been a guest of the Punishment Room three times since he came here. Each time it had gotten worse.

His first visit had been just after he arrived. Two men in hoods and uniforms grabbed him before he'd even gotten off the bus. They dragged him to the Waiting Room and locked him in, confused and afraid.

There were no windows in the Waiting Room, no furniture, and the floor was cold, gray concrete. It had a sharp, acrid odor, beneath the scent of antiseptic. Dominick would later identify it as the smell of fear.

On the walls of the Waiting Room, tacked up in ranks and files and covering every inch of space, were photographs.

Pictures of people being tortured.

Thousands of photos, thousands of faces, each depicting a moment of grotesque agony.

Dominick opened his eyes and they locked onto a picture of himself. He looked so young in the picture, even in the grip of agony. It was taken only a few months ago.

They had used the rack the first time.

He hadn't done anything to warrant it. It was just to get him acquainted with the way things were done here.

He had screamed until his voice gave out.

That was what seemed to be happening to his comrade in the Punishment Room. The screams were becoming hoarser. Not because the pain was lessening, but because he had been in there for over an hour. Poor bastard.

Dominick let his eyes wander around the room until he saw the photo of the second time he'd visited the Punishment Room. For talking to an instructor out of turn. Dominick couldn't even remember what he had said to him.

Dominick's face in the picture was tear-stained and manic.

They had used the screws on him. On his thumbs, his knees, his testicles.

It had taken him ten days in the infirmary to recover.

His third visit to the Punishment Room was the worst, and warranted three Polaroids, all of which hung on the wall. During a two hour period he was strung up by his feet and beaten with a rubber whip over every inch of his naked body.

Then he was beaten again.

And again.

And again.

The pain reached such an intense level he kept blacking out, and a doctor had to be called in to give him amphetamine shots to keep him awake.

That's what the Torture Man thrived on. There was a rumor one poor girl had been in the Punishment Room for fourteen hours, simply because she kept passing out from the pain.

The Torture Man loved that.

What he loved even more was breaking someone tough.

The Torture Man glowed when someone showed anger or hatred; anything other than total submission. Because then the Torture Man got to break the spirit along with the body.

Where they found people like the Torture Man, God only knew.

Another hoarse cry. It would be ending soon, and then it would be Dominick's turn.

This was his fourth visit. That meant the electricity. From what others had told him, electricity made everything else look mild.

He would have current driven into his teeth, and his ears, and up his anus. The Government had not banned this torture, even though it resulted in burns on the contact points. Burns weren't considered permanent damage.

The screaming stopped. The silence that filled the Waiting Room made Dominick dizzy.

It would be only moments now.

He hugged his knees to his chest and touched the bottom of his left heel for the hundredth time. Rules required he strip before he came in, but Dominick had managed to tape a stubby pencil to the bottom of his bare foot.

He tapped the sharpened point, but it offered him no courage. Even if Dominick somehow found the guts to use it as a weapon, he didn't think it would get him very far. The Torture Man would probably be amused.

And after the amusement would come anger.

Thinking about it made Dominick nauseous. But he thought about it anyway.

Maybe it would work, if he was quick. Maybe it would work, if he stabbed the Torture Man somewhere vital, like the face. Maybe…

The door opened.

The Torture Man filled the doorway, steeped in the stench of body odor and fear. He stood almost twenty inches taller than Dominick, a monster of a man, with a barrel chest and strong, thick fingers.

"Nice to see you again, Mr. Pataglia." His voice was like raking leaves. The black cowl left his mouth uncovered, and his crooked brown teeth smiled with power and certainty. There were stains on his gray shirt from his armpits to his flanks, and a large wet spot soaked the front of his black pants.

Though sexual abuse and rape weren't allowed by the law, the government allowed him to masturbate while torturing.

Dominick palmed the pencil and fought to keep his sphincter closed. He could hardly breathe. The Torture Man produced a clip board and glared at it with little rat eyes.

"Attacked a hall monitor, eh Dominick? Haven't you got the balls? We'll have to hook them up to the generator, see if we can light them up."

The Torture Man giggled like a young girl.

Dominick stood on rubbery legs and backed into the corner of the room. Dread soaked him to the core. The Torture Man closed in, huge and looming. He grabbed Dominick by the wrist.

"Please," Dominick pleaded. The pencil felt like a strand of spaghetti in his hand, slick and useless.

The Torture Man brought his face close, so close Dominick could smell his rancid breath.

"You're my last assignment of the day, so we'll have plenty of time together."

Dominick looked away, catching a glimpse of his photo on the wall.

"No we won't."

Dominick's voice surprised him. It was low and hard, steely with resolve.

The Torture Man was surprised as well. He went smiley and wide-eyed.

"Why, Mr. Pataglia, did you just contradict —"

Dominick's hand shot out and plunged the pencil into the center of the Torture Man's right eye.

It went in hard, like stabbing a tire, and there was a sucking-slurping sound.

The Torture Man screamed. He released his grip and stumbled backwards, his meaty hands fluttering around his face like birds afraid to land. Blood and black fluid seeped down his face in gooey trails.

Dominick took three quick steps after him and swung his fist at the pencil, managing to knock it deeper into the socket.

The Torture Man made a keening sound, and then crumpled into a large, fat pile on the concrete. His mouth hung open like an empty sack, and his good eye rolled up into the socket, baring the blood-shot white.

Dominick stood over him for a moment, shocked. Had he done it? Had he killed him?

Run! demanded the voice in his head.

But Dominick remained rooted to the floor.

He had to make sure. He had to make sure the bastard was dead.

The adrenalin was wearing off, leaving Dominick sick and shaky. He forced himself to kneel, and then tentatively stretched out a hand to check the Torture Man's pulse.

It was like willfully putting his hand in a fire.

After an eternity of inching closer and closer, Dominick touched the Torture Man's wet, clammy neck. He probed beneath the fat and the stubble, seeking out the carotid.

There was a pulse.

Dominick yanked his hand back as if shocked.

Run, you idiot! If he wakes up…

But Dominick couldn't run. He embraced a chilling certainty; even if he didn't escape, he couldn't allow this evil man to live. Not just for himself, but for all the others.

He chewed his lower lip and reached for the pencil.

The Torture Man groaned.

Dominick sprang to his feet. He needed a weapon of some kind. Side-stepping the Torture Man, Dominick raced out the door and into the hallway. To the left, the door to the courtyard. To the right, the Punishment Room.

Dominick's reaction was visceral — he didn't want to go in the Punishment Room ever again. But there were weapons…

He went right.

The Punishment Room was straight out of his nightmares. Dark and filthy, illuminated by two bare bulbs hanging from the ceiling by greasy cords. The walls were black, and an underlying stink of urine and excrement fouled the moist air. Chains and shackles were bolted to the floor and walls, a rack sat in one corner, and a cabinet full of the Torture Man's hideous instruments yawned open, revealing his tools of pain.

Dominick heard a noise like wind whistling through the trees. He looked back and saw the Torture Man standing in the doorway, wheezing. The pencil was still poking from his eye, and gooey red tears streaked down his face. He pointed a huge finger at Dominick, and took another labored step forward.

Dominick reached into the Torture Man's cabinet and removed a can of lighter fluid. He popped the top and squirted it at the Torture Man's face.

The Torture Man screamed when the alcohol hit his punctured eye. He stumbled backwards and tripped over the generator.

"You little bastard! When I get you…"

Dominick grabbed the nearest object — a digital camera sitting on the cart — and fell upon the Torture Man. He brought the weapon down on his tormentor's face, again and again, the plastic case cracking and splintering as he used it to knock out teeth and break bone.

The Torture Man lashed out, connecting with the side of Dominick's head. Dominick fell onto his back, landing hard. His vision blurred, and something was poking him behind his left shoulder.

Next to him, the Torture Man sat up. He grabbed the pencil and pulled. His eye slurped out of the socket, looking like a tiny red jellyfish trailing its tentacles. The Torture Man howled, dropping the pencil. The eye swung freely down at cheek level, hanging by a coil of optic nerves.

Dominick reached behind his back, seeking the source of his discomfort. He pulled it into view.

It was a steel clamp, almost the size of his hand. He squeezed the ends and it opened its jaws, baring tiny teeth. A cord was attached to the bottom, and Dominick followed it along the floor to where it plugged into the electric generator.

He glanced at the Torture Man, who had managed to find his rubber whip. He smacked it against Dominick's face, the pain instant and staggering.

Dominick rolled onto his side, still gripping the clamp. The whip lashed across his naked back, and he cried out.

"You think you know pain?!" the Torture Man bellowed. "I'll show you pain!"

Dominick spun around onto his bottom, taking another whip stroke in the face. He thrust the clamp at the Torture Man, securing it to his ankle.

Then he stretched out his hand and hit the switch on the generator.

The reaction was instant.

The Torture Man doubled in half like a book slamming shut, and pitched head-first to the floor. A strong whiff of ozone plumed around him as his grotesque body shook in racking spasms. Blood sprayed from his mouth and a piece of tongue escaped his clenched teeth and tumbled down his chin.

Dominick crab walked backwards, putting distance between them. He watched, wide-eyed, as the clamp on the Torture Man's leg began to smoke, and then ignited the soaked-in lighter fluid.

The Torture Man burned like kindling.

Dominick pulled his gaze away and found the drawer next to the cabinet that held his clothes. He tried to ignore the popping sound of blistering flesh and the Torture Man's gurgling moans. By the time he'd tied his shoes the moans had died along with the monster.

The can of lighter fluid was on the cart, next to a pair of tin snips. Dominick shoved the snips in his back pocket and squirted fluid onto the rack. Then he did the samc to the Torture Man's dreaded cabinet and the instruments it contained.

They burned well.

Finally, he went back into the Waiting Room and doused the walls, staring one last time at the picture of himself on the rack, watching it burn.

They would be coming. Soon. He had to get away.

The door to the courtyard was open, and amazingly, no one was around. It made sense — the Hall Monitors hadn't expected to escort him out of there for another few hours.

Dominick stepped out into the fresh air. The sun winked through the trees like an old friend. A light breeze cleared the stench of urine from his nostrils.

The fence was just beyond the basketball courts, locked and topped with razor wire. Impossible to climb over.

But he wasn't climbing.

Two minutes with the tin snips, and he was though the fence.

Freedom enveloped him like a mother's love.

He ran off into the woods, giddy, yet knowing that someday he would return.

But not as a victim.

Dominick had read the forbidden history books. He knew that a hundred years ago there was no torture in America's Public Schools. There was once a time when eleven-year-olds like himself went to school to learn. When education wasn't Government indoctrination. When children were free.

The Torture Man, evil as he was, was just a symptom of the disease. Both a part of the system, and a product of it.

But Dominick knew there were others like himself. Fighters, who sought change.

He would meet up with these people. Grow strong. And in time, when he returned to this place, it wouldn't be as a victim.

It would be as a liberator.

Dominic Pataglia ran through the woods, not looking back at the Elementary Camp. His footfalls were sure and strong, and as he ran he could swear that he heard the sound of a thousand boys and girls behind him, cheering.

S.A.

I wrote this for the anthology Wolfsbane & Mistletoe, edited by Charlaine Harris and Toni L.P. Kelner. It was one of those stories that practically wrote itself. Werewolves have always been one of my favorite monsters, and I was thrilled to have a chance to cut loose and let my imagination run wild. Some quick notes: The Salvation Army is a wonderful organization with over 3.5 million volunteers, and I'm pretty sure none of them are cough syrup swilling psychotics. The names used in this story are all names of characters from famous werewolf movies. Unless someone tries to sue me, in which case I made all of them up. (L.L. Cool J also did a rocking version of "Who's Afraid of the Big Bad Wolf.") While the modern Bible is missing many of its original passages, the Book of Bob isn't one of them. You're probably getting it confused with the lost Book of Fred. Other than that, everything in this story is 100% true.

ROBERT WESTON SMITH WALKED across the snow-covered parking lot carrying a small plastic container of his poop.

Weston considered himself a healthy guy. At thirty-three years old he still had a six-pack, the result of working out three times a week. He followed a strict macrobiotic diet. He practiced yoga and tai chi. The last time he ate processed sugar was during the Reagan administration.

That's why, when odd things began appearing in his bowel movements, he became more than a little alarmed. So alarmed that he sought out his general practitioner, making an appointment after a particularly embarrassing phone call to his office secretary.

Weston entered the office building with his head down and a blush on his ears, feeling like a kid sneaking out after curfew. He used the welcome mat to stamp the snow off his feet and walked through the lobby to the doctor's office, taking a deep breath before going in. There were five people in the waiting room, two adults and a young boy, plus a nurse in pink paisley hospital scrubs who sat behind the counter.

Weston kept his head down and beelined for the nurse. The poop container was blue plastic, semi-opaque, but it might as well have been a police siren, blinking and howling. Everyone in the room must have known what it was. And if they didn't at first, they sure knew after the nurse said in a loud voice, "Is that your stool sample?"

He nodded, trying to hand it to the woman. She made no effort to take it, and he couldn't really blame her. He carried it, and a clipboard, over to a seat in the waiting room. Setting his poop on a table atop an ancient copy of *Good Housekeeping*, he got to work filling out his insurance information. When it came time to describe the nature of his ailment, he wrote down "intestinal problems." Which was untrue---his intestines felt fine. It's what came out of his intestines that caused alarm.

"What's in the box?"

Weston looked up, staring into the big eyes of a child, perhaps five or six years old.

"It's, um, something for the doctor."

He glanced around the room, looking for someone to claim the boy. Three people had their noses stuck in magazines, one was watching a car commercial on the TV hanging from the ceiling, and the last appeared asleep. Any of them could have been his parent.

"Is it a cupcake?" the boy asked.

"Uh… yeah, a cupcake."

"I like cupcakes."

"You wouldn't like this one."

The boy reached for the container.

"Is it chocolate?"

Weston snatched it up and set it in his lap.

"No. It isn't chocolate."

"Show it to me."

"No."

The boy squinted at the sample. Weston considered putting it behind his back, out of the child's sight, but there was no place to set it other than the chair. It didn't seem wise to put it where he might lean back on it.

"It looks like chocolate. I think I can see peanuts."

"Those aren't peanuts."

In fact, gross and disturbing as it sounded, Weston didn't know what those lumps were. Which is why he was at the doctor's office.

He glanced again at the three people in the waiting room, wondering why no one bothered to corral their son. Weston was single, no children. None of his friends had children. Being a mechanical engineer, he didn't encounter children at his job. Perhaps today's parents had no problems letting their kids walk up to strangers and beg for cupcakes.

"Mr. Smith?" the pink paisley nurse said. "Please come with me."

Weston stood, taking his poop through the door, following the nurse down a short hallway and into an examining room.

"Please put on the gown. I'll be back in a moment."

She closed the door behind him. Weston stared at the folded paper garment, setting on the edge of a beige examination table also lined with paper. He set the container down on next to a jar of cotton swabs. Then he removed his coat, shoes, jeans, boxer shorts, and polo shirt, placed them in a neat pile on the floor, and slipped his arms through the gown's sleeve holes. It felt like wearing a large, stiff napkin.

Weston shivered. It was cold in the room; examination rooms always seemed to be several degrees too cool for comfort. He stood there in his socks, rubbing his bare arms, waiting for the nurse to come back.

She eventually did, taking his temperature and blood pressure, then left him again with the promise that Dr. Waggoner would be there shortly.

A minute passed. Two. Three. Weston stared at the ceiling tiles, thinking about the hours he'd spent on the Internet looking for some sort of clue to what strange disease he had. There was plenty of disturbing content about bowel movements, including a website where people actually sent in pictures of theirs so others could rate them, but he'd found nothing even remotely close to the problem he was having.

The door opened, derailing his train of thought.

"Mr. Smith? I'm Dr. Waggoner. Please, sit down."

Weston sat on the table, the paper chilly under his buttocks. Dr. Waggoner was an older man, portly. Bald, but with enough gray hair growing out of his ears to manage a comb over. He had on trendy round eyeglasses with a faux tortoise shell frame, and a voice that was both deep and nasally.

"Your blood pressure is normal, but your temperature is 100.5 degrees." He snapped on some latex gloves. "How are you feeling right now?"

"Fine."

"Any aches, pains, problems, discomforts?"

"No. I'm a little chilly, but that's all."

Dr. Waggoner removed some sort of scope and checked Weston's eyes and ears as they talked.

"How long have you been having these intestinal problems?"

"Um, on and off for about three months. But they aren't really intestinal problems. I'm finding, uh, strange things in my bowel movements."

"Can you describe them for me?"

"Like little stones. Or things that look like strips of fabric."

Dr. Waggoner raised an eyebrow.

"Well, I have to ask the obvious question first."

Weston waited.

"Have you been eating little stones or strips of fabric?"

The doctor grinned like a Halloween pumpkin. Weston managed a weak smile.

"Not that I'm aware of, Doctor."

"Good to know. Tell me about your diet. Has it changed recently? Eating anything new or exotic?"

"Not really. I eat mostly health foods, have been for the last ten years."

"Been out of the country in the last six months?"

"No."

"Do you eat a lot of rare meat, or raw vegetables?"

"Sometimes. But I don't think I have a tapeworm."

Dr. Waggoner chuckled.

"Ah, the Internet. It gives everyone a doctorate in medicine."

Weston did the open his mouth and say "aaaaah" thing, then said, "I know I'm not a doctor, but I checked a lot of sites, and the things in my stool, they don't look like tapeworm segments."

"Stones and fabric, you said. Can you be more specific?"

"The stones are sort of white. Some very small, like flecks. Other times bigger."

"How big?"

"About the size of my thumb."

"And the fabric?"

"There have been different colors. Sometimes red. Sometimes black. Sometimes blue."

"How closely have you examined these items?"

Weston frowned. "Not too closely. I mean, I never took them out of the toilet and picked them up or anything. Except for that." Weston pointed to the stool on the table.

"We'll have the lab take a look at that. In the meantime, I'm going to have to take a look myself. Can you bend over the table and lift up your gown, please?"

Weston hoped it wouldn't have to come to this, but he assumed the position while Dr. Waggoner applied some chilly lubricating jelly to his hand and the point of entry.

"Just relax. You'll feel some pressure."

It was a hell of a lot worse than pressure, and impossible to relax. Weston clenched his eyes shut and tried to concentrate on something, anything, other than the fat fingers going up the down staircase.

"You said this began three months ago. Has it been non-stop? Intermittent?"

"Only two or three days out of the month," Weston grunted. "Then it goes back to normal."

"When during the month?"

"Usually the last week."

"Have you… wait a second. Stay still for a moment. I think I feel something."

Which is the absolute last thing you want to hear when a doctor has his hand inside you. Weston held his breath, scrunched up his face. He didn't know which was worse, the pain or the humiliation. Blessedly, mercifully, the hand withdrew.

"What is it, Doctor?"

"Hold on. I think there's more. I'm going in again."

Weston groaned, hating his life and everyone in it. The doctor went back in four additional times, so often that Weston was becoming used to it, a fact that disturbed him somewhat.

"I think that's the last of it."

"The last of what?"

Weston turned around, saw the physician staring at several objects on his palm.

Dr. Waggoner said. "A coat button, part of a zipper, and sixty three cents in change. Apparently you're not eating as healthy as you think."

Weston blinked, as if the act would make the objects disappear. They remained.

"This is going to sound like a lie," Weston said. "But I didn't eat those."

"I had a colleague who once examined a man who wanted to get into one of those world record books by eating a bicycle, one piece at a time. He removed a reflector from the man's rectum."

"I'm serious, Doctor. I'm not eating buttons or change. I certainly didn't eat a zipper."

"It looks like a fly from a pair of jeans." Dr. Waggoner chuckled again. "I know an old lady who swallowed a fly."

"I didn't eat a fly."

"Okay. Then there's only one alternative. Are you sexually active?"

Weston sighed. "I'm straight. Currently between girlfriends. And the only person who has been up there in my entire life has been you."

Dr. Waggoner placed the objects in a bedpan and said, "You can sit down now."

Weston got off all fours, but preferred to stand. He didn't think he'd ever sit again.

"You think I'm lying to you."

"These things didn't just materialize inside you from another dimension, Mr. Smith. And you probably don't have a branch of the US Treasury inside you, minting coins."

At least someone seemed to be enjoying this. Weston wondered when he'd ask him to break a dollar.

"I'm telling the truth."

"Do you have a roommate? One who likes practical jokes?"

"I live alone."

"Do you drink? Do any drugs?"

"I have an occasional beer."

"Do you ever drink too much? Have black outs? Periods where you don't remember what happened?"

Weston opened his mouth to say no, but stopped himself. There were a few moments during the last few weeks that seemed sort of fuzzy, memory-wise. He wouldn't call them black-outs. But he'd go to bed, but wake up in a different part of the house. Naked.

"I think I might sleep walk," he admitted.

"Now we're getting somewhere." Dr. Waggoner pulled off his gloves, put them in the hazardous materials bin. "I'm going to refer you to a specialist."

Weston scratched his head. "So you think I'm eating buttons and spare change in my sleep?"

"They're getting inside you, one way or another. Consider yourself lucky. I once had a patient who, while sleepwalking, logged onto an internet casino and blew seventy-eight thousand dollars."

"So he came to see you for help with sleepwalking?"

"He came to see me to set his broken nose, after his wife found out. Don't worry, Mr. Smith. I'm going to prescribe a sleep aid for you tonight, to help curb late-night snacking, and the specialist will get to the root of your problem. Sleepwalking is usually the result of stress, or depression."

Weston frowned. "This doctor you're referring me to. Is he a shrink

"His name is Dr. Glendon. He's a psychiatrist. My nurse will set up an appointment for you. In the meantime, try to lock up all the small, swallowable objects in your home."

Weston walked home feeling like an idiot. An idiot who sat on a cactus. His apartment, only a few blocks away from the doctor's office, seemed like fifty miles because every step stung.

The sun was starting to set, and Naperville had its holiday clothes on. Strands of white lights hung alongside fresh evergreen wreaths and bows, decorating every lamp post and storefront window. The gently falling snow added to the effect, making the street look like a Christmas card.

None of it cheered Weston. Since his job moved him to Illinois, away from his family and friends in Asheville, North Carolina, he'd been down. But not actually depressed. All Weston knew about depression came from watching TV commercials for anti-depressants. He'd never seen a commercial where the depressed person ate nickels, but maybe Dr. Waggoner was on to something.

Fishing his keys from his jeans, he was about to stick them in the lock of the security door when it opened suddenly. Standing there, all four feet of her, was his mean next door neighbor. Weston didn't know her name. She probably didn't know his either. She simply called him "Loud Man." Every twenty minutes she would bang on the wall between their apartments, screaming about him making noise. If he turned on the TV, she'd bang — even when it was at its lowest setting. If the phone rang, she'd bang. When the microwave beeped, she'd bang. She even banged while he was brushing his teeth.

He'd called the landlord about her, three times. Each occasion, Weston got the brush off.

"She's eccentric," he was told. "No family. You should ignore her."

Easy for the landlord to say. How do you ignore someone who won't let you into your own door?

Weston tried to step around her, but the old woman folded her arms and didn't budge. She had light brown skin, and some sort of fabric tied to the top of her head. Weston couldn't help staring at her ears, which had distinctive, gypsy-like gold hoops dangling from them. The ears themselves were huge, probably larger than Weston's hands. Maybe if his ears were that big, he'd complain all the time about noise too.

Her dog, some sort of tiny toy breed with long fur and a mean disposition, saw Weston and began to yap at him, straining against his leash. It had a large gold tag on his collar that read "ROMI."

"Excuse me," Weston said, trying to get by.

The old woman stayed put. So did Romi.

"I said, *excuse me.*"

She pointed a crooked old finger at him.

"Loud Man! You keep noise down!"

"They have these things called earplugs," Weston said. "I think they come in extra large."

She began to scream at him in a high-pitched native tongue that sounded a lot like "Blaaa-laaaa-laaaaa-leeee-laaaa-blaaa!" Romi matched her, yipping right along. Weston took it for about ten seconds, and then pushed past, heading for his apartment. The chorus followed him inside.

Though it was early, Weston yawned, then yawned again. He hung his keys on a hook next to the door, switched the TV on to one setting above MUTE, and sat on the sofa. There was dog hair on the carpet, which made no sense, because Weston had no dog.

But the crazy old lady had a dog.

Could she be getting in my apartment somehow?

Panicked, Weston did a quick tour, looking for anything missing or out of place. He came up empty, but to his shame he realized he was picking up everything smaller than a match book and sticking it in his pockets. He took these items and placed them in a junk drawer in the kitchen.

For some reason, this act drained him of his last drop of energy, and the sun had barely even gone down. He sat back down on the couch, switched to the SciFi Channel, and closed his eyes for just a few seconds.

A ringing sound woke Weston up. He was naked on the kitchen floor, the sun streaming in through the windows. Weston automatically smacked his lips, checking to see if he could taste anything odd. Then he got to his knees and reached for the phone on the counter.

"Mr. Smith? This is Dr. Waggoner's office calling. Please hold for the doctor."

Weston scratched his chest, listening to Neil Diamond singing to a chair who apparently didn't hear him.

"Weston? This is Dr. Waggoner. How did you sleep last night?"

"Not well," he said, noting his nude body.

"Remember to keep your appointment with the psychiatrist today. And also, it wouldn't hurt to see a dentist as well. We got the lab report from your stool sample. It contained three molars."

"Teeth?"

"Yes. Your teeth. There was also a shoelace, and a silver cross on a necklace. The lab is sending the cross over to my office later, in case you'd like to pick it up. It will be cleaned first, of course

"Doctor, I..."

Dr. Waggoner hung up before Weston could finish, "...don't own a silver cross."

He got to his feet and padded over to the bathroom, opening wide for the mirror. Weston wasn't missing any molars. Each of his teeth was in its proper place.

What the hell is going on?

His abdomen grumbled. Weston sat on the toilet and rubbed his temples, trying to make sense of any of this. How could he have swallowed teeth, or a silver cross? Why did he keep waking up naked? What was going on?

He didn't want to look, but before he flushed he forced himself. And gasped.

At the bottom of the toilet bowl were two distinct, unmistakable objects: A gold hoop earring, and a silver tag that said ROMI.

When he stopped running around in a blind panic (which took the good part of twenty minutes) Weston forced himself to the computer and Googled "eating+disorder+neighbor." This led him to sites about anorexia, which certainly wasn't his problem. Next he tried "cannibal" and got hits for bad Italian horror movies and death metal rock bands. "Sleep+eating+people" produced articles about sleeping pills, and "I ate human beings" led to a YouTube video of some drunk Klan member who kept saying "I hate human beings" and apparently posted the video so wasted he misspelled the title of his own rant.

Various other word combination produced pages about Hannibal Lector, Alfred Packer, Sawney Bean, and ultimately Hansel and Gretel.

While on the site about fairy tales, Weston clicked from the old witch who wanted to eat children to the big bad wolf who wanted to eat children. This took him to a site about the history of lycanthropy, which featured several old paintings of wolf people running off with screaming babies in their mouths. Soon Weston was looking up "clinical lycanthropy" which was a real psychiatric term that pretty much meant "batshit crazy."

Could I really be crazy? he thought. *Do I subconsciously think I'm a werewolf?*

A quick click on a lunar calendar confirmed Weston's fears: The only time he'd had blackouts and found weird things in his poop was during the full moon.

Weston sat back, slack-jawed. He wondered if he should call someone. His parents? A doctor? The cops?

He searched his soul for remorse for eating his mean neighbor and her nasty dog, but couldn't find any.

But he must have killed other, nicer people. Right?

Weston slipped on some shorts and attacked the Internet again, looking through back issues of the local newspaper for accounts of murders or disappearances. He found five.

The first was from yesterday. A hand and partial skeleton found near the River Walk, a popular woodsy trail in Naperville. The prints on the hand belonged to Leon Corledo. His death was attributed to the Naperville Ripper.

How could I have missed hearing about that? Weston wondered. Too much work, probably. And the fact that the news depressed him, so he avoided it. Not to mention the fact that every time he turned on his TV, his recently digested neighbor banged.

Weston read on, found that Mr. Corledo was a registered sex offender. No big loss there. Weston followed the links to articles about the Ripper's other known victims. They included:

Waldemar Daminsky, 66, a local businessman with known ties to Polish organized crime.

Tony Rivers, 17, who was decapitated after robbing a liquor store and beating the owner unconscious.

Ginger Fitzgerald, who had recently lost custody of her daughter for locking her in a closet for a week without food or water.

And Marty Coslaw, a lawyer.

Weston felt zero guilt, and breathed a bit easier. But how many criminals and lawyers did Naperville have? Eventually, he'd run out of scumbags to eat. Then what?

He tried the search term "help for real lycanthropy" and, incredibly, got a hit. A single hit, for a website called *Shapeshifters Anonymous.*

Weston went to the site, and found it to be a home for werewolf jokes. After suffering through a spate of awful puns (Where do werewolves go on vacation? A Howliday Inn!) he had about given up when he noticed a tiny hotlink at the bottom of the page that read, "Real therianthropes click here."

He knew from his lycanthropy reading that therianthropes were humans who morphed into animals. He clicked.

The page took him to another site, which had a black background and only five large cryptic words on it.

THERIANTHROPES MUST VIEW THE SOURCE

Weston stared, wondering what it meant. Which source? The source of their affliction? The source of their food?

On a whim, he Googled "view the source" and came up with a bunch of websites about HTML programming. Then he got it.

View the webpage source.

He went back to the werewolf page, opened his Internet Explorer toolbar, and under the PAGE menu clicked VIEW SOURCE. The HTML and Javascript appeared in a new window. Weston read through the computer language gobbledygook until he came to this:

```
&ei=xY0_R6--CZXcigGGoPmBCA"+g}return
true};window.gbar={};(function(){;var
g=window.gbar,a,f,h;functionm(b,e,d){b.display=b.disp
lay=="block"?"none":"block";b.left=e+"px";b.top=d+"px
"}g.tg=function(b){real therianthropes call 1-800-
209-7219}
```

Weston grabbed his phone and dialed with trembling hands.

"Therianthrope hotline, Zela speaking, may I help you?"

"I… uh… is this for real?"

"Are you a therianthrope, sir?"

"I think so. Is this really a werewolf hotline?"

"Is that what you turn into, sir? A wolf?"

"I have no idea. I black out beforehand, can't remember anything."

"Why do you think you're a therianthrope, sir?"

"I'm finding, um, things, in my, uh, toilet."

"Things like bone fragments, jewelry, eyeglasses, bits of clothing, coins, watches, and keys?"

"How did you know?"

"I'm a therianthrope myself, sir. Can I ask where you currently reside?"

"Naperville. Illinois."

"So I'm assuming you just realized you're the Naperville Ripper we've been hearing about?"

"They were all bad people," Weston said quickly. "I'm not sure about the lawyer, but I can make assumptions."

"We've been following the news. He was a defense attorney, defended child molesters. When given a choice, therianthropes usually prefer the wicked over the good. The creatures inside us find evil tastier."

"That's, uh, good to know. So… what are you, exactly? Are you a werewolf too?"

"I'm a weresquirrel, sir."

"When the full moon rises, you turn into a squirrel?"

"Yes."

"A squirrel with buck teeth with a big fluffy tail?

"That's the one."

Weston wasn't sure if he was supposed to laugh or not.

"Do you shrink? Or stay full size?"

"Full size."

"And you eat people?"

"No, sir. Not all therianthropes are carnivores."

"So, if you don't mind me asking, what do you do when you change?"

"I horde nuts."

Weston chose his next words carefully.

"Are they… evil nuts?"

"Sir, I'm going to put your sarcasm down as you being on the edge of a nervous breakdown, so I'll ignore it. Are you interested in getting help for your therianthropy?"

"Yes, please. Thank you, Zela."

"Let me check the meeting schedule. Okay, today, at noon,

there's an SA meeting at St. Lucian's church in Schaumburg, approximately ten miles northwest of you. The secret word to gain entry is Talbot."

"What's SA?"

"Shapeshifters Anonymous."

"So I just go there, and they'll let me join them?"

"If you give the secret word. Yes."

"Do I have to bring anything?"

"Donuts are always nice."

"Donuts. I could bring donuts. Will you be there tonight, Zela? I can bring some with peanuts on them."

"That's very thoughtful of you sir, but I live in New Jersey. And I also think you're kind of a schmuck. Is there anything else I can help you with today?"

"No. Thanks, Zela."

"Thanks for calling the hotline."

Weston hung up, ending what was easily the most surreal conversation he ever had in his life. An hour ago, he'd been a normal guy with some odd bowel movements. Now, he was 99% sure he was some sort of therianthrope.

But what kind?

He went back to the sofa, picked up some of the hair. Long, grayish, fluffy.

Was he a weresheep?

No. He ate people. Had to be a carnivore of some sort.

So what gray animals ate other animals?

Wolves, obviously. Coyotes. Dogs. Cats. Were elephants carnivores?

The Internet told him they were herbivores, which was a relief. But then Weston thought of another gray carnivore.

Rats.

Weston didn't want to be a wererat. He hated rats. Hording nuts was one thing. Swimming in the sewers, eating garbage and feces and dead animals, that was awful. He held his armpit up to his face and sniffed, seeing if he could detect any sort of sewage smell. It seemed okay. Then he checked the time and saw he had two hours to get to the SA meeting. So he hopped in the shower, dressed, and got on his way.

It had snowed during the night, making Naperville seem even more Winter-Wonderlandish. The cold felt good on Weston's bare face. He attributed the slight fever to his condition: Google told him wolves had an average body temperature of 100.5.

His first stop was Dr. Waggoner's, to pick up the silver cross. Weston didn't want to keep it for himself, but it was evidence of a murder, so it was best to get rid of it.

The nurse handed it to him in an envelope.

"Are you going to put it on?" she asked, eyes twinkling.

"Not right now."

But when he stepped outside, he did open the envelope to take a look. It was, indeed, silver. But all of the movies, all the books, said silver killed werewolves. Weston took a deep breath and dumped it into his palm. It didn't burn his skin. Or was that only with vampires?

He was bringing it up to his face, ready to touch it to his tongue, when he remembered where it had been. Besides, it had already passed through his system without killing him. Obviously the legends were wrong.

He tucked the cross into his coat pocket and walked into town, toward the bakery. On his way, he passed a man dressed as Santa Claus, ringing a bell for some charity. Thinking of the cross, Weston approached and dropped it in the steel collection pot.

"Beware," Santa muttered, voice low and sinister.

Weston wasn't sure he heard correctly. "Excuse me?"

"There's a killer on the loose in Naperville." Weston could smell the NyQuil on Santa's breath. "Not an ordinary killer, either. Only comes out when the moon is full."

"Uh, thanks for the warning."

Weston began to walk away, but Santa's hand reached out and snatched his wrist, pinching like a lobster claw.

"Naughty boys get what they deserve," Santa intoned.

"Okay…"

Santa's eyes suddenly lit up, burning with some internal fire.

"They will be torn limb-from-limb! Their heads severed from their unholy bodies! Burned to ash on sacred ground! BURNED! *BURRRRRRRRRRNED!!!!!*"

Weston pulled free, then walked briskly to the other side of the street, badly shaken. What kind of charity allowed cough syrup crazed psychotics out in public? Wasn't there some kind of screening process for volunteers?

He glanced once over his shoulder, and Psycho Santa was talking on a cell phone, still pointing at him like Donald Sutherland at the end of the first *Invasion of the Bodysnatchers* remake. It gave Weston the chills.

The uneasy feeling stayed with him all the way up to Russoff's Bakery, where he bought a dozen assorted donuts and a black coffee. When he stepped back onto the street, Weston considered taking another route home so he wouldn't have to see Looney Claus again, then chided himself for being afraid. After all, he was a werecreature. What did he have to fear? If that Santa was really a bad person, chances were good that Weston's inner therianthrope would eat him tonight during the full moon. Weston allowed himself a small smile at the thought of seeing a white beard in his toilet tomorrow morning.

So he steeled himself, and walked the regular path home. But when he passed the spot where Psycho Santa had been, he saw the volunteer was no longer there. Crazy Kringle had packed up his charity pot and left.

Weston walked to his apartment parking lot, hopped into his car, spent a minute programming his GPS, and headed for the suburb of Schaumburg. During the drive, he tried to get his mind around the events of the past twenty-four hours. But he wasn't able to focus. He kept seeing Santa's face. Kept hearing his threats. Once, in the rearview mirror, he swore he saw someone several car lengths behind him in a pointy red hat.

"You're being paranoid," he said to himself, refusing to drink any more coffee.

Just the same, he drove a little faster.

Ten minutes later he was at St. Lucian's, an unassuming Catholic church with a 1970's vibe to the architecture. It was orange with a black shingle roof, shaped like an upside down V. Two large stained glass windows flanked the double entry doors, and a statue of someone, possibly Jesus, perched atop the steeple. There were only six cars in the parking lot, which Weston appreciated because he wasn't good at remembering names, and no one would be short a donut. He parked behind an SUV and took a deep breath to calm his nerves. It was 10:46.

"Here goes nothing."

Bakery goods in hand, he approached the double doors and let himself into St. Lucian's.

The church was dark, quiet. It smelled of scented candles, many of which were burning on a stand next to a charity box. Weston looked down the aisle, to the altar, seeing no one. Then he caught a handwritten sign taped to the back of a pew that read, "SA MEETING IN BASEMENT."

He did a 360, opened a storage closet, then a confessional booth, before finding the door to the stairs next to a baptism font. The concrete staircase wasn't lit, but at the bottom he heard voices. Weston descended, the temperature getting warmer the lower he went. At the bottom he walked past a large furnace, down a short hall, and over to a meeting room.

A bored looking man whose gray hair and loose skin put him somewhere in the sixties, peered at Weston through thick glasses. He wore jeans and a faded turtleneck sweater. From his stance, and his severe haircut, Weston guessed he was ex-military. He stood guard over the doorway, preventing Weston from seeing inside.

"Sorry, sir. This is a private meeting."

The conversation in the room stopped.

"This is SA, right?"

"Yeah. But it's invitation only."

Weston was momentarily confused, until he remembered the hotline conversation.

"Talbot," he said.

"Tall what?"

"Talbot. Isn't that the password?"

"No."

"It's last week's password," someone from in the room said.

"Sorry, buddy." Old Guy folded his arms. "That was last week's password."

"That's the one I was told to use."

"By whom?"

"The SA hotline woman. Tina or Lena or someone."

"Sorry. Can't let you in."

"I brought you donuts." He meekly held up the box.

Old Guy took them.

"Thanks."

"So I can come in?"

"No."

Weston didn't know what to do. He could call the hotline back, but he didn't have the number handy. He'd have to find Internet access, find the website, and by then the meeting could be over.

"Listen." Weston lowered his voice. "You have to let me in. I'm a thespianthrope."

Several snickers from inside the room.

"Does that mean when the moon rises you start doing Shakespeare?" someone asked.

More laughs. Weston realized what he said.

"A *therianthrope*," he corrected. "I'm the Naperville Ripper."

"I don't care if you're Mother Theresa. You don't get in without the correct password."

Weston snapped his fingers. "Zela. Her name was Zela. She liked to grab people's nuts."

Old Guy remained impassive.

"I mean, she said she was a weresquirrel. She horded nuts."

"I'll call Zela." It was woman's voice. Weston waited, wondering what he would do if they turned him away. For all of his Googling, he'd found precious little information about his condition. He needed to talk to these people, to understand what was going on. And to learn how to deal with it.

"He's okay," the woman said. "Zela gave him the wrong password. Said he's kind of a schmuck, though."

Old Guy stared hard at Weston. "We don't allow for schmuckiness at SA meetings. Got it?"

Weston nodded.

"Oh, lighten up, Scott." The woman again. "Let the poor guy in."

Scott stepped to the side. Weston took his donuts back and entered the room. A standard church basement. Low ceiling. Damp smell. Florescent lights. Old fashioned coffee percolator bubbling on a stand in the corner, next to a trunk. A long, cafeteria style table dominated the center, surrounded by orange plastic chairs. In the chairs were five people, three men and two women. One of the women, a striking blonde, stood up and extended her hand. She had apple cheeks, a tiny upturned nose, and Angelina Jolie lips.

"Welcome to Shapshifters Anonymous. I'm Irena Reed, chapter president."

The one who called Zela. Weston reached his hand out to shake hers, but she bypassed it, grabbing the donuts. She brought them to the table, and everyone gathered round, picking and choosing. Irena selected a jelly filled and bit into, soft and slow. Weston found it incredibly erotic.

"So what's your name?" she purred, mouth dusted with powdered sugar.

"I thought this was anonymous."

Irena motioned for him to come closer, and they walked over to the coffee stand while everyone else ate.

"The founders thought *Shapeshifters Anonymous* had gravitas."

"Gravitas?"

"You know. Depth. Sorry, I'm a school teacher, that's one of our current vocab words. When this group was created, they thought *Shapeshifters Anonymous* sounded better than the other potential names. We were this close to calling ourselves *Shapeshifters R Us*."

"Oh. Okay then." He looked at the group and waved. "My name is Weston."

Weston waited for them all to reply in unison, "Hi, Weston." They didn't.

"You're welcome," Weston tried.

Still no greeting.

"They aren't very social when there's food in front of them," Irena said.

"I guess not. So… you're a therianthrope?"

"A werecheetah. Which is kind of ironic, being a teacher."

He stared blankly, not getting it.

"We expel cheetahs." Irena put a hand to her mouth and giggled.

Weston realized he was already in love with her. "So who is everyone here?"

"The ex-marine, Scott Howard, he's a weretortoise."

Weston appraised the man anew. Long wrinkled neck. Bowed back. "It suits him."

"The small guy with the big head, that's David Kessler. He's a werecoral."

Weston blinked. "He turns into coral?

"Yeah."

"Like a coral reef?"

"Shh. He's sensitive about it."

"How about that older woman?" Weston indicated a portly figure with a huge mess of curly black hair.

"Phyllis Allenby. She's a furry."

"What's that?"

"Furries dress up in animal costumes. Like baseball team mascots."

Weston was confused. "Why?"

"I'm not sure. Might be some sort of weird sex thing."

"So she's not a therianthrope?"

"No. She likes to wear a hippo outfit and dance around. Personally, I don't get it."

"Why is she allowed into meetings?"

"We all kind of feel sorry for her."

A tall man with his mouth around something covered in sprinkles called over to them.

"You two talking about us?"

Irena shot him with her thumb and index finger. "Got it in one, Andy."

Andy strutted over, his grin smeared with chocolate. He shook Weston's hand, pumping enthusiastically.

"Andy McDerrmott, wereboar."

"You… become a pig?" Weston guessed.

"Actually, when the full moon rises, I change into someone vastly self-interested, and I talk incessantly about worthless minutiae going on in my life."

Weston wasn't sure how to answer. Andy slapped him on the shoulder, hard enough to rock him.

"A *bore*! Get it? *Were-bore*!" Andy laughed, flecking Weston with sprinkles. "Actually, kidding, I turn into a pig."

"You mean a bigger pig, right Andy?"

Andy shot Irena a look that was pure letch.

"God, you're so hot, Irena. When are we going to get together, have ourselves a litter of little kiggens?"

"On the first of never, Andy. And they wouldn't be kiggens.

They'd be pities."

"Snap," Phyllis said. "Shoot that pig down, girl."

"So who's the last guy?" Weston asked. "The big one?"

The trio glanced at the heavily muscled man sitting at the end of the table, staring off into space.

"That's Ryan."

"Just Ryan?"

Andy wiped his mouth on the sleeve of his sports jacket. "That's all he's ever told us. Never talks. Never says a word. Comes to every meeting, but just sits there, looking like the Terminator."

"What does he change into?"

"No one knows. Has to be something, though, or Zela wouldn't have sent him here." Andy faced Weston. "So you're the Naperville Ripper, huh? What kind of therianthrope are you? Wererat?"

Andy frowned. "I'm not sure. I think I'm a werewolf."

This provoked laughter from the group.

"What's funny?"

"Everyone thinks they're a werewolf at first," Irena explained, patting him on the arm. "It's because werewolves are the most popular therianthropes."

"They get all the good press," Andy said. "All the books. All the movies. Never gonna see a flick called *An American Wereboar in London*."

"Or *The Oinking*," Phyllis added.

Furry or not, Andy was starting to like Phyllis.

Irena's hand moved up Weston's arm, making him feel a little light-headed.

"Because we can't remember what we do when we've changed, we all first assume we're werewolves."

"So how can I find out what I change into?"

"I set up a video camera and recorded myself." Andy reached into his jacket, took out a CD. "We can pop it in the DVD if you want."

"Don't say yes," Phyllis warned. "The last time he put in a tape of himself and some woman doing the nasty. And it was real nasty."

"An honest mistake." Andy leaned closer to Weston and whispered, "She was a college cheerleader, studying massage therapy. I was bow-legged for a week afterward."

"She was an elderly woman," Phyllis said. "With a walker."

"Mind your own business, you furvert. You're not even a real therianthrope."

Phyllis stuck out her jaw. "I am in my heart."

"When there's a full moon, you don't turn into hippo. You turn into an idiot who puts on a hippo outfit and skips around like a retarded children's show host."

Phyllis stood up, fists clenched.

"I'm 'bout to stick an apple in your talk-hole and roast you on a spit, Ham Boy."

"Enough." Irena raised her hands. "We're adults. Let's act like it."

"Does anyone want the last donut?" It was David, the werecoral, talking. "Weston? You haven't had one yet."

Weston patted his stomach. "No thanks. I just ate my neighbor and her dog."

"I ate a Fuller Brush Salesman once," Andy said.

"Did not," Phyllis countered. "You ate your own toilet brush. And a pack of them *Ty-D-Bowl* tablets. That's why your poo was blue."

"So I can have the last donut?" David had already taken a bite out of it.

Weston looked at Irena, felt his heart flutter.

"Other than video, is there another way to find out what I am?"

Irena's eyes sparkled. "Yes. In fact, there is."

The group, except for Ryan, gathered in front of the chest sitting in the corner of the room.

"Testing equipment." Irena twisted an old fashion key in the lock and opened the lid.

Weston expected some sort of medical supplies, or maybe a chemistry set. Instead, the trunk was filled with dried plants, broken antiques, and assorted worthless-looking junk.

"Hold out your hand."

Weston did as told. Irena held his wrist, and then ran a twig lightly across his palm.

"Feel anything?"

Other than getting a little aroused, Weston felt nothing. He shook his head.

"Cat nip," Irene said. "It's a shame. You would have made a cute kitty."

She brought the branch to her lips, sniffed it, and a tiny moan escaped her throat. Andy took it away from her and tossed it back in the trunk.

"If we let her, she'll play with that all day, and the meeting starts in five minutes. Here, touch this."

Andy handed him a longer, darker twig. Weston touched it, and immediately felt like his entire arm had caught on fire. There was a puff of smoke, and a crackling sound. He recoiled.

"Jesus! What the hell was that, a burning bush?"

Andy cocked his head to the side. "It was wolfsbane. I'll be damned. You are a lycanthrope."

Everyone's expressions changed from surprise to awe, and Weston swore that Irena's pupils got wider. He shrugged.

"Okay, so I'm a werewolf."

"We've never had a werewolf in the group," David said. "How did you become a werewolf?"

"I have no idea."

Weston recalled the masturbation scare tales from his youth, many of which involved hairy palms. He almost asked if that may have caused it, but looked at Irena and decided to keep it to himself.

"Is your mother or father a werewolf?" Scott, the weretortise asked. "I inherited a recessive gene from my mother, Shelly. Been a therianthrope since birth."

"No. This only started three months ago."

"Were you bitten by a therianthrope?" David asked. "That's how they got me."

Weston didn't think that coral could actually bite, but he didn't mention it. Instead he shook his head.

"How about a curse?" Irena asked. "Were you cursed by a gypsy recently?"

"No, I…" Then Weston remembered his evil next door neighbor. He'd been wondering about her ethnic background, and now it seemed obvious. *Of course* she was a gypsy. How could he have missed the signs? His shoulders slumped.

"Oh, boy. I think maybe I was cursed, for brushing my teeth too loudly."

"You're lucky." David smiled. "That's the easiest type of therianthropy to cure."

"Who wants to be cured?" Scott's eyes narrowed. "I like being a weretortise."

"That's because when you change all you do is eat salad and swim around in your bathtub," Andy said. "I root through the garbage and eat aluminum cans. You ever try to crap out a six pack of Budweiser tall boys?"

David put his hands on his hips. "I'm saying that Weston's a carnivore, like Irena. They eat people. It has to weigh heavy on the conscience."

"Do you feel guilty about it?" Weston asked Irena.

"Nope." Irena smiled. "And I have the added benefit of not having to put up with any bad kids in my class for more than a month."

Weston wondered if it was too soon to propose marriage. He squelched the thought and turned to David.

"So, assuming I want to go back to normal, how do I do it?"

"Just go back to the gypsy that cursed you and pay her to take the curse off."

Oops.

"That might be a problem, seeing as how I ate her."

Andy slapped him on the shoulder. "Tough break, man. But you'll get used to it. Until then, it's probably a good idea to get yourself a nice, sturdy leash."

"It's time to begin the meeting. Let's get started." Irena leaned into Weston and softly said, "We can talk more later."

Weston sincerely hoped so.

"Let's begin by joining hands and saying the Shapeshifters Anonymous Credo."

Everyone around the table joined hands, including the silent Ryan. Weston noted that Irena's hand was soft and warm, and she played her index finger along the top of his as she talked. So did Phyllis.

Irena began.

"I, state your name, agree to abide by the rules of ethics as set forth by Shapeshifter's Anonymous."

Everyone, including Weston, repeated it.

"I promise to do my best to use my abilities for the good of man and therianthrope kind."

They repeated it.

"I promise to do my best to help any therianthrope who comes to me in need."

They repeated it. Weston thought it a lot like being in church. Which, technically, they were.

"I promise to do my best to not to devour any nice people."

Weston repeated this verse with extra emphasis.

"I promise to avoid Kris Kringle, the dreaded Santa Claus, and his many evil helpers."

"Hold on," Weston interrupted. "What the hell does that mean?"

"Santa Claus is a therianthrope hunter," David said. "He kills shapeshifters."

"You're kidding. Right?"

An uncomfortable silence ensured. Everyone stopped holding hands. Scott cleared his throat, then pushed away from the table and stood up.

"No one is sure how our kind got started. Some say black magic. Some say interspecies breeding, though I don't buy into that malarkey. Some say therianthropes date back the very beginning, the Garden of Eden, where man and werebeast lived in harmony. But the Bible doesn't tell the whole story. Certain religious leaders over the years have edited it as they see fit. Entire books were taken out. Like the Book of Bob."

Weston looked around to see if anyone was smiling. All faces were serious.

"The Book of Bob?"

"The Book of Bob is a lost chapter of the Old Testament, dating back to the Hellenistic period. It tells the story of God's prophet, Bob, son of Jakeh, who is the first werewolf mentioned in the Bible."

"The first? There aren't any."

"They were edited out. Pay attention, son. You'll learn something. See, Bob was a werewolf, blessed by the Lord with the gift of lycanthropy to do His work by eating evildoers. But after eating his one thousandth sinner, Bob became prideful of his accomplishments, and that angered God."

"Why would that anger God?"

"This was the Old Testament. God got pissed off a lot. Didn't you ever read Job?"

"I'm just saying…"

Irena shushed him. Scott continued.

"So to put Bob in his place, God granted one of Bob's enemies---Christopher, son of Cringle---a red suit of impenetrable armor, and ordered him to smite all therianthropes. God also blessed domesticated beasts with the power to fly through the sky, to pull Christopher's warship of destruction throughout the world."

Weston again looked around the room. Andy was examining his fingernails. Ryan was staring off into space. But David looked like a child listening to his favorite bedtime story.

"Bob and Christopher fought, and Bob proved victorious. Upon triumphing, he begged God to forgive his pridefulness, and God agreed. But Christopher, God's chosen avenger, felt betrayed. So he turned to the other side, begging for assistance."

"The devil?"

"Lucifer himself, the Son of the Morning Star. Lucifer gave Christopher a fearsome weapon, shaped like the talons of an eagle, forged in the fires of hell. He called the weapon Satan's Claws. And Christopher recruited an army of helpers to rid the world of Bob and his kind, claiming he was bringing about salvation."

"Let me see if I got this right," Weston said. "Kris Kringle and his magic red suit are using Satan's Claws---which I'm guessing became *Santa Claus* over time---to kill therianthropes with the help of… *the Salvation Army*?"

Everyone nodded. Weston laughed in disbelief.

"So how did this whole toy thing get started?"

"Kringle has killed millions of therianthropes, leaving many children orphans. He began to feel some remorse, so after he slaughtered their parents he began to leave toys behind, to take away some of the sting."

"And this is for real?"

Scott reached up and pulled down his collar, exposing a terrible scar along is neck.

"Kringle gave this to me when I was seven years old, right after murdering my parents."

"I thought he gave orphans toys."

"He also gave me a train set."

Weston shook his head. "Look, I can accept this whole shape-shifting thing. And touching the wolfsbane, that was creepy. But you want me to believe that every volunteer on the street corners with a bell and a Santa suit is out to murder us? I just saw one of those guys this morning, and while he was kind of odd---"

Scott reached across the table, grabbing Weston by the shirt. His face was pure panic.

"You saw one! Where?"

"Back in Naperville."

"What did he say to you?"

"Something about naughty boys and being beheaded and burned on sacred ground. He was obviously out of his mind."

Irena clutched Weston's hand. "The only way we can die is old age or beheading."

"Think carefully, Weston." Scott actually looked frightened. So did everyone else. "Were you followed here?"

"I don't think so. I mean, maybe I saw him talking on a cell phone. And maybe there was someone in a Santa suit a few cars behind me on the expressway…"

A shrill whistle cut Weston off. It sounded like a teapot.

But it wasn't a teapot. It was an alarm.

"They've found us." David's voice was quavering. "They're here."

"Battle stations!" Irena cried, causing everyone to scurry off in different directions.

Scott hurried to the coffee table, pushed the machine aside, and pressed a red button on the wall. An iron gate slammed closed across the entry door, and three TV monitors rose up on pedestals from hidden panels in the floor.

"Jesus." Phyllis squinted at one of the screens. "There have to be forty of them."

Weston looked, watching as the cameras switch from one view to another around the church. Santa's helpers, dozens of Santa's helpers. Wielding bats and axes and swords. They had the place surrounded.

"We need to call the police." David's voice had gone up an octave.

Irena already had the phone in her hand. "Line's been cut."

"Cell phones?"

"We're in a basement. No signals."

Scott knelt before the trunk, removing the top section and revealing a cache of handguns underneath. He tossed one to Weston, along with an extra clip.

"Are guns safe to throw?"

"Safety is on. Ever used a 9mm before?"

"No."

"Thumb off the safety on the side. Then pull back the top part. That's the slide, loads the bullet into the chamber. Now all you have to do is pull the trigger. Those red suits they're wearing are Kevlar, so aim for the face."

Weston had more questions, but Scott was too busy distributing the guns.

"Place your shots carefully, people. We don't have a lot of ammo. Ryan! Can you fire a weapon?"

Ryan remained sitting, staring into space.

"Dammit, man! We need you!"

Ryan didn't move.

"Can't we escape?" Weston asked Irena.

Irena worked her slide, jacking in a round.

"That's the only door."

"But those are steel bars. They can't get through it."

"They'll get through." Phyllis pointed. "See?"

Weston checked out the monitor, saw a group of Santa's storming down the stairs with a battering ram. The first *CLANG!* made everyone in the room jump.

"The table! Move!"

Weston helped Andy and Scott push the cafeteria table in front of the door. Then the group, except for Ryan, huddled together in the back of the room, guns pointed forward.

"I hope we live through this," Weston told Irena, "because I'd really like to ask you out."

"I'd like that too."

"Living through this, or going out with me?"

"Both."

Another *CLANG!* accompanied by a *CREAK!* which shook the table.

"Wait until you see the whites of their beards, people."

CLANG!

CLANG!

The table lurched forward.

CLANG!

They were in.

The room erupted in gunfire. It was louder than anything Weston had heard in his life, and he'd seen Iron Maiden in concert when he was seventeen. The kick of the gun surprised him, throwing off his aim, but Weston kept his head, kept sighting the targets, kept pulling the trigger.

The first Santa only made it a step inside.

The next three only made it two steps.

Then it got bad. A dozen of Santa's helpers burst into the room, swinging their weapons, their *HO HO HO!* warcries cutting through the cacophony of gunfire.

Weston fired until his pistol was empty. He tried to tug the empty clip out of the bottom of the gun, but it didn't budge. He wasted valuable seconds looking for the button or switch to release it, and then a helper tackled him.

His eyes were crazed, and his breath smelled like cough syrup, and Weston knew that this was the Santa who threatened him on the street corner in Naperville.

"Naughty boy! Naughty boy!" he screamed, both hands clasped on a curved dagger poised above Weston's eye.

Weston blocked with his elbows, trying to keep the knife away, but the crazy old elf possessed some sort of supernatural strength, and the knife inched closer and closer no matter how hard he resisted. Weston saw his terrified expression reflected in the polished steel blade as the tip tickled his eyelashes.

"Hey! Santa! Got some cookies for you!"

Weston watched, amazed, as someone jammed a gun into the Santa's snarling mouth and pulled the trigger. Psycho Santa's hat lifted up off his head, did a pirouette in the air, and fell down onto his limp body.

Weston followed the hand that held the gun, saw Irena staring down at him. She helped him to his feet.

"Thanks."

She nodded, taking his pistol and showing him the button to release the empty clip.

"Where did you learn how to shoot?" he asked.

"I teach high school."

Weston slammed the spare clip home and pulled the slide, firing six times at a Santa's helper swinging, of all things, a Grim Reaper scythe. The neck shot did him in.

"Hold your fire! They're retreating!"

As quickly as it began, the attack stopped. The gun smoke cleared. Weston winced when he saw the piles of dead Santa's helpers strewn around the room. At least two dozen of them. A Norman Rockwell painting it was not.

"Everyone okay?" Scott asked.

Everyone said yes except for Ryan, who remained sitting in the same chair, and David, who had a nasty gash on his shoulder that Phyllis was bandaging with duct tape and paper towels.

"Well, we sure kicked some Santa ass." Andy walked next to one of the fallen helpers and nudged him with his foot. "Try climbing down a chimney now, shit head."

"It's not over."

Everyone turned to look at Ryan.

"Did you saw something, Ryan?" Irena asked.

Ryan pointed to the monitor.

They all stared at a wide angle shot of the parking lot and watched eight reindeer racing down from the sky and using the blacktop like a landing strip. Behind them, a massive sleigh. It skidded to a stop and a hulking figure, dressed in red, climbed out and stared up at the camera.

"It's Santa Claus," Ryan whispered. "He's come to town."

Weston watched, horrified, as Santa headed for the church entrance, his remaining helpers scurrying around him.

"My God," Phyllis gasped. "He's huge."

Weston couldn't really judge perspective, but it seemed like Santa stood at least a foot taller than any of the Salvation Army volunteers.

"Who has ammo left?" Scott yelled.

"I'm out."

"Me too."

"So am I."

Weston checked his clip. "I've got two bullets."

It got very quiet. Scott rubbed his neck.

"Okay. We'll have to make do. Everyone grab a weapon. Kris Kringle is a lot more powerful than his helpers. Maybe, if we all strike at once, we'll have a chance."

From the sound of Scott's voice, he didn't believe his own words.

Andy didn't buy it either. "David is wounded. Ryan is sitting there like a pud. You think three men and two woman can fend off Kringle and his Satan's Claws? He's going to cut us into pieces!"

"We don't have a choice."

"But I don't want to get sliced up!" Andy said. "I'm too pretty to die like that!"

"Calm down, son. You're not helping the situation."

Andy knelt next to one of the helpers and began undressing him.

"You guys fight. I'm going to put on a red suit and pretend to be dead."

Weston locked eyes with Irena, saw fear, wondered if she saw the same in him.

"There's a way."

It was Ryan again, still staring off into space.

"You actually going to get up off your ass and help?" Phyllis asked.

Ryan slowly reached into his pants pocket, pulling out five tiny vials of liquid.

"I've been saving these."

Andy grabbed one, unscrewed the top. "Is it cyanide? Tell me it's cyanide, because I'm so drinking it."

"It's a metamorphosis potion. It will allow you to change into your therianthrope forms, while still retaining your human intellect."

Scott took a vial, squinting at it.

"Where did you get these?"

"I've had them for a long time."

"How do you know they work?"

"I know."

"Guess it can't hurt to try." Irena grabbed the remaining vials. She handed one to Weston, and one to David. She also held one out for Phyllis.

"But I'm not a therianthrope," Phyllis said. "I'm just a furry."

"You're one of us," Irena told her.

Phyllis nodded, and took the vial.

"Are you taking one?" Scott asked Ryan.

Ryan shook his head.

Scott shrugged. "Okay. Here goes nothing."

He downed the liquid. Everyone watched.

At first, nothing happened. Then Scott twitched. The twitching became faster, and faster, until he looked like a blurry photograph. Scott made a small sound, like a sigh, dropped his gun, and fell to all fours.

He'd changed into a turtle. A giant turtle, with vaguely human features. His face, now green and scaled, looked similar to his human face. And his body retained a roughly humanoid shape; so much so that he was able to push off the ground and stand on two stubby legs.

"I'll be damned." Scott reached up and tapped the top of his shell. "And I can still think. Hell, I can even talk."

Irena had already drunk her vial, and her clothes ripped, exposing the spots underneath. While in final werecheetah form she retained her long blonde hair, and---Weston could appreciate this---her breasts. He could suddenly understand the appeal furries saw in anthropomorphic costumes.

"You look great," Weston told her.

Her whiskers twitched, and she licked her arm and rubbed it over her face.

An oink, from behind, and Andy the wereboar was standing next to the overturned table, chewing on the cardboard donut box.

"What?" he said. "There's still some frosting inside."

"This sucks."

Weston turned to David, who had become a greenish, roundish, ball of coral. Weston could make out his face underneath a row of tiny, undulating tentacles.

"I think you're adorable," Irena told him. "Like Humpty Dumpty."

"I don't have arms or legs! How am I supposed to fight Santa?"

"Try rolling on him," Andy said, his snout stuck in the garbage can.

"I guess it's my turn." Phyllis drank the potion.

Everyone waited.

Nothing happened.

"Well, shit," Phyllis said. "And I don't even have my hippo suit here. At least give me the damn gun."

Weston handed it to her, then looked at his vial.

"You'll be fine," Irena said.

She walked a circle around him, then nuzzled against his chest. Weston stroked her chin, and she purred.

"Better hurry," Scott was eyeing the monitor. "Here comes Santa Claus."

Weston closed his eyes and lifted the vial to his lips.

It was kind of like being born. Darkness. Warmth. Then turmoil, sensory overload, a thousand things happening at once. It didn't hurt, but it didn't tickle either. Weston coughed, but it came out harsh. A bark. He looked down at his arms and noted they were covered with long, gray fur. His pants stayed on, but his clawed feet burst through the tops of his shoes.

"Hello, sexy."

Weston stared at Irena and had an overpowering, irrational urge to bark at her. He managed to keep it in check.

"Remember," Scott said. "He's wearing armor. It's claw-proof. Go for his head and neck, or use blunt force."

They formed a semi-circle around the door, except for the immobile David and the still-seated Ryan. Then they waited. Weston heard a licking sound, traced it to Andy, who had his nose buried between his own legs.

"Andy," he growled. "Quit it."

"Are you kidding? I don't think I'm ever going to stop."

Then the crazed Santa's helpers burst into the room, screaming and swinging weapons. Weston recoiled at first, remembered what he was, and then lashed out with a claw. It caught the helper in the side of the head, snapping his neck like a candy cane.

Andy quit grooming — if you could call it that — long enough to gore a helper between his red shirt and pants, right in the belly. What came out looked a lot like a bowlful of jelly.

Phyllis fired twice, then picked up the scythe and started swinging it like a mad woman and swearing like a truck driver with a toothache.

Scott had two helpers backed up against the wall, using his enormous shell to squeeze the life out of them.

Even David had managed to get into the act, snaring a helper with his tiny, translucent tentacles. Judging from the screams, those tentacles had stingers on them.

Weston searched for Irena, and saw her hanging onto a helper's back, biting at his neck.

Two more Santa's helpers rushed in, and Weston lunged at them, surprised by his speed. He kept his arms spread out and caught each one under the chin. His canine muscles flexed, tightened, and their heads came off like Barbie dolls.

And then, there *he* was.

Kris Kringle was even bigger up close than he was on the TV monitors. So tall he had to duck down to fit through the doorway. When he entered the room and reared up, he must have been eight feet tall. And wide, with a chest like a whiskey barrel, arms like tree trunks. His long white beard was flecked with blood, and his tiny dark eyes twinkled with malevolent glee.

But the worst thing were his hands. They ended in horrible metal claws, each blade the length of a samurai sword. One of his helpers, the one Irena had bitten, staggered over to Kringle, clutching his bleeding neck. Kringle lashed out, severing the man into three large pieces, even with the Kevlar suit on.

It was so horrible, so outrageously demonic, that Weston had to laugh when he saw it. In spite of himself.

Scott waddled over to Kringle and pointed his stubby fingers at him.

"Your reign of evil ends today, Kringle."

Kringle laughed, a deep, resonating croak that sounded like thunder. Then his huge black boot shot out, kicking Scott in the chest, knocking him across the room and into the back wall. Scott crashed through it like a turtle-shaped meteor.

Andy said, "Holy shit," then tore ass through the hole in the wall after Scott.

Kringle took a step forward, and Weston had an urge to pee; an urge so strong he actually lifted a leg. There was no way they could defeat Santa Claus. He was a monster. He'd tear through them like tissue paper.

Kringle appraised Weston, eyeing him head to toe, and said, "Robert Weston Smith. Werewolf. You're on my list."

Then he looked at Irena, who'd come to Weston's side, clutching his paw.

"Irena Reed. Werecheetah. You're on my list too. Want to sit on Santa's lap, little girl?"

Irena hissed at him. Kringle's eyes fell upon David next.

"And what the hell are you? A were-onion?"

David released the dead helper. "I'm David Kessler. Werecoral."

"David Kessler. Yes. You're also on my list. Now who is this crazy bitch?"

Phyllis put her hands on her hips and stuck out her jaw. "Phyllis Lawanda Marisha Taleena Allenby. Am I on your stupid ass list too?"

"No."

"No? You sure 'bout that, fat man?"

Kringle smiled. "I checked it twice."

Phyllis's eyes went mean."You saying I'm not one of them? I'm one of them. I'm one of them in my heart, you giant sack of —"

"Enough!"

Ryan stood up and walked over to Kringle.

"And who are you, little human?"

"I'm tired of running, Christopher. I've been running for too long."

Kringle's brow furrowed.

"That voice. I know that voice."

"I had some work done. Changed my human face. But I'm sure you'll recognize this one."

Ryan's body shook, and then he transformed into a werewolf. A giant werewolf, several feet taller than Weston.

Kringle took a step back, his face awash with fear.

"Bob."

Weston watched, awestruck, as this millennia-old battle played out before him.

Kringle snarled, raising up his awful Satan Claws.

Bob bared his teeth and howled, a gut-churning cry that reverberated to the core of Weston's very soul.

But before either of them attacked, before either of them even moved, Kris Kringle's head rolled off his shoulders and onto the floor by Bob's feet.

Phyllis Lawanda Marisha Taleena Allenby, scythe in hand, brought the blade down and speared the tip into Kringle's decapitated head, holding it up so it faced her.

"Am I on your list *now*, mutha fucker?"

Bob peered down at Phyllis, his lupine jaw hanging open.

"You just killed Kris Kringle."

"Damn easy too. Why the hell didn't you do that five thousand years ago?"

Scott, a round green hand pressed to his wrinkled old head, stumbled back into the room.

"What happened?"

"Phyllis killed Kris Kringle," Irena said.

"You go, girl." Scott gave Phyllis a high-five.

"You all fought bravely." Bob stood tall, addressing the group. "Except for the pig. For your courage, you'll now have full control over your therianthrope powers. You can change at will, and shall retain control of your inner creatures."

"So how do we turn back?" Irena asked.

"Concentrate."

Scott went first, morphing back into his human form.

Weston and Irena changed while holding hands.

David's face scrunched up, but nothing happened.

"It's not working," he said. "I'm still coral."

"How about me?" Phyllis asked. "I'm the one that killed that jolly old bastard."

"I can turn you into a werewolf, if you so desire."

"These guys offered me that before. But I don't want to be no wolf, or no cheetah, or no turtle, or no dumb ass coral. No offense, David."

"None taken. I'm concentrating, but nothing's happening."

Phyllis folded her arms. "My inner animal is a hippopotamus. That's what I want to be."

Bob's shoulders slumped. "I'm sorry, Phyllis. That's the extent of my power. But… maybe… just maybe…"

"Maybe what?"

"I don't know if this will work, because he's dead."

"Just spill the beans, Lon Chaney."

"Try sitting on Santa's lap."

Phyllis raised a drawn-on eyebrow. "You serious?"

"He might still have some magic left. Try it."

Phyllis walked over to the fallen Kringle and sat on one of his massive thighs.

"Now what?"

"Make a Christmas wish, Phyllis. Make your most heartfelt Christmas wish ever."

She closed her eyes, and her lips whispered something Weston couldn't hear.

And then Weston felt something. Kind of like a breeze. A breeze made of Christmas magic. It swirled around the room, touching each of them, and them coming to rest on Phyllis.

But nothing happened. She didn't morph into a hippo. She didn't morph into anything. A minute passed, and she was still the same old Phyllis.

"I'm sorry, Phyllis." Bob helped her up. "I wish there was something else I could do."

A sad silence blanketed the room.

Then badboy rapper LL Cool J strutted into the basement, sans shirt. He took Phyllis's hand, gave her a deeply passionate kiss, and cupped her butt.

"Gonna take you back to the crib and make love to you all night, girl. But first we gonna stop by the bank, get your hundred million dollars."

LL picked her up and carried her out.

"See you guys next week," Phyllis called after them.

"Someone push me over to Santa's lap," David said. "This coral wants a house in Hawaii."

"What about all of these corpses?" Scott made a sweeping gesture with his hands. "The police are gonna have a field day."

"I'll take care of it." Bob rubbed his stomach. "I didn't have any of the donuts."

"Little help here." David wiggled in place.

Weston felt a tug on his hand. He stared into Irena's eyes.

"Want to, maybe, grab some coffee?" he asked.

"No."

Weston died a little inside. Irena's nose twitched, showing him a brief glimpse of her inner cheetah.

"Instead of coffee, I want you to come to my place. I've got a leash and a king sized bed."

God bless us, everyone, Weston thought as they walked hand-in-hand out the door.

Serial

by Blake Crouch and Jack Kilborn

1

THE HARDEST THING ABOUT killing a hitchhiker was finding one to pick up.

Donaldson could remember just ten years ago, when interstates boasted a hitcher every ten miles, and a discriminating killer could pick and choose who looked the easiest, the most fun, the juiciest. These days, cops kept the expressways clear of easy marks, and Donaldson was forced to cruise off-ramps, underpasses, and rest areas, prowl back roads, take one hour coffee breaks at oases. Recreational murder was becoming more trouble than it was worth.

He'd finally found one standing in a Cracker Barrel parking lot. The kid had been obvious, leaning against the cement ashtray near the entrance, an oversize hiking pack strapped to his back. He was approaching every patron leaving the restaurant, practicing his grin between rejections.

A ripe plum, ready to pluck.

Donaldson tucked the cell phone into his pocket and got out of the car. He didn't even have to initiate contact. He walked in to use the bathroom and strolled out with his car keys in hand, letting them jingle a bit. The kid solicited him almost immediately.

"Excuse me, sir. Are you heading up north?"

Donaldson stopped, pretending to notice the man for the first time. He was young, maybe mid-twenties. Short, reddish hair, a few freckles on his face, mostly hidden by glasses. His clothing looked worn but of good quality. Donaldson was twice his age, and damn near twice his weight.

Donaldson rubbed his chin, which he knew softened his harsh features.

"In fact I am, son."

The boy's eyes lit up, but he kept a lid on his excitement. Any hitcher worth his salt knew to test the waters before sealing the deal.

"I am, too. If you'd like some company, I can chip in for gas." He hooded his eyes and quickly added, "No funny stuff. I'm just looking for a ride. I was hoping to get to Ogden by midnight. Got family up there. My name's Brett, by the way."

Well played, Donaldson thought. Friendly, a little desperate, making clear this wasn't a sexual hookup and that he had people waiting for him.

As if any of that would keep him safe.

"How do I know you're not some psycho?" Donaldson asked. He knew that was pushing it, but he liked the irony.

"There's a gas station across the street. I can top off the tank, pay with a credit card. All gas stations have cameras these days. Credit card is a paper trail. If anything happens to you, that would link me to your car, and I'd get caught."

Smart kid. But not that smart.

The really smart ones don't hitchhike.

"Won't need gas for a few hundred miles." Donaldson took off his Cubs baseball hat, running a hand over his gray, thinning hair. Another way to disarm the victim. No one feared grandfatherly types. "Until then, if you promise not to sing any show tunes, you got yourself a ride."

Brett smiled, hefted his pack onto his shoulders, and followed his ride into the parking lot. Donaldson unlocked the doors and the kid loaded his pack into the backseat of Donaldson's 2006 black Honda Accord, pausing when he saw the clear plastic covers on the front seats.

"My dog, Neil, usually rides up front with me," Donaldson said, shrugging. "I don't like him messing up the upholstery."

Brett flashed skepticism until he noticed the picture taped to the dash: Donaldson and a furry dachshund.

"Sheds like crazy," Donaldson said. "If you buy a dog, stick with short-haired breeds."

That was apparently reassurance enough, because Brett climbed in.

Donaldson heaved himself into the driver's seat, the car bouncing on its shocks.

"Buckle up for safety." Donaldson resisted the urge to lick his lips, then released the brake, started the car, and pulled onto the highway.

The first ten miles were awkward. Always were. Strangers tended to stay strangers. How often did a person initiate conversation on a plane or while waiting in line? People kept to themselves. It made them feel safe.

Donaldson broke the tension by asking the standard questions. Where'd you go to school? What do you do for a living? Where you headed? When'd you start hitchhiking? Invariably, the conversation turned to him.

"So what's your name?" Brett asked.

"Donaldson." No point in lying. Brett wouldn't be alive long enough to tell anyone.

"What do you do, Donaldson?"

"I'm a courier."

Donaldson sipped from the Big Gulp container in the cup holder, taking a hit of caffeinated sugar water. He offered the cup to Brett, who shook his head. Probably worried about germs. Donaldson smiled. That should have been the least of his worries.

"So you mean you deliver packages?"

"I deliver anything. Sometimes overnight delivery isn't fast enough, and people are willing to pay a premium to get it same day."

"What sort of things?"

"Things people need right away. Legal documents. Car parts for repairs. A diabetic forgets his insulin, guy loses his glasses and can't drive home without them, kid needs his cello for a recital. Or a kidney needs to get to a transplant location on time. That's the run I'm on right now."

Donaldson jerked a thumb over his shoulder, pointing to the backseat floorboard. Brett glanced back, saw a cooler sitting there, a biohazard sticker on the lid.

"No kidding, there's a kidney in there?"

"There will be, once I get it." Donaldson winked at the kid. "By the way, what's your blood type?"

The kid chuckled nervously. Donaldson joined in.

A long stretch of road approaching. No cars in either direction.

"Sounds like an interesting job," Brett said.

"It is. Perfect for a loner like me. That's why it's nice to have company every so often. Gets lonely on the road."

"What about Neil?"

"Neil?"

Brett pointed at the photograph on the dashboard. "Your dog. You said he rode with you sometimes."

"Oh, yeah. Neil. Of course. But it isn't the same as having a human companion. Know what I mean?"

Brett nodded, then glanced at the fuel gauge.

"You're down to a quarter tank," he said.

"Really? I thought I just filled up. Next place we see, I'll take you up on that offer to pay."

It was a bright, sunny late afternoon, clean country air blowing in through the inch of window Donaldson had open. A perfect day for a drive. The road ahead was clear, no one behind them.

"So seriously," Donaldson asked, "What's your blood type?"

Brett's chuckle sounded forced this time, and Donaldson didn't join in. Brett put his hand in his pocket. Going for a weapon, or holding one for reassurance, Donaldson figured. Not many hitchers traveled without some form of reassurance.

But Donaldson had something better than a knife, or a gun. His weapon weighed thirty-six hundred pounds and was barreling down the road at eighty miles per hour.

Checking once more for traffic, Donaldson gripped the wheel, braced himself, and stood on the brake.

The car screeched toward a skidding halt, Brett's seatbelt popping open exactly the way Donaldson had rigged it to, and the kid launched headfirst into the dashboard. The spongy plastic, beneath the veneer, had been reinforced with unforgiving steel.

The car shuddered to a stop, the stench of scorched rubber in the air. Brett was in bad shape. With no seatbelt and one hand in his pocket, he'd banged his nose up pretty good. Donaldson grasped his hair, rammed his face into the dashboard two more times, then opened the glove compartment. He grabbed a plastic zip tie, checked again for oncoming traffic, and quickly secured the kid's hands behind his back. In Brett's coat pocket, he found a tiny Swiss Army knife. Donaldson barked out a laugh.

If memory served, and it usually did, there was an off ramp less than a mile ahead, and then a remote stretch of farmland. Donaldson pulled back onto the highway and headed for it, whistling as he drove.

The farm stood just where he remembered it. Donaldson pulled offroad into a cornfield and drove through the dead stalks until he could no longer see the street. He killed the engine, set the parking brake—the Accord had transmission issues—and tugged out the keys to ensure it wouldn't roll away. Then he picked a few choice tools from his toolbox and stuck them in his pocket.

His passenger whimpered as Donaldson muscled him out of the car and dragged him into the stalks.

He whimpered even more when Donaldson jerked his pants down around his ankles, got him loosened up with an ear of corn, and then forced himself inside.

"Gonna stab me with your little knife?" he whispered in Brett's ear between grunts. "Think that was going to save you?"

When he'd finished, Donaldson sat on the kid's chest and tried out all the attachments on the Swiss Army knife. The tiny scissors worked well on eyelids. The nail file just reached the eardrums. The little two-inch blade was surprisingly sharp and adept at whittling the nose down to the cartilage.

Donaldson also used some tools of his own. Pliers, for cracking teeth and pulling off lips. When used in tandem with some garden shears, he was able to get Brett's tongue out in one piece. And of course, there was the muddler.

Normally wielded by bartenders to mash fruit in the bottom of drink glasses, Donaldson had his own special use for the instrument. People usually reacted strongly to being fed parts of their own face, and even under the threat of more pain, they'd spit those parts out.

Donaldson used the plastic muddler like a ram, forcing those juicy bits down their throats.

After all, it was sinful to waste all of those delectable little morsels like that.

When the fighting and screams began to wind down, the Swiss Army knife's corkscrew attachment did a fine job on Brett's Adam's apple, popping it out in one piece and leaving a gaping hole that poured blood bright as a young cabernet.

Apple was a misnomer. It tasted more like a peach pit. Sweet and stringy.

He shoved another ear of corn into Brett's neck hole, then stood up to watch.

Donaldson had killed a lot of people in a lot of different ways, but suffocation especially tickled his funny bone. When people bled to death they just got sleepy. It was tough to see their expression when they were on fire, with all the thrashing and flames. Damaging internal organs, depending on the organ, was either too fast, too slow, or too loud.

But a human being deprived of oxygen would panic for several minutes, providing quite a show. This kid lasted almost five, his eyes bulging out, wrenching his neck side to side in futile attempts to remove the cob, and turning all the colors of the rainbow before finally giving up the ghost. It got Donaldson so excited he almost raped him again. But the rest of the condoms were in the car, and befitting a man his age, once he got them and returned to the scene of death, his ardor probably would have waned.

He didn't bother trying to take Brett's kidney, or any of his other parts. What the heck could he do with his organs anyway? Sell them on eBay?

Cleanup was the part Donaldson hated most, but he always followed a strict procedure. First, he bagged everything associated with the crime. The rubber, the zip tie, the Swiss Army knife, and the two corn cobs, which might have his prints on them. Then he took a spray bottle of bleach solution and a roll of paper towels and cleaned the muddler, shears, and pliers, and swabbed out the interior of his car. He used baby wipes on himself, paying special attention to his fingernails. He put his tools back into his toolbox. Everything else went into the white plastic garbage bag, along with a full can of gasoline and more bleach spray.

He took the money from Brett's wallet—forty lousy bucks—and found nothing of interest in his backpack. These went into the bag as well, and then he soaked that and the body with lighter fluid.

The fire started easily. Donaldson knew from experience that he had about five minutes before the gas can exploded. He drove out of the cornfield at a fast clip, part of him disappointed he couldn't stay to watch the fireworks.

The final result would be a mess for anyone trying to ID the victim, gather evidence, or figure out what exactly had happened. If the body wasn't discovered right away, and the elements and hungry animals added to the chaos, it would be a crime scene investigator's worst nightmare.

Donaldson knew how effective this particular disposal method was, because he'd used it twenty-six times and hadn't ever been so much as questioned by police.

He wondered if the FBI had a nickname for him, something sexy like *The Roadside Burner*. But he wasn't convinced those jokers had even connected his many crimes. Donaldson's courier route took him all across the country, over a million square miles of hunting ground. He waited at least a year before returning to any particular spot, and he was finding new places to play all the time.

Donaldson knew he would never be caught. He was smart, patient, and never compulsive. He could keep on doing this until he died or his pecker wore out, and they had pills these days to fix that.

He reached I-15 at rush hour, traffic clogging routes both in and out of Salt Lake, and he was feeling happy and immortal until some jerk in a Winnebago decided to drive ten miles under the speed limit. Irritated motorists tagged along like ducklings, many of them using their horns, and everyone taking their good sweet time getting by in the passing lane.

Seriously, they shouldn't allow some people on the road.

Donaldson was considering passing the whole lot of them on the shoulder, and as he surveyed the route and got ready to gun it, he saw a cute chick in pink shoes standing at the cloverleaf. Short, lugging a guitar case, jutting out a hip and shaking her thumb at everyone who passed.

Two in one day? he thought. Do I have the energy?

He cranked open the window to get rid of the bleach smell, and pulled up next to her under the overpass, feeling his arousal returning.

2

SHE SET THE GUITAR case on the pavement and stuck out her thumb. The minivan shrieked by. She turned her head, watched it go—no brakelights. The disappointment blossomed hot and sharp in her gut, like a shot of iced Stoli. Despite the midmorning brilliance of the rising sun, she could feel the cold gnawing through the tips of her gloved fingers, the earflaps of her black woolen hat.

According to her Internet research, 491 (previously 666) ranked as the third least traveled highway in the Lower-Forty-Eight, with an average of four cars passing a fixed point any given hour. Less of course at night. The downside of hitchhiking these little-known thoroughfares was the waiting, but the upside paid generous dividends in privacy.

She exhaled a steaming breath and looked around. Painfully blue sky. Treeless high desert. Mountains thirty miles east. A further range to the northwest. They stood blanketed in snow, and on some level she understood that others would find them dramatic and beautiful, and she wondered what it felt like to be moved by nature.

Two hours later, she lifted her guitar case and walked up the shoulder toward the idling Subaru Outback, heard the front passenger window humming down. She mustered a faint smile as she reached the door. Two young men in the front seats stared at her. They seemed roughly her age and friendly enough, if a little hungover. Open cans of Bud in the center console drink holders had perfumed the interior with the sour stench of beer—a good omen, she thought. Might make things easier.

"Where you headed?" the driver asked. He had sandy hair and an elaborate goatee. Impressive cords of bicep strained the cotton fibers of his muscle shirt. The passenger looked native—dark hair and eyes, brown skin, a thin, implausible mustache.

"Salt Lake," she said.

"We're going to Tahoe. We could take you at least to I-15."

She surveyed the rear storage compartment—crammed with two

snowboards and the requisite boots, parkas, snow pants, goggles, and…she suppressed the jolt of pleasure—helmets. She hadn't thought of that before.

A duffle bag took up the left side of the backseat. A little tight, but then she stood just five feet in her pink crocs. She could manage.

"Comfortable back there?" the driver asked.

"Yes."

Their eyes met in the rearview mirror.

"What's your name?"

"Lucy."

"Lucy, I'm Matt. This is Kenny. We were just about to have us a morning toke before we picked you up. Would it bother you if we did?"

"Not at all."

"Pack that pipe, bro."

They got high as they crossed into Utah and became talkative and philosophically confident. They offered her some pot, but she declined. It grew hot in the car and she removed her hat and unbuttoned her black trench coat, breathing the fresh air coming in through the crack at the top of the window.

"So where you going?" the Indian asked her.

"Salt Lake."

"I already asked her that, bro."

"No, I mean what for?"

"See some family."

"We're going to Tahoe. Do some snowboarding at Heavenly."

"Already told her that, bro."

The two men broke up into laughter.

"So you play guitar, huh?" Kenny said.

"Yes."

"Wanna strum something for us?"

"Not just yet."

They stopped at a filling station in Moab. Matt pumped gas and Kenny went inside the convenience store to procure the substantial list of snacks they'd been obsessing on for the last hour. When Matt walked inside to pay, she opened the guitar case and took out the syringe. The smell wafted out—not overpowering by any means, but she wondered if the boys would notice. She hadn't had a chance to properly clean everything in awhile. Lucy reached up between the seats and tested the weight of the two Budweisers in the drink holders: each about half-full. She eyed the entrance to the store—no one coming—and shot a squirt from the syringe into the mouth of each can.

Kenny cracked a can of Bud and said, "Dude, was that shit laced?"

"What are you talking about?"

They sped through a country of red rock and buttes and waterless arroyos.

"What we smoked."

"I don't think so."

"Man, I don't feel right. Where'd you get it?"

"From Tim. Same as always."

Lucy leaned forward and studied the double yellow line through the windshield. After Matt drifted across for a third time, she said, "Would you pull over please?"

"What's wrong?"

"I'm going to be sick."

"Oh God, don't puke on our shit."

Matt pulled over onto the shoulder and Lucy opened her door and stumbled out. As she worked her way down a gentle embankment making fake retching sounds, she heard Matt saying, "Dude? Dude? Come on, dude! Wake up, dude!"

She waited in the bed of the arroyo for ten minutes and then started back up the hill toward the car. Matt had slumped across the center console into Kenny's lap. The man probably weighed two hundred pounds, and it took Lucy ten minutes to shove him, millimeter by millimeter, into the passenger seat on top of Kenny. She climbed in behind the wheel and slid the seat all the way forward and cranked the engine.

She turned off of I-70 onto 24. According to her map, this stretch of highway ran forty-four miles to a nothing town called Hanksville.

From her experience, it didn't get much quieter than this barren, lifeless waste of countryside.

Ten miles south, she veered onto a dirt road and followed it the length of several football fields, until the highway was almost lost to sight. She killed the engine, stepped out. Late afternoon. Windless. Soundless. The boys would be waking soon, and she was already starting to glow. She opened the guitar case and retrieved the syringe, gave Kenny and Matt another healthy dose.

By the time she'd wrangled them out of the car into the desert, dusk had fallen and she'd drenched herself in sweat. She rolled the men onto their backs and splayed out their arms and legs so they appeared to be making snow angels in the dirt.

Lucy removed their shoes and socks. The pair of scissors was the kind used to cut raw chicken, with thick, serrated blades. She trimmed off their shirts and cut away their pants and underwear.

Kenny and Matt had returned to full, roaring consciousness by 1:15 a.m. Naked. Ankles and wrists tightly bound with deeply scuffed handcuffs, heads helmeted, staring at the small, plain hitchhiker who squatted down facing them at the back of the car, blinding them with a hand held spotlight.

"I didn't think you were ever going to wake up," Lucy said.

"What the hell are you doing?" Matt looked angry.

Kenny said, "These cuffs hurt. Get them off."

She held a locking carabiner attached to a chain that ran underneath the Subaru. She clipped it onto another pair of carabiners. A rope fed through each one, and the ends of the ropes had been tied to the handcuffs on the boys' ankles.

"Oh my God, she's crazy, dude."

"Lucy, please. Don't. We'll give you anything you want. We won't tell anyone."

She smiled. "That's really sweet of you, Matt, but this is what I want. Kind of have my heart set on it."

She stepped over the tangle of chain and rope and moved toward the driver's door as the boys hollered after her.

She left the hatch open so she could hear them. Kept looking back as she drove slowly, so slowly, along the dirt road. They were still begging her, and occasionally yelling when they dragged over a rock or a cactus, but she got them to the shoulder of Highway 24 with only minor injuries.

The moon was up and nearly full. She could see five miles of the road in either direction, so perfectly empty and black, and she wondered if the way it touched her in this moment felt anything like how the beauty of the those mountains she'd seen this morning touched normal people.

Lucy buckled her seatbelt and glanced in the rearview mirror. Matt had climbed to his feet, and he hobbled toward the car.

"Hey, no fair!" she yelled and gave the accelerator a little gas, jerking his feet out from under him. "All right, count of three. We'll start small with half a mile!"

She grasped the steering wheel, heart pumping. She'd done this a half dozen times but never with helmets.

"One! Two! Three!"

She reset the odometer and eased onto the accelerator. Five, ten, fifteen, twenty miles per hour, and the boys already beginning to scream. At four-tenths of a mile, she hit forty, and in the rearview mirror, Kenny's and Matt's pale and naked bodies writhed in full-throated agony, both trying to sit up and grab the rope and failing as they slid across the pavement on their bare backs, dragged by their cuffed ankles, the chains throwing gorgeous yellow sparks against the asphalt.

She eased off the gas and pulled over onto the shoulder. Collected the spray bottle and the artificial leech from the guitar case, unbuckled, jumped out, and went to the boys. They lay on their backs, blood pooling beneath them. Bone and muscle already showing through in many places where the skin had simply been erased, and Kenny must have rolled briefly onto his right elbow, because it had been sanded down to a sharp spire of bone.

"Please," Matt croaked. "Oh, God, please."

"You don't know how beautiful you look," she said, "but I'm gonna make you even prettier."

She spritzed them with pure, organic lemon juice, especially their backs, which looked like raw hamburger, then knelt down with the artificial leech she'd stolen from a medical museum in Phoenix several years ago. Using it always made her think fondly of Luther and Orson.

She stuck each of them twenty times with the artificial leech, and to the heartwarming depth of their new screams, skipped back to the car and hopped in and stomped the gas, their cries rising into something like the baying of hounds, Lucy howling back. She pushed the Subaru past fifty, to sixty, to seventy-five, and in the illumination of the spotlight, the boys bounced along the pavement, on their backs, their sides, their stomachs, and with every passing second looking more and more lovely, and still making those delicious screams she could almost taste, Lucy driving with no headlights, doing eighty under the moon, and the cold winter wind rushing through the windows like the breath of God.

She made it five miles (no one had ever lasted five miles and she credited those well-made snowboarding helmets) before the skeletons finally went quiet.

Lucy ditched what was left of the boys and drove all night like she'd done six blasts of coke, arriving in Salt Lake as the sun edged up over the mountains. She checked into a Red Roof Inn and ran a hot bath and cleaned the new blood and the old blood out of the ropes and let the carabiners and the chains and the handcuffs soak in the soapy water.

In the evening she awoke, that dark weight perched on her chest again. The guitar case items had dried, and she packed them away and dressed and headed out. The motel stood along the interstate, and it came down to Applebee's or Chili's.

She went with the latter, because she loved their Awesome Blossom.

After dinner, she walked outside and stared at the Subaru in the parking lot, the black rot flooding back inside of her, that restless, awful energy that could never be fully sated, those seconds of release never fully quenching, like water tinged with salt. She turned away from the Subaru and walked along the frontage road until she came to a hole in the fence. Ducked through. Scrambled down to the shoulder of the interstate.

Traffic was moderate, the night cold and starry. A line of cars approached, bottled up behind a Winnebago.

She walked under the bridge, set down her guitar case, and stuck out her thumb.

3

DONALDSON PULLED OVER ONTO the shoulder and lowered the passenger window. The girl was young and tiny, wearing a wool cap despite the relative warmth.

"Where you headed?" He winked before he said it, his smile genuine.

"Missoula," Lucy answered.

"Got a gig up there?" He pointed his chin at her guitar case.

She shrugged.

"Well, I'm going north. If you chip in for gas, and promise not to sing any show tunes, you can hop in."

The girl seemed to consider it, then nodded. She opened the rear door and awkwardly fit the guitar case onto the backseat. Before getting in, she stared at the upholstery on the front seats.

"What's with the plastic?" she asked, indicating Donaldson's clear seat covers.

"Sometimes I travel with my dog."

Lucy squinted at the picture taped to the dashboard—the portly driver holding a long-haired dachshund.

"What's its name?"

"Scamp. Loveable little guy. Hates it when I'm away. But I'm away a lot. I'm a courier. Right now, I'm headed up to Idaho Falls to pick up a donor kidney."

Her eyes flitted to the backseat, to a cooler with a biohazard sign on the lid.

"Don't worry," he said, taking off his hat and rubbing a hand through his thinning gray hair. "It's empty for the time being."

The girl nodded, started to get in, then stopped. "Would you mind if I sat in the back? I don't want to make you feel like a chauffeur, but I get nauseated riding up front unless I'm driving."

Donaldson paused. "Normally I wouldn't mind, Miss, but I don't have any seat belts back there, and I insist my passengers wear one. Safety first, I always say."

"Of course. Can't be too careful. Cars can be dangerous."

"Indeed they can. Indeed."

The front passenger door squeaked open, and the girl hopped in.

Donaldson watched her buckle up, and then he accelerated back onto the highway.

Grinning at her, he rubbed his chin and asked, "So what's your name, little lady?"

"I'm Lucy." She looked down at the center console. A Big Gulp sweated in the drink holder. She reached into her pocket and looked at the man and smiled. "I really appreciate you picking me up. I don't think I caught your name."

"Donaldson. Pleased to meet you."

"Is that really your last name, or are you one of those guys who have a last name for a first name?"

"No, that's my first."

They drove in silence for a mile, Donaldson glancing between the girl and the road.

"Highway's packed this time of day. I bet we'd make better time on the county roads. Less traffic. If that's okay with you, of course."

"I was actually just going to suggest that," Lucy said. "Weird."

"Well, I wouldn't want to do anything to make you feel uncomfortable." Donaldson glanced down at Lucy's pocket. "Pretty young thing like yourself might get nervous driving off the main drag. In fact, you don't see many young lady hitchers these days. I think horror movies scared them all away. Everyone's worried about climbing into the car with a maniac."

Donaldson chuckled.

"I love county roads," Lucy said. "Much prettier scenery, don't you think?"

He nodded, taking the next exit, and Lucy leaned over, almost into his lap, and glanced at the gas gauge.

"You're running pretty low there. Your reserve light's on. Why don't we stop at this gas station up ahead. I'll put twenty in the tank. I also need something to drink. This mountain air is making my throat dry."

Donaldson shifted in his seat. "Oh, that light just came on, and I can get fifty miles on reserve. This is a Honda, you know."

"But why push our luck? And I'm really thirsty, Donaldson."

"Here." He lifted his Big Gulp. "It's still half full."

"No offense, but I don't drink after strangers, and I um…this is embarrassing…I have a cold sore in my mouth."

The gas station was coming up fast, and by all accounts it appeared to be the last stop before the county road started its climb into the mountains, into darkness.

"Who am I to say no to a lady?" Donaldson said.

He tapped the brakes and coasted into the station. It had probably been there for forty years, and hadn't updated since then. Donaldson sidled up to an old-school pump—one with a meter where the numbers actually scrolled up, built way back when closed-circuit cameras were something out of a science fiction magazine.

Donaldson peered over Lucy, into the small store. A bored female clerk sat behind the counter, apparently asleep. White trash punching the minimum wage clock, not one to pay much attention.

"The tank's on your side," Donaldson said. "I don't think these old ones take credit cards."

"I can pay cash inside. I buy, you fly."

Donaldson nodded. "Okay. I'm fine with doin' the pumpin'. Twenty, you said?"

"Yeah. You want anything?"

"If they have any gum that isn't older than I am, pick me up a pack. I've got an odd taste in my mouth for some reason."

Lucy got out of the car. Donaldson opened the glove compartment and quickly shoved something into his coat pocket. Then he set the parking brake, pocketed the keys, and followed her out.

While Donaldson stood pumping gas into the Honda, Lucy walked across the oil-stained pavement and into the store. The clerk didn't acknowledge her entrance, just sat staring at a small black-and-white television airing *Jeopardy*, her chin propped up in her hand and a Marlboro Red with a one-inch ash trailing smoke toward the ceiling.

Lucy walked down the aisle to the back of the store and picked a Red Bull out of the refrigerated case. At the drink fountain, she went with the smallest size—sixteen ounces—and filled the cup with ice to the brim, followed by a little Dr. Pepper, Mountain Dew, Pepsi, and Orange Fanta.

She glanced back toward the entrance and through the windows. Donaldson was still fussing with the pump. She reached into her pocket and withdrew the syringe. Uncapped the needle, shot a super-size squirt of liquid Oxycontin into the bubbling soda.

At the counter, she chose a pack of Juicy Fruit and pushed the items forward.

The clerk tore herself away from a video Daily Double and rang up the purchase.

"$24.52."

Lucy looked up from her wallet. "How much of that is gas?"

"Twenty."

"Shit, I told him just do fifteen. Here." She put a Jefferson on the filthy counter. "I'll send him in with the balance, 'cause this is all I've got."

"Don't be trying to steal my gas."

Donaldson was screwing on the gas cap when Lucy walked up. She said, "They still need five bucks. I'm sorry. It came to more than twenty with the drinks and gum. I'm out of cash."

"No ATM?"

"Here? Lucky they have electricity. I'll get you next stop." She flashed a shy grin, sashaying her fingers through the air. "Cross my heart and hope to die."

He just stared at her for a moment, then turned and started toward the store. Lucy opened the front passenger door and traded out Donaldson's Big Gulp for the fresh drink. She tossed the bucket-size cup into a trashcan between the pumps and climbed in.

Donaldson was at the counter. Lucy glanced into the backseat at the cooler with the biohazard sign. She looked into the convenience store, back at the cooler, then spun quickly around in her seat and reached back toward the lid.

Empty. The inside a dull, stained white. She closed it again.

Donaldson's footsteps slapped at the pavement. She settled back into her seat as he opened his door. The chassis bounced when he eased his bulk behind the wheel.

"Sorry about that," Lucy said. "I thought I had another ten. I could swear my snowboarder friend gave me some cash." She stuck out her lower lip, pouting. "I got you some gum. And a new drink."

Donaldson frowned, but he took the Juicy Fruit, ran it under his nose.

"Thank you, kindly. Fresh soda too, huh?"

Lucy cracked open the Red Bull and nodded.

"Cheers. To new friends." She took a sip. A trail of pink liquid dribbled down the corner of her mouth, hugging her chin and neck, dampening her shirt.

Donaldson shifted in his chair and reached for the cup. He sipped on the straw and made a face.

"What flavor is this?"

"I didn't know what you liked," Lucy said. "So I got you a little of everything."

Donaldson chuckled his approval, then turned the key and put the car into gear.

The winding county road ahead was pitch black, like driving through ink. Donaldson sipped his soda. Lucy watched him closely, taking periodic nips at her energy drink. The cool, dry air seemed to crackle with electricity as they climbed into the mountains.

"So is that really a guitar in that case?" Donaldson asked after five miles of silence.

"What do you think?"

"I'll be honest with you, darlin'. You're a bit of a mystery to me. I've been around, but I'm not sure what to make of you."

"How so?"

"You're young. But you've heard of Vietnam, I'm guessing."

"I loved *Platoon*."

Donaldson nodded. "Well then, you were practically there in the rice paddies with me, going toe-to-toe with the Cong."

He drank more soda. Lucy watched.

"Took some shrapnel in my hip in Ca Lu," Donaldson said. "Nicked my sciatic nerve. Biggest nerve in the body. Pain sometimes gets so bad I can chew through a bath towel. Do you understand pain, little girl?"

"More so than you'd think."

"So you should know, then, opiates and I are friends from way back." Donaldson took a big pull off the soda. "So spiking my drink here hasn't done much more than make me a little horny. Actually a lot horny." Donaldson turned to Lucy. "You're about as musical as I am Christian. So you want to tell me what your game is, or do I take you over my knee and spank you right now like the naughty girl you are?"

Lucy said, "It's Oxycontin. Did they have that back in 'Nam, gramps? And you being one fat bastard, I squirted two hundred and fifty milligrams into your drink. I'm not some frat boy trying to roofie up a chunky freshman. I gave you the rhino dose."

She tested the weight of the Styrofoam cup. "Jesus, you've already gone through half of it? I'm actually more concerned you're going to die of a drug overdose instead of the fun I have planned."

She reached across the seat and squeezed his leg. "Look, you will be losing consciousness shortly, so we don't have much time. Pull the car over. I'd like to take you up on that spanking."

Donaldson stared at her, blinked hard twice, and stomped the brake pedal.

Lucy's seatbelt released and she slammed into the metal-reinforced dashboard. Donaldson shook his head, then swiped the zip tie from his pocket. He grabbed a handful of wool cap and the hair beneath it and yanked Lucy up off the floor. She fought hard, but weight and strength won out and he cinched her hands behind her back.

Donaldson glanced through the windshield, then checked the rearview mirror. Darkness.

Lucy laughed through her shattered nose and ran her tongue along her swollen upper lip and gums—two front teeth MIA.

Donaldson blinked and shook his head again. Pulled off the road onto the shoulder.

"We're gonna have some fun, little girl," he said. "And two hundred and fifty milligrams is like candy to me."

He ran a clumsy paw across her breasts, squeezing hard, then turned his attention to the backseat.

The guitar case had two clasps, one on the body, one on the neck.

Donaldson slapped the left side of his face three times and then opened the case.

A waft of foulness seeped out of the velvet-lined guitar lid, although the contents didn't seem to be the source—a length of chain. Four pairs of handcuffs. Three carabiners. Vials of liquid Oxycontin. Cutlery shears. A creepy-looking instrument with six blades at one end. A spotlight. A small spray bottle. Two coils of climbing rope. And a snowboarding helmet.

The front passenger door squeaked open and Donaldson spun around as Lucy fell backward out of the car. He lunged into her seat, but she kicked the door. It slammed into his face, his chin crunching his mouth closed, and as the door recoiled, he saw Lucy struggling onto her feet, her wrists still bound behind her back.

She disappeared into the woods.

Donaldson took a moment, fumbling for the door handle. He found it, but paused.

He adjusted the rearview mirror, grinning to see the blood between his teeth.

"Should we let this one go, sport? Or show the little missus that there are things a lot scarier than a guitar case full of bondage shit?"

Donaldson winked at his reflection, tugged out the keys, yanked up the brake, and shoved his door open. He weaved over to the trunk, a stupid grin on his face, got the right key in on the third try.

Among the bottles of bleach solution, the rolls of paper towels, the gas cans, and the baby wipes, Donaldson grabbed the only weapon an upstanding citizen could legally carry without harassment from law enforcement.

The tire iron clenched in his hand, he bellowed at the woods.

"I'm coming for you, Lucy! And there won't be any drugs to dull *your* pain!"

He stumbled into the forest after her, his erection beginning to blossom.

She crouched behind a juniper tree, the zip tie digging into her wrists. Absolute darkness in the woods, nothing to see, but everything to hear.

Donaldson yelled, "Don't hide from me, little girl! It'll just make me angry!"

His heavy footsteps crunched in the leaves. Lucy eased down onto her butt and leaned back, legs in the air, then slid her bound wrists up the length of them. Donaldson stumbled past her tree, invisible, less than ten feet away.

"Lucy? Where are you?" His words slurred. "I just wanna talk."

"I'm over here, big boy! Still waiting for that spanking!"

His footsteps abruptly stopped. Dead quiet for thirty seconds, and then the footsteps started up again, heading in her general direction.

"Oh, no, please," she moaned. "Don't hurt me, Donaldson. I'm so afraid you'll hurt me."

He was close now, and she turned and started back toward the road, her hands out in front of her to prevent collision with a tree.

A glint of light up ahead—the Honda's windshield catching a piece of moonlight.

Lucy emerged from the woods, her hands throbbing from circulation loss. She stumbled into the car and turned around to watch the treeline.

"Come on, big boy! I'm right here! You can make it!"

Donaldson staggered out of the woods holding a tire iron, and when the moon struck his eyes, they were already half-closed.

He froze.

He opened his mouth to say something, but fell over instead, dropping like an old, fat tree.

Donaldson opened his eyes and lifted his head. Dawn and freezing cold. He lay in weeds at the edge of the woods, his head resting in a padded helmet. His wrists had been cuffed, hands purple from lack of blood flow, and his ankles were similarly bound. He was naked and glazed with dew, and as the world came into focus, he saw that one of those carabiners from Lucy's guitar case had been clipped to his ankle cuffs. A climbing rope ran from that carabiner to another carabiner, which was clipped to a chain which was wrapped around the trailer hitch of his Honda.

The driver-side door opened and Lucy got out, walked down through the weeds. She came over and sat on his chest, giving him a missing-toothed smile.

"Morning, Donaldson. You of all people will appreciate what's about to happen."

Donaldson yawned, then winked at her. "Aren't you just the prettiest thing to wake up to?"

Lucy batted her eyelashes.

"Thank you. That's sweet. Now, the helmet is so you don't die too fast. Head injuries ruin the fun. We'll go slow in the beginning. Barely walking speed. Then we'll speed up a bit when we get you onto asphalt. The last ones screamed for five miles. They where skeletons when I finally pulled over. But you're so heavy, I think you just might break that record."

"I have some bleach spray in the trunk," Donaldson said. "You might want to spritz me with that first, make it hurt even more."

"I prefer lemon juice, but it's no good until after the first half mile."

Donaldson laughed.

"You think this is a joke?"

He shook his head. "No. But when you have the opportunity to kill, you should kill. Not talk."

Donaldson sat up, quick for a man his size, and rammed his helmet into Lucy's face. As she reeled back, he caught her shirt with his swollen hands and rolled on top of her, his bulk making her gasp.

"The keys," he ordered. "Undo my hands, right now."

Lucy tried to talk, but her lungs were crushed. Donaldson shifted and she gulped in some air.

"In…the…guitar case…"

"That's a shame. That means you die right here. Personally, I think suffocation is the way to go. All that panic and struggle. Dragging some poor sap behind you? Where's the fun in that? Hell, you can't even see it without taking your eyes off the road, and that's a dangerous way to drive, girl."

Lucy's eyes bulged, her face turning scarlet.

"Poc…ket."

"Take your time. I'll wait."

Lucy managed to fish out the handcuff keys. Donaldson shifted again, giving her a fraction more room, and she unlocked a cuff from one of his wrists.

He winced, his face getting mean.

"Now let me tell you about the survival of the fittest, little lady. There's a…"

The chain suddenly jerked, tugging Donaldson across the ground. He clutched Lucy.

"Where are the car keys, you stupid bitch?"

"In the ignition…"

"You didn't set the parking brake! Give me the handcuff key!"

The car crept forward, beginning to pick up speed as it rolled quietly down the road.

The skin of Donaldson's right leg tore against the ground, peeling off, and the girl pounded on him, fighting to get away.

"The key!" he howled, losing his grip on her. He clawed at her waist, her hips, and snagged her foot.

Lucy screamed when the cuff snicked tightly around her ankle.

"No! No no no!" She tried to sit up, to work the key into the lock, but they hit a hole and it bounced from her grasp.

They were dragged off the dirt and onto the road.

Lucy felt the pavement eating through her trench coat, Donaldson in hysterics as it chewed through the fat of his ass, and the car still accelerating down the five-percent grade.

At thirty miles per hour, the fibers of Lucy's trench coat were sanded away, along with her camouflage panties, and just as she tugged a folding knife out of her pocket and began to hack at the flesh of her ankle, the rough county road began to grind through her coccyx.

She dropped the knife and they screamed together for two of the longest miles of their wretched lives, until the road curved and the Honda didn't, and the car and Lucy and Donaldson all punched together through a guardrail and took the fastest route down the mountain.

Dear Diary

Here's another old story that I eventually rewrote to flesh it out a bit. It's an epistolary peace, entirely done as journal entries written by a teen girl. I revisited the epistolary form for a section in an upcoming Jack Kilborn book.

Sept 15

Dear Diary,

First day of school! I hope this doesn't turn into a repeat of last year, when Sue Ellen Derbin and Margaret "Superbitch" Dupont decided to try and kick me off of Pom-Pons. When I think about all those things they said about me it makes me soooo mad! Who cares if my parents never had a lot of money or anything, and so what if I don't have any stupid designer clothes, I'm still a better person than them. They were so jealous of my blonde hair and blue eyes and my heritage. I hated those phonies soooo much!!! It's so nice they don't bother me anymore.

My schedule is English, Algebra, Biology, Lunch, Gym, History, Art, and Music. It's nice to finally be an eighth grader and get the classes I want. But I still don't want to be here, and if I ever have kids I'll let them decide if they want to go school or not. I don't care if it's a law, the law stinks and so does school!!!

But it's not all bad. Robert Collins is in my math class and he's sooooo cute! He's got the best butt I've ever seen on a thirteen-year-old, and when he smiles with those dimples I sincerely want to die! We got to choose our own seats and I sat next to him. Tomorrow I'll wear more perfume and see if he notices.

Sept 16

Dear Diary,

Pom-Pon tryouts were today, and I'm Captain of the first squad! With Sue Ellen and Margret Superbitch gone, it was waaaaay too easy. Debbie Baker made squad two leader, and I could tell she was pissed that I beat her out. Tough titties, Deb!!!

But even better than that, Robert commented that he liked my perfume today! I wore a little extra, and while we were doing our problems he wrote me a note that said "Is that you who smells so good?" I almost died, right there in class.

I know I'm going to save that note forever.

Then I did something that was totally unlike me. I asked him if he was still going out with Pam Escher. He said no, Pam was now dating Stu Dorman. It seems Stu dumped Melissa for Pam and Pam dumped poor Robert. I feel bad for him, but not for me. Wouldn't it be great if he asked me out?

Sept 17

Dear Diary,

HE ASKED ME OUT!!!!!!!!!!!!

I couldn't believe it. We were done checking our homework and he leaned over so his lips were almost touching my ear and asked if I wanted to go out after school! So I skipped Pom-Pon practice and we walked over to Barro's Pizza and shared a small pepperoni. I didn't actually eat any, because of my special diet, but he didn't notice. We talked a lot about school and about how everyone is too concerned about appearance rather than being real and he told me about his family that came from New York and I told him that my family actually came from Scandinavian. He was super intelligent and serious. I never would have guessed he was so smart because he's so cute. I wonder if he'll be THE ONE. He's so cute it would be great if he was.

Sept 18

Dear Diary,

I got in BIG trouble for skipping Pom-Pon practice. Debbie Baker kept sucking up to Mrs. Meaker, saying how I shouldn't be squad captain if I didn't show up. The little bitch. Mrs. Meaker didn't say much, other than I had to make sure I didn't miss it again.

Robert and I passed notes back and forth during math. Nothing lovey-dovey, just talk because math is sooooo boring. I wish he had the same lunch period as I did. He said he would ask me out again after school but he has football practice. I told him I had Pom-Pons, and maybe we could meet after. He said great. But my practice ran late (practicing Debbie's stupid new drills) so when I got to Barro's he wasn't there. I hope he isn't mad.

Sept 19

Dear Diary,

Robert looked hurt in Math today, but I wrote him a note in English to explain everything and when he read it he forgave me. He asked me out again after school, and I agreed, even though I would miss another practice. Practicing five times a week is too much, if you ask me. We met at Barro's and got another pepperoni (which I didn't eat), and we talked for two hours. I told him all about runestones and Viking mythology and the Heimskringla and he really seemed interested. Then halfway during our talk he reached out and held my hand. I thought I would die!!!!! His hands are so strong and big. Maybe he is THE ONE.

Sept 20

Dear Diary,

WEEKEND!!!!! I'm gonna spent it all in my basement, getting stronger and watching my diet. If you want to be the best, that's what you have to do.

Sept 22

Dear Diary,

That bitch Debbie got me kicked off as squad one leader!!!!!!!!! I just missed two stupid days! I cried in the bathroom for a half hour. I want to kill her! She talked to Mrs. Meaker and Mrs. Meaker said I wasn't meeting up to my responsibilities. I hate them both.

Robert waited for me after practice so I had a shoulder to cry on. He even kissed me, but it was only on the cheek. He's such a doll. He invited me over to his house for dinner, but I lied to him and said my parents already had plans. I couldn't tell him about the basement. But maybe I will soon.

Sept 23

Dear Diary,

Debbie didn't come to school today. I wonder why? (Ha!) I asked Mrs. Meaker if I could have my squad leader position back, and she said maybe. She'll say yes when Debbie misses another practice.

Robert kissed me on the mouth today, for the first time! It was weird and exciting! He even used his tongue!!!!! He's soooo sophisticated. It was right after practice. He waited for me, and wanted to walk me home. I lied and said my parents didn't allow visitors. He believed me, and then he leaned over and kissed me. I thought my knees turned to Jell-O. I now know that he is THE ONE.

Sept 24

Dear Diary,

I've been thinking about it a lot and I've decided to show Robert the basement. I invited him over after practice and lied and said my parents weren't home. I said I'd make dinner. He was impressed that I could cook. I didn't tell him that I couldn't.

By the time we got to my place it was already getting dark, and Robert said he should call home and check in. But I told him to look at my basement first, because I had a big surprise.

When I turned on the basement light, the hissing started. Robert asked if it was the furnace, and I giggled. Then I pulled the cover off the cages.

Debbie Baker was tied up in the first one, naked, lying in a smelly puddle of her own piss. She twisted and banged her head on the cage door and looked so funny I had to laugh. Robert just stared.

Then I pulled the tarp off the other cage. Margret "Superbitch" Dupont hissed. Sue Ellen Derbin was crying, like always. Sue Ellen had no arms or legs, and was lying naked on the hay I put down for her, which she messed again. Gross! I had to stop feeding her so much dog food.

Superbitch Margret had one stump of an arm left, severed at the elbow. Both had those awful brown scars where I had to burn them to seal the wound after I cut off a limb. I couldn't let them bleed to death. That wouldn't be right.

Robert got really freaked out, and I explained to him they were hissing because I cut out their vocal cords. That way they couldn't attract attention. He turned around and tried to go up the stairs but I had locked the basement door. I told him I thought he was staying for dinner. That's how you get strong. By eating your enemies. One piece at a time. That's what my Viking ancestors did. But the people have to be alive when you eat them, or else you don't ingest their souls. Their souls are what really made you strong. They made me strong. That's why I was Pom-Pon captain. And that's why I was going out with the cutest boy in school.

As I explained this to Robert, he started to yell for help. I tried to tell him not to be scared, because he was THE ONE. THE ONE to share this secret with me. Together we could live forever. It was okay. You didn't have to eat them all at once. You just do it a little bit at a time. I told him I had already eaten my parents. It took two years before I finished the last of Dad.

But Robert just kept on screaming, and I finally had to hit him over the head to shut him up. I guess he wasn't THE ONE after all.

I stripped off his clothes and tied him up and used the long scissors to snip his vocal chords. Then I looked over his trim body and decided what I wanted to eat first. I plugged in the electric saw and built a fire in the pit to heat the cauterizing iron.

I didn't want Robert to bleed to death. That wouldn't be right. I couldn't ingest his strength then. And he looks strong enough to be able to feed me for a loooooooooong time.

The Eagle

This is an old one, written in college. I like to joke than in school, I majored in Budweiser. Which may have been the reason I got Cs in my creative writing classes. Out of the hundreds of short stories I wrote in my teens and twenties, only a handful were actually readable. This is one of the readable ones. Barely.

MY GRANDPA IS EIGHTY-seven years old, which Mom says is really old but I know that people can live to a hundred because I saw it on T.V. Grandpa is in a wheelchair because he had a stroke, and he can't move one side of his body even though he tries real hard. Most of the time he's parked in front of the big window in my Mom and Dad's room, looking out at the woods in our back yard. We own a lot of the woods, but I'm still not allowed to play there by myself because my Mom says the environment is very different from Chicago, where we used to live, and I might get attacked by a bear. We've been here for two months, and I haven't seen a bear yet. Neither has Grandpa, and he spends all of his time looking out the window, so if anyone would have seen a bear it would have been him.

Grandpa came to live with us a long time ago, when I was a little kid. Right after Grandma died. I don't remember Grandma because I was too small, but my Mom has pictures of her holding me. He had the stroke a few years ago, and Mom says it made him crazy. Dad says he isn't crazy, he just likes to kid around sometimes. I really don't have an opinion because I'm not around him much and he spends all his time in my Mom and Dad's room, staring out the window. Grandpa says nature is more educational than watching T.V. I think it's boring.

I don't have to go to school because it's summer. My new best friend is Marty Phipps, who lives about half a mile up the dirt road, and I like to play at his house because his mom lets us go in the woods. My old best friend was Vincey Jackson. I liked Vincey more than Marty, but I don't see Vincey a lot because he lives in Illinois and I'm in Oregon. But Marty is okay. We're building a tree house and we're going to start a club, but we won't let Marty's younger brother join because he's too young and just a baby.

I was putting on my shoes to go to Marty's when Grandpa called me. Grandpa never calls me. If he needs something he calls my mother. So I went to see Grandpa in my Mom and Dad's room, and he was pointing out the window.

"Do you see him, Joey? Do you see him?"

I looked out the window and saw nothing special. Just the woods.

"Ain't it magnificent? Ain't it, Joey?"

Grandpa was kind of smiling, but he couldn't smile all the way because one side of his face wouldn't move, so instead it looked creepy.

I shook my head and said I didn't see anything.

"Well, it's a bald eagle, son! Circling up there! Plain as day!"

I looked out and didn't see anything in the sky at all. But maybe Grandpa had better eyesight than me or something, so I said that I saw it, and I left. Grandpa was starting to drool, and Dad says that he can't help it but I know that only babies drool, and adults shouldn't, and that makes me feel bad. Then I went to Marty Phipps' house to play.

The next day, Grandpa called me in again. He was looking out the window with my Dad's binoculars.

"Come here, Joey. You can see him so close you can count his feathers!"

Grandpa gave me the binoculars and I looked up at the sky and really tried to see the eagle but didn't see anything at all.

"Do you see him, Joey?"

"Yes, Sir."

"Look at him go!"

Mom told me to be nice to Grandpa because when you have a stroke sometimes you see things that aren't really there. I once told Marty Phipp and he said there were no eagles around here, and that Grandpa was crazy. I hit him and he started to cry, but we're friends again now.

I gave Grandpa the binoculars and went over to Marty Phipp's house so we could draw the plans for our tree house.

The next day Grandpa called me again, and wanted me to look at the eagle. He called me again the next day. And the next day. I never saw an eagle, but once I saw a bunch of ducks flying across the sky. Grandpa said the eagle was higher up than the ducks. I didn't see it.

One day when Grandpa called me, he was shaking. I thought he wanted me to look at the eagle again, so I said I saw it. But instead Grandpa grabbed my arm and held on tight.

"The knife! The knife, Joey! Biggest knife I ever seen!"

I got scared and yelled for Mom, who tried to calm Grandpa down. But Grandpa kept screaming.

"He was carrying a head! A head! The knife!"

Mom pulled me away from Grandpa and called the doctor, and two men came and took Grandpa and my mom away in an ambulance. I was over at Marty Phipp's house. He said again that my Grandpa was crazy and I hit him again and we got in a fight but Mrs. Phipp stopped us and we made Rice Crispy treats. I stayed the night at Marty's, and I had bad dreams about Grandpa grabbing me and not letting go.

The next day, Mom and Dad came back from the doctor and told me Grandpa wouldn't be coming home for a while. He was in a special hospital. It didn't bother me at all because I never was close with Grandpa and I was too busy building the club house with Marty Phipp. We went out in the woods to find a good tree. We walked for a while when we got to a creek and then we followed the creek for a while when we saw the shed.

It was a small shed, and it looked like no one had used it for a long time, and Marty said it was great because we could use the wood to build our club house. So we went to the shed and it was really old. I could break the wood just by pushing it. Marty wanted to stand on top so I let him get on my shoulders and he got on and then fell through the roof.

I didn't know what to do. I went in the shed and Marty was on the floor and he wasn't moving. I shook him and yelled his name but he wouldn't wake up. So I ran back along the creek to get my Mom. I was running and running and I looked up in the sky through a break in the trees and I saw something. So I stopped and I squinted in the sun and there it was. An eagle. Circling around the tops of the trees.

Then I began to run again, but I tripped over a human head, and then a very large and dirty man jumped out of the trees and came at me with a knife.

The biggest knife I ever seen.

Sound of Blunder

It's no secret I'm a huge F. Paul Wilson fan. When we were both invited into the Blood Lite anthology, I asked him if he would like to collaborate on a funny horror short. He graciously agreed, and we produced this slapstick bit of schtick. It was a lot of fun to write.

"WE'RE DEAD! WE'RE FREAKIN' DEAD!"

Mick Brady, known by the criminal underground of Arkham, Pennsylvania as "Mick the Mick," held a shaking fist in front of Willie Corrigan's face. Willie recoiled like a dog accustomed to being kicked.

"I'm sorry, Mick!"

Mick the Mick raised his arm and realized that smacking Willie wasn't going to help their situation. He smacked him anyway, a punch to the gut that made the larger man double over and grunt like a pig.

"Jesus, Mick! You hit me in my hernia! You know I got a bulge there!"

Mick the Mick grabbed a shock of Willie's greasy brown hair and jerked back his head so they were staring eye-to-eye.

"What do you think Nate the Nose is going to do to us when he finds out we lost his shit? We're both going to be eating *San Francisco Hot Dogs*, Willie."

Willie's eyes got wide. Apparently the idea of having his dick cut off, boiled, and fed to him on a bun with a side of fries was several times worse than a whack to the hernia.

"We'll…we'll tell him the truth. Maybe he'll understand."

"You want to tell the biggest mobster in the state that your Nana used a key of uncut Columbian to make a pound cake?"

"It was an accident," Willie whined. "She thought it was flour. Hey, is that a spider on the wall? Spiders give me the creeps, Mick. Why do they need eight legs? Other bugs only got six."

Mick the Mick realized that hitting Willie again wouldn't help anything. He hit him anyway, a slap across his face that echoed off the concrete floor and walls of Willie's basement.

"Jesus, Mick! You hit me in my bad tooth! You know I got a cavity there!"

Mick the Mick was considering where he would belt his friend next, even though it wasn't doing either of them any good, when he heard the basement door open.

"You boys playing nice down there?"

"Yes, Nana," Willie called up the stairs. He nudged Mick the Mick and whispered, "Tell Nana yes."

Mick the Mick rolled his eyes, but managed to say, "Yes, Nana."

"Would you like some pound cake? It didn't turn out very well for some reason, but Bruno seems to like it."

Bruno was Willie's dog, an elderly beagle. He tore down the basement stairs, ran eighteen quick laps around Mick the Mick and Willie, and then barreled, full-speed, face-first into the wall, knocking himself out. Mick the Mick watched as the dog's tiny chest rose and fell with the speed of a weed wacker.

"No thanks, Nana," Mick the Mick said.

"It's on the counter, if you want any. Good night, boys."

"Night, Nana," they answered in unison.

Mick the Mick wondered how the hell they could get out of this mess. Maybe there was some way to separate the coke from the cake, using chemicals and stuff. But they wouldn't be able to do it themselves. That meant telling Nate the Nose, which meant San Francisco Hot Dogs. In his twenty-four years since birth, Mick the Mick had grown very attached to his penis. He'd miss it something awful.

"We could sell the cake," Willie said.

"You think someone is going to pay sixty thousand bucks for a pound cake?"

"It's just an idea."

"It's a stupid idea, Willie. No junkie is going to snort baked goods. Ain't gonna happen."

"So what should we do? I — hey, did you hear if the Phillies won? Phillies got more legs than a spider. And you know what? *They catch flies too!* That's a joke, Mick."

"Shaddup. I need to think."

Mick the Mick couldn't think of anything, so he punched Willie again, even though it didn't solve anything.

"Jesus, Mick! You hit my kidney! You know I got a stone there!"

Mick the Mick walked away, rubbing his temples, willing an idea to come.

"That one really hurt, Mick."

Mick the Mick shushed him.

"I mean it. I'm gonna be pissing red for a week."

"Quiet, Willie. Lemme think."

"It looks like cherry Kool-Aid. And it burns, Mick. Burns like fire."

Mick the Mick snapped his fingers. *Fire.*

"That's it, Willie. Fire. Your house is insured, right?"

"I guess so. Hey, do you think there's any pizza left? I like pepperoni. That's a fun word to say. *Pepperoni.* It rhymes with *lonely.* You think pepperoni gets lonely, Mick?"

To help Willie focus, Mick the Mick kicked him in his bum leg, even though it really didn't help him focus much.

"Jesus, Mick! You know I got gout!"

"Pay attention, Willie. We burn down the house, collect the insurance, and pay off Nate the Nose."

Willie rubbed his shin, wincing.

"But where's Nana supposed to live, Mick?"

"I hear the Miskatonic Nursing Home is a lot nicer, now that they arrested the guy who was making all the old people wear dog collars."

"I can't put Nana in a nursing home, Mick!"

"Would you rather be munching on your vein sausage? Nate the Nose makes you eat the whole thing, or else you also get served a side of meatballs."

Willie folded his arms. "I won't do it. And I won't let you do it."

Mick the Mick took aim and punched Willie in his bad knee, where he had the metal pins, even though it did nothing to fix their problem.

"Jesus, Mick! You hit me in the…"

"Woof!"

Bruno the beagle sprang to his feet, ran sixteen laps around the men, then tore up the stairs.

"Bruno!" they heard Nana chide. "Get off the counter! You've had enough pound cake!"

Mick the Mick put his face in his hands, very close to tears. The last time he cried was ten years ago, when Nate the Nose ordered him to break his mother's thumbs because she was late with a loan payment. When he tried, Mom had stabbed Mick the Mick with a meat thermometer. That hurt, but not as much as a wiener-ectomy would.

"Maybe we can leave town," Willie said, putting a hand on Mick the Mick's shoulder.

That left Willie's kidney exposed. Mick the Mick took advantage, even though it didn't help their situation.

Willie fell to his knees. Bruno the beagle tore down the stairs, straddled Willie's calf, and began to hump so fast his little doggie hips were a blur.

Mick the Mick began searching the basement for something flammable. As it often happened in life, arson was really the only way out. He found a can of paint thinner on a dusty metal shelf and worked the top with his thumbnail.

"Mick, no!"

Mick couldn't get it open. He tried his teeth.

"You can't burn my house down, Mick! All my stuff is here! Like my comics! We used to collect comics when we were kids, Mick! Don't you remember?"

Willie reached for a box, dug out a torn copy of Amazing Spiderman #146, and traced his finger up and down Scorpion's tail in a way that made Mick the Mick uncomfortable. So he reached out and slapped Willie's bad tooth. Willie dropped the comic and curled up fetal, and Bruno the beagle abandoned the calf for the loftier possibilities of Willie's head.

Mick managed to pop the top on the can, and he began to sprinkle mineral spirits on some bags labeled *Precious Photos & Memories.*

Willie moaned something unintelligible through closed lips — he was probably afraid to open his mouth until he disengaged Bruno the beagle.

"Mmphp-muummph-mooeoemmum!"

"We don't have a choice, Willie. The only way out of this is fire. Beautiful, cleansing fire. If there's money left over, we'll bribe the orderlies so Nana doesn't get abused. At least not as much as the others."

"Mick!" Willie cried. It came out "Mibb!" because Bruno the beagle had taken advantage. Willie gagged, shoving the dog away. Bruno the beagle ran around Willie seven times then flew up the stairs.

"Bruno!" they heard Nana chide. "Naughty dog! Not when we have company over!"

Willie hacked and spit, then sat up.

"A heist, Mick. We could do a heist."

"No way," Mick the Mick said. "Remember what happened to Jimmy the Spleen? Tried to knock over a WaMu in Pittsburgh. Cops shot his ass off. His whole ass. You want one of them creepy poop bags hanging on your belt?"

Willie wiped a sleeve across his tongue. "Not a bank, Mick. The Arkham Museum."

"The museum?"

"They got all kinds of expensive old stuff. And it ain't guarded at night. I bet we could break in there, get away with all sorts of pricey antiques. I think they got like a T-rex skull. That could be worth a million bucks. If I had a million bucks, I'd buy some scuba gear, so I could go deep diving on shipwrecks and try to find some treasure so I could be rich."

Mick the Mick rolled his eyes.

"You think Tommy the Fence is going to buy a T-rex skull? How we even gonna get it out of there, Willie? You gonna put it in your pocket?"

"They got other stuff too, Mick. Maybe gold and gems and stamps."

"I got a stamp for you."

"Jesus, Mick! My toe! You know I got that infected ingrown!"

Mick the Mick was ready to offer seconds, but he stopped mid-stomp.

"You ever been to the Museum, Willie?"

"Course not. You?"

"Nah."

But maybe it wasn't a totally suck-awful idea.

"What about the alarms?"

"We can get past those, Mick. No problem. Hey, you think I need a haircut? If I look up, I can see my bangs."

Willie did just that. Mick the Mick stared at the cardboard boxes, soaked with paint thinner. He wanted to light them up, watch them burn. But insurance took forever. There were investigations, forms to fill out, waiting periods.

But if they went to the museum and pinched something small and expensive, chances are they could turn it around in a day or two. The faster they could pay off Nate the Nose, the safer Little Mick and the Twins were.

"Okay, Willie. We'll give it a try. But if it don't work, we torch Nana's house. Agreed?"

"Agreed."

Mick the Mick extended his hand. Willie reached for it, leaving his hernia bulge unprotected. Now that they had a plan, it served absolutely no purpose to hit Willie again.

He hit him anyway.

"I don't like it in here, Mick." Willie said as they entered the great central hall of the Arkham Pennsylvania Museum of Natural History and Baseball Cards.

Mick the Mick gave him a look, which was pretty useless since Willie couldn't see his face and he couldn't see Willie's. The only things they could see were whatever lay at the end of their flashlight beams.

Getting in had been a walk. Literally. The front doors were unlocked. And no alarm. Really weird. Unless the museum had stopped locking up because nobody ever came here. Mick the Mick had lived in Arkham all his life and never met anyone who'd ever come here except on a class trip. Made a kind of sense then to not bother with locks. Nobody came during the day when the lights were on, so why would anyone want to come when the lights were out?

Which made Mick the Mick a little nervous about finding anything valuable.

"It's just a bunch of rooms filled with loads of old crap."

Willie's voice shook. "Old stuff scares me. Especially *this* old stuff."

"Why?"

"'Cause it's old and — hey, can we stop at Burger Pile on the way home?"

"Focus, Willie. You gotta focus."

"I like picking off the sesame seeds and making them fight wars."

Mick the Mick took a swing at him and missed in the dark.

Suddenly the lights went on. They were caught. Mick the Mick feared prison almost as much as he feared Nate the Nose. He was small for his size, and unfortunately blessed with perfectly-shaped buttocks. The cons would trade him around like cigarettes.

Mick the Mick ducked into a crouch, ready to run for the nearest exit. He saw Willie standing by a big arched doorway with his hand on a light switch.

"There," Willie said, grinning. "That's better."

Mick wanted to punch his hernia again but he was too far away.

"Put those out!"

Willie stepped away from the wall toward one of the displays. "Hey, look at this."

Mick the Mick realized the damage had been done. Sooner or later someone would come to investigate. Okay, maybe not, but they couldn't risk it. They'd have to move fast.

He looked up and saw a banner proclaiming the name of the exhibit: *Elder Gods and Lost Races of South Central Pennsylvania.*

"What's this?" Willie said, leaning over a display case.

Suddenly a deep voice boomed: *"WELCOME!"*

Willie cried, "Whoa!" and Mick the Mick jumped — high enough so as if he'd been holding a basketball he could have made his first dunk.

Soon as he recovered, he did a thorough three-sixty but saw no one else but Willie.

"*What you see before you,*" the voice continued, "*is a rare artifact that once belonged to an ancient lost race that dwelled in the Arkham area during prehistoric times. This, like every other ancient artifact in this room, was excavated from a site near the Arkham landfill.*"

After recovering from another near dunk, plus a tiny bit of pee-pee, Mick noticed a speaker attached to the underside of the case.

Ah-ha. A recording triggered by a motion detector. But the sound was a little garbled, reminding him of the voice of the aliens in an old black-and-white movie he and Willie had watched on TV last week. The voice always began, "People of Earth …" but he couldn't remember the name of the film.

"*We know little about this ancient lost race but, after careful examination by the eminent archeologists and anthropologists here at the Arkham Pennsylvania Museum of Natural History and Baseball Cards, they arrived at an irrefutable conclusion.*"

"Hey, Willie said, grinning. "Sounds like the alien voice from *Earth versus the Flying Saucers.*"

"*The ancient artifact before you once belonged to an ancient shaman.*"

"What's a shaman, Mick?"

Mick the Mick remembered seeing something about that on TV once. "I think he's a kind of a witch doctor. But forget about —"

"*A shaman, for those of you who don't know, is something of a tribal wise man, what the less sophisticated among you might call a 'witch doctor.'* "

"Witch doctor? Cooool."

Mick the Mick stepped over to see what the voice was talking about. Under the glass he saw a three-foot metal staff with a small globe at each end.

"*The eminent archeologists and anthropologists here at the Arkham Pennsylvania Museum of Natural History and Baseball Cards have further determined that the object is none other an ancient shaman's scepter of power.*"

Willie looked a Mick the Mick with wide eyes. "Did you hear that? A scepter of power! Is that like He-Man's Power Sword? He-Man was really strong, but he had hair like a girl. Is the scepter of power like a power sword, Mick?"

"No, it's more like a magic wand, but forget —"

"*The less sophisticated among you might refer to a scepter of power as a 'magic wand,' and in a sense it functioned as such.*"

"A magic wand! Like in the Harry Potter movies? I love those movies, and I've always wanted a magic wand! Plus I get crazy hot thoughts about Hermoine. She's a real fox. Kinda like Drew Barrymore. In E.T. Hey, why does the wand have a deep groove in it?"

Mick the Mick looked again and noticed the deep groove running its length.

"Note, please, the deep groove running the length of the scepter of power. The eminent archeologists and anthropologists here at the Arkham Pennsylvania Museum of Natural History and Baseball Cards believe that to be what is knows as a fuller…

A fuller? Mick thought. Looks like a blood channel.

"…which the less sophisticated among you might call a 'blood channel.' The eminent archeologists and anthropologists here at the Arkham Pennsylvania Museum of Natural History and Baseball Cards believe this ancient scepter of power might have been used by its shaman owner to perform sacred religious ceremonies — specifically, the crushing of skulls and ritual disemboweling."

Mick the Mick got a chill. He hoped Nate the Nose never got his hands on something like this.

"What's disemboweling, Mick?"

"When someone cuts out your intestines."

"How do you dooky, then? Like squeezing a toothpaste tube?"

"You don't dooky, Willie. You die."

"Cool! Can I have the magic wand, Mick? Can I?"

Mick the Mick didn't answer. He'd noticed something engraved near the end of the far tip. He leaned closer, squinting until it came into focus.

Sears.

What the—?

He stepped back for a another look at the scepter of power and —

"A curtain rod … it's a freakin' curtain rod!"

Willie looked at him like he was crazy. "Curtain rod? Didn't you hear the man? It's, like, a magic wand, and — hey, what's that over there?"

Mick the Mick slapped at Willie's kidney as he passed but missed because he couldn't take his eyes off the Sears scepter of power. Maybe they could steal it, return it to Sears, and get a brand new one. That wouldn't help much with Nate the Nose, but Mick the Mick did need a new curtain rod. His old one had broken, and his drapes were attached to the wall with forks. That made Thursdays — spaghetti night — particularly messy.

"WELCOME!" boomed the same voice as Willie stopped before another display. *"What you see before you is a rare artifact that once belonged to an ancient lost race that dwelled in the Arkham area during prehistoric times. This, like every other ancient artifact in this room, was excavated from a site near the Arkham landfill."*

"Hey, Mick y'gotta see this."

After some biblical thinking, Mick the Mick spared the rod and moved along.

"We know little about this ancient lost race but, after careful examination by the eminent archeologists and anthropologists here at the Arkham Pennsylvania Museum of Natural History and Baseball Cards, they arrived at an irrefutable conclusion: The artifact before you was used by an ancient shaman of this lost race to perform surrogate sacrifices. (For those of you unfamiliar with the term 'shaman,' please return to the previous display.)"

"I know what a shaman is, 'cause you just told me," Willie said. "But what's a surrogate—?"

"A surrogate sacrifice was an image that was sacrificed instead of a real person. Before you is a statuette of a woman carved by the ancient lost race from a yet-to-be-identified flesh-colored substance. Note the head is missing. This is because the statuette was beheaded instead of the human it represented."

Mick the Mick stepped up to the display and immediately recognized the naked pink figure. He'd used to swipe his sister Suzy's and make it straddle his rocket and go for a ride. Only Suzy's had a blonde head.

"That's a freakin' Barbie doll!" He grabbed Willie's shoulder and yanked him away.

"Jesus, Mick! You know I got a dislocating shoulder!"

Willie stumbled, knocking Mick the Mick into another display case, which toppled over with a crash.

"WELCOME! What you see before you is a rare tome of lost wisdom that once belonged —"

Screaming, Mick the Mick kicked the speaker until the voice stopped.

"Look, Mick," Willie said, squatting and poking through the broken glass, "it's not a tome, it's a book. It's supposed to contain lost wisdom. Maybe it can tell us how to keep Nate the Nose off our backs." He rose and squinted at the cover. *"The Really, Really, Really*

Old Ones."

"It's a paperback, you moron. How much wisdom you gonna find in there?"

"Yeah, you're right. It says, 'Do Not Try This at Home. Use Only Under Expert Supervision or You'll Be Really, Really, Really Sorry.' Better not mess with *that.*"

"Oh, yeah?" Mick the Mick had had it — really had it. Up. To. Here. He opened to a random page and read. "'Random Dislocation Spell.' "

Willie winced. "Not my shoulder!"

" 'Use only under expert supervision.' Yeah, right. Look, it's got a bunch of gobbledygook to read."

"You mean like 'Mekka-lekka hi—?"

"Shaddap and I'll show you what bullshit this is."

Mick the Mick started reading, pronouncing the gobbledygook as best he could, going slow and easy so he didn't screw up the words like he normally did when he read.

When he finished he looked at Willie and grinned. "See? No random dislocation."

Willie rolled his shoulder. "Yeah. Feels pretty good. I wonder —"

The smell hit Mick the Mick first, hot and overpowering, reminding him of that time he stuck his head in the toilet because his older brother told him that's where brownies came from. It was followed by the very real sensation of being squeezed. But not squeezed by a person. Squeezed all over by some sort of full-body force like being pushed through a too-small opening. The air suddenly became squishy and solid and pressed into every crack and pore on Mick the Mick's body, and then it undulated, moving him, pushing him, through the solid marble floor of the Arkham Pennsylvania Museum of Natural History and Baseball Cards.

The very fabric of reality, or something like that, seemed to vibrate with a deep resonance, and the timbre rose to become an overpowering, guttural groan. The floor began to dissolve, or maybe he began to dissolve, and then came a horrible yet compelling farting sound and Mick the Mick was suddenly plopped into the middle of a jungle.

Willie landed next to him.

"I feel like shit," Willie said.

Mick the Mick squinted in the sunlight and looked around. They were surrounded by strange, tropical trees and weird looking flowers with big fat pink petals that made him feel sort of horny. A dragonfly the size of a bratwurst hovered over their heads, gave them a passing glance, then buzzed over to one of the pink flowers, which snapped open and bit the bug in half.

"Where are we, Mick?"

Mick the Mick scratched his head. "I'm not sure. But I think when I read that book I opened a portal in the space-time continuum and we were squeezed through one of the eleven imploded dimensions into the late Cretaceous Period."

"Wow. That sucks."

"No, Willie. It doesn't suck at all."

"Yeah it does. The season finale of *MacGyver: The Next Generation* is on tonight. It's a really cool episode where he builds a time machine out of some pocket lint and a broken meat thermometer. Wouldn't it be cool to have a time machine, Mick?"

Mick the Mick slapped Willie on the side of his head.

"Jesus, Mick! You know I got swimmer's ear!"

"Don't you get it, Willie? This book *is* a time machine. We can go back in time!"

Willie got wide-eyed. "I get it! We can get back to the present a few minutes early so I won't miss MacGyver!"

Mick the Mick considered hitting him again, but his hand was getting sore.

"Think bigger than MacGyver, Willie. We're going to be rich. Rich and famous and powerful. Once I figure out how this book works we'll be able to go to any point in history."

"You mean like we go back to summer camp in nineteen seventy-five? Then we could steal the candy from those counselors so they couldn't lure us into the woods and touch us in the bad place."

"Even better, Willie. We can bet on sports and always win. Like that movie."

"Which one?"

"The one where he went to the past and bet on sports so he could always win."

"*The Godfather*?"

"No, Willie. *The Godfather* was the one with the fat guy who slept with horse heads."

"Oh yeah. Hey Mick, don't you think those big pink flowers look like…

"Shut your stupid hole, Willie. I gotta think."

Mick the Mick racked his brain, but he was never into sports, and he couldn't think of a single team that won anything. Plus, he didn't have any money on him. It would take a long time to parlay the eighty-one cents in his pocket into sixty grand. But there *had* to be other ways to make money with a time machine. Probably.

He glanced at Willie, who was walking toward one of those pink flowers, leaning in to sniff it. Or perhaps do something else with it, because Willie's tongue was out.

"Willie! Get away from that thing and try to focus! We need to figure out how to make some money."

"It smells like fish, Mick."

"Dammit, Willie! Did you take your medicine this morning like you're supposed to?"

"I can't remember. Nana says I need a stronger subscription. But every time I go to the doctor to get one I get distracted and forget to ask."

Mick the Mick scratched himself. Another dragonfly — this one shaped like a banana wearing a turtleneck — flew up to one of those pink flowers and was bitten in half too. Damn, those bugs were stupid. They just didn't learn.

Mick the Mick scratched himself again, wondering if the crabs were back. If they were, it made him really angry. When you paid fifty bucks for a massage at Madame Yoko's, the happy ending should be crab-free.

Willie said, "Maybe we can go back to the time when Nate the Nose was a little boy, and then we could be real nice to him so when he grew up he would remember us and wouldn't make us eat our junk."

Or we could push his stroller into traffic, Mick the Mick thought.

But Nate the Nose had bosses, and they probably had bosses too, and traveling through time to push a bunch of babies in front of moving cars seemed like a lot of work.

"Money, Willie. We need to make money."

"We could buy old stuff in the past then sell it on eBay. Hey, wouldn't it be cool to have four hands? I mean, you could touch twice as much stuff."

Mick the Mick thought about those old comics in Willie's basement, and then he grinned wider than a zebra's ass.

"Like Action Comics #1, which had the first appearance of Superman!" Mick the Mick said. "I could buy it with the change in my pocket, and we can sell it for a fortune!"

Come to think of it, he could buy eight copies. Didn't they go for a million a piece these days?

"I wish I could fly, Mick. Could we go back into time and learn to fly like Superman? Then we could have flown away from those camp counselors before they stuck their..."

"Shh!" Mick the Mick tilted his head to the side, listening to the jungle. "You hear something, Willie?"

"Yeah, Mick. I hear you talkin' to me. Now I hear me talkin'. Now I'm singing *a soooong, a haaaaaaaappy soooooong.*"

Mick the Mick gave Willie a smack in the teeth, then locked his eyes on the treeline. In the distance the canopy rustled and parted, like something really big was walking toward them. Something so big the ground shook with every step.

"You hear that, Mick? Sounds like something really big is coming."

A deafening roar from the thing in the trees, so horrible Mick the Mick could feel his curlies straighten.

"Think it's friendly?" Willie asked.

Mick the Mick stared down at his hands, which still held the *Really, Really, Really Old Ones* book. He flipped it open to a random page, forcing himself to concentrate on the words. But, as often happened in stressful situation, or even situations not all that stressful, the words seemed to twist and mash up and go backward and upside-down. Goddamn lesdyxia — shit—*dyslexia.*

"Maybe we should run, Mick."

"Yeah, maybe...wait! No! We can't run!"

"Why can't we run, Mick?"

"Remember that episode of *The Simpsons* where Homer went back in time and stepped on a butterfly and then Bart cut off his head with some hedge clippers?"

"That's two different episodes, Mick. They're both Treehouse of Horror episodes, but from different years."

"Look, Willie, the point is, evolution is a really fickle bitch. If we screw up something in the past it can really mess up the future."

"That sucks. You mean we would get back to our real time but instead of being made of skin and bones we're made entirely out of fruit? Like some kind of juicy fruit people?"

Another growl, even closer. It sounded like a lion's roar — if the lion had balls the size of Chryslers.

"I mean really bad stuff, Willie. I gotta read another passage and get us out of here."

The trees parted, and a shadow began to force itself into view.

"Hey, Mick, if you were made of fruit, would you take a bite of your own arm if you were really super hungry? I think I would. I wonder what I'd taste like?"

Mick the Mick tried to concentrate on reading the page, but his gaze kept flicking up to the trees. The prehistoric landscape lapsed into deadly silence. Then, like some giant monster coming out of the jungle, a giant monster came out of the jungle.

The head appeared first, the size of a sofa — a really big sofa — with teeth the size of daggers crammed into a mouth large enough to tear a refrigerator in half.

"I think I'd take a few bites out of my leg or something, but I'd be afraid because I don't know if I could stop. Especially if I tasted like strawberries, because I love strawberries, Mick. Why are they called strawberries when they don't taste like straw? Hey, is that a T-Rex?"

Now Mick the Mick pee-peed more than just a little. The creature before them was a deep green color, blending seamlessly into the undergrowth. Rather than scales, it was adorned with small, prickly hairs that Mick the Mick realized were thin brown feathers. Its huge nostrils flared and it snorted, causing the book's pages to ripple.

"I really think we should run, Mick."

Mick the Mick agreed. The Tyrannosaur stepped into the clearing on massive legs and reared up to its full height, over forty feet tall. Mick the Mick knew he couldn't outrun it. But he didn't have to. He only had to outrun Willie. He felt bad, but he had no other choice. He had to trick his best friend if he wanted to survive.

"The T-Rex has really bad vision, Willie. If you stay very still, it won't be able to---Willie, come back!"

Willie had broken for the trees, moving so fast he was a blur. Mick the Mick tore after him, swatting dragonflies out of the way as he ran. Underfoot he trampled on a large brown roach, a three-toed lizard with big dewy eyes and a disproportionately large brain, and a small furry mammal with a face that looked a lot like Sal from *Manny's Meats* on 23rd street, which gave a disturbingly human-like cry when its little neck snapped.

Behind them, the T-Rex moved with the speed of a giant two-legged cat shaped like a dinosaur, snapping teeth so close to Mick the Mick that they nipped the eighteen trailing hairs of his comb-over. He chanced a look over his shoulder and saw the mouth of the animal open so wide that Mick the Mick could set up a table for four on the creature's tongue and play Texas Hold 'em, not that he would, because that would be fucking stupid.

Then, just as the death jaws of death were ready to close on Mick the Mick and cause terminal death, the T-Rex skidded to a halt and craned its neck skyward, peering up through the trees.

Mick the Mick continued to sprint, stepping on a family of small furry rodents who looked a lot like the Capporellis up in 5B — so much so that he swore one even said "Fronzo!" when he broke its little furry spine — and then he smacked smack into Willie, who was standing still and staring up.

"Willie! What the hell are you doing? We gotta move!"

"Why, Mick? We're not being chased anymore."

Mick looked back and noticed that, indeed, the thunder lizard had abandoned its pursuit, focusing instead on the sky.

"I think it's looking at the asteroid," Willie said.

Mick the Mick shot a look upward and stared at the very large flaming object that seemed to take up a quarter of the sky.

"I don't think it was there a minute ago," Willie said. "I don't pay good attention but I think I woulda noticed it, don't you think?"

"This ain't good. This ain't no good at all."

"Look how big it's getting, Mick! We should hide behind some trees or something."

"We gotta get out of here, Willie." Mick the Mick said, his voice high-pitched and uncomfortably girlish.

"Feel that wind, Mick? It's hot. I bet that thing is going a hundred miles an hour. Do you feel it?"

"I feel it! I feel it!"

"Do you smell fish, Mick? Hey, look! Those pink flowers that look like —"

Willie screamed. Mick the Mick glanced over and saw his lifelong friend was playing tug of war with one of those toothy prehistoric plants, using a long red rope.

No. Not a red rope. Those were Willie's intestines.

"Help me, Mick!"

Without thinking, Mick the Mick reached out a hand and grabbed Willie's duodenum. He squeezed, tight as he could, and Willie farted.

"It hurts, Mick! Being disemboweled hurts!"

A bone-shaking roar, from behind them. The T-Rex had lost interest in the asteroid and was sniffing at the newly spilled blood, his sofa-sized head only a few meters away and getting closer. Mick the Mick could smell its breath, reeking of rotten meat and bad oral hygiene and dooky.

No, the dooky was coming from Willie. Pouring out like brown shaving cream.

Mick the Mick released his friend's innards and wiped his hand on Willie's shirt. The pink flower made a *pbbbthh* sound and did the same, without the wiping the hand part.

"I gotta put this stuff back in." Willie began scooping up guts and twigs and rocks and shoving them into the gaping hole in his belly.

Mick the Mick figured Willie was in shock, or perhaps even stupider than he'd originally surmised. He considered warning Willie about the infection he'd get from filling himself with dirt, but there were other, more pressing, matters at hand.

The asteroid now took up most of the horizon, and the heat from it turned the sweat on Mick the Mick's body into steam. They needed to get out of here, and fast. If only there was someplace to hide.

Something scurried over Mick the Mick's foot and he flinched, stomping down. Crushed under his heel was something that looked like a beaver. The animal kind. Another proto-beaver beelined around its dead companion, heading through the underbrush into…

"It's a hole, Willie! I think it's a cave!"

Mick the Mick pushed aside a large fern branch and squatted down. The hole led to a diagonalish path, dark and rocky, deep down into the earth.

"It's a hole, Willie! I think it's a cave!"

"You said that, Mick!"

"That's an echo, Willie! Hole must go down deep."

Mick the Mick watched as two more lizards, a giant mosquito, and more beaver things poured into the cave, escaping the certain extinction the asteroid promised.

"That's an echo, Willie! Hole must go down deep."

"You're repeating yourself, Mick!"

"I'm not repeating myself!" Mick yelled.

"Yes you are!"

"No I'm not!"

"I'm not repeating myself!"

"Yes you are!"

"No I'm not!"

"You just did!"

"I'm not, Willie!"

"I'm hurt bad, Mick!"

"I'm not, Willie!"

"I said *I'm* hurt, Mick! Not you!"

Mick the Mick decided not to pursue this line of conversation anymore. Instead, he focused on moving the big outcropping of rock partially obscuring the cave's entrance. If he could budge it just a foot or two, he could fit into the cave and maybe save himself.

Mick the Mick put his shoulder to the boulder, grunting with effort. Slowly, antagonizingly slowly, it began to move.

"You got your cell phone, Mick? You should maybe call 911 for me. Tell them to bring some stitches."

Just a little more. A little bit more…

"I think my stomach just fell out. What's a stomach look like, Mick? This looks like a kidney bean."

Finally, the rock broke away from the base with a satisfying crack. But rather than rolling to the side, it teetered, and then dropped down over the hole, sealing it like a manhole cover.

Mick the Mick began to cry.

"Do kidneys look like kidney beans, Mick?" Willie made a smacking sound. "Doesn't taste like beans. Or kidneys. Hey, the T-Rex is back. He doesn't look distracted no more. You think he took is medication?"

The T-Rex opened its mouth and reared up over Mick the Mick's head, blotting out the sky. All Mick the Mick could see was teeth and tongue and that big dangly thing that hangs in the back of the throat like a punching bag.

"Read to him, Mick. When Nana reads to me, I go to sleep."

The book. They needed to escape this time period. Maybe go into the future, to before Nana baked the cake so they could stop her.

Mick the Mick lifted the *Really, Really, Really Old Ones* and squinted at it. His hands shook, and his vision swam, and all the vowels on the page looked exactly the same and the consonants looked like pretzel sticks and the hair still left on his comb-over was starting to singe and the T-Rex's jaws began to close and another one of those pink flowers leaned in took a big bite out of Little Mick and the Twins but he managed to sputter out:

"OTKIN ADARAB UTAALK!"

Another near-turd experience and then they were excreted into a room with a television and a couch and a picture window. But the television screen was embedded — or growing out of?—a toadstool-like thing that was in turn growing out of the floor. The couch looked funny, like who'd sit on that? And the picture window looked out on some kind of nightmare jungle.

And then again, maybe not so weird.

No, Mick the Mick thought. Weird. Very weird.

He looked at Willie.

And screamed.

Or at least tried to. What came out was more like a croak.

Because it wasn't Willie. Not unless Willie had grown four extra eyes — two of them on stalks — and sprouted a fringe of tentacles around where he used to have a neck and shoulders. He now looked like a conical turkey croquette that had been rolled in seasoned breadcrumbs before baking and garnished with live worms after.

The thing made noises that sounded like, "Mick, is that you?" but spoken by a turkey croquette with a mouth full of linguini.

Stranger still, it sounded a little like Willie. Mick the Mick raised a tentacle to scratch his —

Whoa! *Tentacle?*

Well, of course a tentacle. What did he expect?

He looked down and was surprised to see that he was encased in a breadcrumbed, worm-garnished turkey croquette. No, wait, he *was* a turkey croquette.

Why did everything seem wrong, and yet simultaneously at the same time seem not wrong too?

Just then another six-eyed, tentacle-fringed croquette glided into the room. The Willie-sounding croquette said, "Hi, Nana." His words were much clearer now.

Nana? Was this Willie's Nana?

Of course it was. Mick the Mick had known her for years.

"There's an unpleasant man at the door who wants to talk to you. Or else."

"Or else what?"

A new voice said, "Or else you two get to eat cloacal casseroles, and guess who donates the cloacas?"

Mick the Mick unconsciously crossed his tentacles over his cloaca. In his twenty-four years since budding, Mick the Mick had grown very attached to his cloaca. He'd miss it something awful.

A fourth croquette had entered, followed by the two biggest croquettes Mick the Mick had ever seen. Only these weren't turkey croquettes, these were chipped-beef croquettes. This was serious.

The new guy sounded like Nate the Nose, but didn't have a nose. And what was a nose anyway?

"Oh, no," Willie moaned. "I don't want to eat Mick's cloaca."

"I meant your own, jerk!" the newcomer barked.

"But I have a hernia —"

"Shaddap!"

Mick the Mick recognized him now: Nate the Noodge, pimp, loan shark, and drug dealer. Not the sort you leant your bike to.

Wait … what was a bike?

"What's up, Nate?"

"That brick of product I gave you for delivery. I had this sudden, I dunno, bad feeling about it. A *frisson* of malaise and apprehension, you might say. I just hadda come by and check on it, knome sayn?"

The brick? What brick?

Mick the Mick had a moment of panic — he had no idea what Nate the Noodge was talking about.

Oh, yeah. The *product.* Now he remembered.

"Sure Nate, it's right in here."

He led Nate to the kitchen where the brick of product lay on the big center table.

Nate the Noodge pointed a tentacle at it. One of his guards lifted it, sniffed it, then wriggled his tentacle fringe that it was okay. Mick the Mick had expected him to nod but a nod would require a neck, and the guard didn't have a neck. Then Mick the Mick realized he didn't know what a neck was. Or a nod, for that matter.

What was it with these weird thoughts, like memories, going through his head? They were like half-remembered dreams. Nightmares, more likely. Pink flowers, and giant lizards, and big rocks in the sky, and stepping on some mice that looked like a lot like the Capporellis up in 5B. Except the Capporellis lived in 4B, and looked like jellyfish. What were mice anyway? He looked at Willie to see if he was just as confused.

Willie was playing with his cloaca.

Nate the Noodge turned to them and said, "A'ight. Looks like my frisson of malaise and apprehension was fer naught. Yer cloacas is safe … fer now. But you don't deliver that product like you're apposed to and it's casserole city, knome sayn?

"We'll deliver it, Nate," Willie said. "Don't you worry. We'll deliver it.

"Y'better," Nate said, then left with his posse.

"Where we supposed to deliver it?" Willie said when they were alone again.

Mick the Mick kicked him in his cloaca.

"The same place we always deliver it."

"Ow!" Willie was saying, rubbing his cloaca. "That hurt. You know I got a — hey, look!" He was pointing to the TV. "*The Toad Whisperer* is on! My favorite show!

He settled onto the floor and stared.

Mick the Mick hated to admit it, but he was kind of addicted to the show himself. He settled next to Willie.

Faintly, from the kitchen, he heard Nana say, "Oh dear, I was going to bake a cake but I'm out of flour. Could one of you boys — oh, wait. Here's some. Never mind.

A warning glimp chugged in Mick the Mick's brain and puckered his cloaca. Something bad was about to happen …

What had Nate the Noodge called it? "A *frisson* of malaise and apprehension." Sounded like a dessert, but Mick the Mick had gathered it meant a worried feeling like what he was having right now.

But about what? What could go sour? The product was safe, and they were watching *The Toad Whisperer.* As soon as that was over, they'd go deliver it, get paid, and head on over to Madam Yoko's for a happy ending endoplasmic reticulum massage. And maybe a cloacjob.

The *frisson* of malaise and apprehension faded. Must have been another nightmare flashback.

Soon the aroma of baking cake filled the house. Right after the show he'd snag himself a piece.

Yes, life was good.

Funny Stuff

IF I COULD TURN an unbiased critical eye toward my own work, I'd say the thing that makes it unique is the humor.

My standard author bio says I used to do improv comedy. In college, I wrote and starred in a comedy play called The Caravan O' Laughs, which was a collection of insane skits that had a few shows in Chicago and southern Illinois. I've always been comfortable in front of an audience, and from early on I had the kind of mind that always finds the joke in any situation.

Comedy has its roots in the same part of our brain that responds to fear. We laugh at things that scare us, confuse us, and surprise us. We're wired to recognize and process millions of pieces of incoming information, and when something defies our expectations, laughter is the result. An evolutionary tension breaker to help us deal with being confused.

Most of my writing contains varying degrees of humor. I can't help it. When I'm editing, the thing I spend the most amount of time doing is cutting jokes for the sake of the story. I hate cutting jokes, and if I snip one I'll usually use it later in another tale. My work desk is scattered with little pieces of paper, each containing a joke, many of them awful.

It's a sickness, really.

The following shorts use various forms of humor to varying degrees of success. There's satire, and parody, and black humor, and puns, and inappropriate humor, and one-liners, and slapstick, and a lot of irony. Out of everything I've written, these stories have the most of me in them.

Light Drizzle

The title, and much of the plot, is a nod to my friend Barry Eisler and his John Rain series. But this is also a satire of the entire hitman sub-genre, where tough guy assassins with exotic pasts follow strict codes and kill in bizarre ways with common, everyday objects to get the job done.

THE MARK KNELT NEXT to a garbage can, two hands unsuccessfully trying to plug nine holes in his face, neck, and upper body. A gambler, late in his payments, with one second-chance too many. I didn't have all of the details.

Rule #1: Don't make it personal.

Knowing too much made it personal.

He dropped onto his face and spent a minute imitating a lawn sprinkler—a lawn sprinkler that sprayed blood and cried for his mama. I kept my distance.

Rule #8: Don't get all icky with the victim's fluids.

When all movement ceased, I moved in and planted the killing corkscrew in his left hand. In his right, I placed a bottle of 1997 Claude Chonion Merlot. His death would look like an unfortunate uncorking accident.

Rule #2: Make it look natural.

I ditched the latex gloves in the Dumpster and spun on my heels, practically bumping into the bum entering the mouth of the alley. Ragged clothes. A strong smell of urine. Wide eyes.

I reached into the inner pocket of his trench coat, tugged out another pair of latex gloves.

Rule #3: No witnesses.

"Who're you?" the bum asked.

"I'm John," I lied.

Rule #19: Never give your real name.

My real name was Bob. Bob Drizzle. I'm half Japanese. The other half is also Japanese. I also have a bit of Irish in me, which accounts for my red hair. Plus some Serbo-Croatian, a touch of Samoan, a dab of Nordic, a sprinkling of Cheyenne, and some Masi from my mother's side.

But I blend invisibly into all cultures, where I ply my unique trade. I'm a paid assassin. A paid assassin who kills people for money.

I gave the bum a sad frown and said, "Sorry, buddy."

The gloves didn't go on easy—the previous pair had left my hands sweaty, and my palms fought with the rubber. The bum watched the struggle, his stance unsteady. I considered going back to the dead gambler and retrieving the corkscrew, to make the scene look like a fight for Merlot gone deadly.

Instead, I pulled out a pocketful of skinny balloons.

"I'm unemployed," the bum said.

I shoved the multicolored mélange of latex into his filthy mouth, and while he sputtered and choked I blew up a pink one and expertly twisted it into a horsey. I dropped it by his twitching corpse. Street person dies making balloon animals. We've all seen it on the news many times.

I tugged off the gloves, balled them up inside out, and shot the three pointer at the open can.

Missed.

"What's going on?"

A man. Joe Busybody, sticking his nose in other people's business, watching from the sidewalk. Linebacker body, gone soft with age.

I reached for another pair of gloves. "Sir, this is police business. Would you like to give a statement?"

The guy backpedaled.

"You're no cop."

I didn't bother with the second glove. I removed the aluminum mallet from my holster. That, along with a little seasoning salt and the pork chop I kept in my shoe, would make his death mimic a meat tenderizing gone wrong.

But before I had a chance to tartare his ass, he took off.

I keep in shape.

Rule #13: Stay fit.

Any self-respecting hitman worth his contract fee has to workout these days. Marks were becoming more and more health conscious. Sometimes they ran. Sometimes they refused to die. Sometimes they even had the gall to fight back.

I do Pilates, and have one of those abdominal exercisers they sell on late night television. I bought it at a thrift store, with cash.

Rule #22: Don't leave a paper trail.

The witness had a head start, but I quickly closed the distance. When the guy glanced, wide-eyed, over his shoulder, I was able to smash the mallet on his forehead.

See ya. Wouldn't wanna be ya.

The mark stumbled, and I had to leap over the falling body. I skidded to a stop on thick rubber soles.

Rule #26: Shoes should be silent and have good traction, and good arch support.

I took a moment to scan the street. No one seemed to be watching.

I played Emeril on the mark's face, then put the mallet in his right hand and the pork chop in his left.

I was sprinkling on the Mrs. Dash when I heard something behind me.

My head snapped up at the sound, and I peered over my shoulder. The number 332 commuter bus had stopped at my curb. Right next to the big sign that said BUS STOP.

I cursed under my breath for breaking Rule #86: Don't kill anyone where people are likely to congregate, like bus stops.

I stared. A handful of riders, noses pressed to window glass, stared back.

The bus driver, a heavy-set woman wearing a White Sox hat, scrambled to close the bus door.

But I was fast. In three steps I'd mounted the stairs and withdrawn a can of oven cleaner from my holster. Nasty stuff, oven cleaner. The label is crammed full of warnings. The bus driver stared at the can and got wide-eyed.

"Drive," I told her.

She drove.

I faced the terrified group of riders. Two were children. Three were elderly. One was a nun with an eye patch.

Rule #7: No sympathy.

I snapped on another latex glove.

After counting them twice, I came up with nine people total. Just enough for a soccer team.

Perfect.

I removed the uninflated ball and the bicycle pump from my holster. Soccer games got rowdy. Casualties were common.

After screwing some cleats into the bottoms of my thick, rubber soled shoes, I spent a good ten minutes stomping on the group. The nun was especially tough. But I had training. I was a fuscia belt in Jin Dog Doo, the ancient Japanese art of killing a man using only your hands and feet and edged weapons and blunt weapons and common household appliances and guns.

Eventually, even the nun succumbed. Some torn goal netting and a discarded ref's whistle completed the illusion. Only one last thing left to do.

"Stop the bus!" I yelled at the driver.

The driver didn't stop. She accelerated.

Rule #89: Don't attract attention.

This bus was attracting more than its share. Besides speeding, the driver had just run a red light, prompting honks and screeching brakes from cross-town traffic.

This simple hit had become a bit more complicated than I'd anticipated.

"Slow down!" I ordered the driver.

My command went unheeded. I took a Chilean Sea Bass out of my holster. It used to be called the Pantagonian Toothfish, but some savvy marketers changed its name and it's currently the hottest fish on the five star menus of the world. So hot, that overfishing has brought the Chilean Sea Bass/Pantagonian Toothfish to the brink of extinction.

Beating the driver to death with the fish would look somewhat…well…fishy. At first. But when I planted a deboning knife and a few slices of lemon in her pockets, the cops would get the picture. Just another endangered species taking revenge.

I walked up to the front of the bus and tried to recall if "The Complete Amateur's Guide to Contract Killing" had a rule about whacking a driver while you were a passenger. Nothing sprang to mind.

Still, it didn't seem like a wise idea. I tried another tactic.

"Stop the bus, and I'll let you go."

That was Rule #17: Lie to the mark to put her at ease.

Or was that Rule #18?

I reached for the cheat card that came with the book, folded up in my pants pocket.

Rule #18: Lie to the mark. Rule #17: Get in and out as quickly as possible.

I'd sure blown that rule to hell.

I shook the thought out of my head, recalling Rule #25: Stay focused.

I put the crib sheet back in my pocket and poked the driver in the hat with the bass.

"Stop the bus, and you'll live. I give you my word."

I grinned.

Rule #241: Disarm them with a smile.

The driver hit the brakes, catapulting me forward. I bounced off the front window and into her back. The Sea Bass—my weapon—went flying, which broke Rule #98 and Rule #104 and possibly Rule #206.

Dazed, I sat up, watching as the driver shoved open the door and ran off, screaming.

I did a quick search for the Toothfish, but couldn't find it amid the soccer massacre. I'd have to leave it behind, a blatant disregard for Rule #47. Luckily, the fish had been wiped clean of prints (Rule #11) and was unregistered (Rule #12) so it wouldn't lead back to me.

Now for the driver.

I sprang from the bus and saw her beelining for Comiskey Park, where the White Sox played baseball. There was the usual activity around the stadium; fans, hotdog vendors, people selling programs, and no one seemed to pay any attention to me or the screaming fat lady.

The South Side of Chicago; where screaming fat ladies are commonplace.

Doubling my efforts, I managed to catch up with her just as she reached the ticket counter. I took a 1/10,000th scale replica of the Washington Monument out of my holster and pressed the pointy end to her back. She was about to become another sightseeing souvenir victim. But before I got ram the monolith home, the ticket attendant caught my eye from behind the thick bullet proof glass.

I had a hunch the glass was also souvenir proof, and I couldn't kill the bus driver with someone staring straight into my eyes, practically salivating to be a witness for the prosecution.

So I did the only thing I could in that situation. I whispered to the woman to keep quiet, and then smiled at the attendant.

"Two for the cheap seats," I said.

I paid, then walked arm in arm with the driver through the bustling crowd. The picture presented to me was disheartening. People were everywhere.

There was no private corner to drag the woman into. No secluded nooks. The bathrooms had lines out the door. Every square foot of space was crammed to capacity.

How do you kill a person in a crowded space without anyone seeing you?

I closed my eyes, trying to remember if this situation ever came up in the book. Rule #90? No, that had to do with airplanes. Rule #312? No, that was for killing a mark in a rain forest.

At times like this, I really wished I'd kept my job at the grocery store. Or bought that other book, "The Complete Amateur's Guide to Kidnapping and Extortion."

"Let me go or I'll scream," the bus driver said over the pipe organ music.

"If you scream, I'll kill you," I answered.

A classic stalemate. It happened to me once before, in the Har Dong peninsula, on the isle of Meenee Peepee, in the city of Tini Dik. I was at a hotel (I recall it being the Itsee Wang), and came upon a gorgeous Mossad agent named Desdemona, who I managed to manipulate by engaging in massive quantities of athletic sex with her. Later, when I sobered up, I realized I'd been duped. Rather than a beautiful double agent from Israel, Desdemona had actually been just a large pile of dirty towels.

I had no idea what that had to do with anything, or how it could help me now.

No other options open, the bus driver and I made our way to the seats. They were in Section 542, way up in the nosebleed part of the stadium.

Even that section was full, fans packed shoulder to shoulder. We stepped on several toes and spilled a few beers wading through the crowd.

"These seats suck," said the bus driver.

I told her to shut up.

To keep her quiet, I decided to appeal to her inner overeater, and bought two red hots from a hawking vendor.

She took both of them.

Then we settled in to watch the game.

It was the bottom of the fifth, Sox down two runs.

I chose to make my move at the seventh inning stretch. By then, all of the drunken fans around us would get up to relieve their bladders, and I'd be able to off the bus driver and slip into the stream of moving bodies. Then I could…

The next thing I knew, the bus driver was shoving a hot dog with the works into my face, trying to blind me.

"Help!" she screamed, at the same time trying to get her big ass out of the stadium seat.

First one cheek popped free, then the other, and then her big butt was out and shaking in my face.

I wiped ketchup out of my eyes and looked around.

No one paid any attention to the bus driver. Someone behind us even yelled "Down in front!"

I stood and wrapped an arm around her fat shoulders, under the pretense of helping her back to her seat.

Then I jammed the souvenir monument into her throat. Hard. Six or seven times.

An eerie silence settled over the crowd. Then the stadium exploded in screams.

I looked onto the field, wondering if there had just been a spectacular play.

The game had stopped. Instead of baseball players, I saw myself on the Jumbotron monitor, forty feet high, the bloody Washington

Monument in my hand.

Oops.

I did a quick scan of the ball park. Thirty, maybe thirty-five thousand people.

This was going to be tough.

I reached into my holster for the roll of fabric softener and the Perry Como LP, and got started.

Mr. Spaceman

A humorous horror story that harkens back to the alien invasion movies of the 1950s. I wondered what would happen if an alien landed in modern day California.

"I HAVE TRAVELED MANY billions of light years to mate with an earth woman."

Debbi eyed the john and licked her cherry red lips. *Freak,* she thought. But all the freaks were out tonight. Halloween in LA was crazier than Mardi Gras.

He was dressed up like some kind of gooey alien, and she had to admit his make-up was pretty good. His mask had scales on it, like a fish, and his mouth had little dangly things that moved when he spoke. The spacesuit, made of some kind of metallic silvery fabric, was Hollywood-quality — not surprising, considering they were on the Sunset Strip. It was probably an old movie prop.

The only fake thing about the costume was the eyes; big yellow orbs that were attached to his head on stalks. They looked like tennis balls.

The freak leaned closer to Debbi. "Will you mate with me?"

Any other night, she would have told him to take a hike. Weirdos were best avoided. But rent was due tomorrow, and business had been slow. Besides, her horoscope said today was a day for taking chances, and Debbi always put her faith in the stars. She launched into her pitch.

"Straight is twenty-five, half and half is fifty. And for seventy-five I'll take you around the world, sugar."

"I have already been in orbit around your world eight hundred and forty-two times."

"Couldn't find a parking space, huh?" Debbi smacked her gum. "How much money you got, Mr. Spaceman?"

Mr. Spaceman stuck one of his lobster claws into his tunic and pulled out a roll of cash that would choke a horse.

"Don't flash money like that around here!" Debbi looked up and down the street, scanning for predators. "This isn't a nice neighborhood."

"I thought this was the city of angels."

"The angels carry knives and guns."

She took the john by the claw and led him down the block to the flop house. The desk clerk, a fat, greasy guy named Larry, raised an eyebrow.

"Does Mars need women?"

"Screw you, Larry. Gimme 214 for the rest of the night."

Larry handed her the key and winked.

The room was dark, dingy, the bed still rumpled from the previous rental. Debbi took off her halter top and hot pants, nudifying herself.

"See anything you like, ET?"

The john nodded several times. "I am aroused at the sight of your mammalian infant feeding vessels."

"You should be. They cost six grand."

She sidled up to him, her hand seeking the front of his shiny outfit.

The things I do for a buck…

"So, can Mr. Spock come out and play?"

"Who is this Mr. Spock? My name is Gnerlok. I am from the planet Norbulon in the second quadrant of the Xaldorgia Galaxy."

"A tourist, huh? I had a feeling. Isn't Norbulon somewhere east?"

To a Los Angeleno, everyplace was east.

Gnerlok narrowed his bulbous eyes. "Yes. It is east. Near the state called Florida."

"I can spot an out-of-towner a mile away. How about slipping out of those tin foil pants?"

With the deft move of a pro, Debbi southicated Gnerlok's zipper. His outfit fell with a clanging sound.

"Oh my." Debbi bit her lower lip to keep from laughing, Fire Engine Red #03 rubbing off on her teeth. "I've never seen one that small before."

Gnerlok frowned.

"I assure you, that this is an average size for a male from Norbulon. I'm actually a bit larger than most."

"Go ahead and think that, sugar. You want to take a shower, get all that make-up off?"

"I am fine."

You're about as far from fine as you can get, Debbi thought.

"Okay, Mr. Spaceman. What would you like to do first?"

"Please give my full access to your urteran cavity."

Debbi laid back on the bed. "Like this?"

"That is perfect."

Gnerlok climbed on, then immediately climbed off.

Debbi frowned at him. "What's the matter, sugar?"

"Nothing is the matter. The coupling was most enjoyable."

"You're done?"

"Yes I am. Was our mating pleasurable for you?"

Debbi sighed. She sat up, giving him a pat on the claw. "You're a machine, honey. I'll never have better."

Gnerlok pulled up his pants and dug out his wad O'bills.

"Here is three hundred earth dollars. Thank you for procreating with me."

Debbi reached for the cash. "Anytime, sug —"

Her words were cut off by a rumbling sound. It came from her abdomen, loud enough for them both to hear.

"Excuse me. I had a couple chili dogs for dinner, and it sounds like those dogs are barking."

"That is not the sound of your digestive system."

The sound repeated, louder this time. Debbi looked down, unable to comprehend what she saw.

Her belly was expanding.

"What the hell is going on?"

"We have successfully mated. My brood incubates inside of you."

Her stomach was now the size of a basket ball, and the growth showed no signs of stopping.

Even worse, Debbi felt something deep within.

Something moving.

"You freak!" Debbie screamed. "Take off that stupid mask and tell me what you've done to me!"

She bolted to her feet and reached for Gnerlok's face, her fist closing around one of his eye stalks.

"Please do not tug at my face, earth-woman."

Debbi recoiled. It wasn't a mask.

"My God! What part of Florida are you from?"

"I am not from Florida. I have used deception to gain admission to your birthing portal. Now my progeny shall be born, and we shall enslave the world and —"

"I'm not ready to be a mother!" Debbi cried. "I haven't finished Junior College yet!"

"Nor shall you ever, earth-woman. My species shall destroy —"

Debbi slapped Gnerlok across the face.

"Our agreement was for sex, not motherhood! You owe me a lot more money!"

Gnerlok held his cheek, his bulbous eyes widening.

"But money will not be necessary when we take over —"

There was a popping sound, and a flood of green cascaded down Debbi's legs.

She stared, horrified, as her uterus contracted and a tiny yellow crustacean, the size of a golf ball, shot out of her and plopped onto the floor.

"Waaa," it cried.

Debbi's eyes got moist. She swallowed back the lump forming in her throat. "My baby."

She bent down to pick it up, and the motion caused more creatures to shoot rapid-fire from her womanhood.

"Don't just stand there like an idiot!" she hissed at Gnerlok. "Pick my children up!"

Gnerlok didn't move until Debbi slapped him again. Then he moved as fast as he could.

It was hard to keep up. Debbie's body spit them out like watermelon seeds.

For five minutes, the room was a combat zone. Multi-colored

alien crayfish flew through the air—*BING! BING! BING!*—Gnerlok scurrying after them, mindful where he stepped.

Debbi finally expelled the last child and let out a huge sigh of relief. She felt like an empty corn popper.

"How many is that?" she asked.

Gnerlok placed the final three on the bed and tugged at his dangly mouth thingies.

"One hundred and seventeen."

"Did you get the one that flew behind the TV?"

"Yes I did."

"Check to make sure."

"I am sure."

Debbi clenched her teeth. "Are you sassing back?"

Gnerlok checked behind the TV again.

"None of my progeny reside behind the TV," he said.

"*Your* progeny? Don't you mean *our* progeny? I'm the one that did all the work."

Debbi approached the bed and picked up one of the kids. *Her* kids. It looked like a crawfish, complete with lobster claws and a tail. But its tiny face was almost human.

"They're kind of cute. What do they eat?"

"They are supposed to feast on your rotting corpse until they are large enough to dominate —"

Debbi grabbed Gnerlok by the eye stalk once again, squeezing out a stream of tears.

"Let's get one thing straight, Mr. Spaceman. All this talk of taking over the world, it ends right now. Got it?"

"But I've traveled for billions —"

Debbie yanked. Gnerlok screamed.

"Enough! You're a father now. You have responsibilities. I hope you have a damn good job, because diapers alone are going to cost a fortune."

"My job is to dominate —" Gnerlok cast his free eye, fearfully, at Debbi. "I mean — I currently have no means of employment."

"But you're rich, right? Where did you get that big roll of money?"

Gnerlok mumbled something.

"Speak up, Mr. Spaceman, or I'll tie these eye things into a big bow on your ugly head."

"A scratch-and-win lottery ticket."

Debbi scowled. "So that's how it is. You come up to me all slick, flashing your cash like you're a real player. Then you knock me up, and you don't even have a job. Do you at least have a place to live?"

"I arrived on this planet only two earth hours ago, and have not had a chance to establish a permanent residence."

Debbi sighed. *Ugly, hung like a Chihuahua,* and *a homeless deadbeat.*

"How about a car? No! Wait! A space ship! You've got a space ship, right?"

Gnerlok glanced, one-eyed, at the floor.

"When I landed, a group of three disaffected youths assaulted me and absconded with my interstellar vessel."

Welcome to LA.

Debbi needed to think, and she mentioned as much.

"While you are thinking, could you please release my —"

"I got it! My brother-in-law works for a furniture place. I bet he can get you a job in upholstery. But first, we have to go to City Hall and get married."

"Married? But I am not ready for marriage. I still require a few more years to play the field."

"Should have thought of that before you started mating with earth women. This is your responsibility, Yoda. And you're not weaseling out of it."

Debbi released Gnerlok's eye and turned her attention to the kids on the bed. A feeling of pure joy welled up in her chest, a place she hadn't had much feeling since getting the implants.

"Hello, my darlings. I'm Mama."

"Mama!" several of them cried.

"Yes. Mama. And this is your homeless deadbeat father. He's going to do good by you, or else your Uncle Joey will break his knees. Say hello to your children, Hubbie."

"Hello, children." Gnerlok frowned and gave them a half-hearted wave.

"Tracy! Jerry! Don't eat your brother! Daddy will get you some food." Debbi jabbed a finger at Gnerlok's chest. "There's a pizza place down the street. Get an extra large with anchovies. I bet they'll like anchovies."

"Anchovies," Gnerlok repeated.

"And I'm starving too. Get me a meatball sandwich. And move your alien butt, or I'm picking up the phone and calling the CIA. I'm sure they'd love to hear about your plans to dominate the world."

"Yes, earth-woman."

Gnerlok slunk out the door.

Debbi sat on the bed and tickled little Alphonse under the chin. He giggled.

So did Debbi.

She'd always put her faith in the stars. And for good reason, it turned out.

"You know what, kids?" Debbi's eyes became moist. "I think we can make this work. We can be a big, happy family."

And if it gets too weird, Debbi decided, *I can always make a big pot of gumbo and eat the little buggers.*

"Come to Mama, my delicious little babies. When your father gets home we're going house hunting. We're going to get a nice, big place in Beverly Hills."

With an extra large stove, Debbi decided.

Just in case.

Don't Press That Button!

A Practical Buyer's Guide to James Bond's Gadgets

Written for the essay collection James Bond in the 21st Century. I had a lot of fun with this, being a Bond fan for practically my whole life. Plus, it gave me the opportunity to simply string jokes together, rather than deal with a plot or characters.

IF YOUR FIRST EXPOSURE to James Bond happened before the age of nine, you probably fell in love with the series for one reason: The Gadgets.

The women were hot, but you wouldn't care about that for a few more years. James Bond was tough and could fight, but so could those short guys on UHF's Samurai Saturday, and they had the added appeal of speaking without their lips matching their words. Global politics, espionage, and undercover infiltrations still aren't interesting, years later.

No, the thing that made your pre-pubescent brain scream with unrestrained joy was all the cool stuff Bond picked up in Q Section. You wanted the grappling hook pistol, and the pen filled with acid, and the laser watch, and the hand-held suction cups for climbing walls, and the wrist dart gun, and the rappelling cummerbund—even though you had no idea what a cummerbund was.

But now that you're all grown up, do the gadgets still have the same appeal? Do you still wish you could run to the nearest Wal-Mart and buy an electric razor that can deliver a close shave plus sweep your room for electronic listening devices?

This practical guide will look at some of best of Bond's gadgets, and offer valuable buying advice to those interested in plunking down their hard earned dollars for spy gear.

GADGET	False bottom briefcase which holds a magnetic mine, used by Bond in Octopussy.
USES	Protecting and transporting papers, blowing things up.
COOLNESS	Hidden compartments are always cool. So are mines.
REALITY	These already exist, in a wide variety of colors and payloads.
DO YOU WANT IT?	Yes you do. Think about how memorable your next corporate meeting will be if you're carrying one of these.
SAFETY TIP	Don't try to bring it through airport security.

GADGET	Snorkel that looks like a seagull, used by Bond in Goldfinger.
USES	Fool your friends at the pool, see other seagulls up close, collect change from the bottom of public fountains.
COOLNESS	Uncool. The crocodile submarine in Octopussy has many more applications. In fact, so does simple SCUBA gear. Q Section was apparently hitting the NyQuil when they thought this up.

REALITY	Possible to manufacture, but tough to market, depending on where you put your lips.
DO YOU WANT IT?	Not really, except to amuse yourself while drinking too much.
SAFETY TIP	Boil the bird after every use.

GADGET	Ski pole that fires a rocket, used in Octopussy.
USES	Improve your slalom time, blow up your friends, roast a chicken really fast.
COOLNESS	Very cool.
REALITY	Single use wouldn't be practical, it would be too heavy, and it might go off too soon (many men have this problem, and it's nothing to be embarrassed about.)
DO YOU WANT IT?	Yes, but you should be careful—tucking high explosives under your arm while speeding 70mph downhill isn't for anyone under the age of 14.
SAFETY TIP	Practice on the bunny slope before you take it down that black diamond run.

GADGET	Aston Martin DB5 sports car, used by Bond in Goldfinger and Thunderball.
USES	The ultimate road rage machine/babe magnet. Oil slick sprayer, smoke screens, tire slashing blades, machine guns, and an ejector seat for when your blind date turns out to be a bore.
COOLNESS	This is one pimped out ride.

REALITY	You could probably pay to have this car custom made, but it would cost a lot of money, and you wouldn't be allowed to drive it anywhere, except maybe in Texas.
DO YOU WANT IT?	Hell, yeah. Rush hour would never be the same.
SAFETY TIP	At the dealer, don't be afraid to haggle. And don't get suckered into buying the undercarriage rust protection.

GADGET	Stick-on third nipple, used by Bond in The Man With The Golden Gun.
USES	For those many times in life when you just need a third nipple.
COOLNESS	At first glance, not very cool. But once you consider the possibilities, the coolness factor rises, much more so than the fake fingerprints Bond used in Diamonds Are Forever.
REALITY	Hollywood SPFX guys make these all the time, and you can too with some plaster for an impression cast, and some foam latex. **HINT:** Shave your chest first.
DO YOU WANT IT?	Yes. Put them on sofas, on jewelry, on windows, on fruit, and all over yourself before that visit to the public pool.
SAFETY TIP	Don't use super glue.

GADGET	Little Nellie portable gyrocopter with rocket launchers, machine guns, flamethrower, and heat seeking-missiles.

	Used by Bond in You Only Live Twice.
USES	Fly around, impress the ladies, drop stuff on people.
COOLNESS	Über-cool. Smaller than a helicopter. Not nearly as expensive to use as the Bell-Trexton rocket pack Bond used in Thunderball, but with a lot more fire-power.
REALITY	Available on Ebay for under 20k, but without the weaponry. (Weaponry is available separately on Ebay.)
DO YOU WANT IT?	Of course you want it. Just think about all the stuff you could drop on people.
SAFETY TIP	From three hundred feet, a small honeydew melon can cripple a man.

GADGET	Wrist watch with plastic explosive and detonator, used by Bond in Moonraker.
USES	Blow stuff up, threaten to blow stuff up.
COOLNESS	Cool. Blowing stuff up never gets old.
REALITY	Possible, and cheap to make. But you'd have to buy refills all the time. They always get you on the refills.
DO YOU WANT IT?	Yes. Excuse me, what time is it? It's time to blow stuff up! Let's start with that stupid seagull snorkel.
SAFETY TIP	Don't play with all the dials until you've read the instructions.

GADGET	Keys that open 90% of the world's locks, used by Bond in The Living

	Daylights.
USES	Unlimited. Steal cars. Rob banks. Take the change from parking meters. Shop after hours. And never pay for a vending machine again.
COOLNESS	Opening stuff up: Cool. Walking around like a janitor with a big key ring: Uncool.
REALITY	Master keys exist, and can be found on the Internet. So can lock picks. So can lawyers, which you'll need after you get caught opening up other people's locks.
DO YOU WANT IT?	No. You'd probably just lose them.
SAFETY TIP	Don't keep these in your back pocket while ice skating. Or your front pocket.

GADGET	Surfboard with concealed explosives, combat knife, and mini computer, used by Bond in Die Another Day.
USES	Hang ten, then kill seven.
COOLNESS	Super cool. You can shred that gnarly barrel, and at the same time Google what the hell that means.
REALITY	It's possible to produce, but be careful you don't wax your mini-computer.
DO YOU WANT IT?	Of course. But instead of weapons and electronics, you can fill your board with soda and snacks (that you got for free at the vending machine.)
SAFETY TIP	Make sure the combat knife is properly secured before you hit the waves, or you'll be hanging nine.

GADGET	X-Ray eyeglasses, used by Bond in The World Is Not Enough.
USES	Seeing though things like playing cards, safes, walls, doors, and clothing (to look for concealed weapons and stick-on third nipples.)
COOLNESS	Perhaps Bond's coolest gadget. It would sure make everyday life a lot more interesting.
REALITY	If you ever sent away for a pair of these in the back of a comic book, you know they don't work, but what did you expect for $2.95? Your mother told you they wouldn't work, didn't she? Real versions may exist, but they probably cost big bucks. And cause cancer.
DO YOU WANT IT?	Sure you do. Just don't take them to family reunions. Or retirement homes.
SAFETY TIP	Wear baggy pants.

GADGET	Underwater manta ray cloak, used by Bond in License To Kill.
USES	Pretend you're a manta ray, get close to other manta rays, get sexually assaulted by a manta ray.
COOLNESS	Not cool, unless you have a secret thing for manta rays.
REALITY	Can be made in real life, but for God's sake why?
DO YOU WANT IT?	Only if you're really lonely. You might also consider getting the seagull snorkel as well, and you can pretend you're a ray chasing a seagull. You can play that one for hours and hours.

SAFETY TIP If you spend more than $30 for this, you're a real moron.

GADGET Lotus Esprit sports car that turns into a submarine, complete with mines, missiles, underwater ink jets, and self-destruct mechanism, that Bond used in The Spy Who Loved Me and Moonraker.

USES Never take the ferry again, drive into swimming pool to fetch the quarters Grandpa throws in there.

COOLNESS A hot car, and a hot submersible, all in one. Plus rockets.

REALITY Boat cars do exist in real life, but they're actually dorky looking, and driven by people who can't get dates.

DO YOU WANT IT? You know you do. But when purchasing options, go for an Alpine stereo and Bose speakers instead of a self-destruct button—it's more practical.

UNDERWATER TIP If you drive over a starfish and cut it in half, it will grow into two new starfishes, both of them very pissed off at you.

GADGET Dinner jacket which turns into a black sniper's outfit, used by Bond in The Living Daylights.

USES When black tie events become boring.

COOLNESS Cooler than the light blue tux with the ruffle shirt which turns into an adult diaper, but not by much.

REALITY They already have these for rent at

Gingiss. You'll need two forms of ID, and there's a mandatory 14 day waiting period.

DO YOU WANT IT? You don't want to admit it, but yes you do. But then, you never had much taste in clothing.

FASHION TIP Belts are okay, but the trendy sniper prefers suspenders.

GADGET Cigarette lighter grenade, used by Bond in Tomorrow Never Dies.

USES No smoking means no smoking.

COOLNESS Anything that blows up is cool (see plastic explosive watch.)

REALITY You can put explosives into anything; lighters, bottles, cans, small animals, etc.

DO YOU WANT IT? Absolutely. Think about taking it to a heavy metal concert when the power ballad is playing.

SAFETY TIP Don't get it confused with your real lighter because you might accidentally throw your real lighter at the bad guys and they'll say, "Why'd you throw a lighter at us, stupid? Are we supposed to be scared?" Also, you might blow your face off.

GADGET Piton gun with retractable wire, used by Bond in Diamonds Are Forever and Goldeneye.

USES Climb up buildings and rock faces, retrieve the remote control without get-

	ting up from the couch.
COOLNESS	Climbing, swinging, and shooting things are all cool.
REALITY	Wouldn't actually be strong enough to hold a man's weight, but you could have fun letting your buddies try it out.
DO YOU WANT IT?	Yes. It's like being Spiderman, but without the webby discharge.
SAFETY TIP	Don't point it at your own face, or at family members, unless you're trying to climb them.

GADGET	Exploding talcum powder tear gas, used by Bond in From Russia With Love.
USES	Personal hygiene, making enemies cry.
COOLNESS	Talc isn't very cool. Neither is tear gas. But it does explode, which counts for something.
REALITY	It might already exist. It might not. Who cares?
DO YOU WANT IT?	No. You make your significant other cry all the time without gas, and no one uses talc anymore.
SAFETY TIP	Wear a gas mask before applying to your underarms.

GADGET	Magnetic watch with circular saw, used by Bond in Live And Let Die.
USES	Cutting through rope tied around your wrists, finding screws you dropped on the carpeting.

COOLNESS	Having your watch face spin around really fast is cool. Cutting off your own hand at the wrist is uncool.
REALITY	Buy a chainsaw that tells time instead. It's cheaper and more effective.
DO YOU WANT IT?	No. If you want a cool Bond timepiece, get the plastic explosive watch. Or the laser bean watch from Tomorrow Never Dies. Or the grappling hook watch from The World Is Not Enough. Or the ticker tape message watch from The Spy Who Loved Me. Or the digital radio watch from For Your Eyes Only. Or even the Geiger counter watch from Thunderball—you can't have too many Geiger counters around the house.
SAFETY TIP	Careful you don't lose any fingers when you reset for different time zones.

Remember: You're never too old to play with toys. Especially explosive, potentially deadly, extremely expensive toys. Just think about how envious your friends and family will be when they see you driving around in your sporty new BMW 750 iL with the electrified door handles, bulletproof glass, re-inflating tires, and rear nail ejectors.

Go ahead. Think about it. Because that's as close as you'll ever get to owning one, spy-boy.

Now go boil your seagull snorkel—that thing is riddled with germs.

Piranha Pool

A story about being a writer. It's humorous, but there is a lot of truth behind the jokes.

"WHAT DO YOU THINK?"

I was a cup, waiting to be filled with praise. Instead I got silence. She sat there, my pages in her hands, staring at a point over my shoulder.

"How about that ending?" I prodded. "Weren't your surprised?"

Miranda clucked her tongue. "I guessed the ending."

"You did?"

"Yeah. And I really don't think you need the first few paragraphs."

"Hold on a sec." I motioned time-out with my hands. "The first paragraphs set the scene."

"Sorry—I didn't think you needed them."

I looked away, then back at her. My friend, wife, companion for eight years.

"Did you like anything?"

"Joe, you're a wonderful writer. But this story—I think you were just trying too hard." She brightened. "I thought the middle part was funny."

My eyes narrowed. "When the character died?"

"Yeah. It was cute how you did that."

"That wasn't supposed to be funny."

"Oh."

There was a ticking sound. The hands of my watch. Miranda tried on a smile.

"I like the title."

Great. I remembered how much I loved her, and somehow found the strength to thank her for her opinion. Just because we were man and wife didn't mean we had to agree on everything.

This particular piece didn't speak to her, but that was probably a matter of taste. I was certain that others would view it differently.

"It stinks."

"Excuse me?"

Gerald pinched his nostrils closed. "The story stinks, Joe. Sorry, but it isn't your best."

"What about the surprise ending?"

"Saw it coming."

"You did?"

"It was obvious."

I took the story from my brother's hands and paid too much attention to lining up the sheets of paper.

"You probably guessed it because you know me too well."

"I guessed it because it was cliché. The middle part was kind of funny, though. What did Miranda think of it?"

"She loved it."

"Well, there you go. My opinion probably means nothing, then. I liked that other story you did. The one about the otters."

"I wrote that in second grade."

"Yeah, that was a good one."

I looked at my bare wrist. "Damn, I gotta run, Gerald. Thanks for the input."

"It's a good title, Joe. Maybe you can write a different story using the same title."

"Wow. Great story."

"You liked it?"

"Loved it."

The relief was better than a foot massage.

"How about the ending?"

"Terrific."

"What was your favorite part?"

My mother's smile faltered for a split second. "Oh—there were so many."

Mr. Dubious took over my body. "Mom…?"

"The middle part. I have to say that was my favorite. Very funny."

So much for my relief.

"You thought the death scene was funny?"

Caught in the lie, her demeanor cracked.

"No, not that. But there were some other funny parts."

"What parts were funny, Mom?"

"Well…you had some pretty funny typos."

I rubbed my eyes. "Did you like anything?"

"Joe, I'm your mother. Everything you do is precious to me."

"How about the title?"

Mom shook her head sadly.

"Not even the title?"

"Joe, I'm not a good judge of fiction. You should ask your wife or your brother. I'm sure they'll love it.

"Poopy."

I stared at my four-year-old, a child who is captivated by his own toes.

"Why is it poopy?"

"You should have Spider Man in it."

"I don't want Spider Man in it."

My son looked at me, serious. "Spider Man can climb walls."

"I know he can. But let's talk about Daddy's story. Did you think it was sad when the character died?"

"Does Spider Man tie people up and suck their blood?"

"What?"

"Spiders tie up bugs and suck their blood."

I sighed and looked at Fluffy, the family cat.

Why the hell not?

"Fluffy, dammit, get back in this house!"

But the feline had beat a retreat only two pages into the narrative. Gone to tree, sitting ten feet out of reach in the crook of an elm branch.

"I'm serious, Fluffy."

He stared back down at me with indifferent eyes and then began to groom.

"Fine. Count the days until you get tuna again, cat."

I smoothed out the wrinkled edges of the manuscript and went back to my desk.

A few clicks of the mouse later and I was online. Surely Usenet had fiction forums. Without too much difficulty, I located an amateur fiction newsgroup and posted my tome proudly. Let the compliments commence…

"Joe? What is that sticking out of out computer monitor? Is that a hammer?"

"It slipped."

"You attacked the computer with a hammer? What were you thinking?"

I gave Miranda malice wrapped in a fake grin. "I don't want to talk about it, honey. It's still under warranty."

"I don't think a hammer in the screen is covered by the warranty."

"Miranda…"

"What's wrong with you? Does this have anything to do with that stupid story?"

I stood up, deaf. The story was clenched in my left hand. "I'm going out. I'll be back later."

"So, what did you think?"

The wino held out a filthy hand. "Do I get my five dollars now?"

"First you have to tell me if you liked it."

He brought the paper bag to his lips, took a pull off the unseen bottle.

"It was…"

"Yes?"

"It was wonderful."

His eyes went dreamy, beatific.

I beamed. "Wonderful?"

He hic-cupped. "The loveliest thing I ever heard."

Who would have thought it? I didn't normally endow people who smelled like urine with good taste, but here was an obvious exception.

"What was your favorite part?"

"The chicken."

I stared at my pages, confused.

"Chicken? There's no chicken in this story."

"I ate chicken in Cleveland. Cooked so tender, it fell off the bone. You gonna give me my five bucks?"

Great—he was a lunatic. You can't get an honest opinion from a lunatic. I turned to walk away.

He grabbed my arm. "Man, you owe me five bucks! I stood here listening to that garbage, I want my money!"

I decided, right then, that I'd rather be disemboweled than give this guy five bucks.

I pulled free and hit the street in a sprint. Shouldn't take long to lose him. He was drunk and disheveled and—

"Gimme my damn money!"

—right behind me. For a guy wearing at least four layers of clothing, he could run like the wind. I cut through an alley and hurdled a cluster of garbage cans.

"I listened to that whole crappy story!"

The bum was closing in. I could hear his mismatched shoes slapping the pavement only a few steps back. Just my luck—I'd given a reading to an Olympic sprinter fallen on hard times.

Another turn, between two apartments, into the back parking lot. Dead end.

"Gotcha." The bum grinned, gray teeth winking through a scraggly beard. He gestured with his hand—give it to me.

I sucked in air and nodded submission, my hand producing my wallet.

He shook his head. "All of it."

"You said five bucks."

"I'm gonna need a month's worth of booze, to get that lousy story out of my head."

I left the parking lot forty bucks lighter.

I stared at the page. My story. My child. Why couldn't anyone else see the symbolism? The imagery? This story was perfect! From first word to last, a marvel of narrative genius! What the hell was wrong with the world, was it—

Hmm. Actually, I could probably change this part, here, to make it stronger. And this sentence could be tightened. And perhaps that paragraph is a bit wordy. Where's my pencil?

"Wow, Joe. It doesn't even seem like the same story."

I grinned at my wife. "I took everyone's suggestions into account, and did a little self-editing."

"A little? You practically changed every line. Even the characters are different."

"I kept the title, though."

Miranda nodded, handing back the papers. I could see her searching her thoughts for the right compliment.

I gave her some help. "So it's tighter?"

"Oh, yes. Much tighter."

"Is the death still funny?"

"Not funny at all. Very somber."

I sighed, letting out the tension. "So it's a lot better."

Miranda winced. "Actually, I thought the other version was better."

"See that?" I held my painting in front of my son, keeping it out of reach because the acrylic hadn't dried it. "Daddy made a picture of Spider Man."

My son squinted at my artwork. "It's poopy."

"Joe, you've been staring inside the fridge for ten minutes."

"I want to make a sandwich," I told my wife.

"What are you waiting for?"

"I doubt my ability."

"Joe—it's a slice of ham and two pieces of bread."

I frowned. "I'm having some competency issues."

"Didn't Darren like your cow painting?"

"That wasn't a cow. It was Spider Man."

Miranda rubbed my back. "Go sit down, honey. I'll make you a sandwich."

"Miranda! Come here! What is this?"

She stared at the kitchen table.

"It looks like you've made a big letter A out of pretzel sticks."

"Damn right!"

"Joe—are you okay?"

"I'm fine. Want to see me make a B?"

"I'm calling Dr. Hubbard."

"Many people have feelings of inadequacy. It's natural."

The shrink was old, bespeckled. His gray goatee pointed at me when he talked.

"This is more than inadequacy, Doc. I'm questioning every move I make. I feel totally incompetent."

"All because of one little story?"

"That's how it started."

"May I see it?"

Without getting up off the couch I pulled the crumpled story out of my pants pocket and handed it over. As he read, I could feel body go numb. Ice cold, unfeeling. One more heartless comment couldn't hurt me. I was immune to criticism.

"This is pretty good."

I sat up and spun towards him. "Excuse me?"

He held up a finger, still reading. When he finished the last page, he handed back the story and smiled.

"I liked it."

"Really?"

"Yes. Really."

"You aren't just saying that because I'm paying you three hundred dollars an hour?"

"Really, Joe. I thought it was a nice, touching story. Good structure. Well-defined characters. Interesting subtext. I'd actually like to have a copy to pass around the office."

I sprang to my feet, my blood replaced by helium. "Well, sure, no problem, you can have this copy, absolutely, it's all yours."

"Would you sign it for me?"

Were there clouds above nine?

"Of course. Here, I'll borrow your pen."

"You know," Doc Hubbard said as I scrawled my name on the top margin, "I'm a bit of a writer myself."

"Really?" I added 'To Doc' above my name, and then underlined it.

"Perhaps you'd like to read one of my stories?"

"Sure," I told him, drawing a large circle around my signature. "Be happy to help you with it."

Doc grinned, then opened up his desk drawer. He held out some paper. "Go ahead. Off the clock."

I smiled and accepted his story, pleased to be valued for my opinion.

It was bad. Real bad.

"So? What did you think?"

"Well, Doc, it's interesting."

"Yes. Yes. Go on."

"Um, very few typos."

His grin lost some wattage.

"How about the ending?"

"Actually, I, uh, saw it coming."

The grin was gone now.

"Should have figured," he mumbled.

"What was that?"

"How can you recognize talent, when you have none yourself?"

"But you said…"

"I lied. I said it for three hundos and hour. I've read aspirin bottles with more entertainment value than your stupid story."

"How can you…"

"I'm sorry," Doc Hubbard offered a placid smile. "Our time is up."

"Joe?"

"Hmm?"

"Were you ever planning on going back to work?"

I glanced at Miranda and scratched at my stubble. "I haven't given it much thought."

"You've been lying in bed for three weeks."

"Hmm."

"Work called. I told them you were still sick. They want a doctor's note, or you're going to be fired."

"Bummer."

Miranda's eyes went teary, and she walked off.

"We're leaving."

I stared at my wife and son over the pile of cellophane wrappers cluttering my bed.

"Leaving where?"

"Leaving you, Joe. You're not the man I married. I've been talking to a lawyer."

She handed me a sheaf of papers. The word DIVORCE was on the header. I gave them a token look-through.

"This is terrible," I concluded. "Poor sentence structure, too much legalese, look at this typo…"

But they were already gone.

My story was in front of me, on the table, next to a picture of my family.

I was done dwelling. I'd had enough.

The gun went into my mouth and I pulled the trigger, my last sensation a tremendous BOOM coupled with a sense of perfect relief.

The pitchfork jabbed me in the ass.

"Hey!"

"Keep moving."

I stared out across the inferno, Satan's minions tormenting the damned as they slaved away.

"This room is for rapists. Any rapists in the group?"

Two guys in line with me raised their hands. The devil opened the door for them, and they were seized by a huge goat-like creature and thrust into a cauldron of boiling oil.

"Next room, adulterers."

Four more of my group went in. I winced when the whips began to swing.

"Bad writers. This room here, bad writers."

No one moved.

"That's you, Joe."

I was prodded in, my bowels jelly. But rather than hideous tortures, I found myself in a large classroom, stretching back as far as I could see. People of all races, creeds, and dress sat at undersized desks, rows and rows going off into infinity.

"Hello, Joe." The teacher had a pig snout and tusks, her hair done up in a bun and her pointy tail raised behind her like a question mark.

"What is all this?"

"This is eternity, Joe. Who would like to critique Joe's story first?"

Three million hands went up.

"Who are these people?" I asked.

"Murderers. As punishment for their sins, they were forced to listen to your story. Several times, in fact."

"My story is their torture?"

"Well, I have read it aloud several times. There used to be twice as many people in the room, but a few million elected to go to the boiling oil chamber rather than hear it again."

I shut my eyes. When I opened them, I was still there.

"And I have to listen to their opinions for eternity?"

"Every thirty years you get a one week vacation in the piranha pool."

The teacher made me stand in front of the classroom, and the critiques began.

I counted the days until the piranha pool.

Well Balanced Meal

This is something I wrote back in college. It's the first time I ever did a story using only dialog. I read this at the infamous Gross Out Contest at the World Horror Con, but was pulled off the stage for not being gross enough. The next year I came back with a truly disgusting story and won the contest, becoming the Gross Out Champion of 2004. The story that won the contest will never see print. If you're curious, the ending involved relations with a colostomy bag. This piece is much less extreme.

"HI, WELCOME TO RANALDI'S. You folks ready to order?"

"Not quite yet."

"How about we start you off with some drinks?"

"Sounds good. I'll have a rum and toothpaste."

"Flavor?"

"Pepsident."

"I'm sorry. We only have Aim, Close-Up, Gleem, and Tarter Control Crest."

"Give me the Crest, then."

"And you sir?"

"I'll take a Kahlua and baby oil."

"Miss?"

"Vodka and mayonnaise."

"How about you, Miss?"

"Just hot buttered coffee for me."

"I think I'm ready to order."

"What can I get you sir?"

"A pimpleburger."

"How would you like that cooked?"

"Until it turns brown and starts to bubble."

"You have a choice of soup or salad with that."

"What's the soup?"

"Cream of Menstruation. It's our special — we only get it once a month."

"That sounds good."

"How about you sir, ready to order?"

"Yeah. I'll take boils and eggs."

"Good choice. The chef has several big ones just waiting to be lanced."

"Is the ham fresh?"

"No ma'am."

"Okay, I'll take the ham. Can you cover it with vomit?"

"Of course. What kind?"

"How about from someone who has just eaten chicken?"

"I'll have the cook eat some chicken right now so he can puke it up for you."

"I'd like it to be partially digested, if possible."

"There will be a forty minute wait for that."

"No problem."

"And you miss? Have you decided?"

"Yeah. I think I'll just take a bowl of hot grease with a hair in it."

"Pubic or armpit?"

"Can I get one of each?"

"I think I can arrange that."

"Could we also get an appetizer?"

"Of course sir."

"Fresh rat entrails."

"How many orders?"

"How big are the rats?"

"They're a pretty good size."

"Okay, two. Do we get to dig them out ourselves?"

"Yep. We serve out rat entrails live and squirming."

"Make it three then."

"Can we get a cup of placenta for dipping?"

"Yes you can."

"Is it okay to order dessert now?"

"Of course miss."

"I'd like the sugar fried snot."

"Good choice. One of the busboys has a terrible cold."

"I think I'll have a slice of lung cake."

"Would you like spit sauce on that?"

"On the side."

"Sir, would you like to order your dessert now?"

"A blood sundae."

"What kind?"

"What kind do you have?

"Types A, B, and O."

"No AB?"

"I'm sorry. We're out."

"Could you mix A and B together?"

"It will clot."

"That's okay."

"And you, Miss? Dessert?"

"I think I'll skip dessert and eat my own stool when I get home."

"That's a good idea, honey. Cancel the lung cake, I think I'll just eat my wife's shit too."

"We do serve feces here. Regular and chunky style. We're also running a special on diarrhea. Two cups for the price of one."

"No thanks. Why buy something you can get for free at home?"

"Thrifty thinking, sir. Can I get you folks anything else?"

"Yeah. This fork has got water spots on it. Can I get a new one?"

"Absolutely sir. I'll be right back."

A Newbie's Guide to Thrillerfest

Written for a special edition of the magazine Crimespree, which was given away for free at the first Thrillerfest convention. A variation on this essay also appeared in a special Love Is Murder issue for that conference, using different names and tweaking some of the jokes.

EVERY YEAR THERE ARE dozens of writing conferences. If you're a fan of mysteries and thrillers, 2006 brings you Love is Murder in Chicago, Sleuthfest in Ft. Lauderdale, Bouchercon in Madison, Left Coast Crime in Bristol, Men of Mystery in Los Angeles, Magna Cum Murder in Muncie, and a slew of others, many of which suck.

The best conference of them all is undoubtedly Thrillerfest, presented by the International Thriller Writers. In one short year, the upstart ITW has grown to become the writing organization with the longest website URL: www.internationalthrillerwriters.org.

What can you expect when you attend Thrillerfest? How can you make sure you get your money's worth? Will you have a chance to corner ITW Co-President David Morrell and ask him to blurb your new manuscript, The Speech Impediment Murderererererer? (Answer: Yes. Uncle Davy loves this. The best time to approach him is while he's eating, or in the bathroom.)

Reading and memorizing this carefully compiled article will fully prepare you for anything this conference has to offer. It might even save your life.

REGISTRATION – If possible, buy your conference pass in advance. Bring proof of your registration to the event (a Paypal receipt, a copy of the letter saying you've been confirmed, your hard drive) because there's a 90% chance your registration was lost, and the people running the conference will have no idea who you are. A much easier, and cheaper, tactic is to simply buy a nametag and a black marker. Stick it on your chest when no one is looking, and you're in.

THE HOTEL – If possible, stay at the hotel. After the days' events are through, there are always exclusive parties where you can get free food and drink and meet cool people. You won't get invited to these parties, but you can hang out in the hallway with your ear to the door, and listen to JA Konrath make a fool of himself. Actually, you probably won't need to put your ear to the door to hear that. JA's pretty loud.

WHAT TO WEAR – The fashionable conference-goer wears business casual. Comfortable shoes are a must, because you'll be walking a lot. A book bag is a great accessory. Not only can it hold books, but also an emergency fifth of vodka (do you really want to pay $9 for a martini at the hotel bar?)

AUTHOR SIGHTING – Imagine it: You're in the lobby, putting the cap back on your vodka, and suddenly James Rollins appears out of nowhere. Do you just run up to him, squealing like a schoolgirl, and beg him to sign your paperback copy of Map of Bones that you've read 36 times, the last time aloud to your pet parakeet that you named Sigma?

The answer: NO! Jim is a bigshot author, and they all hate signing paperbacks. Go to the bookroom and buy a hardcover first edition. When you approach him, make sure it's on your hands and knees, because you are not worthy. Address him as "Mr. Rollins" or "Sir" or "Your Highness." And NEVER make direct eye contact. He's far too important to look at you.

In contrast, if you spot James O. Born, feel free to bring him your paperback ex-library copy of Shock Wave. Born will be thrilled to sign that. He'll also sign other authors' books, cocktail napkins, food products, and basically anything but the check.

PANELS – If you're an author, you need to speak on a panel. But it's too late to sign up for one now, bonehead. They've already printed the programs. If you are on a panel, there's only one important rule to follow: Make sure you're on a panel with Barry Eisler. Barry is the one with the gaggle of drooling women following him around, hoping he'll suddenly keel over so they'll get to administer CPR. Don't expect anyone to remember a single thing you've said when you're on a panel with Barry, but at least you'll be speaking to a packed room.

FOOD – Conference food is usually barely edible, but it's expensive to compensate. That's why all of the popular authors usually go out to eat at the trendiest restaurant in the area. It's very easy to get invited to one of these exciting outings, where industry gossips flows fast and loose, and Barry often takes his shirt off and dances the lambada—the dance of love. If you want to go along, all you have to do is write a NYT Bestseller. If you haven't done that, then you're stuck with the hotel food. Be sure to try the potato salad. Is that potato salad? It might be rice pudding. Or lamb. Or a big dish of pus.

ITINERARY – There are many things to see at a conference, and often you'll be tortured by the dilemma of two good panels happening at the same time, with no clue which to attend. The answer is easy. Attend both of them. Authors love seeing scores of people leave the room while they are talking—they believe they're being so effective, the crowd is rushing out to buy their book. Try to do this five or six times per hour, and make sure you open and close the doors loudly. Also, take that extra time between panels to talk on your cell phone. If your conversation carries on into the panel room—it's okay. His Majesty Rollins will forgive you.

WHERE ARE THE AUTHORS? – You've been trying desperately to get F. Paul Wilson's autograph, but he's been missing in action for two days. Where is he? He's in the hotel bar. In fact, all of the authors are in the hotel bar. If you want to chat in depth with your favorite thriller writer, arrive early while they're still coherent. In Paul's case, I challenge you to figure out when that it.

THE BOOKROOM – This is the most important room in the whole conference. Here, you'll find all of the books by all of the authors in attendance, expect for the one book you truly want to buy. They'll be out of that one. But don't worry, there will be plenty of pristine, unsold, unread copies of Bloody Mary by JA Konrath. Plenty of them.

BARGAIN HUNTER TIP – All the paperbacks in the bookroom are free if you simply rip off the cover beforehand! Don't be bashful—the booksellers love it!

ETIQUETTE – It's during one of the delicious buffet-style meals. You've got your plate piled high with something that might be meat in gravy, or it might be a cobbler, and you're searching for a place to eat. While walking around the room, you see an empty chair between Tess Gerritsen and ITW Co-President Gayle Lynds. Do you dare ask to sit there? In a word, NO! They are huge mega bestsellers and that seat belongs to someone a lot more important than you are. Go sit by Jon and Ruth Jordan, who publish this magazine. Always plenty of chairs around them. The surrounding tables are usually free too.

PAID ADVERTISEMENT – Buy the anthology Thriller — Stories To Keep You Up All Night, an ITW collection featuring stories by superstar mega-bestselling authors such as JA Konrath, and others.

ATTENDEES – Conferences are a great place to meet new people who share common interests. They're also a great place to get abducted by some weirdo and killed with a blowtorch. Wise convention goers avoid talking to anyone else, at all times. Try to keep some kind of weapon on you. They sell $59 letter openers in the hotel gift shop, right next to the $42 tee shirts and the $12 bottled water. If you're an author, save the receipt—it's deductible.

Or try carrying around a plate piled high with that stuff they served at lunch—the stuff in the gravy. That way, if someone tries to assault you, you can say, "Stop it! I'm eating!"

AWARDS – At most conferences, the writers like to congratulate themselves by giving each other awards. They usually do this over a nine course meal that takes eleven hours, and a cash bar that charges so much for a Budweiser you'll need to put it on lay-away. In an effort to distinguish itself from the many other conventions and organizations that do this sort of thing, the ITW decided to do this as well.

The star-studded gala begins at 7 P.M. on Saturday, and ends sometime on Thursday morning. When the event has concluded, be sure to congratulate the lucky winners. It's also a lot of fun to go up to the losers and congratulate them for winning, and then pretend to be confused when they tell you they've actually lost. Do this two or three times to the same loser. They'll start to find it funny, eventually.

SIGNINGS – There will be many scheduled signing times, where dozens of authors all sit in the same room and greet the hundreds of fans waiting in line for Lee Child. If you're in Lee's very long line, remember that to keep things moving quickly you aren't allowed to say more than two words to him, and he'll only have time to sign an "L." A lower case "L." Lee's a very busy man.

Lee Goldberg, on the other hand, will have plenty of time to sign his full name. Plenty of time. If you so desire, he'll even sign it using the time-intensive, hand-lettered art of calligraphy. Don't be afraid to ask. He has plenty of time.

SUNDAY – This is the day where everyone sleeps in and/or catches their flight home, and panel attendance is traditionally low. By some dramatic conference oversight, 9 A.M. on Sunday is when JA Konrath has his scheduled panel. He's not sure how this happened. Perhaps he pissed someone off somehow, unlikely as that may sound. But he urges you to attend this panel, on the super-exciting topic of writing for female characters. Never saw that hot-button topic at a convention before, have you? There will be some other high caliber authors on this panel, probably, and JA is bringing some butterscotch schnapps to put in the audience's coffee. Get your lazy butt out of bed and be there. He'll be entertaining. Promise.

CONCLUSION – Remember, if you want to have a memorable conference, responsibility rests squarely on one person's shoulders—the person running the conference. Be sure to complain about every little thing, at any given time, even if it's something they can't fix such as, "The carpet is too soft" or "F. Paul Wilson touched me inappropriately" or "I hear voices in my head." Demand a refund. Threaten to contact an attorney. And above all, remember to have fun.

Inspector Oxnard

A humorous take on the many detectives in crime fiction who are able to glance at a crime scene and brilliantly deduce everything that happened. I wrote this for an anthology, but they rejected it. Too Monty Python-ish, they said.

Special Investigations Inspector J. Gerald Oxnard arrives on the scene moments after the crime has been committed. The usual entourage of detectives from the SI Division of New Bastwick's Police Department accompanies him.

I'm the newly appointed member of this crack investigating team, a reward for my exemplary grades at the Police Academy. It's just my luck that my first case is a murder.

The portly Inspector kneels beside the cooling body of a man in his late twenties. After several minutes of intense scrutiny, he nods and clears his throat, prompting one of the nearby detectives to help him to his feet.

"He was killed by a lion," Inspector Oxnard says. "I'm thoroughly convinced."

The room absorbs the declaration, mulling and silent.

"But…Inspector," I say, "How did a lion get up to Room 715 of the Vandenburg Hotel without anyone seeing it?"

Inspector Oxnard puts a thin and elegantly manicured hand up to his mustache and rolls the waxy end.

"A disguise," he says.

"A disguise?" I ask.

"Of course. Perhaps a long overcoat and some dark glasses. Haven't you ever seen a lion walk on his hind legs at the circus?"

Several of the detectives standing around sound their approval. One writes it down in his note pad.

"But what about the knife?" I ask.

"The knife?" Inspector Oxnard shoots back, eyes sharp and accusing.

"In the deceased's back." I say.

There's a moment of chin-scratching silence.

"Don't lions have an opposable thumb?" Detective Jenkins asks.

"No, you're thinking of monkeys," Detective Coursey says.

"But isn't a lion kind of like a big orange monkey with sharp teeth?" Detective Rumstead asks.

There are several nods of agreement. Inspector Oxnard runs a hand through his gray hair, which is slicked back with mint-smelling gel, and wipes his palm on Detective Coursey's blazer.

"It had to be a lion with a knife," the Inspector says, "wearing an overcoat and dark glasses. Put out an All Points Bulletin, and check to see if a circus is in town."

"But Inspector," I say, "there's no sign of forced entry. How did the lion get into the room?"

"Simple. He had a key."

"Why would he have a key?" I ask.

The silence that follows is steeped in apprehension. After a full minute, Inspector Oxnard makes a self-satisfied yelping sound and thrusts his finger skyward in apparent revelation, poking Detective Graves in the eye.

"The deceased was having an affair with the lion! Thus, the lion had a duplicate key!"

Excited applause sweeps through the group. Inspector Oxnard draws on his pipe, but it does little good because the bowl is upside down, the tobacco speckling his shoes.

"Did the lion prefer the company of men?" Detective Struber says.

"Perhaps," Inspector Oxnard says. "Or perhaps it was…a lioness!"

Several 'ahs' are heard. Someone pipes in, "Of course! The lioness is the one that does the hunting!"

"But what about motive?" I ask, my Police Academy training coming out. "What was the motive?"

"Hunger," the Inspector says. He nods smartly to himself.

"But the body is intact."

"Excuse me?"

"None of it has been eaten!" I say.

"That makes no difference. Maybe the lioness was scared away before she could finish, or perhaps she simply lost her appetite."

"I sometimes have terrible gas, and can't eat at all," Detective Gilbert says.

Nods of acquiescence all around, and several discussions of gas pains ensue.

"But where are the paw prints?" someone shrieks. "Where is the fur? Where is the spoor? Where is the damn reason that this was done by a lion and not a human being?"

Everyone stares at me, and I realize I've been the one shrieking.

Inspector Oxnard frowns and gives me a patronizing pat on the head.

"I know you're only a novice, so I can understand why you cannot grasp all of the subtle intricacies of a murder investigation. But in time, Detective Cornhead, you'll begin to catch on."

"My name is Richards, Inspector. Detective Richards."

"Nothing to be ashamed of." Inspector Oxnard slaps my shoulder. "We were all young once."

Detective Oldendorff runs through the door and trips over the body. He picks himself up, urgency overriding embarrassment.

"There's been another robbery!" he says. "The First New Bastwick Bank!"

Inspector Oxnard thrusts out his lower lip and nods.

"It sounds like that blind panda has struck again. Come, gentlemen!"

Inspector Oxnard gracefully exits the room, his entourage filing behind him like ducklings. I stare at the body for a moment, and then follow.

This police work is a lot harder than I thought.

Appalachian Lullaby

My friend John Weagley asked me if I had any radioactive monkey stories for his collection Requiem For A Radioactive Monkey. Naturally, I did.

AT FIRST, THEY WERE all kind of excited when JoJo got into the Uranium.

"He's gonna mutate, I bet," said Gramps. "Maybe grow another monkey head. Or teats."

"Could easily quadruple in size," said Pops. "Go on a rampage, killin' folks and rapin' women."

Uncle Clem disagreed. "I'm bettin' invisibility. A seeable monkey causes enough trouble, running around, bitin' and chitterin', throwin' feces. An invisible money would be a hunnerd times worse."

"Would the feces be invisible?" Aunt Lula asked.

"Likely so. Wouldn't know it was there 'till you sat in it."

Gramps packed his lower lip with a wad of Skoal and spat brown juice into Aunt Lula's coffee mug.

"Shoulda kept that uranium locked up. Leavin' it on the counter like that, monkey was gonna mess with it sooner or later."

Uncle Clem disagreed. "JoJo ain't never fooled with it before."

"Them glowin' isotopes, they're like a magnet to the lower primates. Shoulda kept it locked up."

Pops scratched his head. "Where'd we get the uranium anyway?"

They all sat around and had a think about that. No one said nothin' for a while, the only sound being the slurp-slurp of Aunt Lula and her coffee.

"Well," Gramps finally said, "whatever strange mutation happens to JoJo, I'm guessin' we all agree it'll be speck-tack-ler."

Somethin' did happen to JoJo, and it happened fast. An hour after messin' with the Uranium, JoJo's hair all fell out, and then he died.

"Didn't see that comin'," Uncle Clem said.

Pops scratched his head. "Where'd we get a monkey anyway?"

No one could answer that. Only one who could have was JoJo, and he didn't say much on account of his deceasedness. Plus, JoJo was a monkey, and monkeys don't talk.

The next day, Gramps lost all of his hair, even the hair growin' from his ears, and got sick something fierce.

"Gramps?" Pops asked him, side-steppin' the chunk-streams gushing from Gramps's dip-hole. "You been messin' with that Uranium?"

Gramps answered between expulsions. "Wanted…another…head."

Later that night, after Gramps hemorrhaged, they buried him in the garden, next to JoJo. The family grieved and grieved, and Aunt Lula made some Uranium cookies to cheer everyone up, but Uncle Clem hoarded them all for himself.

"Thad a dab thine thookie," Uncle Clem said, not speakin' clearly because most of his teeth had worked themselves free of his bleedin' gums.

When Uncle Clem coughed up his pancreas, they buried him in the garden, next to Gramps and JoJo.

Not long after, Aunt Lula's hands turned black and plum fell off, on account she didn't wear no lead gloves when she made the uranium cookies. "Because lead is poisonous," she had said, smartly.

When Aunt Lula died, Pops buried her in another part of the garden, not too close to Uncle Clem and Gramps and JoJo, because that part was all took up.

When he was done, Pops scratched his head. "Where'd we get a garden anyway?"

Convinced the Curse of the Radioactive Uranium would claim him next, which would have been a very bad thing because there was nobody left to bury him in the garden, Pops played it smart.

He buried himself in the garden with the uranium.

When the milkman came by later that week, with the milk and eight ounces of farmer's cheese, he noticed the five new mounds in the garden. Being a curious milkman, he dug them all up.

"Well, will you lookit that," said the mailman. "Where'd they get that uranium?"

He found some tin foil in the kitchen, and wrapped up the Uranium and took it home, for his pet monkey to play with.

ONE NIgHT ONLy

A farce, very much in James Thurber territory. I've always want to write a straight humor novel, but there isn't any market for it.

FRANK STOOD BENEATH THE mismatched letters on the marquee and frowned.

ONE NIgHT ONLy, it proclaimed.

That was still one night too many.

Ahead of him in line, another poor dope with an equally unhappy face was being tugged towards the ticket booth by his significant other.

"He's supposed to be brilliant. Like Marcel Marceau, only he talks," the wife/girlfriend was saying.

The man was having none of it, and neither was Frank. He stared at his own pack leader, his wife Wendy, mushing him forward on the Forced Culture Iditarod. She noted his frown and hugged his arm.

"Stop moping. It'll be fun."

"It's the playoffs."

"It's our anniversary."

"We have another one next year."

Wendy gave him The Look, and he backed down. He glanced at his Seiko, wishing he had a watch like Elroy on The Jetsons, with a mini TV screen. It was ten after nine. Halftime would be almost over, and it was the pivotal fifth game in the Eastern Conference

Finals, the score tied 48-48.

Frank had managed to catch the other four pivotal games, but this one was really pivotal. If the Bulls won, it meant there would only be seven more pivotal games left in the playoffs.

They reached the ticket counter, and Frank noted several divots in the thick glass. Probably made by some other poor bastard forced here by his wife. Tried to shoot his way out, Frank guessed.

He could relate.

His mind wrapped around the fantasy of pulling out an M-16 and taking hostages to avoid seeing the show, but he lost the image when he noted how many twenty dollar bills his wife was setting in the money tray.

"This costs how much?!?"

"It's an exclusive engagement," the cashier said. "Alexandro Mulchahey is only in town for one night."

"And what does he do for this kind of money? Take the whole audience out for dinner in his Rolls Royce?"

Wendy gave him The Elbow. But Frank wasn't finished yet.

"Maybe you folks will finally be able to afford some more capital letters for the marquee."

Now Frank received The Love Handle Pinch; Wendy's fingernails dug into his flab and twisted. He yelped and his wife tugged him aside.

"You're embarrassing me," she said through a forced smile.

"I'm having chest pains. Do you know how many Bulls tickets we could have bought with all that money?"

"If you don't start pretending to have a good time, I'm going to invite GrandMama over for the weekend."

He clammed up. Wendy's grandmother was 160 years old and mean as spit. Her mind had made its grand exit sometime during the Reagan years, and she labored under the delusion that Frank was Rudolph Hess. The last time she visited, GrandMama called the police seven times and demanded they arrest Frank for crimes against humanity.

Plus, she smelled like pee.

Wendy led him into the lobby, and began to point out architecture.

"Ooo, look at the columns."

"Ooo, look at the vaulted ceiling."

"Ooo, look at the mosaic tile. Have you ever seen anything so intricate?"

"Yeah, yeah. Beautiful."

The theater was nice, but it was no Circus Circus. While his wife gaped at the carved railing on the grand staircase, Frank's attention was captivated by a little boy sitting alone near the coat check.

The boy had a Sony Watchman.

"Did you want a drink, dear?"

Wendy smiled at him. "A glass of wine would be wonderful."

Frank got in line—a line that would take him right past the little boy and his portable TV. He made sure Wendy was preoccupied staring at a poster before he made his move.

"Hey, kid! Nice TV. Can you turn on the Bulls Game real fast? Channel 9."

The kid looked up at him, squinting through thick glasses.

"I don't like the Bulls."

"Come on, I just want to check the score." Frank winked, then fished five bucks out of his pocket. "I'll give you five bucks."

"Mom!" The child's voice cut through the lobby like a siren. "An old fat man wants to steal my TV!"

Frank turned away, shielding his face. The bartender gave him the evil eye.

"Merlot," Frank said, throwing down the five.

The bartender raised an eyebrow and told him the price of the wine.

"It's how much?!?"

"Frank, dear…" Wendy was tugging at him as he pulled out more money.

"Hold on, hon. I think I just bought you the last Merlot on earth." Frank watched the bartender pour. "And it's in a plastic cup."

"I want to get a program."

Frank's wife led him past the little boy, who held up his Watchman and stuck out his tongue. The little snot was watching the Bulls. Frank squinted but couldn't make out the score.

They got in line for the programs and Frank momentarily forgot about basketball when he saw the prices.

"For a program?!? Don't they come free with the show?"

"That's a Playbill, Frank."

"What's the difference?"

The difference, apparently, was forty bucks.

"Do they have a layaway?"

"They have sweatshirts, too, Frank. Would you like one?"

"I don't want to have to get a second job."

"Your birthday is coming up."

Wendy grinned at him. Frank couldn't tell if she was joking or not. He forked over the money for a program, and then they walked to the mezzanine and an usher took their tickets.

"Row A, seats 14 and 15."

"Front row center," his wife beamed. "Happy Anniversary, Frank."

She kissed his cheek. Then she began pointing out more architecture.

"Look at the balconies."

"Look at the stage."

"Look at the plasterwork. Have you ever seen anything so beautiful?"

"Yeah, yeah. Beautiful."

The usher showed them their seats and Frank frowned.

"I thought we were front row."

"This is the front row, sir."

"How about all those guys in front of us?"

"That's the orchestra pit, sir."

They took their seats, which were actually pretty nice. Plush red velvet, roomy and comfortable. Too bad they didn't have seats like this at the United Center, where the Bulls played.

Wendy handed him a Playbill, and Frank squinted at the cover. A man in period clothing stared back at him.

"Who is this guy, anyway? Alexandro Mulchahey?"

"He's the famous Irish soliloquist."

"One of those guys who talks with a dummy on his lap?"

"He's a dramatic actor, Frank. He does Shakespearean sonnets."

Frank slumped in his chair. This was worse than he'd thought. When Wendy nagged him about this night, during a pivotal regular season game a few months back, he hadn't heard her mention Shakespeare.

"And this guy's famous?"

"He's the hottest thing in Europe right now. He's in all the papers."

Frank folded his arms. "If he was in all the papers, I would have heard about him."

"He wasn't in the sports section."

Frank frowned. The most pivotal basketball game of the century was playing right now, and Frank was stuck here watching some fruit in tights talk fancy for three hours.

Maybe he could fake a heart attack. Those ambulance guys have radios. They could tune into the game…

Some people needed to get to their seats, and Frank and Wendy had to stand up to let them by.

It was the kid with the Watchman! He stuck his tongue out at Frank as he passed, and then sat three seats away from them, his TV still tuned to the Bulls game.

Frank glanced at Wendy. She was absorbed in her program, gaping at big, color photos of Alexandro, who appeared to be in the throes of agony or ecstasy or a massive bowel movement.

"Look at how passionate he is," Wendy beamed.

"Or constipated," Frank muttered. He turned to look at the kid. The little boy held up the Watchman so Frank could see the game. The screen was tiny, but there was a score in the corner that Frank could almost make out. He leaned closer, straining his eyes.

The little snot switched the channel to Tom and Jerry.

"Goddamn little…"

There was a moaning sound in front of them.

"Orchestra is warming up." Wendy bounced in her seat like an anxious schoolgirl. "It's going to start soon."

The little boy whispered something to his father, and they both got up. Once again Frank and Wendy had to stand. Frank fought the urge to strangle the little monkey as he sashayed past.

The father took the kid by the hand up the aisle.

"Wendy, I have to go to the bathroom."

"The show's about to start."

"It's an emergency." Frank made his Emergency face.

"Hurry back."

Frank stood up and followed the boy into the lobby. As he

guessed, his father led him into the bathroom.

The kid's father was standing by the sink, checking out his hair from three different angles.

"I just joined Hair Club for Men," he told Frank.

"Looks good," Frank told him. It looked like a beaver had died on the man's head.

"Can you see the weave?"

"Hmm? No. Seamless."

Frank eyed the stalls. Only one door was closed. Had to be the kid.

He walked into the nearby stall and closed the door. Removing twenty dollars from his wallet, he slipped the bill under the partition

"Psst. Kid. Twenty bucks if you can give it to me for an hour."

There was no answer. Frank added another bill to the offer.

"How about forty?"

The voice that came from the stall was far to low to belong to a child.

"I normally don't swing that way, man. But for sixty, I'll rock your world."

Frank hurried out of the bathroom and into the lobby. The kid and his dad were going back into the theater.

"Hey! Buddy!"

Several people in the crowd turned to stare at him. He pushed through and caught up with Hair Weave and his kid.

"You think I could check out the game on your son's TV?"

"The game?" Hair Weave scratched his roots.

"Bulls game. Playoffs."

"Clarence, let this man see your TV for a second."

"Batteries are dead."

Clarence switched on the Watchman and nothing happened. He smiled. Malicious little bastard.

"Did you see the score?"

"Yeah—fifty-four to sixty-eight."

"Who was winning?"

"Sixty-eight."

"Come on Clarence, Mommy's waiting."

Clarence stuck out his tongue and followed his father down the aisle.

Frank felt as if his head were about to blow apart. He almost began crying.

"Are you okay, sir?"

An usher, red vest and bow tie, no more than eighteen. Frank grabbed his arms.

"Is there a TV anywhere in this place?"

The boy scrunched his eyebrows. "TV? No. I don't think so."

"How about a radio? It's the Eastern Conference Finals. I have to know the score."

"Sorry. There's a TV in the dressing room, but…"

Frank lit up. "There's one in Evander Mulrooney's room?"

"You mean Alexandro Mulchahey?"

"I went to school with Evander, in Italy."

"Mr. Mulchahey is Irish."

Frank clapped the usher on the shoulder, grinning broadly.

"I should stop in, say hello to the old hound dog. Where's his dressing room?"

"I don't think…"

Frank held the forty dollars under the kid's nose.

"Just tell me where it is."

The usher sniffed the money, then nodded. He led Frank through an unmarked door and down a winding hallway that had none of the frill and pizzazz of the lobby. It barely had ample light.

The hall finally ended at a door to the backstage. Frank half expected to see a jungle of sandbags and painted backdrops, but instead it was very orderly. There were several people milling about, but none of them paid Frank any attention.

"He's the third room on the right. Don't tell him I let you in. I'll lose my job."

Frank didn't bother thanking him. He ran to the door, flinging it open, seeing Evander Fitzrooney sitting in a make-up chair.

The soliloquist turned to him, venom in his eyes.

"I don't allow visitors before a performance! Get out!"

Frank ignored the actor, scanning the room, searching frantically for the…

"Television!"

Frank ran to it, arms outstretched, and Evander stood up and punched Frank square in the nose.

"How many times can I say I'm sorry?"

Wendy stared at Frank through the bars. She didn't seem sympathetic.

"I've decided to let you spend the night in jail, Frank. Maybe it will help you prioritize your life."

"Wendy...please. I need you to bail me out. The game has to be almost over, and I gave my last forty bucks to that pimply usher."

Wendy darkened, then turned on her heels and walked out.

"Wendy! Will you at least find out the score for me? Please!"

After Wendy left, Frank slumped down on the metal bench, alone. Every second seemed to last an hour. Every minute was an eternity. Are the Bulls winning? Will they move on to the finals? What was the score?

Never a religious man, Frank silently begged the Lord to please send someone to give Frank the score.

When Frank finished the prayer and opened his eyes, he was confronted with a wondrous sight.

The cops were bringing in a man—a large, burly man—wearing a Bulls jersey.

"Is the game over?"

The man squinted at Frank. "Yeah, it's over. Most amazing ending I've ever seen. It'll be talked about for decades to come."

"Who won? Who won?"

The door closed, and the cops went away. The burly man looked Frank over, top to bottom.

"You a Bulls fan?"

Frank began to jump up and down.

"Yes, dammit! Who won the game?"

The man smiled. It was an ugly thing.

"How much is it worth to you to know?"

"Name your price. I don't have any money on me, but I'll get it to you. My word is good."

Burly Guy licked his lips. "Don't want no money."

"What is it you want, then?"

Fifteen minutes later, Frank learned a valuable lesson: If you dedicate your life to sports, you'll only get hurt in the end.

Treatment

Written years ago, this eventually sold to Blood Lite 2 edited by Kevin J. Williamson. It's a fun piece where things aren't what they appear to be.

"IT ALL GOES BACK to the time I was bitten by that werewolf."

Dr. Booster's pencil paused for a moment on his notepad, having only written a 'w.'

"A werewolf?"

Tyler nodded. Booster appraised the teenager; pimples, lanky, hair a bit too long for the current style. The product of a well-to-do suburban couple.

"This is the reason your grades have gone down?"

"Yeah. Instead of studying at night, I roam the neighborhood, eating squirrels."

"I see…and how do squirrels taste, Tyler?"

"They go down dry."

Booster wrote 'active imagination' on his pad.

"What makes you say you were bitten by a werewolf?"

"Because I was."

"When did this happen?"

Tyler scratched at the pubescent hairs on his chin. "Two weeks ago. I was out at night, burying this body…"

"Burying a body?"

The boy nodded.

"Tyler, for therapy to work, we have to be honest with each other."

"I'm being honest, Dr. Booster."

Booster made his mouth into a tight line and wrote 'uncooperative' on his pad.

"Fine, Tyler. Whose body were you burying?"

"It was Crazy Harold. He was a wino that hung out in the alley behind the liquor store on Kedzie."

"And why were you burying him?"

Tyler furrowed his brow. "I had to get rid of it. I didn't think digging a grave would be necessary. I thought they disintegrated after getting a stake in the heart."

Booster frowned. "Crazy Harold was a vampire?"

Tyler shifted on the couch to look at him. "You knew? Shouldn't they turn into dust when you kill them?"

Booster glanced the diplomas on his wall. Eight years of education, for this.

"So you're saying you hammered a stake into Crazy Harold —"

"It was actually a broken broom handle."

"—and then buried him."

"In the field behind the house. And just when I finished, that's when the werewolf got me." Tyler lifted up his right leg and hiked up his pants. Above the sock was a raised pink scar, squiggly like an earthworm.

"That's the bite mark?"

Tyler nodded.

"It looks old, Tyler."

"It healed fast."

"Your mother told me you got that scar when you were nine-years-old. You fell off your bike."

Tyler blinked, then rolled his pants leg back down.

"Mom's full of shit."

Booster wrote 'animosity towards mother' in his pad.

"Why do you say that, Tyler? Your mother is the one who recommended therapy, isn't she? It seems as if she wants to help."

"She's not my real mother. Her and Dad were replaced by aliens."

"Aliens?"

"They killed my parents, replaced them with duplicates. They look and sound the same, but they're actually from another planet. I caught them, once, in their bedroom."

Booster raised an eyebrow. "Making love?"

"Contacting the mother ship. They're planning a full scale invasion of earth. But I thought you wanted to know about the werewolf."

Booster pursed his lips. WWSFD? He appealed to the picture of Sigmund hanging above the fireplace. The picture offered no answers.

"Tyler, with your consent, I'd like to try some hypnotherapy. Have you ever been hypnotized?"

"No."

Booster dimmed the lights and sat alongside the couch. He held his pencil in front of Tyler's face at eye level.

"Take a deep breath, then let it out. Focus on the pencil…"

It took a few minutes to bring Tyler to a state of susceptible relaxation.

"Can you hear me, Tyler?"

"Yes."

The boy's jaw was slack, and a thin line of drool escaped the corner of his mouth. Booster was surprised at the child's halitosis — perhaps he had been eating squirrels after all.

"I'd like you to remember back a few weeks, when you told me about burying Crazy Harold."

"Okay."

"Tell me what you see."

"It's cold. There are a lot of rocks in the dirt, and the shovel won't go in very far."

Booster used his pen light to check Tyler's pupils. Slow response. The child was under.

"What were you digging?"

"Grave. For the vampire."

Booster frowned. He'd studied cases of patients lying under hypnosis, but had never had one on his couch.

"What about the werewolf?"

"Came out of the field. It was big, had red eyes, walked on two legs."

"And it bit you?"

"Yeah. I thought it was going to kill me, but Runs Like Stallion saved me."

"Runs Like Stallion?"

"He's a ghost of a Sioux brave. The field is an old Indian burial ground."

Booster decided he'd had enough. He wrote 'treatment' in his notebook and went over to his desk, unlocking the top drawer. The plastic case practically leapt up at him. He took it over to Tyler.

"Tyler, your parents are tired of these stories."

"My parents are dead."

"No, Tyler. They aren't dead. They care about you. That's why they brought you to me."

Booster opened the case. The gnerlock blinked its three eyes and crawled into Booster's hand. It would enter Tyler's mouth and burrow up into his brain, taking over his body.

"Soon, it will all be better. You'll have no more worries. You're going to be a host, Tyler, for the new dominant species on this planet. Are you scared?"

"No."

"Open your mouth, Tyler."

Tyler stretched his mouth wide.

Wider than humanly possible, crammed with sharp teeth.

The gnerlock nesting in Dr. Booster's brain crawled out through his neck after the wolf decapitated the host body.

Its eleven legs beelined for the door, antennae waving hysterically, telepathically cursing that quack Freud.

Halfway there, a green ghostly foot came down on its oblong head, smashing it into the carpeting.

The Indian gave the wolf a thumbs up, but Tyler was already leaping out the window, eyes locked on a juicy squirrel in the grass below.

An Archaeologist's Story

Written for a college anthropology course, as a final project. The Woody Allen influence is obvious. I've always liked this story, but no one ever expressed any interest in publishing it, even though it made the rounds.

DAY 1 — 2:47 P.M.

The funding has come through! As I write this, I am in a plane heading to the Bahamas, on a grant from the University of Sheboygan. With me are my colleagues Dr. Myra Bird and Dr. Jerome Sloan.

I'm thrilled, though my excitement was somewhat dampened when I had some trouble getting my excavation tools through airport security. Jerome's sly joke that I wasn't really an archaeologist, but rather a homicidal maniac, prompted them to conduct an embarrassing and somewhat uncomfortable body-cavity search.

I'm grateful the airport security gentlemen had small hands.

As for the site, none of us knows what to expect. Sure, there have been stories of fossilized Homo erectus skulls just lying on the beach, waiting to be picked up, but archaeological rumors are plentiful. I still remember traveling to the Antarctic six years ago, because of the discovery of what seemed to be an Australopithecus boise tooth, but instead turned out to be just a small white rock. I sorely miss those three toes I lost to frostbite.

But this site seems like the real thing. The authenticated femur of a Homo habilus was found by a vacationing family in a small cave.

Evidently, the children were acting up, and the father had grabbed something lying next to him to beat them with. It turned out to be the fossil in question. Luckily, it remained intact, even though the father used it.

I also believe the children have gotten out of intensive care.

Myra, Jerome and I have been waiting a week now for the go ahead to investigate. My bag was long ago packed and waiting for the word, leaving me pretty much without anything to wear for the last week.

But now we were finally on our way.

Jerome just tapped me on the shoulder, smiling. He is also obviously thrilled about this trip. No, he just wants my martini. I give it to him. I am so high right now I do not need alcohol. This package of peanuts is fine.

DAY 1 — 9:35 P.M.

What a horrible flight! Jerome threw up on the stewardess, who then refused to acknowledge us for the rest of the trip. We didn't even get served our dinner, which as far as I could make out was some kind of meat in brown sauce. When we got to the airport, Customs confiscated Jerome's suitcase, which was filled with liquor. Both Myra and I are appalled at the lack of professionalism on our colleague's part, and we attempted to confront him and express our disappointment.

Unfortunately, he was unconscious.

We managed to get him to the hotel by strapping him to the hood of our taxi, but they charged us fare for three just the same.

The hotel we are staying at is very cheap, and we all must share a room due to budgetary constraints. Myra and I propped Jerome up on the sink, then discussed where we would sleep, there being only one bed. I was willing to be adult about it and share the bed with her, half and half. She agreed, and now I must sleep on the underside of the mattress.

Myra is very sharp, so sharp in fact that I once cut myself shaking her hand. But she has really sexy bone structure, and her teeth are exquisite. I long to run my hands over her illium and ischium, but realize such thoughts are dangerous, as I must work closely with her. Nothing must jeopardize our excavation.

I can barely wait to start work tomorrow.

DAY 2 — 5:43 A.M.

I am awakened in the morning by Jerome retching. The sound was disturbing enough, but the fact that he was retching on me made it impossible to sleep any longer. After a shower, I dressed and went down to the lobby and waited for my colleagues to join me. Myra arrived a few minutes later, without Jerome. When I inquired about him, she told me he was sick and going to stay in bed for the day. I wanted to protest, but realized he probably wouldn't be much help to us anyway, and would only throw up on anything we might find.

We called a cab and took it to the sight. My mind was giddy with anticipation. I could tell Myra was nervous too, because she bit off all her nails and spit them in my face (a cute habit she has.)

When we arrived, it was exactly as I had expected; a clearing in the tropical forest of about eighty square yards. On the edge of it was a rock formation that held a small cave. Myra had brought her camera, and she began to take pictures of the area. Then she gave the camera to me, and asked me to take some pictures of her posing on the rocks.

After shooting three rolls of film, we broke out our equipment and began our excavation. Armed with a flashlight, a horse hair brush, and a small pick, we entered the cave. Myra clutched my arm, afraid of being attacked by vampire bats. Every so often I would flash my light at the ceiling and yell "A bat!" just for fun.

I soon quit, as Myra would slap me repeatedly in the face when she discovered there was no real danger.

A quick inspection of the cave showed no real evidence of primitive man. Though we were unduly excited about seeing something on the wall, which just turned out to be a spray painted picture of a man's genitalia, with "Eat me Jonny" written beside it. Primitive as it may be, it wasn't what we were looking for.

After examining the cave, we went to inspect the area where the femur was found, twenty feet east of the opening. The ground was hard clay, and we discovered the impression of where the discovered femur bone had been lying. Using our picks, we dug roughly six inches down for a square yard of the area encompassing the impression, but got nothing for our efforts except a large pile of clay.

By then it was late afternoon, and we chose to break for lunch. Unfortunately, neither of us had brought anything to eat. But this was a tropical jungle, and there were many edible roots and tubers growing around us. I also noted that several of the rocks were slate, and if need be we could knock off a Mousterian point using the Levallois technique and go hunting for rodents.

Myra, however, wanted a burger and fries, so we had to go back to the hotel.

DAY 2 — 1:46 P.M.

Upon finishing lunch, it was our intention to report our progress to Jerome, then return to the sight. But to our surprise Jerome was not in the room. We begin searching the hotel, and I find him sitting by the pool in a chaise lounge, sipping a Mai-Tai.

I am shocked at his conduct, and threaten to tell our superiors of his insubordination. He flips me the bird.

I find Myra peeking in the Men's room, and tell her of Jerome's attitude. She agrees we should file a report recommending he be dismissed, or at least have his suave safari hat taken away. Then we take a cab back to the sight.

While I continued to excavate the area where the fossil was found, Myra decided to start in another area, closer to the mouth of the cave. It is hard, laborious work, but it is made more bearable by Myra, who sings operettas while she digs.

Four hours into it, I discover something. Rather than get Myra excited over what may be just a rock, I bit off a small portion of my lower lip to keep from yelling with joy. As I dig around it I realize it was smart that I waited, for my discovery was nothing but a long, thin stone. Or perhaps a petrified snake. Either way, it wasn't important.

The sun begins to set, and we know we must go. We aren't discouraged, as neither of us expected to find anything on the first day, but we are a little disappointed. When we get back to the hotel, Jerome is watching "Emmanuelle in Egypt" on pay-per-view, eating what appears to be his third room service filet mignon. He apologizes profusely about earlier, and promises to accompany us tomorrow. We reluctantly forgive him, and Myra lets him sleep next to her that night.

I must sleep on a small wooden chair.

It doesn't bother me, for I have slept in far worse places. Like Detroit. Or that time I was in Cairo, and slept on a bed of camel dung. To this day, I still attract more than the average amount of flies.

DAY 3 — 7:30 A.M.

I awake to the sound of gagging. I then realize that it was me, as Jerome stuffed a small gourd into my mouth as a joke.

He is really beginning to irritate me.

Jerome and Myra had gotten up earlier, so there is no time to change or take a shower, as they are on their way to the sight. I am already in the cab when I realize I am still wearing my Snoopy pajamas.

Myra reassures me not to worry, as the sight is secluded, and they are pretty nice pajamas. Then she takes several pictures, while she and Jerome laugh hysterically. I haven't been so embarrassed since I interned with Leakey, and mislabeled a gracile Australopithecine skull fragment for robust, completely forgetting to take into account the sagittal crest.

I smile politely, and jokingly tell them both to go to hell. We do not talk until we reach the sight. When we get there, Jerome is impressed with our progress. He agrees we should keep at what we are doing, and he'll start work further in the cave. I like this idea, as it keeps Jerome away from me.

Several hours later, I again come upon what appears to be fossil material. But this time it is more definite. I call Myra over, and we begin to dig it out together. It turns out to be a parietal bone, intact! I am so excited I kiss Myra. She surprises me by passionately responding. She then goes into the cave to give the news to Jerome, whom she finds is sleeping. He becomes very excited, and clutches the bone tightly, yelling, "Mine! All mine!"

In the meantime, I excavate the area further, and soon uncover an occipital bone. It begins to get dark, but the prospect of finding a complete skull prompts me to go on. Then I realize my colleagues have already left, and I must walk the seven miles back to the hotel, as I have no cab fare in my pajamas.

DAY 3 — 11:22 P.M.

I make it to the hotel, my feet raw and bloody, and my occipital bone clutched firmly in hand. To my disgust, Myra and Jerome are in bed. Naked. Also in bed with them are several gourds. This sickens me, and I go to the bathroom to clean my feet. I will never eat gourds again.

DAY 4 — 6:45 A.M.

A loud banging on the bathroom door wakes me up. I had fallen asleep on the sink. I open the door and it is Myra, who holds out the parietal bone and demands I examine it. I tell her it is an average Homo erectus parietal. Then she tells me the curvature is too extreme for erectus, yet too round for habilus. I examine my occipital, and then agree. It is possible we may have found the link between the two! It is possible we have found a new species!

In her excitement, Myra kisses me again. I resist at first, after what she did with Jerome, but soon respond to her advances and begin pressing against her body. She falls over backwards, and pulls me down with her. It is then, when we are on the floor, fornicating like animals, that Jerome walks in with the camera. He takes several pictures before I realize what is happening. All the time Myra is laughing and smiling. I finally pull away and hide in the bathroom, humiliated.

Jerome knocks an undetermined time later, and tells me I must give credit for the find to him, or he is sending the pictures to "National Geographic." I am shocked, and cannot speak. He rants on and on, about how he'll call the new species Homo jerome, and how it will make him rich and famous beyond his wildest dreams. I begin to cry.

Myra busts in and takes a picture of this.

DAY 4 — 12:54 P.M.

I am now convinced, after sitting in the bathroom and thinking about it all morning, that Jerome must die. Myra too. I cannot be humiliated in front of the scientific world. Nor can I let the credit for such an important discovery go to someone else. The answer is murder.

I go to Hertz and rent a large SUV. My plan is simple. I will run them over. Then back over them five or six times to make sure they are dead. I park the car behind a palm tree in front of the hotel, then wait for them to come back from the sight. Thoughts of being featured on The Discovery Channel fuel my thirst for vengeance.

The second they step out of the cab, they're pancakes.

DAY 4 — 8:45 P.M.

Myra and Jerome finally return to the hotel. My fingers sweat as I turn the ignition key, and the engine roars to life like a prehistoric beast—perhaps an Indricotherium transsouralicum, or a Doedicurus with a slight cold.

Myra wraps her arms around Jerome and kisses him lovingly, as they both stand innocently on the curb, waiting to be flattened.

I put the car into gear, and slam the accelerator to the floor. My mind is racing, but I foresee everything in slow motion: the look of shock on Jerome's face when he sees me coming at him, the scream Myra will barely have a chance to let out, the crushed, bleeding mess of bone and sinew that was once my colleagues.

I drive past them and keep on going. I cannot bring myself to do it.

I am not a killer. I am an archaeologist.

Who cares if I don't get credit for this find? There will be other excavations. I will find other fossils. There is a big wide world out there, covered in dirt. Somewhere there is bound to be other extraordinary discoveries, and I will be there to make them. I and I alone will go down in history as the man who revolutionized archaeology, even if it takes me the rest of my life. I will bounce back!

Nah…too much work.

I turn the car around and level Jerome and Myra in mid-kiss.

Homo jerome my ass.

After they were flattened, I hit Reverse and backed up over their bodies. Twice.

If only Leakey could see me now.

Could Stephanie Plum Really Get Car Insurance?

I have a dirty little secret. Even though my books are compared to Janet Evanovich's, I'd never read her until after writing Rusty Nail. I was invited into an essay collection about Evanovich's character, called Perfectly Plum, so I read all the books back-to-back, then contributed this piece.

BY MY COUNT, STEPHANIE Plum has been involved in the loss or destruction of twelve vehicles at the time of this writing, which is 8:55 A.M., Eastern Time. But, in all fairness, I'm not very good at counting. Plus, I listened to two of the books on abridged audio, which is known for cutting incidental bits from novels, such as characterization and plot.

Since I had nothing better to do today, other than to donate my kidney to that sick guy who paid me fifty thousand dollars, I decided to find out if, in the real world, could Ms. Plum get insured?

Let's take a moment to look at the phrase "in the real world."

Have you taken a moment? Good. Let's move on.

Since Stephanie Plum is a fictitious character, who lives in a fictitious place called Trenton, New Jersey, she isn't expected to completely conform to all aspects of reality, such as car insurance, or gravity. Since I knew that this task before me would involve a great deal of painstaking research and determination, I immediately went to work. After work, I went to a movie. Then, a nap.

Discouraged by my lack of progress, I called my neighbor Shelby, who knows a lot of stuff, such as why bottled water costs the same as bottled iced tea, even though it doesn't have all the stuff in it that tea has. Such as tea. Quote Shelby:

"Stephanie who?"

The story would end there, except that I have a lot more to tell.

My next course of action was to take my phone off the hook, because I kept getting obnoxious messages along the lines of, "Where's that kidney?" and "You have to get to the hospital immediately!" and "He's dead."

Then I went to the Pleasant Happy Valley Assisted Living Facility (Now with 14% Less Elderly Abuse) to meet with renowned Stephanie Plum Scholar Murray Christmas. That's his real name, and though it may seem odd, it isn't nearly as odd as is sister's name, Groundhog Day. Murray attempted to be cooperative, but being a hundred and three years old, he'd forgotten much of the minutiae, such as his own name. After much patience, and some help from his nurse to understand his drooling wheezes, I got nowhere. So I have no idea why I'm telling you this.

But when the nurse left, I looked through his personal effects, and got a real nice gold watch.

This opens up a large topic for serious discussion, which I am merely going to skip.

After pawning the watch, I pulled out my trusty phone book and began calling insurance companies. After eight calls that went nowhere, I decided I needed a better plan than giggling and making fart sounds when someone answered. So I decided to try talking.

Here are some of the conversations I had. My name has been changed to protect me.

CALL NUMBER ONE

ME: Do you sell car insurance?

INSURANCE MAN #1: Yes.

ME: My name is Julie Pear, and I'm not a fictitious character. I played a hand in destroying twelve cars in my last thirteen books. Will you insure me?

INSURANCE MAN #1: I need more information.

ME: I like the color red, and dogs.

INSURANCE MAN #1: I meant about your driving background.

ME: I also like Rob Schneider movies.

INSURANCE MAN #1: I'm sorry, we can't insure you.

CALL NUMBER TWO

ME: Hello?

INSURANCE MAN #2: Can I help you?

ME: My last four cars have exploded, but it wasn't my fault. Can you insure me?

INSURANCE MAN #2: How did these cars explode?

ME: definition of explosion

INSURANCE MAN #2: Well, you're welcome to come in and we can give you a quote.

ME: How about I give you a quote instead? How about, "This was no boating accident!"

INSURANCE MAN #2: Excuse me?

ME: That was from Jaws. I loved that movie. I still get scared taking baths.

INSURANCE MAN #2: You're an idiot.

CALL NUMBER THREE

INSURANCE MAN #3: Making rude noises like that is very immature. (Pause) I know you're still there. I can here you giggling.

CALL NUMBER FOUR

ME: I want a large thin crust, sausage and extra cheese.

PIZZA GUY: That will be fourteen ninety five.

After all of this hard work, I only knew one thing for certain: if Stephanie Plum were a pound of bacon, she'd sure be a clever one. I'd pay a lot of money to see a talking pound of bacon in high heels. A lot of money.

The next thing on my to do list, after a good scratch, was attend an insurance convention. The convention brought many to tears, due to a chemical leak that gave most attendees second degree burns.

Quote Harold Barnicky, one of the attendees: "Those little crackers they had, the ones with the spinach and cheese—mmmmmmmmmmmm!"

Personally, I preferred the three bean casserole, which was inappropriately named because I counted at least a dozen beans, and counting isn't my strong suit.

But none of this effort brought me any closer to the end of this essay.

Undaunted, superfluous, and proselytical, I decided to try a more direct approach, because even though I'm a writer, I've always wanted to direct.

So I wrote an impassioned, persuasive letter to the largest auto insurer next to my house. The letter brilliantly detailed the whole sordid tale, and was perhaps the greatest thing I've ever written on a cocktail napkin. Without permission, here is the company's reply:

> We CARE Auto Insurance
> WE INSURE EVERYONE!™
> 8866 Haknort Lane
> CHICAGO, IL 60610
> (847) 555 - AUTO

To: Margaret Apples
Re: Recent Insurance Inquiry

Ms. Apples—

When my father began We Care Auto Insurance 64 years ago, he had a grand dream: To supply auto insurance to everyone who needed it, regardless of their driving record or accident history. He wanted to be the insurance company for the common man—-the senior citizens with senility issues, the veterans missing important limbs, the narcoleptics, the mentally retarded, the unrepentant alcoholics.

Father believed everyone—-even those with heroin habits and cataracts the size of dinner plates—-deserved to be insured. For more than six decades, We Care Auto Insurance carried on this proud tradition.

We have insured drivers with organic brain damage of such severity they couldn't count past four. We have insured drivers with quadriplegia, who drove using a suck-and-blow straw. We have insured the legally blind, the morbidly obese, the legally dead, and Mr. Chimpo the Driving Baboon. We've even insured several Kennedys.

Now, for the first time in our history, We Care Auto Insurance must turn down an application.

Yours.

While the law doesn't require us to provide an explanation for the reason you aren't being allowed into the We Care Auto Insurance family, I've chosen to write this letter to make something perfectly clear: We are not to blame, Ms. Apples. You are.

While reviewing insurance applications, we compile statistics from several sources, which allows us to come up with monthly rates and deductible figures. When feeding your information into our computer database, our network promptly froze.

We haven't been able to reboot it.

According to our information, you've been responsible for destroying more cars than any single driver in North America, and possibly South America as well.

You've destroyed more cars than Carzilla, the giant robotic crane that tours with monster truck shows and eats cars.

In layperson's terms; you've destroyed a huge fucking butt-load of cars.

There have been so many, I'm guessing you've lost track of them all. Allow me to refresh your memory.

After your Miata was repossessed (which seems to be the only nice car you've ever owned) you played a hand in the explosion of a Jeep owned by a Detective Gepetto of the Trenton Police Department. This, unfortunately, was not the last automobile casualty Detective Gepetto suffered at your hands.

Your next vehicle, a Jeep, was stolen. You'll be pleased to know that a VIN search has recently located it, in a scrap yard in Muncie, Indiana. The odometer reading was well over 220,000 miles. Having escaped you, this Jeep led a full and possibly interesting life, without explosions, though your insurance company still had to foot the bill for it nonetheless.

The blue Nissan truck you acquired shortly thereafter soon went to the big parking lot in the sky after being blown up with a rocket launcher. I must admit, I had to read the claim report three times before the phrase rocket launcher sunk in. I've insured several CIA operatives, a movie stuntman named Jimmy Rocket who specialized in pyrotechnics, and a scientist who actually worked for a rocket company (I believe they called him a rocket scientist) but none of them ever lost a vehicle to a rocket, missile, or any comparable exploding projectile.

Your replacement car, a Honda CRX, was soaked in gasoline and burned. My record search was unable to turn up the name of the perpetrator, but might I suggest it was one of your previous insurance agents? That wouldn't surprise me.

Your name came up in several claims made by a company cryptically called Sexy Cuban Man. The claims included an exploded Porsche and a stolen BWM. Not content with that, you somehow also managed to burn down a funeral home. Did you get confused in the dark and mistake it for a car somehow?

A Honda Civic, registered to you, was torched, and a Honda CRV registered to you was totaled, and then set ablaze. Why you bought another Honda is beyond my mental capacity, but you did, and it was promptly burned, along with another Sexy Cuban Man vehicle, by—and this is in your own words—a giant rabbit. Was Jimmy Stewart anywhere in the vicinity, pray tell? Or did this rabbit happen to have a basket of brightly colored eggs?

Your next vehicle, a Ford Escape, didn't escape at all. Again it was burned. Perhaps car insurance isn't what you need. Perhaps you simply need a car made of asbestos. Or a Sherman Tank.

Your next victim, a Saturn, was bombed. So was an SUV belonging to the unfortunate Joe Morelli. You also had a hand in the recent explosion of a Ford Escalade.

Records show you just purchased a Mini Cooper. Such an adorable car. I've included it in my nightly prayers.

While the first few explosions might be written off as coincidence, or even bad luck, somewhere around the tenth destroyed vehicle a little light came on inside my head. I finally understood that no one could be this unlucky. There was only one possible explanation.

You're sick in the head.

The psychiatric community calls your specific mental illness Munchausen's by Proxy. A parent, usually the mother, purposely makes her children sick so she can bask in the attention and sympathy of others.

I've decided that this is what you're doing, only with vehicles. Rather than feeding little Molly peanut butter and bleach sandwiches, you've been deliberately destroying your own cars. All because you crave attention.

But your warped scheme to put the spotlight upon yourself isn't without casualties. I'm not speaking of your helpless automotive victims. I'm speaking of my wonderful company.

Writing this letter fills me with sadness, Ms. Apples, for you have destroyed my father's dream. For the first time in our history, we are rejecting an applicant. This comes at a great moral cost, and a great financial cost as well.

Because of you, we have been forced to change our trademarked slogan, We Insure Everyone! Do you have any idea how much letterhead we have with that slogan on it? A warehouse full. And unless we hire someone (perhaps an immigrant, or a homeless person) to cross out the slogan on each individual sheet of paper, it is now land-fill bound.

Ditto our business cards. Our refrigerator magnets. Our full color calendars we give to our loyal customers every holiday season. The large and numerous interstate billboards. And our catchy TV commercials, which feature the jingle written by none other than Mr. Paul Williams, naturally called, "We Insure Everyone."

What will out new slogan be? I'm not sure. There are several in the running. They include: "We Insure Practically Everyone," "We Really Want to Insure Everyone," and "We Insure Everyone But Margaret Apples." I also like the slogan, "Why Can't You Be in the Next Car You Blow Up or At the Very Least Get a Job at the Button Factory," but that has too many words to fit on a business card.

You have crippled us, Ms. Apples. Crippled us worse than many of the people we insure, including the guy with the prosthetic pelvis and the woman born without arms who must steer with her face.

I hope you're happy.

As a public service to the world, I'm sending copies of this letter to every insurance agent in the United States. Hopefully, this will end your reign of terror.

If it takes every cent of my money, every single one of my vast resources, I'll see to it that you never insure another vehicle again. When I get done with you, you won't be able to put on roller skates without the Feds breathing down your neck.

> Whew. There. I feel a lot better now.
>
> And though we aren't able to insure you, Ms. Apples, I do hope you pass our name along to any friends or relatives of yours who are seeking auto insurance.
>
> Sincerely,
> Milton McGlade

So there you have it. Based on the minutes of hard work I've devoted to this topic, Stephanie Plum would not be able to get car insurance.

In conclusion, if I had only ten words to end this essay, I'd have a really hard time thinking of them. Now if you'll excuse me, I've got a kidney to sell on eBay.

Cozy or Hardboiled?

How to Tell the Difference

A fluff piece for Crimespree magazine. I got a big kick out of writing this.

MYSTERY IS A BROAD genre, encompassing thrillers, crime novels, whodunnits, capers, historicals, and police procedurals. Two of its most bi-polar brethren are the tea-cozy, as typified by Agatha Christie, and hardboiled noir, best portrayed by Mickey Spillaine.

But with the constant re-catagorizing and re-inventing of subgenres, how can you, the reader, tell the difference?

Fear no more! Here is a definitive set of criteria to determine if that potential bookstore purchase The Winnipeg Watersports Caper is about a gentleman boat thief, or a serial killer with an overactive bladder.

If the book has an elderly character that solves crimes in her spare time, it is a cozy.

If the book has an elderly character that gets shot seven times in the face and then raped, it is hardboiled.

If the protagonist drinks herbal tea, and eats scones, it is a cozy.

If the protagonist drinks whiskey, and makes other people eat their teeth, it is hardboiled.

If a cat, dog, or other cute domestic animal helps solve the crime, it is a cozy.

If a cat, dog, or other cute domestic animal is set on fire, it is hardboiled.

If the book has a character named Agnes, Dorothy, or Smythe, it is a cozy.

If the book has a character named Hammer, Crotch, or Dickface, it is hardboiled.

If the murder scene involves antiques, it is cozy.

If the murder scene involves entrails, it is hardboiled.

If the hero does any sort of knitting, crafting, or pet-sitting, it is a cozy.

If the hero does any sort of maiming, beating, or humping, it is hardboiled.

If the sidekick is a good natured curmudgeon who collects stamps, it is a cozy.

If the sidekick is a good natured psychopath who collects ears, it is hardboiled.

If the book contains recipes, crossword puzzles, or cross-stitching patterns, it is a cozy.

If the book contains ass-fucking, it is hardboiled.

If cookie crumbs on a Persian rug lead to the villain, it is a cozy.

If semen stains on a stab wound lead to the villain, it is hard-boiled.

If any characters say, "Oh my!" it is a cozy.

If any characters say, "Jesus Goddamn Fucking Christ!" it is hardboiled.

If the murder weapon is a fast-acting poison, it is a cozy.

If the murder weapon is a slow-acting blowtorch, it is hardboiled.

If the main character has a colorful hat that is filled with fruit and flowers, it is a cozy.

If the main character has a colorful vocabulary that is filled with racial slurs and invectives, it is hardboiled.

And finally, if the author picture looks like your grandmother—beware…it could be either.

Addiction

Another humor story about what it's like to be a writer. Like Piranha Pool, this is semi-autobiographical, and pretty much anyone who has ever tried to write for a living can relate to the narrator.

THE FIRST TIME I ever saw it was at a party.

College. Dorm. Walls constructed of Budweiser cases. Every door open, the hallways and rooms crammed with people, six different rock tunes competing for dominance.

Rituals of the young and innocent—and the not so innocent, I found out that night.

I had to give back the beer I'd rented, popped into the first empty room I could find.

He was sitting in the corner, hunched over, oblivious to me.

Curiosity made me forget about my bladder. What was he doing, huddled in the dim light? What unpleasant drug would keep him here, alone and oblivious, when a floor thumping party was kicking outside his door?

"Hey, man, what's up?"

A quick turn, guilty face, covering something up with his hands.

"Nothing. Go away."

"What are you hiding there?"

His eyes were wide, full of secret shame. The shame of masturbation, of cooking heroin needles, of snatching money from Mom's purse.

Then I saw it all—the computer, the notebook full of scrawls, the outline…

"You're writing fiction!"

The guilt melted off his face, leaving it shopworn and heavy.

"Leave me alone. I have to finish this chapter."

"How can you be writing with a party going on?"

He smiled, so subtle that it might have been my beer goggles.

"Have you ever done it?"

"Me?" I tried to laugh, but it sounded fake. "I mean, when I was a kid, you know, drawing pictures and stuff, I used to make up stories…"

"How about lately?"

"Naw. Nothing stronger than an occasional essay."

"You want to try it?"

I took a step back. All of the sudden my bladder became an emergency again.

"No, man…"

The guy stood up. His eyes were as bright as his computer screen.

"You should try it. You'll like it."

"I'm cool. Really."

He smiled, for sure this time, all crooked teeth and condescension.

"You'll be back."

I hurried out of the room.

The clock blinked 3:07 A.M.. I couldn't sleep.

To the left of my bed, my computer.

My mind wouldn't shut off. I kept thinking of the party. Of that guy.

Not me. I wasn't going to go down that path. Sitting alone in my room when everyone else was partying. I wasn't like that.

My computer waited. Patient.

Maybe I should turn it on, make sure it was running okay. Test a few applications.

I crept out of bed.

Everything seemed fine. I should check MS Word, though. Sometimes there are problems.

A look to the side. My roommate was asleep.

What's the big deal, anyway? I could write just one little short short short story. It wouldn't hurt anyone.

I could write it in the dark.

No one would ever know.

One little story.

"Party over at Keenan Hall. You coming?"

"Hmm? Uh, no. Busy."

"Homework?"

"Uh, yeah. Homework."

"That sucks. I'll drink a few for you."

"Sure."

I got back to plotting.

I raised a fist to knock, dropped it, raised it again.

What's the big deal? He probably wasn't in anyway.

One tiny tap, the middle knuckle, barely even audible.

"It's open."

The room was dark, warm. It smelled of old sweat and desperation.

He was at his desk, as I guessed he'd be. Hunched over his computer. The clackety clack of his fingers on the keyboard was comforting.

"I need…I need to borrow a Thesaurus."

His eyes darted over to me, focusing. Then came the condescending smile.

"I knew you'd be back. What are you working on?"

"It, uh, takes place in the future, after we've colonized Jupiter."

"It's impossible to colonize Jupiter. The entire planet is made out of gas."

"In 2572 we discover a solid core beneath the gas…"

I spit out the rest of my concept, so fast my lips kept tripping over one another.

"Sounds interesting. You bring a sample to read?"

How did he know? I dug the disk out of my back pocket.

• • •

I knew it was coming. Short stories weren't enough anymore. The novella seemed hefty at the time, but now those twenty thousand words are sparse and amateurish.

I was ready. I knew I was. I had a great idea, bursting with conflict, and the two main characters were already living in my head, jawing off at each other with dialog that begged to be on paper.

All I lacked was time.

"Hi, Mom. How's Dad? I'm dropping out of college."

I couldn't make much sense of her reply; it was mostly screaming. When my father came on the phone, he demanded to know the reason. Was I in trouble? Was it a girl? Drugs?

"I need the time off to write my novel."

I hadn't ever heard my father cry before.

I don't need understanding. Certainly not sympathy. The orgiastic delight that comes from constructing a perfect paragraph makes up for my crummy apartment and low-paying job at the Food Mart. They let me use the register tape for my notes, and I get a twenty percent discount on instant coffee.

Reality is tenuous, but that's a good sign. It means I'm focused on the book. I'm not really talking to myself. I'm talking to my characters. You see the difference?

Sometimes I need to take days off, like for that problem I had with Chapter 26. But I worked through it. The book is more important than food, anyway. Who needs to eat?

The tears were magic, and the sob was more beautiful than any emotion ever felt by anyone who ever lived.

Helium had replaced the blood in my veins. My hands trembled.

I typed The End and swore I heard the Voice of God.

The alley is cold. I stuff my sweatshirt with newspaper and hunch down by a dumpster, my CD-ROM clutched in a filthy hand that I can barely recognize as my own.

It is my third week on the street. I've made some friends, like Squeaky, who is sitting next to me.

"They locked me out. Sold my stuff to pay the back rent. Even my computer."

Squeaky squeaks. I offer him an empty Dorito bag, and he scurries inside, looking for crumbs. I don't mind him being distracted. He's heard the story before.

"I've still got my novel, though." The CD isn't very shiny anymore, and it has a crack that I pray hasn't hurt the data.

"Best thing I've ever done in my life, Squeaky old pal. Wouldn't change a damn thing about the path I chose."

It starts to rain. I stare at the CD, at my reflection in it. My beard is coming in nicely. It gives me sort of a Hemingway look.

"Did I tell you about the Intervention, Squeaky? Right before I got kicked out. My parents, my brother, the chaplain, and some guy from WA. Tried to get me to quit writing. Follow some stupid 12 step program."

I still feel a twang of guilt, remembering my mother's pleas.

"They wanted me to admit I had a problem. But they don't understand. Writing isn't an addiction. It's a way of life. Like being a rat. Could you stop being a rat, just because your family wanted you to?"

Squeaky didn't answer. The rain was really coming down now.

"I have to write. I don't have a choice. It's who I am."

The CD in my hand got warm to the touch, glowing with an inner spirit that I knew for sure isn't just my imagination. It's worth something. Even if it never sells. Even if I'm the only one who ever reads it.

It validates me.

"I'm no one trick pony, either. I won't rest on my laurels. I've got more books in me."

I pull out my collection of gum wrappers and sort them out, chapter by chapter.

After reading what I wrote that morning, I take my stubby pencil from my shirt pocket and start where I left off.

After all—writer's have to write.

It's what we do.

Weigh To Go

A Personal Essay on Health Clubs

Once upon a time I wanted to write a humor column like Dave Barry. I quickly learned that only Dave Barry was allowed to write humor columns, and newspapers weren't looking for anyone else. This was penned during college, and then tweaked to put on my website.

I WAS WATCHING "THE 20 Minute Workout," sitting back in my easy chair and eating a box of Twinkies. The blonde aerobics instructor (at least I think she was blonde, for I was having trouble seeing over my stomach) was chirping away about how eating healthy and exercising were the keys to a better you, while doing thigh lifts that made me exhausted just looking at her.

Among other health conscious things, she said that if you are truly satisfied with your body, you should be able to stand naked in front of a mirror and like what you see. I accepted the challenge, and after finishing the Twinkies and two bowls of Frosted Sugar-O's Cereal (now with 30% more corn syrup), I disrobed and went straight to the full length mirror.

Much to my dismay, I looked like a giant sack of potatoes with a penis. This did nothing for my self-esteem, and I dove into a Piggo Size Jay's Potato Chips and didn't stop until I hit cellophane.

It was not until later that I realized most of my problems, such as not understanding my income tax return, were directly linked to my overweightedness. I decided at that moment to start a strict regimen of diet and exercise, but soon just limited it to exercise, not wanting to give up my favorite meal, beer and Snickers Bars.

The thing I had to do, as told to me by countless celebrities on TV who can't get work elsewhere, was join a health club. I went to a popular one nearby, housed in a building the size of Rhode Island. Inside was like stepping into The Jetsons: chrome…mirrors…flashing lights…techno music…a running track lined with spongy foam…rows and rows of exercise machines, as far as the eye could see…Elroy, walking Astro…

I was greeted at the door by a very muscular guy who'd been packed into a Spandex outfit so tightly I could see individual corpuscles pumping through his veins. His name was G.

"How do you spell that?" I asked.

"With a G."

"Do you have a last name?"

"It's just G."

"So on your birth certificate…"

"Enough about me." G grinned big, making his neck muscles ping out. "Let's talk about you."

G herded me through a throng of beautiful people, telling each in turn that he was in a meeting and couldn't be disturbed even if Madonna called with a Pilates emergency. We went into his office, which was decorated with pictures of G with his shirt off and smiling, G with his shirt off and scowling, and G with his shirt off and looking apprehensive, probably wondering where he'd left his shirt.

G handed me a bottled water from his personal mini-refrigerator and sat me at his desk. He remained standing.

"It's a good thing you came today, Mr. Konrath, because you're about five beats away from a major myocardial infarction. If you don't join our club right now, I'll ask you to sign this waiver to absolve us of responsibility when you walk out this door and your ventricles explode."

"I actually just had my heart checked, and…"

"Plus, you're so disgustingly fat, no one will ever love you."

"My wife says…"

"Hey, Joanie and Brenda, come in here and meet my new best friend, Mr. Konrath." G motioned for two attractive young women standing in the hall to come in and smile at me. "Don't you think he'd benefit from our programs?"

"I'd love to get him in one of my Prancercize classes," Brenda said, licking her lips. "I'll help you take off that disgusting, icky fat."

Joanie put her head to my chest. "I hear his pulmonary artery crying out like a sick kitty."

"You truly are a disgusting man, Mr. Konrath," G said. "I suggest the Super-Duper Extra Special Presidential Package. That will give you access to all of the club's facilities."

He handed me a color brochure filled with pictures of smiling, healthy people. The Super-Duper Extra Special Presidential Package monthly dues were slightly more than what I earned in a month, but I would have full access to everything, including unlimited use of their one racquetball court, should I ever decide to take up racquetball.

"Sign it and we'll be your friends forever," Joanie said.

"Sign it or you'll get sick and die alone," Brenda said.

G put a hand on my shoulder and squeezed. Hard. "I don't want to sugar coat this—"

"If you did, I'd probably eat it."

"—but if you don't sign this contract you'll be the biggest wussboy I've ever met."

I stared at G and had a momentary delusion that I, too, might be able to look like someone stuck a tube up my ass and inflated me. Sure, his shoulders were so broad that he probably needed help wiping his own ass, but he looked damn good without a shirt.

"Sign," they chanted. "Sign. Sign. Sign…"

I signed, and left the club feeling cheerful about my new commitment to get in shape. The pounds would soon begin to drop off, I was sure. They had to, because I no longer had any money for food.

When I shared the good news with my wife, she was equally excited.

"It cost how much?!?"

"Don't think of it in terms of costs," I said, repeating what G had told me, "think of it in terms of benefits."

"You tell the kids they can't go to college because their father spent all of our savings."

"College is overrated. You don't really learn anything useful. Trade schools—that's where it's at these days. You see that one on TV, teaches you how to repair air conditioners?"

My wife shook her head. "You've got issues, Joe. In fact, you've got a whole damn subscription."

"Why don't you come down to the club, check it out? G said there's a discount for spouses."

"Are you saying I'm fat?"

"I'm saying that your support hose isn't hiding your little pouch like it used to when we were dating."

My wife smiled. She was obviously coming around.

"How long is this stupid contract for?" she asked.

"Three years."

"That's how long you're going without sex. Enjoy the couch."

The couch was close to the refrigerator, so it wasn't too bad.

During my fourth week as an Extra Super Special Guy Member, G called me up.

"Mr. Konrath, you joined a month ago. When are you going to come down and start working out?"

"I can't now, G. I'm waiting for a pizza."

"Come on, Mr. Konrath. Joining was just the first step. Now you've got to start coming in. I'll blend you a fifteen dollar kelp smoothie, personally train you on the equipment for sixty dollars an hour, and give you a nice thirty dollar rub down afterwards."

"I thought all of that was included in my Jumbo Deluxo Mega Membership."

"Did you read the fine print?"

"It was in a different language."

"Don't let money keep you from being the best Mr. Konrath that you can be, Mr. Konrath. Come in today and you can take my Jazz Kwon Do class for half price."

"What do you drive, G?"

"A Mercedes. And my payment is due."

G was right. I'd made the commitment to get in shape. It was time to put up or shut up. Even my wife, after having our lawyer try unsuccessfully to break the heath club contract, had begun encouraging me to go.

"You wasted all that money!" she'd say, encouragingly. "Put

down the cheese wheel, get off your lazy ass, and go work out!"

But, truth be told, I was scared. I knew if I went to the club I'd be surrounded by beautiful people, and I would be alienated and my self-esteem would sink even lower.

My plan was to get in shape before I went to the club. It could happen. I lost four pounds just last week, though I found it later, in my upper thighs.

"G, I feel too uncomfortable to come in. Can we do this over the phone?"

"There's nothing to be ashamed of, Mr. Konrath. There are plenty of fat, ugly people who come here every day. You'll fit right in."

"If they come there every day why are they still fat and ugly?"

"You're disappointing me, Mr. Konrath."

"Sorry, G. I'll drop by later today."

"Great! See you then."

"Are you mad at me, G?"

"No. Not this time."

"Thanks. Bye."

I hung up the phone, happy about recommitting myself to getting into shape. Twenty minutes later I was in the health club parking lot, finishing the last of my pizza. G greeted me warmly, pumping my hand like I was a lat machine. He was bigger than I remembered. I bet he had more definition than Webster's Unabridged.

Well, come on, all the jokes can't be good.

"How's my bestest buddy, Mr. Konrath?"

"Hungry. How about that smoothie?"

"Sure thing. You bring your Visa?"

"My wife took it. But I found some change in the couch."

G led me to the juice bar, and spent five minutes measuring out assorted powders into a stainless steel blender.

"The base is macrobiotic organic yogurt," he told me. "Low fat and sugar free."

"What flavor?"

"Plain."

"Sounds good. Can you add a few scoops of those chocolate chips?"

After the smoothie, G and I hit the equipment. Almost immediately I knew we were going to have problems. First of all, he wanted me to start a program he called "weight training." From what I gathered, this involved picking up weights, and lifting them up and down. G gave me a preview, grabbing a barbell the size of a Cadillac (when they still made them big), and curling it up to his chest several times. I very politely told G that he was out of his freaking mind if he thought I was going to do that. You couldn't pay me to do that. I certainly wasn't go to pay them to let me.

G let out a friendly laugh and then threw me a weight belt and told me to get started while he went to the juice bar for a creatine shake. "For a boost of energy," he said.

"Put in some of those mini marshmallows," I told him. "And some ham."

While I waited for my energy boost, I sat on an exercise bike, content with watching a girl in a string bikini do leg presses. She had a body that could make a priest give up choir boys. When G came back I was sweating like a pig.

"How are we doing, Mr. Konrath?"

"Great, G. I'm glad I signed up."

"Let's not overdo it your first day. Time for your rubdown."

While G rubbed my achy muscles for three dollars a minute, I had to admit that this health club thing was a good idea after all. Sure, I had to take out a second mortgage to pay for it, but seeing that girl do those leg presses gave my heart a workout it hadn't had in years.

And later that night, I actually got in a few minutes of strenuous exercise. With my wife, while thinking of the leg-press girl.

I was so quiet I didn't even wake her up.

Cub Scout Gore Feast

A Bonus Short Story by J.A. Konrath & Jeff Strand

"ISN'T THIS WHEN YOU start telling scary stories, Mr. Hollis?"

Hollis grinned, staring at the boys around the campfire. Cub Scouts, none of them older than ten. For some, the first night they'd ever spent away from their families.

"Are you scouts sure you want to hear a scary story?"

"Yes!" they chorused.

"Even though it's dark and we're all alone in the spooky, menacing forest?"

"Yes! Yes! Yes!"

Hollis sat down on his haunches. His face became serious.

"Okay, I'll tell you a scary story. Scary because it's the absolute, hand-on-my-heart truth. You've all heard rumors about Troop 192, how they disappeared without a trace not too far from here, right?"

Several of the boys nodded.

"Well, the rumors were wrong. There were *lots* of traces of Troop 192. There were traces all over the place…on the ground, up in the trees, by the lake, maybe even under where you're sitting right now. Imagine if you took a blender, like the kind your mothers use to make smoothies, but it was a *giant* blender, maybe…I dunno, eighteen feet high. And then you dropped the entire Troop 192 into it, and accidentally left the lid off, so that when you pressed the 'blend' button they sprayed all over the place. That's what it looked like."

"I heard it was just one kid who went missing," said Anthony.

Hollis shrugged. "If you think one little kid has that many guts inside of his body, more power to you, but I was here. I saw it. It was *gross*."

"My mom said they found him the next morning. He was playing Nintendo."

"Oh, well, I guess your mom is in a position where she was allowed to accompany the law enforcement agencies on their search, huh? Did she somehow become deputized without anybody hearing about it? Do Hooters waitresses typically get to tag along on searches for missing children?"

"She works at Olive Garden."

"Whatever. She wasn't there on the night of the investigation. I'm telling you that it was the entire troop, and their insides were strewn as far as the eye can see." Hollis made a grand gesture with both arms to emphasize the extent of the carnage. "And do you know who got blamed for it?"

Several of the scouts shook their heads.

"Madman Charlie. Oh, they arrested him, and sent him to the electric chair the next morning. But it wasn't Madman Charlie. When Troop 192 was massacred, he was off murdering a young woman in a completely different county. No, Troop 192 wasn't slaughtered by Madman Charlie. They weren't even slaughtered by something … human."

One of the youngest scouts, Billy somebody, raised his hand. No doubt because he was too terrified to hear more.

"Billy, are you too terrified to hear more?" Hollis asked. "Because that's okay. Nobody here will judge you."

"No, Mr. Hollis. I have to go to the bathroom."

Hollis sighed again. "Go ahead, Billy. But don't go too far away. Anyway, there's something inhuman in these woods. Something that hungers for human flesh."

Theolonious raised his hand. Probably wet himself he was so scared.

"Do we have any more hot dogs?" Theolonious asked.

"You already had three."

"Jimmy ate the one I dropped one the ground."

"Jimmy didn't come with us on this trip."

"Well, okay, I ate it, but it wasn't as good as the two that didn't get dropped on the ground. Can I please have another one?"

"This inhuman creature," Hollis said, ignoring him and raising his voice, "slaughtered Troop 192 on a night very much like tonight. It cracked open their bones and sucked out the marrow, and slurped up their intestines like spaghetti, then flossed its sharp fangs with their muscle fibers. And rumor has it this insatiable monster still hunts in these very woods, on the night of…" Hollis paused for dramatic effect, "the *full moon*."

"Was it a Dracula?" Cecil asked.

"Draculas don't rip people up," said Anthony. "Draculas just look unhappy a lot, and kiss girls like in that movie my sister watched seventeen gazillion hundred times."

"Those were dumb Draculas," said Cecil. "But there are cool Draculas, like in *Lord of the Rings*."

"Those were orcs."

"Not those! The other ones!"

"That was a Kraken!"

"The horrible creature," Hollis said, standing tall and raising his arms over his head, "was a werewolf!"

"I thought werewolves just took off their shirts a lot like in that movie with the Draculas."

Hollis shook his head. "In real life, werewolves like to crack open the rib cages of little boys with their sharp claws and bite their still-beating hearts right from their chests. That's what happened to Troop 192."

"If they were attacked by a werewolf," said Anthony, "wouldn't they become werewolves?"

"Not if their bodies were shredded and thrown around all over the trees and lake and ground. If you'd been paying attention when I started telling the story you could have caught that little detail."

"What if a werewolf bit a skunk?" Theolonious asked. "Would it become a werewolfskunk?"

"A werewolf wouldn't bite a skunk," Hollis said.

"Why not?"

"Why *would* it bite a skunk? Would *you* bite a skunk?"

"I wouldn't bite a skunk today," said Mortimer, "but if I was a werewolf, I think I'd bite a skunk if there was one sitting there. You'd have to bite it gently, y'know, so that its whole head doesn't come off, but I think, y'know, werewolves can bite gently when they want to, even though they usually don't. They couldn't use their whole jaw or, y'know, anything like that, but if they just used their front teeth and didn't close them all the way, I think they could bite a skunk without its head coming off."

The other cub scouts murmured their agreement.

"Y'know," Mortimer added.

"And what if the werewolfskunk bit a deer?" asked Theolonious. "Would it turn into a werewolfskunkdeer?"

"I want to know how one werewolf ate all of Troop 192," said Cecil. "How big is a werewolf's stomach?"

"Haven't I already explained that twice?" asked Hollis. "The werewolf didn't eat their whole bodies. He ate the best parts, then scattered the rest of them all over the place so that the kids couldn't turn into little werewolves. Do you want a demerit? Do you?"

"I need toilet paper!" Billy yelled from the woods.

"Use leaves!" Hollis hollered back.

"I tried! They're all stuck to me!"

Fredrick raised his hand. "Would a werewolfskunkdeer try to eat people? Or would it just forage for nuts and berries?"

"You don't even know what 'forage' means," said Silas.

"It means to search for provisions."

"Well, you don't know what 'tourniquet' means!"

"Yes, I do. We learned about them last week. It's that thing you twist around your arm or leg to stop bleeding."

"Well, you don't know what 'hypothesis' means!"

"*Silas*! Enough!" Hollis clenched and unclenched his fists a few times. "Anyway…"

Theolonious frowned. "So is a werewolfskunkdeer a person who changes into something that's a wolf, skunk, and deer all at once, like it has fur and Bambi eyes and sprays skunk spray, or is it a person who can change into a wolf *or* a skunk *or* a deer?"

"I have no idea," Hollis said.

"I think he changes into one of them, but he can't control which one it is. So he'll be fighting Bigfoot and he'll want to change into a wolf because wolves are better at fighting Bigfoot, but he'll change into a skunk instead and Bigfoot just steps on him. That's probably why you don't see many werewolfskunkdeers around anymore."

"What if a werewolf bit a Dracula who bit a zombie who then bit the werewolf?" asked Cecil.

"My baby brother bit the babysitter, but she didn't turn into a baby."

"Shut up!" said Theolonious. "That's not what we're talking about!"

"But what if a werewolfskunkdeer bit a wolf? Is it a werewolfskunkdeerwolf, or does the wolf part just not matter because it was already a wolf?"

"Werewolfwolfskunkdeer sounds better," said Anthony.

"Soon the full moon will rise," Hollis said, raising his arms theatrically. "And then the werewolf takes its supernatural form and…"

"You mean the werewolfwolfskunkdeer."

"No. I mean the werewolf. There's no such thing as a werewolfskunkdeer."

"You forgot the extra wolf. It's werewolf*wolf*skunkdeer."

"I did not forget the extra wolf. We aren't talking about the werewolfskunk deer."

"The werewolf*wolf*skunkdeer."

"We're talking about a werewolf! A regular old werewolf! That's it. Just a man who turns into a goddamn wolf, okay?"

The scouts went silent. Hollis knew he'd gone too far by using the g.d. word, but the punchline to his story was *so* amazing and they were ruining it.

"Mr. Hollis, is this poison oak?" Billy asked, walking back to the campfire holding some leaves.

"Yes, Billy. Put that down."

"I wish I'd picked different leaves. Can I go home?"

"No. There's some baking soda in the tent. Let me finish my story and I'll get it for you."

"Could a werewolf eat a baby whole, in one bite?" asked Anthony.

"I suppose one could," Hollis said. Actually, he *knew* that one could. Firsthand. Heh heh.

"So when it pooped out the baby, would the baby be a werepoopwolf?"

"What if a werepoopwolf bit a werewolfwolfskunkdeer?"

"It would be a werewolfwolfwolfpoopskunkdeer."

"Enough," Hollis said. "The next person who says something gets a bad report to their parents and they won't get to come on any more of these trips. Got it? See that full moon up there? That ties into our little story, doesn't it? Do you see the connection between what happened to Troop 192 and the lunar cycle of today? You get it, right? Do you know what Troop 192 was doing on that fateful night? They were—*irony alert*—sitting around listening to scary stories from their scoutmaster! Do you get where this is going?"

The scouts remained silent.

Hollis stood up.

"That's riiiiiiiiight! The story I was trying to tell you is foreshadowing what's going to happen tonight! Ha! How about that, you little brats? The reason there are so many similarities in the fate of Troop 192 and our situation at this very moment is because *I* am a werewolf!"

He stood there, facing the moonlight, waiting for the inevitable transformation.

"What story did you tell the other kids?" Cecil asked.

"Excuse me?"

"Were you telling them about another werewolf attack before that one?"

"Yes. That's right. It's all a vicious cycle. Each story I tell the scouts is about the previous massacre. I'll tell the next troop about you guys."

"If you killed all of those Cub Scout Troops, who keeps hiring you as a scoutmaster?"

He adjusted his angle. *Change, dammit, change*!

Theolonious raised his hand. "So if you bit a mummy—?"

Screw it, Hollis thought. He'd brought an axe.

Frederick was first, right in the middle of another stupid question when the axe caught him under the chin. It cleaved his jaw in half, his tongue waggling through the gap, blood spurting like a lawn sprinkler.

Hollis pinned Billy under his foot and hacked his arm off, then dangled it above his face, teasing him.

"Stop hitting yourself!" he yelled in Billy's face, slapping him with his own hand. It was good fun until shock set in and Billy stopped screaming.

Cecil got a straight chop to the throat, but the axe wasn't sharp enough to decapitate him fully, and his head flopped backward, still attached to some sinew.

As he'd warned earlier, Hollis drove the axe head into Anthony's ribcage, cracking it open, then diving in the feast on the child's still-beating heart with his razor-sharp werewolf fangs that seemed rather flat and dull for the job. He did manage to bite off a piece of something that could have been a ventricle, but might have been an atrium. Hollis always got those confused.

Theolonius watched, eyes wide, hugging his knees. He was covered in blood that wasn't his own. Hollis raised the axe, ready to make a lupine feast of the boy's small brain, when Theolonious began to scream.

No, not a scream.

That's more like a howl.

First the boy's nose extended, becoming hairy and snoutish.

Then claws burst from his fingertips, curving into the shape of scythes.

Hollis dropped the axe, dumbfounded, as the miniature werewolf then grew…

Antlers?

Theolonious quickly spun around, lifting his giant black tail, one that had a white stripe running down it ala Pepe Le Pew.

"Oh no…"

The werewolfskunkdeer sprayed Hollis with its anal scent glands while the scoutmaster was screaming, and some of the spray got into Hollis's mouth. The smell…the taste…was so bad, Hollis had no choice but to whip out his Swiss Army Knife, thumb open the mini scissors, and immediately begin snipping away at his own nose and tongue, *snip snip snipping* until…

"Mr. Hollis? Is this the baking soda?"

Hollis blinked away the daydream and stared at Billy.

Hollis sighed. "That's it, Billy."

Theolonious raised his hand. "Mr. Hollis? Will we get our fishing merit badges tomorrow?"

"Yes, Theolonious."

"Is storytime over?" Cecil asked.

"I guess."

Silas raised his hand.

"What, Silas? Do you want to ask me what 'transitory' means?"

"I want to know what's wrong with your ears. They're getting longer."

Hollis slapped his hands against the sides of his head. Indeed, his ears were getting longer. Longer and hairier.

He jammed a finger into his mouth, tapping the quick growing fangs.

It's about time.

Hollis leapt onto Silas, taking the boys whole head in his mouth. He squeezed his mighty werewolf jaws closed, feeling the skull bend inward, then crack suddenly, popping open like a walnut, squirting hot brains through Silas's nasal cavity.

With Cecil, he dug his snout into the boy's belly, clenching his teeth down on a length of intestines, holding tight as Cecil ran for the trees. Cecil managed to pull out his intestines, both large and small, his colon, his stomach, and something that might have been a spleen, before keeling over.

With Billy, Hollis dug one of his claws through the child's eye socket, then dug it through his skull and out the other eye, holding him like a six-pack. Then he pulled, tearing off the bridge of Billy's nose.

Theolonious cried out in horror, and Hollis ripped his lungs out of his chest, squeezing them like an accordion, making the scream go on and on and…

"Mr. Hollis? Is that a werewolfskunkdeer?" Cecil asked, pointing at something in the woods.

Hollis shook his head to clear it. The fantasies were getting more and more real. The medication wasn't working like it should.

"It's not?" Cecil asked.

"What are you pointing at, Cecil?"

"That thing, with the horns."

"You mean the tree?"

"No, the…oh, yeah. The branches looked like horns."

And then the transformation began. For real this time? Hollis bit down on the inside of his mouth as hard as he could. It hurt like hell—this was definitely real. Those little bastards were about to see what a *true* werewolf could do.

The scouts stared at him. Their jaws dropped as one.

The inside of his cheek was bleeding pretty badly. He shouldn't have bit so hard.

"That's right," he said. "Just like I've been hinting over and over, I am a werewolf! And on this night of the full moon, I shall enjoy a Cub Scout gore feast!"

Cecil screamed. Hollis laughed and then, transformation complete, let out the howl of the beast he had become.

"That's it?" asked Billy.

"What?"

"You're not very furry."

"My arms are hairy!"

"Not *that* hairy. My dad's arms are hairier."

"Look at my ears! Those aren't normal ears anymore. Look at my fingernails! And my nose sort of looks like a snout now!"

"I thought werewolves were supposed to be a lot scarier," said Theolonious.

"You know what? You kids *suck*! It's not my fault that the werewolf who bit me didn't break the skin all the way, and that I don't do a complete change! You should still be terrified! When's the last time you saw somebody's fingernails grow a full half-inch within ten seconds? Never, that's when? You've never seen somebody's nose change shape like that!"

"My sister got hit in the face with a basketball and—"

"Shut the hell up! I have killed hundreds of Cub Scouts, and if you think your ridiculous werewolfwolfskunkdeermoosepygmy fucker is the height of terror, then you can all just…just…" *No, no, no, I promised myself I wasn't going to do this again. Please, not again. Don't let it happen again…*

It happened again. Hollis succumbed to tears.

There was a long, uncomfortable silence.

"Mr. Hollis, can we go home and play Nintendo?"

"Yes." Mr. Hollis wiped the tears from his eyes. "Yes, we can."

Hint Fiction

A few years ago on my blog, I held a writing contest. The goal was to write a complete story in 25 words or less. I wrote two entries as examples, and the winner wound up getting some free books or something like that. A while later, a writer named Robert Swartwood *told me he'd signed a book deal for a hint fiction anthology. I believe he coined the phrase* hint fiction, *to describe a story written in—you guessed it—25 words or less. He asked me for a story, and I gave him two. Here are the four I've written.*

REFLECTIONS ON REFLECTIONS

Is my hair okay? I can never tell. Is that why you won't invite me in for a bite?

X-JUNKIE

The adrenaline really kicked in when Parker realized he'd forgotten to pack his parachute.

DONOR

Miller watched the TV from his hospital bed, fingers crossed, as the brakes on his son's racecar failed. When he was pronounced dead, Miller smiled.

CHUCK

Flight attendant Sherri was always quick to offer airsick bags. Reverse-bulimia, though a disgusting disease, was bearable when the meals were fresh.

The Days

I'm not a poet. I've written hundreds of funny, often vulgar, poems under the name J. Andrew Haknort, but I mostly shy away from the serious stuff. Except for this one. This poem is special to me, because I wrote it while I was trying to get published. I endured a LOT of rejections while I was struggling to make a go at fiction writing, and those rejections hurt. "The Days" was a pep talk to myself about never giving up…

Let the days stand up
In a single file line
for close inspection.

The time has come, my friends
for some serious reflection
on the way innocence ends.

Life fluttered down
like drooling bats
and fed
upon my hope.

My youthful dreams (or so it seems)
were spontaneously born
to their ever-present state
like the facade of a never ending wall…

One by one I've watched bricks fall.

Faster than I could replace them
Much too fast to even chase them
Too many to count
An ugly amount
My wall became a pile.

Let this be a message sent
Hope is not a good cement.

And so I screamed
at the great mess
Screamed while time slowly
progressed
As time usually does
Burying what never was.

And then I sat
Upon my pile
And cried
For more than quite a while
My dreams had died
Were buried under bricks and bricks and bricks…

A gravesite for the non-essential
The tombstone read, "He had potential."

I sat and sat
and found the hours
were possessed
with magic powers
For they'd turned into weeks.

And when
I finally led my feet
and head to leave
behind the dead
I stumbled into
troubled sleep

leaving brick-dreams far away—
Then I opened my eyes and it was today.

Now how should I continue?

Should I rage against my yesterdays?
Stoke the fire with my hands?
Refight all my private wars
with indignation in command?

Should I pull the stitches
on old wounds
to see if they are healed?

The problem is not mine alone
though selfish I may sometimes be
Impotence is universal
not exclusive to me.

So…
Inspect the days with a jeweler's loupe
Select and keep the precious few
Reject the ones that drip with pain
Elect to have no more that do
Reflect on those that still remain
For those make up the meat of time.
Life in neither good nor bad
Homogenous the paradigm.

And when the shadows of depression
Lead you to your next couch session
Unlock the door before you leave—

You'll back, for this is not
the end of time
as some believe.

Armageddon's far away…
This is simply New Years Eve.

BOOKS BY JA KONRATH

Whiskey Sour
Bloody Mary
Rusty Nail
Dirty Martini
Fuzzy Navel
Cherry Bomb
Afraid
Origin
The List
Disturb
Shot of Tequila
Jack Daniels Stories (Collected Stories)
Crime Stories (Collected Stories)
Horror Stories (Collected Stories)
Truck Stop
Suckers by JA Konrath and Jeff Strand
Serial Uncut by Blake Crouch and Jack Kilborn
Floaters by JA Konrath and Henry Perez
Dumb Jokes & Vulgar Poems
Endurance
Trapped
Shaken
Draculas by JA Konrath, Blake Crouch, Jeff Strand, and F. Paul Wilson
Banana Hammock
Killers by Jack Kilborn and Blake Crouch
Killers Uncut by JA Konrath, Jack Kilborn and Blake Crouch
Wild Night is Calling (short story) by JA Konrath and Ann Voss Peterson

Stirred by Black Crouch and JA Konrath
Flee by JA Konrath and Ann Voss Peterson
A Newbie's Guide to Publishing

Made in the USA
San Bernardino, CA
25 January 2014